THE HISTORY OF VINTAGE

In 2011 Vintage celebrates its 21st birthday. Vintage was created in 1990 to publish paperback editions of the fiction and non-fiction books by the literary imprints, Jonathan Cape, The Bodley Head, Chatto & Windus and Harvill Secker. In 2007 the list expanded to include Vintage Classics. This means that the greatest works from the past are published alongside the best writers of today. We publish 11 Booker Prize winners, 20 Nobel Prize Laureates, 11 Pulitzer Prize winners and one Orange Prize winner.

Love to read · Love Vintage.

THE VINTAGE 21ST BIRTHDAY RAINBOW

Oranges Are Not The Only Fruit by Jeanette Winterson

Trainspotting by Irvine Welsh

Memoirs of a Geisha by Arthur Golden

The Handmaid's Tale by Margaret Atwood

The Time Traveler's Wife by Audrey Niffenegger

American Pastoral by Philip Roth

The Gathering by Anne Enright

Star of the Sea by Joseph O'Connor

Atonement by Ian McEwan

The Road Home by Rose Tremain

Money by Martin Amis

Arthur & George by Julian Barnes

A Week in December by Sebastian Faulks

The Curious Incident of the Dog in the Night-Time by Mark Haddon

Captain Corelli's Mandolin by Louis de Bernières

Midnight's Children by Salman Rushdie

Suite Française by Irène Némirovsky

Possession by A. S. Byatt

Disgrace by J.M. Coetzee

The Woman in Black by Susan Hill

The Wind-Up Bird Chronicle by Haruki Murakami

Haruki Murakami's novels include *Norwegian Wood*, *after the quake*, *Dance Dance Dance*, *Hard-boiled Wonderland and the End of the World*, *A Wild Sheep Chase*, *Kafka on the Shore*, *After Dark*, *South of the Border*, *West of the Sun* and *Sputnik Sweetheart*, as well as two works of non-fiction, *Underground* and *What I Talk About When I Talk About Running*. He has translated into Japanese the work of F. Scott Fitzgerald, Truman Capote, John Irving and Raymond Carver. His new trilogy of novels, *1Q84*, will be published in 2011 by Harvill Secker

Jay Rubin is the author of *Haruki Murakami and the Music of Words*, and he has translated Murakami's *Norwegian Wood* and *after the quake*.

HARUKI MURAKAMI

The Wind-Up Bird Chronicle

TRANSLATED FROM THE JAPANESE BY
Jay Rubin

VINTAGE BOOKS
London

Published by Vintage 2011

2 4 6 8 10 9 7 5 3 1

Copyright © Shindosa Ltd 1994, 1995

English translation © Haruki Murakami 1997, 1998

Translated and adapted from the Japanese by Jay Rubin with the participation of the author

Two chapters of his translation were originally published in the *New Yorker* as 'The Zoo Attack' (31 July 1995) and 'Another Way to Die' (20 January 1997)

Alfred Birnbaum coined the term 'wind-up bird' in his translation of 'The Wind-up Bird and Tuesday's Women' included in the collection, *The Elephant Vanishes.*

Haruki Murakami has asserted his right under the Copyright, Designs and Patents Act 1988 to be identified as the author of this work

First published in Great Britain in three volumes in 1994 and 1995 with the title *Nejimaki-dori kuronikuru* by Sinchosa Ltd, Tokyo

First published in Great Britain in 1998 by The Harvill Press

First published by Vintage in 2003

Vintage
Random House, 20 Vauxhall Bridge Road,
London SW1V 2SA

www.vintage-books.co.uk

Addresses for companies within The Random House Group Limited can be found at: www.randomhouse.co.uk/offices.htm

The Random House Group Limited Reg. No. 954009

A CIP catalogue record for this book is available from the British Library

ISBN 9780099562986

The Random House Group Limited supports the Forest Stewardship Council® (FSC®), the leading international forest certification organisation. All our titles that are printed on Greenpeace approved FSC® certified paper carry the FSC® logo. Our paper procurement policy can be found at www.randomhouse.co.uk/environment

Printed and bound in Great Britain by
CPI Bookmarque, Croydon, CR0 4TD

Contents

THE WIND-UP
BIRD CHRONICLE

Book One: The Thieving Magpie

June and July 1984

1

Tuesday's Wind-up Bird

•

Six Fingers and Four Breasts

When the phone rang I was in the kitchen, boiling a potful of spaghetti and whistling along to an FM broadcast of the overture to Rossini's *The Thieving Magpie*, which has to be the perfect music for cooking pasta.

I wanted to ignore the phone, not only because the spaghetti was nearly done but because Claudio Abbado was bringing the London Symphony to its musical climax. Finally, though, I had to give in. It could have been someone with news of a job. I turned down the gas, went to the living room, and picked up the receiver.

"Ten minutes, please," said a woman on the other end.

I'm good at recognizing people's voices, but this was not one I knew.

"Excuse me? To whom did you wish to speak?"

"To *you*, of course. Ten minutes, please. That's all we need to understand each other." Her voice was low and soft but otherwise nondescript.

"Understand each other?"

"Each other's feelings."

I leaned over and peeked through the kitchen door. The spaghetti pot was steaming nicely, and Claudio Abbado was still conducting *The Thieving Magpie*.

"Sorry, but you caught me in the middle of cooking spaghetti. Could you call back later?"

"Spaghetti!? What are you doing cooking spaghetti at 10.30 in the morning?"

"That's none of your business," I said. "*I* decide what I eat and when I eat it."

"Fair enough. I'll call back," she said, her voice now flat and expressionless. A slight change in mood can do amazing things to the tone of a person's voice.

"Hold on a minute," I said before she could hang up. "If this is some new sales gimmick, you can forget it. I'm out of work. I'm not in the market for anything."

"Don't worry. I know."

"You know? You know what?"

"That you're out of work. I know about that. So, go and cook your precious spaghetti."

"Who the hell –"

She rang off.

Deprived of outlet for my feelings, I stared at the phone in my hand until I remembered the spaghetti. Back in the kitchen, I turned off the gas and poured the contents of the pot into a colander. Thanks to the phone call, the spaghetti was a little softer than *al dente*, but it had not been dealt a mortal blow. I started eating – and thinking.

Understand each other? Understand each other's feelings in ten minutes? What was she talking about? Maybe it was just a hoax call. Or some new sales pitch. In any case, it had nothing to do with me.

After lunch, I went back to my library book on the living room sofa, glancing every now and then at the telephone. What were we supposed to understand about each other in ten minutes? What *can* two people understand about each other in ten minutes? Come to think of it, she seemed awfully sure about those ten minutes: it was the first thing she came out with. As if nine minutes would be too short or eleven minutes too long. Like cooking spaghetti *al dente*.

I couldn't read any more. I decided to iron shirts instead. Which is what I always do when I'm upset. It's an old habit. I divide the job into twelve distinct stages, beginning with the collar (outer surface) and ending with the left-hand cuff. The order is invariable, and I count off each stage to myself. Otherwise, it won't come out right.

I ironed three shirts, checking them for wrinkles and putting them on hangers. Once I had switched off the iron and put it away with the ironing board in the hall cupboard, my mind felt a good deal clearer.

I was on my way to the kitchen for a glass of water when the phone rang again. I hesitated for a second, but decided to answer it. If it was the same woman, I'd tell her I was ironing and hang up.

This time it was Kumiko. The wall clock said 11.30. "How are you?" she asked.

"Fine," I said, relieved to hear my wife's voice.

"What are you doing?"

"Just finished ironing."

"What's wrong?" There was a note of tension in her voice. She knew what it meant for me to be ironing.

"Nothing. I was just ironing some shirts." I sat down and shifted the receiver from my left hand to my right. "What's up?"

"Can you write poetry?" she asked.

"Poetry!?" Poetry? Did she mean . . . poetry?

"I know the publisher of a story magazine for girls. They're looking for somebody to pick and revise poems submitted by readers. And they want the person to write a short poem every month for an opener. Pay's not bad for an easy job. It's part-time of course. But they might add some editorial work if the person –"

"Easy work?" I broke in. "Hang on a minute. I'm looking for something in law, not poetry."

"I thought you did some writing in high school."

"Oh yes, sure, for the school newspaper: which team won the football championship or how the physics teacher fell down the stairs and ended up in the hospital – that kind of stuff. Not poetry. I can't write poetry."

"Sure, but I'm not talking about great poetry, just something for school girls. It doesn't have to earn a place in literary history. You could do it with your eyes shut. Don't you see?"

"Look, I just can't write poetry – eyes open or closed. I've never done it, and I'm not going to start now."

"All right," said Kumiko, a little sadly. "But it's hard to find legal work."

"I know. That's why I've got so many feelers out. I should be hearing something this week. If it's no go, I'll think about doing something else."

"Well, I suppose that's that. By the way, what's today? What day of the week?"

I thought a moment and said, "Tuesday."

"Then will you go to the bank and pay the gas and telephone bills?"

"Sure. I was just about to go shopping for dinner anyway."

"What are you planning?"

"I don't know yet. I'll decide when I'm shopping."

She paused. "Come to think of it," she said, with a new seriousness, "there's no great hurry about your finding a job."

This caught me off guard. "Why's that?" I asked. Had the women of the world chosen today to surprise me on the telephone? "My benefit's going to run out sooner or later. I can't keep hanging around forever."

"True, but with my raise and occasional jobs on the side and our savings, we can get by OK if we're careful. There's no real emergency. Do you hate staying at home like this and doing housework? I mean, is this life so wrong for you?"

"I don't know," I answered honestly. I really didn't know.

"Well, take your time and have a think," she said. "Anyhow, has the cat come back?"

The cat. I hadn't thought about the cat all morning. "No," I said. "Not yet."

"Can you please have a look around the neighbourhood? It's been gone over a week now."

I gave a noncommittal grunt and shifted the receiver back to my left hand. She went on:

"I'm almost certain it's hanging around the empty house at the other end of the alley. The one with the bird statue in the yard. I have often seen it there."

"The alley? Since when have you been going to the alley? You've never said anything –"

"Oops! Got to run. Lots of work to do. Don't forget about the cat."

She hung up. I found myself staring at the receiver again. Then I set it down in its cradle.

I wondered what had taken Kumiko to the alley. To get there from our house, you had to climb over the breeze-block wall. And once you'd made the effort, there was no point in being there.

I went to the kitchen for a glass of water, then out to the veranda to look at the cat's dish. The mound of sardines was untouched from last night. No, the cat had not come back. I stood there looking at our small garden, with the early summer sunshine streaming into it. Not that ours was the kind of garden that gives you spiritual solace to look at. The sun managed to find its way in there for the smallest fraction of each day, so the earth was always black and moist, and all we had by way of garden plants were a few dusty hydrangeas in one corner – and I don't like hydrangeas. There was a small stand of trees nearby, and from it you could hear the mechanical cry of a bird that sounded as if it were winding a spring. We called it the wind-up bird. Kumiko gave it the name. We didn't know what it was really called or what it looked like, but that didn't bother the wind-up bird. Every day it would come to the stand of trees in our neighbourhood and wind the spring of our quiet little world.

So now I had to go cat hunting. I had always liked cats. And I liked this particular cat. But cats have their own way of living. They're not stupid. If a cat stopped living where you happened to be, that meant it had decided to go somewhere else. If it got tired and hungry, it would come back. Finally, though, to keep Kumiko happy, I would have to go looking for our cat. I had nothing better to do.

•

I had left my job at the beginning of April – the law job I had had since graduation. Not that I had left for any special reason. I didn't dislike the work. It wasn't thrilling, but the pay was all right and the office atmosphere was friendly.

My role at the firm was – not to put too fine a point on it – that of office dogsbody. And I was good at it. I might say I have a real talent for the execution of practical duties. I'm a quick learner, efficient, I never complain, and I'm realistic. Which is why, when I said I wanted to leave, the senior partner (the father in this father-and-son law firm) went so far as to offer me a small raise.

But I left anyway. Not that leaving would help me realize any particular hopes or prospects. The last thing I wanted to do, for example, was shut myself up in the house and study for the bar exam. I was surer than ever that I didn't want to become a lawyer. I knew, too, that I didn't want to stay where I was and continue with the job I had. If I was going to get out, now was the time to do it. If I stayed with the firm any longer, I'd be there for the rest of my life. I was thirty years old, after all.

I had told Kumiko at the dinner table that I was thinking of resigning my job. Her only response had been, "I see." I didn't know what she meant by that, but for a while she said nothing more.

I kept silent too, until she added, "If you want to leave, you should leave. It's your life, and you should live it the way you want to." Having said this much, she then became involved in picking out fish bones with her chopsticks and moving them to the edge of her plate.

Kumiko earned pretty good pay as an editor on a health food magazine, and she would occasionally take on illustration commissions from editor friends at other magazines to earn a substantial additional income. (She had studied design in college and had hoped to be a freelance illustrator.) In addition, if I left my job I would have my own income for a while from unemployment insurance. Which meant that even if I stayed home and took care of the house, we would still have enough for extras such as eating out and paying the cleaning bill, and our lifestyle would hardly change.

And so I had left.

•

I was loading groceries into the refrigerator when the phone rang. The ringing seemed to have an impatient edge to it this time. I had just ripped open a plastic pack of tofu, which I set down carefully on the kitchen table to keep the water from spilling out. I went to the living room and picked up the phone.

"You must have finished your spaghetti by now," said the woman.

"You're right. But now I have to go and look for the cat."

"That can wait for ten minutes, I'm sure. It's not like cooking spaghetti."

For some reason, I couldn't just hang up on her. There was something about her voice that demanded my attention. "OK, but no more than ten minutes."

"Now we'll be able to understand each other," she said with quiet certainty. I sensed her settling comfortably into a chair and crossing her legs.

"I wonder," I said. "What can you understand in ten minutes?"

"Ten minutes may be longer than you think," she said.

"Are you sure you know me?"

"Of course I do. We've met hundreds of times."

"Where? When?"

"Somewhere, sometime," she said. "But if I went into that, ten minutes would never be enough. What's important is the time we have now. The present. Don't you agree?"

"Maybe. But I'd like some proof that you know me."

"What kind of proof?"

"My age, say?"

"Thirty," she answered at once. "Thirty and two months. Good enough?"

That shut me up. Obviously she did know me, but her voice meant nothing to me at all.

"Now it's your turn," she said, her voice seductive. "Try picturing me. From my voice. Imagine what I'm like. My age. Where I am. How I'm dressed. Go ahead."

"I have no idea," I said.

"Oh, come on," she said. "Try."

I looked at my watch. Only a minute and five seconds gone. "I have no idea," I said again.

"Then let me help you," she said. "I'm in bed. I've just come out of the shower, and I'm not wearing a thing."

Oh, great. Telephone sex.

"Or would you prefer me with something on? Something lacy. Or stockings. Would that work better for you?"

"I don't give a damn. Do what you like," I said. "Put something on if you want to. Stay naked if you want to. Sorry, but I'm not interested in telephone games like this. I've got a lot of things I have to –"

"Ten minutes," she said. "Ten minutes won't kill you. It won't make a hole in your life. Just answer my question. Do you want me naked or with something on? I've got all kinds of things I could put on. Black lace panties . . ."

"Naked is fine."

"Well, good. You want me naked."

"Yes. Naked. Good."

Four minutes.

"My pubic hair is still wet," she said. "I didn't dry myself very well. Oh, I'm so wet! Warm and moist. And soft. Wonderfully soft and black. Touch me."

"Look, I'm sorry, but –"

"And down below too. All the way down. It's so warm down there, like butter. So warm. Mmm. And my legs. What position do you think my legs are in? My right knee is up, and my left leg is open just enough. Say, five past ten on the clock."

I could tell from her voice that she was not faking it. She really did have her legs open at five past ten, her sex warm and moist.

"Touch the lips," she said. "Slooowly. Now open them. That's it. Slowly, slowly. Let your fingers caress them. Oh so slowly. Now, with your other hand, touch my left breast. Play with it. Caress it. Upward. And give the nipple a little squeeze. Do it again. And again. And again. Until I'm just about to come."

Without a word, I put the receiver down. Stretching out on the sofa, I stared at the clock and released a long, deep sigh. We had been talking for close to six minutes.

The phone rang again ten minutes later, but I left it on the hook. It rang fifteen times. And when it stopped, a deep, cold silence descended on the room.

•

Just before 2, I climbed over the breeze-block wall and down into the alley – or what we called the alley. It was not an "alley" in the proper sense, but then, there was probably no word for what it was. It wasn't a "road" or a "path" or even a "way". Properly speaking, a "way" should be a pathway or channel with an entrance and an exit, which takes you somewhere if you follow it. But our "alley" had neither entrance nor exit. You couldn't call it a cul-de-sac either: a cul-de-sac has at least one open end. The alley had not one dead end but two. The people in the neighbourhood called it "the alley" as an expedient. It was some two hundred yards in length and threaded its way between the back gardens of the houses that lined either side. It was barely over three feet in width, and at several points you had to edge through sideways because of fences sticking out into the path or things that people had left in the way.

About this alley, the story was – the story I heard from my uncle, who rented us our house for next to nothing – that it used to have both an entrance and an exit and served the purpose of providing a shortcut between two streets. But with the rapid economic growth of the mid-fifties, rows of new houses came to fill the empty lots on either side of the road, squeezing it until it was little more than a narrow path. People didn't like strangers passing so close to their houses and yards, so before long one end of the path was blocked off – or, rather, screened off – with an unassertive fence. Then one local citizen decided to enlarge his yard and sealed off his end of the alley with a breeze-block wall. As if in response, a barbed-wire fence went up at the other end, preventing even dogs from getting through. None of the neighbours complained, because none of them used the alley as a passageway, and they were just as happy to have this extra protection against crime. As a result, the alley remained as a kind of abandoned canal, unused, serving as little more than a buffer zone between two rows of houses. Spiders wove their sticky webs in the overgrowth.

Why had Kumiko been frequenting such a place? I myself had walked down that "alley" no more than twice, and Kumiko was afraid of spiders at the best of times. Oh, what the hell – if Kumiko said I should go to the alley and look for the cat, I'd go to the alley and look for the cat. What came later I could think about later. Walking outside like this was far better than sitting in the house waiting for the phone to ring.

The sharp sunshine of early summer dappled the surface of the alley with the hard shadows of the branches that stretched overhead. Without wind to move the branches, the shadows looked like permanent stains, destined to remain imprinted on the pavement for ever. No sounds of any kind seemed to penetrate this place. I could almost hear the blades of grass breathing in the sunlight. A few small clouds floated in the sky, their shapes clear and precise, like the clouds in medieval engravings. I saw everything with such terrific clarity that my own body felt vague and boundless and flowing . . . and hot!

I wore a T-shirt, thin cotton trousers and tennis shoes, but walking in the summer sun, I could feel a light film of sweat forming under my arms and in the hollow of my chest. The T-shirt and trousers had been packed away in a box crammed with summer clothing until I pulled them out that morning, the sharp smell of mothballs penetrating my nostrils.

The houses that lined the alley fell into two distinct categories: older ones and those built more recently. The newer ones were smaller, with smaller yards to match. Their clothes-drying poles often protruded into the alley, making it necessary for me to thread my way through the occasional screen of towels and sheets and undershirts. Over some back walls came the sound of television sets and flushing toilets, and the smell of curry cooking.

The older houses, by contrast, gave hardly any sense of life. These were screened off by well-placed shrubs and hedges, between which I caught glimpses of manicured gardens.

An old, brown, withered Christmas tree stood in the corner of one garden. Another had become the dumping ground for every toy known to man, the apparent refuse of several childhoods. There were tricycles and hoops and plastic swords and rubber balls and tortoise dolls and little baseball bats. One garden had a basketball ring, and another had fine lawn chairs surrounding a ceramic table. The white chairs were caked in dirt, as if they had not been used for some months or even years. The tabletop was coated with lavender magnolia petals, beaten down by the rain.

I had a clear view of one living room through an aluminium storm door. It had a matching leather sofa and chairs, a large TV, a sideboard (on top of which sat a tropical-fish tank and two trophies of some kind), and a decorative floor lamp. The room looked like the set of a TV drama. A huge kennel occupied a large part of another garden, but there was no sign of the dog, and the house door stood open. The screen of the kennel door bulged outward, as if someone had been leaning against it for months at a time.

The vacant house that Kumiko had told me about lay just beyond the place with the huge kennel. One glance was all I needed to see that it was empty – and had been for some time. It was a newish two-story house, yet its wooden storm shutters showed signs of severe aging, and the railings outside the second-story windows were caked with rust. The house had a cozy little garden, in which, sure enough, a stone statue of a bird stood. The statue rested on a base that came to chest height and was surrounded by a thick growth of weeds. Tall fronds of goldenrod were almost touching the bird's feet. The bird – I had no idea what kind of bird it was supposed to be – had its wings open as if it wanted to escape from this unpleasant place as soon as possible. Apart from the statue, the garden had no decorative features. A pile of aging plastic lawn chairs stood against the house, and beside them an azalea bush displayed its bright-red blossoms, their colour strange and unreal. The rest was weeds.

I leaned against the chest-high chain-link fence for a while, contemplating the garden. It should have been a paradise for cats, but there was no sign of cats here now. Perched on the roof's TV aerial, a single pigeon lent its monotonous cries to the scene. The stone bird's shadow fell on the surrounding undergrowth, fragmenting.

I took a lemon drop from my pocket, unwrapped it, and popped it into my mouth. I had regarded my resignation from the firm as an opportunity to give up smoking, but now I was never without a pack of lemon drops. Kumiko said I was addicted to them and warned me that I'd soon have a mouthful of cavities, but I had to have my lemon drops. While I stood there looking at the garden, the pigeon on the TV aerial kept up its regular cooing, like a clerk stamping numbers on a sheaf of papers. I don't know how long I stayed there, leaning against the fence, but I remember spitting my lemon drop on the ground when, half melted, it had filled my mouth with its sticky sweetness. I had just shifted my gaze to the shadow of the stone bird when I sensed that someone was calling to me from behind.

I turned to see a girl standing in the garden on the other side of the alley. She was small and had her hair in a ponytail. She wore dark sunglasses with amber frames and a light-blue sleeveless T-shirt. The rainy season had barely ended, and yet she had already managed to give her slender arms a nice, smooth tan. She had one hand jammed into the pocket of her shorts. The other rested on a waist-high bamboo gate, which could not have been providing much support. Only three feet – maybe four – separated us.

"Hot," she said to me.

"Yeah, right," I answered.

After this brief exchange of views, she stood there looking at me.

Then she took a box of Hope regulars from her pocket, drew out a cigarette, and put it between her lips. She had a small mouth, the upper lip turned slightly upward. She struck a match and lit her cigarette. When she inclined her head to one side, her hair swung away to reveal a beautifully shaped ear, smooth as if just made, its edge aglow with a downy fringe.

She flicked her match away and exhaled smoke through pursed lips. Then she looked up at me as if she had forgotten that I was there. I couldn't see her eyes through the dark, reflective lenses of her sunglasses.

"You live around here?" she asked.

"Uh-huh." I wanted to motion towards our house, but I had turned so many odd angles to get here that I no longer knew just where it was. I ended up pointing at random.

"I'm looking for my cat," I explained, wiping a sweaty palm on my trousers. "It's been gone for a week. Somebody saw it around here somewhere."

"What kind of cat?"

"A big tom. Brown stripes. Tip of the tail a little bent."

"Name?"

"Noboru. Noboru Wataya."

"No, not *your* name. The cat's."

"That *is* my cat's name."

"Oh! Very impressive!"

"Well, actually, it's my brother-in-law's name. The cat reminds us of him. We gave the cat his name, just for fun."

"How does the cat remind you of him?"

"I don't know. Just in general. The way it walks. And it has this blank stare."

She smiled now for the first time, which made her look a lot more childlike than she had seemed at first. She couldn't have been more than fifteen or sixteen. With its slight curl, her upper lip pointed up at a strange angle. I seemed to hear a voice saying "Touch me" – the voice of the woman on the phone. I wiped the sweat from my forehead with the back of my hand.

"A brown-striped cat with a bent tail," said the girl. "Hmm. Does it have a collar or anything?"

"A black flea collar."

She stood there thinking for ten or fifteen seconds, her hand still resting on the gate. Then she dropped what was left of her cigarette and crushed it under her sandal.

"Maybe I did see a cat like that," she said. "I don't know about the bent tail, but it was a brown tiger cat, big, and I think it had a collar."

"When did you see it?"

"When *did* I see it? Hmm. No more than three or four days ago. Our yard is a kind of thoroughfare for the neighbourhood cats. They all cut across here from the Takitanis' to the Miyawakis'."

She pointed towards the vacant house, where the stone bird still spread its wings, the tall goldenrod still caught the early summer sun, and the pigeon went on with its monotonous cooing on top of the TV aerial.

"I've got an idea," she said. "Why don't you wait here? All the cats eventually pass through our place on their way to the Miyawakis'. And somebody's bound to call the police if they see you hanging around like that. It wouldn't be the first time."

I hesitated.

"Don't worry," she said. "I'm the only one here. The two of us can sit in the sun and wait for the cat to show up. I'll help. I've got twenty-twenty vision."

I looked at my watch. Two twenty-six. All I had to do today before it got dark was take in the laundry and make the dinner.

I went in through the gate and followed the girl across the lawn. She dragged her right leg slightly. She took a few steps, stopped, and turned to face me.

"I got thrown from the back of a motorcycle," she said, as if it hardly mattered.

A large oak tree stood at the point where the yard's lawn gave out. Under the tree sat two canvas deck chairs, one draped with a blue beach towel. Scattered on the other were a new box of Hope regulars, an ashtray and lighter, a magazine, and an oversize music machine. The music machine was playing hard-rock music at low volume. She turned the music off and took all the stuff out of the chair for me, dropping it on the grass. From the chair, I could see into the yard of the vacant house – the stone bird, the goldenrod, the chain-link fence. Chances were the girl had been watching me the whole time I was there.

The yard of this house was very large. It had a broad, sloping lawn dotted with clumps of trees. To the left of the deck chairs was a rather large concrete-lined pond, its empty bottom exposed to the sun. Judging by its greenish tinge, it had been without water for some time. We sat with our backs to the house, which was visible through a screen of trees.

The house was neither large nor lavish in its construction. Only the yard gave an impression of largeness, and it was well manicured.

"What a big yard," I said, looking around. "It must be a pain to take care of."

"Must be."

"I used to work for a lawn-mowing company when I was a kid."

"Oh?" She was obviously not interested in lawns.

"Are you always here alone?" I asked.

"Yeah. Always. Except for a maid who comes mornings and evenings. During the day it's just me. Alone. Want a cold drink? We've got beer."

"No, thanks."

"Really? Don't be shy."

I shook my head. "Don't you go to school?"

"Don't you go to work?"

"No work to go to."

"Lost your job?"

"Sort of. I resigned a few weeks ago."

"What kind of job?"

"I was a lawyer's assistant. I'd go to different government offices to pick up documents, put materials in order, check on legal precedents, handle court procedures – that kind of stuff."

"But you resigned."

"Yes."

"Does your wife have a job?"

"She does."

The pigeon across the way must have stopped its cooing and gone off somewhere. I realized just then that a deep silence lay all around me.

"Right over there is where the cats go through," she said, pointing towards the far side of the lawn. "See the incinerator in the Takitanis' yard? They come under the fence at that point, cut across the grass, and go out under the gate to the yard across the way. They always follow exactly the same route."

She perched her sunglasses on her forehead, squinted at the yard, and lowered her glasses again, exhaling a cloud of smoke. In the interval, I saw that she had a two-inch cut next to her left eye – the kind of cut that would probably leave a scar the rest of her life. The dark sunglasses may have been meant to hide the wound. The girl's face was not a particularly beautiful one, but there was something attractive about it, probably the lively eyes or the unusual shape of the lips.

"Do you know about the Miyawakis?" she asked.

17

"Not a thing," I said.

"They're the ones who lived in the vacant house. A very proper family. They had two daughters, both in a private girls' school. Mr Miyawaki owned a few restaurants."

"Why did they leave?"

"Maybe he was in debt. They ran away – just cleared out one night. About a year ago, I think. Left the place to rot and breed cats. My mother's always complaining."

"Are there so many cats in there?"

Cigarette in her lips, the girl looked up at the sky.

"All kinds of cats. Some losing their fur, some with one eye . . . and where the other eye used to be, a lump of raw flesh. Yuck!"

I nodded.

"I've got a relative with six fingers on each hand. She's just a little older than me. Next to her little finger she's got this extra finger, like a baby's finger. She knows how to keep it tucked in so most people don't notice. She's very pretty."

I nodded again.

"You think it's in the family? What do you call it . . . part of the bloodline?"

"I don't know much about heredity."

She stopped talking. I sucked on my lemon drop and looked hard at the cat path. Not one cat had shown itself so far.

"Sure you don't want something to drink?" she asked. "I'm going to have a Coke."

I said I didn't need a drink.

She left her deck chair and disappeared through the trees, dragging her bad leg. I picked up her magazine from the grass and leafed through it. Much to my surprise, it turned out to be a men's magazine, one of the glossy monthlies. The woman in the foldout wore thin panties that showed her slit and pubic hair. She sat on a stool with her legs spread at weird angles. With a sigh, I put the magazine back, folded my hands on my chest, and focused on the cat path again.

•

A very long time went by before the girl came back with a Coke in her hand. The heat was getting to me. Sitting in the sun, I felt my brain fogging over. The last thing I wanted to do was think.

"Tell me," she said, picking up her earlier conversation. "If you were in love with a girl and she turned out to have six fingers, what would you do?"

"Sell her to the circus," I answered.

"Really?"

"No, of course not," I said. "I'm kidding. I don't think it would bother me."

"Even if your kids might inherit it?"

I took a moment to think about that.

"No, I honestly don't think it would bother me. What harm would an extra finger do?"

"What if she had four breasts?"

I thought about that too.

"I don't know."

Four breasts? This kind of thing could go on for ever. I decided to change the subject.

"How old are you?" I asked.

"Sixteen," she said. "Just had my birthday. First year in secondary school."

"Have you been off school long?"

"My leg hurts if I walk too much. And I've got this scar near my eye. My school's very strict. They'd probably start hassling me if they found out I hurt myself falling off a motorcycle. So I'm off sick. I could take a year off. I'm not in any hurry to move up a grade."

"No, I guess not," I said.

"Anyhow, what you were saying before, that you wouldn't mind marrying a girl with six fingers but not four breasts . . ."

"I didn't say that. I said I didn't know."

"Why don't you know?"

"I don't know – it's hard to imagine such a thing."

"Can you imagine someone with six fingers?"

"Yes, I guess so."

"So why not four breasts? What's the difference?"

I took another moment to think it over, but I couldn't find an answer.

"Do I ask too many questions?"

"Do people tell you that?"

"Yes, sometimes."

I turned towards the cat path again. What the hell was I doing here? Not one cat had showed itself the whole time. Hands still folded on my chest, I closed my eyes for maybe thirty seconds. I could feel the sweat forming on different parts of my body. The sun poured into me with a strange heaviness. Whenever the girl moved her glass, the ice clinked inside it like a cowbell.

"Go to sleep if you want," she whispered. "I'll wake you if a cat shows up."

Eyes closed, I nodded in silence.

The air was still. There were no sounds of any kind. The pigeon had long since disappeared. I kept thinking about the woman on the telephone. Did I really know her? There had been nothing familiar about her voice or her manner of speaking. But she definitely knew me. I could have been looking at a De Chirico scene: the woman's long shadow cutting across an empty street and stretching towards me, but she herself in a place far removed from the limits of my consciousness. A bell went on ringing and ringing next to my ear.

"Are you asleep?" the girl asked, in a voice so tiny I could not be sure I was hearing it.

"No, I'm not sleeping," I said.

"Can I get closer? It'll be . . . easier if I keep my voice low."

"Fine with me," I said, eyes still closed.

She moved her chair until it struck mine with a dry, wooden clack.

Strange, the girl's voice sounded quite different, depending on whether my eyes were open or closed.

"Can I talk? I'll keep very quiet, and you won't have to answer. You can even fall asleep. I don't mind."

"OK," I said.

"When people die, it's so cool."

Her mouth was next to my ear now, so the words worked their way inside me along with her warm, moist breath.

"Why's that?" I asked.

She put a finger on my lips as if to seal them.

"No questions," she said. "And don't open your eyes. OK?"

My nod was as small as her voice.

She took her finger from my lips and placed it on my wrist.

"I wish I had a scalpel. I'd cut it open and look inside. Not the corpse . . . the lump of death. I'm sure there must be something like that. Something round and squishy, like a softball, with a hard little core of dead nerves. I want to take it out of a dead person and cut it open and look inside. I've always wondered what it's like. Maybe it's all hard, like toothpaste dried up inside the tube. That's it, don't you think? No, don't answer. It's squishy on the outside, and the deeper you go inside, the harder it gets. I want to cut open the skin and take out the squishy stuff, use a scalpel and some kind of spatula to get through it, and the closer you get to the centre, the harder the squishy stuff gets, until you reach this tiny

20

core. It's sooo tiny, like a tiny ball bearing, and really hard. It must be like that, don't you think?"

She cleared her throat a few times.

"That's all I think about these days. Must be because I have so much time to kill every day. When you don't have anything to do, your thoughts get really, really far out – so far out you can't follow them all the way to the end."

She took the finger from my wrist and drank down the rest of her cola. I knew the glass was empty from the sound of the ice.

"Don't worry about the cat – I'm watching for it. I'll let you know if Noboru Wataya shows up. Keep your eyes closed. I'm sure Noboru Wataya is walking around here somewhere. He'll be here any minute now. He's coming. I know he's coming – through the grass, under the fence, stopping to sniff the flowers along the way, little by little Noboru Wataya is coming closer. Picture him that way, get his image in mind."

I tried to conjure up the image of the cat, but the best I could do was a blurry, backlit photo. The sunlight penetrating my eyelids destabilized and diffused my inner darkness, making it impossible for me to arrive at a precise image of the cat. Instead, what I imagined was a failed portrait, a strange, distorted picture, certain distinguishing features bearing some resemblance to the original but the most important parts missing. I couldn't even recall how the cat looked when it walked.

The girl put her finger on my wrist again, using the tip to draw an odd diagram of uncertain shape. As if in response, a new kind of darkness – different in quality from the darkness I had been experiencing until that moment – began to burrow into my consciousness. I was probably falling asleep. I didn't want this to happen, but there was no way I could resist it. My body felt like a corpse – someone else's corpse – sinking into the canvas deck chair.

In the darkness, I saw the four legs of Noboru Wataya, four silent brown legs above four soft paws with swelling, rubberlike pads, legs that were treading the earth somewhere without a sound.

But where?

"Ten minutes is all it will take," said the woman on the phone. No, she had to be wrong. Sometimes ten minutes is not ten minutes. It can stretch and shrink. That was something I did know for sure.

•

When I woke up, I was alone. The girl had disappeared from the deck chair, which was still touching mine. The towel and cigarettes and magazine were there, but not the glass or the music machine.

The sun had begun to sink in the west, and the shadow of an oak branch had crept across my knees. My watch said it was 4.15. I sat up and looked around. Broad lawn, dry pond, fence, stone bird, goldenrod, TV aerial. Still no sign of the cat. Or of the girl.

I glanced at the cat path and waited for the girl to come back. Ten minutes went by, and neither cat nor girl showed up. Nothing moved. I felt as if I had aged tremendously while I slept.

I stood and glanced towards the house, where there was no sign of a human presence. The bay window reflected the glare of the western sun. I gave up waiting and crossed the lawn to the alley, returning home. I hadn't found the cat, but I had tried my best.

·

At home, I took in the washing and prepared a simple dinner. The phone rang for twelve rings at 5.30, but I didn't answer it. Even after the ringing stopped, the sound of the bell lingered in the indoor evening gloom like dust floating in the air. With the tips of its hard claws, the table clock tapped at a transparent board floating in space.

Why not write a poem about the wind-up bird? The idea struck me, but the first line would not come. How could school girls possibly enjoy a poem about a wind-up bird?

·

Kumiko came home at 7.30. She had been arriving later and later over the past month. It was not unusual for her to return after 8, and sometimes even after 10. Now that I was at home preparing dinner, she no longer had to hurry back. They were understaffed, in any case, and lately one of her colleagues had been off sick.

"Sorry," she said. "The work just went on and on, and that part-time girl is useless."

I went to the kitchen and cooked: fish sautéed in butter, salad, and miso soup. Kumiko sat at the kitchen table and vegged out.

"Where were you at 5.30?" she asked. "I tried to call to say I'd be late."

"The butter ran out. I went to the store," I lied.

"Did you go to the bank?"

"Yes."

"And the cat?"

"Couldn't find it. I went to the vacant house, like you said, but there was no trace of it. I bet it went farther away than that."

She said nothing.

When I finished bathing after dinner, Kumiko was sitting in the living room with the lights out. Hunched in the dark with her grey shirt on, she looked like a piece of luggage that had been left in the wrong place.

Drying my hair with a bath towel, I sat on the sofa opposite Kumiko. In a voice I could barely catch, she said, "I'm sure the cat's dead."

"Don't be silly," I replied. "I'm sure it's having a grand old time somewhere. It'll get hungry and come home soon. The same thing happened once before, remember? When we lived in Koenji . . ."

"This time's different," she said. "This time you're wrong. I know it. The cat's dead. It's rotting in a patch of grass. Did you look in the grass around the vacant house?"

"No, I didn't. The house may be vacant, but it does belong to somebody. I can't just go barging in there."

"Then where *did* you look for the cat? I bet you didn't even try. That's why you didn't find it."

I sighed and wiped my hair again with the towel. I started to speak but gave up when I realized that Kumiko was crying. It was understandable: Kumiko loved the cat. It had been with us since just after our wedding. I threw my towel in the bathroom hamper and went to the kitchen for a cold beer. What a stupid day it had been: a stupid day of a stupid month of a stupid year.

Noboru Wataya, where are you? Did the wind-up bird forget to wind your spring?

The words came to me like lines of poetry.

> Noboru Wataya,
> Where are you?
> Did the wind-up bird
> Forget to wind your spring?

When I was halfway through my beer, the phone started to ring.

"Get it, will you?" I shouted into the darkness of the living room.

"Not me," she said. "You get it."

"I don't want to."

The phone kept on ringing, stirring up the dust that floated in the darkness. Neither of us said a word. I drank my beer, and Kumiko went on crying soundlessly. I counted twenty rings and gave up. There was no point in counting for ever.

2

Full Moon and Eclipse of the Sun
·
On Horses Dying in the Stables

Is it possible, in the final analysis, for one human being to achieve perfect understanding of another?

We can invest enormous time and energy in serious efforts to know another person, but in the end, how close can we come to that person's essence? We convince ourselves that we know the other person well, but do we really know anything important about anyone?

I started thinking seriously about such things a week after I left my job at the law firm. Never until then – never in the whole course of my life – had I grappled with questions like this. And why not? Perhaps because my hands had been full just living. I had simply been too busy to think about myself.

Something trivial got me started, just as most important things in the world have small beginnings. One morning after Kumiko rushed through breakfast and left for work, I threw the laundry into the washing machine, made the bed, washed the dishes and vacuumed. Then, with the cat beside me, I sat on the veranda, checking the wanted ads and the items for sale. At noon I had lunch and went to the supermarket. There I bought food for dinner and, from a discount table, detergent, tissues and toilet paper. At home again, I made preparations for dinner and lay down on the sofa with a book, waiting for Kumiko to come home.

Newly unemployed, I found this kind of life refreshing. No more commuting to work on jam-packed subways, no more meetings with people I didn't want to meet. And best of all, I could read any book I wanted, anytime I wanted. I had no idea how long this relaxed lifestyle would continue, but at that point, at least, after a week, I was enjoying it, and I tried hard not to think about the future. This was my one great vacation in life. It would have to end sometime, but until it did I was determined to enjoy it.

That particular evening, though, I was unable to lose myself in the pleasure of reading, because Kumiko was late coming home from work. She never got back later than 6.30, and if she thought she was going to be delayed by as little as ten minutes, she always let me know. She was like that: almost too conscientious. But that day was an exception. She was still not home after 7, and there was no call. The meat and vegetables were ready and waiting, so that I could cook them the minute she came in. Not that I had a great feast in mind: I would be stir-frying thin slices of beef, onions, green peppers and bean sprouts with a little salt, pepper, soy sauce and a splash of beer – a recipe from my bachelor days. The rice was done, the miso soup was warm, and the vegetables were all sliced and arranged in separate piles in a large dish, ready for the wok. Only Kumiko was missing. I was hungry enough to think about cooking my own portion and eating alone, but I was not ready to make this move. It just didn't seem right.

I sat at the kitchen table, sipping a beer and munching some soggy soda crackers I had found at the back of the cupboard. I watched the small hand of the clock edging towards – and slowly passing – the 7.30 position.

It was after 9 when she came in. She looked exhausted. Her eyes were bloodshot: a bad sign. Something bad had always happened when her eyes were red.

OK, I told myself, stay cool, keep it simple and low-key and natural. Don't get excited.

"I'm so sorry," Kumiko said. "This one job wouldn't go right. I thought of calling you, but things just kept getting in the way."

"Never mind, it's all right, don't let it bother you," I said as casually as I could. And in fact, I wasn't feeling bad about it. I had had the same experience any number of times. Going out to work can be tough, not something sweet and peaceful like picking the prettiest rose in your garden for your sick grandmother and spending the day with her, two streets away. Sometimes you have to do unpleasant things with unpleasant people, and the chance to call home doesn't come up. Thirty seconds is all it would take to say, "I'll be home late tonight," and there are telephones everywhere, but you just can't do it.

I started cooking: turned on the gas, put oil in the wok. Kumiko took a beer from the refrigerator and a glass from the cupboard, did a quick inspection of the food I was about to cook, and sat at the kitchen table without a word. Judging from the look on her face, she was not enjoying the beer.

"You should have eaten without me," she said.

"Never mind. I wasn't that hungry."

While I fried the meat and vegetables, Kumiko went to freshen up. I could hear her washing her face and brushing her teeth. A little later, she came out of the bathroom, holding something. It was the toilet paper and tissues I had bought at the supermarket.

"Why did you buy *this* stuff?" she asked, her voice weary.

Holding the wok, I looked at her. Then I looked at the box of tissues and the package of toilet paper. I had no idea what she was trying to say.

"What do you mean? They're just tissues and toilet paper. We need those things. We haven't run out, but they won't rot if they sit around a little while."

"No, of course not. But why did you have to buy *blue* tissues and *flower-pattern* toilet paper?"

"I don't get it," I said, controlling myself. "They were on sale. Blue tissues are not going to turn your nose blue. What's the big deal?"

"It *is* a big deal. I hate blue tissues and flower-pattern toilet paper. Didn't you know that?"

"No, I didn't," I said. "Why do you hate them?"

"How should I know why I hate them? I just do. *You* hate telephone covers, and thermos bottles with flower decorations, and bell-bottom jeans with rivets, and me having my nails manicured. Not even *you* can say why. It's just a matter of taste."

In fact, I could have explained my reasons for all those things, but of course I did not. "All right," I said. "It's just a matter of taste. But can you tell me that in the six years we've been married you've never once bought blue tissues or flower-pattern toilet paper?"

"Never. Not once."

"Really?"

"Yes, really. The tissues I buy are either white or yellow or pink. And

I *never* buy toilet paper with patterns on it. I'm shocked that you could live with me all this time and not be aware of that."

It was shocking to me, too, to realize that in six long years I had never once used blue tissues or patterned toilet paper.

"And while I'm at it, let me say this," she continued. "I absolutely detest beef stir fried with green peppers. Didn't you know that?"

"No, I didn't," I said.

"Well, it's true. And don't ask me why. I just can't stand the smell of the two of them cooking in the same pan."

"You mean to say that in six years you have never once cooked beef and green peppers together?"

She shook her head. "I'll eat green peppers in a salad. I'll fry beef with onions. But I have never once cooked beef and green peppers together."

I heaved a sigh.

"Haven't you ever thought it strange?" she asked.

"Thought it strange? I didn't even notice," I said, taking a moment to consider whether, since marrying, I had ever eaten anything stir-fried containing beef and green peppers. Of course, it was impossible for me to recall.

"You've been living with me all this time," she said, "but you've hardly paid any attention to me. The only one you ever think about is yourself."

"Now wait just a minute," I said, turning off the gas and setting the wok down on the cooker. "Let's not get carried away here. You may be right. Maybe I haven't paid enough attention to things like tissues and toilet paper and beef and green peppers. But that doesn't mean I haven't paid any attention to *you*. I don't give a *damn* what colour my tissues are. OK, black I'd have trouble with, but white, blue – it just doesn't matter. It's the same with beef and green peppers. Together, apart – who cares? Stir-fried beef and green peppers could disappear from the face of the earth and it wouldn't matter to me. It has nothing to do with you, your essence, what makes Kumiko Kumiko. Am I wrong?"

Instead of answering me, she polished off her beer in two big gulps and stared at the empty bottle.

I dumped the contents of the wok into the garbage. So much for the beef and green peppers and onions and bean sprouts. Weird. Food one minute, garbage the next. I opened a beer and drank from the bottle.

"Why did you do that?" she asked.

"You hate it that much."

"But *you* could have eaten it."

"I suddenly didn't want beef and green peppers any more."

She shrugged. "Whatever makes you happy."

She put her arms on the table and rested her face on them. For a while, she stayed like that. I could see she wasn't crying or sleeping. I looked at the empty wok on the cooker, looked at Kumiko, and drank my beer down. Crazy. Who gives a damn about toilet paper and green peppers?

But I walked over and put my hand on her shoulder. "OK," I said. "I understand now. I'll never buy blue tissues or flowered toilet paper again. I promise. I'll take the stuff back to the supermarket tomorrow and exchange it. If they won't exchange it, I'll burn it in the yard. I'll throw the ashes in the sea. And no more beef and green peppers. Never again. Pretty soon the smell will be gone, and we'll never have to think about it any more. OK?"

But still she said nothing. I wanted to go out for an hour's walk and find her cheery when I got back, but I knew there was no chance of that happening. I'd have to solve this one myself.

"Look, you're tired," I said. "Take a little rest and we'll go out for a pizza. When's the last time we had a pizza? Anchovies and onions. We'll split one. It wouldn't kill us to eat out once in a while."

This didn't do it, either. She kept her face pressed against her arms.

I didn't know what else to say. I sat down and stared at her across the table. One ear showed through her short black hair. It had an earring that I had never seen before, a little gold one in the shape of a fish. Where could she have bought such a thing? I wanted a smoke. I imagined myself taking my cigarettes and lighter from my pocket, putting a cigarette between my lips and lighting up. I inhaled a lungful of air. The heavy smell of stir-fried beef and vegetables struck me hard. I was starving.

My eye caught the calendar on the wall. This calendar showed the phases of the moon. The full moon was approaching. Of course: it was about time for Kumiko's period.

Only after I became a married man did it truly dawn on me that I was an inhabitant of earth, the third planet of the solar system. I lived on the earth, the earth revolved around the sun, and around the earth revolved the moon. Like it or not, this would continue for eternity (or what could be regarded as eternity in comparison with my lifetime). What induced me to see things this way was the absolute precision of my wife's twenty-nine-day menstrual cycle. It corresponded perfectly with the waxing and waning of the moon. And her periods were always difficult. She would

28

become unstable – depressed even – for days before they began. So her cycle became my cycle. I had to be careful not to cause any unnecessary trouble at the wrong time of the month. Before we were married, I hardly noticed the phases of the moon. I might catch sight of the moon in the sky, but its shape at any given time was of no concern to me. Now the shape of the moon was something I always carried around in my head.

I had been with a number of women before Kumiko, and of course each had had her own period. Some were difficult, some were easy, some were finished in three days, others took over a week, some were regular, others could be ten days late and scare the hell out of me; some women had bad moods, others were barely affected. Until I married Kumiko, though, I had never lived with a woman. Until then, the cycles of nature meant the changing of the seasons. In winter I'd get my coat out, in summer it was time for sandals. With marriage I took on not only a cohabitant but a new concept of cyclicity: the phases of the moon. Only once had she missed her cycle for some months, during which time she had been pregnant.

"I'm sorry," she said, raising her face. "I didn't mean to take it out on you. I'm tired, and I'm in a bad mood."

"That's OK," I said. "Don't let it bother you. You should take it out on somebody when you're tired. It makes you feel better."

Kumiko took a long, slow breath, held it in a while, and let it out.

"What about you?" she asked.

"What about me?"

"You don't take it out on anybody when *you're* tired. I do. Why is that?"

I shook my head. "I've never noticed," I said. "Funny."

"Maybe you've got this deep well inside, and you shout into it, 'The king's got donkey's ears!' and then everything's OK."

I thought about that for a while. "Maybe," I said.

Kumiko looked at the empty beer bottle again. She stared at the label, and then at the mouth, and then she turned the neck in her fingers.

"My period's coming," she said. "I think that's why I'm in such a bad mood."

"I know," I said. "Don't let it bother you. You're not the only one. Loads of horses die when the moon's full."

She took her hand from the bottle, opened her mouth, and looked at me.

"Now, where did *that* come from all of a sudden?"

"I read it in the paper the other day. I meant to tell you about it, but I forgot. It was in an interview with a vet. Apparently, horses are tremendously influenced by the phases of the moon – both physically and emotionally. Their brain waves go wild as the full moon approaches, and they start having all kinds of physical problems. Then, on the night itself, a lot of them get sick, and a huge number die. Nobody really knows why this happens, but the statistics prove that it does. Horse vets never have time to sleep on full-moon nights, they're so busy."

"Interesting," said Kumiko.

"An eclipse of the sun is even worse, though. Nothing short of a tragedy for horses. You can't begin to imagine how many horses die on the day of a total eclipse. Anyhow, all I want to say is that right this second, horses are dying all over the world. Compared with that, it's no big deal if you take out your frustrations on somebody. So don't let it bother you. Think about the horses dying. Think about them lying on the straw in some barn under the full moon, foaming at the mouth, gasping in agony."

She seemed to take a moment to think about horses dying in barns.

"Well, I have to admit," she said with a note of resignation, "you could sell anybody anything."

"All right, then," I said. "Change your clothes and let's go out for a pizza."

•

That night, in our darkened bedroom, I lay beside Kumiko, staring at the ceiling and asking myself just how much I really knew about this woman. The clock said 2 a.m. She was sound asleep. In the dark, I thought about blue tissues and patterned toilet paper and beef and green peppers. I had lived with her all this time, unaware how much she hated these things. In themselves they were trivial. Stupid. Something to laugh off, not make a big issue out of. We'd had a little tiff and would have forgotten about it in a couple of days.

But this was different. It was bothering me in a strange new way, digging at me like a little fish bone caught in the throat. Maybe – just maybe – it was more crucial than it had seemed. Maybe this was it: the fatal blow. Or maybe it was just the beginning of what would be the fatal blow. I might be standing at the threshold of something big, and inside lay a world that belonged to Kumiko alone, a vast world that I had never known. I saw it as a big, dark room. I was standing there holding a cigarette lighter, its tiny flame showing me only the smallest part of the room.

Would I ever see the rest? Or would I grow old and die without ever really knowing her? If that was all that lay in store for me, then what was the point of this married life I was leading? What was the point of my life at all if I was spending it in bed with an unknown companion?

•

This was what I thought about that night and what I went on thinking about long afterwards from time to time. Only much later did it occur to me that I had found my way to the core of the problem.

3

Malta Kano's Hat

◆

Sherbet Tone and Allen Ginsberg
and the Crusaders

I was in the middle of preparing lunch when the phone rang again. I had cut two slices of bread, spread them with butter and mustard, filled them with slices of tomato and cheese, set the whole on the chopping board, and I was just about to cut it in half when the bell started ringing.

I let the phone ring three times and cut the sandwich in half. Then I transferred it to a plate, wiped the knife, and put that in the cutlery drawer, before pouring myself a cup of the coffee I had warmed up.

Still the phone went on ringing. Maybe fifteen times. I gave up and answered it. I would have preferred not to answer, but it might have been Kumiko.

"Hello," said a woman's voice, one I had never heard before. It belonged neither to Kumiko nor to the strange woman who had called me the other day when I was cooking spaghetti. "I wonder if I might possibly be speaking with Mr Toru Okada?" said the voice, as if its owner were reading a prepared text.

"You are," I said.

"The husband of Kumiko Okada?"

"That's right," I said. "Kumiko Okada is my wife."

"And Mrs Okada's elder brother is Noboru Wataya?"

"Right again," I said, with admirable self-control. "Noboru Wataya is my wife's elder brother."

"Sir, my name is Kano."

I waited for her to go on. The sudden mention of Kumiko's elder brother had put me on my guard. With the blunt end of the pencil that lay by the phone, I scratched the back of my neck. Five seconds or more went by, during which the woman said nothing. No sound of any kind came from the receiver, as if the woman had covered the mouthpiece with her hand and was talking to someone nearby.

"Hello?" I said, concerned now.

"Please forgive me, sir," blurted the woman's voice. "In that case, I must ask your permission to call you at a later time."

"Now wait a minute," I said. "This is –"

At that point she rang off. I stared at the receiver, then put it to my ear again. No doubt about it: the woman had hung up.

Vaguely dissatisfied, I turned to the kitchen table, drank my coffee, and ate my sandwich. Until the moment the telephone rang, I had been thinking of something, but now I couldn't remember what it was. Knife in my right hand poised to cut the sandwich in half, I had definitely been thinking of something. Something important. Something I had been trying unsuccessfully to recall for the longest time. It had come to me at the very moment when I was about to cut the sandwich in two, but now it was gone. Chewing on my sandwich, I tried hard to bring it back. But it wouldn't come. It had returned to that dark region of my mind where it had been living until that moment.

·

I finished eating and was clearing the dishes when the phone rang again. This time I took it right away.

Again I heard a woman saying "Hello", but this time it was Kumiko.

"How are you?" she asked. "Finished lunch?"

"Yup. What did you have?"

"Nothing," she said. "Too busy. I'll probably buy myself a sandwich later. What did you have?"

I described my sandwich.

"I see," she said, without a hint of envy. "Oh, by the way, I forgot to tell you this morning. You're going to get a call from a Miss Kano."

"She already called," I said. "A few minutes ago. All she did was mention our names – mine and yours and your brother's – and hang up. Didn't said what she wanted. What was that all about?"

"She hung up?"

"Said she'd call again."

"Well, when she does, I want you to do whatever she asks. This is really important. I think you'll have to go and see her."

"When? Today?"

"What's wrong? Do you have something planned? Are you supposed to be seeing someone?"

"Nope. No plans." Not yesterday, not today, not tomorrow: no plans at all. "But who is this Kano woman? And what does she want with me? I'd like to have some idea before she calls again. If it's about a job for me connected with your brother, forget it. I don't want to have anything to do with him. You know that."

"No, it has nothing to do with a job," she said, with a hint of annoyance. "It's about the cat."

"The cat?"

"Sorry, I've got to run. Somebody's waiting for me. I really shouldn't have taken the time to call. Like I said, I haven't even had lunch. I'll get back to you as soon as I'm free."

"Look, I know how busy you are, but give me a break. I want to know what's going on. What's with the cat? Is this Kano woman –"

"Just do what she tells you, will you, please? Understand? This is serious. I want you to stay at home and wait for her call. Must go."

And she went.

•

When the phone rang at 2.30, I was napping on the couch. At first I thought it was the alarm clock. I reached out to push the button, but the clock was not there. I wasn't in bed but on the couch, and it wasn't morning but afternoon. I got up and went to the phone.

"Hello?" I said.

"Hello," said a woman's voice. It was the woman who had called in the morning. "Mr Toru Okada?"

"That's me. Toru Okada."

"Sir, my name is Kano," she said.

"The lady who called before."

"That is correct. I am afraid I was terribly rude. But tell me, Mr Okada, would you by any chance be free this afternoon?"

"You might say that."

"Well, in that case, I know this is terribly sudden, but do you think it might be possible for us to meet?"

"When? Today? Now?"

"Yes."

I looked at my watch. Not that I had to – I had looked at it thirty seconds earlier – but just to make sure. And it was still 2.30.

"Will it take long?" I asked.

"Not so very long, I think. I could be wrong, though. Just at this moment, it is difficult for me to say with complete accuracy. I am sorry."

No matter how long it might take, I had no choice. Kumiko had told me to do as the woman said: that it was serious. If she said it was serious, then it was serious, and I had better do as I was told.

"I see," I said. "Where should we meet?"

"Would you by any chance be acquainted with the Pacific Hotel, across from Shinagawa Station?"

"I would."

"There is a tearoom on the first floor. I shall be waiting there for you at 4 o'clock if that would be all right with you, sir."

"Fine," I said.

"I am thirty-one years old, and I shall be wearing a red vinyl hat."

Terrific. There was something weird about the way this woman talked, something that confused me for a moment. But I could not have said exactly what made it so weird. Nor was there any law against a thirty-one-year-old woman wearing a red vinyl hat.

"I see," I said. "I'm sure I'll find you."

"I wonder, Mr Okada, if you would be so kind as to tell me of any external distinguishing characteristics of your own."

I tried to think of any "external distinguishing characteristics" I might have. Did I have any?

"I'm thirty, I'm five foot nine, ten stone, short hair, no glasses." It occurred to me as I listed these that they hardly constituted external distinguishing characteristics. There could be fifty such men in the Pacific Hotel tearoom. I had been there before, and it was a big place. She needed something more distinctive. But I couldn't think of anything. Which is not to say that I didn't have any distinguishing characteristics. I owned a signed copy of Miles Davis's *Sketches of Spain*. I had a slow resting pulse rate: forty-seven normally, and no higher than seventy with a high fever. I was out of work. I knew the names of all the brothers Karamazov. But none of these characteristics was external.

"What might you be wearing?" she asked.

"I don't know," I said. "I haven't decided yet. This is so sudden."

"Then please wear a polka-dot tie," she said decisively. "Do you think you might have a polka-dot tie, sir?"

"I think I do," I said. I had a navy-blue tie with tiny cream polka dots. Kumiko had given it to me for my birthday a few years earlier.

"Please be so kind as to wear it, then," she said. "Thank you for agreeing to meet me at 4 o'clock." And she hung up.

•

I opened the wardrobe and looked for my polka-dot tie. There was no sign of it on the tie rack. I looked in all the drawers. I looked in all the storage boxes in the wardrobe. No polka-dot tie. There was no way that tie could be in our house without my finding it. Kumiko was such a perfectionist when it came to the arrangement of our clothes, my tie couldn't possibly be in a place other than where it was normally kept. And in fact, I found everything – both her clothes and mine – in perfect order. My shirts were neatly folded in the drawer where they belonged. My sweaters were in boxes so full of mothballs my eyes hurt just from opening the lid. One box contained the clothing she had worn at school: a navy uniform, a flowered minidress, preserved like photos in an old album. What was the point of keeping such things? Perhaps she had simply brought them with her because she hadn't found a suitable opportunity to get rid of them. Or maybe she was planning to send them to Bangladesh. Or donate them oneday as cultural artifacts. Anyway, my polka-dot tie was nowhere to be found.

Hand on the wardrobe door, I tried to recall the last time I had worn the tie. It was a rather stylish tie, in very good taste, but a bit too much for the office. If I had worn it to the firm, somebody would have gone on and on about it at lunch, praising the colour or its sharp looks. Which would have been a kind of warning. In the firm I worked for, it was not good to be complimented on your choice of tie. So I had never worn it there. Rather, I put it on for more private – if somewhat formal – occasions: a concert, or dinner at a good restaurant, when Kumiko wanted us to "dress properly" (not that there were so many such occasions). The tie went well with my navy suit, and she was very fond of it. Still, I couldn't recall when I had last worn it.

I scanned the contents of the wardrobe again and gave up. For one reason or another, the polka-dot tie had disappeared. Oh, well. I put on my navy suit with a blue shirt and a striped tie. I wasn't too worried. She might not be able to spot me, but all I had to do was look for a thirtyish woman in a red vinyl hat.

Dressed to go out, I sat on the sofa, staring at the wall. It had been a long time since I last wore a suit. In normal circumstances, this three-season navy suit would have been a bit too heavy for this time of year, but that particular day was a rainy one, and there was a chill in the air. It was the very suit I had worn on my last day of work (in April). Suddenly it occurred to me that there might be something in one of the pockets. In the inside breast pocket I found a receipt with a date from last autumn. It was some kind of taxi receipt, one I could have been reimbursed for at the office. Now, though, it was too late. I crumpled it up and threw it into the wastebasket.

I had not worn this suit once since resigning, two months earlier. Now, after such a long interval, I felt as if I were in the grip of a foreign substance. It was heavy and stiff, and seemed not to match the contours of my body. I stood and walked around the room, stopping in front of the mirror to yank at the sleeves and the coat-tails in an attempt to make it fit better. I stretched out my arms, took a deep breath, and bent forward at the waist, checking to see if my physical shape might have changed in the past two months. I sat on the sofa again, but still I felt uncomfortable.

Until this spring, I had commuted to work every day in a suit without its ever feeling strange. My firm had had a rather strict dress code, requiring even low-ranking clerks such as myself to wear suits. I had thought nothing of it.

Now, however, just sitting on the couch in a suit felt like an immoral act, like faking one's curriculum vitae or dressing as a woman. Overcome with something very like a guilty conscience, I found it more and more difficult to breathe.

I went to the front hall, took my brown shoes from their place on the shelf, and squeezed myself into them with a shoehorn. A thin film of dust clung to them.

·

As it turned out, I didn't have to find the woman. She found me. When I arrived at the tearoom, I did a quick circuit, looking for the red hat. There were no women with red hats. My watch showed ten minutes to four. I took a seat, drank the water they brought me, and ordered a cup of coffee. No sooner had the waitress left my table than I heard a woman behind me saying, "You must be Mr Toru Okada." Surprised, I spun around. Not three minutes had gone by since my survey of the room.

Under a white jacket she wore a yellow silk blouse, and on her head was a red vinyl hat. By reflex, I stood and faced her. "Beautiful" was a word that might well have been applied to her. At least she was far more beautiful than I had imagined from her telephone voice. She had a slim, lovely build and was sparing in her use of make-up. She knew how to dress – except for the red hat. Her jacket and blouse were finely tailored. On the collar of the jacket shone a gold brooch in the shape of a feather. She could have been taken for a corporate secretary. Why, after having lavished such care on the rest of her outfit, she would have topped it off with that inappropriate red vinyl hat was beyond me. Maybe she always wore it to help people spot her in situations like this. In that case, it was not a bad idea. If the point was to have her stand out in a room full of strangers, it certainly did the job.

She took the seat across the table from mine, and I sat down again.

"I'm amazed you knew it was me," I said. "I couldn't find my polka-dot tie. I *know* I've got it somewhere, but it just wouldn't turn up. Which is why I wore this striped one. I thought I'd find you, but how did you know it was me?"

"Of course I knew it was you," she said, putting her white patent-leather bag on the table. She took off her red vinyl hat and placed it over the bag, covering it from view. I had the feeling she was about to perform a magic trick: when she lifted the hat, the bag would have vanished.

"But I was wearing the wrong tie," I protested.

"The wrong tie?" She glanced at my tie with a puzzled expression, as if to say, What is this odd person talking about? Then she nodded. "It doesn't matter. Please don't be concerned."

There was something strange about her eyes. They had a mysterious lack of depth. They were lovely eyes, but they did not seem to be looking at anything. They were all surface, like glass eyes. But of course they were not glass eyes. They moved, and their lids blinked.

How had she been able to pick me out of the crowd in this busy tearoom? Virtually every chair in the place was taken, and many of them were occupied by men my age. I wanted to ask her for an explanation, but I restrained myself. Better not raise irrelevant issues.

She called to a passing waiter and asked for a Perrier. They had no Perrier, he said, but he could bring her tonic water. She thought about this for a moment and accepted his suggestion. While she waited for her tonic water to arrive, she said nothing, and I did the same.

At one point, she lifted her red hat and opened the clasp of the pocket-book underneath. From the bag she removed a glossy black leather case, somewhat smaller than a cassette tape. It was a business card holder. Like the bag, it had a clasp – the first card holder I had ever seen with a clasp. She drew a card from the case and handed it to me. I reached into my breast pocket for one of my own cards, only then realizing that I did not have any with me.

Her name card was made of thin plastic, and it seemed to carry a light fragrance of incense. When I brought it closer to my nose, the smell grew more distinct. No doubt about it: it was incense. The card bore a single line of small black letters:

```
                    Malta Kano
```

Malta? I turned the card over. It was blank.

While I sat there wondering about the meaning of this name card, the waiter came and placed an ice-filled glass in front of her, then filled it halfway with tonic water. The glass had a wedge of lemon in it. The waitress came with a silver-coloured coffeepot on her tray. She placed a cup in front of me and filled it with coffee. With the furtive movements of someone slipping an unlucky shrine fortune into someone else's hand, she eased the bill onto the table and left.

"It's blank," Malta Kano said to me.

I was still staring at the back of her name card.

"Just my name. There is no need for me to include my address or telephone number. No one ever calls me. I am the one who makes the calls."

"I see," I said. This meaningless response hovered in the air above the table like the floating island in *Gulliver's Travels*.

Holding her glass with both hands, she took one tiny sip through a straw. The hint of a frown crossed her face, after which she thrust the glass aside, as if she had lost all interest in it.

"Malta is not my real name," said Malta Kano. "The Kano is real, but the Malta is a professional name I took from the island of Malta. Have you ever been to Malta, Mr Okada?"

I said I had not. I had never been to Malta, and I had no plans to go to Malta in the near future. It had never even crossed my mind to go there. All I knew about Malta was the Herb Alpert performance of "The Sands of Malta", an authentic stinker of a song.

"I once lived in Malta," she said. "For three years. The water there is terrible. Undrinkable. Like diluted seawater. And the bread there is salty. Not because they put salt in it, but because the water they make it with is salty. The bread is not bad, though. I rather like Malta's bread."

I nodded and sipped my coffee.

"As bad as it tastes, the water from one particular place on Malta has a wonderful influence on the body's elements. It is very special – even mystical – water, and it is available only in one place on the island. The spring is in the mountains, and you have to climb several hours from a village at the base to get there. The water cannot be transported from the spring. If it is taken elsewhere, it loses its power. The only way you can drink it is to go there yourself. It is mentioned in documents from the time of the Crusades. They called it spirit water. Allen Ginsberg once came there to drink it. So did Keith Richard. I lived there for three years, in the little village at the foot of the mountain. I grew vegetables and learned to weave. I climbed to the spring every day and drank the special water. From 1976 to 1979. Once, for a whole week, I drank only that water and ate no food. You must not put anything but that water in your mouth for an entire week. This is a kind of discipline that is required there. I believe it can be called a religious austerity. In this way you purify your body. For me, it was a truly wonderful experience. This is how I came to choose the name Malta when I returned to Japan."

"May I ask what your profession is?"

She shook her head. "It is not my profession, properly speaking. I do not take money for what I do. I am a consultant. I talk with people about the elements of the body. I am also engaged in research on water that has beneficial effects on the elements of the body. Making money is not a problem for me. I have whatever assets I need. My father is a doctor, and he has placed stocks and shares in a trust for my younger sister and myself. An accountant manages them for us. They produce a decent income each year. I have also written several books that bring in a little income. My work on the elements of the body is an entirely nonprofit-making activity. Which is why my card bears neither address nor telephone number. I am the one who makes the calls."

I nodded, but this was simply a physical movement of the head: I had no idea what she was talking about. I could understand the words she spoke, but it was impossible for me to grasp their overall meaning.

Elements of the body?

Allen Ginsberg?

I became increasingly uneasy. I'm not one of those people with special intuitive gifts, but the more time I spent with this woman, the more I seemed to smell trouble.

"You'll have to pardon me," I said, "but I wonder if I could ask you to explain things from the beginning, step by step. I talked to my wife a little while ago, and all she said was that I should see you and talk to you about our missing cat. To be quite honest, I don't really see the point of what you've just been telling me. Does it have anything to do with the cat?"

"Yes, indeed," she said. "But before I go into that, there is something I would like you to know, Mr Okada."

She opened the metal clasp of her pocketbook again and took out a white envelope. In the envelope was a photograph, which she handed to me. "My sister," she said. It was a colour snapshot of two women. One was Malta Kano, and in the photo, too, she was wearing a hat – a yellow knit hat. Again there was an ominous mismatch with her outfit. Her sister – I assumed this was the younger sister whom she had mentioned – wore a pastel-coloured suit and matching hat of the kind that had been popular in the early sixties. I seemed to recall that such colours had been known as "sherbet tone" back then. One thing was certain, however: these sisters were fond of hats. The hairstyle of the younger one was precisely that of Jacqueline Kennedy in her White House days, loaded with hair spray. She wore a little too much make-up, but she could nonetheless be described as beautiful. She was in her early to mid-twenties. I handed the photo back to Malta Kano, who returned it to its envelope and the envelope to the handbag, shutting the clasp.

"My sister is five years my junior," she said. "She was defiled by Noboru Wataya. Violently raped."

Terrific. I wanted to get the hell out of there. But I couldn't just stand up and walk away. I took a handkerchief from my jacket pocket, wiped my mouth with it, and returned it to the same pocket. Then I cleared my throat.

"That's terrible," I said. "I don't know anything about this, but if he did hurt your sister, you have my heartfelt condolences. I must tell you, however, that my brother-in-law and I have virtually nothing to do with each other. So if you are expecting some kind of –"

"Not at all, Mr Okada," she declared. "I do not hold you responsible in any way. If there is someone who should be held responsible for what happened, that person is myself. For being inattentive. For not having protected her as I should have. Unfortunately, certain events made it impossible for me to do so. These things can happen, Mr Okada. As you know, we live in a violent and chaotic world. And within this world, there are places that are still more violent, still more chaotic. Do you understand what I mean, Mr Okada? What has happened has happened. My sister will recover from her injuries, from her defilement. She must. Thank goodness they were not fatal. As I have said to my sister, the potential was there for something much, much worse to happen. What I am most concerned about is the elements of her body."

"Elements of her body," I repeated. This "elements of the body" business was obviously a consistent theme of hers.

"I cannot explain to you in detail how all these circumstances are related. It would be a very long and complicated story, and although I mean no disrespect to you when I say this, it would be virtually impossible for you at this stage, Mr Okada, to attain an accurate understanding of the true meaning of that story, which involves a world that we deal with on a professional basis. I did not invite you here in order to voice any complaint in that regard. You are, of course, in no way responsible for what has happened. I simply wanted you to know that, although it may be a temporary condition, my sister's elements have been defiled by Mr Wataya. You and she are likely to have some form of contact with each other sometime in the future. She is my assistant, as I mentioned earlier. At such time, it would be best for you to be aware of what occurred between her and Mr Wataya and to realize that these things can happen."

A short silence followed. Malta Kano looked at me as if to say, Please think about what I have told you. And so I did. About Noboru Wataya's having raped Malta Kano's sister. About the relationship between that and the elements of the body. And about the relationship between those and the disappearance of our cat.

"Do I understand you to be saying," I ventured, "that neither you nor your sister intends to bring a formal complaint on this matter . . . to go to the police . . . ?"

"No, of course we will do no such thing," said Malta Kano, her face expressionless. "Properly speaking, we do not hold anyone responsible. We would simply like to have a more precise idea of what caused such a thing to happen. Until we solve this question, there is a real possibility that something even worse could occur."

I felt relief on hearing this. Not that it would have bothered me in the least if Noboru Wataya had been convicted of rape and sent to prison. It couldn't happen to a nicer guy. But Kumiko's brother was a rather well-known figure. His arrest and trial would be certain to make the headlines, and that would be a terrible shock for Kumiko. If only for my own mental well-being, I preferred the whole thing to go away.

"Rest assured," said Malta Kano, "I asked to see you today purely about the missing cat. That was the matter about which Mr Wataya sought my advice. Mrs Okada consulted him on the matter, and he in turn consulted me."

That explained a lot. Malta Kano was some kind of clairvoyant or medium, and they had consulted her on the whereabouts of the cat. The Wataya family was into this kind of stuff – divination and house "physiognomy" and such. That was fine with me: people were free to believe anything they liked. But why did he have to go and rape the younger sister of his spiritual counsellor? Why stir up a lot of pointless trouble?

"Is that your area of expertise?" I asked. "Helping people find things?"

She stared at me with those depthless eyes of hers, eyes that looked as if they were staring into the window of a vacant house. Judging from their expression, she had failed to grasp the meaning of my question.

Without answering, she said, "You live in a very strange place, don't you, Mr Okada?"

"I do?" I said. "Strange in what way?"

Instead of replying, she pushed her almost untouched glass of tonic water another six or eight inches away from herself. "Cats are very sensitive creatures, you know."

Another silence descended on the two of us.

"So our place is strange, and cats are sensitive animals," I said. "OK. But we've lived there a long time – the two of us and the cat. Why now, all of a sudden, did it decide to leave us? Why didn't it leave before?"

"That I cannot tell you. Perhaps the flow has changed. Perhaps something has obstructed the flow."

"The flow."

"I do not know yet whether your cat is still alive, but I can be certain of one thing: it is no longer in the vicinity of your house. You will never find the cat in that neighbourhood."

I lifted my cup and took a sip of my now lukewarm coffee. Beyond the tearoom windows, a misty rain was falling. The sky was covered over with dark, low-hanging clouds. A sad procession of people and umbrellas climbed up and down the footbridge outside.

"Give me your hand," she said.

I placed my right hand on the table, palm up, assuming she was planning to read my palm. Instead, she stretched her hand out and put her palm against mine. Then she closed her eyes, remaining utterly still, as if silently rebuking a faithless lover. The waitress came and refilled my cup, pretending not to notice what Malta Kano and I were doing. People at neighbouring tables stole glances in our direction. I kept hoping all the while that there were no acquaintances of mine in the vicinity.

"I want you to picture to yourself one thing you saw before you came here today," said Malta Kano.

"One thing?" I asked.

"Just one thing."

I thought of the flowered minidress that I had seen in Kumiko's clothes storage box. Why that of all things happened to pop into my mind I have no idea. It just did.

We kept our hands together like that for another five minutes – five minutes that felt very long to me, not so much because I was being stared at by people as that the touch of Malta Kano's hand had something unsettling about it. It was a small hand, neither hot nor cold. It had neither the intimate touch of a lover's hand nor the functional touch of a doctor's. It had the same effect on me as her eyes had, turning me into a vacant house. I felt empty: no furniture, no curtains, no rugs. Just an empty container. Eventually, Malta Kano withdrew her hand from mine and took several deep breaths. Then she nodded several times.

"Mr Okada," she said, "I believe that you are entering a phase of your life in which many different things will occur. The disappearance of your cat is only the beginning."

"Different things," I said. "Good things or bad things?"

She tilted her head in thought. "Good things *and* bad things. Bad things that seem good at first, and good things that seem bad at first."

"That sounds very general," I said. "Don't you have any more concrete information?"

"Yes, I suppose what I am saying does sound unspecific," said Malta Kano. "But after all, Mr Okada, when one is speaking of the essence of things, it often happens that one can only speak in generalities. Concrete things capture one's attention, but they are often little more than trivia. Side shows. The more one tries to see into the distance, the more generalized things become."

I nodded silently – without the slightest inkling of what she was talking about.

"Do I have your permission to call you again?" she asked.

"Sure," I said, though in fact I had no wish to be called by anyone. "Sure" was about the only answer I could give.

She snatched her red vinyl hat from the table, took the handbag that had been hidden beneath it, and stood up. Uncertain as to how I should respond, I remained seated.

"I do have one small bit of information that I can share with you," Malta Kano said, looking down at me, after she had put on her red hat. "You will find your polka-dot tie, but not in your house."

4

High Towers and Deep Wells
(Or, Far from Nomonhan)

•

Back at home, I found Kumiko in a good mood. A *very* good mood. It was almost 6 o'clock by the time I arrived home after seeing Malta Kano, which meant I had no time to fix a proper dinner. Instead, I prepared a simple meal from what I found in the freezer, and we each had a beer. She talked about work, as she always did when she was in a good mood: whom she had seen at the office, what she had done, which of her colleagues had talent and which did not. That kind of thing.

I listened, making suitable responses. I heard no more than half of what she was saying. Not that I disliked listening to her talk about these things. Contents of the conversation aside, I loved watching her at the dinner table as she talked with enthusiasm about her work. This, I told myself, was "home". We were doing a proper job of carrying out the responsibilities that we had been assigned to perform at home. She was talking about her work, and I, after having prepared dinner, was listening to her talk. This was very different from the image of home that I had imagined before marriage. But this was *the home I had chosen*. I had had a home, of course, when I was a child. But it was not one I had chosen for myself. I had been born into it, presented with it as an established fact. Now, however, I lived in a world that I had chosen through an act of will. It was my home. It might not be perfect, but the fundamental stance I adopted with regard to my home was to accept it, problems and all, because it was something I myself had chosen. If it had problems, these were almost certainly problems that had originated within me.

"So what about the cat?" she asked. I summarized for her my meeting with Malta Kano in the hotel in Shinagawa. I told her about my polka-dot tie: that there had been no sign of it in the wardrobe. That Malta Kano had nonetheless managed to find me in the crowded tearoom. That she had a unique way of dressing and of speaking, which I described. Kumiko enjoyed hearing about Malta Kano's red vinyl hat, but when I was unable to provide a clear answer regarding the whereabouts of our lost cat, she was deeply disappointed.

"Then she doesn't know where the cat is either?" Kumiko demanded. "The best she could do was tell you it is no longer in our neighbourhood?"

"That's about it," I said. I decided not to mention anything about the "obstructed flow" of the place we lived in or that this could have a connection with the disappearance of the cat. I knew it would bother Kumiko, and for my own part, I had no desire to increase the number of things we had to worry about. We would have had a real problem if Kumiko insisted on moving because this was a "bad place". Given our present economic situation, it would have been impossible for us to move.

"That's what she tells me," I said. "The cat is not around here any more."

"Which means it will never come home?"

"I don't know," I said. "She was vague about everything. All she came up with were hints. She did say she'd get in touch with me when she found out more, though."

"Do you believe her?"

"Who knows? I don't know anything about this kind of stuff."

I poured myself some more beer and watched the head settle. Kumiko rested her elbow on the table, chin in hand.

"She must have told you she won't accept payment or gifts of any kind," she said.

"Uh-huh. That's certainly a plus," I said. "So what's the problem? She won't take our money, she won't steal our souls, she won't snatch the princess away. We've got nothing to lose."

"I want you to understand one thing," said Kumiko. "That cat is very important to me. Or should I say to *us*. We found it the week after we got married. Together. You remember?"

"Of course I do."

"It was so tiny, and soaking wet in the pouring rain. I went to meet you at the station with an umbrella. Poor little baby. We saw him on the way home. Somebody had thrown him into a beer crate next to the off-licence. He's my very first cat. He's important to me, a kind of symbol. I can't lose him."

"Don't worry. I know that."

"So where *is* he? He's been missing for ten days now. That's why I called my brother. I thought he might know a medium or clairvoyant, somebody who could find a missing cat. I know you don't like to ask my brother for anything, but he's followed in my father's footsteps. He knows a lot about these things."

"Ah, yes, the Wataya family tradition," I said as cool as an evening breeze across an inlet. "But what's the connection between Noboru Wataya and this woman?"

Kumiko shrugged. "I'm sure she's just somebody he happened to meet. He seems to have so many contacts these days."

"I'll bet."

"He says she possesses amazing powers but that she's pretty strange." Kumiko poked at her macaroni casserole. "What was her name again?"

"Malta Kano," I said. "She practised some kind of religious austerities on Malta."

"That's it. Malta Kano. What did you think of her?"

"Hard to say." I looked at my hands, resting on the table. "At least she wasn't boring. And that's a good thing. I mean, the world's full of things we can't explain, and somebody's got to fill that vacuum. Better to have somebody who isn't boring than somebody who is. Right? Like Mr Honda, for example."

Kumiko laughed out loud at the mention of Mr Honda. "He was a wonderful old man, don't you think? I liked him a lot."

"Me too," I said.

•

For about a year after we were married, Kumiko and I used to visit the home of old Mr Honda once a month. A practitioner of spirit possession, he was one of the Wataya family's favourite medium types, but he was terrifically hard of hearing. Even with his hearing aid, he could only just make out what we said to him. We had to shout so loud our voices would rattle the shoji paper. I used to wonder if he could hear what the spirits said to him if he was so hard of hearing. But perhaps it worked the other way: the worse your ears, the better you could hear the words of the spirits. He had lost his hearing in the war. A non-commissioned officer with Japan's Manchurian garrison, the Kwantung Army, he had suffered burst eardrums when an artillery shell or a hand grenade or something exploded nearby during a battle with a combined Soviet–Outer Mongolian unit at Nomonhan on the border between Outer Mongolia and Manchuria.

Our visits to Mr Honda's place were not prompted by a belief in his spiritual powers. I had never been interested in such things, and Kumiko placed far less trust in supernatural matters than either her parents or her brother. She did have a touch of superstition, and she could be upset by an ominous prognostication, but she never went out of her way to involve herself in spiritual affairs.

The only reason we went to see Mr Honda was because her father ordered us to. It was the one condition he set for us to marry. True, it was a rather bizarre condition, but we went along with it to avoid complications. Neither of us had expected an easy time from her family. Her father was a government official. The younger son of a not very well-to-do farm family in Niigata, he had attended the prestigious Tokyo University on a scholarship, graduated with honours, and become an elite member of the Ministry of Transport. This was all very admirable. But as is so often the case with men who have made it like this, he was arrogant and self-righteous. Accustomed to giving orders, he harboured not the slightest doubt concerning the values of the world to which he belonged. For him, hierarchy was everything. He bowed to superior authority without question, and he trampled those beneath him without hesitation. Neither Kumiko nor I believed that a man like that would accept a poor, twenty-four-year-old nobody like me, without position or pedigree, decent grades or future promise, as a marriage partner for his daughter. We thought that after her parents turned us down, we'd get married on our own and have nothing to do with them.

Still, I did the right thing. I observed form and went to ask Kumiko's parents for her hand in marriage. To say that their reception was cool would be an understatement. The doors of all the world's refrigerators seemed to have been thrown open at once.

That they gave us their permission in the end – with reluctance, but in a near-miraculous turn of events – was thanks entirely to Mr Honda. He asked them everything they had learned about me, and in the end he declared that if their daughter was going to get married, I was the best possible partner for her; that if she wanted to marry me, they could only invite terrible consequences by opposing the match. Kumiko's parents had absolute faith in Mr Honda at the time, and so there was nothing for it but to accept me as their daughter's husband.

I was always the outsider, though, the uninvited guest. Kumiko and I would visit their home and have dinner with them twice a month with mechanical regularity. This was a truly loathsome experience, situated at the precise midpoint between meaningless mortification of the flesh and brutal torture. Throughout the meal, I had the sense that their dining-room table was as long as a railway station. They would be eating and talking about something way down at the other end, and I was too far away for them to see. This went on for a year, until Kumiko's father and I had a violent argument, after which we never saw each other again. The relief this gave me bordered on ecstasy. Nothing so consumes a person as meaningless exertion.

For a time after our marriage, though, I did exert myself to maintain good relations between us. And without a doubt, the least painful of my exertions were those monthly meetings with Mr Honda.

All payments to Mr Honda were made by Kumiko's father. We merely had to visit Mr Honda's home in Meguro once a month with a big bottle of sake, listen to what he had to tell us, and go home. Simple.

We took to Mr Honda straight away. He was a nice old man, whose face would light up whenever he saw the sake we had brought him. We liked everything about him – except perhaps the way he left his television on full blast because he was so hard of hearing.

We always went to his house in the morning. Winter and summer, he sat with his legs in the sunken hearth. In winter he would have a quilt wrapped around his waist to hold in the heat of the charcoal fire. In summer he used neither quilt nor fire. He was apparently a rather famous fortune-teller, but he lived very simply – ascetically even. His house was small, with a tiny entrance hall barely big enough for one person at a time to tie or untie a pair of shoes. The tatami mats on his floors were badly worn, and cracked windowpanes were patched with tape. Across the way stood a garage, where someone was always yelling at the top of his lungs. Mr Honda wore a kimono that was a cross between a sleeping robe and a traditional workman's jacket. It gave no evidence of having been washed in the recent past. He lived alone and had a woman come in to do the cooking and cleaning. For some reason, though, he never let her launder his robe. Scraggly white whiskers hung on his sunken cheeks.

If there was anything in Mr Honda's house that could be called impressive, it was the huge colour television set. In such a tiny house, its gigantic presence was overwhelming. It was always tuned to the government-supported NHK network. Whether this was because he loved NHK, or he couldn't be bothered to change the channel, or this was a special set that received only NHK, I had no way of telling, but NHK was all he ever watched.

Instead of a flower arrangement or a calligraphic scroll, the living room's ceremonial alcove was filled with this huge television set, and Mr Honda always sat facing it, stirring the divining sticks on the table above his sunken hearth while NHK continued to blast out cooking shows, bonsai care instructions, news updates and political discussions.

"Legal work might be the wrong thing for you, son," said Mr Honda one day, either to me or to someone standing twenty yards behind me.

"It might?"

"Yes, it might. The law presides over things of this world, in the end. The world where shadow is shadow and light is light, yin is yin and yang is yang, I'm me and he's him. 'I am me and / He is him: / Autumn eve.' But *you* don't belong to that world, son. The world you belong to is above that or below that."

"Which is better?" I asked, out of simple curiosity. "Above or below?"

"It's not that either one is better," he said. After a brief coughing fit, he spat a glob of phlegm onto a tissue and studied it closely before crumpling the tissue and throwing it into a wastebasket. "It's not a question of better or worse. The point is, not to resist the flow. You go up when you're supposed to go up and down when you're supposed to go down. When you're supposed to go up, find the highest tower and climb to the top. When you're supposed to go down, find the deepest well and go down to the bottom. When there's no flow, stay still. If you resist the flow, everything dries up. If everything dries up, the world is darkness. 'I am he and / He is me: / Spring nightfall.' Abandon the self, and there you are."

"Is this one of those times when there's no flow?" Kumiko asked.

"How's that?"

"IS THIS ONE OF THOSE TIMES WHEN THERE'S NO FLOW?" Kumiko shouted.

"No flow now," Mr Honda said, nodding to himself. "Now's the time to stay still. Don't do anything. Just be careful of water. Sometime in the future, this young fellow could experience real suffering in connection with water. Water that's missing from where it's supposed to be. Water that's present where it's not supposed to be. In any case, be very, very careful of water."

Kumiko, beside me, was nodding with the utmost gravity, but I could see she was struggling not to laugh.

"What kind of water?" I asked.

"I don't know," said Mr Honda. "Water."

On the TV, some university professor was saying that people's chaotic use of Japanese grammar corresponded precisely to the chaos in their lifestyles. "Properly speaking, of course, we cannot call it chaos. Grammar is like the air: someone higher up might try to set rules for its use, but people won't necessarily follow them." It sounded interesting, but Mr Honda just went on talking about water.

"To tell you the truth, I suffered over water," he said. "There was no water in Nomonhan. The front line was a mess, and supplies were cut off. No water. No rations. No bandages. No bullets. It was awful. The big boys in the rear were interested in only one thing: seizing territory as fast as possible. Nobody was thinking about supplies. For three days, I had almost no water. If you left a flannel out, it'd be wet with dew in the morning. You could wring out a few drops to drink, but that was it. There was no other water at all. I wanted to die, it was so bad. Being thirsty like that is the worst thing in the world. I was ready to run out and stop a bullet. Men who got shot in the stomach would scream for water. Some of them went crazy with the thirst. It was a living hell. We could see a big river flowing right in front of us, with all the water anybody could ever drink. But we couldn't get to it. Between us and the river was a line of huge Soviet tanks with flamethrowers. Machine gun emplacements bristled like pincushions. Sharpshooters lined the high ground. They sent up flares at night. All we had was Model 38 infantry rifles and twenty-five bullets each. Still, most of my buddies went to the river. They couldn't take it. Not one of them made it back. They were all killed. So you see, when you're supposed to stay still, stay still."

He pulled out a tissue, blew his nose loudly, and examined the results before crumpling the tissue and throwing it into the wastebasket.

"It can be hard to wait for the flow to start," he said, "but when you have to wait, you have to wait. In the meantime, assume you're dead."

"You mean I should stay dead for now?" I asked.

"How's that?"

"YOU MEAN I SHOULD STAY DEAD FOR NOW?"

"That's it, son. 'Dying is the only way / For you to float free: / Nomonhan.' "

He went on talking about Nomonhan for another hour. We just sat there and listened. We had been ordered to "receive his teaching", but in a year of monthly visits to his place, he had almost never had a "teaching" for us to "receive". He rarely performed divination. The one thing he talked about was the Nomonhan Incident: how a cannon shell blew off half the skull of the lieutenant next to him, how he leaped onto a Soviet tank and torched it with a Molotov cocktail, how they cornered and shot a downed Soviet pilot. All his stories were interesting, even thrilling, but as with anything else, if you hear them seven or eight times and they tend to lose some of their lustre. Nor did he simply "tell" his stories. He screamed them. He could have been standing on a cliff edge on a windy day, shouting to us across a chasm. It was like watching an old Kurosawa movie from the very front row of a run-down cinema. Neither of us could hear much of anything for a while after we left his house.

Still, we – or at least I – enjoyed listening to Mr Honda's stories. Most of them were bloody, but coming from the mouth of a dying old man in a dirty old robe, the details of battle lost the ring of reality. They sounded more like fairy tales. Almost half a century earlier, Mr Honda's unit had fought a ferocious battle over a barren patch of wilderness on the Manchurian–Mongolian border. Until I heard about it from Mr Honda, I knew almost nothing about the battle of Nomonhan. And yet it had been a magnificent battle. Almost bare-handed, they had defied the superior Soviet mechanized forces, and they had been crushed. One unit after another had been, annihilated. Some officers had, on their own initiative, ordered their troops to retreat to avoid annihilation; their superiors forced them to commit suicide. Most of the troops captured by the Soviets refused to participate in the postwar exchange of prisoners, because they were afraid of being tried for desertion. These men ended up contributing their bones to the Mongolian earth. Sent home with an honourable discharge after he lost his hearing, Mr Honda became a practitioner of divination.

"It was all to the good," he said. "If my hearing hadn't been ruined, I probably would have died in the South Pacific. That's what happened to most of the troops who survived Nomonhan. Nomonhan was a great embarrassment for the Imperial Army, so they sent the survivors where they were most likely to be killed. The commanding officers who made such a mess of Nomonhan went on to have distinguished careers in central command. Some of the bastards even became politicians after the war. But the guys who fought their hearts out for them were almost all snuffed out."

"Why was Nomonhan such an embarrassment for the army?" I asked. "The troops all fought bravely, and a lot of them died, right? Why were the survivors treated so badly?"

But Mr Honda seemed not to hear my question. He stirred and rattled his divining sticks. "You'd better be careful of water," he said.

And so ended the day's session.

·

After my bust-up with Kumiko's father, we stopped going to Mr Honda's. It was impossible for me to continue visiting him knowing it was being paid for by my father-in-law, and we were in no position to pay him ourselves. We could barely keep our heads above water in those days. In time, we forgot about Mr Honda, just as most busy young people tend to forget about most old people.

·

In bed that night, I went on thinking about Mr Honda. Both he and Malta Kano had spoken to me about water. Mr Honda had warned me to be careful. Malta Kano had undergone austerities on the island of Malta in connection with her research on water. Perhaps it was a coincidence, but both of them had been deeply concerned about water. Now it was starting to worry me. I turned my thoughts to images of the battlefield at Nomonhan: the Soviet tanks and machine gun emplacements, and the river flowing beyond them. The unbearable thirst. In the darkness, I could hear the sound of the river.

"Toru," Kumiko said to me in a tiny voice, "are you awake?"

"Uh-huh."

"About the tie. I've just remembered. I took it to the cleaner's in December. It needed pressing. I suppose I forgot."

"December? Kumiko, that's over six months ago!"

"I know. And you know I never do anything like that, forgetting things. It was such a lovely tie, too." She put her hand on my shoulder. "I took it to the cleaner's by the station. Do you think they still have it?"

"I'll go tomorrow. It's probably there."

"What makes you think so? Six months is a long time. Most cleaners will get rid of things that aren't claimed in three months. They can do that. It's the law. What makes you think it's still there?"

"Malta Kano said I'd find it. Somewhere outside the house."

I could feel her looking at me in the dark.

"You mean you believe what she says?"

"I'm starting to."

"Pretty soon you and my brother might even start seeing eye-to-eye," she said, a note of pleasure in her voice.

"We just might," I said.

I kept thinking about the Nomonhan battlefield after Kumiko fell asleep. The soldiers were all asleep there. The sky overhead was filled with stars, and millions of crickets were chirping. I could hear the river. I fell asleep listening to it flow.

5

Hooked on Lemon Drops

◆

Flightless Bird and Waterless Well

After doing the breakfast dishes, I rode my bike to the cleaner's by the station. The owner – a thin man in his late forties, with deep wrinkles in his forehead – was listening to a tape of the Percy Faith orchestra on a music machine that had been placed on a shelf. It was a large JVC, with some kind of extra woofers attached and a mound of cassette tapes standing by. The orchestra was performing "Tara's Theme", making the most of its lush string arrangement. The owner himself was in the back of the shop, whistling along with the music as he ran a steam iron over a shirt, his movements sharp and energetic. I approached the counter and announced with suitable apologies that I had brought a tie in late last year and forgotten to pick it up. To his peaceful little world at 9.30 in the morning, this must have been tantamount to the arrival of a messenger bearing terrible news in a Greek tragedy.

"No ticket, either, I suppose," he said, in a strange, distant voice. He was talking not to me but to the calendar on the wall by the counter. The photo for June showed the Alps – a green valley, cows grazing, a hard-edged white cloud floating against Mont Blanc or the Matterhorn or wherever. Then he looked at me with an expression on his face that all but said, If you were going to forget the damned thing, you should have *forgotten* it! It was a direct and eloquent look.

"End of the year, huh? That's a toughie. We're talking more than six months ago. All right, I'll have a look, but don't expect me to find it."

He switched off his iron, put it on the ironing board, and, whistling along with the theme from *A Summer Place*, started to rummage through the shelves in the back room.

Back in senior school, I had taken my girlfriend to see *A Summer Place*. It starred Troy Donahue and Sandra Dee. We saw it in a rep cinema in a double bill with Connie Francis's *Follow the Boys*. It had been pretty bad, as far as I could remember, but hearing the music now in a cleaner's, thirteen years later, I could recall only good memories from that time.

"A blue polka-dot tie?" asked the owner. "Name Okada?"

"That's it," I said.

"You're in luck."

•

As soon as I got home, I phoned Kumiko at work. "They had the tie," I said.

"Incredible," she said. "Good for you!"

It sounded artificial, like praise for a son bringing home good marks. This made me feel uneasy. I should have waited until her lunch break to phone.

"I'm so relieved," she said. "But I've got someone on hold right now. Sorry. Could you call me back at noon?"

"That I will," I said.

After hanging up, I went out to the veranda with the morning paper. As always, I lay on my stomach with the job ads spread out before me, taking all the time I needed to read them from one end to the other, the columns filled with incomprehensible codes and clues. The variety of professions in this world was amazing, each assigned its place amidst the paper's neat rows, as on a graveyard map.

As happened each morning, I heard the wind-up bird winding its spring in a treetop somewhere. I closed the paper, sat up with my back against a post, and looked out at the garden. Soon the bird gave its rasping cry once more, a long creaking sound that came from the top of the neighbour's pine tree. I strained to see through the branches, but there was no sign of the bird, only its cry. As always. And so the world had its spring wound for the day.

Just before 10, it started to rain. Not a heavy rain. You couldn't really be sure it was raining, the drops were so fine, but if you looked hard, you could tell. The world existed in two states, raining and non-raining, and there should be a line of demarcation between the two. I remained seated on the veranda for a while, staring at the line that was supposed to be there.

What should I do with the time until lunch? Go for a swim at the nearby municipal pool or to the alley to look for the cat? Leaning against the veranda post, watching the rain fall in the garden, I went back and forth between the two.

Pool.

Cat.

The cat won. Malta Kano had said that the cat was no longer in the neighbourhood. But that morning I had an indefinable urge to go out and look for it. Cat hunting had become a part of my daily routine. And, besides, Kumiko might be cheered to learn that I had given it a try. I put on my light raincoat. I decided not to take an umbrella. I put on my tennis shoes and left the house with the key and a few lemon drops in my coat pocket. I cut across the yard, but just as I set one hand on the breeze-block wall, a phone rang. I stood still, straining my ears, but I couldn't tell whether it was our phone or a neighbour's. The minute you leave your house, all phones sound alike. I gave up and climbed over the wall.

I could feel the soft grass through the thin soles of my tennis shoes. The alley was quieter than usual. I stood still for a while, holding my breath and listening, but I couldn't hear a thing. The phone had stopped ringing. I heard no bird cries or street noises. The sky was painted over, a perfect uniform grey. On days like this the clouds seemed to absorb the sounds from the surface of the earth. And not just sounds. All kinds of things. Perceptions, for example.

Hands shoved into the pockets of my raincoat, I slipped down the narrow alley. Where clothes-drying poles jutted out into the lane, I squeezed sideways between the walls. I passed right beneath the eaves of other houses. In this way I made my silent way down this passage reminiscent of an abandoned canal. My tennis shoes on the grass made no noise at all. The only sound I heard on my brief journey was of a radio playing in one house. It was tuned to a talk show discussing callers' problems. A middle-aged man was complaining to the host about his mother-in-law. From the snatches I caught, the woman was sixty-eight and crazy about horse racing. Once I was past the house, the sound of the radio began to fade until there was nothing left, as if what had gradually faded into nothingness was not only the sound of the radio but the middle-aged man and his horse-obsessed mother-in-law, both of whom must exist somewhere in the world.

I finally reached the vacant house. It stood there, hushed as ever. Against the background of grey, low-hanging clouds, its second-story storm shutters nailed shut, the house loomed as a dark, shadowy presence. It could have been a huge freighter caught on a reef one stormy night long ago and left to rot. If it hadn't been for the increased height of the grass since my last visit, I might have believed that time had stopped in this one particular place. Thanks to the long days of rain, the blades of grass glowed with a deep-green lustre, and they gave off the smell of wildness unique to things that sink their roots into the earth. In the exact centre of this sea of grass stood the bird sculpture, in the very same pose I had seen it in before, with its wings spread, ready to take off. This was one bird that could never take off, of course. I knew that, and the bird knew that. It would go on waiting where it stood until the day it was carted off or smashed to pieces. No other possibilities existed for it to leave this garden. The only thing moving in there was a small white butterfly, fluttering across the grass some weeks out of season. It made uncertain progress, like a searcher who has forgotten what he was searching for. After five minutes of this fruitless hunt, the butterfly went off somewhere.

Sucking on a lemon drop, I leaned against the chain-link fence and looked at the garden. There was no sign of the cat. There was no sign of anything. The place looked like a still, stagnant pool in which some enormous force had blocked the natural flow.

I felt the presence of someone behind me and whirled around. But there was no one. There was only the fence on the other side of the alley, and the small gate in the fence, the gate in which the girl had stood. But it was closed now, and in the yard was no trace of anyone. Everything was damp and silent. And there were the smells. Grass. Rain. My raincoat. The lemon drop under my tongue, half melted. They all came together in a single deep breath. I turned to survey my surroundings once more, but there was no one. Listening hard, I caught the muffled chop of a distant helicopter. People were up there, flying above the clouds. But even that sound drew off into the distance, and silence descended once again.

The chain-link fence surrounding the vacant house had a gate, also of chain link, not surprisingly. I gave it a tentative push. It opened with almost disappointing ease, as if it were urging me to come in. "No problem," it seemed to be telling me. "Just walk right in." I didn't have to rely on the detailed knowledge of the law that I had acquired over eight long years to know that it could be a very serious problem indeed. If a neighbour spotted me in the vacant house and reported me to the police, they would show up and question me. I would say I was looking for my cat; it had disappeared, and I was looking for it all over the neighbourhood. They would demand to know my address and occupation. I would have to tell them I was out of work. That would make them all the more suspicious. They were probably nervous about left-wing terrorists, convinced they were all over Tokyo, with hidden arsenals of guns and homemade bombs. They'd call Kumiko at her office to verify my story. She'd be upset.

Oh, what the hell. I went in, pulling the gate shut behind me. If something was going to happen, let it happen. If something *wanted* to happen, let it happen.

I crossed the garden, scanning the area. My tennis shoes on the grass were as soundless as ever. There were several low fruit trees, the names of which I did not know, and a generous stretch of lawn. It was all overgrown now, hiding everything. Ugly passion flower vines had crawled all over two of the fruit trees, which looked as if they had been strangled to death. The row of osmanthus along the fence had turned a ghastly white under a coating of insects' eggs. A stubborn little fly kept buzzing by my ear for a time.

Passing the stone statue, I walked over to a nested pile of white plastic lawn chairs under the eaves. The topmost chair was filthy, but the next one down was not bad. I dusted it off with my hand and sat on it. The overgrown weeds between here and the fence made it impossible for me to be seen from the alley, and the eaves sheltered me from the rain. I sat and whistled and watched the garden receiving its bounty of fine raindrops. At first I was unaware of what tune I was whistling, but then I realized it was the overture to Rossini's *Thieving Magpie*, the same tune I had been whistling when the strange woman called as I was cooking spaghetti.

Sitting here in the garden like this, with no other people around, looking at the grass and the stone bird, whistling a tune (badly), I had the feeling that I had returned to my childhood. I was in a secret place where no one could see me. This put me in a quiet mood. I felt like throwing a stone – a small stone would be OK – at some target. The stone bird would be a good one. I'd hit it just hard enough to make a little clunk. I used to play by myself a lot like that when I was a kid. I'd set up an empty can, retreat, and throw rocks until the can filled up. I could do it for hours. Just now, though, I didn't have any rocks at my feet. Oh, well. Nowhere has everything you need.

I pulled up my feet, bent my knees, and rested my chin on my hand. Then I closed my eyes. Still no sounds. The darkness behind my closed eyelids was like the cloud-covered sky, but the grey was somewhat deeper. Every few minutes, someone would come and paint over the grey with a different-textured grey – one with a touch of gold or green or red. I was impressed with the variety of greys that existed. Human beings were so strange. All you had to do was sit still for ten minutes, and you could see this amazing variety of greys.

Browsing through my book of grey colour samples, I started whistling again, without a thought in my head.

"Hey," said someone.

I snapped my eyes open. Leaning to the side, I stretched to see the gate above the weed tops. It was open. Wide open. Someone had followed me inside. My heart started pounding.

"Hey," the someone said again. A woman's voice. She stepped out from behind the statue and started towards me. It was the girl who had been sunbathing in the yard across the alley. She wore the same light-blue Adidas T-shirt and shorts. Again she walked with a slight limp. The one thing different from before was that she had taken off her sunglasses.

"What are you doing here?" she asked.

"Looking for the cat," I said.

"Are you sure? It doesn't look that way to me. You're just sitting there and whistling with your eyes closed. It'd be hard to find much of anything that way, don't you think?"

I felt myself blushing.

"It doesn't bother me," she went on, "but somebody who doesn't know you might think you were some kind of pervert." She paused. "You're not a pervert, are you?"

"Probably not," I said.

She approached me and undertook a careful study of the nested lawn chairs, choosing one without too much dirt on it and doing one more close inspection before setting it on the ground and lowering herself into it.

"And your whistling's terrible," she said. "I don't know the tune, but it had no melody at all. You're not gay, are you?"

"Probably not," I said. "Why?"

"Somebody told me gays are lousy whistlers. Is that true?"

"Who knows? It sounds like nonsense."

"Anyway, I don't care even if you are gay or a pervert. By the way, what's your name? I don't know what to call you."

"Toru Okada," I said.

She repeated my name to herself several times. "Not much of a name, is it?" she said.

"Maybe not," I said. "I've always thought it sounded like some prewar foreign minister: Toru Okada. See?"

"That doesn't mean anything to me. I hate history. It's my worst subject. Anyhow, never mind. Haven't you got a nickname? Something easier than Toru Okada?"

I couldn't recall ever having had a nickname. Not once in my life. Why was that? "No nickname," I said.

"Nothing? 'Bear'? Or 'Frog'?"

"Nothing."

"Gosh," she said. "Think of something."

"Wind-up bird," I said.

"Wind-up bird?" she asked, looking at me with her mouth open. "What is *that*?"

"The bird that winds the spring," I said. "Every morning. In the treetops. It winds the world's spring. *Creeeak.*"

She went on staring at me.

I sighed. "It just popped into my head," I said. "And there's more. The bird comes over to my place every day and goes *Creeeak* in the neighbour's tree. But nobody's ever seen it."

"That's neat, I guess. So anyhow, you'll be Mr Wind-up Bird. It's not very easy to say, but it's way better than Toru Okada."

"Thank you very much."

She pulled her feet up into the chair and put her chin on her knees.

"How about *your* name?" I asked.

"May Kasahara. May . . . like the month of May."

"Were you born in May?"

"Do you have to ask? Can you imagine the confusion if somebody born in June was named May?"

"I guess you're right," I said. "I suppose you're still off school?"

"I was watching you for a long time," she said, ignoring my question. "From my room. With my binoculars. I saw you go in through the gate. I keep a little pair of binoculars handy, for watching what goes on in the alley. All kinds of people go along there. I'll bet you didn't know that.

And not just people. Animals too. What were you doing here by yourself all that time?"

"Spacing out," I said. "Thinking about the old days. Whistling."

May Kasahara bit a thumbnail. "You're kind of weird," she said.

"I'm not weird. People do it all the time."

"Maybe so, but they don't do it in a neighbour's vacant house. You can stay in your own yard if all you want to do is space out and think about the old days and whistle."

She had a point there.

"Anyhow, I guess Noboru Wataya never came home, huh?"

I shook my head. "And I guess you never saw him, either, after that?" I asked.

"No, and I was on the lookout for him, too: a brown-striped tiger cat. Tail with a slight bend at the tip. Right?"

From the pocket of her shorts she took a box of Hope regulars and lit up. After a few puffs, she stared straight at me and said, "Your hair's thinning a little, isn't it?"

My hand moved automatically to the back of my head.

"Not there, silly," she said. "Your front hairline. It's higher than it should be, don't you think?"

"I've never really noticed."

"Well, *I* have," she said. "That's where you're going to go bald. Your hairline's going to move up and up like this." She grabbed a handful of her own hair and thrust her bare forehead in my face. "You'd better be careful."

I touched my hairline. Maybe she was right. Maybe it had receded a bit. Or was it my imagination? Something new to worry about.

"What do you mean?" I asked. "How can I be careful?"

"You can't, I guess. There's nothing you can do. There's no way to prevent baldness. Guys who are going to go bald go bald. When their time comes, that's it: they just go bald. There's nothing you can do to stop it. They tell you you can keep from going bald with proper hair care, but that's bullshit. Look at the bums who sleep in Shinjuku Station. They've all got great heads of hair. You think they're washing it every day with Clinique or Vidal Sassoon or rubbing Lotion X into it? That's what the cosmetics manufacturers will tell you, to get your money."

"I'm sure you're right," I said, impressed. "But how do you know so much about baldness?"

"I've been working part-time for a wig company. Quite a while now. You know I don't go to school, and I've got all this time to kill. I've been doing surveys and questionnaires, that kind of thing. So I know all about men losing their hair. I'm just loaded with information."

"Gosh," I said.

"But you know," she said, dropping her cigarette butt on the ground and stepping on it, "in the company I work for, they won't let you say anybody's 'bald'. You have to say 'men with a thinning problem'. 'Bald' is discriminatory language. I was joking around once and suggested 'gentlemen who are follically challenged', and boy, did *they* get mad! 'This is no laughing matter, young lady,' they said. They're so damned seeerious. Did you know that? Everybody in the whole damned world is so damned serious."

I took out my lemon drops, popped one in my mouth, and offered one to May Kasahara. She shook her head and took out a cigarette.

"Come to think of it, Mr Wind-up Bird," she said, "you were unemployed. Are you still?"

"Sure am."

"Are you serious about working?"

"Sure am." No sooner had the words left my mouth than I began to wonder how true they were. "Actually, I'm not so sure," I said. "I think I need time. Time to think. I'm not sure myself what I need. It's hard to explain."

Chewing on a nail, May Kasahara looked at me for a while. "Tell you what, Mr Wind-up Bird," she said. "Why don't you come to work with me one day? At the wig company. They don't pay much, but the work's easy, and you can set your own hours. What do you say? Don't think about it too much, just do it. For a change of pace. It might help you figure out all kinds of things."

She had a point there. "You've got a point there," I said.

"Great!" she said. "Next time I go, I'll come and get you. Now, where did you say your house is?"

"Hmm, that's a tough one. Or maybe not. You just keep going and going down the alley, taking all the turns. On the left you'll see a house with a red Honda Civic parked at the back. It's got one of those bumper stickers 'Let There Be Peace for All the Peoples of the World'. Ours is the next house, but there's no gate opening on the alley. It's just a breeze-block wall, and you have to climb over it. It's about chin height on me."

"Don't worry. I can get over a wall that high, no problem."

"Your leg doesn't hurt any more?"

She exhaled smoke with a little sighing kind of sound and said, "Don't worry. It's nothing. I limp when my parents are around because I don't want to go to school. I'm faking. It just turned into a habit. I do it even when nobody's looking, when I'm in my room all by myself. I'm a perfectionist. What is it they say – 'Fool yourself to fool others'? But anyhow, Mr Wind-up Bird, tell me, have you got guts?"

"Not really, no."

"Never had 'em?"

"No, I was never one for guts. Not likely to change, either."

"How about curiosity?"

"Curiosity's another matter. I've got some of that."

"Well, don't you think guts and curiosity are kind of similar?" said May Kasahara. "Where there's guts there's curiosity, and where there's curiosity there's guts. No?"

"Hmm, maybe they are kind of similar," I said. "Maybe you're right. Maybe they do overlap at times."

"Times like when you sneak into somebody's backyard, say."

"Yeah, like that," I said, rolling a lemon drop on my tongue. "When you sneak into somebody's backyard, it does seem that guts and curiosity are working together. Curiosity can bring guts out of hiding at times, maybe even get them going. But curiosity evaporates. Guts have to go for the long haul. Curiosity's like an amusing friend you can't really trust. It turns you on and then it leaves you to make it on your own – with whatever guts you can muster."

She thought this over for a time. "I guess so," she said. "I guess that's one way to look at it." She stood up and brushed off the dirt clinging to the seat of her shorts. Then she looked down at me. "Tell me, Mr Wind-up Bird, would you like to see the well?"

"The well?" I asked. The well?

"There's a dried-up well here. I like it. Kind of. Want to see it?"

•

We cut through the yard and walked around to the side of the house. It was a round well, maybe four-and-a-half feet in diameter. Thick planking, cut to shape and size, had been used to cap the well, and two concrete blocks had been set on the round wooden cap to keep it in place. The well curb stood perhaps three feet high, and close by grew a single old tree, as if standing guard. It was a fruit tree, but I couldn't tell what kind.

Like almost everything else connected with this house, the well looked as though it had been abandoned long before. Something about it felt as if it should be called "overwhelming numbness". Maybe when people take their eyes off them, inanimate objects become even more inanimate.

Close inspection revealed that the well was in fact far older than the objects that surrounded it. It had been made in another age, long before the house was built. Even the wooden cap was an antique. The well surround had been coated with a thick layer of concrete, without a doubt to strengthen a structure that had been built long before. The nearby tree seemed to boast of having stood there far longer than any other tree in the area.

I lowered a concrete block to the ground and removed one of the two half-moons that constituted the wooden cap. Hands on the edge of the well, I leaned over and looked down, but I could not see to the bottom. One could see it was a deep well, its lower half swallowed in darkness. I took a sniff. It had a slight mouldy smell.

"It doesn't have any water," said May Kasahara.

A well without water. A bird that can't fly. An alley with no exit. And –

May picked up a chunk of brick from the ground and threw it into the well. A moment later came a small, dry thud. Nothing more. The sound was dry, desiccated, as if you could crumble it in your hands. I straightened up and looked at May Kasahara. "I wonder why it hasn't got any water. Did it dry up? Did somebody fill it in?"

She shrugged. "When people fill in a well, don't they fill it all the way to the top? There'd be no point in leaving a dry hole like this. Somebody could fall in and get hurt. Don't you think?"

"I think you're right," I said. "Something must have made the water dry up."

I suddenly recalled Mr Honda's words from long before. "When you're supposed to go up, find the highest tower and climb to the top. When you're supposed to go down, find the deepest well and go down to the bottom." So now I had a well if I needed one.

I leaned over the edge again and looked down into the darkness, anticipating nothing in particular. So, I thought, in a place like this, in the middle of the day like this, there existed a darkness as deep as this. I cleared my throat and swallowed. The sound echoed in the darkness, as if someone else had cleared his throat. My saliva still tasted like lemon drops.

•

I put the cover back on the well and set the block on top of it. Then I looked at my watch. Almost 11.30. Time to call Kumiko during her lunch break.

"I'd better go home," I said.

May Kasahara gave a little frown. "Go right ahead, Mr Wind-up Bird," she said. "You fly on home."

When we crossed the yard, the stone bird was still glaring at the sky with its dry eyes. The sky itself was still filled with its unbroken covering of grey clouds, but at least the rain had stopped. May Kasahara tore up a fistful of grass and threw it towards the sky. With no wind to carry them, the blades of grass dropped at her feet.

"Think of all the hours left between now and the time the sun goes down," she said, without looking at me.

"True," I said. "Lots of hours."

6

On the Births of Kumiko Okada
and Noboru Wataya

•

Brought up as an only child, I find it difficult to imagine how grown-up siblings must feel when they meet in the course of their independent lives. In Kumiko's case, whenever the topic of Noboru Wataya came up, she would get a strange look on her face, as if she had put some odd-tasting thing in her mouth by accident, but *exactly* what that look meant I had no way of knowing. In my own feelings towards her elder brother there was not a trace of anything positive. Kumiko knew this and thought it entirely reasonable. She herself was far from fond of the man. It was hard to imagine them ever speaking to each other had the blood relationship not existed between them. But they *were* brother and sister, and this made things somewhat more complicated.

After I had my argument with her father and I severed all contact with her family, Kumiko had virtually no occasion to see Noboru Wataya. The argument had been a violent one. I haven't had many arguments in my life – I'm just not the type – but once I do get going, I go all the way. And so my break with Kumiko's father had been final. Afterwards, when I had got everything off my chest that I needed to, anger was mysteriously absent. I felt only relief. I never had to see him again: it was as if a great burden that I had been carrying for a long time had been lifted from my shoulders. None of the rage or the hatred was left. I even felt a touch of sympathy for the difficulties he had faced in his life, however stupid and repulsive the shape of that life might appear to me. I told Kumiko that I would never see her parents again, but she was free to visit them without me any time she wanted. Kumiko made no attempt to see them. "Never mind," she said. "I wasn't that crazy about visiting them anyway."

Noboru Wataya had been living with his parents at the time, but when the argument started between his father and me, he had simply withdrawn without a word to anyone. This hadn't taken me by surprise. I was a person of no interest to him. He did his best to avoid personal contact with me unless it was really necessary. And so, when I stopped seeing Kumiko's parents, there was no longer any reason for me to see Noboru Wataya. Kumiko herself had no reason to make a point of seeing him. He was busy, she was busy, and they had never been that close to begin with.

Still, Kumiko would phone him from time to time at his campus office, and he would sometimes phone her at her company office (though never at our home). She would announce these contacts to me without detailing the substance of their conversations. I never asked, and she never volunteered the information unless it was necessary.

I didn't care to know what Kumiko and Noboru Wataya were talking about. Which is not to say that I resented the fact that they were talking. I just didn't get it. What was there for two such different human beings to say to each other? Or was it only through the special connection of their blood relationship that this came about?

•

Though brother and sister, Noboru Wataya and Kumiko were separated in age by nine years. Another factor behind the lack of any obvious closeness between the two was Kumiko's having lived for several years with her father's family.

Kumiko and Noboru had not been the only children in the Wataya house. Between them there had been a sister, five years older than Kumiko. At the age of three, however, Kumiko had been sent from Tokyo to distant Niigata, to be raised for a time by her grandmother. Kumiko's parents later told her that this was done because she had been a sickly child and they thought she would benefit from the clean air of the countryside, but she never quite believed this. As far as she herself could remember, she had never been physically weak. She had never suffered from any major illnesses, and no one in her Niigata home seemed especially concerned about her health. "I'm sure it was just some kind of excuse," Kumiko once told me.

Her doubts had been reinforced by something she heard from a relative. Apparently, there had been a long-standing feud between Kumiko's mother and grandmother, and the decision to bring Kumiko to Niigata was the outcome of a truce they had concluded. By offering her up for a time, Kumiko's parents had quelled her grandmother's rage, and by having a grandchild in her possession, the grandmother had obtained concrete confirmation of her ties with her son (Kumiko's father). In other words, Kumiko had been a kind of hostage.

"Besides," Kumiko said to me, "they already had two other children. Their third one was no great loss to them. Not that they were planning to get rid of me: I think they just figured it wouldn't be too hard on such a young child to be sent away. Probably they didn't give it much thought. It was just the easiest solution to the problem. Can you believe it? I don't know why, but they had not the slightest idea what something like that can do to a small child."

She was raised by her grandmother in Niigata from the age of three to six. Nor was there anything sad or twisted about the life she led in the country. Her grandmother was crazy about her, and Kumiko had more fun playing with her cousins, who were closer in age to herself, than with her own brother and sister. She was finally brought back to Tokyo the year she was to enter primary school. Her parents had become nervous about the lengthening separation from their daughter, and they insisted on bringing her back before it was too late. In a sense, though, it was already too late. In the weeks following the decision to send her back, her grandmother became more and more overwrought. She stopped eating and could hardly sleep. One minute she would be hugging and squeezing little Kumiko with all her might, and the next she would be slapping her arm with a ruler, hard enough to raise welts. One minute she would be saying she didn't want to let her go, that she would rather die than lose her, and the next she would tell her to go away, that she never wanted to see her again. In the foulest language imaginable, she would tell Kumiko what a terrible woman her mother was. She even tried to stab herself in the wrist with a pair of scissors. Kumiko could not understand what was happening around her. The situation was simply too much for her to comprehend.

What she did then was to shut herself off from the outer world. She closed her eyes. She closed her ears. She shut her mind down. She put an end to any form of thinking or of hoping. The next several months were a blank. She had no memory of anything that happened in that time. When she emerged, she found herself in a new home. It was the home where she should have been all along. Her parents were there, her brother and her sister. But it was not *her home*. It was simply a *new environment*.

Kumiko became a difficult, taciturn child in these new surroundings. There was no one she could trust, no one she could depend upon unconditionally. Even in her parents' embrace, she never felt entirely at ease. She did not know their smell. It made her uneasy. She even hated it at times. In the family, it was only towards her sister that she began, with difficulty, to open up. Her parents despaired of ever getting through to her; her brother hardly knew she existed. But her sister understood the confusion and loneliness that lay behind her stubborn moods. She stayed with Kumiko through it all, slept in the same room with her, talked with her, read to her, walked with her to school, helped her with her homework. If Kumiko spent hours huddled in the corner of her room in tears, the sister would be there, holding her. She did everything she could to find a way into Kumiko's heart. Had she not died from food poisoning the year after Kumiko returned from Niigata, the situation would have been very different.

"If my sister had lived, things might have been better at home," Kumiko said. "She was just a little girl of eleven, but she was the heart of that household. Maybe if she hadn't died, all of us would have been more normal than we are now. At least *I* wouldn't be such a hopeless case. Do you see what I mean? I felt so guilty after that. Why hadn't I died in my sister's place? I was no good to anybody. I couldn't make anybody happy. Why couldn't I have been the one? My parents and brother knew exactly how I felt, but they said nothing to comfort me. Far from it. They'd talk about my dead sister every chance they got: how pretty she was, how bright, how much everybody liked her, what a thoughtful person she was, how well she played the piano. And then they made *me* take piano lessons! *Somebody* had to use the big grand piano after she died. I didn't have the slightest interest in playing. I knew I could never play as well as she had played, and I didn't need yet another way to demonstrate how inferior I was to her. I couldn't take anyone's place, least of all hers, and I didn't want to try. But they wouldn't listen to me. They *just wouldn't listen*. To this day, I hate the sight of a piano. I hate seeing anyone play."

I felt tremendous anger towards her family when Kumiko told me this. For what they had done to her. For what they had failed to do for her. This was before we were married. We had known each other only a little over two months. It was a quiet Sunday morning, and we were in bed. She

71

talked for a long time about her childhood, as if unravelling a tangled thread, pausing to assess the validity of each event as she brought it forth. It was the first time she told me so much about herself. I hardly knew anything about her family or her childhood until that morning. I knew that she was quiet, that she liked to draw, that she had long, beautiful hair, that she had two moles on her right shoulder blade. And that sleeping with me was her first sexual experience.

She cried a little as she spoke. I could understand why she would need to cry. I held her and stroked her hair. "If she had lived, I'm sure you would have loved her," said Kumiko. "Everybody loved her. Love at first sight."

"Maybe so," I said. "But you're the one I happen to be in love with. It's really very simple, you know. It's just you and me. Your sister's got nothing to do with it."

For a while, Kumiko lay there, thinking. Seven-thirty on Sunday morning: a time when everything sounds soft and hollow. I listened to the pigeons shuffling across my apartment roof, to someone calling a dog in the distance. Kumiko stared at a single spot on the ceiling for the longest time.

"Tell me," she said at last, "do you like cats?"

"Crazy about them," I said. "Always had one when I was a kid. I played with it constantly, even slept with it."

"Lucky you. I was dying to have a cat. But they wouldn't let me. My mother hated them. Not once in my life have I managed to get something I really wanted. Not once. Can you believe it? You can't understand what it's like to live like that. When you get used to that kind of life – of never having anything you want – then you stop knowing what it is you want."

I took her hand. "Maybe it's been like that for you till now. But you're not a kid any more. You have the right to choose your own life. You can start again. If you want a cat, all you have to do is choose a life in which you can have a cat. It's simple. It's your right . . . right?"

Her eyes stayed locked on mine. "Mmm," she said. "Right." A few months later, Kumiko and I were talking about marriage.

•

If the childhood that Kumiko spent in that house was warped and difficult, Noboru Wataya's boyhood there was strangely distorted in another sense. The parents were mad about their only son, but they didn't merely shower him with affection; they demanded certain things of him as well. The father was convinced that the only way to live a full life in Japanese society was to earn the highest possible marks and to shove aside anyone and everyone standing in your path to the top. He believed this with utter conviction.

It was shortly after I had married his daughter that I heard these very words from the man himself. All men are *not* created equal, he said. That was just some righteous-sounding nonsense they taught you in school. Japan might have the political structure of a democratic nation, but it was at the same time a fiercely carnivorous class society in which the weak were devoured by the strong, and unless you became one of the elite, there was no point in living in this country. You'd just be ground to dust. You had to fight your way up every rung of the ladder. This kind of ambition was entirely healthy. If people lost that ambition, Japan would perish. In response to my father-in-law's views, I offered no opinion. He was not looking for my opinion. He had merely been spouting his belief, a conviction that would remain unchanged for all eternity.

Kumiko's mother was the daughter of a high-ranking official. She had been raised in the finest Tokyo neighbourhood, wanting for nothing, and she possessed neither the opinions nor the character to oppose her husband. As far as I could see, she had no opinion at all about anything that was not set directly in front of her (and in fact, she was extremely nearsighted). Whenever an occasion arose in which she needed an opinion on something in the wider world, she borrowed her husband's. If this had been all there was to her, she wouldn't have bothered anyone, but as is so often the case with such women, she suffered from incurable pretentiousness. Lacking any values of their own, such people can arrive at a standpoint only by adopting other people's standards or views. The only principle that governs their minds is the question "How do I look?" And so Mrs Wataya became a narrow, highly strung woman whose only concerns were her husband's place in the government and her son's academic performance. Anything else ceased to have meaning for her.

And so the parents pounded their questionable philosophy and their warped view of the world into the head of the young Noboru Wataya. They egged him on, providing him with the best tutors money could buy. When he took top honours, they rewarded their son by buying him anything he wanted. His childhood was one of extreme material luxury, but when he came to that most sensitive and vulnerable phase of life, he had no time for girlfriends, no chance to go wild with other boys. He had to pour all his energies into maintaining his position as number one. Whether Noboru Wataya was pleased to live that way or not I do not know. Kumiko did not know. Noboru Wataya was not the sort of person

73

to reveal his feelings: not to her, not to his parents, not to anyone. He had no choice anyway. It seems to me that certain patterns of thought are so simple and one-sided that they become irresistible. In any case, Noboru Wataya graduated from his elite private preparatory school, majored in economics at the University of Tokyo, and graduated from this top institution with top grades.

His father expected him to enter the government or a major corporation upon graduation from the university, but Noboru Wataya chose to remain in academe and become a scholar. He was no fool. He knew what he was best suited for: not the real world of communal action but a world that called for the disciplined and systematic use of knowledge, that prized the individual skills of the intellect. He did two years of graduate study at Yale before returning to the graduate school at Tokyo. He followed his parents' promptings and a short time afterwards agreed to an arranged marriage, but that lasted no more than two years. After his divorce, he returned to his parents' home to live with them. By the time I met him, Noboru Wataya was a fully developed oddity, a thoroughly disagreeable character.

About two years after I married Kumiko, Noboru Wataya published a big, thick book. It was an economics study full of technical jargon, and I couldn't understand a thing he was trying to say in it. Not one page made sense to me. I couldn't even tell whether this was because the contents were so difficult or the writing itself was bad. People in the field thought it was great, though. One reviewer declared that it was "an entirely new kind of economics written from an entirely new perspective", but that was as much as I could understand of the review itself. Soon the mass media began to introduce him as a "hero for a new age". Whole books, interpreting his book, appeared. Two expressions he had coined, "sexual economics" and "excretory economics", became the year's buzzwords. Newspapers and magazines carried feature articles on him as one of the intellectuals of the new age. I couldn't believe that anyone who wrote these articles understood what Noboru Wataya was saying in his book. I had doubts whether they had even opened it. But such things were of no concern to them. Noboru Wataya was young and single and smart enough to write a book that nobody could understand.

It made him famous. The magazines all came to him for critical pieces. He appeared on television to comment on political and economic questions. Soon he was a regular panel member on one of the political debate shows. Those who knew Noboru Wataya (including Kumiko and I) had never imagined him to be suited to such glamorous work. Everyone thought of him as the highly strung academic type interested in nothing but his field of specialization. Once he got a taste of the world of mass media, though, you could almost see him licking his chops. He was good. He didn't mind having a camera pointed at him. If anything, he even seemed more relaxed in front of the cameras than in the real world. We watched his sudden transformation with amazement. The Noboru Wataya we saw on television wore expensive suits with perfectly matching ties and glasses with frames of fine tortoiseshell. His hair had been done in the latest style. He had obviously been worked on by a professional. I had never seen him exuding such luxury before. And even if he had been outfitted by the network, he wore the style with perfect ease, as if he had dressed that way all his life. Who was this man? I wondered when I first saw him. Where was the real Noboru Wataya?

In front of the cameras, he played the role of Man of Few Words. When asked for an opinion, his response would be simple, clear and precise. Whenever the debate heated up and everyone else was shouting, he kept his cool. When challenged, he would hold back, let his opponent have his say, and then demolish the person's argument with a single phrase. He had mastered the art of delivering the fatal blow with a purr and a smile. On the television screen, he looked far more intelligent and reliable than the real Noboru Wataya. I'm not sure how he accomplished this. He certainly wasn't handsome. But he was tall and slim and had an air of good breeding. In the medium of television, Noboru Wataya had found the place where he belonged. The mass media welcomed him with open arms, and he welcomed them with equal enthusiasm.

Meanwhile, I couldn't stand the sight of him – in print or on TV. He was a man of talent and ability, to be sure. I recognized that much. He knew how to knock his opponent down quickly and effectively with the fewest possible words. He had an animal instinct for sensing the direction of the wind. But if you paid close attention to what he was saying or what he had written, you knew that his words lacked consistency. They reflected no single worldview based on profound conviction. His was a world that he had fabricated by combining several one-dimensional systems of thought. He could rearrange the combination in an instant, as needed. These were ingenious – even artistic – intellectual permutations and combinations. But to me they amounted to nothing more than a game. If there was any consistency to his opinions, it was the consistent lack of consistency, and if he had a worldview, it was a view that proclaimed his lack of a worldview. But these very absences were what constituted his intellectual assets. Consistency and an established worldview were excess baggage in the intellectual mobile warfare that flared up in the mass media's tiny time segments, and it was his great advantage to be free of such things.

He had nothing to protect, which meant that he could concentrate all his attention on pure acts of combat. He needed only to attack, to knock his enemy down. Noboru Wataya was an intellectual chameleon, changing his colour in accordance with his opponent's, ad-libbing his logic for maximum effectiveness, mobilizing all the rhetoric at his command. I had no idea how he had acquired these techniques, but he clearly had the knack of appealing directly to the feelings of the mass audience. He knew how to use the kind of logic that moved the majority. Nor did it even have to be logic: it had only to appear so, as long as it aroused the feelings of the masses.

Trotting out the technical jargon was another forte of his. No one knew what it meant, of course, but he was able to present it in such a way that you knew it was your fault if you didn't get it. And he was always citing statistics. They were engraved on his brain, and they carried tremendous persuasive power, but if you stopped to think about it afterwards, you realized that no one had questioned his sources or their reliability.

These clever tactics of his used to drive me mad, but I was never able to explain to anyone exactly what upset me. I was never able to construct an argument to refute him. It was like boxing with a ghost: your punches just swished through the air. There was nothing solid for them to connect with. I was shocked to see even sophisticated intellectuals responding to him. It would leave me feeling strangely annoyed.

And so Noboru Wataya came to be seen as one of the most intelligent figures of the day. Nobody seemed to care about consistency any more. All they looked for on the tube were the bouts of intellectual gladiators; the redder the blood they drew, the better. It didn't matter if the same person said one thing on Monday and the opposite on Thursday.

•

I first met Noboru Wataya when Kumiko and I decided to get married. I wanted to talk to him before I saw her father. I figured that as a man closer to my own age, he might be persuaded to smooth the way for me with his father.

"I don't think you should count on his help," Kumiko said to me, with apparent difficulty. "I can't explain it, but he's just not the type."

"Well, I'll have to meet him sooner or later," I said.

"I guess," said Kumiko.

"It's worth a try," I said. "You never know."

"I guess," said Kumiko. "Maybe."

On the phone, Noboru Wataya displayed little enthusiasm at the prospect of meeting me. If I insisted, he said, he could spare me half an hour. We decided to meet at a coffeehouse near Ochanomizu Station. He was just a college instructor at the time, long before he had written his book and long before his sartorial conversion. The pockets of his sports coat bulged from having had fists thrust into them too long. His hair was at least two weeks overdue for a trim. His mustard-colour polo shirt clashed with his blue and grey tweed jacket. He had the look of the typical young assistant professor for whom money was an alien object. His eyes had that sleepy expression of someone who has just slipped out of the library after a day of research in the stacks, but there was a piercing, cold gleam in them too, if you looked closely.

After introducing myself, I said that I was planning to marry Kumiko in the near future. I tried to explain things as honestly as possible. I was working in a law firm, I said, but I knew this was not the right job for me. I was still searching for myself. For such a person to risk marriage might seem to be a reckless act, but I loved his sister, I said, and I believed I could make her happy. The two of us could give each other strength and comfort.

My words appeared lost on Noboru Wataya. He sat with his arms folded, listening in silence. Even after my little speech, he remained perfectly still. He seemed to be thinking about something else.

I had felt awkward in his presence from the start and assumed this was because of the situation. Anybody would feel awkward telling a total stranger, "I want to marry your sister." But as I sat there across from him, an unpleasant feeling began to well up inside me. It was like having some kind of sour-smelling, alien mass growing in the pit of your stomach. Not that there was any particular thing he said or did that rubbed me the wrong way. It was his face: the face of Noboru Wataya itself. It gave me the intuitive sense that it was covered over with a quite different layer of something. Something wrong. It was not his real face. I couldn't shake off this feeling.

I wanted to get the hell out of there. I actually considered getting up and leaving, but I had to see things through to the end. I stayed there, sipping my lukewarm coffee and waiting for him to say something.

When he spoke, it was as if he were deliberately setting the volume of his voice on low to conserve energy. "To tell you the truth," he said, "I can neither understand nor care about what you have been telling me. The things I care about are of an entirely different order, things that I suspect *you* can neither understand nor care about. To state my conclusion as concisely as possible, if you wish to marry Kumiko and she wishes to marry you, I have neither the right nor any reason to stand in your way. Therefore, I shall not stand in your way. I wouldn't even think of doing so. But don't expect anything further from me, either. And most important, don't expect me to waste any more time on this matter than I already have."

He looked at his watch and stood up. His declaration had been concise and to the point. It suffered from neither excess nor omission. I understood with perfect clarity both what he wanted to say and what he thought of me.

And so we parted that day.

After Kumiko and I were married, a number of occasions arose in which it was necessary for Noboru Wataya and me, as brothers-in-law, to exchange words – if not to engage in actual conversation. As he had suggested, there was no common ground between us, and so for all that we might speak words in each other's vicinity, this could never develop into anything that could be called a conversation. It was as though we were speaking in different languages. If the Dalai Lama were on his deathbed and the jazz musician Eric Dolphy were to try to explain to him the importance of choosing one's engine oil in accordance with changes in the sound of the bass clarinet, that exchange might have been more worthwhile and effective than my conversations with Noboru Wataya.

I rarely suffer lengthy emotional distress from contact with other people. A person may anger or annoy me, but not for long. I can distinguish between myself and another as beings of two different realms. It's a kind of talent (by which I do not mean to boast: it's not an easy thing to do, so if you can do it, it *is* a kind of talent – a special power). When someone gets on my nerves, the first thing I do is to transfer the object of my unpleasant feelings to another domain, one having no connection with me. Then I tell myself, Fine, I'm feeling bad, but I've put the source of these feelings into another zone, away from here, where I can examine it and deal with it later in my own good time. In other words, I put a freeze on my emotions. Later, when I thaw them out to perform the examination, I do from time to time find my emotions still in a distressed state, but that is rare. The passage of time will usually extract the venom from most things and render them harmless. Then, sooner or later, I forget about them.

In the course of my life so far, I've been able to keep my world in a more or less stable state by avoiding most useless troubles through activation of this emotional management system. That I have succeeded in maintaining such an effective system all this time is a matter of some pride to me.

When it came to Noboru Wataya, though, my system refused to function. I was unable simply to shove Noboru Wataya into a domain having no connection with me. And that fact itself annoyed the hell out of me. Kumiko's father was an arrogant, unpleasant man, to be sure, but finally he was a small-minded character who had lived by clinging to a simple set of narrow beliefs. I could forget about someone like that. But not Noboru Wataya. He knew what kind of a man he was. And he had a pretty good idea of what made me tick as well. If he had felt like it, he could have crushed me until there was nothing left. The only reason he hadn't was that he didn't give a damn about me. I wasn't worth the time and energy it would have taken to crush me. And that's what got me about him. He was a despicable human being, an egoist with nothing inside him. But he was a far more capable individual than I was.

After that first meeting of ours, I had a bad taste in my mouth that wouldn't go away. I felt as if someone had force-fed me a clump of foul-smelling bugs. Spitting them out did no good: I could still feel them inside my mouth. Day after day, Noboru Wataya was all I could think about. I tried going to concerts and movies. I even went to a baseball game with the guys from the office. I drank, and I read the books that I had been waiting to read when I could find the time. But Noboru Wataya was always there, arms folded, looking at me with those malignant eyes of his, threatening to suck me in like a bottomless swamp. This set my nerves on edge and sent tremors through the ground on which I stood.

The next time I saw her, Kumiko asked about my impressions of her brother. I wasn't able to give an honest reply. I wanted to ask her about the mask he wore and about the twisted "something" that lay behind it. I wanted to tell her everything I had thought about this brother of hers. But I said nothing. I felt that these were things I would never be able to convey to her, that if I couldn't express myself clearly I shouldn't express myself at all – not now.

"He's . . . different, that's for sure," I said. I wanted to add something to this, but I couldn't find the words. Nor did she press me for more. She simply nodded in silence.

My feelings towards Noboru Wataya never changed after that. He continued to set my nerves on edge in the same way. It was like a persistent low-grade fever. I never had a television in the house, but by some uncanny coincidence, whenever I glanced at a TV somewhere, he would be on it, making some pronouncement. If I flipped through the pages of a magazine in a doctor's waiting room, there would be a picture of Noboru Wataya, with an article he had written. I felt as if Noboru Wataya were lying in wait for me just around every corner in the known world.

OK, let's face it. I hated the guy.

7

The Happy Cleaners

•

And Creta Kano Makes Her Entrance

I took a blouse and skirt of Kumiko's to the cleaner's by the station. Normally, I took our laundry to the cleaner's around the corner from us, not because I preferred it but because it was closer. Kumiko sometimes used the station cleaner's in the course of commuting. She'd drop something off in the morning on her way to the office and pick it up on the way home. This place was a little more expensive, but they did a better job than the local cleaner's, according to Kumiko. And her better dresses she would always bring there. Which is why on that particular day I decided to take my bike to the station. I figured she would prefer to have her clothes done there.

I left the house carrying Kumiko's blouse and skirt and wearing a pair of thin green cotton trousers, my usual tennis shoes, and the yellow Van Halen promotional T-shirt that Kumiko had received from a record company. The owner of the shop had his JVC music machine turned up loud, as he had on my last trip. This morning it was an Andy Williams tape. "Hawaiian Wedding Song" was just ending as I walked in and "Canadian Sunset" started. Whistling happily to the tune, the owner was writing in a notebook with a ballpoint pen, his movements as energetic as before. In the pile of tapes on the shelf, I spotted such names as Sergio Mendes, Bert Kaempfert and 101 Strings. So he was an easy-listening freak. It suddenly occurred to me that true believers in hard-driving jazz – Albert Ayler, Don Cherry, Cecil Taylor – could never become owners of cleaning shops in malls across from railroad stations. Or maybe they could. They just wouldn't be happy cleaners.

When I put the green floral-pattern blouse and sage-coloured skirt on the counter, he spread them out for a quick inspection, then wrote on the receipt, "Blouse and Skirt". His writing was clear and carefully formed. I like cleaners who write clearly. And if they like Andy Williams, so much the better.

"Mr Okada, right?" I said he was right. He wrote in my name, tore out the carbon copy, and gave it to me. "They'll be ready next Tuesday, so don't forget to come and get them this time. Mrs Okada's?"

"Uh-huh."

"Very pretty," he said.

A dull layer of clouds filled the sky. The weather forecast had predicted rain. The time was after 9.30, but there were still plenty of men with briefcases and folded umbrellas hurrying towards the station steps. Late commuters. The morning was hot and humid, but that made no difference to these men, all of whom were properly dressed in suits and ties and black shoes. I saw lots of men my age, but not one of them wore a Van Halen T-shirt. Each wore his company's lapel badge and clutched a copy of the *Nikkei News* under his arm. The bell rang, and a number of them dashed up the stairs. I hadn't seen men like this for a long time.

Heading home on my bike, I found myself whistling "Canadian Sunset".

•

Malta Kano called at 11 o'clock. "Hello. I wonder if this might possibly be the home of Mr Toru Okada?" she asked.

"Yes, this is Toru Okada." I knew it was Malta Kano from the first hello.

"My name is Malta Kano. You were kind enough to see me the other day. Would you happen to have any plans for this afternoon?"

None, I said. I had no more plans for the afternoon than a migrating bird has collateral assets.

"In that case, my younger sister, Creta Kano, will come to visit you at 1 o'clock."

"Creta Kano?" I asked in a flat voice.

"Yes," said Malta Kano. "I believe I showed you her photograph the other day."

"I remember her, of course. It's just that –"

"Her name is Creta Kano. She will come to visit you as my representative. Is 1 o'clock a good time for you?"

"Fine," I said.

"She'll be there," said Malta Kano, and hung up.

Creta Kano?

I vacuumed the floors and straightened the house. I tied our old newspapers in a bundle and threw them in a cupboard. I put scattered cassette tapes back in their cases and lined them up by the stereo. I washed the things piled in the kitchen. Then I washed myself: shower, shampoo, clean clothes. I made fresh coffee and ate lunch: ham sandwich and hard-boiled egg. I sat on the sofa, reading the *Home Journal* and wondering what to make for dinner. I marked the recipe for seaweed and tofu salad and wrote the ingredients on a shopping list. I turned on the radio. Michael Jackson was singing "Billy Jean". I thought about the sisters Malta Kano and Creta Kano. What names for a couple of sisters! They sounded like a comedy team. Malta Kano. Creta Kano.

My life was heading in new directions, that was certain. The cat had run away. Strange calls had come from a strange woman. I had met an odd girl and started visiting a vacant house. Noboru Wataya had raped Creta Kano. Malta Kano had predicted I'd find my tie. Kumiko had told me I didn't have to work.

I turned off the radio, returned the *Home Journal* to the bookshelf, and drank another cup of coffee.

·

Creta Kano rang the doorbell at 1 o'clock on the dot. She looked exactly like her picture: a small woman in her early to mid-twenties, the quiet type. She did a remarkable job of preserving the look of the early sixties. She wore her hair in the bouffant style I had seen in the photograph, the ends curled upwards. The hair at the forehead was pulled straight back and held in place by a large, glittering barrette. Her eyebrows were sharply outlined in pencil, mascara added mysterious shadows to her eyes, and her lipstick was a perfect re-creation of the kind of colour popular back then. She looked ready to belt out "Johnny Angel" if you put a mike in her hand.

She dressed far more simply than she made herself up. Practical and businesslike, her outfit had nothing idiosyncratic about it: a white blouse, a tight green skirt, and no accessories to speak of. She had a white patent-leather bag tucked under her arm and wore sharp-pointed white pumps. The shoes were tiny. Their heels thin and sharp as a pencil lead, they looked like a doll's shoes. I almost wanted to congratulate her on having made it this far on them.

So this was Creta Kano. I showed her in, had her sit on the sofa, warmed the coffee, and served her a cup. Had she eaten lunch yet? I asked. She looked hungry to me. No, she said, she had not eaten.

"But don't bother about me," she hastened to add. "I don't eat much for lunch."

"Are you sure?" I asked. "It's nothing for me to fix a sandwich. Don't stand on ceremony. I make snacks and things all the time. It's no trouble at all."

She responded with little shakes of the head. "It's very kind of you to offer, but I'm fine, really. Don't bother. A cup of coffee is more than enough."

Still, I brought out a plate of cookies just in case. Creta Kano ate four of them with obvious pleasure. I ate two and drank my coffee.

She seemed somewhat more relaxed after the cookies and coffee.

"I am here today as the representative of my elder sister, Malta Kano," she said. "Creta is not my real name, of course. My real name is Setsuko. I took the name Creta when I began working as my sister's assistant. For professional purposes. Creta is the ancient name for the island of Crete, but I have no connection with Crete. I have never been there. My sister Malta chose the name to go with her own. Have you been to the island of Crete, by any chance, Mr Okada?"

Unfortunately not, I said. I had never been to Crete and had no plans to visit it in the near future.

"I would like to go there sometime," said Creta Kano, nodding, with a deadly serious look on her face. "Crete is the Greek island closest to Africa. It's a large island, and a great civilization flourished there long ago. My sister Malta has been to Crete as well. She says it's a wonderful place. The wind is strong, and the honey is delicious. I love honey."

I nodded. I'm not that crazy about honey.

"I came today to ask you a favour," said Creta Kano. "I'd like to take a sample of the water in your house."

"The water?" I asked. "You mean the water from the tap?"

"That would be fine," she said. "And if there happens to be a well nearby, I would like a sample of that water also."

"I don't think so. I mean, there *is* a well in the neighbourhood, but it's on somebody else's property, and it's dry. It doesn't produce water any more."

Creta Kano gave me a complicated look. "Are you sure?" she asked. "Are you sure it doesn't have any water?"

I recalled the dry thud that the chunk of brick had made when the girl threw it down the well at the vacant house. "Yes, it's dry, all right. I'm quite sure."

"I see," said Creta Kano. "That's fine. I'll just take a sample of the water from the tap, then, if you don't mind."

I showed her to the kitchen. From her white patent-leather bag she removed two small bottles of the type that might be used for medicine. She filled one with water and tightened the cap with great care. Then she said she wanted to take a sample from the line supplying the bathtub. I showed her to the bathroom. Undistracted by all the underwear and stockings that Kumiko had left drying in there, Creta Kano turned on the tap and filled the other bottle. After capping it, she turned it upside down to make sure it didn't leak. The bottle caps were colour coded: blue for the bath water, and green for the kitchen water.

Back on the living room sofa, she put the two vials into a small plastic freezer bag and sealed it shut. She placed the bag carefully in her white patent-leather bag, the metal clasp of which closed with a dry click. Her hands moved with practised efficiency. It was obvious she had done this many times before.

"Thank you very much," said Creta Kano.

"Is that all?" I asked.

"Yes, for today," she said. She smoothed her skirt, slipped her bag under her arm, and made as if to stand up.

"Wait a minute," I said, with some confusion. I hadn't been expecting her to leave so suddenly. "Wait just a minute, will you, please? My wife wants to know what's happened to the cat. It's been gone for almost two weeks now. If you know anything at all, I'd like you to tell me."

Still clutching the white bag under her arm, Creta Kano looked at me for a moment, then she gave a few quick nods. When she moved her head, the curled-up ends of her hair bobbed with an early-sixties lightness. Whenever she blinked, her long fake eyelashes moved slowly up and down, like the long-handled fans operated by slaves in movies set in ancient Egypt.

"To tell you the truth, my sister says that this will be a longer story than it seemed at first."

"A longer story than it seemed?"

The phrase "a longer story" brought to mind a tall stake set in the desert, where nothing else stood as far as the eye could see. As the sun began to sink, the shadow of the stake grew longer and longer, until its tip was too far away to be seen by the naked eye.

"That's what she says," Creta Kano continued. "This story will be about more than the disappearance of a cat."

"I'm confused," I said. "All we're asking you to do is help us find the cat. Nothing more. If the cat's dead, we want to know for sure. Why does it have to be 'a longer story'? I don't understand."

"Neither do I," she said. She brought her hand up to the shiny barrette on her head and pushed it back a little. "But please put your faith in my sister. I'm not saying that she knows everything. But if she says there will be a longer story, you can be sure there will be a longer story."

I nodded without saying anything. There was nothing more I could say.

Looking directly into my eyes and speaking with a new formality, Creta Kano asked, "Are you busy, Mr Okada? Do you have any plans for the rest of the afternoon?"

No, I said, I had no plans.

"Would you mind, then, if I told you a few things about myself?" Creta Kano asked. She put the white patent-leather bag she was holding down on the sofa and rested her hands, one on top of the other, on her tight green skirt, at the knees. Her nails had been done in a lovely pink colour. She wore no rings.

"Please," I said. "Tell me anything you like." And so the flow of my life – as had been foretold from the moment Creta Kano rang my doorbell – was being channelled in ever stranger directions.

8

Creta Kano's Long Story

•

An Inquiry into the Nature of Pain

"I was born on May 29," Creta Kano began her story, "and on the night of my twentieth birthday I resolved to take my own life."

I put a fresh cup of coffee in front of her. She added cream and gave it a languid stir. No sugar. I drank my coffee black, as always. The clock on the shelf continued its dry rapping on the walls of time.

Creta Kano looked hard at me and said, "I wonder if I should begin at the beginning – where I was born, family life, that kind of thing."

"Whatever you like. It's up to you. Whatever you find most comfortable," I said.

"I was the third of three children," she said. "Malta and I have an elder brother. My father ran his own clinic in Kanagawa Prefecture. The family had nothing you could call domestic problems. I grew up in an ordinary home, the kind you can find anywhere. My parents were very serious people with a strong belief in the value of hard work. They were rather strict with us, but they also gave us a fair amount of autonomy where little things were concerned. We were well off, but my parents did not believe in giving their children extra money for frills. I suppose I had a rather frugal upbringing.

"Malta is five years older than I. There had been something different about her from the beginning. She was able to guess things. She'd

87

know that the patient in room so-and-so had just died, or exactly where they could find a lost wallet, or whatever. Everybody enjoyed this, at first, and often found it useful, but soon it began to bother my parents. They ordered her never to talk about 'things that did not have a clear basis in fact' in the presence of other people. My father had his position as head of the hospital to think about. He didn't want people hearing that his daughter had supernatural powers. Malta put a lock on her mouth after that. Not only did she stop talking about 'things that did not have a clear basis in fact', but she rarely joined in even the most ordinary conversations.

"To me, though, she opened her heart. We grew up very close. She would say, 'Don't ever tell anybody I told you this', and then she'd say something like, 'There's going to be a fire down the street' or 'Auntie So-and-so in Setagaya is going to get worse.' And she was always right. I was still just a little girl, so I thought it was great fun. It never occurred to me to be frightened or to find it eerie. Ever since I can remember, I would always follow my big sister around and expect to hear her 'messages'.

"These special powers of hers grew stronger as she grew older, but she did not know how to use or nurture them, and this caused her a great deal of anguish. There was no one she could go to for advice, no one she could look to for guidance. This made her a very lonely teenager. She had to solve everything by herself. She had to find all the answers herself. In our home, she was unhappy. There was never a time when she could find peace in her heart. She had to suppress her powers and keep them hidden. It was like growing a large, powerful plant in a little pot. It was unnatural. It was wrong. All she knew was that she had to get out of there as soon as possible. She believed that somewhere there was a world that was right for her, a way of life that was right for her. Until she graduated from high school, though, she had to keep herself in check.

"She was determined not to go to college, but rather to go abroad after leaving school. My parents had lived a very ordinary life, of course, and they were not prepared to let her do this. So my sister worked hard to raise the money she would need, and then she ran away. The first place she went to was Hawaii. She lived on Kauai for two years. She had read somewhere that Kauai's north shore had an area with springs that produced marvellous water. Already, back then, my sister had a profound interest in water. She believed that human existence was largely controlled by the elements of water. Which is why she went to live on Kauai. At the time, there was still a hippie commune in the interior of the island.

She lived as a member of the commune. The water there had a great influence on her spiritual powers. By taking that water into her body, she was able to attain a greater harmony between her powers and her physical being. She wrote to me, telling me how wonderful this was, and her letters made me very happy. But soon the area could no longer satisfy her. True, it was a beautiful, peaceful land, and the people there sought only spiritual peace, free of material desires, but they were too dependent on sex and drugs. My sister did not need these things. After two years on Kauai, she left.

"From there she went to Canada, and after travelling around the northern United States, she continued on to Europe. She sampled the water everywhere she went and succeeded in finding marvellous water in several places, but none of it was the perfect water. So she kept travelling. Whenever she ran out of money, she would do something like fortune-telling. People would reward her for helping them find lost things or missing persons. She would have preferred not to take the money. Powers bestowed by heaven should not be exchanged for worldly goods. At the time, though, it was the only way she could keep herself alive. People heard about her divination everywhere she went. It was easy for her to make money. She even helped the police with an investigation in England. A little girl was missing, and she found where the body had been hidden. She also found the murderer's glove nearby. The man was arrested and confessed. It was in all the papers. I'll show you the clippings sometime. Anyhow, she went on wandering through Europe like this until she ended up in Malta. Close to five years had gone by since her departure from Japan, and this place turned out to be her final destination in her search for water. I suppose she must have told you about this herself?"

I nodded.

"All the time she was wandering through the world, Malta would send me letters. Of course, there were times when she couldn't manage to write, but almost every week I would receive a long letter from her about where she was and what she was doing. We were still very close. Even over long distances, we were able to share our feelings with each other through her letters. And what wonderful letters they were! If you could read them, you'd see what a wonderful person she is. Through her letters, I was able to encounter so many different worlds, so many interesting people! Her letters gave me such encouragement! They helped me grow. For that, I will always be deeply grateful to my sister. I don't deny what she did for me in any way. But ultimately, letters are just letters. When

I was in my most difficult teenage years, when I needed my sister more than ever, she was always somewhere far away. I could not stretch out my hand and find her there next to me. At home, I was all alone. Isolated. My teenage years were filled with pain – and later I will tell you more about that pain. There was no one I could go to for advice. In that sense, I was just as lonely as Malta had been. If she had been near me then, my life would have been different from what it is today. She would have given me words of advice and encouragement and salvation. But what's the point of bringing such things up now? Just as Malta had to find her own way, I had to find mine. And when I turned twenty, I decided to kill myself."

Creta Kano took her cup and drank the remaining coffee.

"What delicious coffee!" she said.

"Thanks," I said, as casually as possible. "Can I offer you something to eat? I boiled some eggs a little while ago."

After some hesitation, she said she would have one. I brought eggs and salt from the kitchen and poured her more coffee. With no sense of urgency, Creta Kano and I set about peeling and eating our eggs and drinking coffee. While we were doing this, the phone rang, but I didn't answer it. After fifteen or sixteen rings, it stopped. All that time, Creta Kano seemed unaware of the ringing.

When she finished her egg, Creta Kano took a small handkerchief from her white patent-leather bag and wiped her mouth. Then she tugged at the hem of her skirt.

"Once I had decided to kill myself, I wanted to leave a note behind. I sat at my desk for an hour, trying to write down my reasons for dying. I wanted to make it clear that no one else was to blame, that the reasons were all inside me. I didn't want my family feeling responsible for something that was not their fault.

"But I could not finish the note. I tried over and over again, but each new version seemed worse than the last. When I read what I had written, it sounded foolish, even comical. The more serious I tried to make it, the more ridiculous it came out. In the end, I decided not to write anything at all.

"It was a very simple matter, I felt. I was disappointed with my life. I could no longer endure the many kinds of pain that my life continued to cause me. I had endured the pain for twenty years. My life had been nothing but an unremitting source of pain. But I had tried to bear it as best I could. I have absolute confidence in my efforts to bear the pain. I can declare here with genuine pride that my efforts were second to none. I was not giving up without a fight. But the day I turned twenty, I reached a simple conclusion: life was not worth it. Life was not worth such a struggle."

She stopped speaking and spent some time aligning the corners of the white handkerchief on her lap. When she looked down, her long false eyelashes cast gentle shadows on her face.

I cleared my throat. I felt I ought to say something, but I didn't know what to say, and so I kept silent. In the distance, I heard the wind-up bird cry.

"The pain was what caused me to decide to die," said Creta Kano. "And when I say 'pain', that is exactly what I mean. Nothing mental or metaphorical, but physical pain, pure and simple. Plain, ordinary, direct, physical – and, for that reason, all the more intense – pain: headache, toothache, period pains, lower back pain, stiff shoulders, fever, muscle ache, burns, frostbite, sprains, fractures, blows to the body. All my life I have experienced physical pain with far greater frequency and intensity than other people. Take my teeth, for example. They seemed to have some congenital defect. They would give me pain from one end of the year to the other. No matter how carefully I brushed, or how many times a day, or how strictly I avoided sweets, it did no good. All my efforts ended in cavities. To make matters worse, anaesthetics seemed to have no effect on me. Going to the dentist was always a nightmare. The pain was beyond describing. It scared me to death. And then my terrible periods began. They were incredibly heavy. For a week at a time, I would be in such pain it was as if someone were twisting a drill inside me. My head would throb. You probably can't imagine what it was like, Mr Okada, but the pain would bring tears to my eyes. For a week out of every month, I would be tortured by this unbearable pain.

"If I boarded a plane, my head would feel as if it were splitting open from the change in air pressure. The doctor said it had something to do with the structure of my ears, that this sort of thing happens if the inner ear has a shape that is sensitive to pressure changes. The same thing often happened to me in lifts. I can't take lifts in tall buildings. The pain is so intense, it feels as if my head is going to split in several places and blood gush out. And then there was my stomach. At least once a week it would give me such sharp, piercing pain that I couldn't get up in the morning. The doctors could never find a cause. Some suggested it was psychosomatic. But even if it was, the pain still hurt. As much as I was suffering, though, I could not stay home from school. If I had skipped school every time something hurt me, I would never have gone at all.

"Whenever I bumped into something, it would leave a bruise on my body. Looking at myself in the bathroom mirror always made me want to cry. My body was covered with so many dark bruises I looked like a rotten apple. I hated letting anyone see me in a bathing suit. Ever since I can remember, I've hardly ever gone swimming for that reason. Another problem I had was the difference in the size of my feet. Whenever I bought new shoes, the larger foot would be in terrible pain until the shoe was broken in.

"Because of all these problems, I almost never did sports. In junior school, my friends once dragged me to an ice-skating rink. I fell and hurt my hip so badly that afterwards I would get a terrible ache there every winter. It felt as if I had been jabbed with a big, thick needle. Any number of times, I fell over trying to get up from a chair.

"I suffered from constipation as well. A bowel movement every few days would be nothing but pain for me. And my shoulders would stiffen terribly. The muscles would tighten until they were as hard as a rock. It was so painful, I couldn't stand up, but lying down was no help either. I imagined that my suffering must be much like that of a Chinese punishment I had read about. They would stuff the person in a box for several years. When my shoulders were at their worst, I could hardly breathe.

"I could go on and on listing all the various pains I have suffered in my life, but it would only bore you, Mr Okada, so I will just leave it at this. What I want to convey to you is the fact that my body was a virtual sample book of pain. I experienced every pain imaginable. I began to think I had been cursed, that life was so unfair. I might have been able to go on bearing the pain if other people in the world had had to live the way I did, but they didn't, and I couldn't. Pain was not something that was dealt out fairly. I tried asking people about pain, but nobody knew what real pain was. The majority of people in the world live without feeling much pain – at least not on a daily basis. When this finally hit me (I had just entered junior school at the time), it made me so sad I couldn't stop crying. Why me? Why did *I* have to be the one to bear such a terrible burden? I wanted to die then and there.

"But at the same time, another thought came to me. This could not go on for ever. One morning I would wake up and the pain would have disappeared – suddenly, with no explanation – and a whole new and peaceful life without pain would open up for me. It was not a thought in which I had much faith, however.

"And so I revealed these thoughts to my sister. I told her that I didn't want to go on living in such pain: what was I to do? After she thought about it for a while, she said this: 'There is definitely something wrong with you, I'm sure. But I don't know what it is. And I don't know what you should do about it. I don't have the power yet to make such judgments. All I know is that you should at least wait until you're twenty. Bear it until you turn twenty, and then make your decision. That would be the best thing.'

"This was how I decided to go on living until I was twenty. But no matter how much time went by, the situation did not improve. Far from it. The pain became even more intense. This taught me only one thing: 'As the body develops, the volume of pain increases proportionately.' I endured the pain, however, for eight years. I went on living all that time, trying to see the good side of life. I didn't complain to anyone. I strove to keep smiling, even when the pain was at its worst. I disciplined myself always to present an exterior of calm when the pain was so intense that I could hardly stand. Crying and complaining could not reduce the pain; it could only make me more miserable than before. As a result of my efforts, people loved me. They saw me as a quiet, good-natured girl. I won the confidence of grown-ups and the friendship of people my own age. I might have had a perfect life, a perfect adolescence, if it hadn't been for the pain. But it was always there. It was like my shadow. If I forgot about it for an instant, the pain would attack yet another part of my body.

"In college, I found a boyfriend, and in the summer of my first year I lost my virginity. Even this – as I could have predicted – gave me only pain. An experienced girlfriend of mine assured me that it would stop hurting when I got used to it, but it never did. Whenever I slept with him, the pain would bring tears to my eyes. One day I told my boyfriend that I didn't want to have sex any more. I told him, 'I love you, but I never want to experience this pain again.' He said he had never heard anything so ridiculous. 'You've got an emotional problem,' he said. 'Just relax and it'll stop hurting. It'll even feel *good*. Everybody else does it, so you can too. You're just not trying hard enough. You're babying yourself. You're using this "pain" thing to cover up your problems. Stop complaining; it won't do you any good.'

"When I heard this, after all I had endured over the years, I exploded. 'What do *you* know about pain?' I shouted at him. 'The pain I feel is no ordinary pain. I know what pain is like. I've had them all. When *I* say something hurts, it *really hurts!*' I tried to explain by listing every single pain I had ever experienced, but he didn't understand a thing. It's impossible to understand real pain unless you've experienced it yourself. So that was the end of our relationship.

"My twentieth birthday came soon after that. For twenty long years I had endured the pain, hoping there would be some turning point, but it had never happened. I felt utterly defeated. I wished I had died sooner. My long detour had only protracted the pain."

At this point, Creta Kano took a single deep breath. On the table in front of her sat the dish with eggshells and her empty coffee cup. On her lap lay the handkerchief that she had folded with such care. As if recalling the time, she glanced at the clock on the shelf. "I'm very sorry," she said in a dry little voice. "I hadn't intended to talk so long. I've taken far too much of your time as it is. I won't impose on you any longer. I don't know how to apologize for having bored you at such length."

She grasped the strap of her white patent-leather bag and stood up from the sofa.

This caught me off guard. "Just a minute, please," I said, flustered. I didn't want her to end her story in the middle. "If you're worried about taking my time, then don't worry. I'm free all afternoon. As you've told me this much, why not go on to the end? There's more to your story, I'm sure."

"Of course there is," she said, looking down at me, both hands tightly gripping the strap of her bag. "What I've told you so far is more like an introduction."

I asked her to wait a moment and went to the kitchen. Standing in front of the sink, I gave myself time for two deep breaths. Then I took two glasses from the cabinet, put ice in them, and filled them with orange juice from the refrigerator. Placing the glasses on a small tray, I brought them into the living room. I had gone through these motions with deliberate slowness, but I found her standing as I had left her. When I set the glasses of juice on the table, though, she seemed to have second thoughts. She settled onto the sofa again and placed her bag at her side.

"You want me to tell my story to the very end?" she asked. "Are you sure?"

"Quite sure," I said.

She drank half her orange juice and went on with her story.

"I failed to kill myself, of course. If I had succeeded, I wouldn't be here now, drinking orange juice with you, Mr Okada." She looked into my eyes, and I gave her a little smile of agreement. "If I had died according to plan, it would have been the final solution for me. Dying would have meant the end of consciousness, and I would never have had to feel pain again. Which is exactly what I wanted. Unfortunately, however, I chose the wrong method to die.

"At 9 o'clock on the night of May 29, I went to my brother's room and asked to borrow his car. It was a shiny new Toyota MR2, and the thought of letting me take it made him look very unhappy. But I didn't care. He couldn't refuse, because I had lent him money to help him buy it. I took the key and drove it for half an hour. The car still had barely a thousand miles on it. A touch on the accelerator could make it fly. It was the perfect car for my purpose. I drove as far as the Tama River on the outskirts of the city, where I found a massive stone wall of the kind I had in mind. It was the outer wall of a big condominium building, and it stood at the far end of a cul-de-sac. I gave myself plenty of room to accelerate, and then I pressed the accelerator to the floor. I must have been doing close to a hundred miles an hour when I slammed into the wall and lost consciousness.

"Unfortunately for me, however, the wall turned out to be far less solid than it had appeared. To save money, they had not anchored it properly. The wall simply crumbled, and the front end of the car was crushed flat. That's all that happened. Because it was so soft, the wall absorbed the impact. As if that weren't bad enough, in my confusion I had forgotten to undo my seat belt.

"And so I escaped death. I was hardly even injured. And strangest of all, I felt almost no pain. It was the weirdest thing. They took me to the hospital and patched up my one broken rib. The police came to investigate, but I told them I didn't remember a thing. I said I had probably confused the accelerator and the brake. And they believed me. I had just turned twenty, and it had been only six months since I got my licence. Besides, I just didn't look like the suicidal type. Who would try to kill herself with her seat belt fastened?

"Once I was out of hospital, I had several difficult problems to face. First I had to pay off the outstanding loan on the MR2 that I had turned into scrap metal. Through some error with the insurance company, the car had not been covered.

"Now that it was too late, I realized that to do myself in I should have rented a car with the proper insurance. At the time, of course, insurance was the last thing on my mind. It never occurred to me that my brother's car wouldn't be insured or that I would fail to kill myself. I ran into a stone wall at a hundred miles an hour: it was amazing that I survived.

"A short time later, I received a bill from the condominium association for the repair of the wall. They were demanding 1,364,294 yen. Immediately. In cash. All I could do was borrow it from my father. He was willing to give it to me in the form of a loan, but he insisted that I pay him back. My father was very proper when it came to money matters. He said it was my responsibility for having caused the accident, and he expected me to pay him back in full and on schedule. In fact, at the time, he had very little money to spare. He was in the process of expanding his clinic and was having trouble raising the money for the project.

"I thought again about killing myself. This time I would do it properly. I would jump from the fifteenth floor of the university administration building. There would be no slip-ups that way. I would die for sure. I made several trial runs. I picked the best window for the job. I was on the verge of jumping.

"But something held me back. There was something wrong, something nagging at me. At the last second, that 'something' almost literally pulled me back from the edge. A good deal of time went by, though, before I realized what that 'something' was.

"I didn't have any pain.

"I had felt hardly any pain since the accident. What with one thing and another, I hadn't had a moment to notice, but pain had disappeared from my body. My bowel movements were normal. My period pains were gone. No more headaches or stomach-aches. Even my broken rib caused me hardly any pain. I had no idea why such a thing had happened. But suddenly I was free of pain.

"I decided to go on living for the time being. If only for a little while, I wanted to find out what it meant to live life without pain. I could die whenever I wanted to.

"But to go on living meant I had to pay back my debt. Altogether, I owed more than three million yen. In order to pay it back, I became a prostitute."

"A prostitute?!"

"That's right," said Creta Kano, as if it were nothing at all. "I needed money in the short term. I wanted to pay off my debts as quickly as possible, and that was the only way I knew of raising the money. I didn't have the slightest hesitation. I had seriously intended to die. And I still intended to die, sooner or later. The curiosity I felt about a life without pain was keeping me alive, but strictly on a temporary basis. And compared with death, it would be nothing at all for me to sell my body."

"I see what you mean," I said.

The ice in her orange juice had melted, and Creta Kano stirred it with her straw before taking a sip.

"Do you mind if I ask you a question?" I asked.

"No, not at all. Please."

"Didn't you consult your sister about this?"

"She was practising her austerities on Malta at the time. As long as that went on, she refused to send me her address. She didn't want me to disrupt her concentration. It was virtually impossible for me to write to her during the entire three years she lived on Malta."

"I see," I said. "Would you like some more coffee?"

"Yes, please," said Creta Kano.

I went to the kitchen and warmed the coffee. While I waited, I stared at the extractor fan and took several deep breaths. When it was ready, I poured the coffee into fresh cups and brought it to the living room on a tray, together with a plate of chocolate cookies. We ate and drank for a while.

"How long ago did you try to kill yourself?" I asked.

"I was twenty at the time. That was six years ago, in May 1978."

May 1978 was the month that Kumiko and I had married. So, then, the very month we were married, Creta Kano had tried to kill herself and Malta Kano was practising her austerities in Malta.

"I went to a neighbourhood that had lots of bars, approached the first likely looking man I saw, negotiated a price, went to a hotel, and slept with him," said Creta Kano. "Sex no longer gave me any physical pain at all. Nor any pleasure, either. It was just a physical movement. Neither did I feel guilt about having sex for money. I was enveloped in numbness, an absence of feeling so deep the bottom was lost from view.

"I made very good money this way – close to a million yen in the first month alone. At that rate, I could easily repay what I owed in three or four months. I would come home from campus, go out in the evening, and get home from work by ten at the latest. I told my parents I was working as a waitress, and no one suspected the truth. Of course, they would have thought it strange if I returned so much money all at once, so I decided to give my father 100,000 yen a month and save the rest.

97

"But then one night, when I was propositioning men by the station, two men grabbed me from behind. At first I thought it was the police, but then I realized that they were gangsters. They dragged me into a back street, showed me some kind of knife, and took me to their local head-quarters. They shoved me into a back room, stripped my clothes off, strung me up by the wrists, and proceeded to rape me over and over in front of a video camera. I kept my eyes closed the entire time and tried not to think. Which was not difficult for me, because I felt neither pain nor pleasure.

"Afterwards, they showed me the video and told me that if I didn't want anyone to see it, I should join their organization and work for them. They took my student ID from my purse. If I refused to do what they wanted, they said, they would send a copy of the tape to my parents and blackmail them for all the money they were worth. I had no choice. I told them I would do as they said, that it didn't matter to me. And it really didn't matter. Nothing mattered to me then. They pointed out that my income would go down if I joined their organization, because they would take seventy per cent, but that I would no longer have to take the trouble to find customers by myself or worry about the police. They would send me high-quality customers. If I went on propositioning men indiscriminately, I would end up strangled to death in some hotel room.

"After that, I didn't have to stand on street corners any more. All I had to do was show up at their office in the evening, and they would tell me which hotel to go to. They sent me good customers, as they had promised. I'm not sure why, but I received special treatment. Maybe it was because I looked so innocent. I had an air of breeding about me that the other girls lacked. There were probably a lot of customers who wanted this not-so-professional type. The other girls had three or more customers a day, but I could get away with seeing only one or, at most, two. The other girls carried beepers with them and had to hurry to some run-down hotel when the office called them to sleep with men of uncertain background. In my case, though, I always had a proper appointment in a proper first-class hotel – or sometimes even a condo. My customers were usually older men, rarely young ones.

"The office paid me once a week – not as much as I had made on my own, but not a bad amount boosted by individual tips from customers. Some customers wanted me to do some pretty weird things for them, of course, but I didn't mind. The weirder the request, the bigger the tip. A few of the men started asking for me on a regular basis. These tended to be good tippers. I saved my money in several different accounts. But by then the money didn't matter to me. It was just rows of figures. I was living for one thing only, and that was to confirm my own lack of feeling.

"I would wake up in the morning and lie there, checking that my body was not sensing anything that could be called pain. I would open my eyes, slowly collect my thoughts, and then, one part at a time, check the feeling I had in my body from head to foot. I had no pain at all. Did this mean that there was nothing hurting me or that, even though there was pain, I was not feeling it? I couldn't tell the difference. Either way, it didn't hurt. In fact, I had no sensations at all. After this procedure, I would get out of bed, go to the bathroom, and brush my teeth. Then I would strip off my pyjamas and take a hot shower. There was a terrible lightness to my body. It was so light and airy, it didn't feel like my body. I felt as if my spirit had taken up residence inside a body that was not my own. I looked at it in the mirror, but between myself and the body I saw there I sensed a long, terrible distance.

"A life without pain: it was the very thing I had dreamed of for years, but now that I had it, I couldn't find a place for myself within it. A clear gap separated me from it, and this caused me great confusion. I felt as if I were not anchored to the world – this world that I had hated so passionately; this world that I had reviled for its unfairness and injustice; this world where at least I knew who I was. Now the world had ceased to be the world, and I had ceased to be me.

"I began to cry a lot. In the afternoons I would go to a park – the Shinjuku Imperial Gardens or Yoyogi Park – to sit on the grass and cry. Sometimes I would cry for an hour or two at a time, sobbing out loud. Passers by would stare at me, but I didn't care. I wished that I had died that time, that I had ended my life on the night of May 29. How much better off I would be! But now I could not even die. In my numbness, I lacked the strength to kill myself. I felt nothing: no pain, no joy. All feeling was gone. And I was not even me."

Creta Kano took a deep breath and held it. Then she picked up her coffee cup, stared into it for a while, gave her head a little shake, and put the cup back on the saucer.

"It was around that time that I met Noboru Wataya."

"Noboru Wataya?! As a customer?!"

Creta Kano nodded in silence.

"But –" I began, then stopped to consider my words. "I'm having a little trouble with this. Your sister told me the other day that Noboru Wataya raped you. Was that something separate from what you're telling me now?"

Creta Kano took the handkerchief from her lap and dabbed at her mouth again. Then she looked directly at me. Something about her eyes stirred my heart in a way I found unsettling.

"I'm sorry to bother you," she said, "but I wonder if I might have another cup of coffee."

"Of course," I said. I put her cup on the tray and carried it into the kitchen. Waiting for the coffee to boil, I leaned against the draining-board with my hands thrust in my pockets. When I carried the coffee back into the living room, Creta Kano had vanished from the sofa. Her bag, her handkerchief, every visible sign of her was gone. I went to the hall, from which her shoes were gone as well.

Terrific.

9

Culverts and an Absolute Insufficiency of Electricity

•

May Kasahara's Inquiry into the Nature of Hairpieces

After seeing Kumiko off the next morning, I went to the municipal pool for a swim. Mornings were best, to avoid the crowds. Back home again, I brewed myself some coffee and sat drinking it in the kitchen, going over Creta Kano's weird, unfinished story, trying to recall each event of her life in chronological order. The more I recalled, the weirder the story seemed, but soon the revolutions of my brain slowed down and I began to drift off to sleep. I went to the living room, lay down on the sofa, and closed my eyes. In a moment, I was asleep and dreaming.

I dreamed about Creta Kano. Before she appeared, though, I dreamed about Malta Kano. She was wearing a Tyrolean hat with a big, brightly coloured feather. The place was crowded (it was some kind of large hall), but Malta Kano's hat caught my attention straight away. She was sitting alone at the bar. She had a big tropical drink in front of her, but I couldn't tell whether she was actually drinking it.

I wore my suit and the polka-dot tie. As soon as I spotted Malta Kano, I tried to walk in her direction, but the crowd kept getting in my way. By the time I reached the bar, she was gone. The tropical drink stood there on the bar, in front of her now empty stool. I took the next seat at the bar and ordered a scotch on the rocks. The bartender asked me what kind of scotch I'd like, and I answered Cutty Sark. I really didn't care which brand of scotch he served me, but Cutty Sark was the first thing that came to mind.

Before he could give me my drink, I felt a hand take my arm from behind, the touch as soft as if the person were grasping something that might fall apart at any moment. I turned. There stood a man without a face. Whether or not he actually had no face, I could not tell, but the place where his face was supposed to be was wrapped in a dark shadow, and I could not see what lay beyond it. "This way, Mr Okada," he said. I tried to speak, but before I could open my mouth, he said to me, "Please, come with me. We have so little time. Hurry." Hand still on my arm, he guided me with rapid steps through the crowd and out into a corridor. I followed him down the corridor, unresisting. He did know my name, after all. It wasn't as if I were letting a total stranger take me anywhere he chose. There was some kind of reason and purpose to all this.

After continuing down the corridor for some time, the faceless man came to a stop in front of a door. The number on the door was 208. "It isn't locked. You should be the one to open it." I did as I was told and opened the door. Beyond it lay a large room. It seemed to be part of a suite of rooms in an old-fashioned hotel. The ceiling was high, and from it hung an old-fashioned chandelier. The chandelier was not lit. A small wall lamp gave off a gloomy light, the only source of illumination in the room. The curtains were closed tight.

"If it's whisky you want, Mr Okada," said the faceless man, "we have plenty. Cutty Sark, wasn't it? Drink as much as you like." He pointed to a cabinet beside the door, then closed the door silently, leaving me alone. I stood in the middle of the room for a long time, wondering what to do.

A large oil painting hung on the wall. It was a picture of a river. I looked at it for a while, hoping to calm myself down. The moon was up over the river. Its light fell faintly on the opposite shore, but so very faintly that I could not make out the scenery there. It was all vague outlines, running together.

Soon I felt a strong craving for whisky. I thought I would open the cabinet and take a drink, as suggested by the faceless man, but the cabinet would not open. What looked like doors were actually well-made imitations of doors. I tried pushing and pulling on the various protruding parts, but the cabinet remained firmly shut.

"It's not easy to open, Mr Okada," said Creta Kano. I realized she was standing there – and in her early sixties outfit. "Some time must go by before it will open. Today is out of the question. You might as well give up."

As I watched, she shed her clothes as easily as opening a pea pod and stood naked before me, without warning or explanation. "We have so little time, Mr Okada, let's finish this as quickly as possible. I am sorry for the rush, but I have my reasons. Just getting here was hard enough." Then she came up to me, opened my fly, and, as if it were the most natural thing in the world, took out my penis. Lowering her eyes, with their false lashes, she enclosed my penis with her mouth. Her mouth was far larger than I had imagined. Inside, I immediately came erect. When she moved her tongue, the curled ends of her hair trembled as in a gentle breeze, caressing my thighs. All I could see was her hair and her false eyelashes. I sat on the bed, and she went down on her knees, her face buried in my crotch. "Stop it," I said. "Noboru Wataya will be here any minute. I don't want to see him here."

Creta Kano took her mouth from my penis and said, "Don't worry. We have plenty of time, for this at least."

She ran the tip of her tongue over my penis. I didn't want to come, but there was no way of stopping it. I felt as if it were being sucked out of me. Her lips and tongue held on to me like slippery life forms. I came. I opened my eyes.

Terrific. I went to the bathroom, washed my soiled underpants and took a hot shower, washing myself with care to get rid of the sticky sensations of the dream. How many years had it been since my last wet dream? I tried to recall exactly but couldn't, it had been so long.

I stepped out of the shower and was still drying myself when the phone rang. It was Kumiko. Having just had a wet dream over another woman, I felt a little tense speaking with her.

"Your voice is strange," she said. "What's wrong?" Her sensitivity to such things was frightening.

"Nothing," I said. "I was dozing. You woke me up."

"Oh, really?" she said. I could feel her suspicion coming through the earpiece, which made me all the more tense.

"Anyway, sorry, but I'm going to be a little late today," Kumiko said. "Maybe as late as 9. So I'll eat out."

"That's OK," I said. "I'll find something for myself. Don't worry."

"I really am sorry," she said. It sounded like an afterthought. There was a pause, and then she hung up.

I looked at the receiver for a few seconds. Then I went to the kitchen and peeled an apple.

•

In the six years since I had married Kumiko, I had never slept with another woman. Which is not to say that I never felt the desire for another woman or never had the chance. Just that I had never pursued it when the opportunity arose. I can't explain why, exactly, but it probably has something to do with life's priorities.

I did once happen to spend the night with another woman. She was someone I liked, and I knew she would have slept with me. But, finally, I didn't do it.

We had been working together at the law firm for several years. She was two or three years younger than I. Her job was to take calls and coordinate everyone's schedules, and she was very good at it. She was quick, and she had an outstanding memory. You could ask her anything and she would know the answer: who was working where at what, which files were in which cabinet, that kind of thing. She handled all appointments. Everybody liked her and depended on her. On an individual basis, too, she and I were fairly close. We had gone drinking together several times. She was not what you would call a beauty, but I liked her looks.

When it was time for her to leave her job to get married (she had to move to Kyushu in connection with her husband's work), several colleagues and I invited her out for a last drink together. Afterwards, she and I had to take the same train home, and because it was late, I saw her to her apartment. At the front door, she invited me in for a cup of coffee. I was worried about missing the last train, but I knew we might never see each other again, and I also liked the idea of sobering up with coffee, so I decided to go in. The place was a typical single girl's apartment. It had a refrigerator that was just a little too grand for one person, and a bookshelf stereo. A friend had given her the refrigerator. She changed into something comfortable in the next room and made coffee in the kitchen. We sat on the floor, talking.

At one point when we had run out of things to say, she asked me, as if it had just then occurred to her: "Can you name something – some concrete thing – that you're especially afraid of?"

"Not really," I said, after a moment's thought. I was afraid of all kinds of things, but no one thing in particular. "How about you?"

"I'm scared of culverts," she said, hugging her knees. "You know what a culvert is, don't you?"

"Some kind of ditch, isn't it?" I didn't have a very precise definition of the word in mind.

"Yeah, but it's underground. An underground waterway. A drainage ditch with a lid on. A pitch-dark flow."

"I see," I said. "A culvert."

"I was born and raised in the country. In Fukushima. There was a stream right near my house – a little stream, just the drainage from the fields. It flowed underground at one point into a culvert. I guess I was playing with some of the older kids when it happened. I was just two or three. The others put me in a little boat and launched it into the stream. It was probably something they did all the time, but that day it had been raining, and the water was high. The boat got away from them and carried me straight for the opening of the culvert. I would have been sucked right in if one of the local farmers hadn't happened by. I'm sure they never would have found me."

She ran her left index finger over her mouth as if to check that she was still alive.

"I can still picture everything that happened. I'm lying on my back and being swept along by the water. The sides of the stream tower over me like high stone walls, and overhead is the blue sky. Sharp, clear blue. I'm being swept along in the flow. Swish, swish, faster and faster. But I can't understand what it means. And then all of a sudden I *do* understand – that there's darkness lying ahead. *Real* darkness. Soon it comes and tries to suck me down. I can feel a cold shadow beginning to wrap itself around me. That's my earliest memory."

She took a sip of coffee.

"I'm scared to death," she said. "I'm so scared I can hardly stand it. I feel like I did back then, like I'm being swept along towards *it* and I can't get away."

She took a cigarette from her handbag, put it in her mouth, and lit it with a match, exhaling in one long, slow breath. This was the first time I had ever seen her smoke.

"Are you talking about your marriage?" I asked.

"That's right," she said. "My marriage."

"Is there some particular problem?" I asked. "Something concrete?"

She shook her head. "I don't think so," she said. "Not really. Just a lot of little things."

I didn't know what to say to her, but the situation demanded that I say something.

"Everybody experiences this feeling to some extent when they're about to get married, I think. 'Oh, no, I'm making a terrible mistake!'

You'd probably be abnormal if you *didn't* feel it. It's a big decision, picking somebody to spend your life with. So it's natural to be scared, but you don't have to be *that* scared."

"That's easy to say – 'Everybody feels like that. Everybody's the same,' " she said.

Eleven o'clock had come and gone. I had to find a way to bring this conversation to a successful conclusion and get out of there. But before I could say anything, she suddenly asked me to hold her.

"Why?" I asked, caught off guard.

"To charge my batteries," she said.

"Charge your batteries?"

"My body has run out of electricity. I haven't been able to sleep for days now. The minute I get to sleep I wake up, and then I can't get back to sleep. I can't think. When I get like that, somebody has to charge my batteries. Otherwise, I can't go on living. It's true."

I peered into her eyes, wondering if she was still drunk, but they were once again her usual cool, intelligent eyes. She was far from drunk.

"But you're getting married next week. You can have him hold you all you want. Every night. That's what marriage is for. You'll never run out of electricity again."

"The problem is *now,*" she said. "Not tomorrow, not next week, not next month. I'm out of electricity *now.*"

Lips clamped shut, she stared at her feet. They were in perfect alignment. Small and white, they had ten pretty toenails. She really, truly wanted somebody to hold her, it seemed, and so I took her in my arms. It was all very weird. To me, she was just a capable, pleasant colleague. We worked in the same office, told each other jokes, and had gone out for drinks now and then. But here, away from work, in her apartment, with my arms around her, we were nothing but warm lumps of flesh. We had been playing our assigned roles on the office stage, but stepping down from the stage, abandoning the images that we had been projecting there, we were both just unstable, awkward lumps of flesh, warm pieces of meat kitted out with digestive tracts and hearts and brains and reproductive organs. I had my arms wrapped around her back, and she had her breasts pressed hard against my chest. They were larger and softer than I had imagined them to be. I was sitting on the floor with my back against the wall, and she was slumped against me. We stayed in that position for a long time, holding each other without a word.

"Is this all right?" I asked, in a voice that did not sound like my own. It was as if someone else were speaking for me.

She said nothing, but I could feel her nod.

She was wearing a sweatshirt and a thin skirt that came down to her knees, but soon I realized that she had nothing on underneath. Almost automatically, this gave me an erection, and she seemed to be aware of it. I could feel her warm breath on my neck.

In the end, I didn't sleep with her. But I did have to go on "charging her batteries" until 2 in the morning. She pleaded with me to stay with her until she was asleep. I took her to her bed and tucked her in. But she remained awake for a long time. She changed into pyjamas, and I went on holding and "recharging" her. In my arms, I felt her cheeks grow hot and her heart pound. I couldn't be sure I was doing the right thing, but I knew of no other way to deal with the situation. The simplest thing would have been to sleep with her, but I managed to sweep that possibility from my mind. My instincts told me not to do it.

"Please don't hate me for this," she said. "My electricity is so low I just can't help it."

"Don't worry," I said. "I understand."

I knew I should call home, but what could I have said to Kumiko? I didn't want to lie, but I knew it would be impossible to explain to her what was happening. And after a while, it didn't seem to matter any more. Whatever happened would happen. I left her apartment at 2 o'clock and didn't get home until 3. It was tough finding a cab.

Kumiko was furious, of course. She was sitting at the kitchen table, wide awake, waiting for me. I said I had been out drinking and playing mah-jongg with the guys from the office. Why couldn't I have made a simple phone call? she demanded. It had never crossed my mind, I said. She was not convinced, and the lie became apparent almost immediately. I hadn't played mah-jongg in years, and I just wasn't cut out for lying in any case. I ended up confessing the truth. I told her the entire story from beginning to end – without the erection part, of course – insisting that I had done nothing with the woman.

Kumiko refused to speak to me for three days. Literally. Not a word. She slept in the other room, and she ate her meals alone. This was the greatest crisis our marriage had faced. She was genuinely angry with me, and I understood exactly how she felt.

After her three days of silence, Kumiko asked me, "What would *you* think if you were in *my* position?" These were the very first words she spoke. "What if *I* had come home at 3 o'clock on Sunday morning without so much as a telephone call? 'I've been in bed with a man all this time, but don't worry, I didn't do anything, please believe me. I was just recharging his batteries. OK, great, let's have breakfast and go to sleep.' You mean to say you wouldn't get angry, you'd just believe me?"

I kept quiet.

"And what you did was even worse than that," Kumiko continued. "You *lied* to me! You said you were drinking and playing mah-jongg. A complete lie! How do you expect me to believe you didn't sleep with her?"

"I'm sorry I lied," I said. "I should never have done that. But the only reason I lied was because the truth was so difficult to explain. I want you to believe me: I really didn't do anything wrong."

Kumiko put her head on the table. I felt as if the air in the room were gradually thinning out.

"I don't know what to say," I said. "I can't explain it other than to ask you to believe me."

"All right. If you want me to believe you, I will," she said. "But I want *you* to remember this: I'm probably going to do the same thing to you someday. And when that time comes, I want *you* to believe *me*. I have that right."

Kumiko had never exercised that right. Every once in a while, I imagined how I would feel if she did exercise it. I would probably believe her, but my reaction would no doubt be as complex and as difficult to deal with as Kumiko's. To think that she had made a point of doing such a thing – and for what? Which was exactly how she must have felt about me back then.

•

"Mr Wind-up Bird!" came a voice from the garden. It was May Kasahara.

Still towelling my hair, I went out to the veranda. She was sitting on the edge, biting a thumbnail. She wore the same dark sunglasses as when I had first met her, plus cream-coloured cotton trousers and a black polo shirt. In her hand was a clipboard.

"I climbed it," she said, pointing to the breeze-block wall. Then she brushed away the dirt clinging to her trousers. "I figured I had the right place. I'm glad it was yours! Think if I had come over the wall into the wrong house!"

She took a pack of Hope regulars from her pocket and lit up.

"Anyhow, Mr Wind-up Bird, how are you?"

"OK, I guess."

"I'm going to work now," she said. "Why don't you come along? We work in teams of two, and it'd be *sooo* much better for me to have somebody I know. Some new guy'd ask me all kinds of questions – 'How old are you? Why aren't you in school?' It's such a pain! Or maybe he'd turn out to be a pervert. It happens, you know! Do it for me, will you, Mr Wind-up Bird?"

"Is it that job you told me about – some kind of survey for a wig maker?"

"That's it," she said. "All you have to do is count bald heads on the Ginza from one to four. It's easy! And it'll be good for you. You'll be bald too someday, the way you're going, so you better check it out now while you still have hair."

"Yeah, but how about you? Isn't the truant officer going to get you if they see you doing this stuff on the Ginza in the middle of the day?"

"Nah. I just tell them it's fieldwork for social studies. It always works."

With no plans for the afternoon, I decided to tag along. May Kasahara phoned her company to say we would be coming. On the telephone, she turned into a very proper young woman: Yes, sir, I would like to team up with him, yes, that is correct, thank you very much, yes, I understand, yes, we can be there by noon. I left a note for Kumiko saying I would be back by 6, in case she got home early, then I left the house with May Kasahara.

The wig company was in Shimbashi. On the subway, May Kasahara explained how the survey worked. We were to stand on a street corner and count all the bald men (or those with thinning hair) who walked by. We were to classify them according to the degree of their baldness: C, those whose hair had thinned somewhat; B, those who had lost a lot; and A, those who were totally bald. May took a pamphlet from her folder and showed me examples of the three stages.

"You get the idea pretty much, right – which heads fit which categories? I won't go into details. It'd take all day. But you get it pretty much, which is which?"

"Pretty much," I said, without exuding a great deal of confidence.

On May Kasahara's other side sat an overweight company type – a very definite B – who kept glancing uneasily at the pamphlet, but she seemed not to notice how nervous this was making him.

"I'll be in charge of putting them into categories, and you stand next to me with a survey sheet. You put them in A, B or C, depending on what I tell you. That's all there is to it. Easy, right?"

"I suppose so," I said. "But what's the point of doing a survey like this?"

"I dunno," she said. "They're doing them all over Tokyo – in Shinjuku, Shibuya, Aoyama. Maybe they're trying to find out which neighbourhood has the most bald men. Or they want to know the proportions of A, B and C types in the population. Who knows? They've got so much money, they don't know what to do with it. So they waste it on stuff like this. Profits are huge in the wig business. The employees get *much* bigger bonuses than in just any old company. Know why?"

"No. Why?"

"Wigs don't last long. Bet you didn't know: toupees are good for two, maybe three years max. The better made they are, the faster they get used up. They're the ultimate consumer product. It's because they fit so tightly against the scalp: the hair underneath gets thinner than ever. Once that happens, you have to buy a new one to get that perfect fit again. And think about it: What if you had a toupee and it was no good after two years – what would go through your mind? Would you think, OK, my wig's worn out. Can't wear it any more. But it'll cost too much to buy a new one, so tomorrow I'll start going to work without one? Is that what you'd think?"

I shook my head. "Probably not," I said.

"Of course not. Once a guy starts using a wig, he has to keep using one. It's like his fate. That's why the wig makers make such huge profits. I hate to say it, but they're like drug dealers. Once they get their hooks into a guy, he's a customer for life. Have you ever heard of a bald guy suddenly growing a head of hair? *I* never have. A wig's got to cost half a million yen at least, maybe a million for a tough one. And you need a new one every two years! Wow! Even a car lasts longer than that – four or five years. And then you can trade it in!"

"I see what you mean," I said.

"Plus, the wig makers run their own hairdressing salons. They wash the wigs and cut the customers' real hair. I mean, think about it: you can't just plonk yourself down in an ordinary barber's chair, rip off your wig, and say, 'I'd like a trim,' can you? The income from these places alone is tremendous."

"You know all kinds of things," I said, with genuine admiration. The B-category company type next to May was listening to our conversation with obvious fascination.

"Sure," she said. "The guys at the office like me. They tell me everything. The profits in this business are huge. They make the wigs in South-east Asia and places like that, where labour is cheap. They even get the hair there – in Thailand or the Philippines. The women sell their hair to the wig companies. That's how they earn their dowries in some places. The whole world's so weird! The guy sitting next to you might actually be wearing the hair of some woman in Indonesia."

By reflex, the B-man and I looked around at the others in the car.

•

We stopped off at the company's Shimbashi office to pick up an envelope containing survey sheets and pencils. This company supposedly had a number two market share, but it was utterly discreet, without even a name plaque at the entrance, so that customers could come and go with ease. Neither the envelope nor the survey sheets bore the company name. At the survey department, I filled out a part-time worker's registration form with my name, address, educational background and age. This office was an incredibly quiet place of business. There was no one shouting into the telephone, no one banging away at a computer keyboard with sleeves rolled up. Each individual worker was neatly dressed and pursuing his or her own task with quiet concentration. As might be expected at a wig maker's office, not one man here was bald. Some might even be wearing the company's product, but it was impossible for me to tell those who were from those who weren't. Of all the companies I had ever visited, this had the strangest ambience.

We took the subway to the Ginza. Early and hungry, we stopped at the Dairy Queen for a hamburger.

"Tell me, Mr Wind-up Bird," said May Kasahara, "would you wear a wig if you were bald?"

"I wonder," I said. "I don't like things that take time and trouble. I probably wouldn't try to fight it if I went bald."

"Good," she said, wiping the ketchup from her mouth with a paper napkin. "That's the way. Bald men never look as bad as they think. To me, it's nothing to get so upset about."

"I wonder," I said.

•

For the next three hours, we sat at the subway entrance by the Wako Building, counting the bald-headed men who passed by. Looking down at the heads going up and down the stairs was the most accurate method of determining the degree of baldness of any one head. May Kasahara would say "A" or "B" or "C", and I would write it down. She had obviously done this many times. She never fumbled or hesitated or corrected herself, but assigned each head to its proper category with great speed and precision, uttering the letters in low, clipped tones so as not to be noticed by the passers-by. This called for some rapid-fire naming whenever a large group of bald heads passed by at once: "CCBABCAACCBBB". At one point, an elegant-looking old gentleman (who himself possessed a full head of snow-white hair) stopped to watch us in action. "Pardon me," he said to me after a while, "but might I ask what you two are doing?"

"Survey," I said.

"What kind of survey?" he asked.

"Social studies," I said.

"CACABC," said May Kasahara.

The old gentleman seemed less than convinced, but he went on watching us until he gave up and wandered off somewhere.

When the Mitsukoshi clock across the street signalled 4 o'clock, we ended our survey and went back to the Dairy Queen for a cup of coffee. It had not been strenuous work, but I found that my neck and shoulders were strangely stiff. Maybe it was from the covert nature of the job, a guilty feeling I had about counting bald men in secret. All the time we were on the subway heading back to company headquarters in Shimbashi, I found myself automatically assigning each bald head I saw to category A or B or C, which almost made me queasy. I tried to stop myself, but by then a kind of momentum had set in. We handed in our survey forms and received our pay – rather good pay for the amount of time and effort involved. I signed a receipt and put the money in my pocket. May Kasahara and I took the subway to Shinjuku and from there took the Odakyu Line home. The afternoon rush hour was starting. This was my first ride on a crowded train for some time, but it hardly filled me with nostalgia.

"Pretty good job, don't you think?" said May Kasahara, standing next to me on the train. "It's easy, pay's not bad."

"Pretty good," I said, sucking on a lemon drop.

"Go with me next time? We can do it once a week."

"Why not?" I said.

"You know, Mr Wind-up Bird," May Kasahara said after a short silence, as if a thought had suddenly come to her, "I bet the reason people are afraid of going bald is because it makes them think of the end of life. I mean, when your hair starts to thin, it must feel as if your life is being worn away . . . as if you've taken a giant step in the direction of death, the last Big Consumption."

I thought about it for a while. "That's certainly one way to look at it," I said.

"You know, Mr Wind-up Bird, I sometimes wonder what it must feel like to die little by little over a long period of time. What do you think?"

Unsure exactly what she was getting at, I changed my grip on the hand strap and looked into her eyes. "Can you give me a specific example of what you mean by that – to die little by little?"

"Well . . . I don't know. You're trapped in the dark all alone, with nothing to eat, nothing to drink, and little by little you die. . . ."

"It must be terrible," I said. "Painful. I wouldn't want to die like that if I could help it."

"But finally, Mr Wind-up Bird, isn't that just what life is? Aren't we all trapped in the dark somewhere, and they've taken away our food and water, and we're slowly dying, little by little . . . ?"

I laughed. "You're too young to be so . . . *pessimistic*," I said, using the English word.

"Pessi-what?"

"Pessimistic. It means looking only at the dark side of things."

"Pessimistic . . . pessimistic . . ." She repeated the English to herself over and over, and then she looked up at me with a fierce glare. "I'm only sixteen," she said, "and I don't know much about the world, but I *do* know one thing for sure. If I'm pessimistic, then the adults in this world who are *not* pessimistic are a bunch of idiots."

10

Magic Touch

•

Death in the Bathtub

•

Messenger with Keepsakes

We had moved into our present house in the autumn of the second year we were married. The Koenji apartment we had lived in until then was slated for renovation. We looked for a cheap, convenient apartment to move into, but finding such a place was not easy with our budget. When he heard this, my uncle suggested that we move into a house he owned in Setagaya. He had bought it in his youth and lived there for ten years. He wanted to tear the old place down and put up something more func-tional, but architectural regulations prevented him from building the kind of house he wanted. He was waiting for a rumoured relaxation of the rules to take effect, but if he left the place vacant in the meantime, he would have to pay property taxes, and if he rented it to strangers, there could be trouble when he asked them to vacate. From us, he would take only a nominal rent to cover the taxes, but in return he wanted us to agree to give up the place with three months' notice when the time came. We had no problem with that: the part about the taxes was not entirely clear to us, but we jumped at the chance to live in a real house, if only for a little while, paying the kind of rent we had been paying to live in an apartment (and a very cheap apartment at that). The house was quite far from the nearest station on the Odakyu Line, but it was in a quiet resi-dential neighbourhood, and it had its own small yard. Even though it didn't belong to us, it gave us the feeling, once we moved in, that we were now part of a real "household".

My mother's younger brother, this uncle of mine never made any demands on us. He was kind of a cool guy, I suppose, but there was something almost uncanny about him in the way he left us alone. Still, he was my favourite relative. He had graduated from a college in Tokyo and gone to work as a radio announcer, but when he got sick of the work after ten years, he quit the station and opened a bar on the Ginza. It was an austere little place, but it became widely known for the authenticity of its cocktails, and within a few years my uncle was running a string of bars and restaurants. Every one of his establishments did extremely well: he seemingly had that special spark you need for business. Once, while I was still at college, I asked him why every place he opened was such a success. In the very same location on the Ginza where one restaurant had failed, he might open up the same kind of restaurant and do just fine. Why was that? He held the palms of both hands out for me to see. "It's my magic touch," he said, without a hint of humour. And that was all he said.

Maybe he really did have a "magic touch", but he also had a talent for finding capable people to work for him. He paid them high salaries and treated them well, and they in turn worked hard for him. "When I know I've got the right guy, I put a wad of bills in his hand and let him do his thing," he once told me. "You've got to spend your money on the things that money can buy, not worry about profit or loss. Save your energy for the things that money can't buy."

He married late in life. Only after he had achieved financial success in his mid-forties did he settle down. His wife was a divorcée, three or four years his junior, and she brought her own considerable assets to the marriage. My uncle never told me how he happened to meet her, and all I could tell about her was that she was a quiet sort of woman of good background. They had no children. She had apparently had no children with her first husband, either, which may have been the reason for the divorce. In any case, though not exactly a rich man, my uncle was in a position in his mid-forties where it was no longer necessary for him to break his back over money. In addition to the profits from his restaurants and bars, he had rental income from several houses and condos that he owned, plus a steady income from investments. With its reputation for respectable businesses and modest lifestyles, the family tended to see my uncle as something of a black sheep, and he had never shown much inclination for consorting with relatives. As his only nephew, though, I had always been of some concern to him, especially after my mother died the year I entered college and I had a falling-out with my father, who remarried. When I was living the lonely life of a poor college student in Tokyo, my uncle often treated me to dinner in one or another of his Ginza restaurants.

He and his wife now lived in a condo on a hill in Azabu rather than be bothered with taking care of a house. He was not given to indulging in luxuries, but he did have one hobby, which was collecting rare cars. He kept a Jaguar and an Alfa Romeo in the garage, both of them antiques and extremely well cared for, as shiny as newborn babes.

•

On the phone with my uncle about something else, I took the opportunity to ask him what he knew about May Kasahara's family.

"Kasahara, you say?" He took a moment to think. "Never heard of them. I was a bachelor when I lived there, never had anything to do with the neighbours."

"Actually, it's the house opposite theirs I'm curious about, the vacant house on the other side of the alley from their backyard," I said. "I think somebody named Miyawaki used to live there. Now it's all boarded up."

"Oh, Miyawaki. Sure, I knew him," said my uncle. "He used to own a few restaurants. Had one on the Ginza too. I met him professionally a few times. His places were nothing much, to tell you the truth, but he had good locations. I thought he was doing all right. He was a nice guy, but kind of a spoiled-rich-kid type. He had never had to work hard, or he just never got the hang of it or something, but he never quite grew up. Somebody got him going on the stock market, took him for everything he had – house, land, businesses, everything. And the timing couldn't have been worse. He was trying to open a new place, had his house and land up as collateral. Bang! The whole thing. Had a couple of daughters, I think, college age."

"The house has been empty ever since, I suppose."

"No kidding? I bet the title's a mess and his assets have been frozen or something. You'd better not touch that place, no matter what kind of bargain they're offering you."

"Who? Me?" I laughed. "I could never afford a place like that. But what do you mean?"

"I looked into that house when I bought mine. There's something wrong with it."

"You mean like ghosts?"

"Maybe not ghosts, but I've never heard anything good about the place," my uncle said. "Some fairly well-known army guy lived there till the end of the war, Colonel Somebody-or-other, a real super-elite officer. The troops under his command in North China won all kinds of decorations, but they did some terrible things there – executing five-hundred POWs, forcing tens of thousands of farmers to work for them until half of them dropped dead, stuff like that. These are the stories that were going around, so I don't know how much is true. He was called home just before the end of the war, so he was here for the surrender, and he could see from what was going on that he was likely to be tried as a war criminal. The guys who had gone crazy in China – the generals, the field officers – were being dragged away by the MPs. Well, he had no intention of being put on trial. He was not going to be made a spectacle of and hanged into the bargain. He preferred to take his own life rather than let that happen. So one day when he saw a GI stop a jeep in front of his house, he blew his brains out on the spot. He would have preferred to slit his stomach open the old-fashioned samurai way, but there was no time for that. His wife hanged herself in the kitchen to 'accompany' her husband in death."

"Wow."

"Anyhow, it turned out the GI was just an ordinary GI, looking for his girlfriend. He was lost. He wanted to ask directions. You know how tough it is to find your way around that place. Deciding it's your time to die – that can't be easy for anybody."

"No, it can't be."

"The house was vacant for a while after that, until an actress bought it – a movie actress. You wouldn't know her name. She was around long before your time, and she was never very famous. She lived there, say, ten years or so. Just she and her maid. She was single. A few years after she moved in, she contracted some eye disease. Everything looked cloudy to her, even close up. But she was an actress, after all; she couldn't work with glasses on. And contact lenses were a new thing back then. They weren't very good and almost nobody used them. So before the crew shot a scene, she would always go over the layout and memorize how many steps she had to take from A to B. She managed one way or another: they were pretty simple films, those old Shochiku domestic dramas. Everything was more relaxed in those days. Then one day, after she had checked over the set and gone back to her dressing room, a young cameraman who didn't know what was going on moved the props and things just a little bit."

"Uh-oh."

"She missed her footing, fell over, and couldn't walk after that. And her vision started getting even worse. She was practically blind. It was a shame; she was still young and pretty. Of course her movie-making days were over. All she could do was stay at home. And then the maid took all her money and ran off with some guy. This maid was the one person she knew she could trust, depended on her for everything, and the woman took her savings, her stocks, everything. Boy, talk about terrible stories! So what do you think she did?"

"Well, obviously this story can't have a bright, happy ending."

"No, obviously," said my uncle. "She filled the tub, stuck her face in, and drowned herself. You realize, of course, that to die that way, you have to be pretty damned determined."

"Nothing bright and happy about that."

"No, nothing bright and happy. Miyawaki bought the property soon afterwards. I mean, it's a nice place; everybody wants it when they see it. The neighbourhood is pleasant, the plot is on high ground and gets good sunlight, the lot is big. But Miyawaki had heard the dark stories about the people who had lived there, so he had the whole thing torn down, foundations and all, and put up a new house. He even had Shinto priests come in to do a purification. But that wasn't enough, I guess. Bad things happen to anybody who lives there. It's just one of those pieces of land. They exist, that's all. I wouldn't take it if they gave it to me."

·

After shopping at the supermarket, I organized my ingredients for making dinner. I then took in the laundry, folded it neatly, and put it away. Back in the kitchen, I made myself a pot of coffee. This was a nice, quiet day, without calls from anybody. I stretched out on the sofa and read a book. There was no one to disturb my reading. Every once in a while, the wind-up bird would creak in the backyard. It was virtually the only sound I heard all day.

Someone rang the front doorbell at 4 o'clock. It was the postman. "Registered mail," he said, and handed me a thick envelope. I took it and put my seal on the receipt.

This was no ordinary envelope. It was made of old-fashioned heavy rice paper, and someone had gone to the trouble of writing my name and address on it with a brush, in bold black characters. The sender's name on the back was Tokutaro Mamiya, the address somewhere in Hiroshima Prefecture. I had no knowledge whatsoever of either. Judging from the brushwork, this Tokutaro Mamiya was a man of advanced age. Nobody knew how to write like that any more.

I sat on the sofa and used some scissors to cut the envelope open. The letter itself, just as old-fashioned as the envelope, was written on rolled rice paper in a flowing hand by an obviously cultivated person. Lacking such cultivation myself, I could hardly read it. The sentence style matched the handwriting in its extreme formality, which only complicated the process, but in time I managed to grasp the general meaning. It said that old Mr Honda, the fortune-teller whom Kumiko and I had gone to see so long ago, had died of a heart attack two weeks earlier in his Meguro home. Living alone, he had died without company, but the doctors believed that he had gone quickly and without a great deal of suffering – perhaps the one bright feature of this sad tale. The maid had found him in the morning, slumped forward on the low table of his foot warmer. The letter writer, Tokutaro Mamiya, had been stationed in Manchuria as a first lieutenant and had chanced to share the dangers of war with Corporal Oishi Honda. Now, in compliance with the explicit wishes of the deceased, and in the absence of surviving relatives, Mamiya had undertaken the task of distributing the keepsakes. The deceased had left behind extremely minute written instructions in this regard. "The detailed and meticulous will suggests that Mr Honda had anticipated his own impending death. It states explicitly that he would be extremely pleased if you, Mr Toru Okada, would be so kind as to receive a certain item as a remembrance of him. I can imagine how very busy you must be, Mr Okada, but I can assure you, as an old comrade in arms of the deceased with few years to look forward to myself, that I could have no greater joy than if you were indeed to be so kind as to receive this item as a small remembrance of the late Mr Honda." The letter concluded with the address at which Mr Mamiya was presently staying in Tokyo, care of someone else named Mamiya in Hongo 2-chome, Bunkyo Ward. I imagined he must be in the house of a relative.

I wrote my reply at the kitchen table. I had hoped to keep the postcard short and simple, but once I had pen in hand, those few concise phrases were not forthcoming. "I was fortunate enough to have known the late Mr Honda and benefited from our brief acquaintance. The news that he is no longer living brings back memories of those times. Our ages were very different, of course, and our association lasted but a single year, yet

I always used to feel that there was something about the deceased that moved people deeply. To be quite honest, I would never have imagined that Mr Honda would name me specifically as the recipient of a keepsake, nor am I certain that I am even qualified to receive anything from him, but if such was his wish, then I will certainly do so with all due respect. Please contact me at your earliest convenience."

When I dropped the card into the nearest letter box, I found myself murmuring old Mr Honda's verse: "Dying is the only way / For you to float free: / Nomonhan."

•

It was close to 10 before Kumiko came home from work. She had called before 6 to say that she would be late again today, that I should have dinner without her and she would grab something. Fine, I said, and ate a simple meal. Again I stayed at home alone, reading a book. When she came in, Kumiko said she wanted a few sips of beer. We shared a medium-size bottle. She looked tired. Elbows on the kitchen table, she rested her chin in her hands and said little when I spoke to her. She seemed pre-occupied. I told her that Mr Honda had died. "Oh, really?" she said, with a sigh. "Oh, well, he was getting on in years, and he was almost deaf." When I said that he had left a keepsake for me, though, she was shocked, as if something had suddenly fallen out of the sky.

"For you?!" she exclaimed, her eyebrows twisting into a frown.

"Yeah. Weird, isn't it?"

"He must have liked you."

"How could that be? I never really talked to the guy," I said. "At least *I* never said much. And even if I did, he couldn't hear anything. We used to sit and listen to his stories once a month. And all we ever heard from him was the Battle of Nomonhan: how they threw Molotov cocktails, and which tank caught fire, and which tank didn't, that kind of stuff."

"Don't ask me," said Kumiko. "He must have liked something about you. I don't understand people like that, what's in their minds."

After that, she went silent again. It was a strained silence. I glanced at the calendar on the wall. Her period was not due yet. I imagined that something unpleasant might have happened at the office.

"Working too hard?" I asked.

"A little," Kumiko said, after taking a sip of beer and staring at what was left in her glass. There was an almost defiant tone in her voice. "Sorry I was so late, but you know how it is with magazine work when we get busy. And it's not as if I do this all the time. I get them to give me less overtime than most. They know I have a husband to go home to."

I nodded. "I'm not blaming you," I said. "I know you have to work late sometimes. I'm just worried that you're letting yourself get tired out."

She took a long shower. I drank my beer and flipped through a weekly magazine that she had brought home.

I shoved my hand in my trouser pocket and found the pay there from my recent little part-time job. I hadn't even taken the cash from the envelope. Another thing I hadn't done was tell Kumiko about the job. Not that I had been hiding it from her, but I had let the opportunity to mention it slip by and there had never been another one. As time passed, I found it harder to bring up the subject, for some strange reason. All I would have had to say was, "I met this odd sixteen-year-old girl from down the street and took a job with her doing a survey for a wig maker. The pay was pretty good too." And Kumiko could have said, "Oh, really? Isn't that nice," and that might have been the end of it. Or not. She might have wanted to know more about May Kasahara. She might have been bothered that I was making friends with a sixteen-year-old girl. Then I would have had to tell her about May Kasahara and explain in detail where, when, and how we happened to meet. But I'm not very good at giving people orderly explanations of things.

I took the money from the envelope and put it in my wallet. The envelope itself I crumpled and threw in the wastebasket. So this was how secrets started, I thought to myself. People constructed them little by little. I had not consciously intended to keep May Kasahara a secret from Kumiko. My relationship with her was not that big a deal: whether I mentioned it or not was of no consequence. Once it had flowed down a certain delicate channel, however, it had become cloaked in the opacity of secretiveness, whatever my original intention may have been. The same thing had happened with Creta Kano. I had told Kumiko that Malta Kano's younger sister had come to the house, that her name was Creta, that she dressed in early-sixties style, that she took samples of our tap water. But I had remained silent on the fact that she had afterwards begun to make startling revelations to me and had vanished without a word before reaching the end. Creta Kano's story had been too far-out: I could never have re-created the nuances and conveyed them to Kumiko, and so I had not tried. Or then again, Kumiko might have been less than pleased that Creta Kano had stayed here long after her business was through and made all kinds of troubling personal confessions to me. And so that became another one of my little secrets.

Maybe Kumiko had the same kind of secrets and was keeping them from me. With my own fund of secrets, I was in no position to blame her if she did, of course. Between the two of us, I was surely the more secretive. She tended to say what she was thinking. She was the type of person who thought things through while speaking. I was not like that.

Uneasy with these ruminations, I walked towards the bathroom. The door was wide open. I stood in the doorway and looked at Kumiko from behind. She had changed into blue pyjamas and was standing in front of the mirror, drying her hair with a towel.

"About a job for me," I said. "I *have* been thinking about it. I've asked friends to be on the lookout, and I've tried a few places myself. There *are* jobs out there, so I can work anytime I decide to work. I can start tomorrow if I make up my mind to. It's making up my mind that's hard. I'm just not sure. I'm not sure if it's OK for me to pick a job out of a hat like that."

"That's why I keep telling you to do what you want," she said, while looking at herself in the mirror. "You don't *have* to find a job right away. If you're worried about the economics of it, you don't have to be. If it makes you uneasy not to have a job, if it's a burden to you to have me the only one working while you stay at home and take care of the housework, then take some job – any job – for a while. I don't care."

"Of course, I'll have to find a job eventually. *I* know that. *You* know that. I can't go on hanging around like this for ever. And I *will* find a job sooner or later. It's just that right now, I don't know what kind of a job I should take. For a while after I left, I just figured I'd take some other law-related job. I do have connections in the field. But now I can't get myself into the mood. The more time that passes, the less interest I have in law. I feel more and more that it's simply not the work for me."

Kumiko looked at me in the mirror. I went on:

"But knowing what I *don't* want to do doesn't help me figure out what I *do* want to do. I could do just about anything if somebody made me. But I don't have an image of the *one thing* I really want to do. That's my problem now. I can't find the image."

"So, then," she said, putting her towel down and turning to face me, "if you're tired of law, don't do it any more. Just forget about the bar exam. Don't get all worked up about finding a job. If you can't find the image, wait until it forms by itself. What's wrong with that?"

I nodded. "I just wanted to make sure I had explained to you exactly how I felt."

"Good," she said.

I went to the kitchen and washed my glass. She came in from the bathroom and sat at the kitchen table.

"Guess who called me this afternoon," she said. "My brother."

"Oh?"

"He's thinking of running for office. In fact, he's just about decided to do it."

"Running for office?!" This came as such a shock to me, I could hardly speak for a moment. "You mean . . . for the Diet?"

"That's right. They're asking him to run for my uncle's seat in Niigata."

"I thought it was all set for your uncle's son to succeed him. He was going to resign his directorship at Dentsu or something and go back to Niigata."

She started cleaning her ears with a cotton swab. "That was the plan, but my cousin doesn't want to do it. He's got his family in Tokyo, and he enjoys his work. He's not ready to give up such an important post with the world's largest advertising firm and move back to the wilds of Niigata just to become a Diet member. The main opposition is from his wife. She doesn't want him sacrificing the family to run for office."

The elder brother of Kumiko's father had spent four or five terms in the Lower House, representing that electoral district in Niigata. While not exactly a heavyweight, he had a fairly impressive record, having risen at one point to a minor cabinet post. Now, however, advanced age and heart disease would make it impossible for him to stand at the next election, which meant that someone would have to take over his constituency. This uncle had two sons, but the elder had never intended to go into politics, and so the younger was the obvious choice.

"Now the people in the district are dying to have my brother run. They want somebody young and smart and energetic. Somebody who can serve for several terms, with the talent to become a major power in central government. My brother has a name, he'll attract the young vote: he's perfect. True, he can't schmooze with the locals, but the support organization is strong, and they'll take care of that. Plus, if he wants to go on living in Tokyo, that's no problem. All he has to do is show up for the election."

I had trouble picturing Noboru Wataya as a Diet member. "What do you think of all this?" I asked.

"He's got nothing to do with me. He can become a Diet member or an astronaut, for all I care."

"But why did he make a point of coming to you for advice?"

"Don't be ridiculous," she said, with a dry voice. "He wasn't asking my advice. You know he'd never do that. He was just keeping me informed. As a member of the family."

"I see," I said. "Still, if he's going to run for the Diet, won't it be a problem that he's divorced and single?"

"I wonder," said Kumiko. "I don't know anything about politics or elections or anything. They just don't interest me. But anyway, I'm pretty sure he'll never get married again. To anybody. He should never have got married in the first place. That's not what he wants from life. He's after something else, something completely different from what you or I want. I know that for sure."

"Oh, really?"

Kumiko wrapped two used cotton swabs in a tissue and threw them in the wastebasket. Then she raised her head and looked straight at me. "I once saw him masturbating. I opened a door, and there he was."

"So what? Everybody masturbates," I said.

"No, you don't understand," she said. Then she sighed. "It happened maybe two years after my sister died. He was probably in college, and I was about eight. My mother had wavered between getting rid of my sister's things and stowing them away, and in the end she decided to keep them, thinking I might wear them when I got older. She had put them in a box in a wardrobe. My brother had taken them out and was smelling them and doing it."

I kept silent.

"I was just a little girl then. I didn't know anything about sex. I really didn't know what he was doing, but I could tell that it was something twisted, something I wasn't supposed to see, something much deeper than it appeared on the surface." Kumiko shook her head.

"Does Noboru Wataya know you saw him?"

"Of course. We looked right into each other's eyes."

I nodded. "And how about your sister's clothes?" I asked. "Did you wear them when you got bigger?"

"No way," she said.

"So you think he was in love with your sister?"

"I wonder," said Kumiko. "I'm not even sure he had a sexual interest in her, but he certainly had *something*, and I suspect he's never been able to get away from that something. That's what I mean when I say he should never have got married in the first place."

Kumiko fell silent. For a long time, neither of us said anything. Then she spoke. "In that sense, I think he may have some serious psychological problems. Of course, we all have psychological problems to some extent, but his are a lot worse than whatever you or I might have. They're a lot deeper and more persistent. And he has no intention of letting these scars or weaknesses or whatever they are be seen by anybody else. Ever. Do you understand what I'm saying? This election coming up: it worries me."

"Worries you? How's that?"

"I don't know. It just does," she said. "Anyhow, I'm tired. I can't think any more today. Let's go to bed."

Brushing my teeth in the bathroom, I studied my face in the mirror. For over two months now, since leaving my job, I had rarely entered the "outside world". I had been moving back and forth between the local shops, the swimming pool, and this house. Apart from the Ginza and that hotel in Shinagawa, the farthest point I had travelled from home was the cleaner's by the station. And in all that time, I had hardly seen anyone. Apart from Kumiko, the only people I could be said to have "seen" in two months were Malta and Creta Kano and May Kasahara. It was a narrow world, a world that was standing still. But the narrower it became, and the more it consisted of stillness, the more this world that enveloped me seemed to overflow with things and people that could only be called strange. They had been there all the while, it seemed, waiting in the shadows for me to stop moving. And every time the wind-up bird came to my yard to wind its spring, the world descended more deeply into chaos.

I rinsed my mouth and went on looking at my face for a time.

I can't find the image, I said to myself. I'm thirty, I'm standing still, and I can't find the image.

When I came from the bathroom to the bedroom, Kumiko was asleep.

11

Enter Lieutenant Mamiya

◆

What Came from the Warm Mud

◆

Eau de Cologne

Three days later, Tokutaro Mamiya rang. At 7.30 in the morning. I was eating breakfast with Kumiko.

"I am very, very sorry to call you so early in the morning. I do hope I haven't woken you," said My Mamiya, sounding genuinely apologetic.

I assured him that it was all right: I woke up every morning shortly after 6.

He thanked me for my postcard and explained that he wanted to get me before I left for work this morning, adding that he would be most grateful if I could see him briefly today during my lunch break. He was hoping to take an evening bullet train back to Hiroshima. He had planned to have more time here, he said, but something had come up that made it necessary for him to return home as soon as possible.

I pointed out that I was presently unemployed, that I was free all day, and that I could see him at his convenience, be it morning, noon, afternoon, or whenever.

"But surely you must have something planned at some point in the day?" he inquired with the utmost politeness.

I had no plan at all, I replied.

"That being the case, might I be permitted to call upon you at your residence this morning at 10 o'clock?"

"That would be fine."

Only after I hung up did it occur to me that I had forgotten to tell him how to find our house from the station. Oh, well, I figured, he knows the address; he can make his way here if he wants to.

"Who was that?" asked Kumiko.

"The guy who's distributing Mr Honda's keepsakes. He's going to bring mine here later this morning."

"No kidding?" She took a sip of coffee and spread butter on her toast. "That's very nice of him."

"It is."

"By the way," she said, "shouldn't we – or at least you – go to pay our respects at Mr Honda's: burn a stick of incense, that sort of thing?"

"Good idea. I'll ask him about that."

Preparing to leave the house, Kumiko asked me to zip her dress up. It was a tight fit, and took some doing. She was wearing a lovely fragrance behind her ears – something perfect for a summer morning. "New cologne?" I asked. Instead of answering, she glanced at her watch and reached up to fix her hair.

"I'm late," she said, and took her handbag from the table.

•

I had straightened up the little room that Kumiko used for work and was emptying the wastebasket when I noticed a yellow ribbon she had thrown away. It was peeking out from under a crumpled sheet of writing paper and a few pieces of junk mail. Its bright, glossy yellow was what had caught my eye. It was the kind of ribbon used to wrap presents, the bow tied in the shape of a flower. I picked it up out of the wastebasket and examined it. The ribbon had been discarded along with some wrapping paper from the Matsuya department store. Under the paper was a box bearing the Christian Dior label. The lining inside the box formed the shape of a bottle. Judging from the box, this had been a pretty expensive item. I took it with me to the bathroom and opened Kumiko's cosmetics cabinet. Inside was a virtually unused bottle of Christian Dior eau de cologne, shaped like the hollow in the box. I opened the bottle's gold-coloured cap and took a sniff. It was the same fragrance I had smelled behind Kumiko's ears.

I sat on the sofa, drinking the rest of my morning coffee and collecting my thoughts. Someone had obviously given Kumiko a gift. An expensive gift. Bought it at the Matsuya department store and had it wrapped with a ribbon. If the person who did this was a man, he was someone close to Kumiko. Men didn't give women (especially married women)

127

cologne unless their relationship was a close one. If a woman friend had given it to her . . . But did women give eau de cologne to other women? I could not be sure. One thing I could be sure of, though, was that there was no particular reason for Kumiko to be receiving presents from other people at this time of year. Her birthday was in May. So was our anniversary. She might conceivably have bought herself a bottle of cologne and had it wrapped with a pretty ribbon. But why?

I sighed and looked at the ceiling.

Should I ask her about it directly? "Did somebody give you that cologne?" She might answer: "Oh, that. One of the girls at work had a personal problem I helped her out with. It's too long a story to go into, but she was in a jam. This was a thank-you gift. Wonderful fragrance, don't you think? It's expensive stuff!"

OK, that makes sense. That does it. No need to ask. No need to be concerned.

Except I *was* concerned. She should have said something to me about it. If she had time to go to her room, untie the ribbon, tear off the wrapping paper, open the box, throw all three in the wastebasket, and put the bottle in her cosmetics cabinet, she should have been able to come to me and say, "Look at this present I got from one of the girls at work." Instead, she had said nothing. Maybe she had thought it wasn't worth mentioning. Now, however, it had taken on the thin veil of secrecy. That was what was bothering me.

I looked at the ceiling for a long time. I tried to think about something else, but my mind wouldn't cooperate. I kept thinking about Kumiko at the moment I zipped up her dress: her smooth white back, the fragrance behind her ears. For the first time in months, I wanted a smoke. I wanted to put a cigarette in my mouth, light up, and suck the smoke into my lungs. That would have calmed me down. But I didn't have any cigarettes. I found a lemon drop and sucked on that.

At ten to ten, the phone rang. I assumed it was Lieutenant Mamiya. This house was not easy to find. Even people who had been here more than once sometimes got lost. But the call was not from Lieutenant Mamiya. What I heard coming from the receiver was the voice of the enigmatic woman who had phoned me the other day.

"Hi, honey, it's been a while," she said. "How did you like it last time? Did I get you going a little bit? Why did you hang up on me? And just when things were getting interesting!"

For a split second, I thought she was talking about my recent wet dream about Creta Kano. But that had been a different story. She was talking about the day she called me when I was cooking spaghetti.

"Sorry," I said, "but I'm pretty busy right now. I'm expecting a visitor in ten minutes, and I've got to get the place ready."

"You're awfully busy for somebody who's supposed to be out of work," she said, with a sarcastic edge. The same thing had happened last time: her tone of voice changed from one second to the next. "You're cooking spaghetti, you're expecting a visitor. But that's all right. All we need is ten minutes. Let's talk for ten minutes, just you and me. You can hang up when your guest arrives."

I wanted to hang up without saying a word, but I couldn't do it. I was probably still upset about Kumiko's cologne. Perhaps I felt like talking to someone, and it didn't much matter who.

"Look," I said, "I don't have any idea who you are." I picked up the pencil lying beside the phone and twirled it in my fingers as I spoke. "Are you sure I know you?"

"Of course you do. I told you last time. I know you and you know me. I wouldn't lie about a thing like that. I don't have time to waste calling complete strangers. You must have some kind of blind spot in your memory."

"I don't know about that. Really, though –"

"Enough," she said, cutting me off. "Stop thinking so much. You know me and I know you. The important thing is – well, look at it this way: I'm going to be very nice to you. But you don't have to do a thing. Isn't that marvellous? You don't have to do a thing, you have no responsibilities, and I do everything. *Everything*. Don't you think that's great? So stop thinking so much. Stop making everything so *complicated*. Empty yourself out. Pretend you're lying in some nice, soft mud on a warm spring afternoon."

I kept silent.

"You're asleep. You're dreaming. You're lying in nice, warm mud. Forget about your wife. Forget you're out of work. Forget about the future. Forget about everything. We all emerge from the warm mud, and we all go back to it. Finally – Oh, by the way, Mr Okada, when was the last time you had sex with your wife? Do you remember? Quite some time ago, wasn't it? Yes, indeed, maybe two weeks now."

"Sorry, my visitor is here," I said.

"*More* than two weeks, wasn't it? I can tell from your voice. Three weeks, maybe?"

I said nothing.

"Oh, well, never mind," she said, her voice like a little broom sweeping off the dust that had piled up on the slats of a venetian blind. "That's between you and your wife. But I will give you everything you want. And you, Mr Okada, need have no responsibilities in return. Just go round the corner, and there it is: a world you've never seen. I *told* you you have a blind spot, didn't I? You still don't understand."

Gripping the receiver, I maintained my silence.

"Look around," she said. "Look all around you and tell me what's there. What is it you see?"

Just then the doorbell rang. Relieved, I hung up without a word.

•

Lieutenant Mamiya was a bald old gentleman of exceptional height, who wore gold-rimmed glasses. He had the tanned, healthy look of a man who has done his share of manual labour, without an ounce of excess flesh. Three deep wrinkles marked the corner of each eye with perfect symmetry, as if he were on the verge of squinting because he found the light harsh. It was difficult to tell his age, though he couldn't have been less than seventy. I imagined he must have been a strapping fellow in his prime. This was obvious from his erect carriage and efficient movements. His demeanour and speech showed the utmost respectfulness, but rather than elaborate formality, gave an impression of unadorned precision. The lieutenant appeared to be a man accustomed to making his own decisions and taking responsibility for them. He wore an unremarkable light-grey suit, a white shirt, and a grey and black striped tie. The no-nonsense suit appeared to be made of a material that was a bit too thick for a hot and humid June morning, but the lieutenant was unmarked by a drop of sweat. He had a prosthetic left hand, on which he wore a thin glove of the same light-grey colour as the suit. Encased in this grey glove, the artificial hand looked especially cold and inorganic when compared with the tanned and hairy right hand, from which dangled a cloth-wrapped bundle, knotted at the top.

I showed him to the living room couch and served him a cup of green tea.

He apologized for not having a name card. "I used to teach social studies in a rural public high school in Hiroshima Prefecture, but I haven't done anything since I retired. I grow a few vegetables, more as a hobby than anything, just simple farm work. For that reason, I do not happen to carry a name card, although I realize it is terribly rude of me."

I didn't have a name card, either.

130

"Forgive me, but I wonder how old you might be, Mr Okada?"

"I'm thirty," I said.

He nodded. Then he took a sip of tea. I had no idea what he made of me being thirty years old.

"This is such a nice, quiet home you live in," he said, as if to change the subject.

I told him how I came to be renting it from my uncle for so little. Ordinarily, with our income, we couldn't afford to live in a house half the size, I added. Nodding, he stole a few hesitant glances around the place. I followed his lead and did the same. *Look all around you*, the woman's voice had ordered me. Taking this newly conscious look at my surroundings, I detected a certain coldness in the pervading atmosphere.

"I have been in Tokyo two weeks altogether on this trip," said Lieutenant Mamiya, "and you are the very last person to whom I am distributing a keepsake. Now I feel I can go back to Hiroshima."

"I was hoping I could visit Mr Honda's home and perhaps burn a stick of incense in his memory," I said.

"That is a most laudable intention, but Mr Honda's home – and now his grave – are in Asahikawa, Hokkaido. His family came from Asahikawa to sort out the things he left in his house in Meguro, and now they have gone back. There is nothing left."

"I see," I said. "So Mr Honda was living alone in Tokyo, then, far away from his family."

"That is correct. The eldest son, who lives in Asahikawa, was concerned about leaving his old father to live by himself in the big city, and he knew that it did not look very good. Apparently, he tried to persuade his father to come and live with him, but Mr Honda refused."

"He had a son?" I asked, somewhat taken aback. I had always thought of Mr Honda as utterly alone in the world. "Then I assume Mr Honda's wife must have passed away some time ago."

"Well, that is a rather complicated story. Mrs Honda committed lovers' suicide with another man after the war. In 1950 or 1951, I believe. The details of that event are not something that I would know about. Mr Honda never said too much about it, and of course I was in no position to ask."

I nodded.

"After that, Mr Honda raised his children alone – one son and one daughter. When they became independent, he moved to Tokyo by himself and began his work as a diviner, which is how you knew him."

"What sort of work did he do in Asahikawa?"

"He was partners with his brother in a printing business."

I tried to imagine Mr Honda standing in front of a printing press in overalls, checking proofs, but to me Mr Honda was a slightly grimy old man in a grimy old kimono with a sash more suited to a nightshirt, who sat, winter and summer, with his legs in the sunken hearth, playing with his divining sticks at a low table.

With deft movements, Lieutenant Mamiya used his good hand to untie the cloth bundle he had brought with him. A package emerged, shaped like a small box of candy. It was wrapped in kraft paper and tightly tied in several loops of string. The lieutenant placed it on the table and slid it towards me.

"This is the keepsake that Mr Honda left with me to give to you," he said.

I picked it up. It weighed practically nothing. I couldn't begin to imagine what was inside.

"Shall I open it?" I asked.

Lieutenant Mamiya shook his head. "I am sorry, but Mr Honda indicated that he wished you to open it when you were alone."

I nodded and returned the package to the table.

"In fact," said Lieutenant Mamiya, "I received the letter from Mr Honda exactly one day before he died. It said something like this: 'I am going to die very soon. I am not the least bit afraid of dying. This is the span of life that has been allotted to me by the will of Heaven. Where the will of Heaven is concerned, all one can do is submit to it. There is, however, something that I have left undone. In my cupboard there are various objects – things that I have wanted to pass on to certain people. Now it appears that I will not be able to accomplish that task. Which is why I would be most grateful if you would help me by distributing the keepsakes on the attached list. I fully realize how presumptuous this is of me, but I do hope that you will be so kind as to think of it as my dying wish and exert yourself this one last time for my sake.' I must say, I was utterly shocked to receive such a letter from Mr Honda. I had been out of touch with him for years – perhaps six or seven years without a word. I wrote back immediately, but my reply crossed in the post with the notice from his son that Mr Honda had died."

He took a sip of green tea.

"Mr Honda knew exactly when he was going to die," Lieutenant Mamiya continued. "He must have attained a state of mind that someone like me could never hope to reach. As you said in your postcard, there was something about him that moved people deeply. I felt that from the time I first met him, in the summer of 1938."

"Oh, were you in the same unit with Mr Honda at the time of the Nomonhan Incident?"

"No, I wasn't," said Lieutenant Mamiya, biting his lip. "We were in different units – different divisions, even. We worked together in a small-scale military operation that preceded the Nomonhan battle. Corporal Honda was later wounded at Nomonhan and sent back to Japan. I didn't go to Nomonhan. I lost this hand of mine" – and here Lieutenant Mamiya held up his gloved left hand – "in the Soviet advance of August 1945, the month the war ended. I caught a slug in the shoulder from a heavy machine gun during a battle against a tank unit. I was on the ground, unconscious, when a Soviet tank ran over my hand. I was taken prisoner, treated in a hospital in Chita, and sent to an internment camp in Siberia. They kept me there until 1949. I was on the continent for twelve years altogether from the time they sent me over in 1937. I never set foot on Japanese soil the whole time. My family thought I had been killed fighting the Soviets. They made a grave for me in the village cemetery. I had a kind of understanding with a girl there before I left Japan, but by the time I got back she was married to another man. Twelve years is a long time."

I nodded.

"I'm sorry, Mr Okada," he said. "This talk about the old days must be boring to a young fellow like you. I would like to add one more thing, though. And that is that we were just ordinary young men, the same as you. I never once thought I wanted to be a soldier. I wanted to be a teacher. As soon as I left college, though, they sent me my draft notice, stuck me in officers' training, and I ended up on the continent for twelve years. My life went by like a dream." Lieutenant Mamiya clamped his mouth shut.

"If you wouldn't mind," I said, after some time had passed, "I would very much like to hear the story of how you and Mr Honda came to know each other." I genuinely wanted to know what kind of man Mr Honda had been before I met him.

Hands placed precisely on his knees, Lieutenant Mamiya sat thinking about something. Not that he was uncertain as to what he should do. He was just thinking.

"That story might be a long one," he said.

"I don't mind," I said.

"I've never told it to anyone. And I'm quite certain that Mr Honda never told it to anyone, either. The reason I say that is that we . . . made a pact . . . to keep this one thing secret. But Mr Honda is dead now. I'm the only one left. It wouldn't hurt anyone if I told."

And so Lieutenant Mamiya began to tell me his story.

12

Lieutenant Mamiya's Long Story: Part I

•

I was shipped to Manchuria at the beginning of 1937, Lieutenant Mamiya began. I was a brand-new second lieutenant then, and they assigned me to the Kwantung Army General Staff in Hsin-ching. Geography had been my degree in college, so I ended up in the Military Survey Corps, which specialized in mapmaking. This was ideal for me because, to be quite honest, the duties I was ordered to perform were among the easiest that anyone could hope for in the army.

In addition to this, conditions in Manchuria were relatively peaceful – or at least stable. The recent China Incident had moved the theatre of military operations from Manchuria into China proper. The China Expeditionary Forces were the ones doing the fighting now, while the Kwantung Army had an easy time of it. True, mopping-up operations were still going on against anti-Japanese guerrilla units, but they were confined to the interior, and in general the worst was over. All that the powerful Kwantung Army had to do was police our newly "independent" puppet state of Manchukuo while keeping an eye on the north.

As peaceful as things supposedly were, it was still war, after all, so there were constant manoeuvres. I didn't have to participate in those, either, fortunately. They took place under terrible conditions. The temperature would drop to forty or fifty degrees below zero. One false step in manoeuvres like that, and you could end up dead. Every single time they held such manoeuvres, there would be hundreds of men in the hospital with frostbite or sent to a hot spring for treatment. Hsin-ching was no big city, but it was certainly an exotic foreign place, and if you wanted to have fun there, it provided plenty of opportunities. New single officers like me lived together in a kind of rooming house rather than in barracks. It was more like an extension of student life. I took it easy, thinking that I would have nothing to complain about if my military service ended like this, just one peaceful day after another.

It was, of course, a make-believe peace. Just beyond the edges of our little circle of sunshine, a ferocious war was going on. Most Japanese realized that the war with China would turn into a muddy swamp from which we could never extricate ourselves – or at least any Japanese with a brain in his head realized this. It didn't matter how many battles we won: there was no way Japan could continue to occupy and rule over such a huge country. It was obvious if you thought about it. And sure enough, as the fighting continued, the number of dead and wounded began to multiply. Relations with America went from bad to worse. Even at home, the shadows of war grew darker with every passing day. Those were dark years: 1937, 1938. But living the easy life of an officer in Hsin-ching, you almost wanted to ask, "War? What war?" We'd go out drinking and carousing every night, and we'd visit the cafés where the White Russian girls were.

Then, one day late in April 1938, a senior officer of the general staff called me in and introduced me to a fellow in mufti named Yamamoto. He wore his hair short and had a moustache. He was not a very tall man. I'd say he was in his mid-thirties. He had a scar on the back of his neck that looked as if it might have been made by a blade of some kind. The officer said to me: "Mr Yamamoto is a civilian. He's been hired by the army to investigate the life and customs of the Mongolians who live in Manchukuo. He will next be going to the Hulunbuir Steppe, near the Outer Mongolian border, and we are going to supply him with an armed escort. You will be a member of that detachment." I didn't believe a thing he was telling me. This Yamamoto fellow might have been wearing civilian clothes, but anybody could tell at a glance that he was a professional soldier. The look in his eyes, the way he spoke, his posture: it was obvious. I figured he was a high-ranking officer or had something to do with intelligence and was on a mission that required him to conceal his military identity. There was something ominous about the whole thing.

Three of us were assigned to accompany Yamamoto – too few for an effective armed escort, though a larger group would have attracted the attention of the Outer Mongolian troops deployed along the border. One might have chosen to view this as a case of entrusting a sensitive mission to a few handpicked men, but the truth was far from that. I was the only officer, and I had zero battlefield experience. The only one we could count on for fighting power was a sergeant by the name of Hamano. I knew him well as a soldier who had been assigned to assist the general staff. He was a tough fellow who had worked his way up through the ranks to become a non-commissioned officer, and he had distinguished himself in battle in China. He was big and fearless, and I was sure we could count on him in a pinch. Why they had also included Corporal Honda in our party I had no idea. Like me, he had just arrived from home, and of course he had no battle experience. He was a gentle, quiet soul who looked as if he would be no help at all in a fight. What's more, he belonged to the Seventh Division, which meant that the general staff had gone out of their way to have him sent over to us specifically for this assignment. That's how valuable a soldier he was, though not until much later did the reason for this become clear.

I was chosen to be the commanding officer of the escort because my primary responsibility was the topography of the western border of Manchukuo in the area of the Khalkha River. My job was to make sure that our maps of the district were as complete as possible. I had even been over the area several times in a plane. My presence was meant to help the mission go smoothly. My second assignment was to gather more detailed topographical information on the district and so increase the accuracy of our maps. Two birds with one stone, as it were. To be quite honest, the maps we had in those days of the Hulunbuir Steppe border region with Outer Mongolia were crude things – hardly an improvement over the old Manchu dynasty maps. The Kwantung Army had undertaken several surveys following the establishment of Manchukuo. They wanted to make more accurate maps, but the area they had to cover was huge, and western Manchuria is just an endless desert. National borders don't mean very much in such a vast wilderness. The Mongolian nomads had lived there for thousands of years without the need – or even the concept – of borders.

The political situation had also delayed the making of more accurate maps. Which is to say that if we had gone ahead and unilaterally made an official map showing our idea of the border, it could have caused a full-scale international incident. Both the Soviet Union and Outer Mongolia, which shared borders with Manchukuo, were extremely sensitive about border violations, and there had been several instances of bloody combat over just such matters. In our day, the army was in no mood for war with the Soviet Union. All our force was invested in the war with China, with none to spare for a large-scale clash with the Soviets. We didn't have the divisions or the tanks or the artillery or the planes. The first priority was to secure the stability of Manchukuo, which was still a relatively new political entity. Establishment of the northern and northwestern borders could wait, as far as the army was concerned. They wanted to stall for time by keeping things indefinite. Even the mighty Kwantung Army deferred to this view and adopted a wait-and-see attitude. As a result, everything had been allowed to drift in a sea of vagueness.

If, however, their best-laid plans notwithstanding, some unforeseen event should lead to war (which is exactly what did happen the following year at Nomonhan), we would need maps to fight. And not just ordinary civilian maps, but real combat maps. To fight a war you need maps that show you where to establish encampments, the most effective place to set up your artillery, how many days it will take your infantry to march there, where to secure water, how much feed you need for your horses: a great deal of detailed information. You just couldn't fight a modern war without such maps. Which is why much of our work overlapped with the work of the intelligence division, and we were constantly exchanging information with the Kwantung Army's intelligence section or the military secret service in Hailar. Everyone knew everyone else, but this Yamamoto fellow was someone I had never seen before.

After five days of preparation, we left Hsin-ching for Hailar by train. We took a truck from there, drove it through the area of the Khandur-byo Lamaist temple, and arrived at the Manchukuo Army's border observation post near the Khalkha River. I don't remember the exact distance, but it was something like two-hundred miles. The region was an empty wilderness, with literally nothing as far as the eye could see. My work required me to keep checking my map against the actual landforms, but there was nothing out there for me to check against, nothing that one could call a landmark. All I could see were shaggy, grass-covered mounds stretching on and on, the unbroken horizon, and clouds floating in the sky. There was no way I could have any precise idea where on the map we were. All I could do was guess according to the amount of time we had been driving.

Sometimes, when one is moving silently through such an utterly desolate landscape, an overwhelming hallucination can cause one to feel that oneself, as an individual human being, is slowly unravelling. The surrounding space is so vast that it becomes more and more difficult to keep a balanced grip on one's own being. I wonder if I am making myself clear? The mind expands to fill the entire landscape, becoming so diffuse in the process that one loses the ability to keep it fastened to the physical self. That is what I experienced in the midst of the Mongolian steppe. How vast it was! It felt more like an ocean than a desert landscape. The sun would rise from the eastern horizon, cut its way across the empty sky, and sink below the western horizon. This was the only perceptible change in our surroundings. And in the movement of the sun, I felt something I hardly know how to name: some huge, cosmic love.

At the border post of the Manchukuo Army, we transferred from truck to horseback. They had everything ready for us: four horses to ride, plus two packhorses loaded with food, water, and weapons. We were lightly armed. I and the man called Yamamoto carried only pistols. Hamano and Honda carried Model 38 regulation infantry rifles and two hand grenades each, in addition to their pistols.

The de facto commander of our group was Yamamoto. He made all the decisions and gave us instructions. Since he was supposedly a civilian, military rules required that I act as commanding officer, but no one doubted that he was the one in charge. He was simply that kind of man, for one thing, and although I held the rank of second lieutenant, I was nothing but a pencil pusher without battle experience. Military men can see who holds actual power, and that is the one they obey. Besides, my superiors had ordered me to follow Yamamoto's instructions without question. My obedience to him was to be something that transcended the usual laws and regulations.

We proceeded to the Khalkha River and followed it to the south. The river was swollen with thawed snow. We could see large fish in the water. Sometimes, in the distance, we spotted wolves. They might have been part wild dog rather than purebred wolves, but in any case they were dangerous. We had to post a sentry each night to guard the horses from them. We also saw a lot of birds, most of them migratory fowl on their way back to Siberia. Yamamoto and I discussed features of the topography. Checking our route against the map, we kept detailed notes on every bit of information that came to our notice. Aside from these technical exchanges, however, Yamamoto hardly ever spoke to me. He spurred his horse on in silence, ate separately from the rest of us, and went to sleep without a word. I had the impression that this was not his first trip to the area. He had amazingly precise knowledge of the landforms, directions, and so forth.

After we had proceeded southward for two days without incident, Yamamoto called me aside and told me that we would be fording the Khalkha before dawn the next morning. This came as a tremendous shock to me. The opposite shore was Outer Mongolian territory. Even the bank on which we stood was a dangerous area of border disputes. The Outer Mongolians laid claim to it, and Manchukuo asserted its own claims to the territory, which had led to continual armed clashes. If we were ever taken prisoner by Outer Mongolian troops on this side, the differing views of the two countries gave us some excuse for being there, though in fact there was little danger of encountering them in this season, when melting snow made fording so difficult. The far bank was a different story altogether. Mongolian patrols were there for certain. If we were captured there, we would have no excuse whatever. It would be a clear case of border violation, which could stir up all kinds of political problems. We could be shot on the spot, and our government would be unable to protest. In addition, my superior officer had given me no indication that it would be all right for us to cross the border. I *had*, of course, been told to follow Yamamoto's orders, but I had no way of knowing if this included such a grave offence as a border violation. Secondly, as I said earlier, the Khalkha was quite swollen, and the current was far too strong to make a crossing, in addition to which the water was freezing cold. Not even the nomadic tribes liked to ford the river at this time of year. They usually restricted their crossings to winter, when the river was frozen, or summer, when the flow was down and the water temperature up.

When I said all this to him, Yamamoto stared at me for a moment. Then he nodded several times. "I understand your concern about the violation of international borders," he said to me, with a somewhat patronizing air. "It is entirely natural for you, as an officer with men under your command, to consider the question of responsibility in such a matter. You would never want to put the lives of your men in danger without good cause. But I want you to leave such questions to me. I will assume all responsibility in this instance. I am not in a position to explain a great deal to you, but this matter has been cleared with the highest levels of the army. As regards the fording of the river, we have no technical obstacles. There is a hidden point at which it is possible to cross. The Outer

Mongolian Army has constructed and secured several such points. I suspect that you are fully aware of this as well. I myself have crossed the river a number of times at this point. I entered Outer Mongolia last year at this time at this same place. There is nothing for you to worry about."

He was right about one thing. The Outer Mongolian Army, which knew this area in detail, had sent combat units – though just a few of them – to this side of the river during the season of melting snow. They had made sure they could send whole units across at will. And if *they* could cross, then this man called Yamamoto could cross, and it would not be impossible for the rest of us to cross too.

We stood now at one of those secret fords that had been built by the Outer Mongolian Army. Camouflaged with care, it would not have been obvious to the casual observer. A plank bridge, secured against the swift current by ropes, connected the shallows on either side beneath the surface of the water. A slight drop in the water level would make for an easy crossing by troop transport vehicles, armoured cars, and such. Reconnaissance planes could never spot it underwater. We made our way across the river's strong flow by clinging to the ropes. Yamamoto went first, to be certain there were no Outer Mongolian patrols in the area, and we followed. Our feet went numb in the cold water, but we and our horses struggled across to the far shore of the Khalkha River. The land rose much higher on the far side, and standing there, we could see for miles across the desert expanse from which we had come. This was one reason the Soviet Army would always be in the more advantageous position when the battle for Nomonhan eventually broke out. The difference in elevation would also make for a huge difference in the accuracy of artillery fire. In any case, I remember being struck by how different the view was on either side of the river. I remember, too, how long it took to regain feeling in limbs that had been soaked in the icy water. I couldn't even get my voice to work for a while. But to be quite honest, the sheer tension that came from knowing I was in enemy territory was enough to make me forget about the cold.

We followed the river southward. Like an undulating snake, the Khalkha flowed on below us to the left. Shortly after the crossing, Yamamoto advised us to remove all insignia of rank, and we did as we were told. Such things could only cause trouble if we were captured by the enemy, I assumed. For this reason, I also removed my officer's boots and changed into gaiters.

We were setting up camp that evening when a man approached us from the distance, riding alone. He was a Mongol. The Mongols use an unusually high saddle, which makes it easy to distinguish them from afar. Sergeant Hamano snapped up his rifle when he saw the figure approaching, but Yamamoto told him not to shoot. Hamano slowly lowered his rifle without a word. The four of us stood there, waiting for the man to draw closer. He had a Soviet-made rifle strapped to his back and a Mauser at his waist. Whiskers covered his face, and he wore a hat with earflaps. His filthy robes were the same kind as the nomads', but you could tell from the way he handled himself that he was a professional soldier.

Dismounting, the man spoke to Yamamoto in what I assumed was Mongolian. I had some knowledge of both Russian and Chinese, and what he spoke was neither of those, so it must have been Mongolian. Yamamoto answered in the man's own language. This made me surer than ever that Yamamoto was an intelligence officer.

Yamamoto said to me, "Lieutenant Mamiya, I will be leaving with this man. I don't know how long I will be away, but I want you to wait here – posting a sentry at all times, of course. If I am not back in thirty-six hours, you are to report that fact to headquarters. Send one man back across the river to the Manchukuo Army observation post." He mounted his horse and rode off with the Mongol, heading west.

The three of us finished setting up camp and ate a simple dinner. We couldn't cook or build a campfire. On that vast steppe, with nothing but low sand dunes as far as the eye could see to shield our presence, the least puff of smoke would have led to our immediate capture. We pitched our tents low in the shelter of the dunes, and for supper we ate dry crackers and cold canned meat. Darkness swiftly covered us when the sun sank beneath the horizon, and the sky was filled with an incredible number of stars. Mixed in with the roar of the Khalkha River, the sound of wolves howling came to us as we lay on the sand, recovering from the day's exertions.

Sergeant Hamano said to me, "Looks like a tough spot we've got ourselves in," and I had to agree with him. By then, the three of us – Sergeant Hamano, Corporal Honda and I – had got to know each other pretty well. Ordinarily, a fresh young officer like me would be kept at arm's length and laughed at by a seasoned non-commissioned officer like Sergeant Hamano, but our case was different. He respected the education I had received in a non-military college, and I took care to acknowledge his combat experience and practical judgment without letting rank get in the way. We also found it easy to talk to each other because he was from

Yamaguchi and I was from an area of Hiroshima close to Yamaguchi. He told me about the war in China. He was every bit a soldier, with only grammar school behind him, but he had his own reservations about this messy war on the continent, which looked as if it would never end, and he expressed these feelings honestly to me. "I don't mind fighting," he said. "I'm a soldier. And I don't mind dying in battle for my country, because that's my job. But this war we're fighting now, Lieutenant – well, it's just not right. It's not a real war, with a battle line where you face the enemy and fight to the end. We advance, and the enemy runs away without fighting. Then the Chinese soldiers take their uniforms off and mix with the civilian population, and we don't even know who the enemy *is*. So then we kill a lot of innocent people in the name of flushing out 'renegades' or 'remnant troops', and we commandeer provisions. We have to steal their food, because the line moves forward so fast our supplies can't catch up with us. And we have to kill our prisoners, because we don't have anywhere to keep them or any food to feed them. It's wrong, Lieutenant. We did some terrible things in Nanking. My own unit did. We threw dozens of people into a well and dropped hand grenades in after them. Some of the things we did I can't bring myself to talk about. I'm telling you, Lieutenant, this is one war that doesn't have any Righteous Cause. It's just two sides killing each other. And the ones who get stepped on are the poor farmers, the ones without politics or ideology. For them, there's no Nationalist Party, no Young Marshal Zhang, no Eighth Route Army. If they can eat, they're happy. I know how these people feel: I'm the son of a poor fisherman myself. The little people slave away from morning to night, and the best they can do is keep themselves alive – barely. I can't believe that killing these people for no reason at all is going to do Japan one bit of good."

In contrast to Sergeant Hamano, Corporal Honda had very little to say about himself. He was a quiet fellow, in any case. He'd listen to us talk, without interjecting his own comments. But while I say he was "quiet", I don't mean to imply there was anything dark or melancholy about him. It's just that he rarely took the initiative in conversation. True, that often made me wonder what was on his mind, but there was nothing unpleasant about him. If anything, there was something in his quiet manner that softened people's hearts. He was utterly serene. He wore the same look on his face no matter what. I gathered he was from Asahikawa, where his father ran a small print shop. He was two years younger than I, and when he left school he had joined his

143

brothers, working for his father. He was the youngest of three boys, the eldest of whom had been killed in China two years earlier. He loved to read, and whenever we had a spare moment, you'd see him curled up somewhere, reading a book on some kind of Buddhist topic.

As I said earlier, Honda had absolutely no combat experience, but with only one year of training behind him, he was an outstanding soldier. There are always one or two such men in any platoon, who, patient and enduring, carry out their duties to the letter without a word of complaint. Physically strong, with good intuition, they instantly grasp what you tell them and get the job done right. Honda was one of those. And because he had had cavalry training, he was the one who knew the most about horses; he took care of the six we had with us. And he did this in an extraordinary way. It sometimes seemed to us that he understood every little thing the horses were feeling. Sergeant Hamano immediately acknowledged Corporal Honda's abilities and let him take charge of many things without the slightest hesitation.

So, then, for such an odd, patched-together unit, we attained an extraordinary degree of mutual understanding. And precisely because we were not a regular unit, we had none of that by-the-book military formality. We were so at ease with one another, it was almost as if Karma had brought us together. Which is why Sergeant Hamano was able to say openly to me things that lay far beyond the fixed framework of officer and noncom.

"Tell me, Lieutenant," he once asked, "what do you think of this fellow Yamamoto?"

"Secret service, I'm willing to bet," I said. "Anybody who can speak Mongol like that has got to be a pro. And he knows this area like the back of his hand."

"That's what I think. At first I thought he might be one of those mounted bandits connected with top brass, but that can't be it. I know those guys. They'll talk your ear off and make up half of what they tell you. And they're quick on the trigger. But this Yamamoto guy's no lightweight. He's got guts. He *is* brass – and way up there. I can smell them a mile away. I heard something about some kind of secret tactical unit the army's trying to put together with Mongols from Soviet-trained troops, and that they brought over a few of our pros to run the operation. He could be connected with that."

Corporal Honda was standing sentry a short distance away from us, holding his rifle. I had my Browning lying close by, where I could grab it at any time. Sergeant Hamano had taken his gaiters off and was massaging his feet.

"I'm just guessing, of course," Hamano went on. "That Mongol we saw could be some anti-Soviet officer with the Outer Mongolian Army, trying to make secret contact with the Japanese Army."

"Could be," I said. "But you'd better watch what you say. They'll have your head."

"Come on, Lieutenant. I'm not that stupid. This is just between us." He flashed me a big smile, then turned serious. "But if any of this is true, it's a risky business. It could mean war."

I nodded in agreement. Outer Mongolia was supposedly an independent country, but it was actually more of a satellite state under the thumb of the Soviet Union. In other words, it wasn't much different from Manchukuo, where Japan held the reins of power. It did have an anti-Soviet faction, though, as everyone knew, and through secret contacts with the Japanese Army in Manchukuo, members of that faction had fomented a number of uprisings. The nucleus of the insurgent element consisted of Mongolian Army men who resented the high-handedness of the Soviet military, members of the landowning class opposed to the forced centralization of the farming industry, and priests of the Lama sect, who numbered over a hundred thousand. The only external power that the anti-Soviet faction could turn to for help was the Japanese Army stationed in Manchukuo. And they apparently felt closer to us Japanese, as fellow Asians, than they did to the Russians. Plans for a large-scale uprising had come to light in the capital city of Ulan Bator the previous year, 1937, and there had been a major purge carried out. Thousands of military men and Lamaist priests had been executed as counter-revolutionary elements in secret contact with the Japanese Army, but still anti-Soviet feeling continued to smoulder in one place or another. So there would have been nothing strange about a Japanese intelligence officer crossing the Khalkha River and making contact with an anti-Soviet officer of the Outer Mongolian Army. To prevent such activities, the Outer Mongolian Army had guard units making constant rounds and had declared the entire band of territory ten to twenty kilometres in from the Manchukuo border to be off-limits, but this was a huge area to patrol, and they could not keep a watch on every bit of it.

Even if their rebellion should succeed, it was obvious that the Soviet Army would intervene at once to crush their counter-revolutionary activity, and if that happened the insurgents would request the help of the

Japanese Army, which would then give Japan's Kwantung Army an excuse to intervene. Taking Outer Mongolia would amount to sticking a knife in the guts of the Soviets' development of Siberia. Imperial Headquarters back in Tokyo might be trying to put the brakes on, but this was not an opportunity that the ambitious Kwantung Army General Staff was about to let slip from their fingers. The result would be no mere border dispute but a full-scale war between the Soviet Union and Japan. If such a war broke out on the Manchurian–Soviet border, Hitler might respond by invading Poland or Czechoslovakia. This was the situation that Sergeant Hamano had been referring to in his remark on the potential for war.

The sun rose the next morning, and still Yamamoto had not returned. I was the last one to stand sentry. I borrowed Sergeant Hamano's rifle, sat on a somewhat higher sand dune, and watched the eastern sky. Dawn in Mongolia was an amazing thing. In one instant, the horizon became a faint line suspended in the darkness, and then the line was drawn upward, higher and higher. It was as if a giant hand had stretched down from the sky and slowly lifted the curtain of night from the face of the earth. It was a magnificent sight, far greater in scale, as I said earlier, than anything that I, with my limited human faculties, could comprehend. As I sat and watched, the feeling overtook me that my very life was slowly dwindling into nothingness. There was no trace here of anything as insignificant as human undertakings. This same event had been occurring hundreds of millions – hundreds of billions – of times, from an age long before there had been anything resembling life on earth. Forgetting that I was there to stand guard, I watched the dawning of the day, entranced.

After the sun appeared above the horizon, I lit a cigarette, took a sip of water from my canteen, and urinated. Then I thought about Japan. I pictured my home town in early May – the fragrance of the flowers, the babbling of the river, the clouds in the sky. Friends from long ago. Family. The chewy sweetness of a warm rice puff wrapped in oak leaf. I'm not that fond of sweets, as a rule, but I can still remember how badly I wanted a *mochi* puff that morning. I would have given half a year's pay for one just then. And when I thought about Japan, I began to feel as if I had been abandoned at the edge of the world. Why did we have to risk our lives to fight for this barren piece of earth devoid of military or industrial value, this vast land where nothing lived but wispy grass and biting insects? To protect my homeland, I too would fight and die. But it made no sense at all to sacrifice my one and only life for the sake of this desolate patch of soil from which no shaft of grain would ever spring.

•

Yamamoto came back at dawn the following day. I stood final watch that morning too. With the river at my back, I was staring towards the west when I heard what sounded like a horse's whinny behind me. I spun around but saw nothing. I stared towards where I had heard the sound, gun at the ready. I swallowed, and the sound from my own throat was loud enough to frighten me. My trigger finger was trembling. I had never shot a gun at anyone before.

But then, some seconds later, staggering over the crest of a sand dune, came a horse bearing Yamamoto. I surveyed the area, finger still on the trigger, but no one else appeared – neither the Mongol who had come for him nor enemy soldiers. A large white moon hung in the eastern sky like some ill-omened megalith. Yamamoto's left arm seemed to have been wounded. The handkerchief he had wrapped around it was stained with blood. I woke Corporal Honda to see to the horse. Heavily lathered and breathing hard, it had obviously come a long way at high speed. Hamano stood sentry in my place, and I got the first-aid kit to treat Yamamoto's wound.

"The bullet passed through, and the bleeding stopped," said Yamamoto. He was right: the bullet had missed the bone and gone all the way through, tearing only the flesh in its path. I removed the hand-kerchief, disinfected the openings of the wound with alcohol, and tied on a new bandage. He didn't flinch the whole time, though his upper lip wore a thin film of sweat. He drank deeply from a canteen, lit a cigarette, and inhaled with obvious relish. Then he took out his Browning, wedged it under his arm, removed the clip, and with one hand deftly loaded three rounds into it. "We leave here right away, Lieutenant Mamiya," he said. "Cross the Khalkha and head for the Manchukuo Army observation post."

We struck camp quickly, with hardly a word, mounted the horses, and headed for the ford. I asked Yamamoto nothing about how he had been shot or by whom. I was not in a position to do so, and even if I had been, he probably wouldn't have told me. My only thought at the time was to get out of this enemy territory as quickly as possible, cross the Khalkha River, and reach the relative safety of the opposite bank.

We rode in silence, urging our horses across the grassy plain. No one spoke, but all were thinking the same thing: could we make it across that river? If an Outer Mongolian patrol reached the bridge before we did, it would be the end for us. There was no way we could win in a fight. I remember the sweat streaming under my arms. It never once dried.

147

"Tell me, Lieutenant Mamiya, have you ever been shot?" Yamamoto asked me after a long silence.

"Never," I replied.

"Have you ever shot anyone?"

"Never," I said again.

I had no idea what kind of impression my answers made on him, nor did I know what his purpose was in asking me those questions.

"This contains a document that has to be delivered to headquarters," he said, placing his hand on his saddlebag. "If it can't be delivered, it has to be destroyed – burned, buried, it doesn't matter, but it must not, under any circumstances, be allowed to fall into enemy hands. *Under any circumstances.* That is our first priority. I want to be sure you understand this. It is *very, very* important."

"I understand," I said.

Yamamoto looked me in the eye. "If the situation looks bad, the first thing you have to do is shoot me. Without hesitation. If I can do it myself, I will. But with my arm like this, I may not be able to. In that case, you have to shoot me. And make sure you shoot to kill."

I nodded in silence.

•

When we reached the ford, just before dusk, the fear that I had been feeling all along turned out to be all too well founded. A small detachment of Outer Mongolian troops was deployed there. Yamamoto and I climbed one of the higher dunes and took turns looking at them through the binoculars. There were eight men – not a lot, but for a border patrol they were heavily armed. One man carried a light machine gun, and there was one heavy machine gun, mounted on a rise. It was surrounded by sandbags and aimed at the river. They had obviously stationed themselves there to prevent us from crossing to the other bank. They had pitched their tents by the river and tethered their ten horses nearby. It looked as if they were planning to stay in place until they caught us.

"Isn't there another ford we could use?" I asked.

Yamamoto took his eyes from the binoculars and looked at me, shaking his head. "There is one, but it's too far. Two days on horseback. We don't have that much time. All we can do is cross here, whatever it takes."

"Meaning we ford at night?"

"Correct. It's the only way. We leave the horses here. We finish off the sentry, and the others will probably be asleep. Don't worry, the river will block out most sounds. I'll take care of the sentry. There's nothing for us to do until then, so better get some sleep, rest ourselves now while we have the chance."

We set our fording operation for three in the morning. Corporal Honda took all the packs from the horses, drove the animals to a distant spot, and released them. We dug a deep hole and buried our extra ammunition and food. All that each of us would carry would be a canteen, a day's rations, a gun, and a few bullets. If we were caught by the Outer Mongolians, with their overwhelmingly superior firepower, we could never outfight them, no matter how much ammunition we might carry. For now, we were to get what sleep we could, because if we did make it across the river, there would be no chance to sleep for some time. Corporal Honda would stand sentry first, with Sergeant Hamano taking his place.

Stretching out in the tent, Yamamoto fell asleep immediately. It seemed he hadn't slept at all the whole time. By his pillow was a leather valise, into which he had transferred the important document. Hamano fell asleep soon after him. We were all exhausted, but I was too tense to sleep. I lay there for a long time, dying for sleep but kept awake by imagined scenes of us killing the sentry and being sprayed with machine gun fire as we forded the river. My palms were dripping with sweat, and my temples throbbed. I could not be sure that when the time came I would be able to conduct myself in a manner befitting an officer. I crawled out of the tent and went to sit by Corporal Honda on sentry duty.

"You know, Honda," I said, "we're maybe going to die here."

"Hard to say," he replied.

For a while, neither of us said anything. But there was something in his answer that bothered me – a particular tone that carried a hint of uncertainty. Intuition has never been my strong suit, but I knew that his vague remark was intended to conceal something. I decided to question him about it. "If you have something to tell me, don't hold back now," I said. "This could be the last time we ever talk to each other, so speak."

Biting his lower lip, Honda stroked the sand at his feet. I could see he was wrestling with conflicting feelings. "Lieutenant," he said after some time had passed. He looked me straight in the eye. "Of the four of us here, you will live the longest – far longer than you yourself would imagine. You will die in Japan."

Now it was my turn to look at him. He continued:

"You may wonder how I know this, but it is something that not even I can explain. I just know."

"Are you psychic or something?"

"Maybe although the word doesn't quite match what I feel. It's a little too grandiose. Like I say, I just know, that's all."

"Have you always had this kind of thing?"

"Always," he said with conviction. "Though I've kept it hidden ever since I was old enough to realize what was happening. But this is a matter of life and death, Lieutenant, and *you* are the one who's asking me about it, so I'm telling you the truth."

"And how about other people? Do you know what's going to happen to them?"

He shook his head. "Some things I know, some things I don't know. But you'd probably be better off not knowing, Lieutenant. It may be presumptuous of someone like me to say such big-sounding things to a college graduate like you, but a person's destiny is something you look back at after it's past, not something you see in advance. I have a certain amount of experience where these things are concerned. You don't."

"But anyhow, you say I'm not going to die here?"

He scooped up a handful of sand and let it run between his fingers. "This much I can say, Lieutenant. You won't be dying here on the continent."

I wanted to go on talking about this, but Corporal Honda refused to say anything more. He seemed to be absorbed in his own contemplations or meditations. Holding his rifle, he stared out at the vast prairie. Nothing I said seemed to reach him.

I went back to the low-pitched tent in the shelter of a dune, lay down beside Sergeant Hamano, and closed my eyes. This time sleep came to take me – a deep sleep that all but pulled me by the ankles to the bottom of the sea.

13

Lieutenant Mamiya's Long Story: Part II

◆

What woke me was the metallic click of a rifle's safety being released. No soldier in battle could ever miss that sound, even in a deep sleep. It's a – how can I say it? – a special sound, as cold and heavy as death itself. Almost by instinct, I reached for the Browning next to my pillow, but just then a shoe slammed into my temple, the impact blinding me for a moment. After I had brought my breathing under control, I opened my eyes just enough to see the man who must have kicked me. He was kneeling down and picking up my Browning. I slowly lifted my head, to find the muzzles of two rifles pointed at my face. Beyond the rifles stood two Mongolian soldiers.

I was sure I had fallen asleep in a tent, but the tent was gone now, and a skyful of stars shone overhead. Another Mongolian soldier was pointing a light machine gun at the head of Yamamoto, who was lying beside me. He lay utterly still, as if conserving his energy because he knew it was useless to resist. All of the Mongols wore long overcoats and battle helmets. Two of them were aiming large flashlights at Yamamoto and at me. At first I couldn't grasp what had happened: my sleep had been too deep and the shock too great. But the sight of the Mongolian soldiers and of Yamamoto's face left no doubt in my mind: our tents had been discovered before we had had a chance to ford the river.

Then it occurred to me to wonder what had become of Honda and Hamano. I turned my head very slowly, trying to survey the area, but neither man was there. Either they had been killed already or they had managed to escape.

These had to be the men of the patrol we had seen earlier at the ford. They were few in number, and they were equipped with a light machine gun and rifles. In command was a ruggedly built noncom, the only one of the bunch to be wearing proper military boots. He was the man who had kicked me. He bent over and picked up the leather valise that Yamamoto had had by his head. Opening it, he looked inside, then he turned it upside down and shook it. All that fell to the ground was a pack of cigarettes. I could hardly believe it. With my own eyes, I had seen Yamamoto putting the document into that bag. He had taken it from a saddlebag, put it in this valise, and placed the valise by his pillow. Yamamoto struggled to maintain his cool, but I saw his expression momentarily change. It was obvious he had no idea what had happened to the document. But whatever the explanation might be, its disappearance must have been a great relief to him. As he had said to me earlier, our number one priority was to see that the document never fell into enemy hands.

The soldiers dumped all our belongings on the ground and inspected them in detail, but they found nothing important. Next they stripped us and went through our pockets. They bayoneted our clothing and packs, but they found no documents. They took our cigarettes and pens, our wallets and notebooks and watches, and pocketed them. By turns, they tried on our shoes, and anyone they fit took them. The men's arguments over who got what became pretty intense, but the noncom ignored them. I suppose it was normal among the Mongols to take booty from prisoners of war and enemy dead. The noncom took only Yamamoto's watch, leaving the other items for his men to fight over. The rest of our equipment – our pistols and ammunition and maps and compasses and binoculars – went into a cloth bag, no doubt for sending to Ulan Bator headquarters.

Next they tied us up, naked, with strong, thin rope. At close range, the Mongol soldiers smelled like a stable that had not been cleaned for a long, long time. Their uniforms were shabby, filthy with mud and dust and food stains to the point where it was all but impossible to tell what the original colour had been. Their shoes were full of holes and falling off their feet – quite literally. No wonder they wanted ours. They had brutish faces for the most part, their teeth a mess, their hair long and wild. They looked more like mounted bandits or highwaymen than soldiers, but their Soviet-made weapons and their starred insignia indicated that they were regular troops of the Mongolian People's Republic. To me, of course, their discipline as a fighting unit and their military spirit seemed rather poor. Mongols make for tough, long-suffering soldiers, but they're not much suited to modern warfare.

The night was freezing cold. Watching the white clouds of the Mongolian soldiers' breath bloom and vanish in the darkness, I felt as if a strange error had brought me into the landscape of someone else's nightmare. I couldn't grasp that this was actually happening. It was indeed a nightmare, but only later did I come to realize that it was just the beginning of a nightmare of enormous proportions.

A short time later, one of the Mongolian soldiers came out of the darkness, dragging something heavy. With a big smile, he threw the object on the ground next to us. It was Hamano's corpse. The feet were bare: someone had already taken his boots. They proceeded to strip his clothes off, examining everything they could find in his pockets. Hands reached out for his watch, his wallet and his cigarettes. They divided up the cigarettes and smoked them while looking through the wallet. This yielded a few pieces of Manchukuo paper money and a photo of a woman who was probably Hamano's mother. The officer in charge said something and took the money. The photo was flung to the ground.

One of the Mongolian soldiers must have sneaked up behind Hamano and slit his throat while he was standing guard. They had done to us what we had been planning to do to them. Bright-red blood was flowing from the body's gaping wound, but for such a big wound there was not much blood; most of it had probably been lost by then. One of the soldiers pulled a knife from the scabbard on his belt, its curved blade some six inches long. He waved it in my face. I had never seen such an oddly shaped knife. It seemed to have been designed for some special purpose. The soldier made a throat-slashing motion with the knife and whistled through his teeth. Some of the others laughed. Rather than government issue, the knife seemed to be the man's personal property. Everyone had a long bayonet at his waist, but this man was the only one carrying a curved knife, and he had apparently used it to slit Hamano's throat. After a few deft swirls of the blade, he returned it to its scabbard.

Without a word, and moving only his eyes, Yamamoto sent a glance in my direction. It lasted just an instant, but I knew immediately what he was trying to say: Do you think Corporal Honda managed to get away? Through all the confusion and terror, I had been thinking the same thing:

Where *is* Corporal Honda? If Honda escaped this sudden attack of the Outer Mongolian troops, there might be some chance for us – a slim chance, perhaps, and the question of what Honda could do out there alone was depressing, but some chance was better than no chance at all.

They kept us tied up all night, lying on the sand. Two soldiers were left to watch over us: one with the light machine gun, the other with a rifle. The rest sat some distance away, smoking, talking, and laughing, seemingly relaxed now that they had captured us. Neither Yamamoto nor I said a word. The dawn temperature dropped to freezing in that place, even in May. I thought we might freeze to death, lying there naked. But the cold itself was nothing in comparison with the terror I felt. I had no idea what we were in for. These men were a simple patrol unit: they probably did not have the authority to decide what to do with us. They had to wait for orders. Which meant that we would probably not be killed right away. After that, however, there was no way of telling what would happen. Yamamoto was more than likely a spy, and I had been caught with him, so naturally I would be seen as an accomplice. In any case, we would not get off easily.

Some time after dawn broke, a sound like the drone of an aeroplane engine came out of the distant sky. Eventually, the silver-coloured fuselage entered my field of vision. It was a Soviet-made reconnaissance plane, bearing the insignia of Outer Mongolia. The plane circled above us several times. The soldiers all waved, and the plane dipped its wing in return. Then it landed in a nearby open area, sending up clouds of sand. The earth was hard here, and there were no obstructions, which made it relatively easy to take off and land without a runway. For all I knew, they might have used the same spot for this purpose any number of times. One of the soldiers mounted a horse and galloped off towards the plane with two saddled horses in tow.

When they returned, the two horses carried men who appeared to be high-ranking officers. One was Russian, the other Mongolian. I assumed that the patrol had radioed headquarters about our capture and that the two officers had made the trip from Ulan Bator to interrogate us. They were intelligence officers, without a doubt. I had heard that the GPU was at work behind the scenes in the previous year's mass arrest and purge of anti-government activists.

Both officers wore immaculate uniforms and were clean-shaven. The Russian wore a kind of trench coat with a belt. His boots shone with an unblemished lustre. He was a thin man, but not very tall for a Russian, and perhaps in his early thirties. He had a wide forehead, a narrow nose, and skin almost pale pink in colour, and he wore wire-rim glasses. Overall, though, this was a face that made no impression to speak of. Standing next to him, the short, stout, dark Mongolian officer looked like a little bear.

The Mongolian called the noncom aside, and the three men talked for a while. I guessed that the officers were asking for a detailed report. The noncom brought over a bag containing the things they had confiscated from us and showed them to the others. The Russian studied each object with great care, then put them all back into the bag. He said something to the Mongolian, who in turn spoke to the noncom. Then the Russian took a cigarette case from his breast pocket and opened it for the other two. They went on talking and smoking together. Several times, as he spoke, the Russian slammed his right fist into his left palm. He looked somewhat annoyed. The Mongolian officer kept his arms folded and his face grim, while the noncom shook his head now and then.

At last, the Russian officer ambled over to where we lay on the ground. "Would you like a smoke?" he asked in Russian. As I said earlier, I had studied Russian in college and could follow a conversation pretty well, but I pretended not to understand, so as to avoid any difficulties. "Thanks, but no thanks," said Yamamoto in Russian. He was good.

"Excellent," said the Soviet Army officer. "Things will go more quickly if we can speak in Russian."

He removed his gloves and put them in his coat pocket. A small gold ring shone on his left hand. "As you are no doubt aware, we are looking for a certain something. Looking very hard for it. And we know you have it. Don't ask how we know; we just know. But you do not have it on you now. Which means that, logically speaking, you must have hidden it before you were captured. You haven't transported it over there." He motioned towards the Khalkha River. "None of you has crossed the river. The letter must be on this side, hidden somewhere. Do you understand what I have said to you so far?"

Yamamoto nodded. "I understand," he said, "but we know nothing about a letter."

"Fine," said the Russian, expressionless. "In that case, I have one little question to ask you. What were you men doing over here? As you know, this territory belongs to the Mongolian People's Republic. What was your purpose in entering land that belongs to others? I want to hear your reason."

"Mapmaking," Yamamoto explained. "I am a civilian employee of a map company, and this man and the one they killed were with me for protection. We knew that this side of the river was your territory, and we are sorry for having crossed the border, but we did not think of ourselves as having made a territorial violation. We simply wanted to observe the topography from the vantage point of the plateau on this side."

Far from amused, the Russian officer curled his lips into a smile. "'We are sorry'?" he said slowly. "Yes, of course. You wanted to see the topography from the plateau. Yes, of course. The view is always better from high ground. It makes perfect sense."

For a time he said nothing, but stared at the clouds in the sky. Then he returned his gaze to Yamamoto, shook his head slowly, and sighed.

"If only I could believe what you are telling me! How much better it would be for all of us! If only I could pat you on the shoulder and say, 'Yes, yes, I see, now run along home across the river, and be more careful in future.' I truly wish I could do this. But unfortunately, I cannot. Because I know who you are. And I know what you are doing here. We have friends in Hailar, just as you have friends in Ulan Bator."

He took the gloves from his pocket, refolded them, and put them back. "To be honest, I have no personal interest in hurting you or killing you. If you would simply give me the letter, then I would have no further business with you. You would be released from this place immediately at my discretion. You could cross the river and go home. I promise you that, on my honour. Anything else that happened would be an internal matter for us. It would have nothing to do with you."

The light of the sun from the east was at last beginning to warm my skin. There was no wind, and a few hard white clouds floated in the sky.

A long, long silence followed. No one said a word. The Russian officer, the Mongolian officer, the men of the patrol, and Yamamoto: each preserved his own silence. Yamamoto had seemed resigned to death from the moment of our capture; his face showed not the slightest hint of expression.

"The two of you . . . will . . . almost certainly . . . die here," the Russian went on slowly, a phrase at a time, as if speaking to children. "And it will be a terrible death. They . . ." And here the Russian glanced towards the Mongolian soldiers. The big one, holding the machine gun, looked at me with a snaggle-toothed grin. "They love to kill people in ways that involve great difficulty and imagination. They are, shall we say, aficionados. Since the days of Genghis Khan, the Mongols have enjoyed devising particularly cruel ways of killing people. We Russians are painfully aware of this. It forms part of our history lessons in school. We study what the Mongols did when they invaded Russia. They killed millions. For no reason at all. They captured hundreds of Russian aristocrats in Kiev and killed them all together. Do you know that story? They cut huge, thick planks, laid the Russians beneath them, and held a banquet on top of the planks, crushing them to death beneath their weight. Ordinary human beings would never think of such a thing, don't you agree? It took time and a tremendous amount of preparation. Who else would have gone to the trouble? But they did it. And why? Because it was a form of amusement to them. And they still enjoy doing such things. I saw them in action once. I thought I had seen some terrible things in my day, but that night, as you can imagine, I lost my appetite. Do you understand what I am saying to you? Am I speaking too quickly?"

Yamamoto shook his head.

"Excellent," said the Russian. He paused, clearing his throat. "Of course, this will be the second time for me. Perhaps my appetite will have returned by dinner-time. If possible, however, I would prefer to avoid unnecessary killing."

Hands clasped together behind his back, he looked up at the sky for a time. Then he took his gloves out and glanced towards the plane. "Beautiful weather," he said. "Spring. Still a little cold, but just about right. Any hotter, and there would be mosquitoes. Terrible mosquitoes. Yes, spring is much better than summer." He took out his cigarette case again, put a cigarette between his lips, and lit it with a match. Slowly, he drew the smoke into his lungs, and slowly he let it out again. "I'm going to ask you once more: Do you insist that you really know nothing about the letter?"

Yamamoto said only one word: "*Nyet.*"

"Fine," said the Russian. "Fine." Then he said something in Mongolian to the Mongolian officer. The man nodded and barked an order to the soldiers. They carried over some rough logs and began to sharpen them with their bayonets, quickly turning them into four stakes. Pacing off the distance between the stakes, they pounded them into the ground with rocks at the four corners of a square. All these preparations took some twenty minutes to complete, I guessed, but I had no idea at all what they were for.

The Russian said, "To them, an excellent slaughter is like an excellent meal. The longer they take with their preparations, the more enjoyment they derive from the act. Simply killing a man is no problem: one pistol shot and it's all over. But that would not be" – and here he ran his fingertip slowly over his smooth chin – "very interesting."

They untied Yamamoto and led him to the staked-off area. There they tied his arms and legs to the four stakes. Stretched out on the ground, stark naked, Yamamoto had several raw wounds on his body.

"As you know, these people are shepherds," said the Russian officer. "And shepherds use their sheep in many ways: they eat their flesh, they shear their wool, they take their hides. To them, sheep are the perfect animal. They spend their days with sheep – their whole lives with sheep. They know how to skin them with amazing skill. The hides they use for tents and clothing. Have you ever seen them skin a sheep?"

"Just kill me and get it over with," said Yamamoto.

The Russian brought his palms together and, while rubbing them slowly, nodded to Yamamoto. "Don't worry," he said. "We will be certain to kill you. I guarantee you that. It may take a little time, but you will die. There is nothing to worry about on that score. We are in no hurry. Here we are in the vast wilderness, where there is nothing as far as the eye can see. Only time. All the time we need. And I have many things I wish to tell you. Now, as to the procedure of skinning: every band has at least one specialist – one professional, as it were, who knows everything there is to know about cutting off the skin, a man of miraculous skill. His skinning is a work of art. He does it in the twinkling of an eye, with such speed and dexterity you would think that the creature being skinned alive never noticed what was happening. But of course" – he took the cigarette case from his breast pocket once again, shifted it to his left hand, and tapped upon it with the fingers of his right – "not to notice such a thing would be out of the question. The one being skinned alive experiences terrible pain. Unimaginable pain. And it takes an immense time for death to come. Massive haemorrhaging is what finally does it, but that takes time."

He snapped his fingers. The Mongolian officer stepped forward. From his coat pocket he produced a sheathed knife. It was shaped like the one used before by the soldier who had made the throat-slitting gesture. He pulled the knife from its sheath and held it aloft. In the morning sun, the blade shone with a dull white gleam.

"This man is one of those professionals of whom I spoke," said the Russian officer. "I want you to look at his knife. Closely. It is a very special knife, designed for skinning, and it is extraordinarily well made. The blade is as thin and sharp as a razor. And the technical skill these people bring to the task is extremely high. They've been skinning animals for thousands of years, after all. They can take a man's skin off the way you'd peel a peach. Beautifully, without a single scratch. Am I speaking too quickly for you, by any chance?"

Yamamoto said nothing.

"They do a small area at a time," said the Russian officer. "They have to work slowly if they want to remove the skin cleanly, without any scratches. If, in the meantime, you feel you want to say something, please let me know. Then you won't have to die. Our man here has done this several times, and never once has he failed to make the person talk. Keep that in mind. The sooner we stop, the better for both of us."

Holding his knife, the bearlike Mongolian officer looked at Yamamoto and grinned. To this day, I remember that smile. I see it in my dreams. I have never been able to forget it. No sooner had he flashed this smile than he set to work. His men held Yamamoto down with their hands and knees while he began skinning Yamamoto with the utmost care. It truly was like skinning a peach. I couldn't bear to watch. I closed my eyes. When I did this, one of the soldiers hit me with his rifle butt. He went on hitting me until I opened my eyes. But it hardly mattered: eyes open or closed, I could still hear Yamamoto's voice. He bore the pain without a whimper – at first. But soon he began to scream. I had never heard such screams before: they did not seem part of this world. The man started by slitting open Yamamoto's shoulder and proceeded to peel off the skin of his right arm from the top down – slowly, with care, almost with love. As the Russian officer had said, it was something like a work of art. One would never have imagined there was any pain involved, if it weren't for the screams. But the screams told the horrendousness of the pain that accompanied the work.

Before long, the entire skin of Yamamoto's right arm had come off in a single thin sheet. The skinner handed it to the man beside him, who held it open in his fingertips, circulating among the others to give them a good look. All the while, blood kept dripping from the skin. Then the officer turned to Yamamoto's left arm, repeating the procedure. After that he skinned both legs, cut off the penis and testicles, and removed the ears. Then he skinned the head and the face and everything else. Yamamoto lost consciousness, regained it, and lost it again. The screams would stop whenever he passed out and continue when he came to again. But his voice gradually weakened and finally gave out altogether. All this time, the Russian officer drew meaningless patterns on the ground with the heel of his boot. The Mongolian soldiers watched the procedure in silence. Their faces remained expressionless, showing neither disgust nor excitement nor shock. They watched Yamamoto's skin being removed a piece at a time with the same kind of faces we might have if we were out for a stroll and stopped to have a look at a construction site.

Meanwhile, I did nothing but vomit. Over and over again. Long after it seemed there was nothing more for me to bring up, I continued to vomit. At last, the bearlike Mongolian officer held up the skin of Yamamoto's torso, which he had so cleanly peeled off. Even the nipples were intact. Never to this day have I seen anything so horrible. Someone took the skin from him and spread it out to dry the way we might dry a sheet. All that remained lying on the ground was Yamamoto's corpse, a bloody red lump of meat from which every trace of skin had been removed. The most painful sight was the face. Two large white eyeballs stared out from the red mass of flesh. Teeth bared, the mouth stretched wide open as if in a shout. Two little holes were all that remained where the nose had been removed. The ground was a sea of blood.

The Russian officer spat on the ground and looked at me. Then he took a handkerchief from his pocket and wiped his mouth. "The fellow really didn't know anything, did he?" he said, putting the handkerchief back. His voice sounded somewhat flatter than it had before. "If he had known, he would have talked. Pity. But in any case, the man was a professional. He was bound to have an ugly death sooner or later. Ah, well, can't be helped. And if *he* knew nothing, there's no way that you could know anything."

He put a cigarette between his lips and struck a match. "Which means that you are no longer of any use to us. Not worth torturing for information. Not worth keeping alive as a prisoner. We want to dispose of this affair in the utmost secrecy. There could be complications if we brought you back to Ulan Bator. The best thing, of course, would be to put a bullet in your brain here and now, then bury you or burn you and throw your ashes into the Khalkha. That would be a simple end to the matter. Don't you agree?" He fixed his eyes on mine. I continued to pretend that I could not understand him. "You don't understand Russian, I suppose. It's a waste of time to spell this out to you. Ah, well. I might as well be talking to myself. So hear me out. In any case, I have good news for you. I have decided not to kill you. Think of this as my own small expression of penitence for having pointlessly killed your friend in spite of myself. We've all had our fill of killing this morning. Once a day is more than enough.

And so I will not kill you. Instead, I will give you a chance to survive. If all goes well, you may even come out of this alive. The chances of that happening are not good, of course. Perhaps non-existent. But a chance is a chance. At least it is far better than being skinned alive. Don't you agree?"

He raised his hand and summoned the Mongolian officer. With great care, the man had been washing his knife with water from a canteen and had just finished sharpening it on a whetstone. The soldiers had laid out the pieces of Yamamoto's skin and were standing by them, discussing something. They seemed to be exchanging opinions on the finer points of the skinner's technique. The Mongolian officer put his knife in its scabbard and then into the pocket of his coat before approaching us. He looked me in the face for a moment, then turned to his fellow officer. The Russian spoke a few short Mongolian phrases to him, and without expression the man nodded. A soldier brought two horses for them.

"We'll be going back to Ulan Bator now," the Russian said to me. "I hate to return empty-handed, but it can't be helped. Win some, lose some. I hope my appetite comes back by dinner-time, but I rather doubt it will."

They mounted their horses and left. The plane took off, became a silver speck in the western sky, then disappeared altogether, leaving me alone with the Mongolian soldiers and their horses.

They set me on a horse and lashed me to the saddle. Then, in formation, we moved out to the north. The soldier just in front of me kept singing some monotonous melody in a voice that was barely audible. Apart from that, there was nothing to be heard but the dry sound of the horses' hooves kicking up sand. I had no idea where they were taking me or what they were going to do to me. All I knew was that to them, I was a superfluous being of no value whatever. Over and over in my head I repeated to myself the words of the Russian officer. He had said he would not kill me. He would not kill me, but my chances of surviving were almost non-existent. What could this mean? It was too vague for me to grasp in any concrete way. Perhaps they were going to use me in some kind of horrible game. They wouldn't simply dispatch me, because they planned to enjoy the dreadful contrivance at their leisure.

But at least they hadn't killed me. At least they hadn't skinned me alive like Yamamoto. I might not be able to avoid being killed in the end, but not like *that*. I was alive for now; I was still breathing. And if what the Russian officer had said was true, I would not be killed straight away. The more time that lay between me and death, the more chance I had to survive. It might be a minuscule chance, but all I could do was cling to it.

Then, all of a sudden, the words of Corporal Honda flared to life again in my brain: that strange prognostication of his that I would not die on the continent. Even as I sat there, tied to the saddle, the skin of my naked back burning in the desert sun, I savoured every syllable that he had spoken over and over again. I let myself dwell on his expression, his intonation, the sound of each word. And I resolved to believe him from the bottom of my heart. No, no, I was not going to lie down and die in a place like this! I would come out of this alive! I would tread my native soil once again!

We travelled north for two hours or more, coming to a stop near a Lamaist devotional mound. These stone markers, called *oboo*, serve both as the guardian deity for travellers and as valuable signposts in the desert. Here the men dismounted and untied my ropes. Supporting my weight on either side, two of them led me a short distance. I figured that this was where I would be killed. A well had been dug into the earth here. The mouth of the well was surrounded by a three-foot-high stone curb. They made me kneel down beside it, grabbed my neck from behind, and forced me to look inside. I couldn't see a thing in the impenetrable darkness. The noncom with the boots found a fist-sized rock and dropped it into the well. Some time later came the dry sound of stone hitting sand. So the well was a dry one, apparently. It had once served as a well in the desert, but it must have dried up long before, owing to a movement of the subterranean vein of water. Judging from the time it took the stone to hit the bottom, it seemed to be quite deep.

The noncom looked at me with a big grin. Then he took a large automatic pistol from the leather holster on his belt. He released the safety and fed a bullet into the chamber with a loud click. Then he put the muzzle of the gun against my head.

He held it there for a long time but did not pull the trigger. Then he slowly lowered the gun and raised his left hand, pointing towards the well. Licking my dry lips, I stared at the gun in his fist. What he was trying to tell me was this: I had a choice between two fates. I could have him shoot me now – just die and get it over with. Or I could jump into the well. Because it was so deep, if I landed badly I might be killed. If not, I would die slowly at the bottom of a dark hole. At last it dawned on me that this was the chance the Russian officer had spoken of. The Mongolian noncom pointed at the watch that he had taken from Yamamoto and held up five fingers. He was giving me five seconds to decide. When he got to three, I stepped onto the well curb and leaped inside. I had no choice. I had hoped to be able to cling to the wall and work my way down, but he gave me no time for that. My hands missed the wall, and I tumbled down.

It seemed to take a very long time for me to hit the bottom. In reality, it could not have been more than a few seconds, but I do recall thinking about a great many things on my way down. I thought about my hometown, so far away. I thought about the girl I slept with just once before they shipped me out. I thought about my parents. I recall feeling grateful that I had a younger sister and not a brother: even if I was killed, they would still have her and not have to worry about her being taken by the army. I thought about rice cakes wrapped in oak leaves. Then I slammed into dry ground and lost consciousness for a moment. It felt as if all the air inside me had burst through the walls of my body. I thudded against the well bottom like a sandbag.

I believe that I lost consciousness from the impact, for just a moment. When I came to, I felt some kind of spray hitting me. At first I thought it was rain, but I was wrong. It was urine. The Mongolian soldiers were all peeing on me where I lay in the bottom of the well. I looked up to see them in silhouette far above me, taking turns to come to the edge of the round hole to pee. There was a terrible unreality to the sight, like a drug-induced hallucination. But it was real. I was really in the bottom of the well, and they were spraying me with real pee. Once they had finished, someone shone a torch on me. I heard them laughing. And then they disappeared from the edge of the hole. After that, everything sank into a deep silence.

For a while, I thought it best to lie there face down, waiting to see if they would come back. But after twenty minutes had gone by, then thirty (as far as I could tell without a watch), they did not come back. They had gone away and left me, it seemed. I had been abandoned at the bottom of a well in the middle of the desert. Once it was clear that they would not be returning, I decided to check myself over for injuries. In the darkness, this was not easy. I couldn't see my own body. I couldn't tell with my own eyes what condition it was in. I could only resort to touch, but I could not be sure that the perceptions I was experiencing in the darkness were accurate. I felt that I was being deceived, deluded. It was a very strange feeling.

Little by little, though, and with great attention to detail, I began to grasp my situation. The first thing I realized was that I had been extremely lucky. The bottom of the well was relatively soft and sandy. If it hadn't been, then the impact of falling such a distance would have broken every bone in my body. I took one long, deep breath and tried to move. First I tried moving my fingers. They responded, although feebly. Then I tried to raise myself to a sitting position, but this I was unable to do. My body felt as if it had lost all sensation. My mind was conscious, but there was something wrong with the connection between my mind and my body. My mind would decide to do something, but it was unable to convert the thought into muscular activity. I gave up and, for a while, lay there silent in the dark.

Just how long I remained still I have no idea. But little by little, my perceptions began to return. And along with the recovery of my perceptions, naturally enough, came the sensation of pain. Intense pain. Almost certainly, my leg was broken. And my shoulder might be dislocated or, perhaps, if luck was against me, even broken.

I lay still, enduring the pain. Before I knew it, tears were streaming down my cheeks – tears of pain and, even more, tears of despair. I don't think you will ever be able to understand what it is like – the utter loneliness, the feeling of desperation – to be abandoned in a deep well in the middle of the desert at the edge of the world, overcome with intense pain in total darkness. I went so far as to regret that the Mongolian noncom had not simply shot me and got it over with. If I had been killed that way, at least they would have been aware of my death. If I died here, however, it would be a truly lonely death, a death of no concern to anyone, a silent death.

Now and then, I heard the sound of the wind. As it moved across the surface of the earth, the wind made an uncanny sound at the mouth of the well, a sound like the moan of a woman in tears in a far-off world. That world and this were joined by a narrow shaft, through which the woman's voice reached me, though only at long, irregular intervals. I had been left all alone in deep silence and even deeper darkness.

Enduring the pain, I reached out to touch the earthen floor around me. The well bottom was flat. It was not very wide, maybe five or five-and-a-half feet. As I was groping the ground, my hand suddenly came upon a hard, sharp object. In fear, I drew my hand back, but then slowly and carefully I reached out towards the thing. Again my fingers came into contact with the sharp object. At first I thought it was a tree branch, but soon enough I realized I was touching bones. Not human bones, but those of a small animal, which had been scattered at random, either by the passage of time or by my fall. There was nothing else at the bottom of the well, just sand: fine and dry.

Next I ran my palm over the wall. It seemed to be made of thin, flat stones. As hot as the desert surface became in daytime, the heat did not penetrate to this world below ground. The stones had an icy chill to them. I ran my hand over the wall, examining the gaps between the stones. If I could get a foothold there, I might be able to climb to the surface. But the gaps turned out to be too narrow for that and, in my battered state, climbing seemed all but impossible.

With a tremendous effort, I dragged myself closer to the wall and raised myself against it into a sitting position. Every move made my leg and shoulder throb as if they had been stuck with hundreds of thick needles. For a while after that, each breath made me feel that my body might crack apart. I touched my shoulder and realized it was hot and swollen.

·

How much time went by after that I do not know. But at one point something happened that I would never have imagined. The light of the sun shot down from the opening of the well like some kind of revelation. In that instant, I could see everything around me. The well was filled with brilliant light. A flood of light. The brightness was almost stifling: I could hardly breathe. The darkness and cold were swept away in a moment, and warm, gentle sunlight enveloped my naked body. Even the pain I was feeling seemed to be blessed by the light of the sun, which now warmly illuminated the white bones of the small animal beside me. These bones, which could have been an omen of my own impending fate, seemed in the sunlight more like a comforting companion. I could see the stone walls that encircled me. As long as I remained in the light, I was able to forget about my fear and pain and despair. I sat in the dazzling light in blank amazement. Then the light disappeared as suddenly as it had come. Deep darkness enveloped everything once again. The whole interval had been extremely short. In terms of the clock, it must have lasted ten or, at most, fifteen seconds. No doubt, because of the angles involved, this was all the sun could manage to shine straight down to the bottom of the hole in any single day. The flood of sunlight was gone before I could begin to comprehend its meaning.

After the light faded, I found myself in an even deeper darkness than before. I was all but unable to move. I had no water, no food, not a scrap of clothing on my body. The long afternoon went by, and night came, when the temperature plunged. I could hardly sleep. My body craved sleep, but the cold pricked my skin like a thousand tiny thorns. I felt as if my life's core were stiffening and dying bit by bit. Above me, I could see stars frozen in the sky. Terrifying numbers of stars. I stared up at them, watching as they slowly crept along. Their movement helped me ascertain that time was continuing to flow. I slept for a short while, awoke with the cold and pain, slept a little more, then woke again.

Eventually, morning came. From the round mouth of the well, the sharp pinpoints of starlight gradually began to fade. Still, even after dawn broke, the stars did not completely disappear. Faint almost to the point of imperceptibility, they continued to linger. To slake my thirst, I licked the morning dew that clung to the stone wall. The amount of water was minute, of course, but to me it tasted like a bounty from heaven. The thought crossed my mind that I had had neither food nor water for an entire day. And yet I had no sense of hunger.

I remained there, still, in the bottom of the hole. It was all I could do. I couldn't even think, so profound were my feelings of loneliness and despair. I sat there doing nothing, thinking nothing. Unconsciously, however, I waited for that ray of light, that blinding flood of sunlight that poured straight down to the bottom of the well for one tiny fraction of the day. It must have been a phenomenon that occurred very close to noon, when the sun was at the highest point in the sky and its light struck the surface of the earth at right angles. I waited for the coming of the light and for nothing else. There was nothing else I could wait for.

A very long time went by, it seems. At some point I drifted into sleep. By the time I sensed the presence of something and awoke, the light was already there. I realized that I was being enveloped once again by that overwhelming light. Without thinking, I spread open both my hands and received the sun in my palms. It was far stronger than it had been the first time. And it lasted far longer. At least it felt that way to me. In the light, tears poured out of me. I felt as if all the fluids of my body might turn into tears and come streaming from my eyes, that my body itself might melt away. If it could have happened in the bliss of this marvellous light, even death would have been no threat. Indeed, I felt I *wanted* to die. I experienced a wonderful sense of oneness, an overwhelming sense of unity. Yes, that was it: the true meaning of life resided in that light that lasted for however many seconds it was, and I felt I *ought to die* right then and there.

But of course, before anything could happen, the light was gone. I was still in the bottom of that miserable well. Darkness and cold reasserted their grip on me, as if to declare that the light had never existed at all. For a long time, I remained huddled where I was, my face bathed in tears. As if beaten down by some huge power, I was unable to do – or even to think – anything at all, unable to feel even my own physical existence. I was a dried-up carcass, the cast-off shell of an insect. But then, once again, into the empty room of my mind, returned the prophecy of Corporal Honda: I would not die on the continent. Now, after the light had come and gone, I found myself able to believe his prophecy. I could believe it now because, in a place where I should have died, and at a time when I should have died, I had been unable to die. It was not that I *would not* die: I *could not* die. Do you understand what I am saying, Mr Okada? Whatever heavenly grace I may have enjoyed until that moment was lost for ever.

●

At this point in his story, Lieutenant Mamiya looked at his watch. "And as you can see," he added softly, "here I am." He shook his head as if trying to sweep away the invisible threads of memory. "Just as Mr Honda had said, I did not die on the continent. And of the four of us who went there, I have lived the longest."

I nodded in response.

"Please forgive me for talking at such length. It must have been very boring for you, listening to a useless old man chatter on about the old days." Lieutenant Mamiya shifted his position on the sofa. "My goodness, I'll be late for my train if I stay any longer."

I hastened to restrain him. "Please don't end your story there," I said. "What happened after that? I want to hear the rest."

He looked at me for a moment.

"How about this, then?" he asked. "I really am running late, so why don't you walk with me to the bus stop? I can give you a quick summary along the way."

I left the house with him and walked to the bus stop.

"On the third morning, I was saved by Corporal Honda. He had sensed that the Mongols were coming for us that night, slipped out of the tent, and remained in hiding all that time. He had taken the document from Yamamoto's bag with him. He did this because our number one priority was to see to it that the document did not fall into enemy hands, no matter how great the sacrifice we had to make. No doubt you are wondering why, if he realized that the Mongols were coming, Corporal Honda ran away by himself instead of waking the rest of us so that we could escape together. The simple fact of the matter is that we had no hope of winning in such a situation. They knew that we were there. It was their territory. They had us far outnumbered and outgunned. It would have been the simplest thing in the world for them to find us, kill us, and take the document. Given the situation, Corporal Honda had no choice but to escape by himself. On the battlefield, his actions would have been a clear case of desertion, but on a special assignment like ours, the most important thing is resourcefulness.

"He saw everything that happened. He watched them skinning Yamamoto. He saw the Mongolian soldiers take me away. But he no longer had a horse, so he could not follow right then. He had to come on foot. He dug up the extra supplies that we had buried in the desert, and there he buried the document. Then he came after me. For him to find me down in the well, though, required a tremendous effort. He didn't even know which direction we had taken."

"How *did* he find the well?" I asked.

"I don't know," said Lieutenant Mamiya. "He didn't say much about that. He *just knew,* I'd say. When he found me, he tore his clothing into strips and made a long rope. By then, I was practically unconscious, which made it all the more difficult for him to pull me up. Then he managed to find a horse and put me on it. He took me across the dunes, across the river, and to the Manchukuo Army outpost. There they treated my wounds and put me on a truck sent out by headquarters. I was taken to the hospital in Hailar."

"What ever happened to that document or letter or whatever it was?"

"It's probably still there, sleeping in the earth near the Khalkha River. For Corporal Honda and me to go all the way back and dig it up would have been out of the question, nor could we find any reason to make such an effort. We arrived at the conclusion that such a thing should never have existed in the first place. We coordinated our stories for the army investigation. We decided to insist that we had heard nothing about any document. Otherwise, they would have held us responsible for not bringing it back from the desert. They kept us in separate rooms, under strict guard, supposedly for medical treatment, and they questioned us every day. All these high-ranking officers would come and make us tell our stories over and over again. Their questions were meticulous, and very clever. But they seemed to believe us. I told them every little detail of what I had experienced, being careful to omit anything I knew about the document. Once they got it all down, they warned me that this was a top-secret matter that would not appear in the army's formal records, that I was never to mention it to anyone, and that I would be severely punished if I did. Two weeks later, I was sent back to my original post, and I believe that Corporal Honda was also returned to his home unit."

"One thing is still not clear to me," I said. "Why did they go to the trouble of bringing Mr Honda from his unit for this assignment?"

"He never said much to me about that. He had probably been forbidden to tell anyone, and I suspect that he thought it would be better for me not to know. Judging from my conversations with him, though, I imagine there was some kind of personal relationship between him and the man they called Yamamoto, something that had to do with his special powers. I had often heard that the army had a unit devoted to the study of the occult. Allegedly they gathered people with these spiritual or psychokinetic powers from all over the country and conducted experiments on them. I suspect that Mr Honda met Yamamoto in that connection. In any case, without those powers of his, Mr Honda would never have been able to find me in the well and guide me to the exact location of the Manchukuo Army outpost. He had neither map nor compass, yet he was able to direct us straight there without the slightest uncertainty. Common sense would have told you that such a thing was impossible. I was a professional mapmaker, and I knew the geography of that area quite well, but I could never have done what he did. These powers of Mr Honda were probably what Yamamoto was looking to him for."

We reached the bus stop and waited.

"Certain things will always remain riddles, of course," said Lieutenant Mamiya. "There are many things I still don't understand. I still wonder who that lone Mongolian officer was who met us in the desert. And I wonder what would have happened if we had managed to bring that document back to headquarters. Why did Yamamoto not simply leave us on the right bank of the Khalkha and cross over by himself? He would have been able to move far more freely that way. Perhaps he had been planning to use us as a decoy for the Mongolian troops so that he could escape alone. It is conceivable. Perhaps Corporal Honda realized this from the start and that was why he merely stood by while the Mongolians killed him.

"In any case, it was a very long time after that before Corporal Honda and I had an opportunity to meet again. We were separated from the moment we arrived in Hailar and were forbidden to speak or even to see each other. I had wanted to thank him one last time, but they made that impossible. He was wounded in the battle for Nomonhan and sent home, while I remained in Manchuria until the end of the war, after which I was sent to Siberia. I was only able to find him several years later, after I was repatriated from my Siberian internment. We did manage to meet a few times after that, and we corresponded. But he seemed to avoid talking about what had happened to us at the Khalkha River, and I myself was not too eager to discuss it. For both of us, it had simply been too enormous an experience. We shared it by *not talking about it*. Does this make any sense?

"This has turned into a very long story, but what I wanted to convey to you was my feeling that real life may have ended for me deep in that well in the desert of Outer Mongolia. I feel as if, in the intense light that shone for a mere ten or fifteen seconds a day in the bottom of the well, I burned up the very core of my life, until there was nothing left. That is how mysterious that light was to me. I can't explain it very well, but as honestly and simply as I can state it, no matter what I have encountered, no matter what I have experienced since then, I ceased to feel anything in the bottom of my heart. Even in the face of those monstrous Soviet tank units, even when I lost this left hand of mine, even in the hellish Soviet internment camps, a kind of numbness was all I felt. It may sound strange to say this, but none of that mattered. Something inside me was already dead. Perhaps, as I felt at the time, I should have died in that light, simply faded away. That was the time for me to die. But, as Mr Honda had predicted, I did not die there. Or perhaps I should say that I *could not* die there.

"I came back to Japan, having lost my hand and twelve precious years. By the time I arrived in Hiroshima, my parents and my sister were long since dead. They had put my little sister to work in a factory, which was where she was when the bomb fell. My father was on his way to see her at the time, and he, too, lost his life. The shock sent my mother to her deathbed; she finally passed away in 1947. As I told you earlier, the girl to whom I had been secretly engaged was now married to another man, and she had given birth to two children. In the cemetery, I found my own grave. There was nothing left for me. I felt truly empty, and knew that I should not have come back there. I can hardly remember what my life has been like since then. I became a social studies teacher and taught geography and history in high school, but I was not, in the true sense of the word, alive. I simply performed the mundane tasks that were handed to me, one after another. I never had a single real friend, no human ties with the students in my charge. I never loved anyone. I no longer knew what it meant to love another person. I would close my eyes and see Yamamoto being skinned alive. I dreamed about it over and over. Again and again I watched them peel the skin off and turn him into a lump of flesh. I could hear his heartrending screams. I also had dreams of myself slowly rotting away, alive, in the bottom of the well. Sometimes it seemed to me that that was what had really happened and that my life here was the dream.

"When Mr Honda told me on the bank of the Khalkha River that I would not die on the continent, I was overjoyed. It was not a matter of believing or not believing: I wanted to cling to something then – anything at all. Mr Honda probably knew that and told me what he did in order to comfort me. But there was to be no joy for me. After returning to Japan, I lived like an empty shell. Living like an empty shell is not really living, no matter how many years it may go on. The heart and flesh of an empty shell give birth to nothing more than the life of an empty shell. This is what I hope I have made clear to you, Mr Okada."

"Does this mean," I ventured, "that you never married after returning to Japan?"

"Of course not," answered Lieutenant Mamiya. "I have no wife, no parents or siblings. I am entirely alone."

After hesitating a moment, I asked, "Are you sorry that you ever heard Mr Honda's prediction?"

Now it was Lieutenant Mamiya's turn to hesitate. After a moment of silence, he looked me straight in the face. "Maybe I am," he said. "Maybe he should never have spoken those words. Maybe I should never have heard them. As Mr Honda said at the time, a person's destiny is something you look back at afterwards, not something to be known in advance. I do believe this, however: it now makes no difference either way. All I am doing is fulfilling my obligation to go on living."

The bus came, and Lieutenant Mamiya favoured me with a deep bow. Then he apologized for having taken up my valuable time. "Well, then, I shall be on my way," he said. "Thank you for everything. I am glad in any case that I was able to hand you the package from Mr Honda. This means that my job is done at last. I can go home with an easy mind." Using both his right hand and the artificial one, he deftly produced the necessary coins and dropped them into the fare box.

I stood there and watched as the bus disappeared around the corner.

After it was gone, I felt a strange emptiness inside, a hopeless kind of feeling like that of a small child who has been left alone in an unfamiliar neighbourhood.

Then I went home, and sitting on the living-room couch, I opened the package that Mr Honda had left me as a keepsake. I worked up a sweat removing layer after layer of carefully sealed wrapping paper, until a sturdy cardboard box emerged. It was a fancy Cutty Sark gift box, but it was too light to contain a bottle of whisky. I opened it, to find nothing inside. It was absolutely empty. All that Mr Honda had left me was an empty box.

Book Two: Bird as Prophet

July to October 1984

1

As Concrete as Possible

•

Appetite in Literature

Kumiko didn't come back that night. I stayed up until midnight, reading, listening to music, and waiting for her, but finally I gave up and went to bed. I fell asleep with the light on. It was 6 in the morning when I woke. The full light of day shone outside the window. Beyond the thin curtain, birds were chirping. There was no sign of my wife. The white pillow lay there, high and fluffy. As far as I could make out, no head had rested on it during the night. Her freshly washed, neatly folded summer pyjamas lay on top of the night table. *I* had washed them. *I* had folded them. I turned off the lamp beside my pillow and took a deep breath, as if to regulate the flow of time.

I did a tour of the house in my pyjamas. I went first to the kitchen, then surveyed the living room and looked into Kumiko's room. I checked the bathroom and, just to make sure, tried the cupboards. There was no sign of her anywhere. The house seemed more hushed than usual. I felt as if, by moving around, I alone was to blame for disrupting the quiet harmony of the place, and for no good reason.

There was nothing more for me to do. I went to the kitchen, filled the kettle, and lit the gas. When the water boiled, I made coffee and sat at the kitchen table to take a sip. Then I made toast and ate some potato salad from the refrigerator. This was the first time in years that I had eaten breakfast alone. Come to think of it, apart from a single business trip, we had never once missed breakfast together in all the time since our marriage. We had often missed lunch, and sometimes even dinner, but never breakfast. We had a tacit understanding about breakfast: it was almost a ritual for us. No matter how late we might go to bed, we would always get up early enough to fix a proper morning meal and take the time to enjoy it together.

But that morning Kumiko was gone. I drank my coffee and ate my toast alone, in silence. An empty chair was all I had to look at. I looked and ate and thought about the cologne that she had been wearing the morning before. I thought about the man who might have given it to her. I thought about her lying in a bed somewhere with him, their arms wrapped around each other. I saw his hands caressing her naked body. I saw the porcelain of her back as I had seen it in the morning, the smooth skin beneath the rising zip.

The coffee seemed to have a soapy taste. I couldn't quite believe it. Shortly after the first sip, I sensed an unpleasant aftertaste. I wondered if my feelings were playing tricks on me, but the second sip had the same taste. I emptied the cup into the sink and poured myself more coffee, in a clean cup. Again the taste of soap. I couldn't imagine why. I had washed the pot well, and there was nothing wrong with the water. But the taste – or smell – was unmistakable: it could only have been soap – or possibly moisturizing lotion. I threw away the coffee and started to boil some more water, but it just wasn't worth the trouble. I filled a cup with water from the tap and drank that instead. I really didn't want coffee all that much anyway.

•

I waited until 9.30 and dialled Kumiko's office. A woman answered the phone.

"May I speak to Kumiko Okada?" I asked.

"I'm sorry, but she doesn't seem to be here yet."

I thanked her and hung up. Then I started ironing shirts, as I always did when I felt restless. When I ran out of shirts, I tied up old newspapers and magazines, wiped down the sink and cabinet shelves, cleaned the toilet and bathtub. I polished the mirrors and windows. I unscrewed the ceiling fixtures and washed the frosted glass. I stripped the sheets and threw them in the washing machine, then put on fresh ones.

At 11 o'clock I called the office again. The same girl answered, and again she told me that Kumiko had not come in.

"Was she planning to miss work today?" I asked.

"Not to my knowledge," she said, without a trace of feeling. She was just reporting the facts.

Something was wrong if Kumiko had still not reported to work at 11 o'clock. Most publishers' offices kept irregular hours, but not Kumiko's. Producing magazines on health and natural foods, they had to deal with the kind of writers and other professionals – food producers, farmers, doctors – who went to work early in the morning and came home late in the evening. To accommodate them, Kumiko and her colleagues reported to the company at 9 o'clock sharp and left by 5, unless there was some special reason to stay later.

Hanging up, I went to the bedroom and looked through her wardrobe. If she had run off, Kumiko should have taken her clothes. I checked the dresses and blouses and skirts that were hanging there. Of course, I didn't know every piece of clothing she owned – I didn't know every piece of clothing that I owned – but I often took her things to the cleaner's and picked them up for her, so I had a pretty good grasp of which items she wore most often and which were most important to her, and as far as I could tell, just about everything was there.

Besides, she had had no opportunity to take a lot of clothes with her. I tried to recall as precisely as possible her departure from the house the day before – the clothes she wore, the bag she carried. All she had had with her was the shoulder bag she always carried to work, stuffed with notebooks and cosmetics and her wallet and pens and a handkerchief and tissues. A change of clothing would never have fit inside.

I looked through her drawers. Accessories, stockings, sunglasses, panties, cotton tops: everything was there, arranged in neat rows. If anything had disappeared, it was impossible for me to tell. Panties and stockings, of course, she could have managed to take in her shoulder bag, but come to think of it, why would she have bothered? Those she could have picked up anywhere.

I went back to the bathroom for another look. No sign of change there, either: just a lot of little cosmetics containers and accessories. I opened the bottle of Christian Dior cologne and took another sniff. It smelled the same as before: the fragrance of a white flower, perfect for a summer morning. Again I thought of her ears and her white back.

I went to the living room and stretched out on the sofa. I closed my eyes and listened. Virtually the only sound I could hear was that of the clock ticking off time. There were no car noises or birds chirping. I had no idea what to do now. I decided to call her office again and got as far as lifting the receiver and dialling the first few numbers, but the thought of having to talk to that same girl was too much for me, and I put the receiver back. There was nothing more for me to do. I could only wait. Perhaps Kumiko was leaving me – for what reason I did not know, but it was at least a possibility. Even if it was true, though, she was not the kind of person who would leave without a word. She would do her best to explain her exact reasons as precisely as possible. Of that I was one hundred per cent certain.

Or, then, there might have been an accident. She might have been run over by a car and rushed to hospital. She could be unconscious at that very moment receiving a transfusion. The thought made my heart pound, but I knew that she was carrying her driving license and credit cards and address book. The hospital or the police would have contacted me by now.

I went to sit on the veranda and look at the garden, but didn't look at anything. I tried to think, but I couldn't concentrate on any one thing. All that came to mind, again and again, was Kumiko's back as I raised the zip of her dress – her back, and the smell of the cologne behind her ears.

Just after 1 o'clock, the phone rang. I stood up from the sofa and picked up the receiver.

"Excuse me, but would this be Mr Okada's home?" asked a woman's voice. It was Malta Kano.

"That's right," I said.

"My name is Malta Kano. I am calling about the cat."

"The cat?" I said with some confusion. I had forgotten all about it. Now, of course, I remembered, but it seemed like something from an age ago.

"The cat that Mrs Okada was searching for," Malta Kano explained.

"Sure, sure," I said.

Malta Kano fell silent, as if gauging something. My tone of voice might have put her on the alert. I cleared my throat and shifted the receiver to my other hand.

After a short pause, Malta Kano said, "I must tell you, Mr Okada, I believe that the cat will almost certainly never be found. I hate to say this, but the best you can do is resign yourself to the fact. It is gone for ever. Barring some major change, the cat will never come back."

"Some major change?" I asked. But she did not respond.

Malta Kano remained silent for a long time. I waited for her to say something, but try as I might, I could not hear the smallest breath from her end. Just as I was beginning to suspect that the telephone was out of order, she began to speak again.

"It may be terribly rude of me to say this, Mr Okada, but apart from the cat, isn't there perhaps something else for which I can be of help?"

I could not reply to her immediately. With the receiver in my hand, I leaned back against the wall. It took some time for the words to come.

"Things are still not very clear to me," I said. "I don't know anything for sure. I'm trying to work it out in my own mind. But I think my wife has left me." I explained to her that Kumiko had not come home the night before or reported to work that morning.

She seemed to be mulling this over. "You must be very worried," she said. "There is nothing I can say at this point, but things should become clear before too long. Now all you can do is wait. It must be hard for you, but there is a right time for everything. Like the ebb and flow of the tides. No one can do anything to change them. When it is time to wait, you must wait."

"Look, Miss Kano, I'm grateful for the trouble you've taken with the cat, but right now I'm not in the mood for smooth-sounding generalities. I'm feeling lost. Really lost. Something awful is going to happen: I feel it. But I don't know what to do. I have absolutely no idea what I should do. Is that clear? I don't even know what I should do after this call. What I need right now is facts. Concrete facts. I don't care how stupid and simple they might be, I'll take any facts I can get – am I making myself clear? I need something I can see and touch."

Down the phone I heard the sound of something falling on the floor: something not very heavy – perhaps a single pearl – dropping onto a wooden floor. This was followed by a rubbing sound, as if a piece of tracing paper were being held in someone's fingertips and given a vigorous yank. These movements seemed to be occurring somewhere neither very close to nor far from the telephone, but they were apparently of no interest to Malta Kano.

"I see," she said in a flat, expressionless voice. "Something concrete."

"That's right. As concrete as possible."

"Wait for a phone call."

"Waiting for a phone call is all I've been doing."

"You should be getting a call soon from a person whose name begins with *O*."

"Does this person know something about Kumiko?"

"That I can't say. I'm just telling you this because you said you would take any concrete facts you could get. And here is another one: before very long, a half-moon will last for several days."

"A half-moon?" I asked. "You mean the moon in the sky?"

"Yes, Mr Okada, the moon in the sky. In any case, the thing for you to do is wait. Waiting is everything. Goodbye, then. I'll be talking to you again soon." And she hung up.

•

I fetched our address book from my desk and opened it at the Os. There were precisely four listings, written in Kumiko's neat little hand. The first was my father, Tadao Okada. Then came an old college friend of mine named Onoda, a dentist named Otsuka, and the local Omura off-licence.

I could forget about the off-licence. It was ten minutes' walk from the house, and apart from those rare instances when we would order a case of beer to be delivered, we had no particular dealings with them. The dentist was also irrelevant. I had gone to him for work on a molar two years earlier, but Kumiko had never been there. In fact, she had never been to any dentist since she married me. My friend Onoda I hadn't seen in years. He had gone to work for a bank after college, was transferred to the Sapporo branch in his second year, and had been living in Hokkaido ever since. Now he was just one of those people I exchanged New Year's cards with. I couldn't remember whether he had ever met Kumiko.

That left my father, but it was unthinkable that Kumiko would have some special relationship with him. He had remarried after my mother's death, and I had not seen him or corresponded with him or spoken to him on the telephone in the years since. Kumiko had never even met the man.

Flipping through the address book, I was reminded how little the two of us had had to do with other people. Apart from a few useful meetings with colleagues, we had had almost no relationships outside the house in the six years since our marriage, but instead had lived a withdrawn sort of life, just Kumiko and me.

I decided to make spaghetti for lunch again. Not that I was the least bit hungry. But I couldn't just go on sitting on the sofa, waiting for the phone to ring. I had to move my body, to begin working towards some goal. I put water in a pot, turned on the gas, and until it boiled made tomato sauce while listening to an FM broadcast. The radio was playing an unaccompanied violin sonata by Bach. The performance itself was excellent, but there was something annoying about it. I didn't know whether this was the fault of the violinist or of my own state of mind, but I turned off the music and went on cooking in silence. I heated the olive oil, threw in some garlic and added chopped onions. When these began to brown, I added the tomatoes that I had chopped and strained. It was good to be cutting things and frying things like this. It gave me a sense of accomplishment that I could feel in my hands. I liked the sounds and the smells.

When the water boiled, I put in the salt and a fistful of spaghetti. I set the timer for ten minutes and washed the things in the sink. Even with the finished spaghetti on the plate in front of me, though, I felt no desire to eat. I barely managed to finish half and threw out the rest. The leftover sauce I put in a container and stored in the refrigerator. Oh, well, the appetite had not been there to begin with.

Long before, I seemed to recall, I had read some kind of story about a man who keeps eating while he waits for something to happen. After thinking long and hard about it, I concluded that it was from Hemingway's *A Farewell to Arms*. The hero (I had forgotten his name) manages to escape from Italy to Switzerland by boat, and while waiting in this little Swiss town for his wife to give birth, he constantly goes to the café across the way for something to drink or eat. I could hardly remember anything about the plot. What had stuck in my mind was this one part near the end, in which the hero goes from meal to meal while waiting in a foreign country for his wife to have her baby. The reason I recalled it so clearly, it seemed, was that this part of the book had an intense reality to it. It seemed far more real to me, as literature, for the character's anxiety to cause this abnormal surge in appetite rather than to make him incapable of eating and drinking.

In contrast to *A Farewell to Arms*, though, I developed no appetite at all as I watched the hands of the clock in this quiet house, waiting for something to happen. And soon the thought crossed my mind that my failure to develop an appetite might be owing to the lack within me of this kind of literary reality. I felt as if I had become part of a badly written novel, that someone was taking me to task for being utterly unreal. And perhaps it was true.

•

The phone finally rang, just before 2 in the afternoon.

"Is this the Okada residence?" asked an unfamiliar male voice. It was a young man's voice, low and smooth.

"Yes, it is," I answered, my voice somewhat tense.

"Block two, number twenty-six?"

181

"That's right."

"This is the Omura off-licence calling. Thank you for your continued patronage. I was just about to leave to collect payments, and I wanted to check to see if this was a good time for you."

"Payments?"

"Yes, sir. I have you down for two cases of beer and a case of juice."

"Oh. Fine. I'll be at home for a while yet," I said, bringing our conversation to a close.

After hanging up, I wondered whether that conversation had contained any information regarding Kumiko. But viewed from all possible angles, it had been nothing but a short, practical call from an off-licence. I had ordered beer and juice from them, and they had delivered it, that was certain. Half an hour later, the fellow came to the door, and I paid for two cases of beer and a case of juice.

The friendly young man smiled as he filled out the receipt.

"By the way, Mr Okada, did you hear about the accident by the station this morning? About half past nine."

"Accident?" I asked with a shock. "Who was in an accident?"

"A little girl," he said. "Got run over by a reversing van. Badly hurt, too, I hear. I got there just after it happened. It's awful to see something like that first thing in the morning. Little kids scare the heck out of me: you can't see them in your rear-view mirror. You know the cleaner's by the station? It happened right in front of his place. People park their bikes there, and all these boxes are piled up: you can't see a thing."

After he left, I felt I couldn't stay in the house a minute longer. All of a sudden, the place felt hot and stuffy, dark and cramped. I put on my shoes and got out of there as fast as I could. I didn't even lock the door. I left the windows open and the kitchen light on. I wandered around the neighbourhood, sucking on a lemon drop. As I replayed the words of the young off-licence employee in my mind, it slowly dawned on me that I had left some clothes at the cleaner's by the station. Kumiko's blouse and skirt. The ticket was in the house, but if I just went and asked for them, the man would probably let me have them.

The neighbourhood looked a little different. The people I passed on the street all had an unnatural, even artificial, look. I examined each face as I walked by, and I wondered what kind of people these could be. What kind of houses did they live in? What kind of families did they have? What kind of lives did they lead? Did they sleep with women other than their wives, or men other than their husbands? Were they happy? Did they know how unnatural and artificial they looked?

Signs of the morning's accident were still visible outside the cleaner's: on the ground, the police chalk line; nearby, a few shoppers discussing the accident, with grave expressions on their faces. Inside, the cleaner's shop looked the same as ever. The same black music machine played the same kind of mood music, while in the back an old-fashioned air conditioner roared along and clouds of steam rose from the iron to the ceiling. The song was "Ebb Tide". Robert Maxwell, harp. I thought how wonderful it would be if I could go to the ocean. I imagined the smell of the beach and the sound of waves breaking on the shore. Seagulls. Ice-cold cans of beer.

To the owner, I said only that I had forgotten my receipt. "I'm pretty sure I brought them in last Friday or Saturday: a blouse and a skirt."

"Okada . . . Okada . . . ," he said, and flipped through the pages of a college notebook. "Sure, here it is. One blouse, one skirt. But Mrs Okada picked them up already."

"She did?" I asked, taken aback.

"Yesterday morning. I distinctly remember handing them to her myself. I reckoned she was on her way to work. Brought the receipt in too."

I had no words to answer him with. I could only stare at him.

"Ask the missus," he said. "She's got them, no mistake." He took a cigarette from the box on the register, put it in his mouth, and lit it with a lighter.

"Yesterday morning?" I asked. "Not evening?"

"Morning for sure. Eight o'clock. Your wife was the first customer of the day. I wouldn't forget something like that. Hey, when your very first customer is a young woman, it puts you in a good mood, know what I mean?"

I was unable to fake a smile for him, and the voice that came from me didn't sound like my own. "Oh, well, I guess that takes care of that. Sorry, I didn't know she'd picked them up."

He nodded and glanced at me, crushed out the cigarette, from which he had taken no more than two or three puffs, and went back to his ironing. He seemed to have become interested in me, as if he wanted to tell me something but decided in the end to say nothing. And I, meanwhile, had things I wanted to ask him. How had Kumiko looked when she came for her cleaning? What had she been carrying? But I was confused and very thirsty. What I most wanted was to sit down somewhere and have a cold drink. I felt that was the only way I would ever be able to think about anything again.

I went straight from the cleaner's to the coffeehouse a few doors away and ordered a glass of iced tea. The place was cool inside, and I was the only customer. Small wall-mounted speakers were playing an orchestrated version of the Beatles' "Eight Days a Week". I thought about the seashore again. I imagined myself barefoot and moving along the beach at the water's edge. The sand was burning hot, and the wind carried the heavy smell of the tide. I inhaled deeply and looked up at the sky. Stretching out my hands, palms upward, I could feel the summer sun burning into them. Soon a cold wave washed over my feet.

Whichever way you looked at it, it was odd for Kumiko to have picked things up from the cleaner's on her way to work. For one thing, she would have had to squeeze onto a jam-packed commuter train holding freshly pressed clothes on hangers. Then she would have had to do it again on the way home. Not only would they be something extra to carry, but the cleaner's careful work would have been reduced to a mass of wrinkles. Kumiko being sensitive was about such things, I couldn't imagine she would have done something so pointless. All she had to do was stop by on the way home from work. Or if she was going to be late, she could have asked me to pick them up. There was only one conceivable explanation: she had known she was not coming home. Blouse and skirt in hand, she had gone off somewhere. That way, she would have at least one change of clothing with her, and anything else she needed she could buy. She had her credit cards and her cashpoint card and her own bank account. She could go anywhere she wanted.

And she was with someone – a man. There was no other reason for her to leave home.

This was serious. Kumiko had disappeared, leaving behind all her clothes and shoes. She had always enjoyed buying clothes, to which she devoted considerable care and attention. For her to have left home with little more than the clothes on her back would have required a major act of will. And yet without the slightest hesitation – it seemed to me – she had walked out of the house with nothing more than a blouse and skirt. No, her clothing was probably the last thing on her mind.

Leaning back in my chair, half listening to the painful sanitized background music, I imagined Kumiko boarding a crowded commuter train with her clothes on wire hangers in the cleaner's plastic bags. I recalled the colour of the dress she was wearing, the fragrance of the cologne behind her ears, the smooth perfection of her back. I must have been exhausted. If I shut my eyes, I felt, I would float off somewhere else; I would end up in a quite different place.

2

No Good News in This Chapter

•

I left the coffeehouse and wandered through the streets. The intense heat of the afternoon began to make me feel sick, even feverish. But the one place I didn't want to go was home. The thought of waiting alone in that silent house for a phone call that would probably never come I found suffocating.

All I could think to do was to go and see May Kasahara. I went home, climbed over the wall, and made my way down the alley to the back of her house. Leaning against the fence of the vacant house on the other side of the alley, I stared at the garden with its bird sculpture. May would notice me if I stood here like this. Apart from those few times when she was out working for the wig company, she was always at home, keeping watch over the alley from her room or while sunbathing in the yard.

But I saw no sign of May Kasahara. There was not a cloud in the sky. The summer sunlight was roasting the back of my neck. The heavy smell of grass rose from the ground, invading my lungs. I stared at the bird statue and tried to think about the stories my uncle had recently told me of the fates of those who had lived in this house. But all I could think of was the sea, cold and blue. I took several long, deep breaths. I looked at my watch. I was ready to give up for the day, when May Kasahara finally came out. She ambled slowly through her yard to where I stood. She wore denim shorts, a blue aloha shirt, and red thongs. Standing before me, she seemed to be smiling through her sunglasses.

"Hello there, Mr Wind-up Bird. Find your cat – Noboru Wataya?"

"Not yet," I said. "What took you so long to come out today?"

She thrust her hands into her hip pockets and looked all around, amused. "Look, Mr Wind-up Bird, I may have a lot of free time, but I don't live to stand guard over this alley from morning to night. I have *some* things to keep me busy. But anyhow, I'm sorry. Were you waiting long?"

"Not so long. I got hot standing out here."

May Kasahara stared hard at my face, then wrinkled her eyebrows. "What's wrong, Mr Wind-up Bird? You look terrible – like somebody who's just been dug up out of the ground. Better come over here and rest in the shade for a while."

She took me by the hand and led me into her yard. There she moved a canvas deck chair into the shade of the oak tree and sat me down on it. The thick green branches cast cool shadows that had the fragrance of life.

"Don't worry, there's nobody here, as usual," she said. "You don't have to be the least bit concerned. Take your time. Stop thinking and relax."

"I do have one favour to ask you," I said.

"Try me," she said.

"I want you to make a call for me."

Taking out a notepad and pen, I wrote down the number of Kumiko's office. Then I tore off the page and handed it to her. The little vinyl-covered notepad was warm and damp with sweat. "All I want you to do is call this place and ask if Kumiko Okada is there, and if she's not, ask if she came to work yesterday."

May Kasahara took the paper and looked at it with pursed lips. Then she looked at me. "Fine, I'll take care of it. You just empty your head and get horizontal. You are *not* allowed to move. I'll be right back."

Once she was gone, I stretched out and closed my eyes as ordered. I was soaked with sweat from head to foot. Trying to think, I felt a throbbing deep in my head, and I seemed to have a lump of string in the pit of my stomach. Every once in a while, a hint of nausea came over me. The neighbourhood was absolutely silent. It suddenly occurred to me that I had not heard the wind-up bird for quite some time. When had I last heard it? Probably four or five days ago. But I wasn't certain. By the time I noticed, its cry had been missing too long to tell. Maybe it was a migratory bird. Come to think of it, we had started hearing it about a month before. And for a time, the wind-up bird had continued each day to wind the spring of our little world. That had been the wind-up bird's season.

After ten minutes, May Kasahara came back. She handed me a large glass. Ice clinked when I took it. The sound seemed to reach me from a distant world. There were several gates connecting that world with the place where I was, and I could hear the sound because they all just happened to be open at the moment. But this was strictly temporary. If even one of them closed, the sound would no longer reach my ears. "Drink it," she said. "Lemon juice in water. It'll clear your head."

I managed to drink half and returned the glass to her. The cold water passed my throat and made its way down into my body, after which a violent wave of nausea overtook me. The decomposing lump of string in my stomach began to unravel and rise to the base of my throat. I closed my eyes and tried to let it pass. With my eyes closed, I saw Kumiko boarding the train, with her blouse and skirt in hand. I thought it might be better to vomit. But I did not vomit. I took several deep breaths until the feeling diminished and disappeared altogether.

"Are you OK?" asked May Kasahara.

"Yes, I'm OK," I said.

"I made the call," she said. "Told them I was a relative. That's OK, isn't it?"

"Uh-huh."

"This person, Kumiko Okada, that's Mrs Wind-up Bird, isn't it?"

"Uh-huh."

"They said she didn't come to work – today or yesterday. Just took off without a word. It's a real problem for them. She's not the type to do this kind of thing, they said."

"It's true. She's not the type."

"She's been gone since yesterday?"

I nodded.

"Poor Mr Wind-up Bird," she said. She sounded as if she really did feel sorry for me. She put her hand on my forehead. "Is there anything I can do?"

"Not now," I said. "But thanks."

"Do you mind if I ask more? Or would you rather I didn't?"

"Go ahead," I said. "I'm not sure I can answer, though."

"Did your wife run away with a man?"

"I'm not sure," I said. "Maybe. It's possible."

"But you've been living together all this time. How can you not be sure?"

She was right. How could I not be sure?

"Poor Mr Wind-up Bird," she said again. "I wish I had something to say to help you, but I don't know anything about married life."

I got out of my chair. The effort required to stand was far greater than I would have imagined. "Thanks for everything. You've been a big help. I've got to go now. I should be at home in case word comes. Somebody might call."

"As soon as you get home, take a shower. First thing. OK? Then put on clean clothes. And shave."

"Shave?" I stroked my jaw. It was true: I had forgotten to shave. The thought hadn't crossed my mind all morning.

"The little things are important, Mr Wind-up Bird," May Kasahara said, looking into my eyes. "Go home and take a good look in the mirror."

"I will," I said.

"Mind if I come over later?"

"Fine," I said. Then I added: "You'd be a great help."

May Kasahara nodded in silence.

At home, I looked at my face in the mirror. It was true: I looked terrible. I got undressed, showered, gave myself a good shampoo, shaved, brushed my teeth, put aftershave lotion on my face, and went to the mirror again for a close examination. A little better than before, it seemed. My nausea was gone. My head was still a little foggy, though.

I put on short trousers and a fresh polo shirt. I sat on the veranda, leaning against a pillar and watching the garden while my hair dried. I tried to put the events of recent days in order. First there was the call from Lieutenant Mamiya. That was yesterday morning? Yes, no doubt about it: yesterday morning. Then Kumiko had left the house. I had zipped up her dress. Then I had found the cologne box. Then Lieutenant Mamiya had come and told me his strange war stories: how he had been captured by Outer Mongolian troops and thrown into a well. He had left me the keepsake from Mr Honda. An empty box. Then Kumiko had failed to come home. She had picked up her cleaning that morning by the station and afterwards just disappeared. Without a word to her company. So that was what had happened yesterday.

I could hardly believe that all that had happened in the course of a single day. It was too much for one day.

As I mulled these things over, I began to feel incredibly sleepy. This was not an ordinary kind of sleepiness. It was an intense, even violent, sleepiness. Sleep was stripping me of consciousness the way the clothes might be stripped from the body of an unresisting person. I went to the bedroom without thinking, took everything off except my underwear, and got into bed. I tried to look at the clock on the night table, but I couldn't even turn my head. I closed my eyes and instantly fell into a deep, bottomless sleep.

•

In my sleep, I was zipping up Kumiko's dress. I could see her smooth white back. But by the time I got the zip to the top, I realized it was not Kumiko but Creta Kano. She and I were the only ones in the room.

It was the same room as in the last dream: a room in the same hotel suite. On the table was a bottle of Cutty Sark and two glasses. There was also a stainless-steel ice bucket, full of ice. In the corridor outside, someone was passing by, speaking in a loud voice. I couldn't catch the words, which seemed to be in a foreign language. An unlit chandelier hung from the ceiling. The only illumination in this murky room came from lamps mounted on the wall. Again the windows had thick curtains that were closed tight.

Creta Kano was wearing a summer dress of Kumiko's: pale blue, with an openwork pattern of birds. The skirt came up just above her knees. As always, her make-up was in the Jacqueline Kennedy style. On her left wrist she wore a pair of matching bracelets.

"How did you get that dress?" I asked. "Is it yours?"

Creta Kano looked at me and shook her head. When she did this, the curled tips of her hair moved in a pleasant way. "No, it is not mine," she said. "I'm borrowing it. But don't worry, Mr Okada, this is not causing anyone any difficulty."

"Where are we?" I asked.

Creta Kano didn't answer. As before, I was sitting on the edge of the bed. I wore a suit and my polka-dot tie.

"You don't have to think about a thing, Mr Okada," said Creta Kano. "There is nothing to worry about. Everything is going to be fine."

And again, as before, she unzipped my fly, took out my penis, and put it in her mouth. The one thing different from before was that she did not take off her own clothing. She wore Kumiko's dress the whole time. I tried to move, but it felt as if my body were tied down by invisible threads. I felt myself growing big and hard inside her mouth.

189

I saw her fake eyelashes and curled hair tips moving. Her bracelets made a dry sound against each other. Her tongue was long and soft and seemed to wrap itself around me. Just as I was about to come, all of a sudden she moved away and began slowly to undress me. She took off my jacket, my tie, my trousers, my shirt, my underwear, and made me lie down on the bed. She kept on her own clothes, though. She sat on the bed, took my hand, and brought it under her dress. She was not wearing panties. My hand felt the warmth of her vagina. It was deep, warm, and very wet. My fingers were all but sucked inside.

"Won't Noboru Wataya be here any minute?" I asked. "Weren't you expecting him?"

Instead of answering, Creta Kano touched my forehead. "You don't have to think, Mr Okada. We'll take care of all that. Leave everything to us."

"To *us*?" I asked, but there was no reply.

Then Creta Kano mounted me and used her hand to slip me inside her. Once she had me deep inside, she began a slow rotation of her hips. As she moved, the edges of the pale-blue dress caressed my naked stomach and thighs. With the skirts of the dress spread out around her, Creta Kano, riding me, looked like a soft, gigantic mushroom that had silently poked its face up through the dead leaves on the ground and opened under the sheltering wings of night. Her vagina felt warm and at the same time cold. It tried to envelop me, to draw me in, and at the same time to force me out. My erection grew larger and harder. I felt I was about to burst wide open. It was the strangest sensation, something that went beyond simple sexual pleasure. It felt as if something inside her, something special inside her, were slowly working its way through my organ into me.

With her eyes closed and her chin lifted slightly, Creta Kano rocked quietly back and forth as if she were dreaming. I could see her chest rising and falling with each breath beneath the dress. A few hairs had come loose and hung over her forehead. I imagined myself floating alone in the middle of a vast sea. I closed my eyes and listened, expecting to hear the sound of little waves hitting my face. My body was bathed in lukewarm ocean water. I sensed the gradual flow of the tide. It was carrying me away. I decided to do as Creta Kano had said and not think about anything. I closed my eyes, let the strength go out of my limbs, and gave myself up to the current.

All of a sudden, I noticed that the room had gone dark. I tried to look around, but I could hardly see a thing. The wall lamps had all been extinguished. There was only the faint silhouette of Creta Kano's blue dress rocking on top of me. "Just forget," she said, but it was not Creta Kano's voice. "Forget about everything. You're asleep. You're dreaming. You're lying in nice, warm mud. We all come out of the warm mud, and we all go back to it."

It was the voice of the woman on the telephone. The mysterious woman on the phone had now mounted me and was joining her body with mine. She, too, wore Kumiko's dress. She and Creta Kano had traded places without my being aware of it. I tried to speak. I did not know what I hoped to say, but I at least tried to speak. I was too confused, though, and my voice would not work. All I could expel from my mouth was a hot blast of air. I opened my eyes wide and tried to see the face of the woman mounted on top of me, but the room was too dark.

The woman said nothing more. Instead, she began to move her hips in an even more erotic way. Her soft flesh, itself almost an independent organism, enveloped my erection with a gentle pulling motion. From behind her I heard – or thought I heard – the sound of a knob turning. A white flash went through the darkness. The ice bucket on the table might have shone momentarily in the light from the corridor. Or the flash might have been the glint of a sharp blade. But I couldn't think any more. There was only one thing I could do: I came.

.

I washed myself off in the shower and laundered my semen-stained underwear by hand. Terrific, I thought. Why did I have to be having wet dreams at such a difficult time in my life?

Once again I put on fresh clothing, and once again I sat on the veranda, looking at the garden. Splashes of sunlight danced on everything, filtered through thick green leaves. Several days of rain had promoted a powerful growth of bright-green weeds here and there, giving the garden a subtle shading of ruin and stagnation.

Creta Kano again. Two wet dreams in a short interval, and both times it had been Creta Kano. Never once had I thought of sleeping with her. The desire had not even entered my mind. And yet both times I had been in that room, joining my body with hers. What could possibly be the reason for this? And who was that telephone woman who had taken her place? She knew me, and I supposedly knew her. I went through the various sexual partners I had had in life, but none of them could be the telephone woman. Still, there was *something* about her that seemed familiar. And that was what annoyed me.

Some kind of memory was trying to force its way out. I could feel it in there, bumping around. All I needed was a little hint. If I pulled that one tiny thread, then everything would unravel. The mystery was waiting for me to solve it. But the one slim thread was something I couldn't find.

I gave up trying to think. "Forget everything. You're asleep. You're dreaming. You're lying in nice, warm mud. We all come out of the warm mud, and we all go back to it."

•

Six o'clock came, and still no phone call. Only May Kasahara showed up. All she wanted, she said, was a sip of beer. I took a cold can from the refrigerator and split it with her. I was hungry, so I put some ham and lettuce between two slices of bread and ate that. When she saw me eating, May said she would like the same. I made her a sandwich too. We ate in silence and drank our beer. I kept looking up at the wall clock.

"Don't you have a TV in this house?"

"No TV," I said.

She gave the edge of her lip a little bite. "I thought so. Don't you like TV?"

"I don't *dis*like it. I get along fine without it."

May Kasahara let that sink in for a while. "How many years have you been married, Mr Wind-up Bird?"

"Six," I said.

"And you've got by without TV for six years?"

"Uh-huh. At first we didn't have the money to buy one. Then we got used to living without it. It's nice and quiet that way."

"The two of you must have been happy."

"What makes you think so?"

She wrinkled up her face. "Well, *I* couldn't live a day without television."

"Because you're unhappy?"

May Kasahara did not reply to that. "But now Kumiko is gone. You must be not so happy any more, Mr Wind-up Bird."

I nodded and sipped my beer. "That's about the size of it," I said. That was about the size of it.

She put a cigarette between her lips and, with a practised movement, struck a match to light it. "Now, Mr Wind-up Bird," she said, "I want you to tell me the absolute truth. Do you think I'm ugly?"

I put my beer glass down and took another look at May Kasahara's face. All this time while talking to her, I had been vaguely thinking of other things. She was wearing an oversized black tank top, which gave a clear view of the girlish swell of her breasts.

"You're not the least bit ugly," I said. "That's for sure. Why do you ask?"

"My boyfriend always used to tell me how ugly I was, that I didn't have any boobs."

"The boy who wrecked the bike?"

"Yeah, him."

I watched May Kasahara slowly exhaling cigarette smoke. "Boys that age will say things like that. They don't know how to express exactly what they feel, so they say and do the opposite. They hurt people that way, for no reason at all, and they hurt themselves too. Anyhow, you're not the least bit ugly. I think you're very pretty. No flattery intended."

May Kasahara mulled that one over for a while. She dropped ash into the empty beer can. "Is Mrs Wind-up Bird pretty?"

"Hmm, that's hard for me to say. Some would say she is, and some would say not. It's a matter of taste."

"I see," she said. She tapped on her glass as if bored.

"What's your biker boyfriend doing?" I asked. "Doesn't he come to see you any more?"

"No, he doesn't," said May Kasahara, laying a finger on the scar by her left eye. "I'll never see him again, that's for sure. Two hundred per cent sure. I'd bet my left little toe on it. But I'd rather not talk about that right now. Some things, you know, if you say them, it makes them not true? You know what I mean, Mr Wind-up Bird?"

"I think I do," I said. Then I glanced at the phone in the living room. It sat on the table, cloaked in silence. It looked like a deep-sea creature pretending to be an inanimate object, crouching there in wait for its prey.

"Someday, Mr Wind-up Bird, I'll tell you all about him. When I feel like it. But not now. I just don't feel like it now."

She looked at her watch. "Gotta get home. Thanks for the beer."

I saw her out to the garden wall. A nearly full moon was pouring its grainy light down on the earth. The sight of the full moon reminded me that Kumiko's period was approaching. But that would probably have nothing to do with me any more. The thought sent a sharp pain through my chest. The intensity of it caught me off guard: it resembled sorrow.

With her hand on the wall, May Kasahara looked at me. "Tell me, Mr Wind-up Bird, you do love Kumiko, don't you?"

"I think I do."

"Even though she might have gone off with a lover? If she said she wanted to come back to you, would you take her back?"

I let out a sigh. "That's a tough question," I said. "I'd have to think about it once it really happened."

"Sorry for sticking my nose in," said May Kasahara, with a little click of the tongue. "But don't get angry. I'm just trying to learn. I want to know what it means for a wife to run away. There're all kinds of things I don't know."

"I'm not angry," I said. Then I looked up at the full moon again.

"All right, then, Mr Wind-up Bird. You take care of yourself. I hope your wife comes back and everything works out." Moving with incredible lightness, May Kasahara swung herself over the wall and disappeared into the summer night.

·

With May Kasahara gone, I was alone again. I sat on the veranda, thinking about the questions she had raised. If Kumiko had gone off somewhere with a lover, could I take her back again? I didn't know the answer. I really didn't know. There were all kinds of things that I didn't know.

Suddenly the phone rang. My hand shot out and picked up the receiver.

The voice at the other end belonged to a woman. "This is Malta Kano," she said. "Please forgive me for calling you so often, Mr Okada, but I was wondering if you might happen to have any plans for tomorrow."

I had no plans, I said. Plans were simply something I did not have.

"In that case, I wonder if it might be possible for me to see you in the afternoon."

"Does this have something to do with Kumiko?"

"I believe that it does," said Malta Kano, choosing her words carefully. "Noboru Wataya will also be joining us, most likely."

I almost dropped the receiver when I heard this. "You mean the three of us will be getting together to talk?"

"Yes, I believe that is the case," said Malta Kano. "The present situation makes this necessary. I am sorry, but I cannot go into any further detail on the telephone."

"I see. All right, then," I said.

"Shall we meet at 1 o'clock? In the same place we met before: the tearoom of the Shinagawa Pacific Hotel."

"One o'clock in the tearoom of the Shinagawa Pacific Hotel," I repeated, and hung up.

•

May Kasahara called at 10 o'clock. She had nothing in particular to say; she just wanted to talk to somebody. We chatted about harmless topics for a while. "Tell me, Mr Wind-up Bird," she said in the end. "Have you had any good news since I was there?"

"No good news," I said. "Nothing."

3

Noboru Wataya Speaks

•

The Story of the Monkeys of the Shitty Island

I arrived at the tearoom ten minutes early, but Noboru Wataya and Malta Kano had already found a table and were waiting for me. The lunchtime crowd was thick, but I spotted Malta Kano immediately. Not too many people wore red vinyl hats on sunny summer afternoons. It must have been the same hat she had on the day I met her, unless she owned a collection of vinyl hats, all the same style and colour. She dressed with the same tasteful simplicity as before: a short-sleeved linen jacket over a collarless cotton top. Both pieces were perfectly white and perfectly free of wrinkles. No accessories, no make-up. Only the red vinyl hat clashed with the rest of the outfit, both in tone and in material. As if she had been waiting for my arrival to do so, she removed the hat when I took my seat, placing it on the table. Beside the hat lay a small yellow leather handbag. She had ordered some tonic water but had not touched it, as before. The liquid seemed somehow uncomfortable in its tall glass, as if it had nothing better to do than produce its little bubbles.

Noboru Wataya was wearing green sunglasses. As soon as I sat down, he removed them and stared at the lenses for a while, then he put them back on. He wore what looked like a brand-new white polo shirt under a navy cotton sports jacket. There was a glass of iced tea on the table in front of him, but he too had apparently not touched his drink yet.

I ordered a coffee and took a sip of ice water.

No one spoke. Noboru Wataya appeared not even to have noticed that I had arrived. In order to make sure that I had not suddenly turned transparent, I put a hand on the table and watched it as I turned it over a few times. The waiter came, set a cup in front of me, and filled it with coffee. After he left, Malta Kano made little throat-clearing sounds as if testing a microphone, but still she said nothing.

The first to speak was Noboru Wataya. "I have very little time to spare, so let's make this as simple and straightforward as possible." He seemed to be talking to the stainless-steel sugar bowl in the middle of the table, but of course he was speaking to me. The sugar bowl was just a convenient midpoint between us towards which he could direct his speech.

"Make what as simple and straightforward as possible?" I asked in a straightforward manner.

At last Noboru Wataya took off his sunglasses, folded them, placed them on the table, and looked straight at me. More than three years had gone by since I had last met and spoken to the man, but I felt no sense of the intervening time – thanks, I assumed, to having had his face thrust in front of me so often by the media. Certain kinds of information are like smoke: they work their way into people's eyes and minds whether sought out or not, and with no regard to personal preference.

Forced now to see the man in person, I couldn't help but notice how much the three years had changed the impression his face made. That almost stagnant, muddy look of his had been pushed into the background, to be covered over by something slick and artificial. Noboru Wataya had managed to find for himself a new, more sophisticated mask – a very well-made mask, to be sure: perhaps even a new skin. Whatever it was, mask or skin, I had to admit – yes, even I had to admit – that it had a certain kind of attractive power. And then it hit me: looking at this face was like looking at a television image. He talked the way people on television talked, and he moved the way people on television moved. There was always a layer of glass between us. I was on this side, and he was on that side.

"As I am sure you must realize, we are here today to talk about Kumiko," said Noboru Wataya. "About Kumiko and you. About your future. What you and she are going to do."

"Going to do?" I said, lifting my coffee cup and taking a sip. "Could you be a little more specific?"

Noboru Wataya looked at me with strangely expressionless eyes. "A little more specific? Kumiko has taken a lover. She's left you. Surely you are not suggesting that anyone involved in the present situation wants it to continue for ever. That would not be good for anyone."

"Taken a lover?" I asked.

"Now please, wait just a moment." Malta Kano chose at this point to intervene. "A discussion such as this has its own proper order. Mr Wataya, Mr Okada, it is important to proceed in an orderly fashion."

"I don't see that," said Noboru Wataya, without any sense of life in his voice. "There's no order to this. What kind of order do you mean? This discussion doesn't have any."

"Let him speak first," I said to Malta Kano. "We can impose the proper order afterwards – assuming there is one."

Malta Kano looked at me for a few seconds with her lips lightly pursed, then gave a little nod. "All right, then," she said. "Mr Wataya first. Please."

"Kumiko has another man in her life," he began. "And now she's gone off with him. This much is clear. Which means there would be no point in your continuing to stay married. Fortunately, there are no children involved, and in view of the circumstances, no money need change hands. Everything can be settled quickly. She simply pulls out of your family register. You just have to sign and put your seal on forms prepared by a lawyer, and that takes care of that. And let me add this to avoid any misunderstanding: what I am saying now is the final view of the entire Wataya family."

I folded my arms and mulled over his words for a time. "I have a few questions," I said. "First of all, how do you know that Kumiko has another man?"

"She told me so herself," said Noboru Wataya.

I did not know what to say to that. I put my hands on the table and remained silent. It was hard for me to imagine Kumiko going to Noboru Wataya with such a personal matter.

"She called me a week ago and said she had something to discuss," continued Noboru Wataya. "We met and talked. Face to face. That's when Kumiko told me she was seeing someone else."

For the first time in months, I felt like a smoke. Of course, I had no cigarettes with me. Instead, I took a sip of coffee and put the cup back in the saucer with a loud, dry clash.

"Then she left home," he said.

"I see," I said. "If you say so, it must be true. Kumiko must have had a lover. And she went to you for advice. It's hard for me to believe, but I can't imagine your lying to me about such a thing."

"No, of course I'm not lying," said Noboru Wataya, with the hint of a smile on his lips.

"So is that all you have to tell me? Kumiko left me for another man, so I should agree to a divorce?"

Noboru Wataya responded with a single small nod, as if he were trying to conserve energy. "I suppose you realize that I was not in favour of Kumiko marrying you to begin with. I took no positive steps to interfere, on the assumption that it was a matter that did not concern me, but now I almost wish I had." He took a sip of water and set his glass on the table again. Then he continued: "From the first day I met you, I knew better than to hope you might amount to anything. I saw no sign of promise, nothing in you that suggested you might accomplish something worthwhile or even turn yourself into a respectable human being: nothing there to shine or to shed light on anything. I knew that whatever you set your hand to would end up half-baked, that you would never see anything through to the end. And I was right. You have been married to my sister for six years, and what have you done in all that time? Nothing, right? All you've accomplished in six long years is to leave your job and ruin Kumiko's life. Now you're out of work and you have no plans for the future. There's nothing inside that head of yours but garbage and rocks.

"Why Kumiko ever got together with the likes of you I'll never understand. Maybe she thought the garbage and rocks in your head were interesting. But finally, garbage is garbage and rocks are rocks. You were wrong for her from the start. Which is not to say that Kumiko was perfection, either. She's had her own oddities since childhood, for one reason or another. I suppose that's why she was briefly attracted to you. But that's all over now. In any case, the best thing will be to finish this business as quickly as possible. My parents and I will watch out for Kumiko. We want you to back off. And don't try to find her. You've got nothing to do with her any more. All you can do is cause trouble if you try to get involved. The best thing you can do is to begin a new life in a new place – a life that is better suited to you. That would be best for you and best for us."

To signal that he was finished, Noboru Wataya drained the water in his glass, called the waiter, and ordered more.

"Do you have anything else to say?" I asked.

Noboru Wataya responded this time with a single small shake of the head.

"In that case," I said to Malta Kano, "what is the proper order for this discussion?"

Malta Kano took a small white handkerchief from her bag and used it to wipe the corners of her mouth. Then she picked up her red vinyl hat from the table and set it on top of the bag.

"I'm certain this is all very shocking to you, Mr Okada," she said. "And for my part, I find it extremely painful to be speaking about such things with you face to face, as you can imagine."

Noboru Wataya glanced at his watch in order to ascertain that the world was still spinning on its axis and costing him precious time.

"I see now," Malta Kano continued, "that I must make this as simple and straightforward as possible. Mrs Okada came to see me first. She came to me for advice."

"On my recommendation," interjected Noboru Wataya. "Kumiko came to talk to me about the cat, and I introduced her to Ms Kano."

"Was that before I met you or after?" I asked Malta Kano.

"Before," she said.

"In that case," I said, "to put things in their proper order, it went something like this. Kumiko learned about your existence from Noboru Wataya, and she went to see you about the lost cat. Then, for some reason that is still not clear to me, she hid from me the fact that she had already met you, and arranged for me to see you – which I did, in this very place. Am I right?"

"That is approximately correct," said Malta Kano, with some difficulty. "My first discussion with Mrs Okada was strictly about the cat. I could tell there was something more to it than that, however, which is why I wanted to meet you and speak to you direct. Then it became necessary for me to meet Mrs Okada one more time and to ask about deeper, personal matters."

"Which is when Kumiko told you she had a lover."

"Yes. In short, I believe that is the case. Given my position, it is not possible for me to go into any greater detail than that," said Malta Kano.

I let out a sigh. Not that sighing was going to accomplish anything, but it was something I had to do. "So, then, Kumiko had been involved with this man for some time?"

"Two and a half months or thereabouts, I believe."

"Two and a half months," I said. "How could it have been going on for two and a half months without my noticing anything?"

"Because, Mr Okada, you had no doubts whatsoever about your wife," said Malta Kano.

I nodded. "That's true. It never once crossed my mind. I never imagined Kumiko could lie to me like that, and I still can't really believe it."

"Results aside, the ability to have complete faith in another human being is one of the finest qualities a person can possess."

"Not an easy ability to come by," said Noboru Wataya.

The waiter approached and refilled my coffee cup. A young woman at the next table was laughing out loud.

"So, then," I said to Noboru Wataya, "what is the ultimate purpose of this gathering? Why are the three of us together here? To get me to agree to divorce Kumiko? Or is there some deeper objective? There did seem to be a kind of logic to what you said earlier, but all the important parts are vague. You say Kumiko has a man and has left the house. So where did she go? What is she doing there? Is she by herself or is she with him? Why hasn't Kumiko got in touch with me? If it's true she has another man, that's the end of that. But I won't believe it's true until I hear it directly from her. Do you understand? The only ones who count here are Kumiko and me. We're the ones who have to talk to each other and decide things. You've got nothing to do with this."

Noboru Wataya pushed his untouched glass of iced tea aside. "We are here to inform you of the situation," he said. "I asked Ms Kano to accompany me, thinking it would be better to have a third party present. I don't know who Kumiko's other man is, and I don't know where she is now. Kumiko is grown-up. She can do as she pleases. But even if I knew where she was, I certainly wouldn't tell you. She hasn't been in touch with you because she doesn't want to talk to you."

"She *did* want to talk to *you*, apparently. How much could she have told you? You and she are not very close, as I understand it."

"Well, if *you* and she were so damn close, why did she sleep with another man?" said Noboru Wataya.

Malta Kano gave a little cough.

Noboru Wataya went on: "Kumiko told me she is having a relationship with another man. She said she wants to settle everything once and for all. I advised her to divorce you. She said she would think about it."

"Is that all?" I asked.

"What else is there?"

"I just don't get it," I said. "I don't believe that Kumiko would go to

201

you with something so important. You're the last person she would consult on such a matter. She would either think it out for herself or speak to me. She must have said something else to you. If she had to talk to you in person, it must have been about something else."

Noboru Wataya allowed the faintest possible smile to play over his lips – a thin, cold smile like a sliver of a moon hovering in the dawn sky. "This is what they mean by letting the truth slip out," he said, in a soft but clearly audible voice.

"Letting the truth slip out," I said, testing the expression for myself.

"I'm sure you see my point," he said. "Your wife sleeps with another man. She runs out on you. And then you try to pin the blame on someone else. I've never heard of anything so stupid. Look, I didn't come here for my own pleasure. It was something I had to do. For me, it's just a waste of time. I might as well be throwing my time into the gutter."

When he had finished speaking, a deep silence settled over the table.

"Do you know the story of the monkeys of the shitty island?" I asked Noboru Wataya.

He shook his head, with no sign of interest. "Never heard of it."

"Somewhere, far, far away, there's a shitty island. An island without a name. An island not worth giving a name. A shitty island with a shitty shape. On this shitty island grow palm trees that also have shitty shapes. And the palm trees produce coconuts that give off a shitty smell. Shitty monkeys live in the trees, and they love to eat these shitty-smelling coconuts, after which they shit the world's foulest shit. The shit falls on the ground and builds up shitty mounds, making the shitty palm trees that grow on them even shittier. It's an endless cycle."

I drank the rest of my coffee.

"As I sat here looking at you," I continued, "I suddenly remembered the story of this shitty island. What I'm trying to say is this. A certain kind of shittiness, a certain kind of stagnation, a certain kind of darkness, goes on propagating itself by its own power in its own self-contained cycle. And once it passes a certain point, no one can stop it – even if the person himself wants to stop it."

Noboru Wataya's face wore no expression of any kind. The smile was gone, but neither was there any shadow of annoyance. All I could see was one small wrinkle between his eyebrows, and I could not recall if it was something that had been there before.

"Are you catching my drift, Mr Wataya?" I went on. "I know *exactly* the sort of man you are. You say I'm like garbage or rocks. And you think you could smash me to bits anytime you felt like it. But things are not that simple. To you, with your values, I may well be nothing but garbage and rocks. But I'm not as stupid as you think I am. I know exactly what you've got under that smooth, made-for-TV mask of yours. I know your secret. Kumiko knows and I know: we both know what's under there. If I wanted to, I could tell it to the world. I could bring it out into the light. It might take time, but I could do it. I may be a nobody, but at least I'm not a sandbag. I'm a living, breathing human being. If somebody hits me, I hit back. Make sure you keep that in mind."

Noboru Wataya went on staring at me with that expressionless face of his – a face like a chunk of rock floating in space. What I had said to him was almost pure bluff. I did not know Noboru Wataya's secret. That he had something profoundly warped inside him was not difficult to conceive. But I had no way of knowing with any certainty what that might be. My words, though, seemed to have jabbed at something in there. I could read the effect on his face. He didn't respond to me the way he always did to his opponents in televised panel discussions: he didn't sneer at my words or try to trip me up or find some clever opening. He sat there in silence, without moving a muscle.

Then something very odd began to happen to Noboru Wataya's face. Little by little, it started to turn red. But it did this in the strangest way. Certain patches turned a deep red, while others reddened only slightly, and the rest appeared to have become weirdly pale. This made me think of an autumn wood with blotchy colours where deciduous and evergreen trees grow in a chaotic mix.

Eventually, without a word, Noboru Wataya stood up, took his sunglasses from his pocket, and put them on. The strange, blotchy colours still covered his face. They looked almost permanent now. Malta Kano remained perfectly still in her seat, saying nothing. I myself adopted an expression of complete indifference. Noboru Wataya began to say something to me but, in the end, seemed to have decided against it. Instead, he walked away from the table and disappeared into the crowd.

•

For a while after Noboru Wataya left, Malta Kano and I said nothing to each other. I felt exhausted. The waiter came and offered to refill my coffee cup, but I sent him away. Malta Kano picked up her red hat from the table and stared at it for a few minutes before setting it down on the chair next to her.

I sensed a bitter taste in my mouth. I tried to wash it away by drinking some water, but this did no good.

After another short interval, Malta Kano spoke. "Feelings need to be let out sometimes. Otherwise, the flow can stagnate inside. I'm sure you feel better now that you have said what you wanted to say."

"A little," I said. "But it didn't solve anything. It didn't bring anything to a conclusion."

"You don't like Mr Wataya, do you, Mr Okada?"

"Every time I talk to that guy, I get this feeling of incredible emptiness inside. Every single object in the room begins to look as if it has no substance to it. Everything appears hollow. Exactly why this should be, I could never explain to you with any precision. Because of this feeling, I end up saying and doing things that are simply not me. And I feel terrible about it afterwards. If I could manage never to see him again, nothing would make me happier."

Malta Kano shook her head. "Unfortunately, you will be required to encounter Mr Wataya any number of times again. This is something you will not be able to avoid."

She could well be right. I couldn't get him out of my life so easily.

I picked up my glass and took another drink of water. Where had that awful taste come from?

"There's just one thing I would like to ask you," I said. "Whose side are you on here? Noboru Wataya's or mine?"

Malta Kano put her elbows on the table and brought her palms together before her face. "Neither," she said. "There are no sides in this case. They simply do not exist. This is not the kind of thing that has a top and bottom, a right and left, a front and back, Mr Okada."

"Sounds like Zen," I said. "Interesting enough in itself as a system of thought, but not much good for explaining anything."

She nodded her head. The palms that she was pressing together in front of her face she now pulled three inches apart, holding them at a slight angle and aiming them towards me. They were small, well-shaped palms. "I know that what I am saying does not seem to make a great deal of sense. And I don't blame you for being angry. But if I were to tell you anything now, it would serve no practical purpose. In fact, it would ruin things. You will have to win through your own strength. With your own hands."

"Like in *Wild Kingdom*," I said with a smile. "You get hit, you hit back."

"That's it," said Malta Kano. "Exactly." Then, with all the care of someone retrieving the belongings of a person newly dead, she picked up her handbag and put on her red vinyl hat. When she set the hat on her head, Malta Kano conveyed a strange yet tangible impression that a unit of time had now come to an end.

·

After Malta Kano had left, I went on sitting there alone, with nothing particular on my mind. I had no idea where I should go or what I should do if I were to stand up. But of course I couldn't stay there for ever. When twenty minutes had passed like this, I paid for the three of us and left the tearoom. Neither of the other two had paid.

4

Divine Grace Lost

◆

Prostitute of the Mind

At home, I found a thick letter waiting. It was from Lieutenant Mamiya. My name and address had been written on the envelope in the same bold, handsome characters as before. I changed my clothes, washed my face, and went to the kitchen, where I drank two glasses of cold water. Once I had had a moment to catch my breath, I cut the letter open.

Lieutenant Mamiya had used a fountain pen to fill some ten thin sheets of paper with tiny characters. I flipped through the pages and put them back into the envelope. I was too tired to read such a long letter; I didn't have the powers of concentration just then. When my eyes scanned the rows of handwritten characters, they looked like a swarm of strange blue bugs. And besides, the voice of Noboru Wataya was still echoing faintly in my mind.

I stretched out on the sofa and closed my eyes for a long time, thinking of nothing. It was not hard for me to think of nothing, the way I felt at the moment. In order not to think of any one thing, all I had to do was think of many things, a little at a time: just think about something for a moment and fling it into space.

It was nearly 5 o'clock in the evening when I finally decided to read Lieutenant Mamiya's letter. I went out to the veranda, sat leaning against a pillar, and took the pages from the envelope.

The whole of the first page was filled with conventional phrases: extended seasonal greetings, thanks for my having invited him to my home the other day, and profound apologies for having bored me with his endless stories. Lieutenant Mamiya was certainly a man who knew the civilities. He was a survivor of an age when such civilities occupied a major portion of daily life. I skimmed through those and turned to the second page.

Please forgive me for having gone on at such length with these preliminary matters. My sole purpose in writing this letter today, knowing full well that my presumptuousness in doing so can only burden you with an unwanted task, is to inform you that the events I recently told you about were neither a fabrication of mine nor the dubious reminiscences of an old man, but are the complete and solemn truth in every particular. As you know, the war ended a very long time ago, and memory naturally degenerates as the years go by. Memories and thoughts age, just as people do. But certain thoughts can never age, and certain memories can never fade.

Up to and including this very day, I have never told any of these things to anyone but you, Mr Okada. To most people, these stories of mine would sound like the most incredible fabrications. The majority of people dismiss those things that lie beyond the bounds of their own understanding as absurd and not worth thinking about. I myself can only wish that my stories were, indeed, nothing but incredible fabrications. I have stayed alive all these years clinging to the frail hope that these memories of mine were nothing but a dream or a delusion. I have struggled to convince myself that they never happened. But each time I tried to push them into the dark, they came back stronger and more vivid than ever. Like cancer cells, these memories have taken root in my mind and eaten into my flesh.

Even now I can recall each tiny detail with such terrible clarity, I feel I am remembering events that happened just yesterday. I can hold the sand and the grass in my hands; I can even smell them. I can see the shapes of the clouds in the sky. I can feel the dry, sandy wind against my cheeks. By comparison, it is the subsequent events of my life that seem like delusions on the borderline between dream and reality.

The very roots of my life – those things that I can say once truly belonged to me alone – were frozen stiff or burned away out there, on the steppes of Outer Mongolia, where there was nothing to obstruct one's vision as far as the eye could see. Afterwards, I lost my hand in that fierce battle with the Soviet tank unit that attacked across the border; I tasted unimaginable hardships in a Siberian labour camp in the dead of winter; I was repatriated and served for thirty uneventful years as a social studies teacher in a rural high school; and I have since lived alone, tilling the land. But all those subsequent months and years feel to me like nothing but an illusion. It is as if they never happened. In an instant, my memory leaps across that empty shell of time and takes me back to the wilds of Hulunbuir.

What cost me my life, what turned it into that empty shell, I believe, was something in the light I saw at the bottom of the well – that intense light of the sun that penetrated to the very bottom of the well for ten or twenty seconds. It would come without warning, and disappear just as suddenly. But in that momentary flood of light I saw something – saw something once and for all – that I could never see again as long as I lived. And having seen it, I was no longer the same person I had been.

What happened down there? What did it mean? Even now, more than forty years later, I cannot answer those questions with any certainty. Which is why what I am about to say is strictly a hypothesis, a tentative explanation that I have fashioned for myself without the benefit of any logical basis. I do believe, however, that this hypothesis of mine is, for now, the closest that anyone can come to the truth of what it was that I experienced.

Outer Mongolian troops had thrown me into a deep, dark well in the middle of the steppe, my leg and shoulder were broken, I had neither food nor water: I was simply waiting to die. Before that, I had seen a man skinned alive. Under these special circumstances, I believe, my consciousness had attained such a viscid state of concentration that when the intense beam of light shone down for those few seconds, I was able to descend into a place that might be called the very core of my own consciousness. In any case, I saw the shape of something there. Just imagine. Everything around me is bathed in light. I am in the very centre of a flood of light. My eyes can see nothing. I am simply enveloped in light. But something begins to appear there. In the midst of my momentary blindness, something is trying to take shape. Some thing. *Some* thing *that possesses life. Like the shadow in a solar eclipse, it begins to emerge, black, in the light. But I can never quite make out its form. It is trying to come to me, trying to confer upon me something very much like heavenly grace. I wait for it, trembling. But then, either because it has changed its mind or because there is not enough time, it never comes to me. The moment before it takes full shape, it dissolves and melts once again into the light. Then the light itself fades. The time for the light to shine down into the well has ended.*

This happened two days in a row. Exactly the same thing. Something began to take shape in the overflowing light, then faded before it could reach a state of fullness. Down in the well, I was suffering from hunger and thirst – suffering terribly. But, finally, this was not of primary importance. What I suffered from most down there in the well was the torture of being unable to attain a clear view of that something in the light: the hunger of being unable to see what I needed to see, the thirst of being unable to know what I needed to know. Had I been able to see it clearly,

I would not have minded dying right then and there. I truly felt that way. I would have sacrificed anything for a full view of its form.

Finally, though, the form was snatched away from me for ever. The grace came to an end before it could be given to me. And as I said earlier, the life I led after emerging from that hole in the ground was nothing but a hollow, empty shell. Which is why, when the Soviet Army invaded Manchuria just before the end of the war, I volunteered to be sent to the front. In the Siberian labour camp, too, I purposely strove to have myself placed in the most difficult circumstances. No matter what I did, however, I could not die. Just as Corporal Honda had predicted that night, I was fated to return to Japan and live an amazingly long life. I remember how happy that news made me when I first heard it. But it turned out to be, if anything, a curse. It was not that I would not die: I could not die. Corporal Honda had been right about that too: I would have been better off not knowing.

When the revelation and the grace were lost, my life was lost. Those living things that had once been there inside me, that had been for that reason of some value, were dead now. Not a single thing was left. They had all been burned to ashes in that fierce light. The heat emitted by that revelation or grace had seared away the very core of the life that made me the person I was. Surely I had lacked the strength to resist that heat. And so I feel no fear of death. If anything, my physical death would be, for me, a form of salvation. It would liberate me for ever from this hopeless prison, this pain of being me.

Again I have burdened you with an overlong tale. I beg your forgiveness. But what I want to convey to you, Mr Okada, is this: I happened to lose my life at one particular moment in time, and I have gone on living these forty years or more with my life lost. As a person who finds himself in such a position, I have come to think that life is a far more limited thing than those in the midst of its maelstrom realize. The light shines into the act of life for only the briefest moment – perhaps only a matter of seconds. Once it is gone and one has failed to grasp its offered revelation, there is no second chance. One may have to live the rest of one's life in hopeless depths of loneliness and remorse. In that twilight world, one can no longer look forward to anything. All that such a person holds in his hands is the withered corpse of what should have been.

In any case, I am grateful for the chance to have met you, Mr Okada, and to have told you my story. Whether it will ever be of any use to you, I cannot be certain. But by telling it to you, I feel that I have attained a kind of salvation. Frail and tenuous though it may be, to me any kind of salvation is a treasure. Nor can I help sensing the presence of the subtle threads of fate in the fact that Mr Honda was the one who guided me to it. Please remember, Mr Okada, that there is someone here sending his best wishes to you for a happy life in the years to come.

I read through the letter one more time, with care, and returned it to its envelope.

Lieutenant Mamiya's letter moved my heart in strange ways, but to my mind it brought only vague and distant images. Lieutenant Mamiya was a man I could trust and accept, and I could also accept as fact those things that he declared to be facts. But the very concept of fact or truth had little power to persuade me just then. What most moved me in his letter was the sense of frustration that permeated the lieutenant's words: the frustration of never quite being able to depict or explain anything to his full satisfaction.

I went to the kitchen for a drink of water. Then I wandered around the house. In the bedroom, I sat on the bed and looked at Kumiko's dresses lined up in the wardrobe. And I thought, What has been the point of my life until now? I saw what Noboru Wataya had been talking about. My first reaction to his words had been anger, but I had to admit that he was right. "You have been married to my sister for six years," he had said, "and what have you done in all that time? Nothing, right? All you've accomplished in six long years is to leave your job and ruin Kumiko's life. Now you're out of work and you have no plans for the future. There's nothing inside that head of yours but garbage and rocks." I had no choice but to admit the accuracy of his remarks. Objectively speaking, I had done nothing meaningful in these six years, and what I had in my head was indeed something very like garbage and rocks. I was a zero. Just as he had said.

But was it true that I had ruined Kumiko's life?

For a long time, I looked at her dresses and blouses and skirts. They were the shadows Kumiko had left behind. Bereft of their owner, these shadows could only hang where they were, limp. I went to the bathroom and took out the bottle of Christian Dior cologne that someone had given to Kumiko. I opened it and smelled it. It was the fragrance I had smelled behind Kumiko's ears the morning she had left the house. I slowly poured the entire contents into the sink. As the liquid flowed down the drain, a strong smell of flowers (the exact name of which I tried but failed to recall) hung over the sink, stirring up memories with brutal intensity. In the midst of this intense aroma, I washed my face and brushed my teeth. Then I decided to go to May Kasahara's.

•

As always, I stood in the alley at the back of the Miyawaki house, waiting for May Kasahara to appear, but this time it didn't work. I leaned against the fence, sucked on a lemon drop, looked at the bird sculpture, and thought about Lieutenant Mamiya's letter. Soon, however, it began to grow dark. After waiting close to half an hour, I gave up. May Kasahara must be out somewhere.

I made my way back down the alley to the rear of my house and scaled the wall. Inside, I found the place filled with the hushed, pale darkness of a summer evening. And Creta Kano was there. For one hallucinatory moment, I felt I was dreaming. But no, this was the continuation of reality. A subtle trace of the cologne I had spilled still floated in the air. Creta Kano was sitting on the sofa, her hands on her knees. I drew closer to her, but as if time itself had stopped inside her, she made not the slightest movement. I turned on the light and sat in the chair facing her.

"The door was unlocked," she said at last. "I let myself in."

"That's all right," I said. "I usually leave the door unlocked when I go out."

She wore a lacy white blouse, flouncy mauve skirt, and large earrings. On her left wrist she wore a large pair of matching bracelets. The sight of them sent a shock through me. They were virtually identical to the bracelets I had seen her wearing in my dream. Her hair and make-up were both done in her habitual style. Hair spray held the hair perfectly in place as usual, as if she had just arrived from the beauty salon.

"There is not much time," she said. "I have to return home right away. But I wanted to be sure I had a chance to talk with you, Mr Okada. You saw my sister and Mr Wataya today, I believe."

"I certainly did. Not that it was the most amusing little gathering."

"Isn't there something you would like to ask me in connection with that?" she asked.

All kinds of people were coming to me with all kinds of questions.

"I'd like to know more about Noboru Wataya," I said. "I can't help thinking that I *have* to know more about him."

She nodded. "I would like to know more about Mr Wataya myself. I believe that my sister has already told you that he defiled me once, a very long time ago. I don't have time to go into that today, but I will, on some future occasion. In any case, it was something done to me against my will. It had originally been arranged for me to have relations with him. Which is why it was not rape in the ordinary sense of the word. But he did *defile* me, and that changed me as a person in many important ways. In the end, I was able to recover from the experience. Indeed, it enabled me (with the help of Malta Kano, of course) to bring myself to a whole new, higher level. Whatever the end results may have been, the fact remains that Noboru Wataya violated and defiled me at that time against my will. What he did to me was wrong – and dangerous. The potential was there for me to have been lost for ever. Do you see what I mean?"

I did *not* see what she meant.

"Of course, I had relations with you too, Mr Okada, but it was something done in the correct way, with a correct purpose. I was in no way defiled by that."

I looked straight at her for several seconds, as if staring at a wall with coloured blotches. "You had relations with me?"

"Yes," she said. "The first time I only used my mouth, but the second time we had relations. In the same room both times. You remember, of course? We had so little time on the first occasion, we had to hurry. There was more time to spare on the second occasion."

It was impossible for me to reply to her.

"I was wearing your wife's dress the second time. The blue one. And bracelets like these on my left arm. Isn't that true?" She held her left wrist, with the pair of bracelets, out towards me.

I nodded.

Creta Kano then said, "Of course, we did not have relations in reality. When you ejaculated, it was not into me, physically, but in your own consciousness. Do you see? It was a fabricated consciousness. Still, the two of us share the consciousness of having had relations with each other."

"What's the point of doing something like that?"

"To know," she said. "To know more – and more deeply."

I sighed. This was crazy. But she had been describing the scene of my dream with incredible accuracy. Running my finger around my mouth, I stared at the two bracelets on her left wrist.

"Maybe I'm not very smart," I said, my voice dry, "but I really can't claim to have understood everything you've been telling me."

"In your second dream, when I was in the middle of having relations with you, another woman took my place. Isn't that true? I have no idea who she was. But that event was probably meant to suggest something to you, Mr Okada. This is what I wanted to convey to you."

I said nothing in return.

"You should have no sense of guilt about having had relations with me," said Creta Kano. "You see, Mr Okada, I am a prostitute. I used to be a prostitute of the flesh, but now I am a prostitute of the mind. Things pass through me."

At this point, Creta Kano left her seat and went down on her knees beside me, clutching my hand in both of hers. She had soft, warm, very small hands. "Please hold me, Mr Okada. Right here and now."

We stood up and I put my arms around her. I honestly had no idea whether I should be doing this. But holding Creta Kano just then, just there, did not seem to be a mistake. I could not have explained it, but that was how I felt. I wrapped my arms around her slender body as if I were taking my first lesson in ballroom dancing. She was a small woman. The top of her head came just past the bottom of my chin. Her breasts pressed against my stomach. She held her cheek against my chest. And although she made no sound the whole time, she was crying. I could feel the warmth of her tears through my T-shirt. I looked down, to see her perfectly set hair trembling. I felt I was having a well-made dream. But it was not a dream.

After we had stayed in that position without moving for a very long time, she pulled away from me as if she had suddenly remembered something. Maintaining her distance, she looked at me.

"Thank you so much, Mr Okada," she said. "I will be going home now." She had just been crying with some intensity, but her make-up had hardly been disturbed. A sense of reality was now strangely absent.

"Will you be in my dreams again sometime?" I asked.

"I don't know," she said, with a gentle shake of the head. "Not even I can tell you that. But please have faith in me. Whatever might happen, please don't be afraid of me or feel you must be on your guard where I am concerned. Will you promise me that, Mr Okada?"

I answered with a nod.

Soon afterwards, Creta Kano went home.

The darkness of night was thicker than ever. The front of my T-shirt was soaking wet. I stayed up until dawn, unable to sleep. I didn't feel sleepy, for one thing, and in fact, I was afraid to sleep. I had the feeling that if I were to go to sleep, I would be enveloped in a flow of shifting sand that would carry me off to another world, from which I would never be able to return. I stayed on the sofa until morning, drinking brandy and thinking about Creta Kano's story. Even after the night had ended, the presence of Creta Kano and the fragrance of Christian Dior eau de cologne lingered in the house like captive shadows.

5

Views of Distant Towns

◆

Eternal Half-Moon

◆

Ladder in Place

The telephone rang at almost the exact moment I was falling asleep. I tried to ignore it, but as if it could read my mind, it kept up its stubborn ringing: ten times, twenty times – it was never going to stop. Finally, I opened one eye and looked at the clock. Just after 6 in the morning. Beyond the window shone the full light of day. The call might be from Kumiko. I got out of bed, went to the living room, and picked up the receiver.

"Hello," I said, but the caller said nothing. Somebody was obviously there, but the person did not speak. I, too, kept silent. Concentrating hard, I could just make out the sound of breathing.

"Who is it?" I asked, but the silence continued at the other end.

"If this is the person who's always calling, do me a favour and make it a little later," I said. "No sex talk before breakfast, please."

"The person who's always calling?" blurted out the voice of May Kasahara. "Who do you talk about sex with?"

"Nobody," I said.

"The woman you were holding in your arms last night? Do you talk about sex with her on the telephone?"

"No, she's not the one."

214

"Tell me, Mr Wind-up Bird, just how many women do you have hanging around you – apart from your wife?"

"That would be a very long story," I said. "Anyhow, it's 6 in the morning and I haven't had much sleep. So you came to my house last night, huh?"

"And I saw you with her – holding each other."

"That didn't mean a thing," I said. "How can I put it? It was a kind of little ceremony."

"You don't have to make excuses to me," said May Kasahara. "I'm not your wife. It's none of my business, but let me just say this: you've got a problem."

"You may be right," I said.

"You're having a tough time now, I know that. But I can't help thinking it's something you've brought on yourself. You've got some really basic problem, and it attracts trouble like a magnet. Any woman with any sense would get the hell away from you."

"You may be right," I said again.

May Kasahara maintained a brief silence on her end of the line. Then she cleared her throat once and said, "You came to the alley last night, didn't you? Standing for a long time at the back of my house, like some amateur burglar . . . Don't worry, I saw you there."

"So why didn't you come out?"

"A girl doesn't always want to go out, you know, Mr Wind-up Bird. Sometimes she feels like being nasty – like, if the guy's gonna wait, let him *really* wait."

I grunted.

"But I still felt bad," she went on. "So I dragged myself all the way to your house later – like an idiot."

"And I was holding the woman."

"Yeah, but isn't she a bit cuckoo? Nobody dresses like that any more. And that make-up of hers! She's like in a time-warp or something. She should get her head examined."

"Don't worry," I said, "she's not cuckoo. Different people have different tastes."

"Well, yes. People can have any taste they want. But ordinary people don't go that far just for taste. She's like – what? – right out of an old magazine: everything about her, from head to foot."

To that I did not reply.

"Tell me, Mr Wind-up Bird, did you sleep with her?"

I hesitated a moment and said, "No, I didn't."

"Really?"

"Really. I don't have that kind of *physical* relationship with her."

"So why were you holding her?"

"Women feel that way sometimes: they want to be held."

"Maybe so," said May Kasahara, "but an idea like that can be a little dangerous."

"It's true," I said.

"What's her name?"

"Creta Kano."

May Kasahara fell silent at her end. "You're kidding, right?" she said at last.

"Not at all. And her sister's name is Malta Kano."

"Malta?! That can't be her real name."

"No, it isn't. It's her professional name."

"What are they, a comedy team? Or do they have some connection with the Mediterranean Sea?"

"Actually, there *is* some connection with the Mediterranean."

"Does the sister dress like a normal person?"

"Pretty much," I said. "Her clothing is a lot more normal than Creta's, at least. Except she always wears this red vinyl hat."

"Something tells me she's not exactly normal, either. Why do you always have to go out of your way to hang around with such off-the-wall people?"

"Now, *that* really would be a long story. If everything settles down sometime, I may be able to tell you. But not now. My head is too messed up. And things are even more messed up."

"Yeah, sure," she said, with a note of suspicion in her voice. "Anyway, your wife hasn't come back yet, has she?"

"No, not yet."

"You know, Mr Wind-up Bird, you're a grown man. Why don't you use your head a little bit? If your wife had changed her mind and come home last night, she would have seen you with your arms locked around this woman. Then what?"

"True, that was a possibility."

"And if *she* had been the one making this call, not me, and you started talking about telephone sex, what would she have thought about that?"

"You're right," I said.

"I'm telling you, you've got a problem," she said, with a sigh.

"It's true, I do have a problem."

"Stop agreeing with everything I say! It's not as if you're going to solve everything by admitting your mistakes. Whether you admit them or not, mistakes are mistakes."

"It's true," I said. It *was* true.

"I can't stand it any more!" said May Kasahara. "Anyway, tell me, what did you want last night? You came to my house looking for something, right?"

"Oh, that. Never mind."

"Never mind?"

"Yeah. Finally, it's . . . never mind."

"In other words, she gave you a hug, so you don't need me any more."

"No, that's not it. It just seemed to me –"

At which point May Kasahara hung up. Terrific. May Kasahara, Malta Kano, Creta Kano, the telephone woman, and Kumiko. May Kasahara was right: I had just a few too many women around me these days. And each one came packaged with her own special, inscrutable problem.

But I was too tired to think. I had to get some sleep. And there was something I would have to do when I woke up.

I went back to bed and fell asleep.

•

When I did wake up, I took a knapsack from the drawer. It was the one we kept for earthquakes and other emergencies that might require evacuation. Inside was a water bottle, biscuits, a torch, and a lighter. Kumiko had bought it when we moved into this house, just in case the Big One should hit. The water bottle was empty, though, the biscuits were soggy, and the torch batteries were dead. I filled the bottle with water, threw away the biscuits, and put new batteries in the torch. Then I went to the local hardware store and bought one of those rope ladders they sell as emergency fire escapes. I thought about what else I might need, but nothing came to mind – besides lemon drops. I went through the house, shutting windows and turning off lights. I made sure the front door was locked, but then I reconsidered. Somebody might come looking for me while I was gone. Kumiko might come back. And besides, there was nothing here worth stealing. I left a note on the kitchen table: "Gone for a while. Will return. T."

I wondered what it would be like for Kumiko to find this note. How would she take it? I crumpled it up and wrote a new one: "Have to go out for a while on important business. Back soon. Please wait. T."

Wearing chinos, a short-sleeved polo shirt, and carrying the knapsack, I stepped down into the yard from the veranda. All around me were the unmistakable signs of summer – the genuine article, without reservations or conditions. The glow of the sun, the smell of the breeze, the blue of the sky, the shape of the clouds, the whirring of the cicadas: everything announced the authentic arrival of summer. And there I was, a pack on my back, scaling the garden wall and dropping down into the alley.

Once, as a kid, I had run away from home on a beautiful summer morning just like this. I couldn't recall what had led to my decision to go. I was probably mad at my parents. I left home with a knapsack on my back and, in my pockets, all the money I had saved. I told my mother I would be hiking with some friends and got her to make a lunch for me. There were good hills for hiking just above our house, and kids often went climbing in them without adult supervision. Once I was out of the house, I got on the bus and rode it to the end of the line. To me, this was a strange and distant town. Here I transferred to another bus and rode it to yet another strange and distant – still more distant – town. Without even knowing the name of the place, I got off the bus and wandered through the streets. There was nothing special about this particular town: it was a little more lively than the neighbourhood where I lived, and a little more run-down. It had a street lined with shops, and a commuter train station, and a few small factories. A stream ran through the town, and facing the stream stood a cinema. A board outside announced they were showing a western. At noon I sat on a park bench and ate my lunch. I stayed in the town until early evening, and when the sun began to sink, my heart did too. This is your last chance to go back, I told myself. Once it gets completely dark, you might never be able to leave here. I went home on the same buses that had brought me there. I arrived before 7, and no one noticed that I had run away. My parents had thought I was out in the hills with the other kids.

I had forgotten all about that particular event. But the moment I found myself scaling the wall wearing a knapsack, the feeling came back to me – the indescribable loneliness I had felt, standing by myself amid unfamiliar streets and unfamiliar people and unfamiliar houses, watching the afternoon sun lose its light bit by bit. And then I thought of Kumiko: Kumiko, who had disappeared somewhere, taking with her only her shoulder bag and her blouse and skirt from the cleaner's. She had missed her last chance to turn back. And now she was probably standing by herself in some strange and distant town. I could hardly bear to think of her that way.

But no, she couldn't be by herself. She had to be with a man. That was the only way this made sense.

I stopped thinking about Kumiko.

•

I made my way down the alley.

The grass underfoot had lost the living, breathing greenness it had seemed to possess during the spring rains, and now it wore the dull look typical of summer grass. From among these blades a green grasshopper would leap out now and then as I walked along. Sometimes even frogs would jump away. The alley had become the world of these little creatures, and I was simply an intruder come to upset the prevailing order.

When I reached the Miyawakis' vacant house, I opened the gate and walked in without hesitation. I pressed on through the tall grass to the middle of the yard, passed the dingy bird statue, which continued to stare at the sky, and walked around to the side of the house, hoping that May Kasahara had not seen me come in.

The first thing I did when I got to the well was to remove the stones that held the cap on, then take off one of the two wooden half-circles. To make sure there was still no water at the bottom, I threw in a pebble, as I had done before. And as before, the pebble hit with a dry thud. There was no water. I set down the knapsack, took the rope ladder out, and tied one end of it to the trunk of the nearby tree. I pulled on it as hard as I could to be sure it would hold. This was something on which it was impossible to lavish too much care. If, by some chance, the ladder got loose or came undone, I would probably never make it back to the surface.

Holding the mass of rope in my arms, I began to lower the ladder into the well. The whole, of its length went in, but I never felt it hit the bottom. It couldn't possibly be too short: I had bought the longest rope ladder they made. But the well was a deep one. I shone the torch straight down inside, but I couldn't see whether or not the ladder had reached bottom. The rays of light penetrated only so far, and then they were swallowed up by the darkness.

I sat on the edge of the well curb and listened. A few cicadas were screaming in the trees, as if competing to see which had the loudest voice or the greatest lung capacity. I couldn't hear any birds, though. I recalled the wind-up bird with some fondness. Maybe it didn't like competing with the cicadas and had moved off somewhere to avoid them.

I turned my palms upward in the sunlight. In an instant, they felt warm, as though the light were seeping into the skin, soaking into the very lines of my fingerprints. The light ruled over everything out here. Bathed in light, each object glowed with the brilliant colour of summer. Even intangibles such as time and memory shared the goodness of the summer light. I popped a lemon drop in my mouth and went on sitting there until it had melted away. Then I pulled hard on the ladder one more time to be sure it was firmly anchored.

Making my way down the rope ladder into the well was much harder work than I had imagined it would be. A blend of cotton and nylon, the ladder was unquestionably sturdy, but my footing on the thing was unstable. The rubber bottoms of my tennis shoes would slip whenever I tried to lower my weight onto either leg. My hands had to keep such a tight grip on the rope that my palms started to hurt. I let myself down slowly and carefully, one rung at a time. No matter how far I went, though, there was no bottom. My descent seemed to take for ever. I reminded myself of the sound of the pebble hitting bottom. The well did have a bottom! Working my way down this damned ladder was what took so much time.

When I had counted twenty rungs, a wave of terror overtook me. It came suddenly, like an electric shock, and froze me in place. My muscles turned to stone. Every pore of my body gushed sweat, and my legs began to tremble. There was no way this well could be so deep. This was the middle of Tokyo. It was right behind the house I lived in. I held my breath and listened, but I couldn't hear a thing. The pounding of my heart reverberated in my ears with such force I couldn't even hear the cicadas screaming up above. I took a deep breath. Here I was on the twentieth rung, unable either to proceed farther down or to climb back up. The air in the well was chilling and smelled of the earth. It was a separate world down here, one cut off from the surface, where the sun shone so unstintingly. I looked up to the mouth of the well above me, tiny now. The well's circular opening was cut exactly in half by the half of the wooden cover I had left in place. From below, it looked like a half-moon floating in the night sky. "A half-moon will last for several days," Malta Kano had said. She had predicted it on the telephone.

Terrific. And when the thought crossed my mind, I felt some strength leave my body. My muscles relaxed, and the solid block of breath inside me released and came out.

Summoning one last spurt of strength, I started down the ladder again. Just a little farther down, I told myself. Just a little more. Don't worry, there *is* a bottom. And at the twenty-third rung, I reached it. My foot came in contact with the earth at the bottom of the well.

.

The first thing I did in the darkness was to feel around the surface of the well bottom with the tip of my shoe, still holding onto the ladder in case there was something down there I had to get away from. After making sure there was no water and nothing of a suspicious nature, I stepped onto to the ground. Setting my pack down, I felt for the zip and took out my torch. The glow of the light gave me my first clear view of the place. The surface of the ground was neither very hard nor very soft. And fortunately, the earth was dry. A few rocks lay scattered where people must have thrown them. The one other thing that had fallen to the bottom was an old crisp packet. Illuminated by the torch, the well bottom reminded me of the surface of the moon as I had seen it on television so long ago.

The well's cylindrical concrete wall was blank and smooth, with few irregularities other than some clumps of mosslike stuff growing here and there. It shot straight upward like a chimney, with the little half-moon of light at the opening far above. Looking directly up, I could now grasp how very deep the well was. I gave the rope ladder another hard tug. In my hands, it felt firm and reassuring. As long as it remained in place, I could go back to the surface anytime I wanted. Next I took a deep breath. Apart from a slight smell of mould, there was nothing wrong with the air. My greatest worry had been the air. The air at the bottom of a well tends to stagnate, and dry wells can have poison gases that seep from the earth. Long before, I had read in the paper about a well digger who lost his life from methane gas at the bottom of a well.

Taking a breath, I sat on the floor of the well, with my back against the wall. I closed my eyes and let my body become accustomed to the place. All right, then, I thought: here I am in the bottom of a well.

6

Inheriting Property

•

Inquiry on Jellyfish

•

Something Like a Sense of Detachment

I sat in the dark. Far above me, like a sign of something, floated the perfect half-moon of light defined by the well cap. And yet none of the light from up there managed to find its way to the bottom.

As time passed, my eyes became more accustomed to the darkness. Before long, I could just about make out the shape of my hand if I brought it close to my face. Other things around me began slowly to take on their own dim shapes, like timid little animals letting down their guard in the most gradual stages imaginable. As much as my eyes became used to it, though, the darkness never ceased to be darkness. Anything I tried to focus on would lose its shape and burrow its way soundlessly into the surrounding obscurity. Perhaps this could be called "pale darkness", but pale as it might be, it had its own particular kind of density, which in some cases contained a more meaningful darkness than perfect pitch darkness. In it, you could see something. And at the same time, you could see nothing at all.

Here in this darkness, with its strange sense of significance, my memories began to take on a power they had never had before. The fragmentary images they called up inside me were mysteriously vivid in every detail, to the point where I felt I could grasp them in my hands. I closed my eyes and brought back the time eight years earlier when I had first met Kumiko.

It happened in the visitors' waiting room of the university hospital in Kanda. I had to go to the hospital almost every day back then, to see a wealthy client concerning the inheritance of his property. Kumiko came to the hospital every day between classes in order to tend to her mother, who was there with a duodenal ulcer. She wore jeans or a short skirt and a sweater, her hair in a ponytail. Sometimes she would wear a coat, sometimes not, depending on the early November weather. She had a shoulder bag and always carried a few books that looked like university texts, plus some kind of sketch pad.

The afternoon of the very first day I went to the hospital, Kumiko was there, sitting on the sofa with her legs crossed, wearing black low-heeled shoes and concentrating on a book. I sat opposite her, checking my watch every five minutes until the time for the interview with my client, which had been moved back an hour and a half for some reason I was not aware of. Kumiko didn't raise her eyes from the book. She had very nice legs. Looking at her helped to brighten my spirits somewhat. I found myself wondering what it must feel like to have such a nice (or at least extremely intelligent) face and great legs.

After we had seen each other in the waiting room several times, Kumiko and I began to indulge in small talk – exchanging magazines we had finished reading, or eating fruit from a gift basket someone had brought her mother. We were incredibly bored, after all, and in need of someone our own age to talk to.

Kumiko and I felt something for each other from the start. It was not one of those strong, impulsive feelings that can hit two people like an electric shock when they first meet, but something quieter and gentler, like two tiny lights travelling in tandem through a vast darkness and drawing imperceptibly closer to each other as they go. As our meetings grew more frequent, I felt not so much that I had met someone new as that I had chanced upon a dear old friend.

Soon I found myself dissatisfied with the bitty little conversations we were fitting in between other things in the hospital area. I kept wishing I could meet her somewhere else, so that we could really talk to each other for a change. Finally, one day, I decided to ask her for a date.

"I think both of us could use a change of air," I said. "Let's get out of here and go somewhere else – where there aren't any patients or clients."

Kumiko gave it some thought and suggested, "The aquarium?"

And so the aquarium is where we had our first date. Kumiko brought her mother a change of clothes that Sunday morning and met me in the hospital waiting room. It was a warm, clear day, and Kumiko was wearing a simple white dress under a pale-blue cardigan. I was always struck by how well she dressed even then. She could wear the plainest article of clothing and manage, with the roll of a sleeve or the curl of a collar, to transform it into something spectacular. It was a knack she had. And I could see that she took care of her clothes with an attention bordering on love. Whenever I was with her, walking beside her, I would find myself staring in admiration at her. Her blouses never had a wrinkle. Her pleats hung in perfect alignment. Anything white she wore looked brand-new. Her shoes were never scuffed or smudged. Looking at what she wore, I could imagine her blouses and sweaters neatly folded and lined up in her chest of drawers, her skirts and dresses in plastic wrappers hanging in the wardrobe (which is exactly what I found to be the case after we were married).

We spent that first afternoon together in the aquarium of the Ueno Zoo. The weather was so nice that day, I thought it might be more fun to stroll around the zoo itself, and I hinted as much to Kumiko on the train to Ueno, but it was obvious she had made up her mind to go to the aquarium. If that was what she wanted, it was all right with me. At the aquarium there was a special display of jellyfish, and we went through them from beginning to end, viewing the rare specimens gathered from all parts of the world. They floated, trembling, in their tanks, everything from a tiny cotton puff the size of a fingertip to monsters more than three feet in diameter. For a Sunday, the aquarium was relatively uncrowded. In fact, it was on the empty side. On such a lovely day, anybody would have preferred the elephants and giraffes to jellyfish.

Although I said nothing to Kumiko, I actually hated jellyfish. I had often been stung by jellyfish while swimming in the ocean as a boy. Once, when swimming far out by myself, I wandered into a whole school of them. By the time I realized what I had done, I was surrounded. I never forgot the slimy, cold feeling of them touching me. In the centre of that whirlpool of jellyfish, an immense terror overtook me, as if I had been dragged into a bottomless darkness. I wasn't stung, for some reason, but in my panic I gulped a lot of sea water. Which is why I would have liked to skip the jellyfish display if possible and go to see some ordinary fish, like tuna or flounder.

Kumiko, though, was fascinated. She stopped at every single tank, leaned over the railing, and remained transfixed as if she had lost all sense of time. "Look at this," she'd say to me. "I never knew there

224

were such vivid pink jellyfish. And look at the beautiful way it swims. They just keep wobbling along like this until they've been to every ocean in the world. Aren't they wonderful?"

"Yeah, sure." But the more I forced myself to keep examining jellyfish with her, the more I felt a tightness growing in my chest. Before I knew it, I had stopped replying to her and was counting the change in my pocket over and over, or wiping the corners of my mouth with my handkerchief. I kept wishing we would come to the last of the jellyfish tanks, but there was no end to them. The variety of jellyfish swimming in the oceans of the world was enormous. I was able to bear it for half an hour, but the tension was turning my head into mush. When, finally, it became too painful for me to stand leaning against the railing, I left Kumiko's side and slumped on a nearby bench. She came over to me and, clearly very concerned, asked if I was feeling ill. I answered honestly that looking at the jellyfish was making me dizzy.

She stared into my eyes with a grave expression on her face. "It's true," she said. "I can see it in your eyes. They've gone out of focus. It's incredible – just from looking at jellyfish!" Kumiko took me by the arm and led me out of the gloomy, dank aquarium into the sunlight.

Sitting in the nearby park for ten minutes, taking long, slow breaths, I managed to return to a normal psychological state. The strong autumn sun cast its pleasant radiance everywhere, and the bone-dry leaves of the ginkgo trees rustled softly whenever the breeze picked up. "Are you all right?" Kumiko asked after several minutes had gone by. "You certainly are a strange one. If you hate jellyfish so much, you should have said so right away, instead of waiting until they made you sick."

The sky was high and cloudless, the wind felt good, the people spending their Sunday in the park all wore happy expressions. A slim, pretty girl was walking a large, long-haired dog. An old fellow wearing a felt hat was watching his granddaughter on the swing. Several couples sat on benches, as we were doing. Off in the distance, someone was practising scales on a saxophone.

"Why do you like jellyfish so much?" I asked.

"I don't know. I guess I think they're sweet," she said. "But one thing did occur to me when I was focusing on them. What we see before us is just one tiny part of the world. We get into the habit of thinking, This is the world, but that's not true at all. The real world is in a much darker and deeper place than this, and most of it is occupied by jellyfish and things. We just happen to forget all that. Don't you agree?

Two-thirds of the earth's surface is ocean, and all we can see of it with the naked eye is the surface: the skin. We hardly know anything about what's underneath the skin."

We took a long walk after that. At 5 o'clock, Kumiko said she had to go back to the hospital, so I took her there. "Thank you for a lovely day," she said when we parted. There was a quiet glow in her smile that had not been there before. When I saw it, I realized that I had managed to draw a little closer to her in the course of the day – thanks, no doubt, to the jellyfish.

•

Kumiko and I continued to date. Her mother was discharged from hospital and I no longer had to spend time there working on my client's will, but we would get together once a week for a movie or a concert or a walk. We grew closer to each other each time we met. I enjoyed being with her, and if we should happen to touch, I felt a fluttering in the chest. I often found it difficult to work when the weekend was drawing near. I was sure she liked me. Otherwise, she wouldn't see me every weekend.

Still, I was in no hurry to deepen my relationship with Kumiko. I sensed a kind of uncertainty in her. Exactly what it was I couldn't have said, but it would come out every now and then in her words or actions. I might ask her something, and a single breath would intervene before she answered – just the slightest hesitation, but in that split-second interval I sensed a kind of shadow.

Winter came, and then the new year. We went on seeing each other every week. I never asked about that something, and she never said a word. We would meet and go somewhere and eat and talk about innocuous things.

One day I took a chance and said, "You *must* have a boyfriend, don't you?"

Kumiko looked at me for a moment and asked, "What makes you think so?"

"Just a hunch," I said. We were walking through the wintry and deserted Shinjuku Imperial Gardens.

"What kind of hunch?"

"I don't know. I get the feeling there's something you want to tell me. You should if you can."

The expression on her face wavered the slightest bit – almost imperceptibly. There might have been a moment of uncertainty, but there had never been any doubt about her conclusion. "Thanks for asking," she said, "but I don't have anything that I want to make a special point of talking about."

"You haven't answered my question, though."

"About whether I have a boyfriend?"

"Uh-huh."

Kumiko came to a stop. Then she slipped her gloves off and put them into her coat pocket. She took my gloveless hand in hers. Her hand was warm and soft. When I squeezed her hand in return, it seemed to me that her breaths grew smaller and whiter.

"Can we go to your apartment now?" she asked.

"Sure," I said, somewhat taken aback. "It's not much of a place, though."

I was living in Asagaya at the time, in a one-room apartment with a tiny kitchen and a toilet and a shower the size of a phone booth. It was on the second floor and faced south, overlooking a construction company's storage yard. That southern aspect was the apartment's only good point. For a long time, Kumiko and I sat next to each other in the flood of sunlight, leaning against the wall.

I made love to her for the first time that day. It was what she wanted, I was sure. In a sense, it was she who seduced me. Not that she ever said or did anything overtly seductive. But when I put my arms around her naked body, I knew for certain that she had intended this to happen. Her body was soft and offered no resistance.

It was Kumiko's first experience of sex. For a long time afterwards, she said nothing. I tried several times to talk to her, but she made no reply. She took a shower, put her clothes on, and sat in the sunlight again. I had no idea what to say. I simply joined her in the patch of sunlight and said nothing. The two of us edged along the wall as the sun moved. When evening came, Kumiko said she was leaving. I saw her home.

"Are you sure you don't have something you want to say to me?" I asked again in the train.

She shook her head. "Never mind about that," she murmured.

I never raised the topic again. Kumiko had chosen to sleep with me of her own volition, and if she was indeed keeping something inside that she could not tell me, this would probably be resolved in the course of time.

We continued our weekly dates after that, part of which now included stopping by my apartment for sex more often than not. As we held and touched each other, she began to talk about herself more and more, about the things she had experienced, about the thoughts and feelings these things had given her. And I began to understand the world as Kumiko saw it. I found myself able, too, to talk with Kumiko about the world as I saw it. I came to love her deeply, and she said she never wanted to leave me. We waited for her to graduate from college, and then we got married.

We were happy with our married life and had no problems to speak of. And yet there were times when I couldn't help sensing an area inside Kumiko to which I had no access. In the middle of the most ordinary – or the most excited – conversation, and without the slightest warning, she might sink into silence. It would happen all of a sudden, for no reason at all (or at least no reason I could discern). It was like walking along the road and all of a sudden falling into a pit. Her silences never lasted very long, but afterwards, until a fair amount of time had gone by, it was as if she were not really there.

The first time I went inside Kumiko, I sensed a strange kind of hesitation. Kumiko should have been feeling only pain this first time for her, and indeed she kept her body rigid with the pain she was experiencing, but that was not the only reason for the hesitation I seemed to feel. There was something oddly lucid there, a sense of separation, of distance, though I don't know exactly what to call it. I was seized by the bizarre thought that the body I was holding in my arms was not the body of the woman I had had next to me until a few moments earlier, the two of us engaged in intimate conversation: a switch had been pulled without my noticing, and someone else's flesh had taken its place. While I held her, my hands continued to caress her back. The touch of her small, smooth back had an almost hypnotic effect on me, and yet, at the same time, Kumiko's back seemed to be somewhere far away from me. The entire time she was in my arms, I could have sworn that Kumiko was somewhere else, thinking about something else, and the body I was holding was nothing but a temporary substitute. This might have been the reason why, although I was fully aroused, it took me a very long time to come.

I felt this way only the first time we had intercourse. After that, I felt her much closer to me, her physical responses far more sensitive. I convinced myself that my initial sense of distance had been the result of it being her first experience of sex.

·

Every now and then, while searching through my memories, I would reach out to where the rope ladder was hanging against the wall and give it a tug to make sure it hadn't come loose. I couldn't seem to shake off the fear that it might give way at any moment. Whenever the thought struck me, down there in the darkness, it made me uneasy. I could even hear my own heart pounding. After I had checked a number of times – maybe twenty or thirty – I began to regain a measure of calm. I had done a good job of tying the ladder to the tree, after all. It wasn't going to come loose just like that.

I looked at my watch. The luminous hands showed it to be just before 3 o'clock. Three p.m. I glanced upward. The half-moon slab of light was still floating there. The surface of the earth was flooded with blinding summer light. I pictured to myself a stream sparkling in the sunlight and green leaves trembling in the breeze. The light up there overwhelmed everything, and yet just below it, down here, there existed such darkness. All you had to do was climb a little way underground on a rope ladder, and you could reach a darkness this profound.

I pulled on the ladder one more time to be certain it was anchored firmly. Then I leaned my head against the wall and closed my eyes. At last, sleep overtook me, like a gradual rising tide.

7

Recollections and Dialogue on Pregnancy

•

Empirical Inquiry on Pain

When I woke, the half-moon mouth of the well had taken on the deep blue of evening. The hands of my watch showed 7.30. Seven thirty p.m. Meaning I had been asleep down here for four-and-a-half hours.

The air at the bottom of the well felt chilly. I had experienced too much nervous excitement to think about air temperature when I first climbed down. Now, though, my skin was reacting to the cold air. Rubbing my bare arms to warm them, I realized I should have brought something in the knapsack to put on over my T-shirt. It had never crossed my mind that the temperature in the bottom of the well might be different from the temperature at the surface.

Now I was enveloped by a darkness that was total. No amount of straining could help my eyes to see. I couldn't tell where my own hand was. I felt along the wall to where the ladder hung and gave it a tug. It was still firmly anchored at the surface. The movement of my hand seemed to cause the darkness itself to shift, but that could have been an illusion.

It was the strangest thing not to be able to see my own body with my own eyes, though I knew it must be there. Staying very still in the darkness, I became less and less convinced of the fact that I existed. To cope with that, I would clear my throat now and then, or run my hand over my face. That way, my ears could check on the existence of my voice, my hand could check on the existence of my face, and my face could check on the existence of my hand.

Despite these efforts, my body began to lose its density and weight, like sand gradually being washed away by flowing water. I felt as if a fierce and wordless tug-of-war were going on inside me, a contest in which my mind was slowly dragging my body into its own territory. The darkness was disrupting the proper balance between the two. The thought struck me that my own body was a mere provisional husk that had been prepared for my mind by a rearrangement of the signs known as chromosomes. If the signs were rearranged yet again, I would find myself inside a wholly different body than before. "Prostitute of the mind," Creta Kano had called herself. I no longer had any trouble accepting the phrase. Yes, it was possible for us to couple in our minds and for me to come in reality. In truly deep darkness, all kinds of strange things were possible.

I shook my head and struggled to bring my mind back inside my body.

In the darkness, I pressed the fingertips of one hand against the fingertips of the other – thumb against thumb, index finger against index finger. My right-hand fingers verified the existence of my left-hand fingers, and the fingers of my left hand the existence of the fingers of my right hand. Then I took several slow, deep breaths. OK, then, enough of this thinking about the mind. Think about reality. Think about the real world. The body's world. That's why I'm here. To think about reality. The best way to think about reality, I had decided, was to get as far away from it as possible – a place like the bottom of a well, for example. "When you're supposed to go down, find the deepest well and go down to the bottom," Mr Honda had said. Leaning against the wall, I slowly sucked the mouldy air into my lungs.

•

We didn't have a wedding ceremony. We couldn't afford it, to begin with, and neither of us wanted to feel beholden to our parents. Beginning our life together, any way we could, was far more important to us than a ceremony. We went to the registry office early one Sunday morning, woke the clerk on duty by ringing the bell at the Sunday window, and submitted a registration of marriage. Later, we went to the kind of high-class French restaurant that neither of us could usually afford, ordered a bottle of wine, and ate a three-course dinner. That was enough for us.

At the time, we had practically no savings (my mother had left me a little money when she died, but I made a point of never touching it except in genuine emergencies) and no furniture to speak of. We had no future to speak of, either. Working at a law firm without an attorney's credentials, I had virtually nothing to look forward to, and Kumiko worked for a tiny, unknown publisher. If she had wanted to, she could have found a much better position through her father when she graduated, but she disliked the idea of going to him and instead found a job on her own. Neither of us was dissatisfied, though. We were pleased just to be able to survive without intrusion from anyone.

It wasn't easy for the two of us to build something out of nothing. I had that tendency towards solitude common to only children. When trying to accomplish something serious, I liked to do it myself. Having to check things out with other people and get them to understand seemed to me a great waste of time and energy when it was a lot easier to work alone in silence. And Kumiko, after losing her sister, had closed her heart to her family and grown up as if alone. She never went to them for advice. In that sense, the two of us were very much alike.

Still, little by little, we learned to devote our bodies and minds to this newly created being we called our "home". We practised thinking and feeling about things together. Things that happened to either of us individually we now strove to deal with together as something that belonged to both of us. Sometimes it worked, and sometimes it didn't. But we enjoyed the fresh, new process of trial and error. And even violent collisions we could forget about in each other's arms.

•

In the third year of our marriage, Kumiko became pregnant. This was a great shock to us – or to me, at least – because of the extreme care we had been taking with contraception. A moment of carelessness must have done it; not that we could determine which exact moment it had been, but there was no other explanation. In any case, we simply could not afford the expense of a child. Kumiko was just getting into the swing of her publishing job and, if possible, wanted to keep it. A small company like hers made no provision for anything so grand as maternity leave. A woman working there who wanted to have a child had no choice but to resign. If Kumiko had done that, we would have had to survive on my pay alone, for a while, at least, but this would have been a virtual impossibility.

"I guess we'll have to pass, this time," Kumiko said to me in an expressionless voice the day the doctor gave her the news.

She was probably right. No matter how you looked at it, that was the most sensible conclusion. We were young and quite unprepared for parenthood. Both Kumiko and I needed time for ourselves. We had to establish our own life: that was the first priority. We'd have plenty of opportunities for having children in the future.

·

In fact, though, I did not want Kumiko to have an abortion. Once, in my second year of college, I had made a girl pregnant, someone I had met where I worked part-time. She was a nice kid, a year younger than I, and we got along well. We liked each other, of course, but were by no means serious about each other, nor was there any possibility that we would ever become serious. We were just two lonely youngsters who needed someone to hold.

About the reason for her pregnancy there was never any doubt. I always used a condom, but one day I forgot to have one ready. I had run out. When I told her so, she hesitated for a few seconds and then said, "Oh, well, I think I'm OK today anyway." One time was all it took.

I couldn't quite believe that I had "made a girl pregnant", but I did know that an abortion was the only option. I scraped the money together and went with her to the clinic. We took a commuter train way out to a little town in Chiba, where a friend of hers had put her in touch with a doctor. We got off at a station I had never heard of and saw thousands of tiny houses, all stamped out of the same mould, crowded together and stretching over the rolling hills to the horizon. These were huge new developments that had gone up in recent years for the younger company employees who could not afford housing in Tokyo. The station itself was brand-new, and just across from it stretched huge, water-filled rice fields, bigger than any I had ever seen. The streets were lined with real estate signs.

The clinic waiting room overflowed with huge-bellied young women, most of whom must have been in their fourth or fifth year of marriage and settling down to have children in their newly mortgaged suburban homes. The only young male in the place was me. The pregnant ladies all looked my way with the most intense interest – and no hint of goodwill. Anyone could see at a glance that I was a college student who had accidentally got his girlfriend pregnant and had come with her for an abortion.

After the operation, the girl and I took the train back to Tokyo. Heading into the city in the late afternoon, the train was nearly empty. I apologized to her. My carelessness had got her into this mess, I said.

"Don't take it so hard," she said. "At least you came with me to the clinic, and you paid for the operation."

She and I soon stopped seeing each other, so I never found out what became of her, but for a very long time after the abortion – and even after we drifted apart – my feelings refused to settle down. Every time I recalled that day, the image would flash into my mind of the pregnant young women who filled the clinic waiting room to overflowing, their eyes so full of certainty. And the thought would strike me that I should never have got her pregnant.

In the train on the way back, to comfort me – to comfort *me* – she told me all the details that had made the operation so easy. "It's not as bad as you think," she said. "It doesn't take long, and it doesn't hurt. You just take your clothes off and lie there. Yeah, I suppose it's kind of embarrassing, but the doctor was nice, and so were the nurses. Of course, they did lecture me a little, said to be more careful from now on. So don't feel so bad. It's partly my fault too. I was the one who said it'd be OK. Right? Cheer up."

All during the long train ride to the little town in Chiba, and all the way back again, though, I felt I had become a different person. Even after I had seen her home and returned to my room, to lie in bed and look at the ceiling, I could sense the change. I was a new me, and I could never go back to where I had been before. What was getting to me was the awareness that I was no longer innocent. This was not a moralistic sense of wrongdoing, or the workings of a guilty conscience. I knew that I had made a terrible mistake, but I was not punishing myself for it. It was a *physical fact* that I would have to confront with coolness and logic, beyond any question of punishment.

.

The first thing that came to mind when I heard that Kumiko was pregnant was the image of those pregnant young women who filled the clinic waiting room. Or rather, it was the special smell that seemed to hang in the air there. I had no idea what that smell was – if it was the actual smell of something at all. Perhaps it had been something *like* a smell. When the nurse called her name, the girl slowly raised herself from the hard plastic chair and walked straight for the door. Just before she stood up, she glanced at me with the hint of a smile on her lips – or what was left of a smile that she had changed her mind about.

I knew that it was unrealistic for us to have a child, but I didn't want Kumiko to have an abortion, either. When I said this to her, she replied,

"We've been through all this. If I have a baby now, that's the end of working for me, and you'll have to find a better-paid job to support me and the baby. We won't have money for anything extra. We won't be able to do anything we want to do. From now on, the realistic possibilities for us will be narrowed down to nothing. Is that OK with you?"

"Yes," I said. "I think it is OK with me."

"Really?"

"If I put my mind to it, I can probably find work – with my uncle, say: he's looking for help. He wants to open up a new place, but he can't find anybody he can trust to run it. I'm sure I'd make a lot more with him than I'm making now. It's not a law firm, but so what? I'm not so crazy about the work I'm doing now."

"So you'd run a restaurant?"

"I'm sure I could if I gave it a try. And in an emergency, I've got a little money my mother left me. We wouldn't starve to death."

Kumiko fell silent and stayed that way, thinking for a long time and making tiny wrinkles at the corners of her eyes. She had these little expressions that I liked. "Does this mean you want to have a baby?" she asked.

"I don't know," I said. "I know you're pregnant, but it hasn't really hit me that I might become a father. And I don't really know how our life would change if we had a baby. You like your job, and it seems like a mistake to take that away from you. On the one hand, I think the two of us need more time with each other, but I also think that having a baby would expand our world. I don't know what's right. I've just got this feeling that I don't want you to have an abortion. So I can't make any guarantees. I'm not one hundred per cent sure about any of this, and I don't have any amazing solutions. All I've got is this feeling."

Kumiko thought about this for a while, rubbing her stomach every now and then. "Tell me," she said. "Why do you think I got pregnant? Nothing comes to mind?"

I shook my head. "Not really. We've always been careful. This is just the kind of trouble I wanted to avoid. So I don't have any idea how it happened."

"You don't think I might have had an affair? Haven't you thought about that possibility?"

"Never."

"Why not?"

"I don't know. I can't claim a sixth sense or anything, but I'm sure of that much."

We were sitting at the kitchen table, drinking wine. It was late at night and all was silent. Kumiko narrowed her eyes and stared at the last sip of wine in the bottom of her glass. She almost never drank, though she would have a glass of wine when she couldn't get to sleep. It always worked for her. I was just drinking to keep her company. We didn't have anything so sophisticated as real wine glasses. Instead, we were drinking from little beer glasses we got free at the local off-licence.

"*Did* you have an affair?" I asked, suddenly concerned.

Kumiko smiled and shook her head. "Don't be silly. You know I wouldn't do anything like that. I just brought it up as a theoretical possibility." Then she turned serious and put her elbows on the table. "Sometimes, though, I can't tell about things. I can't tell what's real and what's not real . . . what things really happened and what things didn't. . . . Just *sometimes*, though."

"Is this one of those sometimes?"

"Well, sort of. Doesn't this kind of thing ever happen to you?"

I thought about it for a minute. "Not that I can recall, no," I said.

"How can I put this? There's a kind of gap between what I think is real and what's really real. I get this feeling like some kind of little something-or-other is there, somewhere inside me . . . like a burglar is in the house, hiding in a wardrobe . . . and it comes out every once in a while and messes up whatever order or logic I've established for myself. The way a magnet can make a machine go crazy."

"Some kind of little something-or-other? A burglar?" I said. "Wow, talk about vague!"

"It *is* vague. Really," said Kumiko, then drank down the rest of her wine.

I looked at her for a time. "And you think there's some kind of connection between that 'some kind of little something-or-other' and the fact that you're pregnant?"

She shook her head. "No, I'm not saying the two things are related or not related. It's just that sometimes I'm not really sure about the order of things. That's all I'm trying to say."

There was a growing touch of impatience in her words. The moment had arrived to end this conversation. It was after 1 o'clock in the morning. I reached across the table and took her hand.

"You know," said Kumiko, "I wish you'd let me decide this for myself. I realize it's a big problem for both of us. I really do. But this one

236

I want you to let *me* decide. I feel bad that I can't explain very well what I'm thinking and feeling."

"Basically, I think the right to make the decision is yours," I said, "and I respect that right."

"I think there's a month or so left to decide. We've been talking about this together all along now, and I think I have a pretty good idea how you feel about it. So now let me do the thinking. Let's stop talking about it for a while."

·

I was in Hokkaido when Kumiko had the abortion. The firm never sent its lackeys out of town on business, but on that particular occasion no one else could go, so I ended up being the one sent north. I was supposed to deliver a briefcase stuffed with papers, give the other party a simple explanation, take delivery of their papers, and come straight home. The papers were too important to mail or entrust to a courier. Because all return flights to Tokyo were full, I would have to spend a night in a Sapporo business hotel. Kumiko went for the abortion that day, alone. She phoned me after 10 at the hotel and said, "I had the operation this afternoon. Sorry to be informing you after the fact like this, but an appointment arose at short notice, and I thought it would be easier on both of us if I made the decision and took care of it by myself while you were away."

"Don't worry," I said. "Whatever you think is best."

"I want to tell you more, but I can't do it yet. I'll have to tell you some other time."

"We can talk when I get back."

After the call, I put on my coat and went out to wander through the streets of Sapporo. It was still early March, and both sides of the road were lined with high mounds of snow. The air was almost painfully cold, and your breath would come out in white clouds that vanished in an instant. People wore heavy coats and gloves and scarves wrapped up to their chins and made their way down the icy pavements with careful steps. Taxis ran back and forth, their studded tyres scratching at the road. When I couldn't stand the cold any longer, I stepped into a bar for a few quick shots and went out to walk some more.

I stayed on the move for a very long time. Snow floated down every once in a while, but it was frail snow, like a memory fading into the distance. The second bar I visited was below street level. It turned out to be a much bigger place than the entrance suggested. There was a small stage next to the bar, and on it was a slim man with glasses, playing a guitar and singing. He sat on a metal chair with his legs crossed, guitar case at his feet.

I sat at the bar, drinking and half listening to the music. Between songs, the man explained that the music was all his own. In his late twenties, he had a face with no distinguishing characteristics, and he wore glasses with black plastic frames. His outfit consisted of jeans, high lace-up boots, and a checked flannel work shirt that hung loose around his waist. The type of music was hard to define – something that might have been called "folk" in the old days, though a Japanese version of folk. Simple chords, simple melodies, unremarkable words. Not the kind of stuff I'd go out of my way to listen to.

In normal circumstances, I wouldn't have paid any attention to music like that. I would have had my whisky, paid my bill, and left the place. But that night I was chilled to the bone, and had no intention of going outside again until I had warmed up through and through. I drank one shot and ordered another. I made no attempt to remove my coat or my scarf. When the barman asked if I wanted a snack, I ordered some cheese and ate a single slice. I tried to think, but I couldn't get my head to work right. I didn't even know what it was I wanted to think about. I was a vacant room. Inside, the music produced only a dry, hollow echo.

When the man finished singing, there was scattered applause, neither enthusiastic nor yet perfunctory. There were no more than ten or fifteen customers in the place. The fellow stood and bowed. He seemed to make some funny remarks that caused a few of the customers to laugh. I called the barman and ordered my third whisky. Then, at last, I took off my coat and my scarf.

"That concludes my show for tonight," announced the singer. He paused and surveyed the room. "But there must be some of you here tonight who didn't like my songs. For you, I've got a little something extra. I don't do this all the time, so you should consider yourselves very lucky."

He set his guitar on the floor and, from the guitar case, took a single thick white candle. He lit it with a match, dripped some wax into a plate, and stood the candle up. Then, looking like a Greek philosopher, he held the plate aloft. "Can I have the lights down, please?" One of the employees dimmed the lights. "A little darker, if you don't mind." Now the place became much darker, and the candle flame stood out clearly. Palms wrapped around my whisky glass to warm it, I kept my eyes on the man and his candle.

"As you are well aware," the man continued, his voice soft but penetrating, "in the course of life we experience many kinds of pain. Pains of the body and pains of the heart. I know I have experienced pain in many different forms, and I'm sure you have too. In most cases, though, I'm sure you've found it very difficult to convey the truth of that pain to another person: to explain it in words. People say that only they themselves can understand the pain they are feeling. But is this true? I for one do not believe that it is. If, before our eyes, we see someone who is truly suffering, we do sometimes feel his suffering and pain as our own. This is the power of empathy. Am I making myself clear?"

He broke off and looked around the room once again.

"The reason that people sing songs for other people is because they want to have the power to arouse empathy, to break free of the narrow shell of the self and share their pain and joy with others. This is not an easy thing to do, of course. And so tonight, as a kind of experiment, I want you to experience a simpler, more physical kind of empathy. Lights please."

Everyone in the place was hushed now, all eyes fixed on the stage. Amid the silence, the man stared off into space, as if to insert a pause or to reach a state of mental concentration. Then, without a word, he held his left hand over the lighted candle. Little by little, he brought the palm closer and closer to the flame. Someone in the audience made a sound like a sigh or a moan. You could see the tip of the flame burning the man's palm. You could almost hear the sizzle of the flesh. A woman let out a hard little scream. Everyone else just watched in frozen horror. The man endured the pain, his face distorted in agony. What the hell was this? Why did he have to do such a stupid, senseless thing? I felt my mouth going dry. After five or six seconds of this, he slowly removed his hand from the flame and set the dish with the candle in it on the floor. Then he clasped his hands together, the right and left palms pressed against each other.

"As you have seen tonight, ladies and gentlemen, pain can actually burn a person's flesh," said the man. His voice sounded exactly as it had earlier: quiet, steady, cool. No trace of suffering remained on his face. Indeed, it had been replaced by a faint smile. "And the pain that must have been there, you have been able to feel as if it were your own. That is the power of empathy."

The man parted his clasped hands. From between them he produced a thin red scarf, which he opened for all to see. Then he stretched his palms out towards the audience. There were no burns at all. A moment of silence followed, and then people expressed their relief in wild applause. The chatter of voices replaced the tension that had filled the room. As if the whole thing had never happened, the man put his guitar into the case, stepped down from the stage, and disappeared.

When I paid my bill, I asked the girl at the door if the man sang here often and whether he usually performed the trick.

"I'm not sure," she said. "As far as I know, this was his first time here. I never heard of him until today. And nobody told me he did magic tricks. Wasn't that amazing, though? I wonder how he does it. I bet he'd be a hit on TV."

"It's true," I said. "It looked like he was really burning himself."

I walked back to the hotel, and the minute I got into bed, sleep came to me as if it had been waiting all this time. As I drifted off, I thought of Kumiko, but she seemed very far away, and after that it was impossible for me to think of anything. Through my mind flashed the face of the man burning his palm. He really seemed to be burning himself, I thought. And then I fell asleep.

8

The Root of Desire
◆
In Room 208
◆
Passing Through the Wall

Before dawn, in the bottom of the well, I had a dream. But it was not a dream. It was something that happened to take the form of a dream.

I was walking alone. The face of Noboru Wataya was being projected on the screen of a large television in the centre of a broad lobby. His speech had just begun. He wore a tweed suit, striped shirt, and navy-blue tie. His hands were folded on the table before him, and he was talking into the camera. A large map of the world hung on the wall behind him. There must have been over a hundred people in the lobby, and each and every one of them stopped what they were doing to listen to him, with serious expressions on their faces. Noboru Wataya was about to announce something that would determine people's fates.

I, too, stopped and looked at the television screen. In practised – but utterly sincere – tones, Noboru Wataya was addressing millions of people he could not see. That unbearable something I always felt when I was face to face with him was now hidden in some deep, invisible place. He spoke in his uniquely persuasive style – the pauses timed with precision, the ringing of the voice, the variety of facial expressions, all giving rise to an effective sense of reality. Noboru Wataya seemed to have been growing more polished as an orator with each day that passed. Much as I hated to, I had to grant him that.

"And so you see, my friends," he was saying, "everything is both complicated and simple. This is the fundamental rule that governs the world. We must never forget it. Things that appear to be complicated – and that, in fact, *are* complicated – are very simple where motives are concerned. It is just a matter of *what we are looking for*. Motive is the root of desire, so to speak. The important thing is to seek out the root. Dig beneath the complicated surface of reality. And keep on digging. Then dig even more until you come to the very tip of the root. If you will only do that" – and here he gestured towards the map – "everything will eventually become clear. That is how the world works. The stupid ones can never break free of the apparent complexity. They grope through the darkness, searching for the exit, and die before they are able to comprehend a single thing about the way of the world. They have lost all sense of direction. They might as well be deep in a forest or down in a well. And the reason they have lost all sense of direction is because they do not comprehend the fundamental principles. They have nothing in their heads but garbage and rocks. They understand nothing. Nothing at all. They can't tell front from back, top from bottom, north from south. Which is why they can never break free of the darkness."

Noboru Wataya paused at that point to give his words time to sink into the minds of his audience.

"But let's forget about people like that," he went on. "If people want to lose all sense of direction, the best thing that you and I can do is let them. We have more important things to do."

The more I heard, the angrier I became, until my anger was almost choking me. He was pretending to talk to the world at large, but in fact he was talking to me alone. And he must have had some kind of twisted, distorted motive for doing so. But nobody else realized that. Which is precisely why Noboru Wataya was able to exploit the gigantic system of television in order to send me secret messages. In my pockets, I clenched my hands into fists, but I had no way to vent my anger. And my inability to share this anger with anybody in the lobby aroused in me a profound sense of isolation.

The place was filled with people straining to catch every word that Noboru Wataya spoke. I cut across the lobby and headed straight for a corridor that connected with the guest rooms. The faceless man was standing there. As I approached, he looked at me with that faceless face of his. Then, without a sound, he moved to block my way.

"This is the wrong time," he said. "You don't belong here now."

But the deep, slashing pain caused by Noboru Wataya now urged me on. I reached out and pushed the faceless man aside. He wobbled like a shadow and fell away.

"I'm saying this for your sake," he called from behind me, his every word lodging in my back like a piece of shrapnel. "If you go any farther, you won't be able to come back. Do you understand?"

I ignored him and moved ahead with rapid steps. I wasn't afraid of anything now. I had to know. I had lost all sense of direction, but I couldn't stay like that for ever.

I walked down the familiar-looking corridor. I assumed the man with no face would follow and try to stop me, but when I looked back, there was no one coming. The long, winding corridor was lined with identical doors. Each door had a number, but I couldn't recall the number of the room to which I had been taken the last time. I was sure I had been aware of the number back then, but now my attempts to recall it yielded nothing, and there was no question of my opening every one.

I wandered up and down the corridor until I passed a room-service waiter carrying a tray. On it was a new bottle of Cutty Sark, an ice bucket, and two glasses. I let the waiter go by, then followed after him. Every now and then, the polished tray caught the light of a ceiling fixture with a bright flash. The waiter didn't look back. Chin drawn in purposefully, he moved straight ahead, his steps in a steady rhythm. Sometimes he would whistle a few lines of music. It was the overture to *The Thieving Magpie*, the opening where the drums come in. He was good.

The corridor was a long one, but I encountered no one else in it all the time I was following the waiter. Eventually, he stopped in front of a door and gave three gentle knocks. After a few seconds had passed, someone opened the door and the waiter carried the tray in. I pressed against the wall, hiding behind a large Chinese-style vase, and waited for the waiter to come out. The room number was 208. Of course! Why hadn't I been able to remember it until now?

The waiter was taking a very long time. I glanced at my watch. At some point, though, the hands had stopped moving. I examined the flowers in the vase and smelled each one. The flowers seemed to have been brought from a garden only moments before, so fresh were they, retaining every bit of their colour and aroma. Most likely they still hadn't noticed that they had been severed from their roots. A tiny winged insect had worked its way into the core of a red rose with thick, fleshy petals.

Five minutes or more went by before the waiter came out of the room, empty-handed. With his chin pulled in as before, he went back the same way he had come. As soon as he had disappeared around a corner, I walked over to the door. I held my breath and listened, expecting to hear something. But there was no sound, no indication that anyone was inside. I took a chance and knocked. Three times. Gently. As the waiter had done. But no one answered. I let a few seconds pass and knocked three times again, this time a little more forcefully than before. Still no response.

Next, I tried the knob. It turned, and the door opened without a sound. The room seemed pitch dark at first, but some light was managing to find its way in around the thick curtains. With effort, I could just make out the window itself and a table and sofa. This was the room in which I had coupled with Creta Kano. It was a suite: the living room here and the bedroom in back. On the table were the dim forms of the Cutty Sark bottle, the glasses, and the ice bucket. When I opened the door, the stainless-steel ice bucket had caught the light from the corridor and sent back a knife-sharp flash. I entered the darkness and closed the door quietly behind me. The air in the room felt warm, and it carried the heavy scent of flowers. I held my breath and listened, keeping my left hand on the knob so that I could open it at any time. There had to be a person in here, somewhere. Someone had ordered the whisky, ice, and glasses from room service and had opened the door to let the waiter in.

•

"Don't turn on the light," said a woman's voice. It came from the bedroom. I recognized it immediately. It was the voice of the enigmatic woman who had made those strange calls to me. I let go of the knob and began to feel my way towards the voice. The darkness of the inner room was more nearly opaque than that of the outer room. I stood in the doorway between the two and strained to see into the darkness.

I could hear the sound of bedsheets shifting. A black shadow moved in the darkness. "Leave it dark," said the woman's voice.

"Don't worry," I said. "I won't turn on the light."

I kept a firm grip on the doorjamb.

"Did you come here alone?" the woman asked, sounding vaguely tired.

"Of course," I said. "I thought I'd find you here. You or Creta Kano. I've got to know where Kumiko is. I mean, everything started with that first call from you. You opened Pandora's box. Then it was one weird thing after another, until finally Kumiko disappeared. That's why I'm here.

Alone. I don't know who you are, but you hold some kind of key. Am I right?"

"Creta Kano?" the woman asked in guarded tones. "Never heard of her. Is she here too?"

"I don't know where she is. But I've met her here more than once."

Each breath I took brought with it the strong smell of flowers. The air was thick and heavy. Somewhere in this room was a vase full of flowers. Somewhere in this same darkness, they were breathing, swaying. In the darkness filled with their intense fragrance, I began to lose track of my own physicality. I felt as if I had become a tiny insect. Now I was working my way in among the petals of a giant flower. Sticky nectar, pollen and soft hairs awaited me. They needed my invasion and my presence.

"You know," I said to the woman, "the very first thing I want to do is find out who you are. You tell me I know you, and I've tried as hard as I can to recall you, but without success. Who *are* you?"

"Who *am* I?" the woman parroted, but without a hint of mockery. "I'd like a drink. Pour two on the rocks, will you? You will drink with me, I suppose?"

I went back to the living room, opened the new bottle of whisky, put ice in the glasses, and poured two drinks. In the dark, this took a good deal of time. I carried the drinks into the bedroom. The woman told me to put one on the night table. "And you sit on the chair by the foot of the bed."

I did as I was told, placing one glass on the night table and sitting in an upholstered armchair some distance away, drink in hand. My eyes had perhaps grown more used to the darkness. I could see shadows shifting there. The woman seemed to have raised herself on the bed. Then there was the clink of ice as she drank. I, too, took a sip of whisky.

For a long time, she said nothing. The longer the silence continued, the stronger the smell of flowers seemed to become.

"Do you really want to know who I am?" the woman asked.

"That's why I'm here," I said, but my voice sounded uneasy in the darkness.

"You came here specifically to learn my name, did you?"

Instead of answering, I cleared my throat, but this also had a strange reverberation.

The woman jiggled the ice in her glass a few times. "You want to know my name," she said, "but unfortunately, I can't tell you what it is. I know you very well. You know me very well. But *I* don't know me."

I shook my head in the darkness. "I don't get it," I said. "And I'm sick

245

of riddles. I need something concrete that I can get my hands on. Hard facts. Something I can use as a lever to pry the door open. That's what I want."

The woman seemed to wring a sigh out of the core of her body. "Toru Okada, I want *you* to discover my name. But no: you don't have to discover it. *You know it already.* All you have to do is remember it. If you can find my name, then I can get out of here. I can even help you find your wife: help you find Kumiko Okada. If you want to find your wife, try hard to discover my name. That is the *lever* you want. You don't have time to stay lost. Every day you fail to find it, Kumiko Okada moves that much farther away from you."

I put my whisky glass on the floor. "Tell me," I said, "where is this place? How long have you been here? What do you do here?"

"You have to leave now," said the woman, as if she had just recalled what she was doing. "If *he* finds you here, there'll be trouble. He's even more dangerous than you think. He might kill you. I wouldn't put it past him."

"Who is this 'he'?"

The woman didn't answer, and I didn't know what else to say. I felt lost. Nothing stirred in the room. The silence was deep and thick and suffocating. My head felt feverish. The pollen might have been doing it. Mixed with the air, the microscopic grains were penetrating my head and sending my nerves haywire.

"Tell me, Toru Okada," said the woman, her voice suddenly very different. The quality of her voice could change in an instant. Now it had become one with the room's thick, heavy air. "Do you ever think you'd like to hold me again? That you'd like to get inside me? That you'd like to kiss me all over? You can do anything you want to me, you know. And I'll do anything you want . . . anything . . . things that your wife . . . Kumiko Okada . . . would never do for you. I'll make you feel so good you'll never forget it. If you –"

With no warning at all, there was a knock on the door. It had the hard, precise sound of a nail being driven straight in – an ominous sound in the dark.

The woman's hand came out of the darkness and took me by the arm. "Come this way," she whispered. "Hurry." Her voice had lost the dreamy quality now. The knocking started again: two knocks with precisely the same force. It occurred to me that I hadn't locked the door.

"Hurry," she said. "You have to get out of here. This is the only way."

I moved through the darkness as the woman drew me on. I could hear the doorknob turning slowly. The sound sent chills down my spine. At the very moment the light from the corridor pierced the darkness, we slipped into the wall. It had the consistency of a gigantic mass of cold gelatin; I clamped my mouth shut to prevent it entering. The thought struck me: I'm passing through the wall! In order to go from one place to another, I was passing through a wall. And yet, even as it was happening, it seemed like the most natural thing to do.

I felt the woman's tongue entering my mouth. Warm and soft, it probed every crevice and it wound around my own tongue. The heavy smell of flower petals stroked the walls of my lungs. Down in my loins, I felt a dull need to come. Clamping my eyes closed, I fought it. A moment later, I felt a kind of intense heat on my right cheek. It was an odd sensation. I felt no pain, only the awareness of heat. I couldn't tell whether the heat was coming from the outside or boiling up inside me. Soon everything was gone: the woman's tongue, the smell of flowers, the need to come, the heat on my cheek. And I passed through the wall. When I opened my eyes I was on the other side of the wall – at the bottom of a deep well.

9

The Well and Stars

•

How the Ladder Disappeared

The sky was already bright just after 5 in the morning, but even so, I could make out a lot of stars overhead. It was just as Lieutenant Mamiya had told me: from the bottom of a well, you can see stars in the daylight. Into the perfect half-moon slice of sky, faintly glowing stars were packed neatly, like specimens of rare minerals.

Once before, when camping on a mountaintop with some friends when I was ten or eleven, I had seen stars in such numbers that they filled the sky. It almost seemed as if the sky would break under the weight of all those things and come tumbling down. Never had I seen such an amazing skyful of stars. Unable to sleep after the others had drowsed off, I crawled out of the tent and lay on the ground, looking at the sky. Now and then, a shooting star would trace a bright arc across the heavens. The longer I watched, though, the more nervous it made me. There were simply too many stars, and the sky was too vast and deep. A huge, overpowering foreign object, it surrounded me, enveloped me, and made me feel almost dizzy. Until that moment, I had always thought that the earth on which I stood was a solid object that would last for ever. Or rather, I had never thought about such a thing at all. I had simply taken it for granted. But in fact, the earth was nothing but a chunk of rock floating in one little corner of the universe: a temporary foothold in the vast emptiness of space. It – and all of us with it – could be blown away tomorrow by a momentary flash of something or a tiny shift in the universe's energy. Beneath this breathtaking skyful of stars, the uncertainty of my own existence struck me with full force (though not in so many words, of course). It was a stunning discovery for a young boy.

Looking up at the dawn stars from the bottom of a well was a special experience very different from looking at the full, starry sky on a mountaintop, as if my mind – my self – my very existence – were firmly bonded through my narrow window to each one of those stars in the sky. I felt a deep sense of intimacy towards them: they were my stars, visible to no one but me, down here in the dark well. I embraced them as my own, and they in turn showered me with energy and warmth.

As time passed and the sky fell more and more under the sway of the bright morning sun of summer, one star at a time would obliterate itself from my field of view. They did this with the utmost gentleness, and I studied the process of obliteration with wide-open eyes. The summer sun did not, however, erase every star from the sky. A few of the strongest ones remained. No matter how high the sun climbed, they stubbornly refused to disappear. This made me very happy: apart from the occasional cloud that drifted by, the stars were the only things I could see from down there.

I had sweated in my sleep, and now the sweat was beginning to grow cold and chill me. I shuddered several times. The sweat made me think of that pitch-dark hotel room and the telephone woman there. Still ringing in my ears were the words she had spoken – every one of them – and the sound of the knocking. My nostrils retained the heavy smell of flowers. And Noboru Wataya was still talking from the other side of the television screen. The memory of these impressions remained, undimmed by the passage of time. And this was because *it had not been a dream*, my memory told me.

Even after I was fully awake, I continued to feel an intense warmth in my right cheek. Mixed with the warmth was a mild sensation of pain, as if the skin had been chafed with rough sandpaper. I pressed my palm against the spot through my one-day stubble, but this did nothing to reduce the heat or the pain. Down in the bottom of the dark well, without a mirror, it was impossible for me to examine what was happening to my cheek.

I reached out and touched the wall, tracing the surface with my fingertips and then pressing my palm against it for a time, but I found nothing unusual: it was just an ordinary concrete wall. I made a fist and gave it a few taps. The wall was hard, expressionless, and slightly damp. I still had a clear impression of the strange, slippery sensation it had given me when I passed through it – like tunnelling through a mass of gelatin.

I groped in my knapsack for the canteen and took a drink of water. I had gone a full day now without eating. The thought itself gave me intense hunger pangs, but these began to fade soon enough as they were absorbed into a limbo-like numbness. I brought my hand to my face again and tried to gauge the growth of my beard. My jaw now wore a day's worth of stubble. No doubt about it: a whole day had gone by. But my one-day absence was probably not affecting anybody. Not one human being would have noticed that I was gone. I could disappear from the face of the earth, and the world would go on moving without the slightest hiccup. Things were tremendously complicated, to be sure, but one thing was clear: no one needed me.

I looked up again at the stars. The sight of them gradually calmed the beating of my heart. Then it occurred to me to grope along the wall for the ladder. Where it should have been, my hand encountered nothing. I felt over a broad area, checking with the utmost care, but there was no ladder. It no longer existed in the place where it belonged. I took a deep breath, took the torch from the knapsack, and switched it on. But there was no sign of the ladder. Standing, I shone the light on the floor and then the wall above me, as far as the beam could reach. The ladder was nowhere. Cold sweat crept down my sides like some kind of living creature. The torch slipped from my hand, fell to the ground, and switched off from the impact. It was a sign. In that instant, my mind snapped: it was a grain of sand, absorbed into the surrounding darkness. My body stopped functioning, as if its plug had been pulled. A perfect nothingness came over me.

This lasted perhaps a few seconds, until I retrieved myself. My physical functions returned bit by bit. I bent over and picked up the torch lying at my feet, gave it a few taps, and switched it on again. The light returned without a problem. I needed to calm myself and put my thoughts in order. Fear and panic would solve nothing. When had I last checked the ladder? Yesterday, late at night, just before I fell asleep. I had made certain it was there and only then let myself sleep. No mistake. The ladder had disappeared while I was sleeping. It had been pulled up. Taken away.

I switched off the torch and leaned against the wall. Then I closed my eyes. The first thing I felt was hunger. It swept towards me out of the distance, like a wave, washed over me and glided away. Once it was gone, I stood there, hollow, empty as a gutted animal. After the initial panic had passed, I no longer felt either terror or despair. Strangely enough, all I felt at that moment was a kind of resignation.

·

Back from Sapporo, I held Kumiko and comforted her. She was feeling lost and confused. She had taken the day off from work. "I couldn't sleep a wink last night," she said. "The clinic had a slot at just the right time, so I went ahead and decided by myself." She cried a little after saying this.

"It's finished now," I said. "No point thinking about it any more. We talked it over, and this was how it worked out. If there's anything else you want to talk about, better do it here and now. Then let's just put it out of our minds. Forget about it. You said on the phone you had something to tell me."

Kumiko shook her head. "Never mind," she said. "You're right. Let's forget about it."

We went on with our lives for a while, avoiding all mention of Kumiko's abortion. But this wasn't easy to do. We could be talking about something entirely different, when suddenly both of us would fall silent. At weekends, we'd go to movies. In the dark, we could concentrate on the movie, but we could just as easily be thinking about things that had nothing to do with the movie, or we might be resting our brains by thinking about nothing at all. Often I knew that Kumiko, sitting next to me, was thinking about something entirely different from what I was thinking about. I could sense it.

After the movie, we'd go somewhere for a beer or a snack. Sometimes we wouldn't know what to talk about. This went on for six weeks – a very long six weeks, at the end of which Kumiko said to me, "What do you say we take a trip tomorrow, go away for a little holiday, just the two of us? Tomorrow's Friday: we can take off until Sunday. People need that kind of thing once in a while."

"I know what you mean," I said, smiling, "but I wonder if anybody at my office even knows what a holiday is."

"Call in sick, then. Say it's flu or something. I'll do the same."

We took the train to Karuizawa. I picked that destination because Kumiko said she wanted a quiet place in the mountains where we could walk as much as we liked. It was off-season there in April; the hotel was hushed, most of the shops were closed, but that was exactly what we wanted. We did nothing but go out for walks every day, from morning to evening.

·

It took a full day and a half for Kumiko to release her feelings. And once she did, she sat in the hotel room, crying, for nearly two hours. I said nothing the whole time, just held her and let her cry.

Then, little by little, in fragments, she began to tell me things. About the abortion. About her feelings at the time. About her extreme sense of loss. About how alone she had felt while I was in Hokkaido – and how she could have done what she did only while feeling so alone.

"And don't get me wrong," she concluded. "I'm not regretting what I did. It was the only way. I'm quite clear about that. What really hurts, though, is that I want to tell you everything – every last thing – but I just can't do it. I can't tell you exactly how I feel."

Kumiko pushed her hair up, revealing a small, shapely ear, and she gave her head a shake.

"I'm not hiding it from you. I'm planning to tell you sometime. You're the only one I *can* tell. But I just can't do it now. I can't put it into words."

"Something from the past?"

"No, that's not it."

"Take all the time you need," I said. "Until you're ready. Time is the one thing we've got plenty of. I'll be right here with you. There's no rush. I just want you to keep one thing in mind: anything of yours – anything at all, as long as it belongs to you – I will accept as my own. That is one thing you will never have to worry about."

"Thank you," she said. "I'm so glad I married you."

But we did not have as much time as I thought we had. Just what was it that Kumiko had been unable to put into words? Did it have something to do with her disappearance? Perhaps, if I had tried dragging it out of her then, I could have avoided losing her now. But no, I concluded after mulling it over: I could never have forced her. She had said she couldn't put it into words. Whatever it was, it was more than she had the strength for.

·

"Hey, down there! Mr Wind-up Bird!" shouted May Kasahara. In a shallow sleep at the time, I thought the voice was part of a dream. But it was not a dream. When I looked up, there was May Kasahara's face, small and far away. "I know you're down there! C'mon, Mr Wind-up Bird! Answer me!"

"I'm here," I said.

"What on earth for? What are you doing down there?"

"Thinking," I said.

"I don't get it. Why do you have to go to the bottom of a well to think? It must be so uncomfortable!"

"This way, you can really concentrate. It's dark and cool and quiet."

"Do you do this a lot?"

"No, not a lot. I've never done it before in my life – getting into a well like this."

"Is it working? Is it helping you to think?"

"I don't know yet. I'm still experimenting."

She cleared her throat. The sound reverberated loudly to the bottom of the well.

"Anyway, Mr Wind-up Bird, did you notice the ladder's gone?"

"Sure did," I said. "A little while ago."

"Did you know it was me who pulled it up?"

"No, that I didn't know."

"Well, who did you think did it?"

"I didn't know," I said. "I don't know how to put this, but that thought never really crossed my mind – that somebody took it. I thought it had just disappeared, to tell you the truth."

May Kasahara fell silent. Then, with a note of caution in her voice, as if she thought my words contained a trap, she said, "Just disappeared. Hmm. What do you mean, 'it just disappeared'? That, all by itself, it . . . just . . . disappeared?"

"Maybe so."

"You know, Mr Wind-up Bird, it's funny for me to bring this up now, but you're pretty weird. There aren't too many people out there as weird as you are. Did you know that?"

"I'm not so weird to me," I said.

"Then what makes you think that ladders can just disappear?"

I rubbed my face with both hands and tried to concentrate all my attention on this conversation with May Kasahara. "*You* pulled it up, didn't you?"

"Of course I did. It wouldn't have taken much brainwork to figure that one out. *I* did it. I sneaked out in the night and pulled the ladder up."

"But why?"

"Why not? Do you know how many times I went to your house yesterday? I wanted you to go to work with me again. You weren't there, of course. Then I found that note of yours in the kitchen. So I waited a long time, but you never came back. So then I thought you just might be at the empty house again. I found the well cover half open and the ladder hanging down. Still, it never occurred to me you could be down there. I just figured some workman or somebody had been there and left his ladder. I mean, how many people go to sit at the bottom of a well when they want to think?"

"You've got a point there," I said.

"Anyhow, so then I sneaked out at night and went to your place, but you still weren't there. That's when it popped into my mind. That maybe you were down in the well. Not that I had any idea what you'd be doing down there, but you know, like I said, you're kinda weird. I came to the well and pulled the ladder up. Bet *that* got you going."

"Yeah, you're right."

"Do you have anything to eat or drink down there?"

"A little water. I didn't bring any food. I've got three lemon drops, though."

"How long have you been down there?"

"Since late yesterday morning."

"You must be hungry."

"I guess so."

"Don't you need to pee or anything?"

Now that she mentioned it, I realized I hadn't peed once since coming down here. "Not really," I said. "I'm not eating or drinking much."

"Say, Mr Wind-up Bird, you know what? You might die down there, depending on my mood. I'm the only one who knows you're in there, and I'm the one who hid the rope ladder. Do you realize that? If I just walked away from here, you'd end up dead. You could yell, but no one would hear you. No one would think you were at the bottom of a well. I bet no one would even notice that you were gone. You don't work for any company, and your wife ran away. I suppose someone would notice eventually that you were missing and report it to the police, but you'd be dead by then, and they'd never find your body."

"I'm sure you're right. I could die down here, depending on your mood."

"How do you feel about that?"

"Scared," I said.

"You don't sound scared."

I was still rubbing my cheeks. These were my hands and my cheeks. I couldn't see them in the dark, but they were still here: my body still existed. "That's because it hasn't really sunk in," I said.

"Well, it has with *me*," said May Kasahara. "I bet it's a lot easier to kill somebody than people think."

254

"Probably depends on the method."

"It'd be so easy! I'd just have to leave you there. I wouldn't have to do a thing. Think about it, Mr Wind-up Bird. Just imagine how much you'd suffer, dying little by little of hunger and thirst down in the darkness. It wouldn't be easy."

"I'm sure you're right," I said.

"You don't really believe me, do you, Mr Wind-up Bird? You think I couldn't do anything so cruel."

"I don't really know," I said. "It's not that I believe you could do it, or that I believe you couldn't. Anything could happen. The possibility is there. That's what I think."

"I'm not talking about possibility," she said in the coldest tone imaginable. "Hey, I've got an idea. It just occurred to me. You went to all the trouble of climbing down there so you could think. Why don't I fix it so you can concentrate on your thoughts even better?"

"How can you do that?" I asked.

"How? Like this," she said, closing the open half of the well cover. Now the darkness was total.

10

May Kasahara on Death and Evolution

•

The Thing Made Elsewhere

I was crouching down in total darkness. All I could see was nothingness. And I was part of this nothingness. I closed my eyes and listened to the sound of my heart, to the sound of the blood circulating through my body, to the bellows-like contractions of my lungs, to the slippery undulations of my food-starved gut. In the deep darkness, every movement, every throb, was magnified enormously. This was my body: my flesh. But in the darkness, it was all too raw and physical.

Soon my conscious mind began to slip away from my physical body.

I saw myself as the wind-up bird, flying through the summer sky, alighting on the branch of a huge tree somewhere, winding the world's spring. If there really was no more wind-up bird, someone would have to take on its duties. Someone would have to wind the world's spring in its place. Otherwise, the spring would run down and the delicate mechanism would grind to a halt. The only one who seemed to have noticed that the wind-up bird was gone, however, was me.

I tried my best to imitate the cry of the wind-up bird in the back of my throat. It didn't work. All I could produce was a meaningless, ugly sound like the rubbing together of two meaningless, ugly things. Only the real wind-up bird could make the sound. Only the wind-up bird could wind the world's spring the way it was supposed to be wound.

Nonetheless, as a voiceless wind-up bird unable to wind the world's spring, I decided to go flying through the summer sky – which turned out to be fairly easy. Once you were up, all you had to do was flap your wings at the right angle to adjust direction and altitude. My body mastered the art in a moment and sent me flying effortlessly wherever I wanted to go. I looked at the world from the wind-up bird's vantage point. Whenever I had had enough flying, I would land on a branch and peer through the green leaves at rooftops and roads. I watched people moving over the ground, carrying on the functions of life. Unfortunately, though, I could not see my own body. This was because I had never once seen the wind-up bird and had no idea what it looked like.

For a long time – how long could it have been? – I remained the wind-up bird. But being the wind-up bird never got me anywhere. The flying part was fun, of course, but I couldn't go on having fun for ever. There was something I had to accomplish down here in the darkness at the bottom of the well. I stopped being the wind-up bird and returned to being myself.

•

May Kasahara paid her second visit a little after 3. Three in the afternoon. When she opened half the well, light flooded in overhead – the blinding glare of a summer day. To protect my eyes, so accustomed now to total darkness, I closed them and kept my head down for a while. The mere thought of light up there caused a thin film of tears to ooze.

"Hi there, Mr Wind-up Bird," said May Kasahara. "Are you still alive? Mr Wind-up Bird? Answer if you're still alive."

"I'm alive," I said.

"You must be hungry."

"I think so."

"Still just 'I think so'? It'll be a while before you starve to death, then. Starving people don't die so easily, as long as they've got water."

"That's probably true," I said, the uncertainty in my voice echoing in the well. The echo probably amplified any hint of anything contained in my voice.

"I know it's true," said May Kasahara. "I did a little research in the library this morning. All about hunger and thirst. Did you know, Mr Wind-up Bird, somebody once lived underground for twenty-one days? During the Russian Revolution."

"No kidding," I said.

"He must have suffered a lot."

"Yes, he must."

"He survived, but he lost all his hair and teeth. Everything. Even though he lived, it must have been terrible."

"Yes, it must."

"Even if you lose your teeth and hair, though, I suppose you can live a pretty normal life if you've got a decent wig and false teeth."

"Yes, and wigs and dentures have made great strides since the time of the Russian Revolution, too. That might make things a little easier."

"You know, Mr Wind-up Bird . . . ," said May Kasahara, clearing her throat.

"What?"

"If people lived for ever – if they never got any older – if they could just go on living in this world, never dying, always healthy – do you think they'd bother to think hard about things, the way we're doing now? I mean, we think about just about everything, more or less – philosophy, psychology, logic. Religion. Literature. I think, if there were no such thing as death, that complicated thoughts and ideas like that would never come into the world. I mean –"

May Kasahara cut herself short and remained silent for a while, during which her "I mean" hung in the darkness of the well like a hacked-off fragment of thought. Maybe she had lost the will to say any more. Or maybe she needed time to think of what came next. I waited in silence for her to continue, my head lowered as from the beginning. The thought crossed my mind that if May Kasahara wanted to kill me right away, it would be no trouble for her at all. She could just drop a big rock down the well. If she tried a few times, one was bound to hit me on the head.

"I mean . . . this is what I think, but . . . people have to think seriously about what it means for them to be alive here and now because they know they're going to die sometime. Right? Who would think about what it means to be alive if they were just going to go on living for ever? Why would they bother? Or even if they *should* bother, they'd probably just reckon, 'Oh, well, I've got plenty of time for that. I'll think about it later.' But we can't wait till later. We've got to think about it right this second. I might get run over by a truck tomorrow afternoon. And you, Mr Wind-up Bird: you might starve to death. One morning three days from now, you could be dead in the bottom of a well. See? Nobody knows what's going to happen. So we need death to make us evolve. That's what I think. Death is this huge, bright thing, and the bigger and brighter it is, the more we have to drive ourselves crazy thinking about things."

May Kasahara paused.

"Tell me, Mr Wind-up Bird . . ."

"What?"

"Down there in the darkness, have you been thinking about your own death? About how you would die down there?"

I took a moment to think about her question. "Nope," I said. "That's one thing I haven't been thinking about."

"Why *not*?" May Kasahara asked, with a note of disgust, as if she were speaking to a deformed animal. "Why *haven't* you been thinking about it? You're literally facing death right now. I'm not kidding around. I told you before, it's up to *me* whether you live or die."

"You could drop a rock," I said.

"A rock? What are you talking about?"

"You could find a big rock and drop it on me."

"Well, sure, I could do that." But she didn't seem to like the idea. "Anyhow, Mr Wind-up Bird, you must be starving. It's just gonna get worse and worse. And you'll run out of water. So how can you *not* think about death? Don't you think it's weird?"

"Yes, I suppose it's kind of weird," I said. "But I've been thinking about other things the whole time. I'll probably think about death, too, when I start to get really hungry. I've still got three weeks before I die, right?"

"That's if you have water," said May Kasahara. "That's what happened with that Russian guy. He was a big landowner or something. The revolutionary guard threw him down an old mine shaft, but there was water seeping through the wall, so he licked it and kept himself alive. He was in total darkness, just like you. But you don't have much water, do you?"

"No," I said truthfully. "Just a little left."

"Then you'd better be careful with it," said May Kasahara. "Take little sips. And take your time thinking. About death. About how you're dying. You've still got plenty of time."

"Why are you so determined to make me think about death? What's in it for you?"

"Nothing's in it for me," May Kasahara shot back. "What makes you think there's anything in it for me for *you* to think about your own death? It's *your* life. It's got nothing to do with me. I'm just . . . interested."

"Out of curiosity?"

"Yeah. Curiosity. About how people die. About how it feels to die. Curiosity."

May Kasahara fell silent. When the conversation broke off, a deep stillness filled in the space around me, as if it had been waiting for this opportunity. I wanted to raise my face and look up. To see whether May Kasahara was visible from down here. But the light was too strong. I was sure it would burn my eyes out.

"There's something I want to tell you," I said.

"OK. Tell me."

"My wife had a lover," I said. "At least I'm pretty sure she did. I never realized it, but for months, while she was still living with me, she was sleeping with this guy. I couldn't believe it at first, but the more I thought about it, the more convinced I became. Now, looking back, I can see there were all kinds of little clues. She'd come home at crazy hours, or she'd flinch when I touched her. But I couldn't read the signals. I trusted her. I never thought she'd have an affair. It just never occurred to me."

"Wow," said May Kasahara.

"So then one day she just left the house and never came back. We had breakfast together that morning. She went off to work in her usual outfit. All she had with her was her handbag, and she picked up a blouse and skirt at the cleaner's. And that was it. No goodbye. No note. Nothing. Kumiko was gone. Left all her things – clothes and everything. And she'll probably never come back here – back to me. Not of her own accord, at least. That much I know."

"Is Kumiko with the other guy now, do you think?"

"I don't know," I said, shaking my head. As my head moved slowly through it, the surrounding air felt like some kind of heavy water, without the watery feel. "They probably are together."

"And so now you're crushed, Mr Wind-up Bird, and that's why you went down in the well."

"Of course I was crushed when I realized what was happening. But that's not why I'm here. I'm not hiding from reality. Like I said before, I needed a place where I could be alone and concentrate on my thinking. Where and how did my relationship with Kumiko go wrong? That's what I can't understand. Not that I'm saying everything was perfect until that point. A man and a woman in their twenties, with two distinct personalities, just happen to meet somewhere and start living together. There's not a married couple anywhere without their problems. But I thought we were doing OK, that any little problems would solve themselves over time. But I was wrong. I was missing something big, making some kind of mistake on a basic level, I suppose. That's what I came here to think about."

May Kasahara said nothing. I swallowed once.

"I wonder if this'll make any sense to you. When we got married, six years ago, the two of us were trying to make a brand-new world – like building a new house on an empty lot. We had this clear image of what we wanted. We didn't need a fancy house or anything, just something to keep the weather out, as long as the two of us could be together. We didn't need any extras. Things would just get in the way. It all seemed so simple to us. Have you ever had that feeling – that you'd like to go to a whole different place and become a whole different self?"

"Sure," said May Kasahara. "I feel that way all the time."

"Well, that's what we were trying to do when we got married. I wanted to get outside myself: the me that had existed until then. And it was the same for Kumiko. In that new world of ours, we were trying to get hold of new selves that were better suited to who we were deep down. We believed we could live in a way that was more perfectly suited to who we were."

May Kasahara seemed to shift her centre of gravity in the light. I could sense her movement. She seemed to be waiting for me to continue. But I had nothing more to say at that point. Nothing came to mind. I felt tired from the sound of my own voice in the concrete tube of the well.

"Does this make any sense to you?" I asked.

"Sure it does."

"What do you think about it?"

"Hey, I'm still a kid, you know. I don't know anything about marriage. I don't know what was in your wife's mind when she started fooling around with another man or when she left you. But from what you just told me, I think you had the wrong idea from the very beginning. You know what I mean, Mr Wind-up Bird? What you were just talking about . . . it's kind of impossible for anybody to *do* that stuff, like, 'OK, now I'm gonna make a whole new world' or 'OK, now I'm gonna make a whole new self.' That's what I think. You might *think* you made a new world or a new self, but your old self is always gonna be there, just below the surface, and if something happens, it'll stick its head out and say 'Hi'. You don't seem to realize that. You were made somewhere

261

else. And even this idea you have of remaking yourself: even *that* was made somewhere else. Even *I* know that much, Mr Wind-up Bird. You're a grown-up, aren't you? How come you don't get it? That's a *big problem*, if you ask me. And that's what you're being punished for – by all kinds of things: by the world you tried to get rid of, or by the self you tried to get rid of. Do you see what I'm saying?"

I remained silent, staring at the darkness that enveloped my feet. I didn't know what to say.

"OK, Mr Wind-up Bird," she said softly. "You go ahead and think. Think. Think."

The cover snapped into place, and the well opening was blocked once again.

·

I took the canteen from my knapsack and gave it a shake. The light sloshing sound echoed in the darkness. Maybe a quarter left. I leaned my head against the wall and closed my eyes. May Kasahara was probably right. This person, this self, this me, was made somewhere else. Everything had come from somewhere else, and it would all go somewhere else. I was nothing but a pathway for the person known as me.

Even *I* know that much, Mr Wind-up Bird. How come you don't get it?

11

Hunger as Pain

•

Kumiko's Long Letter

•

Bird as Prophet

I fell asleep a few times and woke up just as often. These were short, unsettled snatches of sleep, as on an aeroplane. Whenever deep sleep was looming, I would shrink back and wake up; whenever full wakefulness was about to arrive, I would drift off into sleep, in endless repetition. Without changes in the light, time wobbled by like a wagon with a loose axle. My cramped, unnatural posture robbed my body of rest. Each time I woke, I would check the time on my watch. Its pace was heavy and uneven.

With nothing better to do, I would pick up the torch and shine it at random – at the ground, at the walls, at the well cover. What I found there was always the same ground, the same walls, the same well cover. The shadows cast by the moving beam would sway, stretch and shrink, swell and contract. When I tired of this, I would spend time feeling my face, probing every line and crevice, examining my features anew to learn their shape. I had never been seriously concerned about the shape of my ears before this. If someone had told me to draw a picture of my own ears – even a rough sketch – I would have been at a loss. Now, though, I would have been able to reproduce every hollow and curve in accurate detail. I found it odd how different the ears were. I had no idea how this had come about or what effect this lack of symmetry might have (it probably had some effect).

The hands of my watch showed 7.28. I must have looked at my watch some two thousand times since coming down here. Now it was 7.28 at night, that much was certain; at a baseball game, it would be the bottom of the third inning or the top of the fourth. When I was a kid, I used to like to sit up high in the outfield stands and watch the summer day trying not to end. The sun had sunk below the western horizon, but the afterglow was still brilliant and beautiful. The stadium lights stretched their long shadows across the field as if to hint at something. First one and then another light would be turned on with the utmost caution shortly after the game got going. Still there was enough light in the sky to read a newspaper by. The memory of the long day's glow remained at the door to keep the summer night from entering.

With patience and persistence, though, the artificial illumination was winning its quiet victory over the light of the sun, bringing forth a flood of festive colours. The brilliant green of the playing field, the handsome black earth, the straight white lines newly drawn upon it, the glinting varnish on the bats of players waiting for their turn at the plate, the cigarette smoke floating in the beams of light (looking, on windless days, like souls wandering in search of someone to take them in) – all these would begin to show up with tremendous clarity. The young beer sellers would hold their hands up in the light, flashing bills tucked between their fingers. The crowd would rise from their seats to follow the path of a high-fly ball, their voices rising with its arc or dissolving into a sigh. Small flocks of birds returning to their roosts would fly past towards the sea. This was the stadium at 7.30 in the evening.

I thought about the baseball games I had seen over the years. The Saint Louis Cardinals had come to Japan once, when I was little, for a friendly game. I had seen that one with my father from an infield seat. Before the game itself, the Cardinals players stood along the perimeter of the field with baskets full of autographed tennis balls, throwing them into the stands as fast as they could. People went crazy trying to grab a ball for themselves, but I just stayed in my seat without moving, and before I knew it, I had a ball in my lap. It was a magical happening: strange and sudden.

I looked at my watch again. Seven thirty-six. Eight minutes had gone by since the last look. Just eight minutes. I took the watch off and held it against my ear. It was ticking away just fine. I shrugged my shoulders in the darkness. Something strange was happening to my sense of time. I decided not to look at my watch for a while. Maybe I didn't have anything else to do, but it wasn't healthy to be looking at a watch this often. I had to make a tremendous effort to keep myself from looking, though. The pain was like what I had felt when I quit smoking. From the moment I decided to give up thinking about time, my mind could think of nothing else. It was a kind of contradiction, a schizoid split. The more I tried to forget about time, the more I was compelled to think about it. Before I knew it, my eyes would be seeking out the watch on my left wrist. Whenever this happened, I would avert my face, close my eyes, and struggle not to look. I ended up taking the watch off and stuffing it into my knapsack. Even so, my mind went on groping for the watch inside the pack, where it continued to tick off the time.

And so time flowed on through the darkness, even without advancing watch hands: time undivided and unmeasured. Once it lost its points of demarcation, time ceased being a continuous line and became instead a kind of formless fluid that expanded or contracted at will. Within this kind of time, I slept and woke and slept and woke, and became slowly more accustomed to life without timepieces. I trained my body to realize that I no longer needed time. But soon I was feeling tremendous anxiety. True, I had been liberated from the nervous habit of checking my watch every five minutes, but once the frame of reference of time faded completely away, I began to feel as if I had been flung into the ocean at night from the deck of a moving ship. No one noticed my screams, and the boat continued its forward advance, moving farther and farther away until it was about to fade from view.

Abandoning the effort, I took the watch from the knapsack and returned it to my wrist. The hands were pointing to 6.15. Probably 6.15 a.m. The last time I had looked at my watch, it had been 7.36. Seven thirty-six at night. It seemed reasonable to conclude that eleven hours had gone by since then. It could hardly have been twenty-three hours. But I could not be sure. What was the essential difference between eleven hours and twenty-three hours? Whichever it was – eleven or twenty-three – my hunger had become far more intense. The sensation was nothing like what I had imagined an intense hunger to be. I had assumed that hunger would be a feeling of absence. Instead, it was closer to pure physical pain – utterly physical and direct, like being stabbed or throttled. And the pain was uneven. It lacked consistency. It would rise like a swelling tide until I was on the verge of fainting, and then little by little it would recede.

To divert my attention from the intense pain of these hunger pangs,

I tried to concentrate on something else. But it was no longer possible for me to do any serious thinking. Fragmentary thoughts would drift into my mind, then disappear as quickly as they had come. Whenever I tried to grab one, it would slip through my fingers like some slimy, shapeless animal.

I stood up and stretched and took a deep breath. Every part of my body hurt. Every muscle and joint cried out in pain from having been in an awkward position for so long. I stretched myself slowly upward, then did some knee bends, but after ten of those I felt dizzy. Sitting down again on the well floor, I closed my eyes. My ears were ringing, and sweat streamed down my face. I wanted to hold on to something, but there was nothing to hold on to. I felt like throwing up, but there was nothing inside me that I could have thrown up. I tried deep breathing, hoping to refresh my mind by renewing the air inside my body and giving my circulation a charge, but the clouds in my mind refused to clear. My body's so weak now, I thought, and in fact I tried saying the words aloud – "My body's so weak now" – but my mouth had difficulty forming the words. If only I could see the stars, I thought, but I could not see stars. May Kasahara had sealed the mouth of the well.

I assumed that May Kasahara would come to the well again sometime during the morning, but she didn't. I spent the time waiting for her to arrive leaning against the wall. The sick feeling stayed with me all morning, and my mind had lost the power to concentrate on anything, for however short a time. The hunger pangs continued to come and go, and the darkness around me grew thicker and thinner. With each new wave another chunk of my ability to concentrate would be taken away, like furniture being stripped a piece at a time by burglars in an empty house.

Noon passed, and still May Kasahara did not appear. I closed my eyes and tried to sleep, hoping to dream of Creta Kano, but my sleep was too shallow for dreams. Not long after I gave up any effort to concentrate. All kinds of fragmentary memories began to visit me. They arrived in silence, like water slowly filling an underground cavern. Places I had gone, people I had met, wounds I had received, conversations I had had, things I had bought, things I had lost: I was able to recall them all with great vividness and in amazing detail. I thought of houses and apartments in which I had lived. I thought of their windows and closets and furniture and lighting fixtures. I thought of teachers and professors I had had, all the way from elementary school through to college. Few if any of these memories had any connection with each other. They were minute and meaningless and came in no chronological order. Now and then, my recollections would be interrupted by another painful wave of hunger. But each memory was incredibly vivid, causing me a physical jolt like the force of a tornado.

I sat there watching my mind pursue these memories, until it brought to life an incident that had occurred in the office some three or four years earlier. It had been a stupid, pointless event, but the more time I spent with re-creating its absurd details, the more annoyed I felt, until the annoyance turned to outright anger. The anger that seized me was so intense that it blotted out everything else – my fatigue, my hunger, my fear – causing me to tremble and my breath to come in gasps. I could hear my heart pounding, and the anger pumped my bloodstream full of adrenaline. It had been an argument that started from a minor misunderstanding. The other guy had flung some nasty phrases at me, and I had managed to have my say as well, but we both realized how pointless the whole thing had been and apologized to each other, putting an end to the matter without any lingering hard feelings. These things happen: you're busy, you're tired, and you let some careless remark slip out. I just forgot about the whole thing. Down in the pitch blackness at the bottom of the well, though, far removed from reality, the memory came back to life with searing vividness. I could feel the heat of it against my skin, hear it sizzling my flesh. Why had my response to such an outrageous comment been so feeble? Now I came up with all kinds of things I should have said to the guy. I polished them, sharpened them, and the sharper they got, the angrier I got.

Then, all of a sudden, the possessing demon slipped away, and none of this mattered any more. Why did I have to revive stale memories like this? What good did it do? The other guy had probably forgotten about the argument long since. *I* certainly had until this moment. I took a deep breath, let my shoulders droop and my body sink back into the darkness. I tried pursuing another memory, but once the intense anger passed, I had run out of memories. My head was now as empty as my stomach.

Then, before I knew it, I was talking to myself, mumbling fragmentary thoughts that I didn't know I was having. I couldn't stop myself. I heard my mouth forming words, but I could hardly understand a thing I was saying. My mouth was moving by itself, automatically, spinning long strings of words through the darkness, words the meaning of which I could not grasp. They came out of one darkness, to be sucked into the next. My body was nothing but an empty tunnel, a conduit for moving the words from there to here. They were definitely fragments of thought, but thought that was happening outside my consciousness.

What was going on? Were my nerves beginning to crack? I looked at my watch. The hands said 3.42. Probably 3.42 in the afternoon. I pictured to myself what the light looked like at 3.42 on a summer afternoon. I imagined myself in that light. I listened for any sound my ears might pick up, but there was nothing: no cicada or bird cries, no children's voices. Maybe, while I was down here in the well, the wind-up bird had not wound the spring, and the world had stopped moving. Bit by bit, the spring had run down, and at a certain point in time, all movement – the rivers' flow, the stirring of leaves, birds flying through the sky – had stopped.

What was May Kasahara doing? Why didn't she come? She hadn't shown up here for a very long time. The thought struck me that something terrible might have happened to her – a traffic accident, say. In which case, there was no longer anyone in the world who knew I was down here. And I really would die a slow death at the bottom of the well.

I decided to take a different look at things. May Kasahara was not such a careless person. She was not about to let herself get run over. She was probably in her room now, scanning this yard once in a while with her binoculars and imagining me down here in the well. She was doing this on purpose: letting a lot of time go by to give me a scare, to make me feel abandoned. That was my guess. And if she was purposely letting a lot of time go by, then her plan was a grand success. I really was scared. I did feel abandoned. Whenever the thought struck me that I might very well just rot down here in the dark, I could hardly breathe with the fear that gripped me. The more time that went by, the more I would weaken, until my hunger pangs became violent enough to kill me. Before that happened, though, I might lose the ability to move my body at will. Even if someone were to lower the rope ladder to me, I might not be able to climb it. All my hair and teeth might fall out.

Then it occurred to me to worry about the air. I had been down in the bottom of this deep, narrow concrete tube over two days now, and to make matters worse, the top had been sealed. There was no air circulation to speak of. The air around me suddenly began to feel heavy and oppressive. I couldn't tell whether this was my imagination playing tricks on me or if the air really was heavier because of the lack of oxygen. To find out, I made several deep inhalations and exhalations, but the more I breathed, the worse it felt. Fear made the sweat gush out of me. Once I started thinking about the air, death invaded my mind as something real and imminent. It rose like silent, black water, seeping into every corner of my consciousness. Until now, I had been thinking about the possibility of starvation, for which there was still plenty of time. Things would happen much more quickly if the oxygen gave out.

What would it feel like to die of asphyxiation? How long would it take? Would it be a slow, agonizing process, or would I gradually lose consciousness and die as if falling asleep? I imagined May Kasahara coming to the well and finding me dead. She would call out to me several times, and when there was no answer she would drop a few pebbles into the well, thinking I was asleep. But I would not wake up. Then she would realize that I was dead.

I wanted to shout for someone. I wanted to scream that I was shut up inside here. That I was hungry. That the air was going bad. I felt as if I had reverted to being a helpless little child. I had run away on a whim and couldn't find my home again. I had forgotten the way. It was a dream I had had any number of times. It was the nightmare of my youth – going astray, losing the way home. I had forgotten all about those nightmares years ago. But now, at the bottom of this deep well, they came to life again with terrible vividness. Time moved backward in the dark, to be swallowed by a different kind of time.

I took the canteen from my knapsack, unscrewed the top, and, with the greatest care, so not to spill a single drop, let a small amount of water find its way into my mouth. I kept it there for a long time, savouring the moisture, then swallowed it as slowly as possible. A loud sound came from my throat as the water passed through, as if some hard, heavy object had fallen to the floor, but it was just the sound I made swallowing a few drops of water.

•

"Mr Okada!"

Someone was calling me. I heard the voice in my sleep. "Mr Okada! Mr Okada! Please wake up!"

It sounded like Creta Kano. I managed to open my eyes, but nothing had changed. I was still surrounded by darkness and couldn't see a thing. There was no clear border between sleep and wakefulness. I tried to raise myself, but there was not enough strength in my fingers. My body felt cold and shrivelled and dull, like a long-forgotten cucumber at the back of the refrigerator. My mind was wrapped tight in exhaustion and weakness. I don't care, do what you want, I'll get a hard-on in my mind again and come in reality. Go ahead, if that's what you want. In my clouded consciousness, I waited for her hands to loosen my belt. But Creta Kano's voice was coming from somewhere far overhead. "Mr Okada! Mr Okada!" it called. I looked up, to find half the well cover open and above it a beautiful, starry sky, a sky shaped like a half-moon.

"I'm here!"

I raised myself and managed to stand. Looking up, I shouted again, "I'm here!"

"Mr Okada!" said the *real* Creta Kano. "Are you down there?"

"Yes, I'm here!"

"How did *that* happen?"

"It's a long story."

"I'm sorry, I can't hear you very well. Can you speak a little louder?"

"It's a long story!" I shouted. "I'll tell you about it after I get out of here. Right now, I can't speak very loudly."

"Is this your rope ladder?"

"Yes, it is."

"How did you manage to raise it from there? Did you throw it?"

"Of course not!" Why would I have done such a thing? *How* could I have done such a thing? "Of course not! Somebody pulled it up without telling me."

"But that would make it impossible for you to get out."

"Of course it would," I said, as patiently as I could manage. "That's what happened. I can't get out of here. Can you do me a favour and let the ladder down? That way, I *can* get out."

"Yes, of course. I'll do it now."

"Wait a minute! Before you let it down, can you make sure it's anchored to the base of the tree? Otherwise –"

But she didn't respond. It seemed there was no one there any more. I focused as hard as I could on the well mouth, but I couldn't see anyone. I took the torch from my sack and aimed it upward, but the light caught no human form. What it did reveal was the rope ladder, hanging where it belonged, as if it had been there all the time. I let out a deep sigh, and as it left me, I felt a hard knot at the core of my body relax and melt away.

"Hey, there! Creta Kano!" I shouted, but still there was no answer.

The hands on my watch showed 1.07. One seven at night, of course. The stars twinkling overhead told me that much. I slipped my knapsack on my back, took one deep breath, and started up. The unstable rope ladder was difficult to climb. With each exertion, every muscle, every bone and joint in my body, creaked and cried out. I took one careful step at a time, and soon there was a hint of warmth in the surrounding air, and then a distinct smell of grass. The cries of insects reached me now. I got my hands on the edge of the well curb and with one last effort pulled myself over, all but rolling onto the soft surface of the earth. That was it: I was above ground again. For a while, I simply lay there on my back, thinking of nothing. I looked up at the sky and sucked the air deep into my lungs over and over again – the thick, warmish air of a summer night, filled with the fresh smell of life. I could smell the earth, smell the grass. The smell alone was enough to give my palms the soft sensation of touching the earth and the grass. I wanted to take them both in my hands and devour them.

There were no longer any stars to be seen in the sky: not one. The stars up there were visible only from the bottom of a well. All that hung in the sky was a nearly full, corpulent moon.

How long I went on lying there I had no idea. For a long time, all I did was listen to the beating of my heart. I felt that I could go on living for ever, doing just that – listening to the beating of my heart. At last, though, I raised myself from the ground and surveyed my surroundings. No one was there. The garden stretched out into the night, with the statue of the bird staring off at the sky, as always. No lights shone inside May Kasahara's house. There was only one mercury lamp burning in her yard, casting its pale, expressionless light as far as the deserted alley. Where could Creta Kano have disappeared to?

In any case, the first thing to do was to go home – go home, drink something, eat something, and take a nice, long shower. I probably stank something awful. I had to get rid of that smell before anything else. Then I had to fill my empty stomach. Everything else would come later.

I followed the usual route back home, but to my eyes the alley looked different, unfamiliar. Maybe because of the naked moonlight, signs of stagnation and putrefaction stood out with unusual intensity, and I could smell something like the rotting flesh of dead animals and the very definite stink of faeces and urine. In many of the houses, people were still up, talking or eating while they watched television. From one window drifted the smell of greasy food, assaulting my brain and stomach.

I passed by a groaning air-conditioning unit and received a bath of lukewarm air. I heard the sound of a shower and saw the blurred shadow of a body on a bathroom window.

I managed to scale the wall behind my house and dropped down into the yard. From here, the house looked pitch dark and almost seemed to be holding its breath. It retained no sense of warmth or intimacy. It was supposed to be the house where I was carrying on my life day after day, but now it was just an empty building without a trace of humanity. If I had any home to go back to, though, this was it.

I stepped up to the veranda and slid open the glass door. Having been shut up for so long, the air was heavy and stagnant. It smelled like a mixture of overripe fruit and insecticide. The short note I had left on the kitchen table was still there. The dishes I had washed remained stacked on the draining board. I took a glass and filled it over and over again, drinking water from the tap. The refrigerator had nothing special in it – a haphazard collection of leftovers and partly used ingredients: eggs, ham, potato salad, aubergine, lettuce, tomatoes, tofu, cream cheese, milk. I poured some of the milk onto a bowl of cornflakes and ate that. I should have been starving, but after seeing actual food in the refrigerator, I felt hardly any hunger. If anything, I was a little nauseated. Still, to soften the pain of my empty stomach, I followed the cornflakes with a few biscuits. These did nothing to make me want to eat more.

I went to the bathroom, took all my clothes off and threw them into the washing machine. Stepping under a hot shower, I scrubbed every inch of my body and washed my hair. Kumiko's nylon shower cap still hung in the bathroom. Her special shampoo was there, her conditioner, and the plastic brush she used for shampooing. Her toothbrush. Her floss. Everything looked the same as it had before she left. The only change brought about by her absence was that one simple fact: Kumiko was no longer there.

I stood before the mirror and examined my face. It was covered with black stubble. After a moment of hesitation, I decided not to shave. If I shaved now, I would probably cut myself. Tomorrow morning would be fine. I didn't have to see anybody. I brushed my teeth, rinsed my mouth out several times, and left the bathroom. Then I opened a beer, took a tomato and a lettuce from the refrigerator, and made a salad. Once I had eaten that, I began to feel a desire for more food, so I took out some potato salad, spread it between two pieces of bread, and ate it. I looked at the clock only once.

How many hours had I been down in the well? But just thinking about time made my head throb. No, I did not want to think about time. That was one thing I most definitely wanted to avoid thinking about now.

I went to the toilet and took a long pee with my eyes closed. I could hardly believe how long it lasted. I felt I might pass out while I was standing there. Afterwards, I went to the living room, stretched out on the sofa, and stared at the ceiling. It was the strangest feeling: my body was tired, but my mind was wide awake. I didn't feel the least bit sleepy.

•

It suddenly occurred to me to check the mail. Somebody might have written to me while I was in the well. I went to the hall and found that a single letter had arrived. The envelope bore no return address, but the handwriting on the front was obviously Kumiko's, each tiny character written – almost drawn – with great precision, like a design. It was a time-consuming style of writing, but it was the only way she knew. My eyes went straight to the postmark. It was smudged and barely legible, but I could make out the character *taka* and possibly *matsu*. Takamatsu in Kagawa Prefecture? Kumiko didn't know anyone in Takamatsu, as far as I was aware. The two of us had never gone there, and she had never said anything about having taken the ferry to Shikoku or crossed the new bridge. The name Takamatsu had simply never entered any of our conversations. Maybe it wasn't Takamatsu.

In any case, I took the letter to the kitchen, sat down at the table, and used scissors to open the envelope, taking care not to cut the stationery within. To calm myself, I took a swallow of my leftover beer.

"You must have been shocked and worried when I disappeared so suddenly without a word," Kumiko had written in her usual Mont Blanc blue-black ink. The paper was the standard thin letter paper sold everywhere.

I meant to write to you sooner and do a proper job of explaining everything, but time slipped by while I went on brooding over how I could express my feelings precisely and explain my present situation so that you would understand. I feel very bad about this for you.

You may have begun to suspect by now that I was seeing a man. I was sexually involved with him for close to three months. He was someone I met through work, someone you don't know at all. Nor does it matter very much who he was. I will never see him again. For me, at least, it is over. This may or may not be of some comfort to you.

Was I in love with him? There is no way I can answer that question. The question itself seems irrelevant. Was I in love with you? To that I can answer without hesitation: Yes. I was always extremely glad that I had married you. And I still feel that way. So why, you might ask, did I have to have an affair and, to top it off, run away from home? I asked myself the same question over and over again even while it was happening: Why do I have to do this?

There is no way I can explain it. I never had the slightest desire to take a lover or have an affair. Such thoughts were the farthest thing from my mind when I first started seeing him. We met a few times in connection with business, and though we found it easy to talk to each other, the most that happened after that was an occasional remark on the phone that went beyond business. He was much older than I, had a wife and children, and was not particularly attractive to me as a man: it never occurred to me that I might become involved with him.

This is not to say that I was entirely free of thoughts about getting even with you. It still rankled with me that you had once spent the night with a certain woman. I believed you when you said that you hadn't done anything with her, but the mere fact that you hadn't done anything with her didn't make it right. It was just how I felt. But still, I didn't have an affair in order to get even with you. I remember I once said I would, but that was only a threat. I slept with him because I wanted to sleep with him. Because I couldn't bear not to sleep with him. Because I couldn't suppress my own sexual desire.

We had not seen each other for some time when we had to meet on a business matter. We followed this with dinner and then went somewhere for a quick drink. Since I can't drink, of course, all I had, to be sociable, was a glass of orange juice without a drop of alcohol in it. So alcohol had nothing to do with what happened. We were just talking and eating in the most ordinary way. But then one moment, by accident, we touched, and all I could think of was that I wanted to be in his arms. The instant we touched, I knew that he wanted my body, and he seemed to sense that I wanted his. It was a totally irrational, overwhelming charge of electricity that passed between us. I felt as if the sky had fallen on me. My cheeks were burning, my heart was pounding, and I had a heavy, melting feeling below the waist. I could hardly sit straight on the barstool, it was so intense. At first I didn't realize what was happening inside me, but soon I realized it was lust. I had such a violent desire for him that I could hardly breathe. Without either of us being the first to suggest it, we walked to a nearby hotel and had wild sex.

Spelling it out as graphically as this is probably going to hurt you, but I believe that, in the long run, an honest, detailed account will be the best thing. It may be hard, but I want you to bear the pain and read on.

What I did with him had virtually nothing to do with "love". All I wanted was to be held by him and have him inside me. Never in my life had I experienced such a suffocating need for a man's body. I had read about "unbearable desire" in books, but until that day I could never really imagine what such a phrase meant.

Why this need arose in me so suddenly, why it happened not with you but with someone else, I have no idea. But the desire I felt then was impossible to suppress, nor did I even try. Please understand: not for a moment did it occur to me that I was betraying you in any way. The sex I had in that hotel bed with him was something close to madness. To be quite honest, I had never in my life felt anything so good. No, it wasn't that simple: it didn't just "feel good". My flesh was rolling in hot mud. My mind sucked in the sheer pleasure to the point of bursting – and then it burst. It was miraculous. It was one of the most wonderful things that had ever happened to me.

And then, as you know, I kept it hidden all that time. You never realized that I was having an affair. You never doubted me, even when I began coming home late. I'm sure you trusted me completely. You thought I could never betray you. And for betraying this trust of yours, I had no sense of guilt. I would call you from the hotel room and say that work was going to keep me out late. I piled one lie on top of another, but they caused me no pain. It seemed like the most natural thing in the world to do. My heart needed my life with you. The home I shared with you was the place where I belonged. It was the world I belonged to. But my body had this violent need for sex with him. Half of me was here, and half there. I knew that sooner or later the break would have to come, but at the time, it felt as if this double life would go on for ever. Over here I was living peacefully with you, and over there I was making violent love with him.

I want you to understand one thing, at least. This was never a matter of your being sexually inferior to him or lacking in sex appeal, or my being tired of sex with you. It was just that, at that time, my body experienced this violent, irrepressible hunger. I could do nothing to resist it. Why such things happen I have no idea. All I can say is that it did happen. A few times during the weeks that I was sleeping with him, I thought about having sex with you too. It seemed unfair to me, for your sake, that I should be sleeping with him but not with you. But in your arms, I had ceased to feel anything at all. You must have noticed. For close to two months, I made up all kinds of excuses to avoid having sexual relations with you.

But then one day, he asked me to leave you for him. We were such a perfect match, he said, that there was no reason for us not to be together. He would leave his family, he said. I asked him to give me time to think about it. But on the train home after I left him that night, I realized that I no longer felt a thing for him. I don't understand it myself, but the moment he asked me to join him, that special something inside me disappeared as if a strong wind had come up and blown it away. My desire for him was gone without a trace.

That was when I started to feel guilty towards you. As I wrote earlier, I had felt nothing of the sort the whole time I was feeling intense desire for him. All I had felt was how convenient it was that you had noticed nothing. I thought I could get away with anything, as long as you failed to notice. My connection with him belonged to a different world from my connection with you. After my desire for him evaporated, though, I no longer knew where I was.

I have always thought of myself as an honest person. True, I have my faults. But where important things were concerned, I had never lied to anyone or deceived myself. I had never hidden anything from you. That had been one small source of pride for me. But then, for months, I went on telling you those fatal lies without a twinge of regret.

That very fact is what started to torment me. It made me feel as if I were an empty, meaningless, worthless person. And in fact, that is probably what I am. But there is one other thing, in addition, that continues to bother me, and that is: how did I suddenly come to feel such intense, abnormal sexual desire for a man I didn't even love? This is what I simply cannot grasp. If it hadn't been for that desire, I would still be enjoying my happy life with you. And that man would still be a nice friend to chat with on occasion. But that feeling, that incredible, over-whelming lust, tore down everything we had built up over the years. It took away everything that was mine: it took away you, and the home that we had made together, and my work. Why did such a thing have to happen?

After I had my abortion three years ago, I told you that there was something I had to say to you. Do you remember? Perhaps I should have said it. Perhaps I should have told you everything that was in my heart before things came to this. This might never have happened if I had done so. But now that it has happened – even now – I don't believe that I would be able to tell you what I was feeling then. And that is because it seems to me that once I put it into words, things would be even more decisively ruined than they are now. Which is why I came to feel that the best thing I could do was to swallow it all and disappear.

I am sorry to have to tell you this, but the fact is that I was never able to have true sexual pleasure with you, either before or after we were married. I loved it when you held me in your arms, but all I ever felt was a vague, far-off sense that almost seemed to belong to someone else. This is in no way your fault. My inability to feel was purely and simply my own responsibility. There was some kind of blockage inside me, which would always hold any sexual feeling I had in check. When, for reasons I cannot grasp, that blockage was swept away by sex with him, I no longer had any idea what I should do.

There was always something very close and delicate between us, you and me. It was there from the very beginning. But now it has been lost for ever. That perfect meshing of the gears, that mythical something, has been destroyed. Because I destroyed it. Or more accurately, something made me destroy it. I am terribly sorry it ever happened. Not everyone is lucky enough to have such a chance as I had with you. I hate the thing that caused all this to happen. You have no idea how much I hate it. I want to know precisely what it is. I have to know precisely what it is. I have to search out its roots and judge and punish it. I cannot be sure that I have the strength to do so. But one thing is certain: this is my problem alone. It has nothing to do with you.

I have only one thing to ask of you, and that is this: please don't concern yourself about me any more. Please don't try to find me. Just forget about me and think about beginning a new life. Where my family is concerned, I will do the proper thing: I will write to them and explain that this is all my fault, that you are in no way responsible. They will not cause you any trouble. Formal divorce proceedings will begin quite soon, I think. That will be best for both of us. So please don't protest. Just go along with them. As far as the cloths and other things I have left behind are concerned, I'm sorry, but please just dispose of them or donate them somewhere. Everything belongs to the past now. Anything I ever used in my life with you I have no right to use now.

Goodbye.

I read the letter one more time from beginning to end and returned it to its envelope. Then I took another can of beer from the refrigerator and drank it.

If Kumiko was planning to institute divorce proceedings, that meant she had no intention of killing herself right away. That gave me some relief. But then I ran up against the fact that I had not had sex with anyone for almost two months. As she had said in her letter, Kumiko had resisted sleeping with me all that time. She had symptoms of a mild bladder infection, she said, and the doctor had told her to refrain from sex for a while. And of course I had believed her. I had no reason not to.

During those two months, I had had relations with women in my dreams – or in some world that, within the limits of my vocabulary, I could only call a dream – with Creta Kano and with the telephone woman. But now that I thought about it, two months had gone by since the last time I had slept with a real woman in the real world. Lying on the sofa, staring at my own hands resting on my chest, I thought about the last time I had seen Kumiko's body. I thought about the soft curve of her back when I zipped her dress up, and the smell of cologne behind her ears. If what she said in the letter was the irrevocable truth, however, I would probably never sleep with Kumiko again. She had written it with such clarity and finality: what else could it be but the irrevocable truth?

The more I thought about the possibility that my relationship with

Kumiko had become a thing of the past, the more I began to miss the gentle warmth of that body that had once belonged to me. I had enjoyed sleeping with her. Of course, I had enjoyed it before we were married, but even after some years had gone by and the initial thrill had faded, I enjoyed having sex with Kumiko. Her slender back, the nape of her neck, her legs, her breasts – I could recall the touch of every part of her with total vividness. I could recall all the things I had done for her and she had done for me in the course of our sexual union.

But now Kumiko had joined her body with that of someone I did not know – and with an intensity I could hardly imagine. She had discovered a pleasure she had been unable to obtain from sex with me. While she was doing it with him, she had most likely squirmed and writhed enough to make the bed shake and had released groans loud enough to be audible in the next room. She had probably done things with him that she would never have done with me. I went and opened the refrigerator, took out a beer, and drank it. Then I ate some potato salad. Wanting to hear music, I turned on the FM radio, tuning in to a classical station at low volume. "I'm so tired today," Kumiko would say. "I'm just not in the mood. I'm sorry. Really." I'd answer, "That's OK, no big deal." When Tchaikovsky's *Serenade for Strings* ended, a little piano piece came on that sounded like something by Schumann. It was familiar, but I couldn't recall the title. When it was over, the female announcer said it had been the seventh of Schumann's *Forest Scenes*, titled "Bird as Prophet". I imagined Kumiko twisting her hips beneath the other man, raising her legs, planting her fingernails in his back, drooling on the sheets. The announcer explained that Schumann had created a scene of fantasy in which a mysterious bird lived in the forest, foretelling the future.

What had I ever known about Kumiko? Soundlessly, I crushed the empty beer can in my hand and threw it into the bin. Could it be true that the Kumiko I had thought I understood, the Kumiko I had held close to me and joined my body with over the years – that Kumiko was nothing but the most superficial layer of the person Kumiko herself, just as the greater part of this world belongs to the realm of the jellyfish? If so, what about those six years we had spent together? What had they been? What had they meant?

•

I was reading Kumiko's letter yet again when the phone rang. The sound shot me out of the sofa. Who could possibly be calling at 2 in the morning? Kumiko? No, she would never call here. Probably May Kasahara.

She had seen me leave the empty house and decided to give me a call. Or possibly Creta Kano. She wanted to explain why she had disappeared. It could be the telephone woman. She might be trying to convey a message to me. May Kasahara had been right: there were just a few too many women around me. I wiped the sweat from my face with a towel that lay nearby, and when I was ready I picked up the receiver. "Hello," I said. "Hello," came the voice from the other end. It did not belong to May Kasahara. Neither was it Creta Kano's voice, or the voice of the enigmatic woman. It was Malta Kano.

"Hello," she said, "is that Mr Okada? My name is Malta Kano. I wonder if you remember me?"

"Of course. I remember you very well," I said, trying to still the pounding of my heart. How could I not have remembered her?

"I must apologize for telephoning you so late at night. This is something of an emergency, however. I fully recognized what a rude intrusion this would be and how angry it would make you, but I felt compelled to call nevertheless. I am terribly sorry."

She need not be concerned, I assured her: I was up, in any case, and not the least bit bothered.

12

Discovered When Shaving

•

Discovered When Waking

"The reason I am calling you so late at night, Mr Okada, is that I felt I ought to reach you at the earliest possible opportunity," said Malta Kano. Listening to her speak, I had the impression that she was choosing and arranging each word into well-ordered sentences according to strict principles of logic – which was what she always did. "If you have no objection, there are several questions that I wish to be permitted to ask you, Mr Okada. May I proceed?"

Receiver in hand, I lowered myself onto the sofa. "Go right ahead, ask me anything you like," I said.

"Have you by any chance been away these past two days, Mr Okada? I tried telephoning you any number of times, but you seemed always to be out."

"Well, yes, I was out. I wanted to get away from the house for a while. I needed to be alone to do some thinking. I've got lots of things I need to think about."

"Yes, Mr Okada, I am very much aware of that. I understand how you feel. A change of scene can be a very good thing when one wishes to think clearly and carefully about something. In this case, however, Mr Okada – and I know this will sound as if I am prying – were you not somewhere *very* far away?"

"Well, not so *very* far away," I said, with deliberate ambiguity. I switched the receiver from my left hand to my right. "How can I put this? I was in a somewhat cut-off place. I really can't go into it, though, in great detail. I have my reasons. And I only got back a little while ago. I'm too tired for long explanations."

"Of course, Mr Okada. I understand. Everyone has their reasons. I will not press you to explain. You must be very tired indeed: I can tell from the sound of your voice. Please do not concern yourself about me. I should not be bothering you with a lot of questions at a time like this. I am terribly sorry. We can always discuss this matter at a more appropriate time. I know it was terribly rude of me to ask such a personal question, but I did so only because I was worried that something very bad had happened to you over the past few days."

I tried to make an appropriate response, but the little noise that came from my throat sounded less like a response than the gasp of an aquatic animal that had breathed the wrong way. *Something very bad*, I thought. Of all the things that were happening to me, which were bad and which were not bad? Which were all right and which were not all right?

"Thank you for being so concerned about me," I said, getting my voice to work properly, "but I'm fine at the moment. I can't say that something good has happened to me, but there's been nothing especially bad, either."

"I am glad to hear that."

"I'm just tired, that's all," I added.

Malta Kano made a dainty little sound of clearing her throat. "By the way, Mr Okada, I wonder if you might have noticed any major physical change during the past few days?"

"A physical change? In me?"

"Yes, Mr Okada. Some kind of change in your body."

I raised my face and looked at my reflection in the glass patio door, but I couldn't make out anything that could be called a physical change. I had scrubbed every part of my body in the shower but had noticed nothing then, either. "What kind of change did you have in mind?" I asked.

"I have no idea what it might be, but it should be very obvious to anyone who looks at you."

I stretched my left hand open on the table and stared at the palm, but it was just my usual palm. It had not changed in any way that I could perceive. It had not become covered in gold foil, nor had it developed webs between the fingers. It was neither beautiful nor ugly. "When you say that it should be very obvious to anyone who looks at me, what do you mean? Something like wings sprouting on my back?"

"It could be something like that," said Malta Kano, in her usual even tone. "Of course, I mean that as *one possibility*."

"Of course," I said.

"So, then, *have* you noticed some such change?"

"Not really. Not so far, at least. I mean, if wings had sprouted on my back, I couldn't help but notice, don't you think?"

"Of course," said Malta Kano. "But do be careful, Mr Okada. To know one's own state is not a simple matter. One cannot look directly at one's own face with one's own eyes, for example. One has no choice but to look at one's reflection in the mirror. Through experience, we come to believe that the image is correct, but it is just a belief."

"I'll be careful," I said.

"I do have one more thing I would like to ask you, Mr Okada. For some time now, I have been unable to establish contact with my sister Creta – just as I lost contact with you. It may be a coincidence, but I find it very strange. I was wondering if, perhaps, you might have some knowledge of the circumstances behind this."

"Creta Kano?!"

"Yes," said Malta Kano. "Does anything come to mind in that regard?"

No, nothing came to mind, I replied. I had no clear basis for thinking so, but I felt that for the time being, it would be better if I said nothing to Malta Kano about the fact that I had not long ago spoken with Creta Kano in person and that, immediately afterwards, she had disappeared. It was just a feeling.

"Creta was worried about having lost contact with you, Mr Okada. She went out last night, saying that she planned to visit your home and see what she could find there, but even at this late hour she has not returned. And for some reason, I can no longer sense her presence."

"I see. Well, if she should happen to come here, I'll tell her to contact you right away," I said.

Malta Kano remained silent for some time. "To tell you the truth, Mr Okada, I am worried about Creta. As you know, the work that she and I do is far from ordinary. But she is not as well versed in matters of that world as I am. I do not mean to imply that she is not gifted. In fact, she is very gifted. But she is not yet fully acclimatized to her gift."

"I see."

Malta Kano fell silent once again. This silence was longer than the last one. I sensed a certain indecision on her part.

"Hello. Are you still there?" I asked.

"Yes, Mr Okada, I am still here," she replied.

"If I see Creta, I'll be sure to tell her to get in touch with you," I said again.

"Thank you very much," said Malta Kano. Then, after apologizing for the late-night call, she hung up. I hung up, too, and looked at my reflection in the glass one more time. Then the thought struck me: I might never speak with Malta Kano again. This could be the last contact I would ever have with her. She could disappear from my life for ever. I had no special reason for thinking this: it was just a feeling that came to me.

•

Suddenly I thought about the rope ladder. I had left it hanging down the well. The sooner I retrieved it, the better. Problems could arise if someone found it there. And then there was the sudden disappearance of Creta Kano. I had last seen her at the well.

I shoved my torch into my pocket, put on my shoes, stepped down into the garden, and climbed over the wall again. Then I passed down the alley to the vacant house. May Kasahara's house was pitch dark. The hands of my watch were nearing 3 a.m. I entered the yard of the vacant house and headed straight for the well. The rope ladder was still anchored to the base of the tree and hanging down into the well, which was still just half open.

Something prompted me to peer down into the well and call Creta Kano's name in a kind of whispered shout. There was no answer. I pulled out my torch and aimed it down the well. The beam did not reach bottom, but I heard a tiny moaning sound. I tried calling the name again.

"It's all right. I'm here," said Creta Kano.

"What are you *doing* in a place like this?" I asked, in a low voice.

"What am I *doing*? I'm doing the same thing *you* were doing, Mr Okada," she replied, with obvious puzzlement. "I'm thinking. This really *is* a perfect place for thinking, isn't it?"

"Well, yes, I guess it is," I said. "But your sister called me at home a little while ago. She's very worried about you. It's the middle of the night and you're still not home, and she says she can't feel your presence. She wanted me to tell you to get in touch with her right away if I heard from you."

"I see. Well, thank you for taking the trouble."

"Never mind about that, Creta Kano. Will you do me a favour and come out of there? I have to talk to you."

She did not reply.

I switched off my torch and returned it to my pocket.

"Why don't you come down here, Mr Okada? The two of us could sit here and talk."

It might not be a bad idea, I thought, to climb down into the well again and talk with Creta Kano, but then I thought about the mouldy darkness at the bottom of the well and got a heavy feeling in my stomach.

"No, sorry, but I'm not going down there again. And you ought to come out, too. Somebody might pull the ladder up again. And the air is stale."

"I know that. But I want to stay down here a little longer. Don't worry yourself about me."

There was nothing I could do as long as Creta Kano had no intention of coming out of the well.

"When I talked to your sister on the phone, I didn't tell her I saw you here. I hope that was the right thing to do. I just had this feeling that it'd be better to say nothing."

"You were right," said Creta Kano. "Please don't tell my sister I am here." A moment later, she added, "I don't want to worry her, but I need a chance to think sometimes too. I will come out as soon as I am done. I would like to be alone now, if you would be so kind. I will not cause you any trouble."

I decided to leave her and go back to the house for the time being. I could come in the morning and check up on her. If May Kasahara pulled the ladder up again during the night, I could deal with the situation then and help Creta Kano climb out of the well one way or another. I went home, undressed, and stretched out in bed. Picking up the book I had been reading, I opened it. I was too much on edge to get to sleep right away, but before I had read two full pages, I realized I was dozing off. I closed the book, turned out the light, and the next moment was sound asleep.

•

It was 9.30 in the morning by the time I awoke. Concerned about Creta Kano, I dressed without bothering to wash my face and hurried down the alley to the vacant house. The clouds hung low in the sky, and the humid morning air seemed to threaten rain at any moment. The rope ladder was gone from the well. Someone must have untied it from the base of the tree and carried it off somewhere. Both halves of the well cover were set tightly in place, with a stone on each half. Opening one side and peering down into the well, I called Creta Kano's name. There was no answer. I tried a few more times, waiting after each call. Thinking she might be asleep, I tossed a few pebbles inside, but there no longer seemed to be anybody at the bottom of the well. Creta Kano must have climbed out of the well when morning came, untied the ladder, and taken it with her. I set the cover in place and moved away from the well.

In the alley again, I leaned against the fence of the vacant house, watching May Kasahara's house for a time. I thought she might notice me there, as she usually did, and come out, but there was no sign of her. All around was silence – no people, no noises of any kind, not even the cry of a cicada. I passed the time digging at the surface of the ground with the toe of my shoe. Something felt different about the neighbourhood, unfamiliar – as if, in the days I was down in the well, the old reality of this place had been supplanted by a new reality, which had settled in and taken over. I had been feeling this, somewhere deep down, ever since I had emerged from the well and gone home.

Walking back down the alley to my house, I went into the bathroom and brushed my teeth. Several days' worth of black stubble covered my face. I looked like a newly rescued shipwreck victim. This was the first time in my life I had ever let my beard grow so long. I toyed with the idea of really letting it grow but after a few moments' thought decided to shave it. For some reason, it just seemed better to keep the face I had had when Kumiko left.

I softened up my beard with a hot towel and covered my face with a thick layer of shaving cream. I then proceeded to shave, slowly and carefully, so as to avoid cutting myself: first the chin, then the left cheek, then the right cheek. As I was finishing the right cheek, what I saw in the mirror made me catch my breath. It was a blue-black stain of some kind. At first I thought I might have smeared myself with something by accident. I wiped off the remaining traces of shaving cream, gave my face a good wash with soap and water, and scrubbed at the stained area with a flannel. But still the stain would not come off. It seemed to have penetrated deep into the skin. I stroked it with a finger. That one patch of skin felt just a little warmer than the rest of my face, but otherwise it had no particular feeling. It was a mark. I had a mark on my cheek in the exact location where, in the well, I had had the sensation of heat.

I brought my face up to the mirror and examined the mark with the utmost care. Located just beyond the right cheekbone, it was about the size of an infant's palm. Its bluish colour was close to black, like the blue-black Mont Blanc ink that Kumiko always used.

One possible explanation was that this was an allergic reaction. I might have come in contact with something in the well that caused an eruption of the skin, the way lacquer can do. But what could there have been down there, in the bottom of the well, to cause such a thing? I had examined every nook and cranny of the place with my torch, finding nothing there but the dirt bottom and the concrete wall. Besides, did allergies or eruptions ever leave such well-defined marks?

A mild panic overtook me. For a few moments, I lost all sense of direction, as when a huge wave crashes over you on the beach, dragging you in. The flannel fell from my hand. I knocked over the wastebasket and stubbed my foot against something, mumbling meaningless syllables all the while. Then I managed to regain my composure and, leaning against the sink, began thinking calmly about how to deal with this fact.

The best thing I could do for now was to wait and see. I could always go to a doctor later. It might be a temporary condition, something that would heal itself, like a lacquer eruption. It had formed in a few short days, so it might disappear just as quickly. I went to the kitchen and made myself some coffee. I was hungry, but whenever I tried to eat anything, my appetite would vanish like water in a mirage.

I stretched out on the sofa and watched the rain that had begun to fall. Every now and then I would go to the bathroom and look in the mirror, but I could see no change in the mark. It had dyed that area of my cheek a deep, dark – almost handsome – blue.

I could think of only one thing that might have caused this, and that was my having passed through the wall in my predawn dreamlike illusion in the well, with the telephone woman leading me by the hand. She had pulled me through the wall so that we could escape from the dangerous *someone* who had opened the door and was coming into the room. The moment I passed through the wall, I had had the clear sensation of heat on my cheek – in the exact spot where I now had this mark. Of course, whatever causal connection there might be between my passing through the wall and the forming of a mark on my face remained unestablished.

The man without a face had spoken to me in the hotel lobby. "This is the wrong time," he had warned me. "You don't belong here now." But I had ignored his warning and continued on. I was angry at Noboru

Wataya, angry at my own confusion. And as a result, perhaps, I had received this mark.

Or the mark could be a brand that had been left on me by that strange dream or illusion or whatever it was. *That was no dream,* they were telling me through the mark: *It really happened. And every time you look in the mirror now, you will be forced to remember it.*

I shook my head. Too many things were being left unexplained. The one thing I understood for sure was that I didn't understand a thing. A dull throbbing started in my head. I couldn't think any more. I felt no urge to do anything. I took a sip of lukewarm coffee and went on watching the rain.

•

That afternoon, I called my uncle for a chat. I needed to talk to someone – it didn't matter much who – about this feeling I had that I was being ripped away from the world of reality.

When he asked how Kumiko was doing, I said fine and let it go at that. She was on a short business trip at the moment, I added. I could have told him what had really been happening, but to put recent events into some kind of order that would make sense to a third party would have been impossible. They didn't make much sense to me, so how could I explain them to someone else? I decided to keep the truth from my uncle for the time being.

"You used to live in this house, didn't you?" I asked.

"Sure did," he said. "Six or seven years altogether. Wait a minute . . . I bought the place when I was thirty-five and lived there till I was forty-two. Seven years. Moved into this condo when I got married. I lived there alone all that time."

"I was just wondering, did anything bad happen to you while you were here?"

"Anything bad? Like what?"

"Like you became ill or you split up with a woman or something."

My uncle gave a hearty laugh. "I split up with more than one woman, that's for sure. But not just while I was living there. Nah, I couldn't count that as anything especially bad. Nobody I hated to lose, tell you the truth. As far as illness goes . . . hmm. No, I don't think so. I had a small growth removed from the back of my neck, but that's about all I remember. The barber found it, said I ought to have it removed just to be safe. So I went to the doctor, but it turned out to be nothing much. That was the first time I went to see the doctor while I was living in that house – and the last. I ought to get a rebate on my health insurance!"

"No bad memories you associate with the place, then?"

"Nope, none," said my uncle, after he had thought about it for a moment. "But what's this about, all of a sudden?"

"Nothing much," I said. "Kumiko saw a fortune-teller the other day and came home with an earful about this house – that it's unlucky, things like that," I lied. "*I* think it's nonsense, but I promised to ask you about it."

"Hmm. What do they call it? 'House physiognomy'? I don't know anything about that stuff. But I've lived in the place, and my impression is that it's OK, it doesn't have any problems. Miyawaki's place is another matter, of course, but you're pretty far away from there."

"What kind of people lived here after you moved out?" I asked.

"Let's see: after me a school teacher and his family lived there for three years, and then a young couple for five years. He ran some kind of business, but I don't remember what it was. I can't swear that everybody lived a happy life in that house: I had a property agent managing the place for me. I never met the people, and I don't know why they moved out, but I never heard about anything bad that happened to any of them. I just assumed the place got a little small for them and they wanted to build their own homes, that kind of thing."

"Somebody once told me that the flow of this place has been obstructed. Does that ring a bell?"

"The flow has been obstructed?"

"I don't know what it means, either," I said. "It's just what they told me."

My uncle thought it over for a while. "No, nothing comes to mind. But it might have been a bad idea to fence off both ends of the alley. A road without an entrance or exit is a strange thing, when you stop to think about it. The fundamental principle of things like roads and rivers is for them to flow. Block them and they stagnate."

"I see what you mean," I said. "Now, there's one more thing I need to ask you. Did you ever hear the cry of the wind-up bird in this neighbourhood?"

"The wind-up bird?" said my uncle. "What's that?"

I explained about the wind-up bird, how it came to the tree at the back once a day and made that spring-winding cry.

"That's news to me," he said. "I've never seen or heard one. I like birds, and I've always made a point of listening to their calls, but this is the first time I've ever heard of such a thing. You mean it has something to do with the house?"

"No, not really. I was just wondering if you'd ever heard of it."

"You know, if you really want the lowdown on things like this – the people who lived there after me and that kind of stuff – you ought to talk to old Mr Ichikawa, the property agent across from the station. That's Setagaya Dai-ichi Realtors. Tell him I sent you. He handled that house for me for years. He's been living in the neighbourhood since the year dot, and he just might tell you everything you'd ever want to know. He's the one who told me about the Miyawaki house. He's one of those old guys that love to talk. You ought to go see him."

"Thanks. I will," I said.

"So anyway, how's the job hunt going?"

"Nothing yet. To tell you the truth, I haven't been looking very hard. Kumiko's working, and I'm taking care of the house, and we're managing for now."

My uncle seemed to be thinking about something for a few moments. Then he said, "Let me know if it ever gets to the point where you just can't make it. I might be able to give you a hand."

"Thanks," I said. "I will." And so our conversation ended.

I thought about calling the old property agent and asking him about the background of this house and about the people who had lived here before me, but it seemed ridiculous even to be thinking about such nonsense. I decided to forget it.

The rain kept falling at the same gentle rate throughout the afternoon, wetting the roofs of the houses, wetting the trees in the yards, wetting the earth. I had toast and soup for lunch and spent the rest of the afternoon on the sofa. I wanted to do some shopping, but the thought of the mark on my face made me hesitate. I was sorry I hadn't let my beard grow. I still had some vegetables in the refrigerator, and there were some cans in the cupboard. I had rice and I had eggs. I could feed myself for another two or three days if I kept my expectations low.

Lying on the sofa, I didn't think about anything. I read a book, I listened to a classical music tape, I stared out at the rain falling in the garden. My cogitative powers seemed to have reached an all-time low, thanks perhaps to that long period of all-too-concentrated thinking in the dark well bottom. If I tried to think seriously about anything, I felt a dull ache in my head, as if it were being squeezed in the jaws of a padded vice. If I tried to recall anything, every muscle and nerve in my body seemed to creak with the effort. I felt I had turned into the tin man from *The Wizard of Oz*, my joints rusted and in need of oil.

Every now and then I would go to the lavatory and examine the mark on my face, but it remained unchanged. It neither spread nor shrank. The intensity of its colour neither increased nor decreased. At one point, I noticed that I had left some hair unshaved on my upper lip. In my confusion at discovering the mark on my right cheek, I had forgotten to finish shaving. I washed my face again, spread on shaving cream, and took off what was left.

In the course of my occasional trips to the mirror, I thought of what Malta Kano had said on the phone: that I should be careful; that through experience, we come to believe that the image in the mirror is correct. To make certain, I went to the bedroom and looked at my face in the full-length mirror that Kumiko used whenever she got dressed. But the mark was still there. It was not just something caused by the other mirror.

I was unaware of any physical abnormality apart from the mark. I took my temperature, but it was the same as always. Other than the fact that I felt little hunger, for someone who had not eaten in almost three days, and that I experienced slight nausea every now and then (which was probably a continuation of what I had felt at the bottom of the well), my body was entirely normal.

The afternoon was a quiet one. The phone never rang. No letters arrived. No one came down the alley. No voices of neighbours disturbed the stillness. No cats crossed the garden, no birds came and called. Now and then a cicada would cry, but not with the usual intensity.

I began to feel hungry just before 7 o'clock, so I fixed myself a dinner of tinned food and vegetables. I listened to the evening news on the radio for the first time in ages, but nothing special had been happening in the world. Some teenagers had been killed in an accident on the expressway when the driver of their car had failed in an attempt to pass another car and crashed into a wall. The branch manager and staff of a major bank were under police investigation in connection with an illegal loan they had made. A thirty-six-year-old housewife from Machida had been beaten to death with a hammer by a young man in the street. But these were all events from some other, distant world. The only thing happening in my world was the rain falling in the yard. Soundlessly. Gently.

When the clock showed 9, I moved from the sofa to bed, and after finishing a chapter of the book I had started, I turned out the light and went to sleep.

I awoke with a start in the middle of some kind of dream. I could not remember what had been happening in the dream, but it was clear it had been filled with tension, because my heart was pounding. The room was still pitch dark. For a while after I awoke, I could not remember where I was. It was quite some time before I realized that I was in my own house, in my own bed. The hands of the alarm clock showed it to be just after 2 in the morning. My irregular sleeping habits in the well were probably responsible for these unpredictable cycles of sleep and wakefulness. Once my confusion died down, I felt the need to pee. It was probably the beer I'd drunk. I would have preferred to go back to sleep, but I had no choice in the matter. When I resigned myself to the fact and sat up in bed, my hand brushed against the skin of the person sleeping next to me. This came as no surprise. That was where Kumiko always slept. I was used to having someone sleeping by my side. But then I realized that Kumiko was no longer with me. She had left. *Some other person was sleeping next to me.*

I held my breath and turned on the light by the bed. It was Creta Kano.

13

Creta Kano's Story Continued

•

Creta Kano was stark naked. Facing my side of the bed, she lay there asleep, with nothing on, not even a cover, revealing two well-shaped breasts, two small pink nipples, and, below a perfectly flat stomach, a black triangle of pubic hair, looking like a shaded area in a drawing. Her skin was very white, with a newly minted glow. At a loss to explain her presence here, I nevertheless went on staring at her beautiful body. She had her knees tight together and slightly bent, her legs in perfect alignment. Her hair fell forward, covering half her face, which made it impossible for me to see her eyes, but she was obviously in a deep sleep: my turning on the bedside lamp had caused not the slightest tremble, and her breathing was quiet and regular. I was now wide awake through. I took a thin summer spread from the wardrobe and placed it over her. Then I turned out the lamp and, still in my pyjamas, went to the kitchen to sit at the table for a while.

I recalled my mark. That patch on my cheek was still warm to the touch. The mark was still there, all right – I had no need to look in the mirror. It wasn't the kind of insignificant thing that just disappears by itself overnight. I thought about looking up a nearby dermatologist in the phone book when it become light, but how could I answer if a doctor asked me what I thought the cause might be? I was in a well for two or three days. No, it had nothing to do with work or anything; I was just there to do a little thinking. I reckoned the bottom of a well would be a good place for that. No, I didn't take any food with me. No, it wasn't on my property; it belonged to another house. A vacant house in the neighbourhood. I went in without permission.

I sighed. I could never say these things to anyone, of course.

I rested my elbows on the table and, without really intending to, found myself thinking in vivid detail about Creta Kano's naked body. She was sound asleep in my bed. I thought about the time in my dream when I joined my body with hers as she wore Kumiko's dress. I still had a clear impression of the touch of her skin, the weight of her flesh. Without a step-by-step investigation of that event, I would not be able to distinguish the point at which the real ended and the unreal took over. The wall separating the two regions had begun to melt. In my memory, at least, the real and the unreal seemed to be residing together with equal weight and vividness. I had joined my body with Creta Kano's, and at the same time, I had not.

To clear my head of these jumbled sexual images, I had to go to the basin and splash my face with cold water. A little while later, I looked in on Creta Kano. She was still sound asleep. She had pushed the cover down to her waist. From where I stood, I could see only her back. It reminded me of my last view of Kumiko's back. Now that I thought about it, Creta Kano's figure was strikingly similar to Kumiko's. I had failed to notice the resemblance until now because their hair and their taste in clothes and their make-up were so utterly different. They were the same height and appeared to be about the same weight. They probably wore the same dress size.

I carried my own summer quilt to the living room, stretched out on the sofa, and opened my book. I had been reading a history book from the library. It was all about Japanese management of Manchuria before the war and the battle with the Soviets in Nomonhan. Lieutenant Mamiya's story had aroused my interest in continental affairs of the period, and I had borrowed several books on the subject. Now, however, less than ten minutes into the detailed historical narrative, I was falling asleep. I laid the book on the floor, intending to rest my eyes for a few moments, but I fell into a deep sleep, with the lights still on.

A sound from the kitchen woke me up. When I went to investigate, Creta Kano was there, making breakfast, wearing a white T-shirt and blue shorts, both of which belonged to Kumiko.

"Where are your clothes?" I demanded, standing in the kitchen door.

"Oh, I'm sorry. You were asleep, so I took the liberty of borrowing some of your wife's clothing. I know it was terribly forward of me, but I didn't have a thing to wear," said Creta Kano, turning just her head to look at me. At some point since I last saw her, she had reverted to her usual sixties style of hair and make-up, lacking only the fake eyelashes.

"That's no problem," I said. "What I want to know is what happened to your clothes."

"I lost them," she said simply.

"Lost them?"

"Yes. I lost them somewhere."

I stepped into the kitchen and watched, leaning against the table, as Creta Kano made an omelette. With deft movements, she cracked the eggs, added seasoning, and beat the mixture.

"Meaning you came here naked?"

"Yes, that is correct," said Creta Kano, as if it were the most natural thing in the world. "I was completely naked. You know that, Mr Okada. You put the cover on me."

"True enough," I mumbled. "But what I'd like to know is, where and how did you lose your clothing, and how did you manage to get here with nothing on?"

"I don't know any more than you do," said Creta Kano, shaking the frying pan to fold the omelette over on itself.

"You don't know any more than I do," I repeated.

Creta Kano slipped the omelette onto a plate and garnished it with a few stalks of freshly steamed broccoli. She had also made toast, which she set on the table, along with coffee. I put out the butter and salt and pepper. Then, like a newly married couple, we sat down to breakfast, facing each other.

It was then that I remembered my mark. Creta Kano had shown no surprise when she looked at me, and she asked me nothing about it. I reached up to touch the spot and found it slightly warm, as before.

"Does that hurt, Mr Okada?"

"No, not at all," I said.

Creta Kano stared at my face. "It looks like a mark," she said.

"It looks like a mark to me too," I said. "I'm wondering whether I should show it to a doctor or not."

"It strikes me as something that a doctor would not be able to help with."

"You may be right," I said. "But I can't just ignore it."

Fork in hand, Creta Kano thought for a moment. "If you have

shopping or other business, I could do it for you. You can stay inside as long as you like, if you would rather not go out."

"I'm grateful for the offer, but you must have your own things to do, and I can't just stay holed up here for ever."

Creta Kano thought about that for a while too. "Malta Kano would probably know how to deal with this."

"Would you mind getting in touch with her for me, then?"

"Malta Kano gets in touch with other people, but she does not allow people to get in touch with her." Creta Kano bit into a piece of broccoli.

"But *you* can get in touch with her, I'm sure?"

"Of course. We're sisters."

"Well, next time you talk to her, why don't you ask her about my mark? Or you could ask her to get in touch with me."

"I am sorry, but that is something I cannot do. I am not allowed to approach my sister on someone else's behalf. It's a sort of rule we have."

Buttering my toast, I let out a sigh. "You mean to say, if I have something I need to talk to Malta Kano about, all I can do is wait for her to get in touch with me?"

"That is exactly what I mean," said Creta Kano. Then she nodded. "But about that mark. Unless it hurts or itches, I suggest that you forget about it for a while. I never let things like that bother me. And you should not let it bother you, either, Mr Okada. People just get these things sometimes."

"I wonder," I said.

For several minutes after that, we went on eating our breakfast in silence. I hadn't eaten breakfast with another person for quite a while now, and this breakfast was particularly delicious. Creta Kano seemed pleased when I told her this.

"Anyhow," I said, "about your clothes . . ."

"Does it bother you that I put on your wife's clothing without permission?" she asked, with obvious concern.

"No, not at all. I don't care what you wear of Kumiko's. She left them here, after all. What I'm concerned about is how you lost your own clothes."

"And not just my clothes. My shoes too."

"So how did it happen?"

"I can't remember," said Creta Kano. "All I know is I woke up in your bed with nothing on. I can't remember what happened before that."

"You *did* go down into the well, didn't you – after I left?"

"That I do remember. And I fell asleep down there. But I can't remember anything after that."

"Which means you don't have any recollection of how you got out of the well?"

"None at all. There is a gap in my memory." Creta Kano held up both index fingers, about eight inches apart. How much time that was supposed to represent I had no idea.

"I don't suppose you remember what you did with the rope ladder, either. It's gone, you know."

"I don't know anything about the ladder. I don't even remember if I climbed it to get out of the well."

I stared at the coffee cup in my hand for a time. "Do you mind showing me the bottoms of your feet?" I asked.

"No, not at all," said Creta Kano. She sat down in the chair next to mine and stretched her legs out in my direction so that I could see the soles of her feet. I took her ankles in my hands and examined her soles. They were clean. Beautifully formed, the soles had not a mark on them – no cuts, no mud, nothing at all.

"No mud, no cuts," I said.

"I see," said Creta Kano.

"It was raining all day yesterday. If you lost your shoes somewhere and walked here from there, you should have mud on your feet. And you must have come in through the garden. But your feet are clean, and there's no mud anywhere."

"I see."

"Which means you didn't walk here barefoot from anywhere."

Creta Kano inclined her head to one side as if impressed. "This is all logically consistent," she said.

"It may be logically consistent, but it's not getting us anywhere," I said. "Where did you lose your clothes, including your shoes, and how did you walk here from there?"

Creta Kano shook her head. "I have no idea," she said.

•

While she stood at the sink, absorbed in washing the dishes, I stayed at the kitchen table, thinking about these things. Of course, I had no idea, either.

"Do these things happen to you often – that you can't remember where you've been?" I asked.

"This is not the first time that something like this has happened to me, when I can't recall where I have been or what I was doing. It doesn't happen often, but it does happen to me now and then. I once lost some clothes, too. But this is the first time I've lost all my clothes and my shoes and everything."

Creta Kano turned off the water and wiped the table with a dish cloth.

"You know, Creta Kano," I said, "you haven't told me your whole story. Last time, you broke off in the middle and disappeared. Remember? If you don't mind, I'd like to hear the rest. You told me how the mob got hold of you and made you work as one of their prostitutes, but you didn't tell me what happened after you met Noboru Wataya and slept with him."

Creta Kano leaned against the kitchen sink and looked at me. Drops of water on her hands ran down her fingers and fell to the floor. The shape of her nipples showed clearly through the white T-shirt, a vivid reminder of the naked body I had seen the night before.

"All right, then. I'll tell you everything that happened after that. Right now."

Creta Kano sat down once again in the seat opposite mine.

"The reason I left that day when I was in the middle of my story, Mr Okada, is that I was not prepared to tell it all. I had started my story because I felt I ought to tell you, as honestly as possible, what really happened to me. But I found I could not go all the way to the end. You must have been shocked when I disappeared so suddenly."

Creta Kano put her hands on the table and looked straight at me as she spoke.

"Well, yes, I was shocked, though it was not the most shocking thing that's happened to me lately."

•

"As I told you before, the very last customer I had as a prostitute of the flesh was Noboru Wataya. The second time I met him, as a client of Malta Kano's, I recognized him immediately. It would have been impossible for me to forget him. Whether he remembered me or not I cannot be certain. Mr Wataya is not a person who shows his feelings.

"But let me go back and put things in order. First I will tell you about the time I had Noboru Wataya as a customer. That would be six years ago.

"As I told you before, I was in a state at that time in which I had no perception of pain at all. And not only pain: I had no sensations of any kind. I lived in a bottomless numbness. Of course, I don't mean to say that I was unable to feel any sensations at all – I knew when something was hot or cold or painful. But these sensations came to me as if from a distance, from a world that had nothing to do with me. Which is why I felt no resistance to the idea of having sexual relations with men for money. No matter what anyone did to me, the sensations I felt did not belong to me. My unfeeling flesh was not my flesh.

"Now, let's see, I told you about how I had been recruited by the mob's prostitution ring. When they told me to sleep with men I did it, and when they paid me I accepted it. I left off at that point."

I nodded to her.

"That day they told me to go to a room on the sixteenth floor of a downtown hotel. The client had the unusual name of Wataya. I knocked on the door and went in to find the man sitting on the sofa. He appeared to have been drinking room-service coffee while reading a book. He wore a green polo shirt and brown cotton trousers. His hair was short, and he wore brown-framed glasses. On the coffee table in front of him were his cup and a coffeepot and the book. He seemed to have been deeply absorbed in his reading: there was a kind of excitement still in his eyes. His features were in no way remarkable, but those eyes of his had an energy that was almost weird. When I first saw them, I thought for a moment that I was in the wrong room. But it was not the wrong room. The man told me to come inside and lock the door.

"Still seated on the sofa, without saying a word, he ran his eyes over my body. From head to foot. That was what usually happened when I entered a client's room. Most men would look me over. Excuse me for asking, Mr Okada, but have you ever been with a prostitute?"

I said that I had not.

"It's as if they were looking over merchandise. It doesn't take long to get used to being looked at like that. They are paying money for flesh, after all; it makes sense for them to examine the goods. But the way that man looked at me was different. He seemed to be looking through my flesh to something on the other side. His eyes made me feel uneasy, as if I had become a half-transparent human being.

"I was a little confused, I suppose. I dropped my handbag on the floor. It made a small sound, but I was in such an abstracted state that, for a time, I was almost unaware of what I had done. Then I stooped down to pick up the bag. The clasp had opened when it hit the floor, and some of my cosmetics had fallen out. I picked up my eyebrow pencil and lip cream and a small bottle of eau de cologne, returning each of them to my bag. He kept those eyes of his trained on me the whole time.

"When I had finished gathering up my things from the floor and putting them back in the bag, he told me to undress. I asked him if it would be all right for me to take a shower first, because I had been perspiring quite a bit. The weather was hot that day, and I had been sweating on the subway. He didn't care about that, he said. He didn't have much time. He wanted me to undress right away.

"Once I was naked, he told me to lie face down on the bed, which I did. He ordered me to stay still, to keep my eyes closed, and not to speak until I was spoken to.

"He sat down next to me with his clothes on. That was all he did: sit down. He did not lay a finger on me. He just sat and looked at my naked body. He kept this up for some ten minutes, while I lay there, unmoving, face down. I could feel his eyes boring into the nape of my neck, my back, my buttocks, and my legs, with almost painful intensity. It occurred to me that he might be impotent. Customers like that turn up now and then. They pay for a prostitute, have her undress, and they look at her. Some will undress the woman and finish themselves off in her presence. All kinds of men go to prostitutes, for all kinds of reasons. I just assumed he was one of those.

"After a while, though, he reached out and began to touch me. His ten fingers moved down my body, from my shoulders to my back, from my back to my buttocks, in search of something. This was not foreplay. Neither, of course, was it a massage. His fingers moved over my body with the utmost care, as if tracing a route on a map. And all the while he touched my flesh, he seemed to be thinking – not in any ordinary sense of the word, but *seriously thinking* about something with the utmost concentration.

"One minute his fingers would seem to be wandering here and there at random, and the next they would come to a stop and remain for a long time in one place. It felt as if the fingers themselves were going from confusion to certainty. Am I making myself clear? Each finger seemed to be alive and thinking, with a will of its own. It was a very strange sensation. Strange and disturbing.

"And yet the touch of his fingers aroused me sexually. For the first time in my life. Sex had been nothing but a source of pain for me until I became a prostitute. The mere thought of it had filled me with fear – fear of the pain I knew I would have to endure. Just the opposite happened after I became a prostitute: I felt nothing. I no longer felt pain, but I felt no other sensations, either. I would sigh and pretend to be aroused for the pleasure of the customer, but it was all fake, a professional act. When *he* touched me, though, my sighs were real. They came out of my body's innermost depths. I knew that something inside me had begun to move, as if my centre of gravity were changing location in my body, first to one place and then to another.

"At last, the man stopped moving his fingers. With his hands on my waist, he seemed to be thinking. Through his fingertips, I could tell that he was steadying himself, quietly regularizing his breathing. Then he began to remove his clothing. I kept my eyes closed and my face buried in the pillow, waiting for what would come next. Once he was naked, he spread my arms and legs open wide.

"The room was almost frighteningly quiet. The only sound was the soft rush of the air conditioner. The man himself made almost no perceptible sounds. I couldn't even hear him breathing. He placed his palms on my back. I went limp. His penis touched my buttocks, but it was still soft.

"Just then the phone on the night table began to ring. I opened my eyes and turned my head to look at the man's face, but he seemed unaware that the phone was ringing. It rang eight or nine times and then stopped. Again the room became silent."

Creta Kano paused at that point for a few measured breaths. She remained silent, looking at her own hands. "I'm sorry," she said, "but do you mind if I take a short break?"

"Not at all," I said. I refilled my coffee cup and took a sip. She drank her cold water. We sat there without speaking for a good ten minutes.

"His fingers began to move again, touching every part of my body," Creta Kano continued, "every part without exception. I lost the power to think. My ears were filled with the sound of my own heart, pounding but with a strange slowness. I could no longer control myself. I cried out aloud again and again as he caressed me. I tried to keep my voice in check, but another someone was using my voice to moan and shout. I felt as if every screw in my body had come loose. Then, after a very long time, and with me still lying face down, he put something inside me from behind. What it was, I still have no idea. It was huge and hard, but it was not his penis. I am certain of that. I remember thinking that I had been right: he was impotent, after all.

"Whatever it was that he put inside me, it made me feel pain for the first time since my failed suicide attempt – real, intense pain that belonged to me and to no one else. How can I put this? The pain was almost

300

impossibly intense, as if my physical self were splitting in two from the inside out. And yet, as terrible as it felt, I was writhing as much in pleasure as in pain. The pleasure and pain were one. Do you see what I mean? The pain was founded on pleasure, and the pleasure on pain. I had to swallow the two as a single entity. In the midst of this pain and pleasure, my flesh went on splitting in two. There was no way for me to prevent it from happening. Then something very weird occurred. From between the two split halves of my physical self came crawling a thing that I had never seen or touched before. How large it was I could not tell, but it was as wet and slippery as a newborn baby. I hadn't the slightest idea what it was. It had always been inside me, and yet it was something of which I had no knowledge. This man had drawn it out of me.

"I wanted to know what it was. I wanted to see it with my own eyes. It was a part of me, after all, I had a right to see it. But this was impossible. I was caught in the torrent of pleasure and pain. An entirely physical being, I could only cry out, and drool, and churn my hips. The mere act of opening my eyes was an impossibility.

"I then reached a sexual peak – although, rather than a peak, it felt more as if I were being thrown from a high cliff. I screamed, and I felt as if every piece of glass in the room had shattered. I not only felt it: I actually saw and heard the windows and drinking glasses shattering into powdered fragments and felt them raining down on me. I then felt sick to my stomach. My consciousness began to slip away, and my body turned cold. I know this will sound strange, but I felt as if I had turned into a bowl of cold porridge – all sticky and lumpy, and the lumps were throbbing, slowly and hugely, with each beat of my heart. I recognized this throbbing: it had happened to me before. Nor did it take very long for me to remember what it was. I knew it as that dull, fatal, never-ending pain that I had experienced before my failed suicide attempt. And, like a crowbar, the pain was prying open the lid of my consciousness – prying it open with an irresistible force and dragging out the jellied contents of my memory without the consent of to my will. Strange as it may sound, I was like a dead person watching her own autopsy. Do you see what I mean? I felt as if I were watching from some vantage point as my body was being cut open and one slimy organ after another was being pulled out of me.

"I continued to lie there, drooling on the pillow, my body racked with convulsions, incontinent. I knew that I should try to control myself, but I had lost the power for such control. Every screw in my body had not only come loose but had fallen out. In my clouded brain, I felt with incredible intensity exactly how alone and how powerless I was. Everything came gushing out of me. Things both tangible and intangible turned to liquid and flowed out through my flesh like saliva or urine. I knew that I should not let this happen, that I should not allow my very self to spill out this way and be lost for ever, but there was nothing I could do to staunch the flow. I could only watch it happen. How long this continued, I have no idea. It seemed as if all my memories, all my consciousness, had just slipped away. Everything that had been inside me was outside now. At last, like a heavy curtain falling, darkness enveloped me in an instant.

"And when I regained consciousness, I was a different person."

Creta Kano stopped speaking at that point and looked at me.

"That is what happened," she said softly.

I said nothing but waited instead for the rest of her story.

14

Creta Kano's New Departure

•

Creta Kano went on with her story.

"For some days after that, I lived with the feeling that my body had fallen apart. Walking, I had no sense that my feet were touching the ground. Eating, I had no sense that I was chewing on anything. Sitting still, I had the terrifying feeling that my body was either endlessly falling or floating up beneath a big balloon, through infinite space. I could no longer connect my body's movements or sensations with my own self. They were functioning as they wished, without reference to my will, without order or direction. And yet I knew no way to bring calm to this intense chaos. All I could do was wait for things to settle down in their own good time. I locked myself in my room from morning to night, hardly eating a thing, and telling my family that I was not feeling well.

"Some days went by like this – three or four, I would say. And then, all of a sudden, everything quietened down, as if a wild wind had blown through and gone on its way. I looked around, and I examined myself, and I realized that I had become a new person, quite different from what I had been until then. This was my third self. My first self had been the one that lived in the endless anguish of pain. My second self had been the one that lived in a state of pain-free numbness. The first

303

one had been me in my original state, unable to shift the heavy yoke of pain from my neck. And when I did attempt to shift it – which is to say, when I tried to kill myself and failed – I became my second self: an interim me. True, the physical pain that had tortured me until then had disappeared, but all other sensations had retreated with it into the haze. My will to live, my physical vitality, my mental powers of concentration: all these had disappeared along with the pain. After I passed through that strange period of transition, what emerged was a brand-new me. Whether this was the me that should have been there all along I could not yet tell. But I did have the sense, however vague and undefined it might be, that I was at least heading in the right direction."

Creta Kano raised her eyes and looked at me, as if she wanted to hear my impressions of her story. Her hands still rested on the table.

"So, then," I said, "what you're saying is that the man gave you a new self, am I right?"

"Perhaps he did," said Creta Kano, nodding. Her face was as expressionless as the bottom of a dried-up pond. "Being caressed by that man, and held by him, and made to feel such intense sexual pleasure for the first time in my life, I experienced some kind of gigantic physical change. Why it happened, and why, of all people, it had to be *that man* who made it happen, I have no idea. Whatever the process may have been, the fact remains that at the end of it, I found myself in a whole new container. And once I had passed through the deep confusion I mentioned earlier, I sought to accept this new self as something truer – if for no other reason than that I had been enabled to escape from my profound numbness, which had been such a suffocating prison to me.

"Still, the bad aftertaste remained with me for a long time, like a dark shadow. Each time I recalled those ten fingers of his, each time I recalled that thing he put inside me, each time I recalled that slimy, lumpish thing that came (or felt as if it came) out of me, I felt terribly uneasy. I felt a sense of anger – and despair – that I had no means of dealing with. I tried to erase that day from my memory, but this I was unable to do, because the man had *pried open* something inside my body. The sensation of having been pried open stayed with me, inseparably bonded to the memory of that man, along with an unmistakable sense of defilement. It was a contradictory feeling. Do you see what I mean? The transformation that I had experienced was undoubtedly something right and true, but the transformation had been caused by something filthy, something wrong and false. This contradiction – this split – would torment me for a very long time."

Again Creta Kano stared at her hands as they lay on the table.

"After that, I stopped selling my body. There was no longer any point to it." Creta Kano's face remained expressionless.

"You could quit just like that?" I asked.

She nodded. "Just like that," she said. "I didn't say anything to anybody, just stopped selling myself, but this caused no problem. It was almost disappointing how easy it was. I had thought they would at least call me, and I was bracing myself for the day, but it never came. They never said a thing to me. They knew my address. They knew my phone number. They could have threatened me. But nothing happened.

"And so, on the surface at least, I had become an ordinary girl again. By that time, I had repaid my parents everything I owed them, and I had put away a good deal of money. With what I gave him, my brother had bought another new car to waste his time driving around in, but he could never have imagined what I had done to pay him back.

"I needed time to get used to my new self. What kind of a being was this self of mine? How did it function? What did it feel – and how? I had to grasp each of these things through experience, to memorize and stockpile them. Do you see what I am saying? Virtually everything inside me had spilled out and been lost. I was completely new, but I was also completely empty. I had to fill in that blank, little by little. With my own hands, I had to construct this thing I called 'I' – or, rather, make *the things that constituted me*.

"I was still officially a student, but I had no intention of returning to university. I would leave the house in the morning, go to a park, and sit by myself on a bench all day, doing nothing. Or I would wander up and down the paths in the park. When it rained, I would go to the library, put a book on the table in front of me, and pretend to be reading. I sometimes spent the whole day in a cinema or riding round and round the city on the Yamanote Circle Line. I felt as if I were floating in a pitch-black space, all by myself. There was no one I could go to for advice. If my sister Malta had been there, I could have shared everything with her, but at that time, of course, she was in seclusion far away on the island of Malta, performing her austerities. I did not know her address. I had no way of contacting her. And so I had to solve these problems by myself. No book explained the kind of thing that I had experienced. Still, although I was lonely, I was not unhappy. I was able to cling to myself. At least now I *had* a self to cling to.

"My new self was able to feel pain, though not with that earlier intensity. I could feel it, but at the same time I had learned a method of escaping from it. Which is to say, I was able to disconnect from the physical self that was feeling the pain. Do you see what I am saying? I was able to divide myself into a physical self and a non-physical self. It may sound difficult when I describe it like this, but once you learn the method, it is not difficult at all. When pain comes to me, I leave my physical self. It's just like quietly slipping into the next room when someone you don't want to meet comes along. It is very natural. I recognize that pain has come to my body; I feel the existence of the pain; but I am not there. I am in the next room. And so the yoke of the pain is not able to burden me."

"And you can separate from yourself like that anytime you please?"

"No," said Creta Kano, after thinking it for a moment. "At first I could do it only when my body was experiencing physical pain. Pain was the key to the splitting of my consciousness. Later, with Malta Kano's help, I learned to do it at will to some extent. But that was much later.

"Before long, a letter arrived from Malta Kano. She told me that she had finally finished three years of training on Malta and within a week would be returning to Japan. She planned to live in Japan permanently from then on. I was thrilled at the prospect of seeing her again. We had been apart for nearly eight years. And as I mentioned earlier, Malta was the only person in the world to whom I could freely tell everything that was in my heart.

"On the day she came back to Japan, I told Malta everything that had happened to me. She listened to my long, strange story to the very end without comment, without asking a single question. And when I was finished, she heaved a deep sigh and said to me, 'I know I should have been with you, I should have been watching over you all this time. For some reason, I never realized that you had such profound problems. Perhaps it was because you were simply too close to me. But in any case, there were things I had to do. There were places I had to go, alone. I had no choice in the matter.'

"I told her that she should not let it bother her. These were *my* problems, after all, and I was improving little by little. She thought about this for a while, saying nothing, and then she said, 'All the things you have been through ever since I left Japan have been painful and bitter for you, but as you say, you have been moving towards the proper state, step by step. The worst is over for you, and it will never come back. Such things will never happen to you again. It will not be easy, but you will be able to forget many things once a certain amount of time has passed. Without a true self, though, a person cannot go on living. It is like the ground we stand on. Without the ground, we can build nothing.

" 'There is one thing, however, which you must never forget, and that is that your body has been defiled by that man. It is a thing that should never have happened. You could have been lost for ever; you might have had to wander for ever through nothingness. Fortunately, the state of your being just happened not to be the real, original you, and so it had the reverse effect. Instead of trapping you, it liberated you from your transitory state. This happened through sheer good luck. The defilement, however, remains inside you, and at some point you will have to rid yourself of it. This is something that I cannot do for you. I cannot even tell you how to do it. You will have to discover the method for yourself, and do it by yourself.'

"My sister then gave me my new name: Creta Kano. Newly reborn, I needed a new name, she said. I liked it from the start. Malta Kano then began to use me as a spiritual medium. Under her guidance, I learned more and more how to control my new self and how to divide the flesh from the spirit. Finally, for the first time in my life, I became capable of living with a sense of peace. Of course, my true self was still something that lay beyond my grasp. I was still lacking too much for that to happen. But now, in Malta Kano, I had a companion by my side, someone I could depend upon, someone who understood me and accepted me. She became my guide and my protector."

"But then you met Noboru Wataya again, didn't you?"

Creta Kano nodded. "That is true," she said. "I did meet Noboru Wataya again. It happened early in March of this year. More than five years had passed since I had been taken by him and undergone my transformation and begun to work with Malta Kano. We came face to face again when he visited our home to see Malta. We did not speak to each other. I merely caught a glimpse of him in the hallway, but one glimpse was all it took to freeze me in my tracks as if I had been struck by lightning. It was *that man* – the last man to buy me.

"I called Malta Kano aside and told her that he was the man who had defiled me. 'Fine,' she said. 'Just leave everything to me. Don't worry. You keep out of sight. Make sure he doesn't see you.' I did as I was told. Which is why I do not know what he and Malta Kano discussed."

"What could Noboru Wataya have possibly wanted from Malta Kano?"

Creta Kano shook her head. "I am sorry, Mr Okada, I have no idea."

"People come to your house because they want something, isn't that usually the case?"

"Yes, it is."

"What kinds of things do they come for?"

307

"All kinds of things."

"But *what* kinds of things? Can you give me an example?"

Creta Kano bit her lip for a moment. "Lost things. Their destinies. The future. Everything."

"And you two know about those things?"

"We do. Not absolutely everything, but most of the answers are in here," said Creta Kano, pointing at her temple. "You just have to go inside."

"Like going down into a well?"

"Yes, like that."

I put my elbows on the table and took a long, deep breath.

"Now, if you don't mind, there's something I'd like you to tell me. You showed up in my dreams a few times. You did this consciously. You willed it to happen. Am I right?"

"Yes, you are right," said Creta Kano. "It was an act of will. I entered your consciousness and joined my body with yours."

"You can do things like that?"

"Yes, I can. That is one of my functions."

"You and I joined our bodies together in my mind." When I heard myself speaking these words, I felt as if I had just hung a bold surrealistic painting on a white wall. And then, as if looking at the painting from a distance to make sure it was not hanging crooked, I said the words again: "You and I joined our bodies together in my mind. But I never asked you two for anything. It never even crossed my mind to find out anything from you. Right? So why did you take it upon yourself to do such a thing?"

"Because I was ordered to by Malta Kano."

"Meaning that Malta Kano used you as a medium to hunt around inside my mind. What was she looking for? Answers for Noboru Wataya? Or for Kumiko?"

Creta Kano said nothing for a time. She seemed confused. "I don't really know," she said. "I was not given detailed information. That way, I can function more spontaneously as a medium. My only job is to have people's minds pass through me. It is Malta Kano's job to assign meaning to what I find there. But please understand, Mr Okada: Malta Kano is fundamentally on your side. I hate Noboru Wataya, you see, and Malta Kano's first concern is for me. She did this *for your sake*, Mr Okada. That is what I believe."

•

Creta Kano went out to the local supermarket. I gave her money and suggested that as she was going out, she should change into more respectable clothing. She nodded and went to Kumiko's room, where she put on a white cotton blouse and a floral-pattern skirt.

"It doesn't bother you, Mr Okada, for me to put on your wife's clothing?"

I shook my head. "Her letter told me to get rid of it all. No one's going to be bothered if you wear her things."

Just as I expected, everything fitted her perfectly – uncannily so. Even her shoe size was the same. Creta Kano left the house wearing a pair of Kumiko's sandals. The sight of Creta Kano in Kumiko's clothing made me feel once again that reality was changing its direction, the way a huge passenger ship lumbers into a new course.

After Creta Kano had gone out, I lay on the sofa staring at the garden, my mind a blank. She came back by taxi thirty minutes later, holding three large bags stuffed with groceries. Then she made me ham and eggs and a sardine salad.

"Tell me, Mr Okada, do you have any interest in Crete?" Creta Kano asked without warning after we had eaten.

"Crete?" I said. "You mean the island of Crete, in the Mediterranean?"

"Yes."

I shook my head. "I don't know," I said. "I'm not *un*interested, I suppose. I've never thought much about it."

"Would you like to go to Crete with me?"

"Go to Crete with you?" I echoed.

"I would like to get away from Japan for a while. That is what I was thinking about the whole time I was in the well after you left. Ever since Malta gave me the name Creta, I have felt that I would like to go to Crete someday. As preparation, I read many books about the island. I even studied Greek, so that I would be able to live there when the time came. I have fairly substantial savings, enough for us to live on for a good length of time without difficulty. You would not have to worry about money."

"Does Malta Kano know you're planning to go to Crete?"

"No. I haven't said anything to her about it, but I am sure she would not be opposed to the idea. She would probably think it was a good thing for me. She has been using me as a medium for the past five years, but it is not as if she has merely been exploiting me as some kind of tool. She has been doing it to aid my recovery as well. She believes that by passing the minds or egos of a variety of people through me, she will make it possible for me to obtain a firm grasp on my own self. Do you see what I mean? It works for me as a kind of vicarious experience of what it feels like to have an ego.

"Come to think of it, I have never once in my life said unambiguously to anybody, 'I want to do this.' I have never even thought to myself, 'I want to do this.' From the moment of my birth, I lived with pain at the centre of my life. My only purpose in life was to find a way to coexist with intense pain. And after I turned twenty and the pain disappeared when I attempted to kill myself, a deep numbness came to replace the pain. I was like a walking corpse. A thick veil of unfeeling was draped over me. I had nothing – not a sliver – of what could be called my own will. And then, when my flesh was violated and my mind pried open by Noboru Wataya, I obtained my third self. Even so, I was still not myself. All I had managed to do was get a grasp on the minimum necessary container for a self – a mere container. And as a container, under the guidance of Malta Kano, I passed many egos through myself.

"This, then, is how I have spent the twenty-six years of my life. Just imagine if you will: for twenty-six years, I was nothing. This is the thought that struck me with such force when I was alone in the well, thinking. During all this long time, the person called 'me' was in fact nothing at all, I realized. I was nothing but a prostitute. A prostitute of the flesh. A prostitute of the mind.

"Now, however, I am trying to get a grasp on my new self. I am neither a container nor a medium. I am trying to establish myself here on the face of the earth."

"I understand what you are saying to me, but still, why do you want to go to Crete with *me?*"

"Because it could be a good thing for both of us: for you, Mr Okada, and for me," said Creta Kano. "For the time being, there is no need for either of us to be here. And if that is the case, I feel, it would be better for us not to be here. Tell me, Mr Okada, do you have some course of action you must follow – some plan for what you are going to do from this point on?"

"The one thing I need to do is talk to Kumiko. Until we meet face to face and she tells me that our life together is finished, I can't do anything else. How I'm going to go about finding her, though, I have no idea."

"But if you *do* find her and your marriage is, as you say, 'finished', would you consider coming to Crete with me? Both of us would have to start something new at some point," said Creta Kano, looking into my eyes. "It seems to me that going to the island of Crete would not be a bad beginning."

"Not bad at all," I said. "Sudden, maybe, but not a bad beginning."

Creta Kano smiled at me. When I thought about it, I realized this was the first time she had ever done so. It made me feel that, to some extent, history was beginning to head in the right direction. "We still have time," she said. "Even if I hurry, it will take me at least two weeks to get ready. Please use the time to think it over, Mr Okada. I don't know if there is anything I can give you. It seems to me that I don't have anything to give right now. I am quite literally empty. I am just getting started, putting some contents into this empty container little by little. I can give you myself, Mr Okada, if you say that is good enough for you. I believe we can help each other."

I nodded. "I'll think about it," I said. "I'm very pleased that you made me this offer, and I think it would be great if we could go together. I really do. But I've got a lot of things I have to think about and a lot of things I have to straighten out."

"And if, in the end, you say you don't want to go to Crete, don't worry. I won't be hurt. I will be sorry, but I want your honest answer."

·

Creta Kano stayed in my house again that night. As the sun was going down, she invited me out for a stroll in the local park. I decided to forget about my bruise and leave the house. What was the point of worrying about such things? We walked for an hour in the pleasant summer evening, then came home and ate.

After our supper, Creta Kano said she wanted to sleep with me. She wanted to have physical sex with me, she said. This was so sudden, I didn't know what to do, which is exactly what I said to her: "This is so sudden. I don't know what to do."

Looking directly at me, Creta Kano said, "Whether or not you go with me to Crete, Mr Okada, I want you to take me one time – just one time – as a prostitute. I want you to buy my flesh. Here. Tonight. It will be my last time. I will cease to be a prostitute, whether of the flesh or of the mind. I will abandon the name of Creta Kano as well. In order to do that, however, I want to have a clearly visible point of demarcation, something that says, 'It ends here.' "

"I understand your wanting a point of demarcation, but why do you have to sleep with me?"

"Don't you see, Mr Okada? By sleeping with the real you, by joining

311

my body with yours in reality, I want to pass through you, this person called Mr Okada. By doing that, I want to be liberated from this feeling of defilement inside me. That will be the point of demarcation."

"Well, I'm sorry, but I don't buy people's flesh."

Creta Kano bit her lip. "How about this, then? Instead of money, give me some of your wife's clothing. And shoes. We'll make that the price of my flesh. That should be all right, don't you think? Then I will be saved."

"Saved. By which you mean that you will be liberated from the defilement that Noboru Wataya left inside you?"

"Yes, that is just what I mean," said Creta Kano.

I stared at her. Without false eyelashes, Creta Kano's face had a much more childish look. "Tell me," I said, "who is this Noboru Wataya guy, really? He's my wife's brother, but I hardly know him. What is he thinking? What does he want? All I know for sure is that he and I hate each other."

"Noboru Wataya is a person who belongs to a world that is the exact opposite of yours," said Creta Kano. Then she seemed to be searching for the words she needed to continue. "In a world where you are losing everything, Mr Okada, Noboru Wataya is gaining everything. In a world where you are rejected, he is accepted. And the opposite is just as true. Which is why he hates you so intensely."

"I don't get it. Why would he even notice that I'm alive? He's famous, he's powerful. Compared to him, I'm an absolute zero. Why does he have to take the time and trouble to hate *me*?"

Creta Kano shook her head. "Hatred is like a long, dark shadow. In most cases, not even the person it falls upon knows where it comes from. It is like a two-edged sword. When you cut the other person, you cut yourself. The more violently you hack at the other person, the more violently you hack at yourself. It can often be fatal. But it is not easy to dispose of. Please be careful, Mr Okada. It is very dangerous. Once it has taken root in your heart, hatred is the most difficult thing in the world to eradicate."

"And you were able to feel it, weren't you? – the root of the hatred that was in Noboru Wataya's heart."

"Yes, I was. I am," said Creta Kano. "That is the thing that split my flesh in two, that defiled me, Mr Okada. Which is why I do not want him to be my last customer as a prostitute. Do you understand?"

That night I went to bed with Creta Kano. I took off what she was wearing of Kumiko's and joined my body with hers. Quietly and gently. It felt like an extension of my dream, as if I were re-creating in reality the very acts I had performed with Creta Kano in my dream. Her body was real and alive. But there was something missing: the clear sense that this was actually happening. Several times the illusion overtook me that I was doing this with Kumiko, not Creta Kano. I was sure I would wake up the moment I came. But I did not wake up. I came inside her. It was reality. True reality. But each time I recognized that fact, reality felt a little less real. Reality was coming undone and moving away from reality, one small step at a time. But still, it was reality.

"Mr Okada," said Creta Kano, with her arms wrapped around my back, "let's go to Crete together. This is not the place for us any more: not for you and not for me. We have to go to Crete. If you stay here, something bad is going to happen to you. I know it. I am sure of it."

"Something bad?"

"Something very, very bad," Creta Kano prophesied – in a small but penetrating voice, like the prophet bird that lived in the forest.

15

The Only Bad Thing That Ever Happened
in May Kasahara's House

•

May Kasahara on the Gooshy Source of Heat

"Hello, Mr Wind-up Bird," said the woman's voice. Pressing the receiver to my ear, I looked at my watch. Four o'clock in the afternoon. When the phone rang, I had been asleep on the sofa, drenched in sweat. It had been a short, unpleasant nap. And now there remained with me the physical sensation of someone having been sitting on top of me the whole time I was asleep. Whoever it was had waited until I was asleep, come to sit on top of me, and got up and gone away just before I woke.

"Hel-looo," cooed the woman's voice in a near whisper. The sound seemed to have to pass through some extra-thin air to reach me. "This is May Kasahara calling. . . ."

"Hey," I tried to say, but my mouth still wasn't moving the way I wanted it to. The word may have come out like some kind of groan.

"What are you doing now?" she asked, in an insinuating tone.

"Nothing," I said, moving the mouthpiece away to clear my throat. "Nothing. Napping."

"Did I wake you?"

"Sure you did. But that's OK. It was just a nap."

May Kasahara seemed to hesitate a moment. Then she said, "How about it, Mr Wind-up Bird: will you come over to my house?"

I closed my eyes. In the darkness hovered lights of different colours and shapes.

"I don't mind," I said.

"I'm sunbathing in the yard, so just let yourself in the back."

"OK."

"Tell me, Mr Wind-up Bird, are you mad at me?"

"I'm not sure," I said. "Anyhow, I'm going to take a shower and change, and then I'll come over. I've got something I want to talk to you about."

I took a quick cold shower to clear my head, turned on the hot water to wash, and finished off cold again. This did manage to wake me up, but my body still felt dull and heavy. My legs would begin trembling, and at several points during the shower I had to grab the towel bar or sit on the edge of the tub. Maybe I was more fatigued than I had thought.

After I stepped out of the shower and wiped myself down, I brushed my teeth and looked at myself in the mirror. The dark-blue mark was still there on my right cheek, neither darker nor lighter than before. My eyeballs had a network of tiny red lines, and there were dark circles under my eyes. My cheeks looked sunken, and my hair was in need of a trim. I looked like a fresh corpse that had just come back to life and dug its way out of the grave.

I put on a T-shirt and shorts, a hat and dark glasses. Out in the alley, I found that the hot day was far from over. Everything alive above ground – everything visible – was gasping in the hope of a sudden shower, but there was no hint of a cloud in the sky. A blanket of hot, stagnant air enveloped the alley. The place was deserted, as always. Good. On a hot day like this, and with my face looking so awful, I didn't want to meet anyone.

In the yard of the empty house, the bird sculpture was glaring at the sky, as usual, its beak held aloft. It looked far more grimy than when I had last seen it, more worn down. And there was something more strained in its gaze. It seemed to be staring hard at something extraordinarily depressing that was floating in the sky. If only it could have done so, the bird would have liked to avert its gaze, but with its eyes locked in place the way they were, it had no choice except to look. The tall weeds surrounding the sculpture remained motionless, like a chorus in a Greek tragedy waiting with bated breath for an oracle to be handed down. The TV aerial on the roof apathetically thrust its silver feelers into the suffocating heat. Under the harsh summer light, everything was dried out and exhausted.

After I had surveyed the yard of the vacant house, I walked into May Kasahara's yard. The oak tree cast a cool-looking shadow over the lawn, but May Kasahara had obviously avoided that, to stretch out in the harsh sunlight. She lay on her back in a deck chair, wearing a tiny chocolate-coloured bikini, its little cloth patches held in place by bits of string. I couldn't help wondering if a person could actually swim in a thing like that. She wore the same sunglasses she had on when we first met, and large beads of sweat dotted her face. Under her deck chair were a white beach towel, a container of suntan cream, and a few magazines. Two empty Sprite cans lay nearby, one serving as an ashtray. A plastic hose with a sprinkler lay out on the lawn, where no one had bothered to reel it in after it was last used.

When I drew near, May Kasahara sat up and reached out to turn off her radio. She had a far deeper tan than last time. This was no ordinary tan from a weekend at the beach. Every bit of her body – from head to toe – had been beautifully roasted. Sunning was all she did all day, it seemed – including the whole time I was in the well, no doubt. I took a moment to glance at the yard. It looked pretty much as it had before, the broad lawn well manicured, the pond still unfilled and looking parched enough to make you thirsty.

I sat on the deck chair next to hers and took a lemon drop from my pocket. The heat had caused the paper wrapper to stick to the sweet.

May Kasahara looked at me for some time without saying anything. "What happened to you, Mr Wind-up Bird? What's that mark on your face? It is a mark, isn't it?"

"I think it is. Probably. But I don't know how it happened. I looked, and there it was."

May Kasahara raised herself on one elbow and stared at my face. She brushed away the drops of sweat beside her nose and gave her sunglasses a little push up to where they belonged. The dark lenses all but hid her eyes.

"You have no idea at all? No clue where it happened or how?"

"None at all."

"None?"

"I got out of the well, and a little while later I looked in the mirror, and there it was. Really. That's all."

"Does it hurt?"

"It doesn't hurt, it doesn't itch. It *is* a little warm, though."

"Have you been to the doctor?"

I shook my head. "It'd probably be a waste of time."

"Probably," said May Kasahara. "I hate doctors too."

I took off my hat and sunglasses and used my handkerchief to wipe the sweat from my forehead. The armpits of my grey T-shirt were already black with sweat.

"Great bikini," I said.

"Thanks."

"Looks like they put it together from scraps – making the maximum use of our limited natural resources."

"I take off the top when nobody's around."

"Well, well," I said.

"Not that there's all that much underneath to uncover," she said, as if by way of excuse.

True, the breasts inside her bikini top were still small and undeveloped. "Have you ever swum in that thing?" I asked.

"Never. I don't know how to swim. How about you, Mr Wind-up Bird?"

"Yeah, I can swim."

"How far?"

"Far."

"Ten kilometres?"

"Probably. . . . Nobody home now?"

"They left yesterday, for our summer house in Izu. They all want to go swimming for the weekend. 'All' is my parents and my little brother."

"Not you?"

She gave a tiny shrug. Then she took some Hope regulars and matches from the folds of her beach towel and lit up.

"You look terrible, Mr Wind-up Bird."

"Of course I look terrible – after days at the bottom of a well with almost nothing to eat or drink, who wouldn't look terrible?"

May Kasahara took off her sunglasses and turned to face me. She still had that deep cut next to her eye. "Tell me, Mr Wind-up Bird. Are you mad at me?"

"I'm not sure. I've got tons of things I have to think about before I start getting mad at you."

"Has your wife come back?"

I shook my head. "She sent me a letter. Says she's never coming back."

"Poor Mr Wind-up Bird," said May Kasahara. She sat up and reached out to place her hand lightly on my knee. "Poor, poor Mr Wind-up Bird. You know, Mr Wind-up Bird, you may not believe this, but I was planning to save you from the well at the very end. I just wanted to frighten you a little, torment you a little. I wanted to see if I could make you scream. I wanted to see how much it would take until you were so mixed up you lost your world."

I didn't know how to reply to this, so I just nodded.

"Did you think I was serious when I said I was going to let you die down there?"

Instead of answering right away, I rolled the lemon drop wrapper into a ball. Then I said, "I really wasn't sure. You sounded serious, but you sounded like you were just trying to scare me too. When you're down in a well, talking to somebody at the top, something weird happens to the sound: you can't really catch the expression in the other person's voice. But finally, it's not a question of which is right. I mean, reality is made up of these different layers. So maybe in *that* reality you were serious about trying to kill me, but in *this* reality you weren't. It depends on which reality *you* take and which reality *I* take."

I pushed my rolled-up sweet wrapper into the hole of a Sprite can.

"Say, could you do me a favour, Mr Wind-up Bird?" said May Kasahara, pointing at the hose on the lawn. "Would you spray me with that? It's sooo hot! My brain's going to fry if I don't wet myself down."

I left my deck chair and walked over to pick up the blue plastic hose on the lawn. It was warm and limp. I reached behind the bushes and turned on the tap. At first only hot water that had been warmed inside the hose came out, but it cooled down until it was spraying cold water. May Kasahara stretched out on the lawn, and I aimed a good, strong spray at her.

She closed her eyes and let the water wash over her body. "Oh, that feels so good! You should do it too, Mr Wind-up Bird."

"This isn't a bathing suit," I said, but May Kasahara looked as if she was enjoying the water a lot, and the heat was just too intense for me to resist. I took off my sweat-soaked T-shirt, bent forward, and let the cold water run over my head. While I was at it, I took a swallow of the water: it was cold and delicious.

"Hey, is this well water?" I asked.

"Sure is! It comes up through a pump. Feels great, doesn't it? It's so cold. You can drink it too. We had a guy from the health department do a water quality inspection, and he said there's nothing wrong with it, you almost never get water this clean in Tokyo. He was amazed. But still, we're a little afraid to drink it. With all these houses packed together like this, you never know what's going to get into it."

"But don't you think it's weird? The Miyawakis' well is bone dry, but yours has all this nice, fresh water. They're just across the alley. Why should they be so different?"

"May Kasahara cocked her head. "Maybe something caused the underground water flow to change just a little bit, so their well dried up and ours didn't. Of course, I don't know what the exact reason would be."

"Has anything bad happened in your house?" I asked.

May Kasahara wrinkled up her face and shook her head. "The only bad thing that's happened in this house in the last ten years is that it's so damned boring!"

May Kasahara wiped herself down and asked if I wanted a beer. I said I did. She brought two cold cans of Heineken from the house. She drank one, and I drank the other.

"So tell me, Mr Wind-up Bird, what's your plan from now on?"

"I haven't really decided," I said. "But I'll probably get out of here. I might even get out of Japan."

"Get out of Japan? Where would you go?"

"To Crete."

"Crete? Does this have something to do with that Creta What's-her-name woman?"

"Something, yeah."

May Kasahara thought this over for a moment.

"And was it Creta What's-her-name that saved you from the well?"

"Creta Kano," I said. "Yeah, she's the one."

"You've got a lot of friends, haven't you, Mr Wind-up Bird?"

"Not really. If anything, I'm famous for having so few friends."

"Still, I wonder how Creta Kano found out you were down in the well. You didn't tell anybody you were going down there, right? So how did she figure out where you were?"

"I don't know," I said.

"But anyhow, you're going to Crete?"

"I haven't really decided I'm going to go. It's just one possibility. I have to settle things with Kumiko first."

May Kasahara put a cigarette in her mouth and lit up. Then she touched the cut next to her eye with the tip of her little finger.

"You know, Mr Wind-up Bird, just about the whole time you were down in the well, I was out here sunbathing. I was watching the garden of the vacant house, and baking myself, and thinking about you in the well, that you were starving and moving closer to death little by little. I was the only one who knew you were down there and couldn't get out. And when I thought about that, I had this incredibly clear sense of what you were feeling: the pain and anxiety and fear. Do you see what I mean? By doing that, I was able to get sooo close to you! I really wasn't going to let you die. This is true. Really. But I wanted to keep going. Right down to the wire. Right down to where you would start to fall apart and be scared out of your mind and you couldn't take it any more. I really felt that that would be the best thing – for me and for you."

"Well, I'll tell you what," I said. "I think that if you really had gone down to the wire, you might have wanted to go all the way. It might have been a lot easier than you think. If you went that far, all it would have taken was one last push. And then afterwards you would have told yourself that it was the best thing – for me and for you." I took a swig of beer.

May Kasahara thought about that for a time, biting her lip. "You may be right," she said. "Not even I know for sure."

I took my last swallow of beer and stood up. I put on my sunglasses and slipped into my sweat-soaked T-shirt. "Thanks for the beer."

"You know, Mr Wind-up Bird," said May Kasahara, "last night, after my family left for the summer house, I went down into the well. I stayed there five or maybe six hours altogether, just sitting still."

"So you're the one who took the rope ladder away."

"Yeah," said May Kasahara, with a little frown. "I'm the one."

I turned my eyes to the broad lawn. The moisture-laden earth was giving off a vapour that looked like heat haze. May Kasahara pushed the butt of her cigarette into an empty Sprite can.

"I didn't feel anything special for the first few hours. Of course, it bothered me a little bit to be in such total darkness, but I wasn't terrified or scared or anything. I'm not one of those ordinary girls that scream their heads off over every little thing. But I knew it wasn't just dark. You were down there for days, Mr Wind-up Bird. You know there's nothing down there to be afraid of. But after a few hours, I knew less and less who I was. Sitting still down there in the darkness, I could tell that something inside me – inside my body – was getting bigger and bigger. It felt like this *thing* inside me was growing, like the roots of a tree in a pot, and when it got big enough it would break me apart. That would be the

320

end of me, like the pot splitting into a million pieces. Whatever this thing was, it stayed put inside me when I was under the sun, but it sucked up some special kind of nourishment in the darkness and started growing *sooo* fast it was scary. I tried to hold it down, but I couldn't. And that's when I really got scared. It was the scaredest I've ever been in my life. This thing inside me, this gooshy white thing like a lump of fat, was taking over, taking *me* over, eating me up. This gooshy thing was really small at first, Mr Wind-up Bird."

May Kasahara stopped talking for a little while and stared at her hands, as if she were remembering what had happened to her that day. "I was *really* scared," she said. "I guess that's what I wanted *you* to feel. I guess I wanted you to hear the sound of the *thing* chewing you up."

I lowered myself into a deck chair and looked at the body of May Kasahara, hardly covered by her little bikini. She was sixteen years old, but she had the build of a girl of thirteen or fourteen. Her breasts and hips were far from fully matured. Her body reminded me of those drawings that use the absolute minimum of line yet still give a vivid sense of reality. But still, at the same time, there was something about it that gave an impression of extreme old age.

Then, all of a sudden, it occurred to me to ask her, "Have you ever had the feeling that you've been defiled by something?"

"Defiled?" She looked at me, her eyes narrowed. "You mean physically? You mean raped?"

"Physically. Mentally. Either."

May Kasahara looked down at her own body, then returned her gaze to me. "Physically, no. I mean, I'm still a virgin. I've let a boy feel me up. But just through my clothes."

I nodded.

"Mentally, hmm, I'm not sure. I don't really know what it means to be defiled mentally."

"Neither do I," I said. "It's just a question of whether you *feel* it's happened to you or not. If you don't feel it, that probably means you haven't been defiled."

"Why are you asking me about this?"

"Because some of the people I know have that feeling. And it causes all kinds of complicated problems. There's one thing I want to ask you, though. Why are you always thinking about death?"

She put a cigarette between her lips and nimbly struck a match with one hand. Then she put on her sunglasses.

"You mean you don't think much about death, Mr Wind-up Bird?"

"I *do* think about death, of course. But not all the time. Just once in a while. Like most people."

"Here's what I think, Mr Wind-up Bird," said May Kasahara. "Everybody's born with some different thing at the core of their existence. And that thing, whatever it is, becomes like a heat source that runs each person from the inside. I have one too, of course. Like everybody else. But sometimes it gets out of hand. It swells or shrinks inside me, and it shakes me up. What I'd really like to do is find a way to communicate that feeling to another person. But I can't seem to do it. They just don't get it. Of course, the problem could be that I'm not explaining it very well, but I think it's because they're not listening very well. They pretend to be listening, but they're not really. So I get worked up sometimes, and I do some crazy things."

"Crazy things?"

"Like, say, trapping you in the well, or, like, when I'm riding on the back of a motorcycle, putting my hands over the eyes of the guy who's driving."

When she said this, she touched the wound next to her eye.

"And that's how the motorcycle accident happened?" I asked.

May Kasahara gave me a questioning look, as if she had not heard me. I couldn't make out the expression in her eyes behind the dark glasses, but a kind of numbness seemed to have spread over her face, like oil poured on still water.

"What happened to the guy?" I asked.

With her cigarette between her lips, May Kasahara continued to look at me. Or rather, she continued to look at my mark. "Do I have to answer that question, Mr Wind-up Bird?"

"Not if you don't want to. You're the one who brought it up. If you don't want to talk about it, then don't."

May Kasahara grew very quiet. She seemed to be having trouble deciding what to do. Then she drew in a chestful of cigarette smoke and let it out slowly. With a heavy movement, she dragged her sunglasses off and turned her face to the sun, eyes closed tight. Watching her, I felt as if the flow of time were slowing down little by little – as if time's spring were beginning to run down.

"He died," she said at last, in a voice with no expression, as though she had resigned herself to something.

"He died?"

May Kasahara tapped the ash off her cigarette. Then she picked up her towel and wiped the sweat from her face over and over again. Finally, as if recalling a task that she had forgotten, she said in a clipped, businesslike way, "We were going pretty fast. It happened near Enoshima."

I looked at her without a word. She held an edge of the beach towel in each hand, pressing the edges against her cheeks. White smoke was rising from the cigarette between her fingers. With no wind to disturb it, the smoke rose straight up, like a miniature smoke signal. She seemed to be having trouble deciding whether to cry or to laugh. At least it looked that way to me. She wavered on the narrow line that divided one possibility from the other, but in the end she fell to neither side. May Kasahara pulled her expression together, put the towel on the ground, and took a drag on her cigarette. The time was nearly 5 o'clock, but the heat showed no sign of abating.

"I killed him," she said. "Of course, I didn't mean to kill him. I just wanted to push the limits. We did stuff like that all the time. It was like a game. I'd cover his eyes or tickle him when we were on the bike. But nothing ever happened. Until that day . . ."

May Kasahara raised her face and looked straight at me.

"Anyway, Mr Wind-up Bird, no, I don't feel as if I've been defiled. I just wanted to get close to that gooshy thing if I could. I wanted to trick it into coming out of me and then crush it to bits. You've got to really push the limits if you're going to trick it into coming out. It's the only way. You've got to offer it good bait." She shook her head slowly. "No, I don't think I've been defiled. But I haven't been saved, either. There's nobody who can save me right now, Mr Wind-up Bird. The world looks totally empty to me. Everything I see around me looks fake. The only thing that isn't fake is that gooshy thing inside me."

May Kasahara sat there for a long time taking small, regular breaths. There were no other sounds, no bird or insect cries. A terrible quiet settled over the yard, as though the world had become empty.

May Kasahara turned to face me. She seemed just then to have remembered something. Now all expression was gone from her face, as if she had been washed clean. "Tell me, Mr Wind-up Bird, did you sleep with that Creta Kano person?"

I nodded.

"Will you write to me from Crete?" asked May Kasahara.

"Sure I will. If I go."

"You know, Mr Wind-up Bird," she said after some hesitation, "I think I might be going back to school."

"Oh, so you've changed your mind about school?"

She gave a little shrug. "It's a different one. I refuse to go back to my old school. The new one's far from here. So anyway, I probably won't see you for a while."

I nodded. Then I took a lemon drop from my pocket and put it into my mouth. May Kasahara glanced around and lit up a cigarette.

"Tell me, Mr Wind-up Bird, is it fun to sleep with a bunch of different women?"

"That's beside the point."

"Yeah, I've heard that one already."

"Right," I said, but I didn't know what else to say.

"Oh, forget it. But you know, Mr Wind-up Bird, it's because I met you that I finally decided to go back to school. No kidding."

"Why's that?" I asked.

"Yeah, why is that?" May Kasahara said. Then she wrinkled up the corners of her eyes and looked at me. "Maybe I wanted to go back to a more normal world. But really, Mr Wind-up Bird, it's been a lot of fun being with you. No kidding. I mean, you're such a supernormal guy, but you do such *un*normal things. And you're so – what? – unpredictable. So hanging around with you hasn't been boring in any way. You have no idea how much good that's done me. Not being bored means not having to think about a lot of stupid stuff. Right? So where that's concerned, I'm glad you've been around. But to tell you the truth, it's made me nervous too."

"In what way?"

"Well, how can I put this? Sometimes, when I'm looking at you, I get this feeling like maybe you're fighting real hard against something *for me*. I know this sounds weird, but when that happens, I feel like I'm right with you, sweating with you. See what I mean? You always look so cool, like no matter what happens, it's got nothing to do with you, but you're not really like that. In your own way, you're out there fighting as hard as you can, even if other people can't tell by looking at you. If you weren't, you wouldn't have gone into the well like that, right? But anyhow, you're not fighting for me, of course. You're falling all over yourself, trying to wrestle with this big whatever-it-is, and the only reason you're doing it is so you can find Kumiko. So there's no point in me getting all sweaty for you. I know all that, but still, I can't help feeling that you *are* fighting for me, Mr Wind-up Bird – that, in a way, you are probably fighting for a lot of other people at the same time you're fighting for Kumiko. And that's maybe why you look like an absolute idiot sometimes. That's what I think, Mr Wind-up Bird. But when I see you doing this, I get all tense and nervous, and I end up feeling totally drained. I mean, it looks like you can't possibly win. If I had to bet on the match, I'd bet on you to lose. Sorry, but that's how it is. I like you a lot, but I don't want to go broke."

"I understand completely."

"I don't want to watch you going under, and I don't want to sweat any more for you than I already have. That's why I've decided to go back to a world that's a little more normal. But if I hadn't met you here – here, in front of this vacant house – I don't think things would have turned out this way. I never would have thought about going back to school. I'd still be hanging around in some not-so-normal world. So in that sense, it's all because of you, Mr Wind-up Bird. You're not *totally* useless."

I nodded. It was the first time in a long time anyone had said anything nice about me.

"Come here, Mr Wind-up Bird," said May Kasahara. She raised herself up in her deck chair.

I got out of my chair and went to hers.

"Sit down right here, Mr Wind-up Bird," said May Kasahara.

I did as I was told and sat down next to her.

"Show me your face, Mr Wind-up Bird."

She stared at me for a time. Then, placing one hand on my knee, she pressed the palm of the other against the mark on my cheek.

"Poor Mr Wind-up Bird," said May Kasahara, in a near whisper. "I know you're going to take on all kinds of things. Even before you know it. And you won't have any choice in the matter. The way rain falls in a field. And now close your eyes, Mr Wind-up Bird. Really tight. Like they're glued shut."

I closed my eyes tight.

May Kasahara touched her lips to my mark – her lips were small and thin, like an extremely well-made imitation. Then she parted those lips and ran her tongue across my mark – very slowly, covering every bit of it. The hand she had placed on my knee remained there the whole time. Its warm, moist touch came to me from far away, from a place still farther than if it had passed through all the fields in the world. Then she took my hand and touched it to the wound beside her eye. I caressed the half-inch

325

scar. As I did so, the waves of her consciousness pulsed through my fingertips and into me – a delicate resonance of longing. Someone should take this girl in his arms and hold her tight, I thought. Probably someone other than me. Someone qualified to give her something.

"Goodbye, Mr Wind-up Bird. See you again sometime."

16

The Simplest Thing

•

Revenge in a Sophisticated Form

•

The Thing in the Guitar Case

The next day I called my uncle and told him I might be moving out of the house sometime in the next few weeks. I apologized for springing it on him so suddenly but explained that it was because Kumiko had left me, with just as little warning. There was no point in covering up any more. I told him that she had written to say she would not be coming back, and that I wanted to get away from this place, though exactly for how long I could not be sure. My summary explanation was followed by a thoughtful silence at my uncle's end of the line. He seemed to be mulling something over. Then he said, "Mind if I come over there for a visit sometime soon? I'd like to see with my own eyes what's going on. And I haven't been to the house for quite a while now."

•

My uncle came to the house two evenings later. He looked at my mark but had nothing to say about it. He probably didn't know what to say. He just gave it a funny look, with his eyes narrowed. He had brought me a good bottle of scotch and a pack of fish-paste cakes that he had bought in Odawara. We sat on the veranda, eating the cakes and drinking the whisky.

"What a pleasure it is to be sitting on a veranda again," my uncle said, nodding several times. "Our condo doesn't have one, of course.

Sometimes I really miss this place. There's a special feeling you get on a veranda that you just can't get anywhere else."

For a while, he sat there gazing at the moon, a slim white crescent of a moon that looked as if someone had just finished sharpening it. That such a thing could go on floating in the sky seemed almost miraculous to me.

Then, in an utterly offhand manner, my uncle asked, "How'd you get that mark?"

"I really don't know," I said, and took a gulp of whisky. "All of a sudden, it was there. Maybe a week ago? I wish I could explain it better, but I just don't know how."

"Did you go to the doctor?"

I shook my head.

"I don't want to stick my nose in where I'm not wanted, but just let me say this: you really ought to sit down and think hard about what it is that's most important to you."

I nodded. "I *have* been thinking about that," I said. "But things are so complicated and tangled up. I can't seem to separate them out and do one thing at a time. I don't know how to untangle things."

My uncle smiled. "You know what I think? I think what you ought to do is start by thinking about the simplest things and go from there. For example, you could stand on a street corner somewhere day after day and look at the people who come by. You're not in any hurry to decide anything. It may be tough, but sometimes you've got to just stop and take time. You ought to train yourself to look at things with your own eyes until something becomes clear. And don't be afraid of putting some time into it. Spending plenty of time on something can be the most sophisticated form of revenge."

"Revenge?! What do you mean, 'revenge'? Revenge against whom?"

"You'll understand soon enough," said my uncle, with a smile.

·

All told, we sat on the veranda, drinking together, for something over an hour. Then, announcing that he had stayed too long, my uncle stood up and left. Alone again, I sat on the veranda, leaning against a pillar and staring out at the garden under the moon. For a time, I was able to breathe deeply the air of realism or whatever it was that my uncle left behind, and to feel, for the first time in a very long time, a sense of genuine relief.

Within a few hours, though, that air began to dissipate, and a kind of cloak of pale sorrow came to envelop me once again. In the end, I was in my world again, and my uncle was in his.

My uncle had said that I should think about the simplest things first, but I found it impossible to distinguish between what was simple and what was difficult. And so the next morning, after the rush hour had ended, I took the train to Shinjuku. I decided just to stand there and look at people's faces. I didn't know if it would do any good, but it was probably better than doing nothing. If looking at people's faces until you got sick of them was an example of a simple thing, then it couldn't hurt to give it a try. If it went well, it just might give me some indication of what constituted the "simple" things for me.

The first day, I spent two full hours sitting on the low brick wall that ran along the edge of the raised flower bed outside Shinjuku Station, watching the faces of the people who passed by. But the sheer numbers of people were too great, and they walked too quickly. I couldn't manage a good look at any one person's face. To make matters worse, some homeless guy came over to me after I had been there for a while and started haranguing me about something. A policeman came by several times, glaring at me. So I gave up on the busy area outside the station and decided to look for a place better suited to the leisurely study of passers-by.

I went along the passageway under the tracks on the west side of the station, and after I had spent some time walking around, I found a small, tiled plaza outside a glass high-rise. It had a little sculpture and some handsome benches where I could sit and look at people as much as I liked. The numbers were nowhere near as great as outside the main entrance of the station, and there weren't any homeless guys here with bottles of whisky stuck in their pockets. I spent the day there, making do for lunch with some doughnuts and coffee from Dunkin' Donuts, and going home before the evening rush.

At first the only ones who caught my eye were the men with thinning hair, thanks to the training I had received doing surveys with May Kasahara for the toupee maker. Before I knew it, my gaze would lock onto a bald head and I'd have the man classified as A, B or C. At this rate, I might just as well have called May Kasahara and volunteered to join her for work again.

After a few days had gone by, though, I found myself capable of just sitting and watching people's faces without a thought in my head. Most of the ones who passed by were men and women who worked in offices in the high-rise. The men wore white shirts and ties and carried briefcases, the women mostly wore high-heeled shoes. Others I saw included patrons of the building's restaurants and shops, family groups headed for the observation deck on the top floor, and a few people who were just passing through, walking from point A to point B. Most of the people tended not to walk very quickly. I just let myself watch them all, without any clear purpose. From time to time there would be people who attracted my interest for some reason or other, and then I would concentrate on their faces and follow them with my eyes.

Every day, I would take the train to Shinjuku at 10 o'clock, after the rush hour, sit on the bench in the plaza, and stay there almost motionless until 4, staring at people's faces. Only after I had tried this out did I realize that by training my eyes on one passing face after another, I was able to empty my head completely, like pulling the cork from a bottle. I spoke to no one, and no one spoke to me. I thought nothing, I felt nothing. I often had the sense that I had become part of the stone bench.

Someone did speak to me once, though – a thin, well-dressed middle-aged woman. She wore a bright-pink, tight-fitting dress, dark sunglasses with tortoiseshell frames, and a white hat, and she carried a white mesh handbag. She had nice legs and had on expensive-looking spotless white leather sandals. Her make-up was thick, but not offensively so. She asked me if I was in some kind of difficulty. Not at all, I replied. I seem to see you here every day, she said, and asked what I was doing. I said I was looking at people's faces. She asked if I was doing it for some purpose, and I said I was not.

Sitting down beside me, she took a pack of Virginia Slims from her bag and lit up with a small gold lighter. She offered me one, but I shook my head. Then she took off her sunglasses and, without a word, stared at my face. More precisely, she stared at the mark on my face. In return, I stared back into her eyes. But I was unable to read any emotion stirring there. I saw nothing but two dark pupils that seemed to be functioning as they were meant to. She had a small, pointed nose. Her lips were thin, and colour had been applied to them with great care. I found it hard to guess her age, but I supposed she was in her mid-forties. She looked younger than that at first glance, but the lines on either side of her nose had a special kind of weariness about them.

"Do you have any money?" she asked.

This caught me off guard. "Money? What do you mean, do I have any money?"

"I'm just asking do you have any money? Are you broke?"

"No. At the moment, I'm not broke," I said.

She drew her lips to one side, as if examining what I had said, and continued to concentrate all her attention on me. Then she nodded. And then she put her sunglasses on, dropped her cigarette to the ground, rose gracefully from her seat, and, without a glance in my direction, slipped away. Amazed, I watched her disappear into the crowd. Maybe she was a little crazy. But her immaculate grooming made that hard to believe. I stepped on her discarded cigarette, crushing it out, and then I did a slow scan of my surroundings, which turned out to be filled with the normal real world. People were moving from one place to another, each with his or her own purpose. I didn't know who they were, and they didn't know who I was. I took a deep breath and went back to my task of looking at the faces of these people, without a thought in my head.

I went on sitting there for eleven days altogether. Every day, I had my coffee and doughnuts and did nothing but watch the faces of the people passing by. Aside from the meaningless little conversation with the well-dressed woman who approached me, I spoke with no one for the whole eleven days. I did nothing special, and nothing special happened to me. Even after this eleven-day vacuum, however, I was unable to come to any conclusion. I was still lost in a complex maze, unable to solve the simplest problem.

But then, on the evening of the eleventh day, something very strange occurred. It was a Sunday, and I had stayed there watching faces until later than usual. The people who came to Shinjuku on a Sunday were different from the weekday crowd, and there was no rush hour. I caught sight of a young man with a black guitar case. He was of average height. He wore glasses with black plastic frames, had hair down to his shoulders, was dressed in blue denim jacket and jeans, and trudged along in worn-out trainers. He walked past me looking straight ahead, a thoughtful expression in his eyes. When I saw him, something struck me. My heart gave a thump. *I know that guy*, I thought. I've seen him some-where. But it took me a few seconds to remember who he was – the singer I had seen that night in the snack bar in Sapporo. No doubt about it: it was him.

I leapt from my bench and hurried after him. Given his leisurely pace, it was not difficult to catch up with him. I followed ten steps behind, adjusting my pace to his. I considered the possibility of speak-ing to him. I would say something like, "You were singing three years ago in Sapporo, weren't you? I heard you there." "Oh, really?" he would say. "Thank you very much." And then what? Should I say, "My wife had an abortion that night. And she left me not too long ago. She had been sleeping with another man"? I decided just to follow him and see what happened. Maybe as I walked along I would figure out a way to handle it.

He was walking away from the station. He passed beyond the string of high-rises, crossed the Ome Highway, and headed for Yoyogi. He seemed to be deep in thought. Apparently at home in the area, he never once hesitated or looked around. He kept walking at the same pace, facing straight ahead. I followed after him, thinking about the day that Kumiko had her abortion. Sapporo in early March. The earth was hard and frozen, and now and then a few snowflakes had fluttered down. I was back in those streets, my lungs full of frozen air. I saw the white breath coming from people's mouths.

Then it hit me: that was when things had started to change. Yes, definitely. That had been a turning point. After that, the flow around me had begun to show signs of change. Now that I thought about it, that abortion had been an event of great significance for the two of us. At the time, however, I had not been able to perceive its true importance. I had been too distracted by the *act* of abortion itself, while the genuinely important thing may have been something else entirely.

I had to do it, she said. *I felt it was the right thing to do, the best thing for both of us. But there's something else, something you don't know about, something I can't put into words just yet. I'm not hiding anything from you. I just can't be sure whether or not it's something real. Which is why I can't put it into words yet.*

Back then, she couldn't be sure that that *something* was real. And that *something*, without a doubt, had been more connected with the pregnancy than with the abortion. Maybe it had had something to do with the child in her womb. What could it have been? What had sent her into such confusion? Had she had relations with another man and refused to give birth to his baby? No, that was out of the question. She herself had declared that it was out of the question. It had been my child, that was certain. But still, there had been *something* she was unable to tell me. And that *something* was inextricably connected to her decision to leave me. Everything had started from that.

But what the secret was, what had been concealed there, I had no idea. I was the only one left alone, the only one in the dark. All I knew for certain was that as long as I failed to solve the secret of that *something*, Kumiko would never come back to me. I began to sense a quiet anger growing inside my body, an anger directed towards that *something* that remained invisible to me. I stretched my back, drew in a deep breath, and calmed the pounding of my heart. Even so, the anger, like water, seeped into every corner of my body. It was an anger steeped in sorrow. There was no way for me to smash it against something, nothing I could do to dispel it.

.

The man went on walking at the same steady pace. He crossed the Odakyu Line tracks, passed a block of shops, through a shrine, through a labyrinth of alleys. I followed after him, adjusting my distance so as to keep him from spotting me. And it was clear that he had not spotted me. He never once looked around. There was definitely something about this man that made him different from ordinary people. Not only did he never look back, he never once looked to either side. He was so utterly concentrated: what could he be thinking about? Or was he, rather, thinking about absolutely nothing?

Before long, the man entered a hushed area of deserted streets lined with two-story wood-frame houses. The road was narrow and twisted, and the run-down houses were jammed up against each other on either side. The lack of people here was almost weird. More than half the houses were vacant. Boards were nailed across the front doors of the vacant houses, and applications for planning permission were posted outside. Here and there, like missing teeth, were vacant lots filled with summer weeds and surrounded by chain-link fences. There was probably a plan to demolish this whole area in the near future and put up some new high-rises. Pots of morning glories and other flowers crammed the little space outside one of the few houses that were occupied. A tricycle lay on its side, and a towel and a child's bathing suit were being dried in the second-story window. Cats lay everywhere – beneath the windows, in the doorway – watching me with weary eyes. Despite the early-evening hour, there was no sign of people. The geography of this place confounded me. I couldn't tell north from south. I guessed that I was in the triangular area between Yoyogi and Sendagaya and Harajuku, but I could not be sure.

It was, in any case, a forgotten section of the city. It had most likely been overlooked because the roads were so narrow that cars could hardly pass through. The hands of the developers had not reached this far. Stepping in here, I felt as if time had turned back twenty or thirty years. I realized that at some point, the constant roar of car engines had been swallowed up and was now gone. Carrying his guitar case, the man had made his way through the maze of streets until he came to a wood-frame apartment house. He opened the front door, went inside, and closed the door behind him. As far as I could see, the door had not been locked.

I stood there for a time. The hands of my watch showed 6.20. I leaned against the chain-link fence of the vacant lot across the street, observing the building. It was a typical two-floor wood-frame apartment building. The look of the entrance and the layout of the rooms gave it away. I had lived in a building like this for a time when I was a student. There had been a shoe cabinet in the hallway, a shared toilet, a little kitchen, and only students or single working people lived there. This particular building, though, gave no sense of anyone living there. It was devoid of sound or movement. The plastic-veneer door bore no nameplate. Where it had been removed, there was a long, narrow blank. All the windows of the place were shut tight, with curtains drawn, despite the lingering afternoon heat.

This apartment house, like its neighbours, was probably scheduled for demolition soon, and no one lived there any longer. But if that was true, what was the man with the guitar case doing here? I expected to see a window slide open after he went inside, but still nothing moved.

I couldn't just go on hanging around for ever in this deserted alley. I walked over to the front door and gave it a push. I had been right: it was not locked, and it opened in easily. I stood in the doorway a moment, trying to get a sense of the place, but I could hardly make out anything in the gloomy interior. With the windows all closed, the place was filled with hot, stale air. The mouldy smell reminded me of the air at the bottom of the well. My armpits were streaming in the heat. A drop of sweat ran down behind my ear. After a moment's hesitation, I stepped inside and quietly closed the door behind me. By checking the name tags (if there were any) on the mailboxes or the shoe cabinet, I intended to find out if anyone was still living here, but before I could do so I realized that someone was there. Someone was watching me.

To the right of the entrance stood a tall shoe cabinet or some such thing, and the *someone* was standing just beyond it, as if hiding. I held my breath and peered into the gloomy warmth. The person standing there was the young man with the guitar case. It was obvious he had been hiding behind the shoe cabinet from the time he entered. My heart pounded at the base of my throat like a hammer smashing a nail. What was he doing there? Waiting for me? "Hello there," I forced myself to say. "I was hoping to ask you –"

But the words were barely out of my mouth when something slammed into my shoulder. Hard. I couldn't tell what was happening. All I felt at that moment was a physical impact of blinding intensity. I went on standing there, confused. But the next second, I realized what was going on. With the agility of a monkey, the man had leaped out from behind the shoe cabinet and hit me with a baseball bat. While I stood there in shock, he raised the bat again and swung it at me. I tried to dodge, but I was too late. This time the bat hit my left arm. For a moment, the arm lost all feeling. There was no pain, nothing at all. It was as if the whole arm had just melted into space.

Before I knew it, though, almost as a reflex action, I was kicking at him. I had never had formal training in martial arts, but a friend of mine in high school with some proficiency in karate had taught me a few elementary moves. Day after day, he had had me practising kicks – nothing fancy: just training to kick as hard and high and straight as possible. This was the single most useful thing to know in an emergency, he had said. And he was right. Absorbed with swinging his bat, the man had never anticipated the possibility that he might be kicked. Just as frantic as he was, I had no idea where my kick was aimed, nor was it very strong, but the shock of it seemed to take the wind out of him. He stopped swinging his bat, and as if a break in time had occurred at that point, he stared at me with vacant eyes. Given this opportunity, I aimed a stronger, more accurate kick at his groin, and when he curled up with the pain, I wrenched the bat from his hands. Then I kicked him hard in the ribs. He tried to grab my leg, so I kicked him again. And then again, in the same place. Then I smashed his thigh with the bat. Emitting a dull scream, he fell to the floor.

At first I kicked and beat him out of sheer terror, so as to prevent myself from being hit. Once he fell on the floor, though, I found my terror turning to unmistakable anger. The anger was still there, the quiet anger that had welled up in my body earlier while I was walking along and thinking about Kumiko. Released now, it flared up uncontrollably into something close to intense hatred. I smashed the man's thigh again with the bat. He was drooling from the corner of his mouth. My shoulder and left arm were beginning to throb where he had hit me. The pain aroused my anger all the more. The man's face was distorted with pain, but he struggled to raise himself from the floor. I couldn't make my left arm work, so I threw the bat down and stood over him, smashing his face with my right hand. I punched him again and again. I punched him until the fingers of my right hand grew numb and then started to hurt. I was going to beat him until he was unconscious. I grabbed his neck and smashed his head against the wooden floor. Never in my life had I been involved in a fistfight. I had never hit another person with all my strength. But now hitting was all I could do, and I couldn't seem to stop. My mind was telling me to stop: this was enough. Any more would be too much. The man could no longer get to his feet. But I couldn't stop. There were two of me now, I realized. I had split in two, but *this* me had lost the power to stop the other me. An intense chill ran through my body.

Then I realized the man was smiling. Even as I went on hitting him, the man kept smiling at me – the more I hit him, the bigger the smile, until finally, with blood streaming from his nose and lips, and choking on his own spit, the man gave out a high, thin laugh. He must be crazy, I thought, and I stopped punching him and stood up straight.

I looked around and saw the black guitar case propped against the side of the shoe cabinet. I left the man where he lay, still laughing, and approached the guitar case. Lowering it to the floor, I opened the clasps and lifted the cover. There was nothing inside – no guitar, no candles. The man looked at me, laughing and coughing. I could hardly breathe. All of a sudden, the hot, steamy air inside this building became unbearable. The smell of mould, the feel of my own sweat, the smell of blood and saliva, my own sense of anger and hatred: all became more than I could bear. I pushed the door open and went outside, closing the door behind me. As before, there was no sign of anyone in the area. All that moved was a large brown cat, slowly making its way across the vacant lot, oblivious of me.

I wanted to get out of there before anyone spotted me. I wasn't sure which way I should go, but I started walking and before long managed to find a bus stop with a sign reading "To Shinjuku Station". I hoped to calm my breathing and straighten my head out before the next bus came, but failed to do either. Over and over, I told myself: All I was trying to do was look at people's faces! I was just looking at the faces of people passing by on the street, the way my uncle had said. I was just trying to untangle the simplest complications in my life, that's all. When I got on the bus, the passengers turned towards me. Each of them gave me the same shocked look and then averted his eyes. I assumed it was because of the mark on my face. Some time passed before I realized it was because of the splatters on my white shirt of the man's blood (mostly blood from his nose) and the baseball bat I was still clutching in my hands.

I ended up taking the bat all the way home with me and throwing it in a cupboard.

That night I stayed awake until the sun came up. The places on my shoulder and left arm where the man had hit me with the bat began to swell and to throb with pain, and my right fist retained the sensation of punching the man over and over and over again. The hand was still a fist, I realized, still clutched into a ball and ready to fight. I tried to relax it, but the hand would not cooperate. And where sleeping was concerned, it was less a matter of being unable to sleep than of not wanting to sleep. If I went to sleep in my present state, there was no way I could avoid having terrible dreams. Trying to calm myself, I sat at the kitchen table, taking sips of the whisky my uncle had left with me and listening to quiet music on the cassette player. I wanted to talk to someone. I wanted someone to talk to me. I put the telephone on the table and stared at it for hours. Call me, somebody, please, anybody – even the mysterious phone woman; I didn't care. It could be the most filthy and meaningless talk, the most disgusting and sinister conversation. It didn't matter. I just wanted someone to talk to me.

But the telephone didn't ring. I finished the remaining half-bottle of scotch, and after the sky grew light, I crawled into bed and went to sleep. Please don't let me dream, please just let my sleep be a blank, if only for today.

But of course I did dream. And as I had expected, it was a terrible dream. The man with the guitar case was in it. I performed the same actions in the dream as I had in reality – following him, opening the front door of the apartment building, feeling the impact of the bat, and hitting and hitting and hitting the man. But after that it was different. When I stopped hitting him and stood up, the man, drooling and laughing wildly as he had in reality, pulled a knife from his pocket – a small, sharp knife. The blade caught the faint evening glow that spilled in through the curtains, reflecting a white glimmer reminiscent of bone. But the man did not use the knife to attack me. Instead, he took all his clothes off and started to peel his own skin as if it were the skin of an apple. He worked quickly, laughing aloud all the while. The blood gushed out of him, forming a black, menacing pool on the floor. With his right hand, he peeled the skin of his left arm, and with his bloody, peeled left hand he peeled the skin of his right arm. In the end, he became a bright-red lump of flesh, but even then, he went on laughing from the dark hole of his open mouth, the white eyeballs moving spasmodically against the raw lump of flesh. Soon, as if in response to the unnatural loudness of his laughter, the man's peeled skin began to slither across the floor towards me. I tried to run away, but my legs would not move. The skin reached my feet and began to crawl upward. It crept over my own skin, the man's blood-soaked skin clinging to mine and forming an overlay. The heavy smell of blood was everywhere. Soon my legs, my body, my face, were entirely covered by the thin membrane of the man's skin. Then my eyes could no longer see, and the man's laughter reverberated in the hollow darkness. At that point, I woke up.

Confusion and fear overtook me. For a while, I even lost hold of my own existence. My fingers were trembling. But at the same time, I knew that I had reached a conclusion.

I could not – and should not – run away, not to Crete, not to anywhere. I had to get Kumiko back. With my own hands, I had to pull her back into this world. Because if I didn't, that would be the end of me. This person, this self that I thought of as "me", would be lost.

Book Three: The Birdcatcher

October 1984 to December 1985

1

The Wind-up Bird in Winter

•

Between the end of that strange summer and the approach of winter, my life went on without change. Each day would dawn without incident and end as it had begun. It rained a lot in September. October had several warm, sweaty days. Apart from the weather, there was hardly anything to distinguish one day from the next. I worked at concentrating my attention on the real and useful. I would go to the pool almost every day for a long swim, take walks, make myself three meals.

But even so, every now and then I would feel a violent stab of loneliness. The very water I drank, the very air I breathed, would feel like long, sharp needles. The pages of a book in my hands would take on the threatening metallic gleam of razor blades. I could hear the roots of loneliness creeping through me when the world was hushed at 4 o'clock in the morning.

•

And yet there were a few people who wouldn't leave me alone – people from Kumiko's family, who wrote me letters. Kumiko could not go on being married to me, they said, and so I should agree to an immediate divorce. That would supposedly solve all problems. The first few letters tried to exert pressure on me in a businesslike manner. When I failed to answer, they resorted to threats and, in the end, turned to pleading. All were looking for the same thing.

Eventually, Kumiko's father called.

"I am not saying that I will never agree to a divorce," I said. "But first I want to see Kumiko and talk to her, alone. If she can convince me it's what she wants, then I will give her a divorce. Only then will I agree to it."

I turned towards the kitchen window and looked at the dark, rain-filled sky stretching away into the distance. It had been raining for four straight days, into a wet, black world.

"Kumiko and I talked everything over before we decided to get married, and if we are going to end that marriage, I want to do it the same way."

Kumiko's father and I went on making parallel statements, arriving nowhere – or nowhere fruitful, at least.

Several questions remained unanswered. Did Kumiko really want to divorce me? And had she asked her parents to try to convince me to go along with it? "Kumiko says she doesn't want to see you," her father had told me, exactly as her brother, Noboru Wataya, had said. This was probably not an out-and-out lie. Kumiko's parents were not above interpreting things in a manner convenient to themselves, but as far as I knew, they were not the sort to manufacture facts out of nothing. They were, for better or worse, realistic people. If what her father had said was true, then, was Kumiko now being "sheltered" by them?

But that I found impossible to believe. Love was simply not an emotion that Kumiko had felt for her parents and brother from the time she was a little girl. She had struggled for years to keep herself independent of them. It could well be that Kumiko had chosen to leave me because she had taken a lover. Even if I could not accept the explanation she had given me in her letter, I knew that it was not out of the question. But what I could not accept was that Kumiko should have gone straight from me to them – or to some place they had prepared for her – and that she should be communicating with me through them.

The more I thought about it, the less I understood. One possibility was that Kumiko had experienced an emotional breakdown and could no longer look after herself. Another was that she was being held against her will. I spent several days arranging and rearranging a variety of facts and words and memories, until I had to give up thinking. Speculation was getting me nowhere.

342

Autumn was drawing to a close, and a touch of winter hung in the air. As I always did at that season, I raked the dead leaves in the garden and stuffed them into plastic bags. I set a ladder against the roof and cleaned the leaves out of the gutters. The little garden of the house I lived in had no trees, but the wind carried leaves in abundance from the broad-spreading deciduous trees in the gardens on both sides. I didn't mind the work. The time would pass as I watched the withered leaves floating down in the afternoon sunshine. One big tree in the neighbour's to the right put out bright-red berries. Flocks of birds would perch there and chirp as if in competition with each other. These were brightly coloured birds, with short, sharp cries that stabbed the air.

I wondered about how best to store Kumiko's summer clothes. I could do as she had said in her letter and get rid of them. But I remembered the care that she had given to each item. And it was not as if I had no place to keep them. I decided to leave them for the time being where they were.

Still, whenever I opened the wardrobe, I was confronted by Kumiko's absence. The dresses hanging there were the husks of something that had once existed. I knew how she looked in these clothes, and to some of them were attached specific memories. I would find myself sitting on the edge of the bed, staring at the rows of dresses or blouses or skirts. I would have no idea how long I had been sitting there. It could have been ten minutes or an hour.

Sometimes, as I sat staring at a dress, I would imagine a man I didn't know helping Kumiko out of it. His hands would slip the dress off, then go on to remove the underwear beneath. They would caress her breasts and press her thighs apart. I could see those breasts and thighs in all their white softness, and the other man's hands touching them. I didn't want to think about such things, but I had no choice. They had probably happened in reality. I had to get used to such images. I couldn't just shove reality aside.

Now and then, I would recall the night I slept with Creta Kano, but the memory of it was vague. I held her in my arms that night and joined my body with hers any number of times: that was an undeniable fact. But as the weeks passed by, the feeling of certainty began to disappear. I couldn't bring back concrete images of her body or of the ways in which it had joined with mine. If anything, the memories of what I had done with her earlier, in my mind – in unreality – were far more vivid than the memories of the reality of that night. The image of her mounted on me, wearing Kumiko's blue dress, in that strange hotel room, came back to me over and over again with amazing clarity.

•

Early October saw the death of the uncle of Noboru Wataya who had served as Niigata's representative to the Lower House. He suffered a heart attack shortly after midnight in his hospital bed in Niigata, and by dawn, despite the doctors' best efforts, he was dead. The death had long been anticipated, of course, and a general election was expected shortly, so the uncle's supporters lost no time in formalizing their earlier plan to have Noboru Wataya inherit the constituency. The late representative's vote-gathering machinery was solidly based and solidly conservative. Barring some major unforeseen event, Noboru Wataya's election was assured.

The first thing that crossed my mind when I read the article in a library newspaper was how busy the Wataya family was going to be from now on. The farthest thing from anybody's mind would be Kumiko's divorce.

•

The black-and-blue mark on my face neither grew nor shrank. It produced neither fever nor pain. Little by little, I forgot I even had it. I stopped trying to hide the mark by wearing sunglasses or a hat with the brim pulled down low. I would be reminded of it now and then when I went out shopping and people would stare at me or look away, but even these reactions stopped bothering me after a while. I wasn't harming them by having a mark on my face. I would examine it each morning when I washed and shaved, but I could see no change. Its size, colour and shape remained the same.

The number of individual human beings who voiced concern about the sudden appearance of a mark on my cheek was exactly four: the owner of the cleaning shop by the station, my barber, the young man from the Omura off-licence, and the woman at the counter of the local library. In each case, when asked about it, I made a show of annoyance and said something vague like "I had a little accident." They would mumble, "My, my" or "That's too bad", as if apologizing for having mentioned it.

I seemed to be growing more distant from myself with each day that went by. If I stared at my hand for a while, I would begin to feel that I was looking through it. I spoke with hardly anybody. No one wrote to me or called. All I found in my mailbox were bills and junk mail, and most of the junk mail consisted of designer-brand catalogues addressed to Kumiko, full of colourful photos of spring dresses and blouses and skirts. The winter was a cold one, but I sometimes forgot to turn on the heat, unsure whether the cold was real or just something inside me. I would throw the switch only after a look at the thermometer had convinced me that it really was cold, but even so, the cold I felt did not diminish.

·

I wrote to Lieutenant Mamiya with a general description of what had been happening to me. He might be more embarrassed than pleased to receive the letter, but I couldn't think of anyone else I could write to. I opened with that exact apology. Then I told him that Kumiko had left me on the very day he had visited my house, that she had been sleeping with another man for some months, that I had spent almost three days at the bottom of a well, thinking, that I was now living here all alone, and that the keepsake from Mr Honda had been nothing but an empty whisky box.

Lieutenant Mamiya sent me an answer a week later.

To tell you the truth, you have been in my thoughts to an uncanny degree since we last met. I left your home feeling that we really ought to go on talking, to "spill our guts" to each other, so to speak, and the fact that we did not has been no small source of regret to me. Unfortunately, however, some urgent business had come up, which required me to return to Hiroshima that night. Thus, in a certain sense, I was very glad to receive a letter from you. I wonder if it was not Mr Honda's intention all along to bring the two of us together. Perhaps he believed that it would be good for me to meet you and for you to meet me. The division of keepsakes may well have been an excuse to have me visit you. This may explain the empty box. My visit to you itself would have been his keepsake.

I was amazed to hear that you had spent time down in a well, for I, too, continue to feel myself strongly attracted to wells. Considering my own close call, one would think that I would never have wanted to see another well, but quite the contrary, even to this day, whenever I see a well, I can't help looking in. And if it turns out to be a dry well, I feel the urge to climb down inside. It may be that I continue to hope I will encounter something down there, that if I go down inside and simply wait, it will be possible for me to encounter a certain something. Not that I expect it to restore my life to me. No, I am far too old to hope for such things. What I hope to find is the meaning of the life that I have lost. By what was it taken away from me, and why? I want to know the answers to these questions with

absolute certainty. And I would go so far as to say that if I could have those answers,
I would not mind being even more profoundly lost than I am already. Indeed, I would
gladly accept such a burden for whatever years of life may be left to me.

I was truly sorry to hear that your wife had left you, but that is a matter on
which I am unable to offer you any advice. I have lived far too long a time with-
out the benefit of love or family and am thus unqualified to speak on such matters.
I do believe, however, that if you feel the slightest willingness to wait a while
longer for her to come back, then you should probably continue to wait there as
you are doing now. That is my opinion, for what it is worth. I realize full well how
hard it must be to go on living alone in a place from which someone has left you,
but there is nothing so cruel in this world as the desolation of having nothing to
hope for.

If possible, I would like to come to Tokyo in the near future and see you again,
but unfortunately I am having a little problem with one leg, and the treatment for
it will take some time. Please take care and be well.

Sometimes I climbed the garden wall and went down the winding
alley to where the vacant Miyawaki house had stood. Dressed in a
three-quarter-length coat, a scarf wrapped under my chin, I trod the
alley's dead winter grass. Short puffs of frozen winter wind whistled
through the electric lines overhead. The house had been completely
demolished, the yard now surrounded by a high plank fence. I could
look in through the gaps in the fence, but there was nothing to see –
no house, no paving stones, no well, no trees, no TV aerial, no bird
sculpture: just a flat, black stretch of cold-looking earth, compacted by
the tracks of a bulldozer, and a few scattered clumps of weeds. I could
hardly believe there had once been a deep well in the yard and that I had
climbed down into it.

I leaned against the fence, looking up at May Kasahara's house, to
where her room was, on the second floor. But she was no longer there.
She wouldn't be coming out any more to say, "Hi, Mr Wind-up Bird."

.

On a bitter-cold afternoon in mid-February, I dropped in at the estate
agents' office by the station that my uncle had told me about, Setagaya
Dai-ichi Realtors. When I walked in, the first person I saw was a middle-
aged female receptionist. Several desks were lined up near the entrance,
but their chairs were empty, as if all the brokers were out on appointments.
A large gas heater glowed bright red in the middle of the room. On a sofa in
a small reception area towards the back sat a slightly built old man,
engrossed in a newspaper. I asked the receptionist if a Mr Ichikawa might

be there. "That's me," said the old man, turning in my direction. "Can I help you?"

I introduced myself as my uncle's nephew and mentioned that I lived in one of the houses that my uncle owned.

"Oh, I see," said the old man, laying his paper down. "So *you're* Mr Tsuruta's nephew!" He folded his reading glasses and gave me a head-to-toe inspection. I couldn't tell what kind of impression I was making on him. "Come in, come in. Can I offer you a cup of tea?"

I told him not to bother, but either he didn't hear me or he ignored my refusal. He asked the receptionist to make tea. It didn't take her long to bring it to us, but by the time he and I were sitting opposite each other, drinking tea, the stove had gone out and the room was getting chilly. A detailed map showing all the houses in the area hung on the wall, marked here and there in pencil or felt-tip pen. Next to it hung a calendar with Van Gogh's famous bridge painting: a bank calendar.

"I haven't seen your uncle in quite a while. How is he doing?" the old man asked after a sip of tea.

"I think he's fine, busy as ever. I don't see him much myself," I said.

"I'm glad to hear he's doing well. How many years has it been since I last saw him? I wonder. At least it *seems* like years." He took a cigarette from his jacket pocket, and after taking careful aim, he struck a match with a vigorous swipe. "I was the one who found that house for him, and I managed it for him for a long time too. Anyhow, it's good to hear he's keeping busy."

Old Mr Ichikawa himself seemed anything but busy. I imagined he must be semi-retired, showing up at the office now and then to take care of longtime clients.

"So how do you like the house? No problems?"

"No, none at all," I said.

The old man nodded. "That's good. It's a nice place. Maybe on the small side, but a nice place to live. Things have always gone well for the people who lived there. For you too?"

"Not bad," I said to him. At least I'm alive, I said to myself. "I had something I wanted to ask you about, though. My uncle says you know more than anybody about this area."

The old man chuckled. "This area is one thing I *do* know," he said. "I've been dealing in property here for close to forty years."

"The thing I want to ask you about is the Miyawaki place behind ours. They've bulldozed it, you know."

"Yes, I know," said the old man, pursing his lips as though rummaging through the drawers in his mind. "It sold last August. They *finally* got all the mortgage and title and legal problems straightened out and put it on the market. A speculator bought it, to tear down the house and sell the land. Leave a house vacant that long, I don't care how good it is, it's not going to sell. Of course, the people who bought it are not local. Nobody local would touch the place. Have you heard some of the stories?"

"Yes, I have, from my uncle."

"Then you know what I'm talking about. I suppose we could have bought it and sold it to somebody who didn't know any better, but we don't do business that way. It just leaves a bad taste in your mouth."

I nodded in agreement. "So who did buy it, then?"

The old man knit his brow and shook his head, then told me the name of a well-known property corporation. "They probably didn't do any research, just snapped it up when they saw the location and the price, figured they'd turn a quick profit. But it's not going to be so easy."

"They haven't been able to sell it?"

"They came close a few times," the old man said, folding his arms. "It's not cheap, buying a piece of land. It's a lifetime investment. People are careful. When they start looking into things, any number of stories come out, and in this case, not one of them is good. You hear stories like that, and the ordinary person is not going to buy. Most of the people who live around here know the stories about that place."

"What are they asking?"

"Asking?"

"The price of the land where the Miyawaki house was."

Old Mr Ichikawa looked at me in a way that showed I had aroused his curiosity. "Well, let's see. The lot is a little over thirty-five hundred square feet. Not quite a hundred *tsubo*. The market price would be one and a half million yen per *tsubo*. I mean, that's a first-rate lot – wonderful setting, southern exposure. A million and a half, no problem, even with the market as slow as it is. You might have to wait a little while, but you'd get your price at that location. *Ordinarily*. But there's nothing ordinary about the Miyawaki place. That's not going to move, no matter how long you wait. So the price has to go down. It's already down to a million ten per *tsubo*, so with a little more bargaining you could probably get the whole place for an even hundred million."

"Do you think the price will continue to fall?"

The old man gave a sharp nod. "Of course it's going to fall. To nine hundred thousand per *tsubo* easy. That's what they bought it for. They're really getting worried now. They'd be happy just to break even. I don't know if they'd go any lower. They might take a loss if they're hurting for cash. Otherwise, they could afford to wait. I just don't know what's going on inside the company. What I do know is that they're sorry they bought the place. Getting mixed up with that piece of land is not going to do anybody any good." He tapped ash into the ashtray.

"The yard has a well, doesn't it?" I asked. "Do you know anything about the well?"

"Hmm, it does have a well, doesn't it," said Mr Ichikawa. "A deep well. But I think they filled it in. It was dry, after all. Useless."

"Do you have any idea when it dried up?"

The old man glared at the ceiling for a while, with his arms folded. "That was a *long* time ago. I can't remember, really, but I'm sure I heard it had water sometime before the war. It must have dried up after the war. I don't know when, exactly. But I know it was dry when the actress moved in. There was a lot of talk then about whether or not to fill in the well. But nobody ever did anything about it. I guess it was too much bother."

"The well in the Kasahara place across the alley still has plenty of water – good water, I'm told."

"Maybe so, maybe so. The wells in that area always produced good-tasting water. It's got something to do with the soil. You know, water veins are delicate things. It's not unusual to get water in one place and nothing at all right close by. Is there something about that well that interests you?"

"To tell you the truth, I'd like to buy that piece of land."

The old man raised his eyes and focused them on mine. Then he lifted his teacup and took a silent sip. "You want to buy that piece of land?"

My only reply was a nod.

The old man took another cigarette from his pack and tapped it against the tabletop. But then, instead of lighting it, he held it between his fingers. His tongue flicked across his lips. "Let me say one more time that that's a place with a lot of problems. No one – and I mean *no* one – has ever done well there. You *do* realize that? I don't care how cheap it gets, that place can never be a good buy. But you want it just the same?"

"Yes, I still want it, knowing what I know. But let *me* point out one thing: I don't have enough money on hand to buy the place, no matter how far the price falls below market value. But I intend to raise the money, even if it takes me a while. So I would like to be kept informed of any new developments. Can I count on you to let me know if the price changes or if a buyer shows up?"

For a time, the old man just stared at his unlit cigarette, lost in thought. Then, clearing his throat with a little cough, he said, "Don't worry, you've got time; that place is not going to sell for a while, I guarantee you. It's not going to move until they're practically giving it away, and that won't happen for a while. So take all the time you need to raise the money. *If you really want it.*"

I gave him my phone number. The old man wrote it down in a little sweat-stained black notebook. After returning the notebook to his jacket pocket, he looked me in the eye for a while and then looked at the mark on my cheek.

·

February came to an end, and March was half gone when the freezing cold began to relent somewhat. Warm winds blew from the south. Buds appeared on the trees, and new birds showed up in the garden. On warm days I began to spend time sitting on the veranda, looking at the garden. One evening I got a call from Mr Ichikawa. The Miyawaki land was still unsold, he said, and the price had dropped.

"I *told* you it wouldn't move for a while," he added, with a touch of pride. "Don't worry, from now on it's just going to creep down. Meanwhile, how are you doing? Funds coming together?"

·

I was washing my face at 8 o'clock that night when I noticed that my mark was beginning to run a slight fever. When I laid my finger against it, I could feel a touch of warmth that had not been there before. The colour, too, seemed more intense than usual, almost purplish. Barely breathing, I stared into the mirror for a long time – long enough for me to begin to see my own face as something other than mine. The mark was trying to tell me something: it *wanted* something from me. I went on staring at my self beyond the mirror, and that self went on staring back at me from beyond the mirror without a word.

I have to have that well. Whatever happens, I have to have that well.

This was the conclusion I had reached.

2

Waking from Hibernation

◆

One More Name Card

◆

The Namelessness of Money

Just wanting the land was not going to make it mine, of course. The amount of money I could realistically raise was close to zero. I still had a little of what my mother had left me, but that would evaporate soon in the course of living. I had no job, nothing I could offer as collateral. And there was no bank in the world that would lend money to someone like me out of sheer kindness. I would have to use magic to produce the money from thin air. And soon.

One morning I walked to the station and bought ten fifty-million-yen lottery tickets, with continuous numbers. Using drawing pins, I covered a section of the kitchen wall with them and looked at them every day. Sometimes I would spend a whole hour in a chair staring hard at them, as if waiting for a secret code to rise out of them that only I could see. After several days of this, the thought struck me from nowhere: *I'm never going to win the lottery.*

Before long, I knew this without a doubt. Things were not going to be solved so easily – by just buying a few lottery tickets and waiting for the results. I would have to get the money through my own efforts. I tore up the lottery tickets and threw them away. Then I stood in front of the washbasin mirror and peered into its depths. There has to be a way, I said to myself in the mirror, but of course there was no reply.

•

Tired of always being shut up in the house with my thoughts, I began to walk around the neighbourhood. I continued these aimless walks for three or four days, and when I tired of the neighbourhood, I took the train to Shinjuku. The impulse to go downtown came to me when I happened to pass the station. Sometimes, I thought, it helps to think about things in a different setting. It occurred to me, too, that I hadn't been on a train for a very long time. Indeed, while putting my money in the ticket machine, I experienced the nervousness one feels when doing something unfamiliar. When had I last been the streets of the city? Probably not since I followed the man with the guitar case from the Shinjuku west entrance – more than six months earlier.

The sight of the crowds in Shinjuku Station I found overwhelming. The flow of people took my breath away and even made my heart pound – and this wasn't even rush hour! I had trouble making my way through the crush of bodies at first. This was not so much a crowd as a raging torrent – the kind of flood that tears whole houses apart and sweeps them away. I had been walking only a few minutes when I felt the need to calm my nerves. I entered a café that faced the avenue and took a seat by one of its large glass windows. Late in the morning, the café was not crowded. I ordered a cup of cocoa and half-consciously watched the people walking by outside.

I was all but unaware of the passage of time. Perhaps fifteen minutes had gone by, perhaps twenty, when I realized that my eyes had been following each polished Mercedes-Benz, Jaguar and Porsche that crept along the jam-packed avenue. In the fresh morning sunlight after a night of rain, these cars sparkled with almost painful intensity, like symbols of something. They were absolutely spotless. *Those guys have money.* Such a thought had never crossed my mind before. I looked at my reflection in the glass and shook my head. This was the first time in my life I had a desperate need for money.

When the lunchtime crowd began to fill the café, I decided to take a walk. I had no particular goal other than to walk through the city I had not seen for so long. I walked from one street to another, my only thought being to avoid bumping into the people coming towards me. I turned right or left or went straight ahead, depending on the changing of the traffic signals or the whim of the moment. Hands in pockets, I concentrated on the physical act of walking – from the avenues with their rows of department stores and display windows, to the back alleys with their garishly decorated porno shops, to the lively streets with cinemas, through the hushed precincts of a Shinto shrine, and back to the avenues. It was a warm afternoon, and nearly half the crowd had left their coats indoors. The occasional breeze felt pleasant for a change. Before I realized it, I found myself standing in familiar surroundings. I looked at the tiles beneath my feet, at the little sculpture that stood there, and at the tall glass building that towered over me. I was standing in the middle of the small plaza outside the high-rise, the very one where I had gone last summer to watch the people passing by, as my uncle had advised me to do. I had kept it up for eleven days then, at the end of which I had followed the weird man with the guitar case into the strange apartment house lobby, where he attacked me with the bat. Aimless walking around Shinjuku had brought me to the very same place.

As before, I bought myself coffee and a doughnut at Dunkin' Donuts and took them with me to the plaza bench. I sat and watched the faces of the people passing by, which put me in an increasingly calm and peaceful mood. It felt good for some reason I could not fathom, as though I had found a comfortable niche in a wall where people would not notice me watching them. It had been a very long time since I had had such a good look at people's faces. And not only people's faces, I realized. I had hardly looked – really looked – at anything at all over these past six months. I sat up straight on the bench and poised myself to look at things. I looked at the people, I looked at the buildings towering overhead, I looked at the spring sky where the clouds had parted, I looked at the colourful billboards, I picked up a newspaper lying close by and looked at it. Colour seemed gradually to be returning to things as evening approached.

•

The next morning I took the train to Shinjuku again. I sat on the same bench and looked at the faces of the people passing by. Again for lunch I had a doughnut and coffee. I took the train home before the evening rush hour started. I made myself dinner, drank a beer, and listened to music on the radio. The next day I did exactly the same thing. Nothing happened that day, either. I made no discoveries, solved no riddles, answered no questions. But I did have the vague sense that I was, little by little, moving closer to something. I could detect this movement, this increasing closeness, whenever I looked at myself in the mirror above the sink. The colour of my mark was more vivid than before, warmer than before. *My mark is alive* I told myself. Just as I am alive, my mark is alive.

I repeated the routine every day, as I had done the previous summer, boarding the train for the city just after 10, sitting on the bench in the plaza by the high-rise, and looking at the people passing back and forth all day, without a thought in my head. Now and then, the real sounds around me would grow distant and fade away. The only thing I heard at those times was the deep, quiet sound of water flowing. I thought of Malta Kano. She had talked about listening to the sound of water. Water was her main motif. But I could not recall what Malta Kano had said about the sound of water. Nor could I recall her face. All that I could bring back was the red colour of her vinyl hat. Why had she always worn that red vinyl hat?

But then sounds little by little came back to me, and once again I returned my gaze to the faces of the people.

•

On the afternoon of the eighth day of my going into town, a woman spoke to me. At that moment, I happened to be looking in another direction, with an empty coffee cup in my hand. "Excuse me," she said. I turned and raised my eyes to the face of the woman standing in front of me. It was the same middle-aged woman I had encountered here last summer – the only person who had spoken to me during the time I spent in the plaza. It had never occurred to me that we would meet again, but when she spoke to me, it seemed like the natural conclusion of a great flow.

As before, the woman was immaculately dressed, in terms of both the quality of the individual items of clothing and the style with which she had combined them. She wore dark tortoiseshell sunglasses, a smoky blue jacket with padded shoulders, and a red flannel skirt. Her blouse was of silk, and on the collar of her jacket shone a finely sculpted gold brooch. Her red high heels were simple in design, but I could have lived several months on what they must have cost her. My own outfit was a mess, as usual: the baseball jacket I bought the year I entered college, a grey sweat-shirt with a stretched-out neck, frayed jeans, and formerly white tennis shoes that were now of indeterminate colour.

Despite the contrast, she sat down next to me, crossed her legs, and, without a word, took a box of Virginia Slims from her handbag. She offered me a cigarette as she had last summer, and again I declined. She put one between her lips and lit it, using a long, slender gold lighter the size of an eraser. Then she took off her sunglasses, put them in her jacket pocket, and stared into my eyes as if searching for a coin she had dropped into a shallow pond. I studied her eyes in return. They were strange eyes, of great depth but expressionless.

She narrowed her eyes slightly and said, "So. You're back."

I nodded.

I watched the smoke rise from the tip of her narrow cigarette and drift away on the wind. She turned to survey the scene around us, as if to ascertain with her own eyes just what it was I had been looking at from the bench. What she saw didn't seem to interest her, though. She turned her eyes to me again. She stared at my mark for a long time, then at my eyes, my nose, my mouth, and then my mark again. I had the feeling that what she really wanted to do was inspect me like a dog in a show: prise my lips open to check my teeth, look into my ears, and whatever else they do.

"I guess I need some money now," I said.

She paused a moment. "How much?"

"Eighty million yen should do it."

She took her eyes from mine and peered up at the sky as if calculating the amount: let's see, if I take that from there, and move this from here . . . I studied her make-up all the while – the eye-shadow faint, like the shadow of a thought, the curl of the eyelashes subtle, like some kind of symbol.

"That's not a small amount of money," she said, with a slight diagonal twist of the lips.

"*I'd* say it's enormous."

Her cigarette was only one-third smoked when she dropped it to the ground and carefully crushed it beneath the sole of her high-heeled shoe. Then she took a leather calling-card case from her slim handbag and thrust a card into my hand.

"Come to this address at exactly 4 o'clock tomorrow afternoon," she said.

The address – an office building in the wealthy Akasaka district – was the only thing on the card. There was no name. I turned it over to check the back, but it was blank. I brought the card to my nose, but it had no fragrance. It was just a normal white card.

"No name?" I said.

She smiled for the first time and gently shook her head from side to side. "I believe that what you need is money. Does money have a name?"

I shook my head as she was doing. Money had no name, of course. And if it did have a name, it would no longer be money. What gave money its true meaning was its dark-night namelessness, its breathtaking interchangeability.

She stood up from the bench. "You can come at 4 o'clock, then?"

"If I do, you'll put money in my hand?"

"I wonder," she said, a smile at the corners of her eyes like wind patterns in the sand. She surveyed the surrounding scene one more time, then smoothed her skirt with a perfunctory sweep of the hand.

With quick steps, she disappeared into the flow of people. I went on looking at the cigarette she had crushed out, at the lipstick colouring its filter. The bright red reminded me of Malta Kano's vinyl hat.

If I had anything in my favour, it was that I had nothing to lose. Probably.

3

What Happened in the Night

•

The boy heard the hard-edged sound in the middle of the night. He woke up, reached out for the floor lamp, and, once it was on, sat up and looked around the room. The time on the wall clock was just before 2. The boy could not imagine what might be happening in the world at a time like this.

Then the sound came again – from outside the window, he was sure. It sounded like someone winding a huge spring. Who could be winding a spring in the middle of the night? No, wait: it was *like* someone winding a spring, but it was not really a spring. It was the cry of a bird. The boy carried a chair over to the window and climbed up onto it. He pulled the curtains back and opened the window a crack. In the middle of the sky hung a large white moon, the full moon of late autumn, filling the yard below with its light. The trees out there looked very different at night from how they did in the daylight. They had none of their usual friendliness. The evergreen oak looked almost annoyed as it trembled in the occasional puff of wind with an unpleasant creaking sound. The stones in the garden looked whiter and smoother than they ordinarily did, staring up at the sky impassively like the faces of dead people.

The cry of the bird seemed to be coming from the pine tree. The boy leaned out of the window and looked up, but from this low angle, the large, heavy branches of the pine hid the bird. He wanted to see what it looked like. He wanted to memorize its colour and shape so that tomorrow he could find it in his illustrated encyclopedia. His intense desire to know had brought him fully awake now. Finding birds and fish and other animals in his encyclopedia was his greatest joy. Its thick volumes lined one shelf of his room. He had yet to enter elementary school, but he already knew how to read.

The bird fell silent after winding the spring several times in succession. The boy wondered whether anyone else had heard the cry. Had his father and mother heard it? His grandmother? If not, he could tell them all about it in the morning: a bird that sounded *just* like the winding of a spring was sitting in the pine tree last night at 2 o'clock. If only he could catch a glimpse of it! Then he could tell everybody its name.

But the bird never raised its cry again. It fell silent as a stone, up there in the branches of the pine bathed in moonlight. Soon a chill wind blew into the room, as if delivering some kind of warning. The boy shuddered and closed the window. This was a different kind of bird, he knew, not some sparrow or pigeon, which showed itself to people without hesitation. He had read in his encyclopedia that most nocturnal birds were cunning and cautious. The bird probably knew that he was on the lookout for it. It would never come out as long as he waited for it to appear. The boy wondered if he should go to the bathroom. That would mean walking down the long, dark corridor. No, he would just go back to bed. It was not so bad that he couldn't wait until morning.

The boy turned the light out and closed his eyes, but thoughts of the bird in the pine tree kept him awake. The bright moonlight spilled in from beneath the curtains as if in invitation. When the wind-up bird cried one more time, the boy leaped out of bed. This time he did not turn on the light, but slipping a cardigan over his pyjamas, he climbed onto the chair by the window. Parting the curtains just the tiniest bit, he peered up into the pine tree. This way, the bird would not notice that he was there.

•

What the boy saw this time, though, was the outline of two men. He caught his breath. The men knelt like two black shadows at the base of the pine tree. Both wore dark clothing. One had no hat on, the other wore what looked like a felt hat with a brim. Why are these strange men here in our garden in the middle of the night? the boy wondered. Why wasn't the dog barking at them? Maybe he ought to tell his parents right away.

But his curiosity him at the window. He wanted to see what the men were doing.

Then, without warning, the wind-up bird cried out again. More than once, it sent its long, creaking sound out into the night. But the men did not seem to notice. They never budged, never looked up. They remained kneeling at the base of the tree, face to face. They seemed to be discussing something in low tones, but with the branches blocking the moonlight, the boy could not make out their faces. Before long, the two men stood up at the same moment. There was a good eight-inch difference in their heights. Both men were thin, and the tall one (the one with the hat) wore a long coat. The short one had on tighter-fitting clothes.

The shorter man approached the pine tree and stood there, looking up into the branches. After a while, he began patting and grabbing the trunk with both hands as if inspecting it, until, all at once, he jumped up onto it. Then, with no effort whatever (or so it seemed to the boy), he went racing up the tree like a circus performer. The boy knew this tree like an old friend. He knew that climbing it was no easy feat. Its trunk was smooth and slippery, and there was nothing to hold on to until you got fairly high up. But why was the man climbing the tree in the middle of the night? Was he trying to catch the wind-up bird?

The tall man stood at the base of the tree, looking up. Soon after, the small man disappeared from view. The branches rustled now and then, which meant that he must still be climbing up the tall pine. The wind-up bird would be sure to hear him coming and fly away. The man might be good at climbing trees, but the wind-up bird would not be that easy to capture. If he was lucky, though, the boy was hoping he might be able to catch a glimpse of the wind-up bird as it took off. He held his breath, waiting for the sound of wings. But the sound of wings never came, nor was there any cry.

•

There was no sound or movement for a very long time. Everything was bathed in the white, unreal light of the moon, the yard like the wet bottom of a sea from which the water has just been removed. Entranced, motionless, the boy went on staring at the pine tree and the tall man left behind. He could not have torn his eyes away if he had tried. His breath clouded the glass. Outdoors, it must be cold. The tall man stood looking up, hands on hips, never moving, as if frozen to the spot. The boy imagined that he was worried about his shorter companion, waiting for him to accomplish some mission and come climbing down out of the

359

pine tree. Nor would it have been strange for the man to be worried: the boy knew that the tall tree was harder to climb down than up. But then, all of a sudden, the tall man stalked off into the night, as if abandoning the whole project.

The boy felt that now he was the only one left behind. The small man had disappeared into the pine tree, and the tall one had gone off somewhere. The wind-up bird maintained its silence. The boy wondered if he should wake his father. But he knew he would not get him to believe this. "I'm sure you've just had another dream," his father would say. It was true, the boy did often dream, and he often mistook his dreams for reality, but he didn't care what anybody said: this was *real* – the wind-up bird and the two men in black. They had just disappeared all of a sudden, that was all. His father would believe him if he did a good job of explaining what had happened.

It was then that the boy realized: the small man looked a lot like his father. Of course, he was too short to be his father, but apart from that, he was exactly the same: the build, the movements. But no, his father could never climb a tree that way. He wasn't that agile or strong. The more he thought about it, the more confused the boy became.

The tall man came back to the base of the tree. Now he had something in his hands – a shovel and a large cloth bag. He set the bag down on the ground and started digging near the roots of the tree. The shovel cut into the earth with a sharp, clean sound. Now everybody was bound to wake up, the boy thought. It was such a big, clear sound!

But no one woke up. The man went on digging without a break, seemingly unconcerned that anyone might hear him. Though tall and thin, he was much more powerful than he looked, judging from the way he used that shovel. He worked steadily, without wasted effort. Once he had the size of hole he wanted, the man leaned the shovel against the tree and stood there looking down. He never once looked up, as though he had forgotten all about the man who had climbed the tree. The only thing on his mind now was the hole, it seemed. The boy did not like this. *He* would have been worried about the man in the tree.

The boy could tell from the mound of earth the man had dug that the hole itself was not very deep – maybe just above his own knees. The man seemed satisfied with the shape and size of the hole. He turned to the bag and gently lifted a blackish, cloth-wrapped object from inside it. The way the man held it, it seemed soft and limp. Maybe the man was about to bury some kind of corpse in the hole. The thought made the boy's heart race. But the thing in the cloth was no bigger than a cat. If human, it could only be an infant. But why did he have to bury something like that in *my yard*? thought the boy. He swallowed the saliva that he had unconsciously allowed to collect in his mouth. The loud gulp he made frightened the boy himself. It might have been loud enough for the man to hear outside.

Just then, as if aroused by the boy's gulp, the wind-up bird cried out, winding an even bigger spring than before: *Creeeak. Creeeak.*

When he heard this cry, the boy intuitively felt that something very important was about to happen. He bit his lip and without realizing scratched the skin of his arms. He should never have seen any of this, he felt. But now it was too late. Now it was impossible for him to tear his eyes away from the scene before him. He parted his lips and pressed his nose against the cold windowpane, transfixed by the strange drama that was now unfolding in his yard. He was no longer hoping for other members of the family to get out of bed. *No one would wake up anyway, no matter how big a sound they made out there. I'm the only person alive who can hear these sounds. It was that way from the start.*

The tall man bent over and, handling it with the utmost care, laid the thing in the black cloth in the bottom of the hole. Then he rose to his full height and stared down at it lying there. The boy could not make out the look on the man's face beneath the brim of his hat, but he seemed somehow to be wearing a grim, even a solemn, expression. Yes, it had to be some kind of corpse, thought the boy. Before long, the man reached a decision, lifted the shovel, and began filling in the hole. When he had finished shovelling, he lightly tamped the earth beneath his feet and smoothed it over. Then he set the shovel against the trunk of the tree and, with the cloth bag in his hand, moved away with slow steps. He never looked back. He never looked up into the tree. And the wind-up bird never cried again.

The boy turned to look at the clock on his wall. Squinting in the darkness, he could just make out the time as 2.30. He kept watch on the pine tree for another ten minutes through the opening in the curtains, in case something should move out there, but an intense sleepiness overtook him all at once, as if a heavy iron lid were closing over his head. He wanted to know what would happen to the short man up in the tree and the wind-up bird, but he couldn't keep his eyes open any longer. Struggling to slip off the cardigan before he lost consciousness, he burrowed under the covers and sank into sleep.

4

Buying New Shoes

◆

The Thing That Came Back Home

I walked from the Akasaka subway station down a lively street lined with restaurants and bars to the place where the office building stood, a short way up a gentle slope. It was an unremarkable building, neither new nor old, big nor small, elegant nor dilapidated. A travel agency occupied part of the ground floor, its large window displaying posters of Mykonos and a San Francisco cable car. Both posters looked faded from long duty in the window. Three members of the firm were hard at work on the other side of the glass, talking on the telephone or typing at a computer keyboard. Pretending to be looking at the posters, I killed time watching the office scene while waiting for the hour to strike 4. For some reason, both Mykonos and San Francisco seemed light years from where I stood.

The more I looked at this building, the more I realized how ordinary it was, as if it had been built to match the pencil sketch a small child might do if told to draw a building, or as if it had been consciously designed to be inconspicuous in its surroundings. As careful as I had been in checking the addresses during my search for the place, I came close to passing it by, it was so plain. The building's unobtrusive main entrance stood near the door of the travel agency. Skimming the nameplates, I got the impression that most of the offices were occupied by small-scale businesses – law offices, architects, importers, dentists. Several of the nameplates were shiny enough for me to be able to see my face in them, but the one for Room 602 had faded with age to an indistinct colour. The woman had obviously had her office here for some time. "Akasaka Fashion Design", read the inscription. The sheer age of the nameplate helped to temper my misgivings.

A locked glass door stood between the lobby and the lift. I rang the bell for 602 and looked around for the closed-circuit TV camera I assumed must be transmitting my image to a monitor inside. There was a small, camera-like device in a corner of the lobby ceiling. Soon the buzzer sounded, unlocking the door, and I went inside.

I took the absolutely unadorned lift to the sixth floor and, after a few uncertain moments in the absolutely unadorned corridor, found the door of 602. First checking to be certain that the sign on the door said "Akasaka Fashion Design", I gave the bell exactly one short ring.

The door was opened by a slim young man with short hair and regular features. He was possibly the handsomest man I had ever seen in my life. But even more than his features, what caught my eye was his clothing. He wore a shirt of almost painful whiteness and a deep-green tie with a fine pattern. Not only was the tie itself stylish, but it had been tied in a perfect knot, every twist and dip exactly as one might see in a men's fashion magazine. I could never have tied a tie so well, and I found myself wondering how he did it. Was it a talent or was he born with the fruits of disciplined practice? His trousers were dark grey, and he wore brown tasselled loafers. Everything looked brand-new, as if he had just put it on for the first time a few minutes before.

He was shorter than me. The hint of a smile played about his lips, as if he had just heard a joke and was now smiling in the most natural way. Nor had the joke been a vulgar one: it was the kind of elegant pleasantry that the minister of foreign affairs might have told the crown prince at a garden party a generation ago, causing the surrounding listeners to titter with delight. I began to introduce myself, but he gave his head a slight shake to signal that it was unnecessary for me to say anything. Holding the door open inward, he ushered me forward, and after a quick glance up and down the hall, he closed the door, saying nothing all the while. He looked at me with eyes narrowed as if to apologize for being unable to speak because of the nervous black panther sleeping by his side. Which is not to say that there *was* a black panther sleeping by his side: he just looked as if there were.

I was standing now in a reception room with a comfortable-looking leather sofa and chair, an old-fashioned wooden coat-rack, and a floor lamp. There was a single door in the far wall, which looked as if it must lead to the next room. Beside the door, facing away from the wall, was a simple oak desk that supported a large computer. The table standing in front of the sofa might have been just large enough to hold a telephone book. A pleasant pale-green carpet covered the floor. From hidden speakers, at low volume, came the strains of a Haydn string quartet. The walls bore several lovely prints of flowers and birds. One glance told you this was an immaculate room, with no hint of disorder. Shelves on one wall held fabric samples and fashion magazines. The office's furnishings were neither lavish nor new, but had the comforting warmth of the old and familiar.

The young man showed me to the sofa, then went around to the other side of the desk and sat down facing me. Holding his palms out towards me, he signalled for me to wait a while. Instead of saying "Sorry to keep you waiting," he produced a slight smile, and instead of saying "It will not take long," he held up one finger. He seemed to be able to express himself without words. I nodded once to signal that I under-stood. To have spoken in his presence would have seemed inappropriate and vulgar.

As if holding a broken object, he picked up a book lying next to the computer and opened it to where he had left off. It was a thick black book without a dust jacket, so I could not make out the title. From the moment he opened it, you could see that the young man's concentration on his book was total. He seemed to have forgotten that I was there. I would have liked to read something too, to pass the time, but nothing had been provided. I crossed my legs, settled into the sofa, and listened to Haydn (though if pressed, I could not have sworn it was Haydn). It was nice music, but the kind that seems to melt into air the moment it emerges from its source. On the young man's desk, apart from the computer, was an ordinary black telephone, a pencil tray, and a calendar.

I was wearing virtually the same outfit I had had on the day before – baseball jacket, hooded sweatshirt, blue jeans, and tennis shoes. I had just grabbed whatever came to hand before leaving the house. In this immaculate, orderly room, in the presence of this immaculate, handsome youth, my tennis shoes looked especially dirty and worn out. No, they *were* dirty and worn out, the heels practically gone, the colour an indeter-minate grey, the uppers full of holes. Those shoes had been through a lot, soaking up everything in their path with fatal certainty. I had worn them every day for the past year, climbing over the back wall countless times, stepping in dog shit now and then on trips down the alley, climbing down to the bottom of the well. No wonder they were dirty and worn out. Not since quitting my job had it occurred to me to think about what shoes I had on. Studying them so closely like this, I felt with new intensity just how alone I was, just how far the world had left me behind. It was time for me to buy a new pair of shoes, I told myself. These were just too awful.

Before long, the Haydn came to an end – an abrupt and messy end. After a short pause, some kind of Bach harpsichord piece started (though I couldn't have sworn this was Bach, either). I crossed and recrossed my legs. The telephone rang. The young man marked the place he was reading with a slip of paper, pushed his book aside, and picked up the receiver. He held it to his ear and gave a slight nod. Focusing on his desktop calendar, he marked it with a pencil. Then he held the receiver near the surface of the desk and rapped his knuckles twice against the wood as if knocking on a door. After this, he hung up. The call had lasted some twenty seconds, during which the young man had not spoken a word. In fact, he had not made a sound with his voice since letting me into the room. Was he unable to talk? Certainly he could hear, judging from the way he had answered the phone and listened to what was being said at the other end.

He sat looking at his phone for a while as if in thought. Then he rose without a sound, walked around his desk, making straight for where I was sitting, and sat down next to me. He then placed his hands on his knees in perfect alignment. They were slim, refined hands, as one might have imagined from his face. His knuckles and finger joints did have a few wrinkles; there was no such thing as fingers without wrinkles: they needed a few, at least, to move and bend. But his fingers did not have many wrinkles – no more than the minimum necessary. I looked at his hands as unobtrusively as I could. This young man must be the woman's son, I thought. His fingers were shaped like hers. Once that thought entered my mind, I started to notice other points of resemblance: the small, rather sharp nose, the crystalline clarity of the eyes. The pleasant smile had begun to play about his lips again, appearing and disappearing with all the naturalness of a seaside cave at the mercy of the waves. Soon he rose to his feet, in the same swift manner with which he had sat down beside me, and his lips silently formed the words "This way, please." Despite the absence of sound, it was clear to me what he wanted to say.

I stood and followed him. He opened the inner door and guided me through it.

Beyond the door was a small kitchen and basin, and beyond that yet another room, much like the reception room in which I had been sitting, but a size smaller. It had the same kind of well-aged leather sofa and a window of the same shape. The carpet on the floor was the same colour as the other one as well. In the middle of the room was a large work-bench, with scissors, toolboxes, pencils, and design books laid out in an orderly fashion. There were two tailor's dummies. The window had not merely a blind but two sets of curtains, cloth and lace, both shut tight. With the ceiling light off, the room was gloomy, as on the evening of a cloudy day. One bulb of the floor lamp near the sofa had been turned off. A glass vase holding gladiolus blossoms stood on the coffee table in front of the sofa. The flowers were fresh, as if cut only moments before, the water in the vase clear. The music was not audible in this room, nor were there any pictures or clocks on the walls.

The young man gestured silently again, this time for me to sit on the sofa. Once I had seated myself in accordance with his instructions, he took something like a pair of swimming goggles from his trousers pocket and stretched them out before my eyes. They *were* swimming goggles, just ordinary goggles made of rubber and plastic, much the same as the ones I used when swimming in the ward pool. Why he had brought them out here I had no idea. I couldn't even imagine.

"Don't be afraid," the young man said to me. Properly speaking, he "said" nothing. He simply moved his lips and fingers ever so slightly. Still, I had an accurate understanding of what he was saying to me. I nodded.

"Please put these on. Don't take them off yourself. I will take them off. You mustn't move them, either. Do you understand?"

I nodded again.

"I will not harm you in any way. You will be fine. Don't worry."

I nodded.

The young man walked behind the sofa and put the goggles over my eyes. He stretched the rubber strap around to the back of my head and adjusted the eye cups so that the foam pads fitted around my eyes. The one way these goggles were different from the ones I always used was that I couldn't see anything through them. A thick layer of some-thing had been painted over the transparent plastic. A complete – and artificial – darkness surrounded me. I couldn't see a thing. I had no idea where the light of the floor lamp was shining. I had the illusion that I myself had been painted over with a thick layer of something.

The young man rested his hands lightly on my shoulders as if to encourage me. He had slim, delicate fingers, but they were in no way fragile. They had the assertive presence of the fingers of a pianist resting on the keyboard, and coming through them I could sense a kind of good-will – or, if not precisely goodwill, something very close to it. "You'll be fine. Don't worry," they conveyed to me. I nodded. Then he left the room. In the darkness, I could hear his footsteps drawing into the distance, and then the sound of a door opening and closing.

·

I went on sitting in the same position for some time after the young man left the room. The darkness in which I sat had something strange about it. The fact of being unable to see anything was the same as what I had experienced in the well, but otherwise this darkness had a certain quality that made it quite different. It had no direction or depth, no weight or tangibility. It was less like darkness than nothingness. I had merely been rendered temporarily blind by artificial means. I felt my muscles stiffen-ing, my mouth and throat going dry. What was going to happen to me? But then I recalled the touch of the young man's fingers. *Don't worry*, they had told me. For no clear reason, I felt that those "words" of his were something I could believe in.

The room was so utterly still that when I held my breath I was overcome by a sense that the world had stopped in its tracks and every-thing would in time be swallowed up by water, sinking to eternal depths. But no, the world was apparently still moving. Before long, a woman opened the door and stepped quietly into the room.

I knew it was a woman from the delicate fragrance of her perfume. This was not a scent a man would wear. It was probably expensive perfume. I tried to recall the scent, but I could not do so with confidence. Robbed of my sight, I found my sense of smell had also been thrown off balance. The one thing I could be sure of was that the perfume I was smelling now was different from that of the well-dressed woman who had directed me to this place. I could hear the sound of the woman's clothes rustling as she crossed the room and gently lowered herself onto the sofa, to my right. So lightly did she settle into the cushions of the sofa that it was clear she was a small woman.

Sitting there, the woman stared straight at me. I could feel her eyes focused on my face. You really can feel someone looking at you, even if you can't see, I realized. The woman, never moving, went on staring at me for a long time. I sensed her slow, gentle breathing but could not hear a sound. I remained in the same position, facing straight ahead. The mark on my cheek felt slightly feverish. The colour was probably more vivid than usual. Eventually, the woman reached out and placed her fingertips on my mark, very carefully, as if inspecting some valuable, fragile thing. Then she began to caress it.

I didn't know how to react to this, or how I was expected to react. I had only the most distant sense of reality. I felt a strange detachment, as if I were trying to leap from one moving vehicle to another that was moving at a different speed. I existed in the empty space between the two, a vacant house. I was now a vacant house, just as the Miyawaki house had once been. This woman had come into the vacant house and, for some unknown reason, was running her hands all over the walls and pillars. Whatever her reason might be, vacant house that I was (and I was that and nothing more), I could do nothing (I *needed* to do nothing) about it. Once that thought crossed my mind, I was able to relax somewhat.

The woman said nothing. Apart from the sound of rustling clothes, the room was enveloped in a deep silence. The woman traced her fingertips over my skin as if trying to read some minute secret script that had been engraved there ages ago.

Finally, she stopped caressing my mark. She stood up, came around behind me, and, instead of her fingertips, used her tongue. Just as May Kasahara had done in the garden last summer, she licked my mark. The way she did it, however, was far more mature than the way May Kasahara had done it. Her tongue moved and clung to my flesh with far greater skill. With varying pressure, changing angles, and different movements, it tasted and sucked and stimulated my mark. I felt a hot, moist throbbing below the waist. I didn't want to have an erection. To do so would have been too meaningless. But I couldn't stop myself.

I struggled to superimpose my own image upon that of a vacant house. I thought of myself as a pillar, a wall, a ceiling, a floor, a roof, a window, a door, a stone. It seemed the most reasonable thing to do.

I close my eyes and separate from this flesh of mine, with its filthy tennis shoes, its weird goggles, its clumsy erection. Separating from the flesh is not so difficult. It can put me far more at ease, allow me to cast off the discomfort I feel. I am a weed-choked garden, a flightless stone bird, a dry well. I know that a woman is inside this vacant house that is myself. I cannot see her, but it doesn't bother me any more. If she is looking for something inside here, I might as well give it to her.

The passage of time becomes more and more unclear. Of all the kinds of time available to me here, I lose track of which kind I am using. My consciousness goes gradually back into my flesh, and in turn the woman seems to be leaving. She leaves the room as quietly as she came in. The rustle of clothing. The shimmering smell of perfume. The sound of a door opening, then closing. Part of my consciousness is still *there* as an empty house. At the same time, I am still *here*, on this sofa, as me. I think, What should I do now? I can't decide which one is reality. Little by little, the word "here" seems to split in two inside me. I am *here*, but I am also *here*. Both seem equally real to me. Sitting on the sofa, I steep myself in this strange separation.

•

Soon the door opened and someone came into the room. I could tell from the footsteps that it was the young man. He came around behind me and took off the goggles. The room was dark, the only light the single bulb of the floor lamp. I rubbed my eyes with my palms, accustoming them to the world of reality. The young man was now wearing a suit. Its deep grey, with hints of green, was a perfect match for the colour of his tie. With a soft smile, he took my arm, helped me to stand, and guided me to the back door of the room. He opened the door to reveal a bathroom on the other side. It had a toilet and, beyond the toilet, a small shower stall. The toilet lid was down, and he had me sit on top of it while he turned the shower on. He waited for the hot water to begin flowing, then he gestured for me to take a shower. He unwrapped a fresh bar of soap and handed it to me. Then he went out of the bathroom and closed the door. Why did I have to take a shower? I didn't get it.

I finally understood as I was undressing. I had come in my underpants. I stepped into the hot shower and washed myself with the new green soap. I rinsed away the semen sticking to my pubic hair. I stepped out of the shower and dried myself with a large towel. Beside the towel I found a pair of Calvin Klein boxer shorts and a T-shirt, both still in their wrappers and both my size. Maybe they had planned for me to come in my trousers. I stared at myself in the mirror for a while, but my head was not working properly. I threw my soiled underwear into a wastebasket and put on the clean, white new underpants, the clean, white new T-shirt. Then I put on my jeans and slipped my sweatshirt over my head. I put on my socks and my dirty tennis shoes and finally my baseball jacket. Then I stepped out of the bathroom.

•

The young man was waiting for me outside and guided me to the original waiting room.

The room looked as it had earlier. On the desk lay the same opened book, next to which stood the computer. Anonymous classical music flowed from the speakers. The young man had me sit on the sofa and brought me a glass of chilled mineral water. I drank half the glass. "I seem to be tired," I said. The voice didn't sound like mine. Nor had I been intending to say any such thing. The words had come out of nowhere, without my will. The voice was definitely mine, though.

The young man nodded. He took a white envelope from the inner pocket of his jacket and slipped it into the inner pocket of my baseball jacket. Then he nodded once again. I looked outside. The sky was dark, and the street was aglow with neon signs, the light from office building windows, streetlamps, and headlights. The thought of staying in this room any longer became intolerable. Without a word, I stood up, crossed the room, opened the door, and went out. The young man watched me from where he stood by his desk, but he remained as silent as ever and made no attempt to stop me from leaving.

•

On the return commute Akasaka Mitsuke Station was churning. In no mood for the bad air of the subway, I decided to go as far as I could on foot. I walked past the palace for foreign dignitaries as far as Yotsuya Station. Then I walked along Shinjuku Boulevard and went into a small place without too many people to have a glass of beer. My first swallow made me notice how hungry I was, so I ordered a snack. I looked at my watch and realized it was almost 7 o'clock. Come to think of it, though, the time of day was of no concern to me.

At some point, I noticed there was something in the inner pocket of my jacket. I had forgotten all about the envelope the young man had given me on my way out. It was just an ordinary white envelope, but holding it, I realized it was much heavier than it looked. More than just heavy, though, its weight had something strange about it, as though there were something inside holding its breath. After a moment's indecision, I tore it open – which was something I would have to do sooner or later. Inside was a neat bundle of ten-thousand-yen notes. Brand-new ten-thousand-yen notes, without a crease or wrinkle. They didn't look real, they were so new, though I could find no reason to believe them not to be new. There were twenty bills in all. I counted them again to be sure. Yes, no doubt about it: twenty bills. Two-hundred-thousand yen.

I returned the money to the envelope and the envelope to my pocket.

Then I picked up the fork from the table and stared at it for no reason. The first thing that came into my head was that I would use the money to buy myself a new pair of shoes. That was the one thing I needed most. I paid my bill and went back out to Shinjuku Boulevard, where there was a large shoe shop. I chose some very ordinary blue trainers and told the salesman my size without asking the price. I would wear them home if they fit, I said. The salesman (who might have been the owner) threaded white laces through the eyelets of both shoes and asked, "What shall I do with your old shoes?" I said he could throw them away, but then I reconsidered and said I would take them home.

He flashed me a nice smile. "An old pair of good shoes can come in handy, even if they're a little messy," he said, as if to imply that he was used to seeing such dirty shoes all the time. Then he put the old ones in the box the new ones had come in and put the box in a shopping bag. Lying in their new box, the old tennis shoes looked like tiny animal corpses. I paid the bill with one of the crisp new ten-thousand-yen notes from the envelope, and for change received a few not-so-new thousand-yen notes. Taking the bag with the old shoes, I got on the Odakyu train and went home. I hung on to the strap, mingling with homebound commuters, and thought about the new items I was wearing – my new underpants and T-shirt and shoes.

•

Home again, I sat at the kitchen table as usual, drinking a beer and listening to music on the radio. It then occurred to me that I wanted to talk to someone – about the weather, about political stupidity; it didn't matter what. I just wanted to talk to somebody, but I couldn't think of anyone, not one person I could talk to. I didn't even have the cat.

•

Shaving the next morning, I inspected the mark on my face, as usual. I couldn't detect any change. I sat on the veranda and, for the first time in a long time, spent the day just looking at the garden out back. It was a nice morning, a nice afternoon. The leaves of the trees fluttered in the early-spring breeze.

I took the envelope containing the nineteen ten-thousand-yen notes out of my jacket pocket and put it in my desk drawer. It still felt strangely heavy in my hand. Some kind of meaning seemed to be implied by the heaviness, but I could not understand what it was. It reminded me of something, I suddenly realized. What I had done reminded me of something. Staring hard at the envelope in the drawer, I tried to remember what it was, but I couldn't do it.

I closed the drawer, went to the kitchen, made myself some tea, and was standing by the sink, drinking the tea, when I remembered what it was. What I had done yesterday was just like the work Creta Kano had done as a call girl. You go to a designated place, sleep with someone you don't know, and get paid. I had not actually slept with the woman (just come in my pants), but apart from that, it was the same thing. In need of a certain amount of money, I had offered my flesh to someone to get it. I thought about this as I drank my tea. A dog barked in the distance. Shortly afterwards, I heard a light aircraft. But my thoughts would not come together. I went out to the veranda again and looked at the garden, wrapped in afternoon sunlight. When I tired of doing that, I looked at the palms of my hands. To think that *I* should have become a prostitute! Who could have imagined that I would have sold my body for money? Or that my first purchase would have been new trainers?

I wanted to breathe the air outside, so I decided to go shopping. I walked down the street, wearing my new trainers. I felt as if these new shoes had transformed me into a new being, different from what I had been before. The street scene and the faces of the people I passed looked different too. In the local supermarket, I picked up vegetables and eggs and milk and fish and coffee beans, paying for them with the bills I had received as change at the shoe shop the night before. I wanted to tell the round-faced, middle-aged woman at the till that I had made this money the previous day by selling my body. I had earned two-hundred-thousand yen. Two-hundred-thousand yen! I could slave away at the law office where I used to work, doing overtime every day for a month, and I might come home with a little over one-hundred-and-fifty-thousand yen. That's what I wanted to say to her. But of course I said nothing. I handed over the money and received a paper bag filled with groceries in return.

One thing was certain: things had started to move. I told myself this as I walked home clutching my bag of groceries. Now all I had to do was hold on tight to keep from being knocked off. If I could do that, I might end up somewhere – somewhere different from where I was now, at least.

·

My premonition was not false. When I got home, the cat came out to greet me. Just as I opened the front door, he let out a loud meow as if he had been waiting all day and came up to me, his tail with the bent tip held high. It was Noboru Wataya, missing now for almost a year. I put the bag of groceries down and scooped him up in my arms.

5

A Place You Can Figure Out
If You Think About It Really, Really Hard
(May Kasahara's Point of View: 1)

•

Hi, Mr Wind-up Bird.

I bet you think I'm in a classroom somewhere, studying with a textbook open in front of me, like any ordinary school kid. Sure, last time we met I told you myself that I was going to go to "another school," so it would be natural for you to think so. And in fact, I did go to another school, a private boarding school for girls, far, far away, a fancy one, with big, clean rooms like hotel rooms, and a cafeteria where you could choose whatever you wanted to eat, and big, shiny new tennis courts and a swimming pool, so naturally it was pretty expensive, a place for rich girls. Problem rich girls. You can imagine what it was like – an honest-to-goodness refined-country-school kind of thing in the mountains. It was surrounded by a high wall topped with barbed wire, and it had this huge iron gate that Godzilla himself couldn't have kicked in and round-the-clock guards clunking around like robots – not so much to keep people on the outside from getting in as to keep people on the inside from getting out.

So now you're going to ask me, "Why go to such an awful place if you know it's so awful?" You're right, but I had no choice. The main thing I wanted was to get out of the house, but after all the problems I had caused, that was the only school "charitable" enough to accept me as a transfer student. So I made up my mind to stick it out. But it really was awful! People use the word "nightmarish", but it was worse than that. I really did have nightmares in that place – all the time — and I'd wake up soaked in sweat, but even then I'd wish I could have kept dreaming, because my nightmares were way better than reality in that place. I wonder if you know what that's like, Mr Wind-up Bird. I wonder if you've ever been in the pits like that.

So finally, I stayed in this high-class hotel/jail/country school for only one term. When I got home for the spring break, I announced to my parents that if I had to go back there, I was going to kill myself. I'd stuff three tampons down my throat and drink tons of water; I'd slash my wrists; I'd dive headfirst off the school roof. And I meant what I said. I wasn't kidding. Both my parents put together have the imagination of a tree frog, but they knew — from experience — that when I got going like that, it wasn't an empty threat.

So anyhow, I never went back to the place. Throughout March and April, I shut myself up in the house, reading, watching TV, and just plain vegging out. And a hundred times a day, I'd think, I want to see Mr Wind-up Bird. I wanted to slip down the alley, jump over the fence, and have a nice long talk with you. But it wasn't that easy. It would've been a replay of the summer. So I just watched the alley from my room and wondered to myself, What's Mr Wind-up Bird up to now? Spring is slowly, quietly taking over the whole world, and Mr Wind-up Bird is in it too, but what's happening in his life? Has Kumiko come home to him? What's going on with those strange women Malta Kano and Creta Kano? Has Noboru Wataya the cat come back? Has the mark disappeared from Mr Wind-up Bird's cheek . . . ?

After a month of living like that, I couldn't take it any more. I don't know how or when it happened, but for me that neighbourhood is nothing now but "Mr Wind-up Bird's world", and when I'm in it, I'm nothing but "the me contained in Mr Wind-up Bird's world". And it's not just a sort-of-kind-of thing. It's not your fault, of course, but still . . . So I had to find my own place.

I thought about it and thought and thought, and finally it hit me where I had to go.

(Hint) It's a place you can figure out if you think about it really, really hard. You'll be able to imagine where I am if you make the effort. It's not a school, it's not a hotel, it's not a hospital, it's not a jail, it's not a house. It's a kind of special place way far away. It's . . . a secret. For now, at least.

I'm in the mountains again, in another place surrounded by a wall (but not such a huge wall), and there's a gate and a nice old man who guards the gate, but you can go in and out anytime you like. It's a huge piece of land, with its own little woods and a pond, and if you go for a walk when the sun comes up you see lots of animals: lions and zebras and – no, I'm kidding, but you can see cute little animals like badgers and pheasants. There's a dormitory, and that's where I live.

I'm writing this letter in a tiny room at a tiny desk near a tiny bed next to a tiny bookcase beside a tiny wardrobe, none of which have the slightest decoration, and all of which are designed to meet the minimum functional requirements. On the desk is a fluorescent lamp, a teacup, the stationery for writing this letter, and a dictionary. To be honest, I almost never use the dictionary. I just don't like dictionaries. I don't like the way they look, and I don't like what they say inside. Whenever I use a dictionary, I make a face and think, Who needs to know that? People like me don't get along well with dictionaries. Say I look up "transition" and it says: "passage from one state to another". I think, So what? It's got nothing to do with me. So when I see a dictionary on my desk I feel like I'm looking at some strange dog leaving a twisty piece of poop on our lawn out back. But anyway, I bought a dictionary because I figured I might have to look something up while I was writing to you, Mr Wind-up Bird.

Also I've got a dozen pencils, all sharpened and laid out in a row. They're brand-new. I just bought them at the stationery store – especially for writing to you (not that I'm trying to make you feel grateful or anything: just-sharpened, brand-new pencils are really nice, don't you think?). Also I've got an ashtray and cigarettes and matches. I don't smoke as much as I used to, just once in a while for a mood change (like right now, for instance). So that's everything on my desk. The desk faces a window, and the window has curtains. The curtains have a sweet little flower design – not that I picked them out or anything: they came with the window. That flower design is the only thing here that doesn't look plain and simple. This is a perfect room for a teenage girl – or maybe not. No, it's more like a model jail cell designed with good intentions for first offenders. My music machine is on the shelf (the big one – remember, Mr Wind-up Bird?), and I've got Bruce Springsteen on now. It's Sunday afternoon and everybody's out having fun, so there's nobody to complain if I turn it up loud.

The only thing I do for fun these days is go to the nearby town at weekends and buy the cassette tapes I want at a record store. (I almost never buy books. If there's something I want to read, I can get it at our little library.) I'm pretty friendly with the girl next door. She bought a used car, so when I want to go to town, I go with her. And guess what? I've been learning to drive it. There's so much open space here, I can practise all I want. I don't have a licence yet, but I'm a pretty good driver.

To tell you the truth, though, apart from buying music tapes, going to town is not all that much fun. Everybody says they have to get out once a week or they'll go nuts, but I get my relief by staying here when everybody's gone and listening to my favourite music like this. I once went on a kind of double date with my friend with the car. Just to give it a try. She's from around here, so she knows a lot of people. My date was a nice enough guy, a college student, but I don't know, I still can't really get a clear sense of all kinds of things. It's as if they're out there, far away, lined up like dolls in a shooting gallery, and all these transparent curtains are hanging down between me and the dolls.

To tell you the truth, when I was seeing you that summer, Mr Wind-up Bird, when we were sitting at the kitchen table talking and drinking beer and things, I would think, What would I do if Mr Wind-up Bird all of a sudden pushed me down and tried to rape me? I didn't know what I would do. Of course, I would have resisted and said, "No, Mr Wind-up Bird, you shouldn't do this!" But I also would have been thinking I had to explain why it was wrong and why you shouldn't be doing it, and the more I thought, the more mixed up I would get, and by that time you probably would have finished raping me. My heart would pound like crazy when I thought about this, and I would think the whole thing was kind of unfair. I bet you never had any idea I had thoughts like this going on in my head. Do you think this is stupid? You probably do. I mean, it is stupid. But at the time, I was absolutely, tremendously serious about these things. Which, I think, is why I pulled the rope ladder out of the well and put the cover on with you down inside there that time, kind of like sealing you off. That way, there would be no more Mr Wind-up Bird around, and I wouldn't have to be bothered by those thoughts for a while.

I'm sorry, though. I know I should never have done that to you (or to anybody). But I can't help myself sometimes. I know exactly what I'm doing, but I just can't stop. That's my greatest weakness.

I don't believe that you would ever rape me, Mr Wind-up Bird. I know that now, somehow. It's not that you would never, ever do it (I mean, nobody knows for sure what's going to happen), but maybe that you would at least not do it to confuse me. I don't know how to put it exactly, but I just sort of feel that way.

All right, enough of this rape stuff.

Anyhow, even though I might go out on a date with a boy, emotionally I just wouldn't be able to concentrate. I'd be smiling and chatting away, and my mind would be floating around somewhere else, like a balloon with a broken string. I'd be thinking about one unrelated thing after another. I don't know, I guess I just want to be alone a little while longer. And I want to let my thoughts wander freely. In that sense, I guess, I'm probably still "on the road to recovery".

I'll write again soon. Next time, I'll probably be able to go a little further into all kinds of things.

P.S. Before the next letter comes, try to guess where I am and what I'm doing.

6

Nutmeg and Cinnamon

•

The cat was covered from nose to tailtip with clumps of dried mud, his fur stuck together in little balls, as if he had been rolling around on a filthy patch of ground for a long time. He purred with excitement as I picked him up and examined him all over. He might have been a bit emaciated, but apart from that, he looked little different from when I had last seen him: face, body, fur. His eyes were clear, and he had no wounds. He certainly didn't seem like a cat that had been missing for a year. It was more as if he had come home after a single night of carousing.

I fed him on the veranda: a plateful of sliced mackerel that I had bought at the supermarket. He was obviously starving. He polished off the fish slices so quickly he would gag now and then and spit pieces back into the plate. I found the cat's water dish under the sink and filled it to the brim. He came close to emptying it. Having accomplished this much, he started licking his mud-caked fur, but then, as if suddenly recalling that I was there, he climbed into my lap, curled up, and went to sleep.

The cat slept with his forelegs tucked under his body, his face buried in his tail. He purred loudly at first, then more quietly, until he entered a state of complete and silent sleep, all defences down. I sat in a sunny spot on the veranda, stroking him gently so as not to wake him. I had not thought about the cat's special soft, warm touch for a very long time. So much had been happening to me that I had all but forgotten that the cat had disappeared. Holding this soft, small living creature in my lap this way, though, and seeing how it slept with complete trust in me, I felt a warm rush in my chest. I put my hand on the cat's chest and felt his heart beating. The pulse was faint and fast, but his heart, like mine, was ticking off the time allotted to his small body with all the restless earnestness of my own.

Where had this cat been for a year? What had he been doing? Why had he chosen to come back now, all of a sudden? And where were the traces of the time he had lost? I wished I could ask him these questions. If only he could have answered me!

·

I brought an old cushion out to the veranda and set the cat down on top of it. He was as limp as a load of washing. When I picked him up, the slits of his eyes opened, and he opened his mouth, but he made no sound. He settled himself onto the cushion, gave a yawn, and fell back to sleep. Once I was satisfied he was resting, I went to the kitchen to put away the groceries I had brought home. I placed the tofu and vegetables and fish in their compartments in the refrigerator, then glanced out to the veranda again. The cat was sleeping in the same position. We had always called him Noboru Wataya because the look in his eyes resembled that of Kumiko's brother, but that had just been our little joke, not the cat's real name. In fact, we had let six years go by without giving him a name.

Even as a joke, though, Noboru Wataya was no name for a cat of ours. The real Noboru Wataya had simply become too great a presence in the course of those six years – especially now that he had been elected to the House of Representatives. Saddling the cat with that name for ever was out of the question. As long as he remained in this house, it would be necessary to give him a new name, a name of his own – and the sooner the better. It should be a simple, tangible, realistic name, something you could see with your eyes and feel with your hands, something that could erase the sound and memory and meaning of the name Noboru Wataya.

I brought in the plate that had held the fish. It looked as clean as if it had just been washed and wiped. The cat must have enjoyed his meal. I was glad I had happened to buy some mackerel just at the time the cat had chosen to come home. It seemed like a good omen, fortunate for both me and the cat. Yes, that was it: I would call him Mackerel. Rubbing him behind the ears, I informed him of the change: "You're not Noboru Wataya any more," I said. "From now on, your name is Mackerel." I wanted to shout it to the world.

I sat on the veranda next to Mackerel the cat, reading a book until the sun began to set. The cat slept as soundly as if he had been knocked unconscious, his quiet breathing like a distant bellows, his body rising and falling with the sound. I would reach out now and then to feel his warmth and make sure the cat was really there. It was wonderful to be able to do that: to reach out and touch something, to feel something warm. I had been missing that kind of experience.

•

Mackerel was still there the next morning. He had not disappeared. When I woke up, I found him sleeping next to me, on his side, legs stretched straight out. He must have woken up during the night and licked himself clean. The mud and hair balls were gone. He looked almost like his old self. He had always had a handsome coat of fur. I held him for a while, then fed him his breakfast and changed his water. Then I moved away from him and tried calling him by name: "Mackerel". Finally, on the third try, he turned towards me and gave a little meow.

Now it was time for me to begin my new day. The cat had come back to me, and I had to begin to move forward too. I took a shower and ironed a freshly laundered shirt. I put on a pair of cotton trousers and my new trainers. The sky was hazy and overcast, but the weather was not especially cold. I decided to wear a thickish sweater without a coat. I took the train to Shinjuku, as usual, went through the subway passageway to the west exit plaza, and took a seat on my usual bench.

•

The woman showed up a little after 3 o'clock. She didn't seem astonished to see me, and I reacted to her approach without surprise. Our encounter was entirely natural. We exchanged no greetings, as if this had all been prearranged. I raised my face, and she looked at me with a flicker of the lips.

She wore a springlike orange cotton top, a tight skirt the colour of topaz, and small gold earrings. She sat down next to me and, as always, took a pack of Virginia Slims from her purse. She put a cigarette in her mouth and lit up with a slim gold lighter. This time she knew better than to offer me a cigarette. And after taking two or three leisurely puffs herself, with an air of deep thought, she dropped her cigarette on the ground as if testing gravity conditions for the day. She then patted me on the knee and said, "Come with me", after which she stood to leave. I crushed her cigarette out and did as she said. She raised her hand to stop a passing taxi and climbed in. I climbed in beside her. She then announced very clearly an address in Aoyama, after which she said nothing at all until the

379

cab had threaded its way through thick traffic to Aoyama Boulevard. I watched the sights of Tokyo passing by the window. There were several new buildings that I had never seen before. The woman took a notebook from her bag and wrote something in it with a small gold pen. She looked at her watch now and then, as if checking on something. The watch was set in a gold bracelet. All the little accessories she carried with her seemed to be made of gold. Or was it that they turned to gold the moment she touched them?

She took me into a boutique on Omote Sando that sold designer brands. There she picked out two suits for me, both of thin material, one blue grey, the other dark grey. These were not suits I could have worn to the law firm: they even *felt* expensive. She did not offer any explanations, and I did not ask for them. I simply did as I was told. This reminded me of several so-called art films I had seen in college. Movies like that never explained what was going on. Explanations were rejected as some kind of evil that could only destroy the films' "reality". That was one way of thinking, one way to look at things, no doubt, but it felt strange for me, as a real, live human being, to enter such a world.

I am of average build, so neither suit had to be altered other than to adjust the sleeves and trouser legs. The woman picked out three dress shirts and three ties to match each shirt, then two belts and half a dozen pairs of socks. She paid with a credit card and asked them to deliver everything to my place. She seemed to have a clear image in her mind of how I should look. It took her no time to pick out what she bought me. I would have spent more time at a stationer's choosing a new eraser. But I had to admit that her good taste in clothes was nothing short of astounding. The colour and style of every shirt and tie she chose seemingly at random were perfectly coordinated, as if she had selected them after long, careful consideration. Nor were the combinations she came up with the least bit ordinary.

Next, she took me to a shoe store and bought me two pairs of shoes to go with the suits. This took no time, either. Again she paid with a credit card and asked for the items to be delivered to my house. Delivery hardly seemed necessary for a couple of pairs of shoes, but this was apparently her way of doing things: pick things out fast, pay with a credit card, and have the stuff delivered.

Next, we went to a watchmaker's and repeated the process. She bought me a stylish, elegant watch with a crocodile-skin strap to go with the suits, and again she took almost no time choosing it. The price was somewhere up around fifty- to sixty-thousand yen. I had a cheap plastic watch, but this was apparently not good enough for her. The watch, at least, she did not have delivered. Instead, she had them wrap it and handed it to me without a word.

Next, she took me to a unisex hair salon. The place was like a dance studio, with shiny wooden floors, and mirrors covering the walls. There were fifteen chairs, and everywhere technicians were coming and going with shears and hairbrushes and whatnot in their hands. Potted plants stood at various points on the floor, and from two black Bose speakers on the ceiling came the faint sounds of one of those meandering Keith Jarrett piano solos. I was shown to a chair straight away. The woman must have set up an appointment for me from one of the stores we had visited. She gave detailed instructions to the thin man who would be cutting my hair. They seemed to know each other. As he responded to each of her instructions, he kept his eyes on my face in the mirror with an expression he might have worn studying a bowlful of celery sticks he was expected to eat. He had a face like the young Solzhenitsyn. The woman said to him, "I'll be back when you've finished," and left the salon with quick steps.

The man said very little as he cut my hair – "This way, please," when it was time for my shampoo, "Excuse me," when he brushed off clippings. When he moved away, I would reach out from under the cloth and touch the mark on my right cheek. This was the first time I had ever seen it in a mirror other than my own at home. The wall-sized mirrors reflected the images of many people, my image among them. And on my face shone this bright blue mark. It didn't seem ugly or unclean to me. It was simply part of me, something I would have to accept. I could feel people looking at it now and then – looking at its reflection in the mirror. But there were too many images in the mirror for me to be able to tell who. I just felt their eyes trained on the mark.

My haircut took half an hour. My hair, which had been growing longer and longer since I left my job, was short once again. I moved to one of the chairs along the wall and sat there listening to music and reading a magazine in which I had no interest until the woman came back. She seemed pleased with my new hairstyle. She took a ten-thousand-yen note from her purse, paid, and led me outside. There she came to a stop and studied me from head to toe, exactly the same way I always examined the cat, as if to see whether there was something she had forgotten to do. Apparently, there was not. Then she glanced at her gold watch and released a kind of sigh. It was nearly 7 o'clock.

"Let's have dinner," she said. "Can you eat?"

I had had one slice of toast for breakfast and one doughnut for lunch. "Probably," I said.

She took me to a nearby Italian restaurant. They seemed to know her there. Without a word, we were shown to a quiet table in the back. As soon as I sat down opposite from her, she ordered me to put the entire contents of my trouser pockets on the table. I did as I was told, saying nothing. My reality seemed to have left me and was now wandering around nearby. I hope it can find me, I thought. There was nothing special in my pockets: keys, handkerchief, wallet. She observed them with no show of interest, then picked up the wallet and looked inside. It contained about fifty-five-hundred yen in cash, a telephone card, a cashpoint card, and my swimming-pool card, nothing else. Nothing unusual. Nothing to prompt anyone to smell it or measure it or shake it or dip it in water or hold it up to the light. She handed it back to me with no change in her expression.

"I want you to go out tomorrow and buy a dozen handkerchiefs, a new wallet and key holder," she said. "That much you can choose yourself, I'm sure. And when was the last time you bought yourself new underwear?"

I thought about it for a moment but couldn't remember. "I can't remember," I said. "It's been a while, I think, but I'm a little clean-crazy, and for a man living alone, I'm good about doing my laund —"

"Never mind. I want you to buy a dozen vests and pants."

I nodded without speaking.

"Just bring me a receipt. I'll pay for them. And make sure you buy the best they have. I'll pay your cleaning bills too. Don't wear a shirt more than once without sending it to the cleaner's. All right?"

I nodded again. The cleaner by the station would be happy to hear this. But, I thought to myself, proceeding to extend this one, concise conjunction, clinging to the window by surface tension, into a proper, full-length sentence: "But why are you doing all this – buying me a whole new wardrobe, paying for my haircuts and cleaning?"

She did not answer me. Instead, she took a Virginia Slim from the packet and put it in her mouth. A tall waiter with regular features appeared from nowhere and, with a practised gesture, lit her cigarette with a match. He struck the match with a clean, dry sound – the kind of sound that could stimulate a person's appetite. When he was through, he presented us with menus. She did not bother to look, however, and she told the waiter not to bother with the day's specials. "Bring me a salad and a bread roll, and some kind of fish with white meat. Just a few drops of dressing on the salad, and a dash of pepper. And a glass of sparkling water, no ice." I didn't want to bother looking at the menu. "I'll have the same," I said. The waiter bowed and withdrew. My reality was still having trouble locating me, it seemed.

"I'm asking purely out of curiosity," I said, trying once more to elicit an explanation from her. "I don't mean to criticise after you've bought me all these things, but is it really worth all the time and trouble and money?"

Still she would not answer.

"I'm just curious," I said again.

Again no answer. She was too busy looking at the oil painting on the wall to answer my question. It was a picture of what I assumed was an Italian landscape, with a well-pruned pine tree, and several reddish farm-houses lining the hills. The houses were all small but pleasant. I wondered what kind of people might live in such houses: probably normal people living normal lives. None of them had inscrutable women coming out of nowhere to buy them suits and shoes and watches. None of them had to calculate the huge funds they would need to gain possession of some dried-up well. I felt a stab of envy for people living in such a normal world. Envy is not an emotion I feel very often, but the scene in the painting aroused that sense in me to a surprising degree. If only I could have entered the picture right then and there! If only I could have walked into one of those farmhouses, enjoyed a glass of wine, then crawled under the covers and gone to sleep without a thought in my head!

The waiter came before long and placed glasses of sparkling water in front of the woman and me. She crushed out her cigarette in an ashtray.

"Why don't you ask me something else?" she said.

While I was thinking about something else to ask, she took a sip of her sparkling water.

"Was that young man in the office in Akasaka your son?" I asked.

"Of course," she answered without hesitation.

"Is he unable to speak?"

The woman nodded. "He never spoke much to begin with, but all of a sudden, at the age of six, he stopped speaking entirely. He stopped using his voice in any way."

"Was there a reason for that?"

She ignored this question. I tried to think of another. "If he doesn't talk, how does he manage to take care of business?"

She wrinkled her brow just the slightest bit. She had not ignored my question, but she obviously had no intention of answering it.

"I'll bet you chose everything he was wearing, from head to foot. The way you did with me."

"I do not like it when people wear the wrong thing. That is all. It is something I simply cannot – *cannot* – abide. I at least want the people around me to dress as well as possible. I want everything about them to look right, whether or not it can be seen."

"I guess you don't like my appendix, then," I said, trying to make a joke.

"Do you have some problem with the shape of your appendix?" she asked, looking straight at me with an utterly serious expression. I regretted the joke.

"Nothing at the moment," I said. "I didn't really mean anything by it. It was just a kind of 'for instance'."

She kept her questioning stare fixed on me a while longer – she was probably thinking about my appendix.

"So anyhow, I want the people around me to look right, even if I have to pay for it myself. That is all there is to it. Don't let it worry you. I am doing this entirely for myself. I feel a personal, almost physical, revulsion for messy clothing."

"The way a musician can't stand hearing music played off key?"

"Something like that."

"Do you buy clothing this way for all the people around you?"

"I suppose I do. Not that I have so many people around me. I mean, I may not like what they wear, but I can't buy clothing for all the people in the world now, can I?"

"Everything has its limits," I said.

"Exactly."

•

Soon our salads arrived, and we ate them. As the woman had specified, each salad had no more than a few drops of dressing – so few you could have counted them on one hand.

"Do you have anything else you want to ask me?" she asked.

"I'd like to know your name," I said. "I mean, it would be helpful if you had a name or something I could use."

She said nothing for a few moments, as she crunched on a radish. Then she formed a deep wrinkle between her eyebrows, as if she had just found something bitter in her mouth by mistake. "Why would you have to use my name? You won't be writing me any letters, I'm sure. Names are, if anything, irrelevant."

"But what if I have to attract your attention, for example? I'd need your name for that."

She laid her fork on her plate and dabbed at her mouth with her napkin. "I see what you mean," she said. "That never crossed my mind. You're right, though. You might very well need my name in a situation like that."

She sat there thinking for a long time. While she was thinking, I ate my salad.

"Let's see, now: you need a suitable name you can use for things like attracting my attention, correct?"

"That's pretty much it."

"So it doesn't have to be my real name, correct?"

I nodded.

"A name, a name . . . what kind of name would be best?"

"Something simple, something easy to call out, I would think. If possible, something concrete, something real, some *thing* you can really touch and see. That way, it would be easy to remember."

"For example?"

"For example, I call my cat Mackerel. In fact, I named him just yesterday."

"Mackerel," she said aloud, as if to confirm the sound of the word. Then she stared at the salt and pepper shakers on the table for a while, raised her face to me, and said, "Nutmeg".

"Nutmeg?"

"It just popped into my head. You can call me that, if you don't mind."

"No, I don't mind at all. So what should I call your son?"

"Cinnamon."

"Parsley, sage, rosemary and thyme," I said, with a hint of melody.

"Nutmeg Akasaka and Cinnamon Akasaka. Not bad, don't you think?"

Nutmeg Akasaka and Cinnamon Akasaka: wouldn't May Kasahara have been shocked if she knew that I had made the acquaintance of such people! "For heaven's sake, Mr Wind-up Bird, why can't you ever get involved with people who are a little more normal?" Indeed, why not, May Kasahara? It was a question I could not have answered.

"Come to think of it," I said, "last year I met two women named Malta Kano and Creta Kano. As a result of which, all kinds of things happened to me. Neither of them is around any more, though."

Nutmeg gave a little nod in response but offered no opinion.

"They just disappeared somewhere," I added feebly. "Like the dew on a summer morning." Or like a star at daybreak.

She brought a forkful of something that looked like chicory to her mouth. Then, as if suddenly recalling a promise made long before, she shot her hand out and took a drink of water.

"Don't you want to know about that money? The money you got the day before yesterday? Am I wrong?"

"No, you are not wrong. I would very much like to know about that."

"I don't mind telling you, but it could be a very long story."

"One that would end by dessert?"

"Probably not," said Nutmeg Akasaka.

7

The Mystery of the Hanging House

•

SETAGAYA, TOKYO: THE MYSTERY OF THE HANGING HOUSE
Who Bought Jinxed Land After Family Suicide?
What's Going On in Posh Neighbourhood?

[From *The* – – – *Weekly*, October 7]

Locals call this plot in ——— 2-chome, Setagaya, the "hanging house". Located in a quiet residential neighbourhood, this 3,500-square-foot piece of prime property with fine southern exposure is a virtually ideal location for a home, but those in the know agree on one thing: they wouldn't take it if you gave it to them. And the reason for this is simple: every known owner of this property, without exception, has met with a terrible fate. Our investigations have revealed that, since the start of the Showa Period, in 1926, no fewer than seven owner-occupants of this property have ended their lives in suicide, the majority by hanging or asphyxiation.

[Details on suicides omitted here]

Bogus Firm Buys Jinxed Land

The most recent in what can hardly be considered a coincidental string of tragedies is the murder-suicide of the family of Kojiro Miyawaki [photo], owner of the long-established Rooftop Grill restaurant chain, headquartered in the Ginza. Miyawaki sold all his restaurants and declared bankruptcy two years ago in the face of massive debt, but thereafter he was pursued by several lenders with links to organized crime. Finally, in January of this year, Miyawaki used his belt to strangle his fourteen-year-old daughter, Yukie, in her sleep at an inn in Takamatsu City, after which he and his wife, Natsuko, hanged themselves with ropes they had brought with them for the purpose. The Miyawakis' eldest daughter, a college student at the time, is still missing.

When he bought the property in April 1972, Miyawaki knew of the ominous rumours surrounding the place, but he laughed them off, declaring, "Those were just coincidences." After purchasing the land, he had the long-vacant house demolished and the lot graded. To be on the safe side, he called in a Shinto priest to exorcise any evil spirits that might still be lurking there, and only then did he have his new, two-story home built. Things went well after that. The family led a tranquil life. Neighbours agree that the Miyawaki home appeared to be harmonious, the daughters bright and happy. But after ten years, the family fortunes took that sudden, disastrous turn.

Miyawaki lost the house, which he had put up as collateral, in the autumn of 1983, but squabbling among his creditors with regard to the order of reimbursement kept final disposal of it in abeyance until a court-mediated settlement last summer, which opened the way for sale of the land. It was purchased initially by a major Tokyo property firm, ——— Land and Buildings, at a price far below current market value. The company proceeded to demolish the Miyawakis' house and tried to sell it as an empty lot. A prime piece of Setagaya property, it attracted much interest, but every deal fell through when buyers heard about the jinx attached to the land. According to Mr M, head of ——— Land and Buildings' sales division:

"Yes, of course we had heard some of the bad stories connected with the property, but ultimately it's a great location, and everybody's so desperate for prime property these days, we figured if we set the price low enough somebody was bound to buy it. We were being optimistic. It hasn't budged since we put it on the market. People don't care about the price – they back out as soon as they hear the stories. And talk about bad timing! The poor Miyawakis committed suicide in January, and all the news reports mentioned the land. Quite frankly, we didn't know what to do with it."

The lot finally sold in April of this year. "Please don't ask me the buyer or the price," says Mr M, so details are hard to come by, but according to the property grapevine, ——— Land and Buildings had to let it go for something far below the asking price. Better to take a fair-sized loss than continue paying the bank interest on a property that would never sell. "The purchasers knew exactly what they were getting into, of course," says Mr M. "We are not in the habit of deceiving our customers. We explained everything beforehand. They bought it knowing the entire history of the place."

Which leads us to the question of who would choose to buy such a jinxed piece of land. Our investigation has been far more difficult than we had imagined. According to the ward office registry, the purchaser is a company with offices in Minato Ward known as Akasaka Research, which claims to be involved in "economic research and consulting", their purpose in buying the land being listed as "construction of corporate residence". The "corporate residence" was, in fact, built this spring, but the firm itself is a typical "paper company". We visited the Akasaka 2-chome address listed in the documents but found only a small plaque, "Akasaka Research", on the door of one apartment in a small condominium building, and no one answered when we rang the bell.

Tight Security and Secrecy

The present "former Miyawaki residence" is surrounded by a wall far higher than any other in the neighbourhood. It has a huge, solid, black iron fence built to discourage peeping (see photo) and a video camera mounted on the gate pillar. We tried ringing the bell, but there was no response. Neighbours have seen the electric gate open and a black Mercedes 500SEL with tinted windows go in and out several times a day, but there has been no other sign of entry or egress, and no sounds are ever heard from the place.

Construction began in May, but always behind high fences, so neighbours have no idea what the house looks like. It was built with incredible speed: two-and-a-half months from start to finish. A local caterer who delivered lunches to the construction site told us: "The building itself was always hidden behind a canvas screen, so I really can't say, but it wasn't a big house – just one story, like a concrete box, real plain. I remember thinking they were building a kind of air-raid shelter. It didn't look like an ordinary house that ordinary people live in – too small and not enough windows. But it wasn't an office building, either. The landscapers came in and planted some really impressive trees all over the place. The yard probably cost a bundle."

We tried calling every major landscaping firm in Tokyo, until we came up with the one who had worked on the "former Miyawaki residence", but the owner could tell us nothing about the party who had ordered the job. The construction company had supplied them with a map of the garden and written orders calling for a good assemblage of mature, well-shaped trees. "Our bid was high, but they accepted it and never tried to bargain."

The landscaper also told us that while they were at work on the garden, a well-digging company was called in and dug a deep well.

"They erected scaffolding in one corner of the garden to bring up the dirt. I got a good look at the job because I was planting a persimmon tree close by. They were digging out an old well that had been filled in. It still had the original concrete tube. They seemed to have an easy time of it, because it had been filled in not long before. The weird thing is, they didn't strike water. I mean, it was a dry well to begin with, and they were just restoring it to its original condition, so there was no way they were going to find water. I don't know, it was weird, like they had some special reason for doing it."

Unfortunately, we have been unable to locate the company that dug the well, but we have been able to determine that the Mercedes 500SEL is the property of a major leasing company with headquarters in Chiyoda Ward and that the vehicle was leased for a year beginning in July by a company in Minato Ward. The identity of their customer could not be revealed to us by the leasing company, but judging from the confluence of events, it is almost certainly Akasaka Research. We might point out that the estimated annual leasing fee for a Mercedes 500SEL is ——— yen. The company offers a chauffeur with every car, but we have been unable to determine whether this particular 500SEL came with a driver or not.

People in the neighbourhood were not anxious to speak with us about the "hanging house". This is not an area known for its neighbourhood socializing, and most people probably do not want to become involved. Local resident Mr A said to us:

"I used to keep my eyes open and tried to figure them out when they first came here, but I'm sure these aren't mobsters or a political organization. Too few people go in and out of the place for that. I don't really get it. It's true they take some pretty impressive security measures, but I have no reason to complain, and I don't think any of the other neighbours are concerned. This is a whole lot better than having that vacant house with all the weird rumours."

Still, we'd like to know who the new owner is and what this "Mr X" is using the place for. The mystery only deepens.

8

Down in the Well

◆

I climb down the steel ladder anchored to the side of the well, and in the darkness at the bottom, I feel for the bat I always leave propped against the wall – the bat I unthinkingly brought home with me from the house where I had followed the man with the guitar case. The touch of the scarred old bat in the darkness at the bottom of the well fills me with a strange sense of peace. It also helps me to concentrate.

When I find the bat, I take a tight grip of the handle, like a baseball player entering the batter's box, assuring myself that this is *my* bat. I go on from there to check that nothing has changed down here in the darkness, where there is nothing to see. I listen hard for anything new; I take a lungful of air; I scrape the ground with the sole of my shoe; I check the hardness of the wall with a few taps of the bat's tip. These are just rituals designed to calm me down. The well bottom is like the bottom of the sea. Things down here stay very still, keeping their original forms, as if under tremendous pressure, unchanging from day to day.

A round slice of light floats high above me: the evening sky. Looking up at it, I think about the October evening world, where "people" must be going about their lives. Beneath that pale autumn light, they must be walking down streets, going to the shop for things, preparing dinner, boarding trains for home. And they think – if they think at all – that these things are too obvious to think about, just as I used to do (or not do). They are the vaguely defined "people", and I used to be a nameless one among them. Accepting and accepted, they live with one another beneath that light, and whether it lasts for ever or for a moment, there must be a kind of closeness while they are enveloped in the light. I am no longer one of them, however. They are up there, on the face of the earth; I am down here, at the bottom of a well. They possess the light, while I am in the process of losing it. Sometimes I feel that I may never find my way back to that world, that I may never again be able to feel the peace of being enveloped in the light, that I may never again be able to hold the cat's soft body in my arms. And then I feel a dull ache in the chest, as if something inside there is being squeezed to death.

But as I dig at the soft earth of the bottom of the well with the rubber sole of my tennis shoe, scenes from the surface of the earth grow ever more distant. The sense of reality subsides bit by bit, and the closeness of the well envelops me in its place. Down here, the well is warm and silent, and the softness of the inner earth caresses my skin. The pain inside me fades like ripples on water. The place accepts me, and I accept the place. I tighten my grip on the bat. I close my eyes, then open them again to gaze upward.

I pull on the rope to close the well lid, using a pulley arrangement constructed for me by the clever young Cinnamon. The darkness is now complete. The well mouth is closed, and all light gone. Not even the occasional sound of the wind can be heard any longer. The break between "people" and me is now total. I don't even have a torch with me. This is like a confession of faith. I mean to show "them" that I am trying to accept the darkness in its entirety.

I lower my bottom to the earth, lean my back against the concrete wall, grip the bat between my knees, and close my eyes, listening to the sound of my heart. There is no need for me to close my eyes, of course, down here in the darkness, but I do it anyway. Closing the eyes has its own significance, in darkness or otherwise. I take several deep breaths, letting my body grow accustomed to this deep, dark, cylindrical space. The smell here is the same as always, the feel of the air against my skin is the same. The well was completely filled in for a time, but the air here is the same as before. With its mouldy smell and its trace of dampness, the air smells exactly as it did when I first climbed inside. Down here there are no seasons. Not even time exists.

•

I always wear my old tennis shoes and my plastic watch, the one I had on the first time I came down into the well. Like the bat, they calm me. I check to see in the darkness that these objects are in firm contact with my body. I check to see that I am not separated from myself. I open my eyes and, after a time, close them again. This is to help bring the pressure of the darkness inside me more into line with the pressure of the darkness around me. Time passes by. Soon, as always, I lose the ability to distinguish between the two kinds of darkness. I can no longer tell if my eyes are open or closed. The mark on my cheek begins to run a slight fever. I know that it is taking on a more vivid purple.

In the two increasingly intermingled darknesses, I concentrate on my mark and think about the room. I try to separate from myself, just as I do whenever I am with the women. I try to get out of this clumsy flesh of mine, which is crouching here in the dark. Now I am nothing but a vacant house, an abandoned well. I try to go outside, to change vehicles, to leap from one reality to another that moves at a different speed, and I keep a firm grip on the bat all the while.

Now a single wall is the only thing separating me from the strange room. I ought to be able to pass through that wall. I should be able to do it with my own strength and with the power of the deep darkness in here.

If I hold my breath and concentrate, I can see what is in the room. I myself am not in there, but I am looking at what is. This is the hotel suite: Room 208. Thick curtains cover the windows. The room is dark. A vase holds a massive bouquet of flowers, and the air is heavy with their suggestive fragrance. A large floor lamp stands beside the entrance, but its bulb is white and dead as the morning moon. Still, if I stare hard enough, after a time I can just make out the shapes of things in the hint of light that manages to find its way into the room, the way the eyes become used to the darkness in a cinema. On the small table in the middle of the room stands a nearly full bottle of Cutty Sark. The ice bucket contains newly cracked chunks of ice (judging from their clear, hard edges), and someone has made a scotch on the rocks in the glass that is standing there. A stainless-steel tray forms a still, cold pool on the table-top. There is no way of knowing the time. It could be morning or evening or the middle of the night. Or perhaps this place simply has no time. On the bed at the back of the suite lies a woman. I hear her moving between the sheets. The ice makes a pleasant clinking in her glass. Minuscule grains of pollen suspended in the air shudder with the sound, like living organisms. Each tiny ripple of sound passing through the air brings more of them to sudden life. The pale darkness opens itself to the pollen, and the pollen, taken in, increases the density of the darkness. The woman brings the whisky glass to her lips, allows a few drops of the liquid to trickle down her throat, and then she tries to speak to me. The bedroom is dark. I can see nothing but the faint movement of shadows. But she has something to say to me. I wait for her to speak. I wait to hear her words.

They are there.

•

Like a make-believe bird hanging in a make-believe sky, I see the rooms from above. I enlarge the view, pull back, and survey the whole, then zoom in on the details. Each detail carries much significance, of course. I check each in turn, examining it for shape and colour and texture. Between one detail and the next, there is no connection, no warmth. All I am doing at that point is a mechanical inventory of details. But it's worth a try. Just as the rubbing together of stones or sticks will eventually produce heat and flame, a connected reality takes shape little by little. It works in the same way that the piling up of random sounds produces a single syllable from the monotonous repetition of what at first glance appears to be meaningless.

I can feel the growth of this faint connection in the farthest depths of the darkness. Yes, that's it, that will do fine. It's very quiet here, and "they" still haven't noticed my presence. I sense the wall that separates me from that place melting, turning into jelly. I hold my breath. *Now!*

But the moment I step towards the wall, a sharp knock resounds, as if they know what I am trying to do. Someone is pounding on the door. It's the same knocking I heard before, a hard, decisive hammering, as if someone is trying to drive a nail straight through the wall. It comes in the same pattern: two knocks, a pause, two knocks. The woman gasps. The floating pollen shudders, and the darkness gives a great lurch. The invasive sound slams shut the passageway that was at last beginning to take shape for me.

It happens this way *every time.*

•

Once again I am myself inside my own body, sitting at the bottom of the well, my back against the wall, my hands gripping the baseball bat. The touch of the world on "this side" returns to my hands slowly, the way an image comes into gradual focus. I feel the slight dampness of sweat on my palms. My heart is pounding in my throat. My ears retain the living sound of that harsh, world-stabbing knock, and I can still hear the slow turning of the doorknob in the darkness. Someone (or some *thing*) outside is opening the door, preparing to enter, but at that very instant, all images evaporate. The wall is as hard as ever, and I am flung back to this side.

In the darkness, I tap the wall in front of me with the end of the bat – the same hard, cold, concrete wall. I am enclosed by a cylinder of cement. Almost made it that time, I tell myself. I'm getting closer. I'm sure of it. At some point, I'm going to break through the barrier and get "inside". I will slip into the room and be standing there, ready, when the knock comes. But how long is it going to take for this to happen? And how much time is there left?

At the same time, I am afraid that it really is going to happen. Because then I will have to confront whatever it is that must be there.

I remain curled up in the darkness. I have to let my heart quiet down. I have to peel my hands from the bat. Before I can rise to my feet on the earthen floor of the well, then climb the steel ladder to the surface, I will need more time, and more strength.

9

The Zoo Attack
(or, A Clumsy Massacre)

•

Nutmeg Akasaka told the story of the tigers, the leopards, the wolves, and the bears that were shot by soldiers on a miserably hot afternoon in August 1945. She narrated with the order and clarity of a documentary film projected on a stark white screen. She left nothing vague. Yet she herself had not witnessed the spectacle. While it was happening, she was standing on the deck of a transport ship carrying refugee settlers home to Japan from Manchuria. What she had actually witnessed was the surfacing of an American submarine.

Like everyone else, she and the other children had come up from the unbearable steam bath of the ship's hold to lean against the deck rail and enjoy the gentle breezes that moved across the calm, unbroken sea, when, all at once, the submarine came floating to the surface as if it were part of a dream. First the aerial and the radar beacon and periscope broke the surface. Then the conning tower came up, raising a wake as it cut through the water. And finally, the entire dripping mass of steel exposed its graceful nakedness to the summer sun. Although in form and shape the thing before her could have been nothing but a submarine, it looked instead like some kind of symbolic sign – or an incomprehensible metaphor.

The submarine ran parallel to the ship for a while, as if stalking its prey. Soon a hatch opened, and one crew member, then another and another, climbed onto the deck, moving in a slow, almost sluggish manner. From the conning tower deck, the officers examined every detail of the transport ship through enormous binoculars, the lenses of which would flash every now and then in the sunlight. The transport ship was full of civilians heading back to Japan, their destination the port of Sasebo. The majority were women and children, the families of Japanese officials in the puppet Manchukuo government and of high-ranking personnel of the Japanese-owned South Manchuria Railway, fleeing to the homeland from the chaos that would follow the imminent defeat of Japan in the war. Rather than face the inevitable horror, they were willing to accept the risk of attack by an American submarine on the open sea – until now, at least.

•

The submarine officers were checking to see if the transport ship was unarmed and without a naval escort. They had nothing to fear. The Americans now had full command of the air as well. Okinawa had fallen, and few if any fighter planes remained on Japanese soil. No need to panic: time was on their side. A petty officer barked orders, and three sailors spun the cranks that turned the deck gun until it was aimed at the transport ship. Two other crewmen opened the rear-deck hatch and hauled up heavy shells to feed the gun. Yet another squad of crewmen was loading a machine gun the men had set on a raised part of the deck near the conning tower. All the crewmen preparing for the attack wore combat helmets, although a few of the men were naked from the waist up and nearly half were wearing shorts. If she stared hard at them, Nutmeg could see brilliant tattoos inscribed on their arms. If she stared hard, she could see lots of things.

One deck gun and one machine gun constituted the submarine's total firepower, but this was more than enough to sink the rotting old freighter that had been refitted as a transport ship. The submarine carried only a limited number of torpedoes, and these had to be reserved for encounters with armed convoys – assuming there *were* armed convoys left in Japan. This was the iron rule.

Nutmeg clung to the ship's handrail and watched as the deck gun's black barrel pivoted in her direction. Dripping wet only moments earlier, it had been baked dry in the summer sun. She had never seen such an enormous gun before. Back in Hsin-ching, she had often seen some kind of regimental gun belonging to the Japanese Army, but there was no comparison between it and the submarine's enormous deck gun. The submarine flashed a signal lamp at the freighter: *Heave to. Attack to commence. Immediately evacuate all passengers to lifeboats.* (Nutmeg could not read the signal lamp, of course, but in retrospect she understood it perfectly.) Aboard the transport ship, which in the chaos of war had undergone minimal conversion from an old freighter on army orders, there were not enough lifeboats. In fact, there were only two small boats for more than five-hundred passengers and crew. There were hardly any life jackets or life buoys aboard.

Gripping the rail and holding her breath, Nutmeg stared, transfixed by the streamlined submarine. It shone as if brand-new, without a speck of rust. She saw the white-painted numerals on the conning tower. She saw the radar aerial rotating above it. She saw the sandy-haired officer with dark glasses. This submarine has come up from the bottom of the ocean to kill us all, she thought, but there's nothing strange about that, it could happen anytime. *It has nothing to do with the war; it could happen to anyone anywhere.* Everybody thinks it's happening because of the war. But that's not true. The war is just *one of the things that could happen.*

Face to face with the submarine and its huge gun, Nutmeg felt no fear. Her mother was shouting at her, but the words made no sense. Then she felt something grab her wrists and pull on them. But her hands stayed locked on the rail. The roar of voices all around her began to move far away, as if someone were turning down the volume on a radio. I'm so sleepy, she thought. So sleepy. Why am I so sleepy? She closed her eyes, and her consciousness rushed away, leaving the deck far behind.

.

Nutmeg was seeing Japanese soldiers as they moved through the extensive zoo shooting any animal that could attack human beings. The officer gave his order, and the bullets from the Model 38 rifles ripped through the smooth hide of a tiger, tearing at the animal's guts. The summer sky was blue, and from the surrounding trees the screams of cicadas rained down like a sudden shower.

The soldiers never spoke. The blood was gone from their sunburned faces, which made them look like pictures painted on ancient urns. A few days from now – a week at most – the main force of the Soviet Far East Command would arrive in Hsin-ching. There was no way to stop the advance. Ever since the war began, the crack troops and once abundant equipment of the Kwantung Army had been drained away to support the widening southern front, and now the greater part of both had sunk to the bottom of the sea or was rotting in the depths of the jungle. The tanks were gone. The anti-tank guns were gone. All but a handful of the troop transport trucks had broken down, and there were no spare parts. A general mobilization could still bring together large numbers of troops, but there were not even enough old-model rifles left to arm every man, or bullets enough to load every rifle. And so the great Kwantung Army, "Bulwark of the North", had been reduced to a paper tiger. The proud Soviet mechanized units that had crushed the German Army were completing their transfer by rail to the Far Eastern front, with plenty of equipment and with spirits high. The collapse of Manchukuo was imminent.

Everyone knew this to be the truth, the Kwantung Army Command most of all. And so they evacuated their main force to the rear, in effect abandoning both the small border garrisons and the Japanese civilian smallholders. These unarmed farmers were slaughtered by the Soviet Army, which was advancing too rapidly to take prisoners. Many women chose – or were forced to choose – mass suicide over rape. The border garrisons locked themselves into the concrete bunker dubbed "Fortress for the Ages" and put up a fierce resistance, but without support from the rear, they were annihilated by the Soviets' overwhelming firepower. Members of the general staff and other high-ranking officers arranged to have themselves "transferred" to new headquarters in Tonghua, near the Korean border, and the puppet emperor Henry Pu-yi and his family threw their possessions together and escaped from the capital by private train. Most of the Chinese soldiers in the Manchukuo Army assigned to defend the capital deserted as soon as they heard the Soviets were invading, or else they staged revolts and shot their Japanese commanding officers. They had no intention of laying down their lives for Japan in a struggle against superior Soviet troops.

As a result of these interrelated developments, the capital city of Manchukuo, the "Special New Capital City, Hsin-ching", which the modern Japanese state had constructed in the wilderness and staked its reputation on, was left floating in a strange political vacuum. In order to avoid needless chaos and bloodshed, the high-ranking Chinese bureaucrats of Manchukuo argued that Hsin-ching should be declared an open city and surrendered without armed resistance, but the Kwantung Army rejected this.

The soldiers dispatched to the zoo had resigned themselves to their fate. In a mere few days, they assumed, they would die fighting the Soviet Army (though in fact, after disarmament, they would be sent to work –

and, in the case of three of the men, to die – in Siberian coal mines). All they could do was pray that their deaths would not be too painful. None of them wanted to be crushed under the tracks of a slow-moving tank or roasted in a trench by flamethrowers or die by degrees with a bullet in the stomach. Better to be shot in the head or the heart. But first they had to kill these zoo animals.

.

If possible, they were to kill the animals with poison in order to conserve what few bullets they had left. The young lieutenant in charge of the operation had been so instructed by his superior officer and told that the zoo had been given enough poison to do the job. The lieutenant led eight fully armed men to the zoo, a twenty-minute walk from head-quarters. The zoo gates had been closed since the Soviet invasion, and two soldiers were standing guard at the entrance, with bayonets on their rifles. The lieutenant showed them his orders and led his men inside.

The zoo's director confirmed that he had indeed been ordered to "liquidate" the fiercer animals in case of an emergency and to use poison, but the shipment of poison, he said, had never arrived. When the lieutenant heard this, he became confused. He was an accountant, assigned to the paymaster's office, and until he was dragged away from his desk at headquarters for this emergency detail, he had never once been put in charge of a detachment of men. He had had to rummage through his drawer to find his pistol, which had not been serviced for years now, and he was not even sure it would fire.

"Bureaucratic work is always like this, Lieutenant," said the zoo director, a man several years his senior, who looked at him with a touch of pity. "The things you need are never there."

To inquire further into the matter, the director called in the zoo's chief veterinary surgeon, who told the lieutenant that the zoo had only a very small amount of poison, probably not enough to kill a horse. The vet was a tall, handsome man in his late thirties, with a blue-black mark on his right cheek, the size and shape of a baby's palm. The lieutenant imagined it had been there since birth.

From the zoo director's office, the lieutenant telephoned headquar-ters, seeking further instructions, but Kwantung Army Headquarters had been in a state of extreme confusion ever since the Soviet Army crossed the border several days earlier, and most of the high-ranking officers had disappeared. The few remaining officers had their hands full, burning stacks of important documents in the courtyard or leading troops to the edge of town to dig anti-tank trenches. The major who had given the lieutenant his orders was nowhere to be found. So now the lieutenant had no idea where they were to obtain the poison they needed. Who in the Kwantung Army would have been in charge of poisons? His call was transferred from one office to another, until a medical corps colonel got on the line, only to scream at the lieutenant, "You stupid son of a bitch! The whole goddamn country's going down the drain, and you're asking me about a goddamn fucking *zoo*?! Who gives a shit?"

Who indeed, thought the lieutenant. Certainly not the lieutenant himself. With a dejected look, he rang off and decided to give up on the poison. Now he was faced with two options. He could forget about killing any animals and lead his men out of there, or they could use bullets to do the job. Either way would constitute a violation of the orders he had been given, but in the end he decided to do the shooting. That way, he might later be torn down a strip for having wasted valuable ammunition, but at least the goal of "liquidating" the more dangerous animals would have been met. If, on the other hand, he chose not to kill the animals, he might be court-martialled for having failed to carry out orders. There was some doubt whether there would even *be* any courts-martial at this late stage of the war, but ultimately, orders were orders. So long as the army continued to exist, its orders had to be carried out.

If possible, I'd rather not kill any animals, the lieutenant told himself, in all honesty. But the zoo was running out of things to feed them, and most of the animals (especially the big ones) were already suffering from chronic starvation. Things could only get worse – or at least they were not going to get any better. Shooting might even be easier for the animals themselves – a quick, clean death. And if starving animals were to escape into the city streets during intense fighting or air strikes, a disaster would be unavoidable.

The director handed the lieutenant a list of animals for "emergency liquidation" that he had been instructed to compile, along with a map of the zoo. The vet with the mark on his cheek and two Chinese workers were assigned to accompany the firing squad. The lieutenant glanced at the list and was relieved to find it shorter than he had imagined. Among the animals slated for liquidation, though, were two Indian elephants. Elephants? the lieutenant thought with a frown. How in the hell are we supposed to kill elephants?

Given the layout of the zoo, the first animals to be liquidated were the tigers. The elephants would be left for last, in any case. The plaque on the tiger cage explained that the pair had been captured in Manchuria in the Greater Khingan Mountains. The lieutenant assigned four men to each tiger and told them to aim for the heart – the whereabouts of which was just another mystery to him. Oh, well, at least one bullet was bound to hit home. When eight men together pulled back on the levers of their Model 38s and loaded a cartridge into each chamber, the ominous dry clicking transformed the whole atmosphere of the place. The tigers stood up at the sound. Glaring at the soldiers through the iron bars, they let out huge roars. As an extra precaution, the lieutenant drew his automatic pistol and released the safety. To calm himself, he cleared his throat. This is nothing, he tried to tell himself. Everybody does stuff like this all the time.

The soldiers knelt down, took careful aim, and, at the lieutenant's command, pulled their triggers. The recoil shook their shoulders, and for a moment their minds went empty, as if flicked away. The roar of the simultaneous shots reverberated through the deserted zoo, echoing from building to building, wall to wall, slicing through wooded areas, crossing water surfaces, a stab to the hearts of all who heard it, like distant thunder. The animals held their breath. Even the cicadas stopped crying. Long after the echo of gunfire faded into the distance, there was not a sound to be heard. As if they had been whacked with a huge club by an invisible giant, the tigers shot up into the air for a moment, then landed on the floor of the cage with a great thud, writhing in agony, vomiting blood. The soldiers had failed to finish the tigers off with a single volley. Snapping out of their trance, the soldiers pulled back on their rifle levers, ejecting spent shells, and took aim again.

•

The lieutenant sent one of his men into the cage to be certain that both tigers were dead. They certainly *looked* dead – eyes closed, teeth bared, all movement gone. But it was important to make sure. The vet unlocked the cage, and the young soldier (he had just turned twenty) stepped inside fearfully, thrusting his bayonet ahead of him. It was an odd performance, but no one laughed. He gave a light kick to one tiger's hindquarters with the heel of his boot. The tiger remained motionless. He kicked the same spot again, this time a little harder. The tiger was dead without a doubt. The other tiger (the female) lay equally still. The young soldier had never visited a zoo in his life, nor had he ever seen a real tiger before. Which was partly why he couldn't quite believe that they had just succeeded in killing a real, live tiger. He felt only that he had been dragged into a place that had nothing to do with him and had been forced to perform an act that had nothing to do with him. Standing in an ocean of black blood, he stared down at the tigers' corpses, entranced. They looked much bigger dead than they had when alive. Why should that be? he asked himself, mystified.

The cage's concrete floor was suffused with the piercing smell of the big cats' urine, and mixed with it was the warm odour of blood. Blood was still gushing from the holes torn in the tigers' bodies, forming a sticky black pond around his feet. All of a sudden, the rifle in his hands felt heavy and cold. He wanted to fling it away, bend down, and vomit the entire contents of his stomach onto the floor. What a relief it would have been! But vomiting was out of the question – the squad leader would beat his face out of shape. (Of course, this soldier had no idea that he would die seventeen months later when a Soviet guard in a mine near Irkutsk would split his skull open with a shovel.) He wiped the sweat from his forehead with the back of his wrist. His helmet was weighing down upon him. One cicada, then another, began to cry again, as if finally revived. Soon their cries were joined by those of a bird – distinctive cries, like the winding of a spring: *Creeeak. Creeeak.* The young soldier had moved from a mountain village in Hokkaido across the sea to China with his parents at the age of twelve, and together they had tilled the soil of a frontier village in Bei'an until a year ago, when he had been drafted into the army. Thus he knew all the birds of Manchuria, but he had never heard a bird with that particular cry. Perhaps it was a bird imported from a distant land, crying in its cage in another part of the zoo. Yet the sound seemed to come from the upper branches of a nearby tree. He turned and squinted in the direction of the sound, but he could see nothing. A huge elm tree with dense leaves cast its cool, sharp shadow on the ground below.

He looked towards the lieutenant, as if requesting instructions. The lieutenant nodded, ordered him out of the cage, and spread open the zoo map again. So much for the tigers. Next we'll do the leopards. Then maybe the wolves. We've got bears to deal with too. We'll think about the elephants when the others are finished off, he thought. And then he realized how hot it was. "Take a breather," he said to his men. "Have some water." They drank from their canteens. Then they shouldered their rifles, took their places in formation, and headed for the leopard cage. Up in a tree, the unknown bird with the insistent call went on winding its spring. The chests and backs of the men's short-sleeved military shirts were stained black with sweat. As this formation of fully armed soldiers strode along, the clanking of all kinds of metallic objects sent hollow echoes throughout the deserted zoo. The monkeys clinging to the bars of their cages rent the air with ominous screams, sending frantic warnings to all the other animals in the zoo, who in turn joined the chorus in their own distinctive ways. The wolves sent long howls skyward, the birds contributed a wild flapping of wings, some large animal somewhere was slamming itself against its cage, as if to issue a threat. A chunk of cloud shaped like a fist appeared out of nowhere and hid the sun for a time. On that August afternoon, people, animals – everyone was thinking about death. Today the men would be killing animals; tomorrow Soviet troops would be killing the men. Probably.

·

We always sat across from each other at the same table in the same restaurant, talking. She was a regular there, and of course she always paid the bill. The back part of the restaurant was divided into private compartments, so that the conversation at any one table could not be heard at another. There was only one seating per evening, which meant that we could talk at our leisure, right up to closing time, without interference from anyone – including the waiters, who approached the table only to bring or clear a dish. She would always order a bottle of Burgundy of one particular vintage and always leave half the bottle unconsumed.

"A bird that winds a spring?" I asked, looking up from my food.

"A bird that winds a spring?" said Nutmeg, repeating the words exactly as I had said them, then curling her lips just a little. "I don't understand what you're saying. What are you talking about?"

"Didn't you just say something about a bird that winds a spring?"

She shook her head slowly. "Hmm. Now I can't remember. I don't *think* I said anything about a bird."

I could see it was hopeless. She always told her stories like this. I didn't ask her about the mark, either.

"So you were born in Manchuria, then?" I asked.

She shook her head again. "I was born in Yokohama. My parents took me to Manchuria when I was three. My father was teaching at a school of veterinary medicine, but when the Hsin-ching city administrators wanted someone sent over from Japan as chief veterinary surgeon for the new zoo they were going to build, he volunteered for the job. My mother didn't want to abandon the settled life they had in Japan and go off to the ends of the earth, but my father insisted. Maybe he wanted to test himself in a place bigger and more open than Japan. I was so young, it didn't matter where I was, but I really enjoyed living at the zoo. It was a wonderful life. My father always smelled like the animals. All the different animal smells would mix together into one, and it would be a little different each day, like changing the blend of ingredients in a perfume. I'd climb up onto his lap when he came home and make him sit still while I smelled him.

"But then the war took a turn for the worse, and we were in danger, so my father decided to send my mother and me back to Japan before it was too late. We went with a lot of other people, taking the train from Hsin-ching to Korea, where a special boat was waiting for us. My father stayed behind in Hsin-ching. The last time I ever saw him, he was standing in the station, waving to us. I stuck my head out the window and watched him growing smaller and smaller until he disappeared into the crowd on the platform. No one knows what happened to him after that. I think he must have been taken prisoner by the Soviets and sent to Siberia to do forced labour and, like so many others, died over there. He's probably buried in some cold, lonely patch of earth without anything to mark his grave.

"I still remember everything about the Hsin-ching zoo in perfect detail. I can bring it all back inside my head – every pathway, every animal. We lived in the chief veterinary surgeon's official residence, inside the grounds. All the zoo workers knew me, and they let me go anywhere I wanted – even on holidays, when the zoo was closed."

Nutmeg closed her eyes to bring back the scene inside her mind. I waited, without speaking, for her to continue her story.

"Still, I can't be sure if the zoo as I recall it was *really* like that. How can I put it? I sometimes feel that it's *too* vivid, if you know what I mean. And when I start having thoughts like this, the more I think about it, the less I can tell how much of the vividness is real and how much of it my imagination has invented. I feel as if I've wandered into a labyrinth. Has that ever happened to you?"

It had not. "Do you know if the zoo is still there in Hsin-ching?" I asked.

"I wonder," said Nutmeg, touching the end of her earring. "I heard that the place was closed down after the war, but I have no idea if it's still closed."

·

For a very long time, Nutmeg Akasaka was the only person in the world that I could talk to. We would meet once or twice a week and talk to each other across the table at the restaurant. After we had met several times like that, I discovered that she was an extremely accomplished listener. She was quick on the uptake, and she knew how to direct the flow of the story by means of skilful questions and responses.

So as to avoid upsetting her in any way, I always took great care whenever we met to see that my outfit was neat and clean and well chosen. I would put on a shirt fresh from the cleaner's and choose the tie that best matched it. My shoes were always shined and spotless. The first thing she would do when she saw me was examine me from top to bottom, with the eyes of a chef choosing vegetables. If anything displeased her, she would take me straight to a shop and buy me the proper article of clothing. If possible, she would have me change into it then and there. When it came to clothing, she would accept nothing less than perfection.

As a result, my wardrobe began to fill up. Slowly but steadily, new suits, new jackets, and new shirts invaded the territory that had once been occupied by Kumiko's skirts and dresses. Before long, the wardrobe was becoming cramped, and so I folded Kumiko's things, packed them in boxes with mothballs, and put them in a storage area. If she ever came back, I knew she would wonder what in the world had happened in her absence.

I took a long time to explain, little by little, about Kumiko to Nutmeg – that I had to save her and bring her back here. She put her elbow on the table, propping her chin in her hand, and looked at me for a while.

"So where is it that you're going to save Kumiko *from*? Does the place have a name or something?"

I searched for the words in space. But they were not in space. Neither were they underground. "Somewhere far away," I said.

Nutmeg smiled. "It's like *The Magic Flute*. You know: Mozart. Using a magic flute and magic bells, they have to save a princess who's being held captive in a faraway castle. I love that opera. I don't know *how* many times I've seen it. I know the lines by heart: 'As the birdcatcher I am known by young and old through the land.' Ever seen it?"

I shook my head. I had never seen it.

"In the opera, the prince and the birdcatcher, Papageno, are led to the castle by three children riding on a cloud. But what's really happening is a battle between the land of day and the land of night. The land of night is trying to recapture the princess from the land of day. Halfway through the opera, the heroes can't tell any longer which side is right – who is being held captive and who is not. Of course, at the end, the prince gets the princess, Papageno gets Papagena, and the villains fall into hell." Nutmeg ran her finger along the rim of her glass. "Anyhow, at this point you don't have a birdcatcher or a magic flute or bells."

"But I do have a well," I said.

•

Whenever I grew tired of talking or was unable to go on telling my story because I lacked the words I needed, Nutmeg would give me a rest by talking about her own early life, and her stories turned out to be far more lengthy and convoluted than mine. And also, unlike me, she would impose no order on her stories but would leap from topic to topic as her feelings dictated. Without explanation, she would reverse chronological order or introduce as a major character someone she had never mentioned before. In order to know which period of her life the fragment that she was presently narrating belonged to, it was necessary to make careful deductions, though no amount of deduction would work in some cases. She would narrate events she had witnessed with her own eyes, as well as events that she had never witnessed.

•

They killed the leopards. They killed the wolves. They killed the bears. Shooting the bears took the most time. Even after the two gigantic animals had taken dozens of rifle slugs, they continued to crash against the bars of their cage, roaring at the men and slobbering, fangs bared. Unlike the cats, who were more willing to accept their fate (or who at least appeared to accept it), the bears seemed unable to comprehend the fact that they were being killed. Possibly for that reason, it took them far longer than was necessary to reach a final parting with that temporary condition known as life. When the soldiers at last succeeded in extinguishing all signs of life in the bears, they were so exhausted they were ready to collapse on the spot. The lieutenant reset his pistol's safety catch and used his hat to wipe the sweat dripping from his brow. In the deep silence that followed the killing, several of the soldiers seemed to be trying to mask their sense of shame by spitting loudly on the ground. Spent shells were scattered about their feet like so many cigarette butts. Their ears still rang with the crackling of their rifles. The young soldier who would be beaten to death by a Soviet soldier seventeen months later in a coal mine near Irkutsk took several deep breaths in succession, averting his gaze from the bears' corpses. He was engaged in a fierce struggle to force back the nausea that had worked its way up to his throat.

In the end, they did not kill the elephants. Once they confronted them, it became obvious that the beasts were simply too large. The soldiers' rifles looked like silly toys in their presence. The lieutenant thought it over for a while and decided to leave the elephants alone. Hearing this, the men breathed a sigh of relief. Strange as it may seem – or perhaps it does not seem so strange – they all had the same thought: it was so much easier to kill humans on the battlefield than animals in cages, even if, on the battlefield, one might end up being killed oneself.

Those animals that were now nothing but corpses were dragged from their cages by the Chinese workers, loaded onto carts, and hauled to an empty warehouse. There, the animals, which came in so many shapes and sizes, were laid out on the floor. Once he had seen the operation through to its conclusion, the lieutenant returned to the zoo director's office and had the man sign the necessary documents. Then the soldiers lined up and marched away in formation, with the same metallic clanking they had made when they came. The Chinese workers used hoses to wash off the black stains of blood on the floors of the cages, and with brushes they scrubbed away the occasional chunk of animal flesh that clung to the walls. When this job was finished, the workers asked the vet with the blue-black mark on his cheek how he intended to dispose of the corpses. The doctor was at a loss for an answer. Ordinarily, when an animal died at the zoo, he would call a professional to do the job. But with the capital now bracing itself for a bloody battle, with people now struggling to be the first to leave this doomed city, you couldn't just make a phone call and get someone to run over to dispose of an animal corpse for you. Summer was at its height, though, and the corpses would soon begin to decompose. Even now, black swarms of flies were massing. The best thing would be to bury them – an enormous job even if the zoo had access to heavy equipment, but with the limited help available to them now, it would be impossible to dig holes large enough to take all the corpses.

The Chinese workers said to the vet: Doctor, if you will let us take the corpses whole, we will dispose of them for you. We have plenty of friends to help us, and we know exactly where to do the job. We will take them outside the city and get rid of every last trace. We will not cause you any problems. But in exchange, we want the hides and meat. Especially the bear meat: everybody will want that. Parts of bear and tiger are good for medicine – they will command a high price. And though it's too late now to say this, we wish you had aimed only at their heads. Then the hides would have been worth a good deal more. The soldiers were such amateurs! If you had let us take care of it from the beginning, we wouldn't have done such a clumsy job. The vet agreed to the bargain. He had no choice. After all, it was *their* country.

Before long, ten Chinese appeared, pulling several empty carts behind them. They dragged the animals' corpses out of the warehouse, piled them onto the carts, tied them down, and covered them with straw mats. They hardly said a word to each other the whole time. Their faces were expressionless. When they had finished loading the carts, they dragged them off somewhere. The old carts creaked with the strain of supporting the animals' weight. And so ended the massacre – what the Chinese workers called a clumsy massacre – of zoo animals on a hot August afternoon. All that was left were several clean – and empty – cages. Still in an agitated state, the monkeys kept calling out to one another in their incomprehensible language. The badgers rushed back and forth in their narrow cage. The birds flapped their wings in desperation, scattering feathers all around. And the cicadas kept up their grating cry.

•

After the soldiers had finished their killing and returned to headquarters, and after the last two Chinese workers had disappeared somewhere, dragging their cart loaded with animal corpses, the zoo took on the hollow quality of a house emptied of furniture. The vet sat on the rim of a waterless fountain, looked up at the sky, and watched the group of hard-edged clouds that were floating there. Then he listened to the cicadas crying. The wind-up bird was no longer calling, but the vet did not notice that. He had never heard the wind-up bird to begin with. The only one who had heard it was the poor young soldier who would be beaten to death in a Siberian coal mine.

The vet took a sweat-dampened pack of cigarettes from his breast pocket, put a cigarette in his mouth, and struck a match. As he lit up, he realized that his hand was trembling – so much that it took him three matches to light the cigarette. Not that he had experienced an emotional trauma. A large number of animals had been "liquidated" in a moment before his eyes, and yet, for some inexplicable reason, he felt no particular shock or sadness or anger. In fact, he felt almost nothing. He was just terribly puzzled.

He sat there for a while, watching the smoke curl upward from his cigarette and trying to sort out his feelings. He stared at his hands resting on his lap, then looked once again at the clouds in the sky. The world he saw before him looked as it always had. He could find in it no signs of change. And yet it ought to have been a world distinctly different from the one he had known until then. After all, the world in which he lived now was a world in which bears and tigers and leopards and wolves had been "liquidated". Those animals had existed this morning, but now, at 4 o'clock in the afternoon, they had ceased to exist. They had been massacred by soldiers, and even their dead bodies were gone.

There should have been a decisive gap separating those two different worlds. There *had* to be a gap. But he could not find it. The world looked the same to him as it always had. What most puzzled the vet was the lack of feeling inside himself.

He realized that he was exhausted. Come to think of it, he had hardly slept at all the night before. How wonderful it would be, he thought, if he could find the cool shade of a tree somewhere, to stretch out and sleep, if only for a little while – to stop thinking, to sink into the silent darkness of unconsciousness. He glanced at his watch. He had to find food for the surviving animals. He had to treat the baboon that was running a high fever. There were a thousand things he had to do. But now, more than anything, he had to sleep. What came afterwards he could think about afterwards.

The vet walked into the neighbouring wooded area and stretched out on the grass where no one would notice him. The shaded grass felt cool and good. The smell was something he remembered fondly from childhood. Several large Manchurian grasshoppers bounded over his face making an agreeable, loud hum. He lit another cigarette as he lay there, and he was pleased to see that his hands were no longer trembling so badly. Inhaling the smoke deep into his lungs, he pictured the Chinese men stripping the hides off all those freshly killed animals somewhere and cutting up the meat. He had often seen Chinese doing work like that, and he knew they were anything but clumsy. In a matter of moments, an animal would be reduced to hide, meat, organs, and bones, as if those elements had originally been quite separate and had just happened to come together for a little while. By the time I wake from my nap, I'm sure, those pieces of meat will be out there in the marketplace. That's reality for you: quick and efficient. He tore up a handful of grass and toyed with its softness a while. Then he stubbed his cigarette and, with a deep sigh, expelled all the smoke left in his lungs. When he closed his eyes, the grasshoppers' wings sounded much louder in the darkness. The vet was overtaken by the illusion that huge grasshoppers the size of bullfrogs were leaping all around him.

Maybe the world was like a revolving door, it occurred to him as his consciousness was fading away. And which section you ended up in was just a matter of where your foot happened to fall. There were tigers in one section, but no tigers in another. Maybe it was as simple as that. And there was no logical continuity from one section to another. And it was precisely because of this lack of logical continuity that choices didn't mean very much. Wasn't that why he couldn't feel the gap between one world and another? But that was as far as his thoughts would go. He wasn't able to think more deeply than that. The fatigue in his body was as heavy and suffocating as a sodden blanket. No more thoughts came to him, and he just lay there, inhaling the aroma of the grass, listening to the grasshoppers' wings, and feeling through his skin the dense membrane of shadow that covered him.

And in the end his mind was sucked into the deep sleep of afternoon.

•

The transport ship cut its engines as ordered, and soon came to a standstill on the surface of the ocean. There was less than one chance in ten thousand that it would outrun such a swift, modern submarine. The submarine's deck gun and machine gun were still trained on the transport ship, its crew in a state of readiness to attack. Yet a strange sense of tranquillity hovered over the two ships. The submarine's crew stood in full view on deck, lined up and watching the transport ship with an air of having time to kill. Many of them had not even bothered to strap on battle helmets. There was hardly any wind that summer afternoon, and now, with both engines cut, the only sound was the languid slap of waves against the two ships' hulls. The transport ship signalled to the submarine: "We are a transport ship carrying unarmed civilians. We have neither munitions nor military personnel on board. We have few lifeboats." The submarine's response was brusque: "That is not our problem. Evacuation or no, we commence firing in precisely ten minutes." This ended the exchange of messages between the two ships. The captain of the transport ship decided not to convey the communication to his passengers. What good would it do? A few of them might be lucky enough to survive, but most would be dragged to the bottom of the sea with this miserable old washtub. The captain longed for one last drink, but the whisky bottle – some fine old scotch he had been saving – was in a desk drawer in his cabin, and there was no time to get it now. He took off his hat and looked up at the sky, hoping that, through some miracle, a squadron of Japanese fighter planes might suddenly appear there. But this was not to be a day for miracles. The captain had done all he could. He thought about his whisky again.

As the ten-minute grace period was running out, strange movements began on the deck of the submarine. There were hurried exchanges among the officers lined up on the conning-tower deck, and one of the officers scrambled down to the main deck and ran among the crew, shouting orders of some kind. Wherever he went, ripples of movement spread among the men at their battle stations. One sailor shook his head from side to side and punched the barrel of the deck gun with a clenched fist. Another took his helmet off and stared up at the sky. The men's actions might have been the expression of anger or joy or disappointment or excitement. The passengers on the transport ship found it impossible to tell what was happening or what this was leading to. Like an audience watching a pantomime for which there was no programme (but which contained a very important message), they held their breaths and kept their eyes fixed on the sailors' every movement, hoping to find some small hint of meaning. Eventually, the waves of confusion that had spread among the sailors began to subside, and in response to an order from the bridge, the shells were removed from the deck gun with great dispatch. The men turned cranks and swung the barrel away from the transport ship until the gun was pointing straight ahead again, then they plugged the horrid black hole of the muzzle. The gun shells were returned below decks, and the crew ran for the hatches. In contrast to their earlier movements, they did everything now with speed and efficiency. There was no chatting or wasted motion.

The submarine's engines started with a definite growl, and at almost the same moment the siren screeched to signal "All hands below decks!" The submarine began to move forward, and a moment later it was plunging downward, churning up a great white patch of foam, as if it had hardly been able to wait for the men to get below and fasten the hatches. A membrane of seawater swallowed the long, narrow deck from front to rear, the gun sank below the surface, the conning tower slipped downward, cutting through the dark-blue water, and finally the aerial and the periscope plunged out of sight, as if to wipe the air clean of any evidence they had ever been there. Ripples disturbed the surface of the ocean for a short while, but soon they also subsided, leaving only the calm afternoon sea.

Even after the submarine had plunged beneath the surface, with the same amazing suddenness that had marked its appearance, the passengers stood frozen on deck, staring at the watery expanse. Not a throat was cleared among them. The captain recovered his presence of mind and gave his order to the navigator, who passed it onto the engine room, and eventually, after a long fit of grinding, the antique engine started up like a sleeping dog kicked by its master.

The crew of the transport ship held their breaths, waiting for a torpedo attack. The Americans might have simply changed their plans, deciding that sinking the ship with a torpedo would be faster and easier than a time-consuming volley from the gun. The ship ran in short zigzags, the captain and navigator scanning the ocean's surface with their binoculars, searching for the deadly white wake of a torpedo. But there was no torpedo. Twenty minutes after the submarine had disappeared beneath the waves, people at last began to break free of the death curse that had hung over them. They could only half believe it at first, but little by little they came to feel that it was true: they had come back alive from the verge of death. Not even the captain knew why the Americans had abandoned their attack. What could have changed their minds? (Only later did it become clear that instructions had arrived from headquarters just moments before the attack was to have begun, advising them to suspend all hostilities unless attacked by the enemy. The Japanese government had telegraphed the Allied powers that they were prepared to accept the Potsdam Declaration and surrender unconditionally.) Released now from the unbearable tension, several passengers plopped down on the deck where they stood and began to wail, but most of them could neither cry nor laugh. For several hours – and, in the case of some, for several days – they remained in a state of total abstraction, the spike of a long and twisted nightmare thrust mercilessly into their lungs, their hearts, their spines, their brains, their wombs.

Little Nutmeg Akasaka remained sound asleep in her mother's arms all the time this was happening. She slept for a solid twenty hours, as if she had been knocked unconscious. Her mother shouted and slapped her cheeks to no avail. She might as well have sunk to the bottom of the sea. The intervals between her breaths grew longer and longer, and her pulse slowed. Her breathing was all but inaudible. But when the ship arrived in Sasebo, she woke without warning, as if some great power had dragged her back into this world. And so Nutmeg did not herself witness the events surrounding the aborted attack and disappearance of the American submarine. She heard everything much later, from her mother.

The freighter limped into the port of Sasebo a little past ten in the morning on August 16, the day after the non-attack. Over the port hung a weird silence, and no one came out to greet the ship. Not even at the anti-aircraft emplacement by the harbour mouth were there signs of humanity. The summer sunlight baked the ground with dumb intensity. The whole world seemed caught in a deep paralysis, and some on board felt as if they had stumbled by accident into the land of the dead. After years spent abroad, they could only stare in silence at the country of their ancestors. At noon on August 15, the radio had broadcast the Emperor's announcement of the war's end. Six days before that, the nearby city of Nagasaki had been incinerated by a single atomic bomb. The phantom empire of Manchukuo was disappearing into history. And caught unawares in the wrong section of the revolving door, the vet with the mark on his cheek would share the fate of Manchukuo.

10

So, Then, the Next Problem
(May Kasahara's Point of View: 2)

•

Hi, again, Mr Wind-up Bird.

Have you thought about where I am and what I'm doing, the way I told you to at the end of my last letter? Were you able to imagine anything at all?

Oh, well, I guess I'll just go on assuming that you couldn't figure out a thing – which I'm sure is true.

So let me just get it over with and tell you right from the start.

I'm working in – let's say – a certain factory. A big factory. It's in a certain provincial city – or, should I say, in the mountains on the outskirts of a certain provincial city that faces the Sea of Japan. Don't let the word "factory" fool you, though. It's not what you'd imagine: one of those macho places full of big, high-tech machines grinding away and conveyor belts running and smoke pouring out of smokestacks. It's big, all right, but the grounds are spread out over a wide area and it's bright and quiet. It doesn't produce any smoke at all. I never imagined the world had such widely spread-out factories. The only other factory I've ever seen was the Tokyo caramel factory our class visited on a field trip in elementary school, and all I remember is how noisy and cramped it was and how people were just slaving away with gloomy expressions on their faces. So to me, a "factory" was always like some illustration you'd see in a textbook under "Industrial Revolution".

The people working here are almost all girls. There's a separate building nearby, a laboratory, where men in white coats work on product development,

415

wearing very serious looks on their faces, but they make up a very small proportion of the whole. All the rest are girls in their late teens or early twenties, and maybe seventy per cent of those live in the dorms inside the company compound, like me. Commuting to this place from the town every day by bus or car is a real pain, and the dorms are nice. The buildings are new, the rooms are all singles, the food is good and they let you choose what you want, the facilities are excellent, and room and board is cheap. There's a heated pool and a library, and you can do things like tea ceremony and flower arranging if you want (but I don't want), and they even have an active programme of sports teams, so a lot of girls who start out commuting end up moving into a dorm. All of them return home at weekends to eat with their families or go to the movies or go on dates with their boyfriends and stuff, so on Saturday the place turns into an empty ruin. There aren't too many people like me, without a family to go home to at weekends. But like I said before, I like the big, hollow, empty feeling of the place at weekends. I can spend the day reading, or listening to music with the volume turned up, or walking in the hills, or, like now, sitting at my desk and writing to you, Mr Wind-up Bird.

The girls who work here are all locals – which means farmers' daughters. Well, maybe not every single one, but they're mostly happy, healthy, optimistic, hardworking girls. There aren't many big industries in this district, so before, girls would go to the city to find jobs when they graduated from school. That meant the guys left in town couldn't find anybody to marry, which only added to the depopulation problem. So then the town got together and offered businesses this big tract of land to set up a factory, and the girls didn't have to leave. I think it was a great idea. I mean, look, they got somebody like me to come all the way out here. So now, when they graduate from school (or drop out, like me), the girls all go to work at the factory and save their pay and get married when they're old enough and leave their jobs and have a couple of kids and turn into fat walruses that all look alike. Of course, there are a few who go on working here after they get married, but most of them leave.

This should give you a pretty good idea of what this place is like. OK?

So now the next question for you is this: What do they make in this factory?

Hint: You and I once went out on a job connected with it. Remember? We went to the Ginza and did a survey.

Oh, come on. Even you must have figured it out by now, Mr Wind-up Bird! That's it! I'm working in a wig factory! Surprised?

I told you before how I got out of that high-class hotel/jail/country school after six months and just hung around at home, like a dog with a broken leg. Then, all of a sudden, the thought of the wig company's factory popped into my head. I remembered something my boss at the company had once said to me, more as a joke than anything, about how they never had enough girls for the factory and they'd hire me anytime I wanted to go work there. He even showed me a pamphlet from the place, and I remember thinking it looked like a really cool factory and I wouldn't mind working there. My boss said the girls all did hand labour, implanting hairs into the toupees. Making a hairpiece is a very delicate business, not like some aluminium pot you can stamp out one two three. You have to plant little bunches of real hair very very very carefully, one bunch at a time, to make a quality hairpiece. Doesn't it make you faint, just thinking about it? I mean, how many hairs do you think there are on a human head? You have to count them in the hundreds of thousands! And to make a wig you have to plant them all by hand, the way they plant seedlings in a rice field. None of the girls here complain about the work, though. They don't mind because this region is in the snow country, where it has always been the custom for the farm women to do detailed handiwork to make money during the long winters. That's supposed to be why the company chose this area for its factory.

To tell you the truth, I've never minded doing this kind of hand labour. I know I don't look it, but I'm actually pretty good at sewing. I always impressed my teachers. You still don't believe me? It's true, though! That's why it occurred to me that I might enjoy spending part of my life in a factory in the mountains, keeping my hands busy from morning to night and never thinking about anything upsetting. I was sick of school, but I hated the thought of just hanging around and letting my parents take care of me (and I'm sure they hated the thought of it too), but I didn't have any one thing that I was dying to do, so the more I thought of it, the more it seemed that the only thing I could do was go to work in this factory.

I got my parents to act as my sponsors and my boss to give me a reference (they liked my survey work), I passed my interview at company headquarters, and the very next week I was all packed (not that I took anything more than my clothes and my music machine). I got on the bullet train by myself, transferred to a cute little train that goes up into the hills, and made it all the way to this nothing little town. But it was like I'd come to the other side of the earth. I was sooo bummed off when I got off the train! I thought I had made a terrible mistake. But finally, no: I've been here six months now without any special problems, and I feel settled in.

I don't know what it is, but I've always been interested in wigs. Or maybe I should say I've always been "attracted" to them, the way some guys are attracted to motorcycles. You know, I hadn't really been aware of it before, but when I went out to do that market research and I had a chance to see all those bald men (or what the company calls "men with a thinning problem"), it really struck me what a lot of guys like that there are in the world! Not that I have personal feelings one way or another towards men who are bald (or have a thinning problem). I don't especially "like" them or "dislike" them. Take you, for example, Mr Wind-up Bird. Even if your hair were thinner than it is now (and it will be before too long), my feelings towards you would absolutely not change in any way. The only strong feeling I have when I see a man with a thinning problem is that sense I think I mentioned to you before of life being worn away. Now, that is something I'm really interested in!

I once heard that people reach the peak of their growth at a certain age (I forget whether it was nineteen or twenty or what), after which the body starts to wear out. If that's the case, then it's just one part of the "wearing away" of the body for the hair to fall out and grow thinner. There's nothing strange about it at all. It's normal and natural. If there's any problem in all this, it's the fact that some guys go bald young and others never go bald, even when they're old. I know if I were bald, I'd think it was unfair. I mean, it's a part of the body that really sticks out! Even I understand how they feel, and the problem of thinning hair has nothing to do with me.

In most cases, the person losing his hair is in no way responsible for whether the volume of hair he loses is greater or less than anybody else's. When I was working part-time, my boss told me that the genes determine ninety per cent of whether a person is going to go bald or not. A man who has inherited a gene for thinning hair from his grandfather and father is going to lose his hair sooner or later, no matter what he does to prevent it. "Where there's a will there's a way" just doesn't apply to baldness. When the time comes for the gene to stand up and say, "All right, now, let's get this show on the road" (that is, if genes can stand up and say "Let's get this show on the road"), the hair has no choice but to start falling out. It is unfair, don't you think? I know I think it is.

So now you know I'm out here in this factory, far away from where you are, working hard every day. And you know about my deep personal interest in the toupee and its manufacture. Next I'm going to go into somewhat greater detail on my life and work here.

Nah, forget it. Bye-bye.

11

Is This Shovel a Real Shovel?
(What Happened in the Night: 2)

•

After he fell into a deep sleep, the boy had a vivid dream. He knew it was a dream, though, which came as some comfort to him. *I know this is a dream, so what happened before was not a dream. It really, really happened. I can tell the difference between the two.*

In his dream, the boy had gone out to the garden. It was still the middle of the night, and he was alone. He picked up the shovel and started digging out the hole that the tall man had filled in. The man had left the shovel leaning against the trunk of the tree. Freshly filled in, the hole was not that hard to dig, but just picking up the heavy shovel was enough to take the boy's breath away. And he had no shoes on. The soles of his feet were freezing cold. Even so, he went on panting and digging until he had uncovered the cloth bundle that the man had buried.

The wind-up bird no longer cried. The man who had climbed the tree never came down. The night was so silent it almost hurt the boy's ears. The man had just disappeared, it seemed. *But finally, this is a dream*, the boy thought. It was not a dream that the wind-up bird had cried and the man who looked like his father had climbed the tree. Those things had really happened. So there couldn't be any connection between this and that. Strange, though: here he was, in a dream, digging out the real hole. So how was he to distinguish between what was a dream and what was not a dream? Was this shovel a real shovel? Or was it a dream shovel?

The more he thought, the less he understood. And so the boy stopped thinking and put all his energy into digging the hole. Finally, the shovel came up against the cloth bundle.

The boy took great care after that to remove the surrounding dirt so as not to damage the cloth bundle. Then he went down on his knees and lifted the bundle from the hole. There was not a cloud in the sky, and there was no one there to block the moist light of the full moon that poured down on the ground. In the dream, he was free of fear. Curiosity was the feeling that dominated him with its power. He opened the bundle, to find a human heart inside. He recognized its shape and colour from the picture he had seen in his encyclopedia. The heart was still fresh and alive and moving, like a newly abandoned infant. True, it was sending no blood out through its severed artery, but it continued to beat with a strong pulse. The boy heard a loud throbbing in his ears, but it was the sound of his own heart. The buried heart and the boy's own heart went on pounding in perfect unison, as if communicating with each other.

The boy steadied his breathing and told himself firmly, "You are not afraid of this. This is just a human heart, that's all. Just like in the encyclopedia. Everybody has one of these. *I* have one." With steady hands, the boy wrapped the beating heart in the cloth again, returned it to the bottom of the hole, and covered it over with earth. He smoothed the earth with his bare foot so that no one could tell a hole had been dug there, and he stood the shovel against the tree as he had found it. The ground at night was like ice. Climbing over the sill of his window, the boy returned to his own warm, friendly room. He brushed the mud from his feet into his wastebasket so as not to dirty his sheets, and he started to crawl into bed. But then he realized that someone was already lying there. Someone was sleeping in his bed, under the covers, in his place.

Angry now, the boy stripped the covers back. "Hey, you, get out of there! This is *my* bed!" he wanted to shout at the person. But no sound came out, because the person he found in the bed was himself. He was already in his bed, asleep, breathing peacefully. The boy stood frozen in place, at a loss for words. If I am already sleeping here, then where should *this* me sleep? Now, for the first time, the boy felt afraid, with a fear that seemed as if it would chill him to the marrow. The boy wanted to shout. He wanted to scream as loud as he could to wake up his sleeping self and everyone else in the house. But his voice would not come. He strained with all his might, but he could produce no sound.

Nothing at all. So he put his hand on the shoulder of his sleeping self and shook it as hard as he could. But the sleeping boy would not wake up.

There was nothing more he could do. The boy stripped off his cardigan and flung it on the floor. Then he pushed his other, sleeping self as hard as he could away from the centre of the bed and crammed himself into the small space that was left for him at the edge. He had to secure a spot for himself here. Otherwise, he might be pushed out of this world where he belonged. Cramped and without a pillow, the boy nevertheless felt incredibly sleepy as soon as he lay down. He could not think any more. The next moment, he was sound asleep.

•

When he woke up in the morning, the boy was in the middle of the bed, alone. His pillow was under his head, as always. He raised himself slowly and looked around the room. At first glance, the room seemed unchanged. It had the same desk, the same bureau, the same wardrobe, the same floor lamp. The hands of the wall clock pointed to 6.20. But the boy knew something was strange. It might all look the same, but this was not the same place where he had gone to sleep the previous night. The air, the light, the sounds, the smells, were all just a little bit different from before. Other people might not notice, but the boy knew. He stripped off the covers and looked at himself. He held his hands up and moved each of his fingers in turn. They moved as they should. And his legs moved. He felt no pain or itching. He slipped out of bed and went to the toilet. When he had finished peeing, he stood at the sink and looked at his face in the mirror. He pulled off his pyjama top, stood on a chair, and looked at the reflection of his fair-skinned little body. He found nothing unusual.

Yet something was different. He felt as if his self had been put into a new container. He knew that he was still not fully accustomed to this new body of his. There was something about this one, he felt, that just didn't match his original self. A sudden feeling of helplessness overtook him, and he tried to call for his mother, but the word would not emerge from his throat. His vocal cords were unable to stir the air, as if the very word "mother" had disappeared from the world. Before long, the boy realized that the word was not what had disappeared.

12

M's Secret Cure

•

SHOW BUSINESS WORLD TAINTED BY OCCULT

[From *The* ——— *Monthly,* November]

. . . These occult cures, which have become a kind of craze among members of the entertainment world, are spread primarily by word of mouth, but in some cases they bear the mark of certain secret organizations.

Take, for example, "M": 33, started out ten years ago as supporting actress in a television drama series, well received, leading roles ever since in TV and films, six years ago married "boy wonder" property developer, no problems in first two years of marriage. His business did well, and she recorded some fine performances on film. But then the dinner club and boutique he opened in her name ran into trouble and he started bouncing cheques, for which she became liable. Never eager to go into business to begin with, M had more or less had her arm twisted by her husband, who wanted to expand. One view has it that the husband was taken in by a kind of scam. In addition, there had always been a serious rift between M and her in-laws.

Soon the gossip spread about the trouble M was having with her husband, and before long the two were living separately. They concluded formal divorce proceedings two years ago after an arbitrator helped them settle their debts, but after that M started showing signs of depression, and the need for therapy put her into virtual retirement. According to one source at the studio she worked for, M was regularly plagued by serious delusions after the divorce. She ruined her health with antidepressants, and it got to the point where people were saying, "She's had it as an actress." Our source observed, "She had lost the powers of concentration you need to act, and it was shocking what happened to her looks. It didn't help, either, that she was basically a serious person who would dwell on things to the point where it would affect her mentally. At least her financial settlement had left her in pretty good shape, so she could make it for a while without working."

One distant relative of M's was the wife of a famous politician and former cabinet minister. M was practically a daughter to this person, who introduced her to a woman who practised a form of spiritual healing for a very limited, upper-class clientele. M went to her for a year on a regular basis for treatment of her depression, but exactly what this treatment consisted of, no one knows. M herself kept it absolutely secret. Whatever it was, it seems to have worked. It wasn't long before M was able to stop taking antidepressants, as a result of which she lost the strange puffiness the medicine had caused, her hair regained its fullness, and her beauty returned. She recovered mentally, as well, and grad-

ually began acting again. At that point, she stopped the treatments.

In October of this year, however, just as the memory of her nightmare was beginning to fade, M had one episode during which, for no apparent reason, her symptoms flared up again. The timing couldn't have been worse: she had a major acting job just a few days ahead of her, something she could not have carried off in her present state. M contacted the woman and requested the usual treatment, but the woman told her that she was no longer in practice. "I'm sorry," she said, "but I can't do anything for you. I'm not qualified any more. I've lost my powers. There *is* someone I can introduce you to, but you'll have to swear absolute secrecy. If you say *one word* about it to anyone, you'll be sorry. Is that clear?"

M was instructed to go to a certain place, where she was brought into the presence of a man with a bluish mark on his face. The man, around thirty, never spoke while she was there, but his treatment was "incredibly effective". M refused to divulge what she paid for the session, but we can imagine that the "consultation fee" was quite substantial.

This is what we know about the mysterious treatment, as told by M to a trusted "very close" friend. She first had to go to "a certain hotel", where she met a young man whose job it was to guide her to the healer. They left from a special underground VIP parking lot in "a big black car" and went to the place where the treatment was performed. As far as the treatment itself is concerned, however, we have been able to learn nothing. M is said to have told her friend, "Those people have awesome powers. Something terrible could happen to me if I broke my promise."

M paid only one visit to the place, and she has not since suffered any seizures. We tried approaching M directly for more information on the treatment and the mysterious woman, but as expected, she refused to see us. According to one well-informed source, this "organization" generally avoids contacts with the entertainment world and concentrates on the more secretive worlds of politics and finance. Our contacts in the performing arts have, so far, yielded no more information. . . .

13

The Waiting Man

•

What Couldn' t Be Shaken Off

•

No Man Is an Island

Eight o'clock came and went and everything was dark when I opened the back gate and stepped out into the alley. I had to squeeze through sideways. Less than three feet high, the gate had been cleverly camouflaged in the corner of the fence so as to be undetectable from the outside. The alley emerged from the night, illuminated as always by the cold white light of the mercury lamp in the garden of May Kasahara's house.

I clicked the gate shut and slipped down the alley. Through one fence after another, I caught glimpses of people in their dining rooms and living rooms, eating and watching TV dramas. Food smells drifted into the alley through kitchen windows and exractor fans. One teenage boy was practising a fast passage on his electric guitar, with the volume turned down. In a second-floor window, a tiny girl was studying at her desk, an earnest expression on her face. A married couple having a heated argument sent their voices out into the alley. A baby was screaming. A telephone rang. Reality spilled out into the alley like water from an overfilled bowl – as sound, as smell, as image, as plea, as response.

I wore my usual tennis shoes to keep my steps silent. My pace could be neither too fast nor too slow. The important thing was not to attract people's attention, not to let that "reality" pick up on my passing presence. I knew every corner, each obstacle. Even in the dark I could slip down the alley without bumping into anything. When I reached the back of my house, I stopped, looked around, and climbed over the low wall.

The house crouched in the darkness like the shell of a giant animal. I unlocked the kitchen door, turned on the light, and changed the cat's water. I took a tin of cat food from the cupboard and opened it. Mackerel heard the sound and appeared from nowhere. He rubbed his head against my leg a few times, then started to tear into his food. While he was eating, I took a cold beer from the refrigerator. I always had supper in the "residence" – something that Cinnamon had prepared for me – and so the most I ever had here was a salad or a slice of cheese. Drinking my beer, I took the cat on my knees and confirmed his warmth and softness with my hands. Having spent the day in separate places, we both confirmed the fact that we were home.

•

Tonight, however, when I slipped my shoes off and reached out to turn the kitchen light on, I felt a presence. I stopped in the darkness and listened, inhaling quietly. I heard nothing, but I caught the faint scent of tobacco. There was someone in the house, someone waiting for me to come home, someone who, a few moments earlier, had probably given up the struggle and lit a cigarette, taking no more than a few puffs and opening a window to let the smoke out, but still the smell remained. This could not be a person I knew. The house was still locked up, and I didn't know anyone who smoked, apart from Nutmeg Akasaka, who would hardly be waiting in the dark if she wanted to see me.

Instinctively, my hand reached out in the darkness, feeling for the bat. But it was no longer there. It was at the bottom of the well now. The sound my heart had started making was almost unreal, as if the heart itself had escaped from my chest and was beating beside my ear. I tried to keep my breathing regular. I probably didn't need the bat. If someone was here to hurt me, he wouldn't be sitting around inside. Still, my palms were itching with anticipation. My hands were seeking the touch of the bat. Mackerel came from somewhere in the darkness and, as usual, started meowing and rubbing his head against my leg. But he was not as hungry as usual. I could tell from the sounds he made. I reached out and turned on the kitchen light.

"Sorry, but I went ahead and gave the cat his supper," said the man on the living room sofa, with an easy lilt to his voice. "I've been waiting a very long time for you, Mr Okada, and the cat was all over my feet and meowing, so – I hope you don't mind – I found a tin of cat food in the cupboard and gave it to him. To tell you the truth, I'm not very good with cats."

He showed no sign of standing up. I watched him sitting there and said nothing.

"I'm sure this was quite a shock to you – finding somebody in your house, waiting for you in the dark. I'm sorry. Really. But if I had turned the light on, you might not have come in. I'm not here to do you any harm, believe me, so you don't have to look at me that way. I just need to have a little talk with you."

He was a short man, dressed in a suit. It was hard to guess his height while he was seated, but he couldn't have been five feet tall. Somewhere between forty-five and fifty years old, he looked like a chubby little frog with a bald head – a definite A in May Kasahara's classification system. He did have a few clumps of hair clinging to his scalp over his ears, but their odd black presence made the bare area stand out all the more. He had a large nose, which may have been a bit blocked, judging by the way it expanded and contracted like a bellows with each noisy breath he took. Above that nose sat a pair of thick-looking wire-rim glasses. He had a way of pronouncing certain words so that his upper lip would curl, revealing a mouthful of crooked, tobacco-stained teeth. He was, without question, one of the ugliest human beings I had ever encountered. And not just physically ugly: there was a certain clammy weirdness about him that I could not put into words – the sort of feeling you get when your hand brushes against some big, strange insect in the darkness. He looked less like a human being than like something from a long-forgotten nightmare.

"Do you mind if I have a smoke?" he asked. "I was trying not to before, but sitting and waiting without a cigarette is like torture. It's a very bad habit."

Finding it difficult to speak, I simply nodded. The strange-looking man took an unfiltered Peace from his jacket pocket, put it between his lips, and made a loud, dry scratching sound as he lit it with a match. Then he picked up the empty cat food tin at his feet and dropped the match into it. So he had been using the tin as an ashtray. He sucked the smoke into his lungs with obvious pleasure, drawing his thick eyebrows into one shaggy line and letting out little moans. Each long puff made the end of the cigarette glow bright red like burning coal. I opened the patio door and let the outside air in. A light rain was falling. I couldn't see it or hear it, but I knew it was raining from the smell.

The man had on a brown suit, white shirt, and red tie, all of the same cheap quality, and all worn out to the same degree. The colour of the suit was reminiscent of an amateur paint job on an old car. The deep wrinkles in the trousers and jacket looked as permanent as valleys in an aerial photograph. The white shirt had taken on a yellow tinge, and one button on the chest was ready to fall off. It also looked one or two sizes too small, with its top button open and the collar crooked. The tie, with its strange pattern of ill-formed ectoplasm, looked like a leftover from the days of the Osmond brothers. Anyone looking at him would have seen straight off that this was a man who paid no attention whatsoever to the phenomenon of clothing. He wore what he wore because he had no choice but to put something on when dealing with other people, as if he were hostile to the idea of wearing clothes at all. He might have been planning to wear these things the same way every day until they fell apart – like a highland farmer driving his donkey from morning to night until he kills it.

Once he had sucked all the nicotine he needed into his lungs, he gave a sigh of relief and a strange look, that hovered somewhere between a smile and a smirk, appeared on his face. Then he opened his mouth.

"Well, now, let me not forget to introduce myself. I am not usually so rude. The name is Ushikawa. That's *ushi* for 'bull' and *kawa* for 'river'. Easy enough to remember, don't you think? Everybody calls me Ushi. Funny: the more I hear that, the more I feel like a real bull. I even feel a kind of affinity whenever I happen to see a bull out in a field somewhere. Names are funny things, don't you think, Mr Okada? Take Okada, for example. Now, there's a nice, clean name: 'hill-field'. I sometimes wish I had a normal name like that, but unfortunately, a surname is not something you're free to pick. Once you're born into this world as Ushikawa, you're Ushikawa for life, like it or not. They've been calling me Ushi since the day I started nursery school. There's no way around it. You get a guy named Ushikawa, and people are bound to call him Ushi, right? They say a name expresses the thing it stands for, but I wonder if it isn't the other way around – the thing gets more and more like its name. Anyhow, just think of me as Ushikawa, and if you feel like it, call me Ushi. I don't mind."

I went to the kitchen and brought back a can of beer from the refrigerator. I did not offer any to Ushikawa. I hadn't invited him here, after all. I said nothing and drank my beer, and Ushikawa said nothing and drew deeply on his cigarette. I did not sit in the chair across from him but rather stood leaning against a pillar, looking down at him. Finally, he stubbed his butt out in the empty cat food tin and looked up at me.

"I'm sure you're wondering how I got in here, Mr Okada. True? You're sure you locked the door. And in fact, it *was* locked. But I have a key. A real key. Look, here it is."

He thrust his hand into his jacket pocket, pulled out a key ring with one key attached, and held it up for me to see. It certainly did look like the key to this house. But what attracted my attention was the key holder. It was just like Kumiko's – a simple-styled green leather key holder with a ring that opened in an unusual way.

"It's the real thing," said Ushikawa. "As you can see. And the holder belongs to your wife. Let me say this to avoid any misunderstanding: this was given to me by your wife, Kumiko. I did not steal it or take it by force."

"Where is Kumiko?" I asked, my voice sounding somewhat mangled.

Ushikawa took his glasses off, seemed to check on the cloudiness of the lenses, then put them back on. "I know exactly where she is," he said. "In fact, I am taking care of her."

" 'Taking care of her'?"

"Now, don't get me wrong. I don't mean it that way. Don't worry," Ushikawa said, with a smile. When he smiled, his face broke up asymmetrically from side to side, and his glasses went up at an angle. "Please don't glare at me like that. I'm just helping her as part of my work – running errands, doing odd jobs. I'm a dogsbody, that's all. You know how she can't go outside."

" 'Can't go outside'?" I parroted his words again.

He hesitated a moment, his tongue flicking across his lips. "Well, maybe you don't know. That's all right. I can't really say whether she *can't* go out or *doesn't want* to go out. I'm sure you would like to know, Mr Okada, but please don't ask me. Not even I know all the details. But there's nothing for you to worry about. She is not being held against her will. I mean, this is not a movie or a novel. We can't really do that sort of thing."

I set my beer can down with care at my feet. "So anyway, tell me, what did you come here for?"

After patting his knees several times with outstretched palms, Ushikawa gave one deep, sharp nod. "Ah, yes. I forgot to mention that, didn't I? I go to all the trouble of introducing myself, and then I forget to tell you what I'm here for! That has been one of my most consistent flaws over the years: to go on and on about foolish things and leave out the main point. No wonder I'm always doing the wrong thing! Well, then, belated though it may be, here it is: I work for your wife Kumiko's elder brother. Ushikawa's the name – but I already told you that, about the Ushi and everything. I work for Dr Noboru Wataya as a kind of private secretary – though not the usual 'private secretary' that a member of the Diet might have. Only a certain kind of person, a superior kind of person, can be a real 'private secretary'. The term covers a wide range of types. I mean, there are private secretaries, and then there are private secretaries, and I'm as close to the second kind as you can get. I'm down there – I mean, way, way down there. If there are spirits lurking everywhere, I'm one of the dirty little ones down in the corner of a bathroom or a cupboard. But I can't complain. If somebody this messy came right out in the open, think of what it could do to Dr Wataya's clean-cut image! No, the ones who face the cameras have to be slick, intelligent-looking types, not bald midgets. 'How-dee-doo, folks, it's me, Dr Wataya's private sec-ruh-teh-ree.' What a laugh! Right, Mr Okada?"

I kept silent as he prattled on.

"So what I do for the Doctor are the unseen jobs, the 'shadow' jobs, so to speak, the ones that aren't out in the open. I'm the fiddler under the porch. Jobs like that are my speciality. Like this business with Ms Kumiko. Now, don't get me wrong: don't think that taking care of her is just some busywork for a lowly hack. If what I've said has given you that impression, it couldn't be further from the truth. I mean, Ms Kumiko is the Doctor's one and only dear little sister, after all. I consider it a consummate honour to have been allowed to take on such an important task, believe me!

"Oh, by the way, this may seem very rude, but I wonder if I could ask you for a beer? All this talking has made me very thirsty. If you don't mind, I'll just grab one myself. I know where it is. While I was waiting, I took the liberty of peeking into the refrigerator."

I nodded to him. Ushikawa went to the kitchen and took a bottle of beer from the refrigerator. Then he sat down on the sofa again, drinking straight from the bottle with obvious relish, his huge Adam's apple twitching above the knot of his tie like some kind of animal.

"I tell you, Mr Okada, a cold beer at the end of the day is the best thing life has to offer. Some choosy people say that a too cold beer doesn't taste good, but I couldn't disagree more. The first beer should be so cold

430

you can't even taste it. The second one should be a little less chilled, but I want that first one to be like ice. I want it to be so cold my temples throb with pain. This is my own personal preference, of course."

Still leaning against the pillar, I took another sip of my own beer. Lips closed tight in a straight line, Ushikawa surveyed the room for some moments.

"I must say, Mr Okada, for a man without a wife, you do keep the house clean. I'm very impressed. I myself am completely hopeless, I'm embarrassed to say. My place is a mess, a garbage heap, a pigsty. I haven't washed the bathtub for a year or more. Perhaps I neglected to tell you that I was also deserted by my wife. Five years ago. So I can feel a certain sympathy for you, Mr Okada, or to avoid the risk of misinterpretation, let me just say that I can understand how you feel. Of course, my situation was different from yours. It was only natural for my wife to leave me. I was the worst husband in the world. Far from complaining, I have to admire her for having put up with me as long as she did. I used to beat her. No one else: she was the only one I could beat up. You can tell what a weakling I am. Got the heart of a flea. I would do nothing but grovel outside the house; people would call me Ushi and order me around, and I would just suck up to them all the more. So when I got home I would take it out on my wife. Heh heh heh – pretty bad, eh? And I knew just how bad I was, but I couldn't stop. It was like a sickness. I'd beat her face out of shape until you couldn't recognize her. And not just beat her: I'd slam her against the wall and kick her, pour hot tea on her, throw things at her, you name it. The kids would try to stop me, and I'd end up hitting them. Little kids: seven, eight years old. And not just push them around: I'd wallop them with everything I had. I was an absolute devil. I'd try to stop myself, but I couldn't. I couldn't control myself. After a certain point, I would tell myself that I had done enough damage, that I had to stop, but I didn't know how to stop. Do you see what a horror I was? So then, five years ago, when my daughter was five, I broke her arm – just snapped it. That's when my wife finally got fed up with me and left with both kids. I haven't seen any of them since. Haven't even heard from them. But what can I do? It's my own fault."

I said nothing to him. The cat came over to me and gave a short meow, as if looking for attention.

"Anyway, I'm sorry, I wasn't planning to exhaust you with all these boring details. You must be wondering if I have any business that has brought me here this evening. Well, I have. I didn't come here for small talk, Mr Okada. The Doctor – which is to say, Dr Wataya – ordered me to come to see you. I will now tell you exactly what he told me, so please listen.

"First of all, Dr Wataya is not opposed to the idea of reconsidering a relationship between you and Ms Kumiko. In other words, he would not object if both of you decided that you wanted to go back to your previous relationship. At the moment, Ms Kumiko herself has no such intention, so nothing would happen right away, but if you were to reject any possibility of divorce and insist that you wanted to wait as long as it took, he could accept that. He will no longer insist upon a divorce, as he has in the past, and so he would not mind if you wanted to use me as a conduit if there was something you wished to communicate to Ms Kumiko. In other words, no more locking horns on every little thing: a renewal of diplomatic relations, as it were. This is the first item of business. How does it strike you, Mr Okada?"

I lowered myself to the floor and stroked the cat's head, but I said nothing. Ushikawa watched me and the cat for a time, then continued to speak.

"Well, of course, Mr Okada, you can't say a word until you've heard everything I have to say. All right, then, I will continue through to the end. Here is the second item of business. This gets a little complicated, I'm afraid. It has to do with an article called 'The Hanging House', which appeared in one of the weekly magazines. I don't know if you have read it or not, Mr Okada, but it is a very interesting piece. Well written. 'Jinxed land in posh Setagaya residential neighbourhood. Many people met untimely deaths there over the years. What mystery man has recently bought the place? What is going on behind that high fence? One riddle after another . . .'

"Anyhow, Dr Wataya read the piece and realized that the 'hanging house' is very close to the house you live in, Mr Okada. The idea began to gnaw at him that there might be some connection between it and you. So he investigated . . . or, should I say, the lowly Ushikawa, on his short little legs, took the liberty of investigating the matter, and – bingo! – there you were, Mr Okada, just as he had predicted, going back and forth down that back passageway every day to the other house, obviously very much involved with whatever it is that is going on inside there. I myself was truly amazed to see such a powerful display of Dr Wataya's penetrating intelligence.

"There's been only one article so far, with no follow-up, but who knows? Dying embers can always rekindle. I mean, that's a pretty fascinating story. So Dr Wataya is more than a little nervous. What if his brother-in-law's name were to come out in some unpleasant connection? Think of the scandal that could erupt! Dr Wataya is the man of the moment, after all. The media would have a field day. And then there's this difficult business with you and Ms Kumiko. They would blow it up out of all proportion. I mean, everybody has something he would rather not have aired in public, right? Especially when it comes to personal affairs. This is a delicate moment in the Doctor's political career, after all. He has to proceed with the utmost caution until he's ready to take off. So what he has in mind for you is a little deal of sorts he's cooked up. If you will cut all connection with this 'hanging house', Mr Okada, he will give some serious thought to bringing you and Ms Kumiko back together again. That's all there is to it. How does that strike you, Mr Okada? Have I set it out with sufficient clarity?"

"Probably," I said.

"So what do you think? What is your reaction to all this?"

Stroking the cat's neck, I thought about it for a while. Then I said, "I don't get it. What made Noboru Wataya think that I had anything to do with that house? How did he make the connection?"

Ushikawa's face broke into one of his big smiles, but his eyes remained as cold as glass. He took a crushed pack of cigarettes from his pocket and lit up with a match. "Ah, Mr Okada, you ask such difficult questions. Remember, I am just a lowly messenger. A stupid carrier pigeon. I carry slips of paper back and forth. I think you understand. I can say this, however: the Doctor is no fool. He knows how to use his brain, and he has a kind of sixth sense, something that ordinary people do not possess. And also let me tell you this, Mr Okada: he has a very real kind of power that he can exercise in this world, a power that grows stronger every day. You had better not ignore it. You may have your reasons for not liking him – and that is fine as far as I am concerned, it's none of my business – but things have gone beyond the level of simple likes and dislikes. I want you to understand that."

"If Noboru Wataya is so powerful, why doesn't he just stop the magazine from publishing any more articles? That would be a whole lot simpler."

Ushikawa smiled. Then he inhaled deeply on his cigarette.

"Dear, dear Mr Okada, you mustn't say such reckless things. You and I live in Japan, after all, one of the world's most truly democratic states. Correct? This is no dictatorship where all you see around you are banana plantations and soccer fields. No matter how much power a politician may have in this country, quashing an article in a magazine is not a simple thing. It would be far too dangerous. You might succeed in getting the company top brass in your pocket, but someone is going to be left dissatisfied. And that could end up attracting all the more attention. It just doesn't pay to try pushing people around when such a hot story is involved. Believe me.

"And just between you and me, there may be some vicious players interested in this affair, types you don't know anything about, Mr Okada. If that's the case, this is eventually going to involve more than our dear Doctor. Once that happens, we could be talking about a whole new ball game. Let's compare this to a visit to the dentist. So far, we're at the stage of poking a spot where the novocaine's still working. Which is why no one's complaining. But soon the drill is going to hit a nerve, and then somebody's going to jump out of the chair. Somebody could get seriously angry. Do you see what I'm saying? I'm not trying to threaten you, but it seems to me – to old Ushikawa here – that you are little by little being dragged into dangerous territory without even realizing it."

Ushikawa seemed at last to have made his point.

"You mean I should pull out before I get hurt?" I asked.

Ushikawa nodded. "This is like playing catch in the middle of the expressway, Mr Okada. It's a very dangerous game."

"In addition to which, it's going to cause Noboru Wataya a lot of trouble. So if I just throw in my hand, he'll put me in touch with Kumiko."

Ushikawa nodded again. "That about sums it up."

I took a swallow of beer. Then I said, "First of all, let me tell you this. I'm going to get Kumiko back, but I'm going to do it myself, without help from Noboru Wataya. I don't want his help. And you're right about one thing: I don't like Noboru Wataya. As you say, though, this is not just a question of likes and dislikes. It's something more basic than that. I don't simply dislike him: I cannot accept the fact of his very existence. And so I refuse to make any deals with him. Please be so kind as to convey that to him for me. And don't you ever come into this house again without my permission. It is *my* house, not some hotel lobby or train station."

Ushikawa narrowed his eyes and stared at me from behind his glasses. His eyes remained motionless. As before, they were devoid of emotion. Not that they were expressionless. But all that was there was something fabricated temporarily for the occasion. At that point, he held his disproportionately large right palm aloft, as if checking for rain.

"I understand completely," he said. "I never thought this would be easy, so I'm not surprised by your answer. Besides, I don't surprise very easily. I understand how you feel, and I'm glad everything is out in the open like this, no hemming and hawing, just a simple yes or no. Makes it easier for everybody. The last thing I need as a carrier pigeon is another convoluted answer where you can't tell black from white! The world has too many of those as it is! Not that I'm complaining, but all I seem to get every day are sphinxes giving me riddles. This job is bad for my health, let me tell you. Living like this, before you know it, you become devious by nature. Do you see what I mean, Mr Okada? You become suspicious, always looking for ulterior motives, never able to put your faith in anything that's clear and simple. It's a terrible thing, Mr Okada, it really is.

"So, fine, Mr Okada, I will let the Doctor know that you have given him a very clear-cut answer. But don't expect things to end there. *You* may want to finish this business, but it's not that simple. I will probably have to come to see you again. I'm sorry to put you through this, having to deal with such an ugly, messy little fellow, but please try to accustom yourself to *my* existence, at least. I don't harbour any ill feelings towards you as an individual, Mr Okada. Really. But for the time being, whether you like it or not, I'm going to be one of those things that you can't just sweep away. I know it's an odd way to put it, but please try to think of me like that. I can promise you one thing, though. I will not be letting myself into your house again. You are quite right: that is not a proper way to behave. I should go down on my knees and beg to be let in. This time I had no choice. Please try to understand. I am not always so reckless. Appearances to the contrary, I am an ordinary human being. From now on, I will do as other people do and call beforehand. That should be all right, don't you think? I will ring once, hang up, then ring again. You'll know it's me that way, and you can tell yourself, 'Oh, it's that stupid Ushikawa again' when you pick up the phone. But *do* pick up the phone. Otherwise, I will have no choice but to let myself in again. Personally, I would rather not do such a thing, but I am being paid to wag my tail, so when my boss says 'Do it!' I have to try my best to do it. You understand."

I said nothing to him. Ushikawa crushed what was left of his cigarette in the bottom of the cat food tin, then glanced at his watch as if suddenly remembering something. "Oh, my, my, my – look how late it is! First I come barging in, then I talk you to death and take your beer. Please excuse me. As I said earlier, I don't have anybody to go home to, so when I find someone I can talk to, I settle in for the night. Sad, don't you think? I tell you, Mr Okada, living alone is not something you should do for long. What is it they say? 'No man is an island.' Or is it 'The devil finds mischief for idle hands'?"

After sweeping some imaginary dust from his lap, Ushikawa stood up slowly.

"No need to see me out," he said. "I let myself in, after all; I can let myself out. I'll be sure to lock the door. One last word of advice, though, Mr Okada, though you may not want to hear this. There are things in this world it is better not to know about. Of course, those are the very things that people most want to know about. It's strange. I know I'm being very general. . . . I wonder when we'll meet again? I hope things are better by then. Oh, well, good night."

The quiet rain continued through the night, tapering off towards dawn, but the sticky presence of the strange little man, and the smell of his unfiltered cigarettes, remained in the house as long as the lingering dampness.

14

Cinnamon's Strange Sign Language

•

The Musical Offering

"Cinnamon stopped talking once and for all just before his sixth birthday," Nutmeg said to me. "It was the year he should have entered junior school. All of a sudden, that February, he stopped talking. And strange as it may seem, it was night before we noticed that he hadn't said a word all day. True, he was never much of a talker, but *still*. When it finally occurred to me what was happening, I did everything I could to make him speak. I talked to him, I shook him; nothing worked. He was like a stone. I didn't know whether he had suddenly lost the power to speak or he had decided on his own that he would stop speaking. And I still don't know. But he's never said another word – never made another *sound*. He'll never scream if he's in pain, and you can tickle him but he'll never laugh out loud."

Nutmeg took her son to several different ear, nose, and throat specialists, but none of them could locate the cause. All they could determine was that it was not physical. Cinnamon could *hear* perfectly well, but he wouldn't speak. All the doctors concluded that it must be psychological in origin. Nutmeg took him to a psychiatrist friend of hers, but he also was unable to establish a cause for Cinnamon's continued silence. He administered an IQ test, but there was no problem there. In fact, Cinnamon turned out to have an unusually high IQ. The doctor could find no evidence of emotional problems, either. "Has he experienced some kind of shock?" the psychiatrist asked Nutmeg. "Try to think. Could he have witnessed something abnormal or been subjected to violence at home?" But Nutmeg could think of nothing. One day her son had been normal in every way: he had eaten his meals in the normal way, had normal conversations with her, gone to bed when he was supposed to, had no trouble falling asleep. And the next morning he had sunk into a world of deep silence. There had been no problems at home. The child was being brought up under the ever watchful gaze of Nutmeg and her mother, neither of whom had ever raised a hand to him. The doctor concluded that the only thing they could do was observe him and hope that something would turn up. Unless they knew the cause, there was no way of treating him. Nutmeg should take Cinnamon to see the doctor once a week, in the course of which they might figure out what had happened. It was possible that he would just start speaking again, like someone waking from a dream. All they could do was wait. True, the child was not speaking, but there was nothing else wrong with him. . . .

And so they waited, but Cinnamon never again rose to the surface of his deep ocean of silence.

•

Its electric motor producing a low hum, the front gate began to swing inwards at 9 o'clock in the morning, and Cinnamon's Mercedes-Benz 500SEL pulled into the driveway. The car phone's aerial protruded from the back window like a newly sprouted tentacle. I watched through a crack in the blinds. The car looked like some kind of huge migratory fish, afraid of nothing. The brand-new black tyres traced a silent arc over the concrete surface and came to a stop in the designated spot. They traced exactly the same arc every morning and stopped in exactly the same place with probably no more than two inches' variation.

I was drinking the coffee that I had brewed for myself a few minutes earlier. The rain had stopped, but grey clouds covered the sky, and the ground was still black and cold and wet. The birds raised sharp cries as they flitted back and forth in search of worms on the ground. The driver's door opened after a short pause, and Cinnamon stepped out, wearing sunglasses. After a quick scan of the area, he took the glasses off and slipped them into his breast pocket. Then he closed the car door. The precise sound of the big Mercedes' door latch was different from the sounds other car doors made. For me, this sound marked the beginning of another day at the Residence.

I had been thinking all morning about Ushikawa's visit the night

438

before, wondering whether I should tell Cinnamon that Ushikawa had been sent by Noboru Wataya to get me to pull out of the activities conducted at this house. In the end, though, I decided not to tell him – for the time being, at least. This was something that had to be settled between Noboru Wataya and me. I didn't want to have any third parties involved.

Cinnamon was stylishly dressed, as always, in a suit. All his suits were of the finest quality, tailored to fit him like a glove. They tended to be rather conservative in cut, but on him they looked youthful, as if transformed by magic into the latest fashion.

He wore a new tie, of course, one to match that day's suit. His shirt and shoes were different as well. His mother, Nutmeg, had picked everything out for him, in her usual way. His outfit was as spotless, top to bottom, as the Mercedes he drove. Each time he showed up in the morning, I found myself admiring him – or, I might even say, moved by him. What kind of being could possibly lie hidden beneath that perfect exterior?

•

Cinnamon took two paper shopping bags full of food and other necessaries out of the trunk and held them in his arms as he entered the Residence. Embraced by him, even these ordinary paper bags from the supermarket looked elegant and artistic. Maybe he had some special way of holding them. Or possibly it was something more basic than that. His whole face lit up when he saw me. It was a marvellous smile, as if he had just emerged into a bright opening after a long walk in a deep wood. "Good morning," I said to him. "Good morning," he did not say to me, though his lips moved. He proceeded to take the groceries out of the bags and arrange them in the refrigerator like a bright child committing newly acquired knowledge to memory. The other supplies he arranged in the cupboards. Then he had a cup of coffee with me. We sat across from each other at the kitchen table, just as Kumiko and I had done every morning long before.

•

"Cinnamon never spent a day at school," said Nutmeg. "Ordinary schools wouldn't accept a child who didn't speak, and I felt it would be wrong to send him to a school with nothing but handicapped children. The reason for his being unable to speak – whatever it was – I knew to be different from other children's reasons. And besides, he never showed any sign of wanting to go to school. He seemed to like best staying at home on his own, reading or listening to classical music or playing in the yard with the dog we had then. He would go out for walks too, sometimes, but not with much enthusiasm, because he didn't like to be with children his own age."

Nutmeg studied sign language and used that to talk with Cinnamon. When sign language was not enough, they would converse in writing. One day, though, she realized that she and her son were able to convey their feelings to each other perfectly well without resorting to such indirect methods. She knew exactly what he was thinking or requesting with only the slightest gesture or change of expression. From that point on, she ceased to be concerned about Cinnamon's inability to speak. It certainly wasn't obstructing any mental exchange between mother and son. The absence of spoken language did, of course, give her an occasional sense of physical inconvenience, but it never went beyond the level of inconvenience, and in a sense it was this very factor that purified the quality of the communication between the two.

During lulls between jobs, Nutmeg would teach Cinnamon how to read and write and do arithmetic. But beyond that, there was not that much that she was required to teach him. He liked books, and he would use them to teach himself what he needed to know. She was less a teacher for him than the one who chose the books. He liked music and wanted to play the piano, but after learning the basic finger movements in a few months with a professional piano teacher, he used only manuals and recorded tapes to bring himself to a high level of technical accomplishment for one so young. He loved to play Bach and Mozart, and apart from Poulenc and Bartók, he showed little inclination to play anything beyond the Romantics. During his first six years of study, his interests were concentrated on music and reading, but from the time he reached middle school age, he turned to the acquisition of languages, beginning with English and then French. In both cases, he taught himself enough to read simple books after six months of study. He had no intention of learning to converse in either language, of course; he wanted only to be able to read books. Another activity he loved was tinkering with complicated machinery. He bought a complete collection of professional tools, with which he was able to build radios and valve amplifiers, and he enjoyed taking clocks apart and fixing them.

Everyone around him – which is to say, his mother, his father, and his grandmother (Nutmeg's mother) – became accustomed to the fact that he never spoke, and ceased to think of it as unnatural or abnormal. After a few years, Nutmeg stopped taking her son to the psychiatrist. The weekly consultations were doing nothing for his "symptoms", and as the doctors had noted in the beginning, apart from his not speaking, there was nothing wrong with him. Indeed, he was an almost perfect child. Nutmeg could not recall ever having had to force him to do anything or to scold him for doing anything he shouldn't have done. He would decide for himself what he had to do and then he would do it, flawlessly, in his own way. He was so different from other children – ordinary children – that comparing him with them was meaningless. He was twelve when his grandmother died (an event that caused him to go on crying, soundlessly, for several days), after which he took it upon himself to do the cooking, laundry and cleaning while his mother was at work. Nutmeg wanted to hire a housekeeper when her mother died, but Cinnamon would not hear of it. He refused to have a stranger come in and disrupt the order of the household. It was Cinnamon, then, who ran the house, and he did so with a high degree of precision and discipline.

•

Cinnamon spoke to me with his hands. He had inherited his mother's slender, well-shaped fingers. They were long, but not too long. He held them up near his face and moved them without hesitation, and like a species of sensible, living creature they communicated his messages to me. "A client will be coming at 2 o'clock this afternoon. That is all for today. There is nothing you have to do until she gets here. I will take the next hour to finish my work, and then I will pick her up and bring her back. The weather forecast predicts overcast skies all day. You can spend time in the well while it is still light out without hurting your eyes."

As Nutmeg had said, I had no trouble understanding the words that his fingers conveyed. I was unacquainted with sign language, but it was easy for me to follow his complex, fluid movements. It may have been Cinnamon's skill that brought his meaning out so naturally, just as a play performed in a foreign language can still be moving. Or then again, perhaps it only seemed to me that I was watching his fingers move but was not actually doing so. The moving fingers were perhaps no more than a decorative facade, and I was half-consciously watching some other aspect of the building behind it. I would try to catch sight of the boundary between the facade and the background whenever we chatted across the breakfast table, but I could never quite manage to discern it, as if any line that might have marked the border between the two kept moving and changing its shape.

After our short conversations – or communications – Cinnamon would take his suit jacket off, put it on a hanger, tuck his tie inside the front of his shirt, and then do the cleaning or cooking. As he worked, he would listen to music on a compact stereo. One week he would listen to nothing but Rossini's sacred music, and another week Vivaldi's concertos for wind instruments, repeating them so often that I ended up memorizing the melodies.

Cinnamon worked with marvellous dexterity and no wasted motion. I used to offer to lend him a hand at first, but he would only smile and shake his head. Watching how he went about his chores, I became convinced that things would progress far more smoothly if I left everything to him. It became my habit after that to avoid getting in his way. I would read a book on the "fitting room" sofa while he was doing his morning chores.

The Residence was not a big house, and it had minimal furnishings. No one actually lived there, so it never got particularly dirty or untidy. Still, every day Cinnamon would vacuum every inch of the place, dust the furniture and shelves, clean the windowpanes, wax the table, wipe the light fixtures, and put everything in the house back where it belonged. He would arrange the dishes in the china cabinet and line up the pots according to size, align the edges of the linen and towels, point all coffee cup handles in the same direction, reposition the bar of soap on the bathroom sink, and change the towels even if they showed no sign of having been used. Then he would gather the rubbish into a single bag, close it up, and take it out. He would adjust the time on the clocks according to his watch (which, I would have been willing to bet, was no more than three seconds out). If, in the course of his cleaning, he found anything the slightest bit out of place, he would put it back where it belonged with precise and elegant movements. I might test him by shifting a clock half an inch to the left on its shelf, and the next morning he would be sure to move it half an inch back to the right.

In none of this behaviour did Cinnamon give the impression of obsessiveness. He seemed to be doing only what was natural and "right". Perhaps in Cinnamon's mind there was a vivid imprint of the way this world – or at least this one little world here – was supposed to be, and for him to keep it that way was as natural as breathing. Perhaps he saw himself as lending just the slightest hand when things were driven by an intense inner desire to return to their original forms.

Cinnamon prepared food, stored it in the refrigerator, and indicated to me what I ought to have for lunch. I thanked him. He then stood before the mirror, straightened his tie, inspected his shirt, and slipped into his suit coat. Finally, with a smile, he moved his lips to say goodbye, took one last look around, and went out through the front door. Sitting behind the wheel of the Mercedes-Benz, he slipped a classical tape into the deck, pressed the remote-control button to open the front gate, and drove away, tracing back over the same arc he had made when he arrived. Once the car had passed through, the gate closed. I watched through a crack in the blind, holding a cup of coffee, as before. The birds were no longer as noisy as they had been when Cinnamon arrived. I could see where the low clouds had been broken up and carried off by the wind, but above them was yet another, thicker layer of cloud.

·

I sat at the kitchen table, putting my cup down and surveying the room upon which Cinnamon's hands had imposed such a beautiful sense of order. It looked like a large, three-dimensional still life, disturbed only by the quiet ticking of the clock. The clock's hands showed 10.20. Looking at the chair that Cinnamon had occupied earlier, I asked myself once again whether I had done the right thing by not telling them about Ushikawa's visit the night before. Might it not impair whatever sense of trust there might be between Cinnamon and me or Nutmeg and me?

I preferred, though, to wait for a while to see how things would develop. What was it about my activities here that disturbed Noboru Wataya so? Which of his tails was I stepping on? And what kind of countermeasures would he adopt? If I could find the answers to these questions, I might be able to draw a little closer to his secret. And as a result, I might be able to draw closer to where Kumiko was.

As the hands of the clock were coming up to 11 (the clock that Cinnamon had slid half an inch to the right, back to its proper place), I went out to the yard to climb down into the well.

·

"I told Cinnamon the story of the submarine and the zoo when he was lit-tle – about what I had seen from the deck of the transport ship in August 1945 and how the Japanese soldiers shot the animals in my father's zoo at the same time as an American submarine was training its cannon on us and preparing to sink our ship. I had kept that story to myself for a very long time and never told it to anyone. I had wandered in silence through the gloomy labyrinth that spread out between illusion and truth. When Cinnamon was born, though, it occurred to me that he was the one I could tell my story to. And so, even before he could understand words, I began telling it to him over and over again, in a near whisper, telling him everything I could remember, and as I spoke, the scenes would come alive to me, in vivid colours, as if I had prised off a lid and let them out.

"As he began to understand language, Cinnamon asked me to tell him the story again and again. I must have told it to him a hundred, two-hundred, five-hundred times, but not just repeating the same thing every time. Whenever I told it to him, Cinnamon would ask me to tell him some other little story contained in the main story. He wanted to know about a different branch of the same tree. I would follow the branch he asked for and tell him *that* part of the story. And so the story grew and grew.

"In this way, the two of us went on to create our own interlocking system of myths. Do you see what I mean? We would get carried away telling each other the story every day. We would talk for hours about the names of the animals in the zoo, about the sheen of their fur or the colour of their eyes, about the different smells that hung in the air, about the names and faces of the individual soldiers, about their birth and child-hood, about their rifles and the weight of their ammunition, about the fears they felt and their thirst, about the shapes of the clouds floating in the sky. . . .

"I could see all the colours and shapes with perfect clarity as I told the story to Cinnamon, and I was able to put what I saw into words – the exact words I needed – and convey them all to him. There was no end to it. There were always more details that could be filled in, and the story kept growing deeper and deeper and bigger and bigger."

Nutmeg smiled as she spoke of those days long ago. I had never seen such a natural smile on her face before.

"But then one day it ended," she said. "Cinnamon stopped sharing stories with me that February morning when he stopped talking."

Nutmeg paused to light a cigarette.

"I know now what happened. His words were lost in the labyrinth, swallowed up by the world of the stories. Something that came out of those stories snatched his tongue away. And a few years later, the same thing killed my husband."

•

The wind grew stronger than it had been in the morning, sending one heavy grey cloud after another on a course due east. The clouds looked like silent travellers headed for the edge of the earth. In the bare branches of the trees in the yard, the wind would give a short, wordless moan now and then. I stood by the well, looking up at the sky. Kumiko was probably somewhere looking at the clouds too. The thought crossed my mind for no reason. It was just a feeling I had.

I climbed down the ladder to the bottom of the well and pulled the rope to close the lid. After taking two or three deep breaths, I gripped the bat and gently lowered myself to a sitting position in the darkness. The total darkness. Yes, that was the most important thing. This unsullied darkness held the key. It was like a TV cooking programme. "Everybody got that now? The secret to *this* recipe is total darkness. Make sure you use the thickest kind you can buy." And the strongest bat you can lay your hands on, I added, smiling for a moment in the darkness.

I could feel a certain warmth in the mark on my cheek. It told me that I was drawing a little closer to the core of things. I closed my eyes. Still echoing in my ears were the strains of the music that Cinnamon had been listening to repeatedly as he worked that morning. It was Bach's "Musical Offering", still there in my head like the lingering murmur of a crowd in a high-ceilinged auditorium. Silence descended and began to burrow its way into the folds of my brain, one after another, like an insect laying eggs. I opened my eyes, then closed them again. The darknesses inside and out began to blend, and I began to move outside of my self, the container that held me.

As always.

15

This Could Be the End of the Line
(May Kasahara's Point of View: 3)

•

Hi, again, Mr Wind-up Bird.

*Last time, I got as far as telling you about how I'm working in this wig factory
in the mountains far away with a lot of local girls. This is the continuation of that
letter.*

*Lately, it's really been bothering me that, I don't know, the way people work
like this every day from morning to night is kind of weird. Hasn't it ever struck
you as strange? I mean, all I do here is do the work that my bosses tell me to do
the way they tell me to do it. I don't have to think at all. It's like I just put my
brain in a locker before I start work and pick it up on the way home. I spend seven
hours a day at a workbench, planting hairs into wig bases, then I eat dinner in
the cafeteria, take a bath, and of course I have to sleep, like everybody else, so out
of a twenty-four-hour day, the amount of free time I have is nothing. And because
I'm so tired from work, the "free time" I have I mostly spend lying around in a fog.
I don't have any time to sit and think about anything. Of course, I don't have to
work at weekends, but then I have to catch up on the laundry and cleaning, and
sometimes I go into town, and before I know it the weekend is over. I once made
up my mind to keep a diary, but I had nothing to write, so I gave up after a week.
I mean, I just do the same thing over and over again, day in, day out.*

*But still – but still – it does not bother me at all that I'm now just a part
of the work I do. I don't feel the least bit alienated from my life. If anything, I*

sometimes feel that by concentrating on my work like this, with all the mindless determination of an ant, I'm getting closer to the "real me". I don't know how to put it, but it's as if by not thinking about myself I can get closer to the core of my self. That's what I mean by "kind of weird".

I'm giving this job everything I've got. Not to boast, but I've even been named worker of the month. I told you, I may not look it, but I'm really good at handiwork. We divide up into teams when we work, and any team I join improves its figures. I do things like helping the slower girls when I'm finished with my part of a job. So now I'm popular with the other girls. Can you believe it? Me, popular! Anyway, what I wanted to tell you, Mr Wind-up Bird, is that all I've been doing since I came to this factory is work, work, work. Like an ant. Like the village blacksmith. Have I made myself clear so far?

Anyway, the place where I do my work is really weird. It's huge, like a hangar, with a great, high roof, and wide open. A hundred-and-fifty girls sit lined up working there. It's quite a sight. Of course, they didn't have to put up such a monster factory. It's not as if we're building submarines or anything. They could have divided us up into separate rooms. But maybe they figured it would increase our sense of communal solidarity to have that many people working together in one place. Or maybe it's just easier for the bosses to oversee the whole bunch of us at once. I'll bet they're using whatchamacallit psychology on us. We're divided up into teams, surrounding workbenches just like the ones in science class where you dissect frogs, and one of the older girls sits at the end as team leader. It's OK to talk as long as you keep your hands moving (I mean, you can't just shut up and do this stuff all day long), but if you talk or laugh too loud or get too engrossed in your conversation, the team leader will come over to you with a frown and say, "All right, Yumiko, let's keep the hands moving, not the mouth. Looks like you're falling behind." So we all whisper to each other like burglars in the night.

They pipe music into the factory. The style changes, depending on the time of day. If you're a big fan of Barry Manilow or Air Supply, Mr Wind-up Bird, you might like this place.

It takes me a few days to make one of "my" wigs. The time differs according to the grade of the product, of course, but you have to measure the time it takes to make a wig in days. First you divide the base into checkerboard squares, and then you plant hair into one square after another in order. It's not assembly line work, though, like the factory in Chaplin's movie, where you tighten one bolt and then the next one comes; each wig is "mine". I almost feel like signing and dating each one when I'm through with it. But I don't, of course: they'd just get mad at me. It's a really nice feeling to know, though, that someone out there in the world is

447

wearing the wig I made on his head. It gives me a sense of, I don't know, connectedness.

Life is so strange, though. If somebody had said to me three years ago, "Three years from now, you're going to be in a factory in the mountains making wigs with a lot of country girls," I would have laughed in their face. I could never have imagined this. And as for what I'll be doing three years from now: nobody knows the answer to that one, either. Do you know what you're going to be doing three years from now, Mr Wind-up Bird? I'm sure you don't. Forget about three years: I'd be willing to bet all the money I've got here that you don't know what you'll be doing a month from now!

The girls around me, though, know pretty much where they'll be in three years. Or at least they think they do. They think they're going to save the money they make here, find the right guy after a few years, and be happily married.

The guys these girls are going to marry are mostly farmers' sons or guys who will inherit the store from their fathers or guys working in small local companies. Like I said before, there's a chronic shortage of young women here, so they get bought up pretty quickly. It would take some really bad luck for anybody to be left over, so they all find somebody or other to marry. It's really something. And as I said in my last letter, most people leave work when they get married. Their job in the wig factory is just a stage that fills the few years' gap between leaving school and getting married – like a room they come into, stay in a little while, then leave.

Not only does the wig company not mind this, they seem to prefer to have the girls work just a few years and leave when they get married. It's a lot better for them to have a constant turnover of workers rather than to have to worry about salaries and benefits and unions and stuff like that. The company takes better care of the girls with ability who become team leaders, but the other, ordinary girls are just consumer goods to them. There's a tacit understanding, then, between the girls and the company that they will get married and leave. So for the girls, imagining what is going to happen three years from now involves only one of two possibilities: they'll either be looking for a mate while they go on working here, or they will have left to get married. Talk about simplicity!

There just isn't anybody around here like me, who is thinking to herself, I don't know what's going to happen to me three years from now. They are all good workers. Nobody does a botched job or complains about the work. Now and then, I'll hear somebody griping about the cafeteria food, that's all. Of course, this is work we're talking about, so it can't be fun all the time; you might have somebody putting in her hours from 9 to 5 because she has to, even though she really wants to run off for the day, but for the most part, I think they're enjoying the work.

It must be because they know this is a finite period suspended between one world and another. That's why they want to have as much fun as possible while they're here. Ultimately, this is just a transition point for them.

Not for me, though. This is no time of suspension or transition for me. I have no idea at all where I'm going from here. For me, this could be the end of the line. Do you see what I mean? So strictly speaking, I am not enjoying the work here. All I'm doing is trying to accept the work in every possible way. When I'm making a wig, I don't think about anything but making that wig. I'm deadly serious – enough so that I break out in a sweat all over.

I don't quite know how to put this, but lately I've been thinking about the boy who got killed in the motorcycle accident. To tell you the truth, I haven't thought too much about him before. Maybe the shock of the accident twisted my memory or something in a weird way, because all I remembered about him were these weird kinds of things, like his smelly armpits or what a totally dumb guy he was or his fingers trying to get into strange places of mine. Every once in a while, though, something not so bad about him comes back to me. Especially when my mind is empty and I'm just planting hairs in a wig base, these things come back to me out of nowhere. Oh, yeah, I'll think, he was like that. I guess time doesn't flow in order, does it – A, B, C, D? It just sort of goes where it feels like going.

Can I be honest with you, Mr Wind-up Bird? I mean, really, really, really honest? Sometimes I get sooo scared! I'll wake up in the middle of the night all alone, hundreds of miles away from anybody, and it's pitch dark, and I have no idea what's going to happen to me in the future, and I get so scared I want to scream. Does that happen to you, Mr Wind-up Bird? When it happens, I try to remind myself that I am connected to others – other things and other people. I work as hard as I can to list their names in my head. On the list, of course, is you, Mr Wind-up Bird. And the alley, and the well, and the persimmon tree, and that kind of thing. And the wigs that I've made here with my own hands. And the little bits and pieces I remember about the boy. All these little things (though you're not just another one of those little things, Mr Wind-up Bird, but anyhow . . .) help me to come back "here" little by little. Then I start to feel sorry I never let my boyfriend see me naked or touch me. Back then, I was determined not to let him put his hands on me. Sometimes, Mr Wind-up Bird, I think I'd like to stay a virgin the rest of my life. Seriously. What do you think about that?

Bye-bye, Mr Wind-up Bird. I hope Kumiko comes back soon.

16

The World's Exhaustion and Burdens
•
The Magic Lamp

The phone rang at 9.30 at night. It rang once, then stopped, and started ringing again. This was to be Ushikawa's signal.

"Hello, Mr Okada," said Ushikawa's voice. "Ushikawa here. I'm in your neighbourhood and thought I might drop by, if it's all right with you. I know it's late, but there's something I wanted to talk to you about in person. What do you say? It has to do with Ms Kumiko, so I thought you might be interested."

I pictured Ushikawa's expression at the other end of the line as I listened to him speaking. He had a self-satisfied smile on his face, lips curled and filthy teeth exposed, as if to say, I know this is an offer you can't refuse; and unfortunately, he was right.

•

It took him exactly ten minutes to reach my house. He wore the same clothes he'd had on three days earlier. I could have been mistaken about that, but he wore the same kind of suit and shirt and tie, all grimy and wrinkled and baggy. These disgraceful articles of clothing looked as if they had been forced to accept an unfair portion of the world's exhaustion and burdens. If, through some kind of reincarnation, it were possible to be reborn as Ushikawa's clothing, with a guarantee of rare glory in the *next* rebirth, I would still not want to do it.

After asking my permission, Ushikawa helped himself to a beer in the refrigerator, checking first to see that the bottle felt properly chilled before he poured the contents into a glass he found nearby. We sat at the kitchen table.

"All right, then," said Ushikawa. "In the interest of saving time, I will dispense with the small talk and plunge directly into the business at hand. You would like to talk with Ms Kumiko, wouldn't you, Mr Okada? Directly. Just the two of you. I believe that is what you have been wanting for some time now. Your first priority. Am I right?"

I gave this some thought. Or I paused for a few moments, as if giving it some thought.

"Of course I want to talk with her if that is possible."

"It is not impossible," said Ushikawa softly, with a nod.

"But there are conditions attached . . . ?"

"There are *no* conditions attached." Ushikawa took a sip of his beer. "I do have a new proposition for you this evening, however. Please listen to what I have to say, and give it careful consideration. It is something quite separate from the question of whether or not you talk to Ms Kumiko."

I looked at him without speaking.

"To begin with, then, Mr Okada, you are renting that land, and the house on it, from a certain company, are you not? The 'hanging house', I mean. You are paying a rather large sum for it each month. You have not an ordinary lease, however, but one with an option to buy some years hence. Correct? Your contract is not a matter of public record, of course, and so your name does not appear anywhere – which is the point of all the machinations. You are, however, the de facto owner of the property, and the rent you pay accomplishes the same thing as mortgage payments. The total sum you are to pay – let's see – including the house, comes to something in the region of eighty-million yen, does it not? At this rate, you should be able to assume ownership of the land and the building in something less than two years. That is *very* impressive! Very fast work! I have to congratulate you."

Ushikawa looked at me for confirmation of everything he had been saying, but I remained silent.

"Please don't ask me how I know all these details. You dig hard enough, you find what you want to know – if you know how to dig. And I have a pretty good idea who is behind the dummy company. Now, *that* was a tough one! I had to crawl through a labyrinth for it. It was like looking for a stolen car that's been repainted and had new tyres put on and the seats re-covered and the serial number filed off the engine. They covered all their traces. They're real pros. But now I have a pretty good idea of what's going on – probably better than you do, Mr Okada. I'll bet you don't even know who it is you're paying the money back to, right?"

"That's all right. Money doesn't come with names attached."

Ushikawa laughed. "You're absolutely right, Mr Okada. Money does *not* come with names attached. Very well said! I'll have to write that down. But Mr Okada, things don't always go the way you want them to. Take the boys at the tax office, for example. They're not very bright. They only know how to squeeze taxes out of places that have names attached. So they go out of their way to stick names on where there aren't any. And not just names, but numbers too. They might as well be robots, for all the emotion that's involved in the process. But that is exactly what this capitalist society of ours is built on. . . . Which leads us to the conclusion that the money you and I are now talking about does indeed have a name attached, and a very excellent name it is."

I looked at Ushikawa's head as he spoke. Depending on the angle, the light created some strange dents in his scalp.

"Don't worry," he said, with a laugh. "The tax man won't be coming here. And even if he did come, with this much of a labyrinth to crawl through, he'd be bound to smash into something. Wham! He'd raise a huge bump on his head. And finally, it's just a job for him: he doesn't want to hurt himself doing it. If he can get his money, he'd rather do it the easy way than the hard way: the easier the better. As long as he gets what he's looking for, the brownie points are the same. Especially if his boss tells him to take the easy way, any ordinary person is going to choose that. I managed to find what I did because it was me doing the searching. Not to boast or anything, but I'm good. I may not look it, but I'm really good. I know how to avoid injury. I know how to slip down the road at night when it's pitch black out.

"But to tell you the truth, Mr Okada (and I know you're one person I can really open up to), not even I know what you're doing in that place. I do know the people who visit you there are paying an arm and a leg. So you must be doing something special for them that's worth all that money. That much is as clear as counting crows on snow. But exactly what it is you do, and why you're so stuck on that particular piece of land, I have no idea. Those are the two most important points in all this, but they are the very things most hidden, like the centre of a palmist's signboard. That worries me."

452

"Which is to say, that's what worries Noboru Wataya," I said.

Instead of answering, Ushikawa started pulling on the matted fuzz above his ears.

"This is just between you and me, Mr Okada, but I have to confess I really admire you. No flattery intended. This may sound odd, but you're basically a really ordinary guy. Or to put it even more bluntly, there's nothing at all special about you. Sorry about that, but don't take it the wrong way. It's true, though, in terms of how you fit in society. Meeting you face to face and talking with you like this, though, I'm very, very impressed with you – with how you handle yourself. I mean, look at the way you've managed to shake up a man like Dr Wataya! That's why I'm just the carrier pigeon. A completely ordinary person couldn't pull this off.

"That's what I like about you. I'm not making this up. I may be worthless scum, but I don't lie about things like that. And I don't think of you in totally objective terms, either. If there's nothing special about you in terms of how you fit in society, I'm a hundred times worse. I'm just an uneducated twerp from an awful background. My father was a tatami maker in Funabashi, an alcoholic, a real bastard. I used to wish he'd die and leave me alone, I was such a miserable kid, and I ended up getting my wish, for better or worse. Then I went through storybook poverty. I don't have a single pleasant memory from childhood, never had a kind word from either parent. No wonder I went bad! I managed to squeak through high school, but after that it was the school of hard knocks for me. Lived on my wits, what little I had. That's why I don't like members of the elite or official government types. All right: I hate them. Walk right into society through the front door, get a pretty wife, self-satisfied bastards. I like guys like you, Mr Okada, who've done it all on their own."

Ushikawa struck a match and lit another cigarette.

"You can't keep it up for ever, though. You're going to burn out sooner or later. Everybody does. It's the way people are made. In terms of evolutionary history, it was only yesterday that men learned to walk around on two legs and get in trouble thinking complicated thoughts. So don't worry, you'll burn out. Especially in the world that you're trying to deal with: everybody burns out. There are too many tricky things going on in it, too many ways of getting into trouble. It's a world *made* of tricky things. I've been working in that world since the time of Dr Wataya's uncle, and now the Doctor has inherited it, lock, stock and barrel. I used to do risky stuff for a living. If I had kept it up, I'd be in jail now – or dead. No kidding. The Doctor's uncle picked me up in the nick of time. So these little eyes of mine have seen a hell of a lot. Everybody burns out in this world: amateur, pro, it doesn't matter, they all burn out, they all get hurt, the OK guys and the not-OK guys both. That's why everybody takes out a little insurance. I've got some too, here at the bottom of the heap. That way, you can manage to survive if you burn out. If you're all by yourself and don't belong anywhere, you go down once and you're out. Finished.

"Maybe I shouldn't say this to you, Mr Okada, but you're ready to go down. It's a sure thing. It says so in my book, in big, black letters about two or three pages ahead: 'TORU OKADA READY TO FALL.' It's true. I'm not trying to scare you. I'm a whole lot more accurate in this world than weather forecasts on TV. So all I want to tell you is this: there's a time when things are right for pulling out."

Ushikawa closed his mouth at that point and looked at me. Then he went on:

"So let's stop all this sounding each other out, Mr Okada, and get down to business. . . . Which brings us to the end of a very long introduction, so now I can make you the offer I came here to make."

Ushikawa put both hands on the table. Then he flicked his tongue over his lips.

"So let's say I've just told you that you ought to cut your ties with that land and pull out of the deal. But maybe you can't pull out, even if you want to. Maybe you're stuck until you pay off your loan." Ushikawa cut himself short and gave me a searching look. "If money's a problem, we've got it to give you. If you need eighty-million yen, I can bring you eighty-million yen in a nice, neat bundle. That's eight-thousand ten-thousand-yen bills. You can pay off whatever you owe and pocket the rest, free and clear. Then it's party time! Hey, what do you say?"

"So then the land and building will belong to Noboru Wataya? Is that the idea?"

"Yes, I guess that's the way things work. I suppose there are a lot of annoying details that will have to be taken care of, though. . . ."

I gave his proposal some thought. "You know, Ushikawa, I really don't get it. I don't see why Noboru Wataya is so eager to get me away from that property. What does he plan to do with it once he owns it?"

Ushikawa slowly rubbed one cheek with the palm of his hand. "Sorry, Mr Okada, I don't know about things like that. As I mentioned to you at first, I'm just a stupid carrier pigeon. My master tells me what to do, and I do it. And most of the jobs he gives me are unpleasant. When I used to read the story of Aladdin, I'd always sympathize with the genie, the way they worked him so hard, but I never dreamed I'd grow up to be like him. It's a sad story, let me tell you. But in the end, everything I have said to you is a message I was sent to deliver. It comes from Dr Wataya. The choice is up to you. So what do you say? What kind of answer should I carry back?"

I said nothing.

"Of course, you will need time to think. That is fine. We can give you time. I don't mean you to decide right now, on the spot. I would *like* to say take all the time you want, but I'm afraid we can't be that flexible. Now, let me just say this, Mr Okada. Let me give you my own personal opinion. A nice, fat offer like this is not going to sit on the table for ever. You could look away for a second, and it might be gone when you look back. It could evaporate, like mist on a windowpane. So please give it some serious thought – in a hurry. I mean, it's not a bad offer. Do you see what I mean?"

Ushikawa sighed and looked at his watch. "Oh, my, my, my – I've got to be going. Overstayed my welcome again, I'm afraid. Enjoyed another beer. And as usual, I did all the talking. Sorry about that. I'm not trying to make excuses, but, I don't know, when I come here I just seem to settle in. You have a comfortable house here, Mr Okada. That must be it."

Ushikawa stood up and carried his glass and beer bottle and ashtray to the kitchen sink.

"I'll be in touch with you soon, Mr Okada. And I'll make arrangements for you to talk with Ms Kumiko, that I promise. You can look forward to it soon."

·

After Ushikawa left, I opened the windows and let the accumulated cigarette smoke out. Then I drank a glass of water. Sitting on the sofa, I cuddled the cat, Mackerel, on my lap. I imagined Ushikawa removing his disguise when he was one step beyond my door, and flying back to Noboru Wataya. It was a stupid thing to imagine.

17

The Fitting Room

•

A Successor

Nutmeg knew nothing about the women who came to her. None of them offered information about herself, and Nutmeg never asked. The names with which they made their appointments were obviously made up. But around them lingered that special smell produced by the combination of power and money. The women themselves never made a show of it, but Nutmeg could tell from the style and fit of their clothes that they came from backgrounds of privilege.

She rented space in an office building in Akasaka – an inconspicuous building in an inconspicuous place, out of respect for her clients' extreme concern for their privacy. After careful consideration, she decided to make it a fashion design studio. She had, in fact, been a fashion designer, and no one would have found it suspicious for substantial numbers of a variety of women to be coming to see her. Her clients were all in their thirties to fifties. Nutmeg stocked the room with clothing and design sketches and fashion magazines, brought in the tools and workbenches and mannequins needed for fashion design, and even went so far as to design a few outfits to give the place an air of authenticity. The smaller of the two rooms she designated as the fitting room. Her clients would be shown to this "fitting room", and on the sofa they would be "fitted" by Nutmeg.

Her client list was compiled by the wife of the owner of a major department store. The woman had chosen a strictly limited number of trustworthy candidates from among her wide circle of friends, convinced that in order to avoid any possibility of scandal, she would have to make this a club with an exclusive membership. Otherwise, news of the arrangement would be sure to spread quickly. The women chosen to become members were warned never to reveal anything about their "fitting" to outsiders. Not only were they women of great discretion, but they knew that if they broke their promise they would be permanently expelled from the club.

Each client would telephone to make an appointment for a "fitting" and show up at the designated time, knowing that she need not fear encountering any other client, and that her privacy would be guaranteed. Honoraria were paid on the spot, in cash, their size having been determined by the department store owner's wife – at a level much higher than Nutmeg would have imagined, though this never became an obstacle. Any woman who had been "fitted" by Nutmeg always called for another appointment, without exception. "You don't have to let the money be a burden to you," the department store owner's wife explained to Nutmeg. "The more they pay, the more assured these women feel." Nutmeg would go to her "office" three days a week and do one "fitting" a day. That was her limit.

Cinnamon became his mother's assistant when he turned sixteen. By then, it had become difficult for Nutmeg to handle all the clerical tasks herself, but she had been reluctant to hire a complete stranger. When, after much deliberation, she asked her son to help her with her work, he agreed immediately without even asking what kind of work it was she did. He would go to the office each morning at 10 o'clock by cab (unable to bear being with others on buses or tube trains), clean and dust, put everything where it belonged, fill the vases with fresh flowers, make coffee, do whatever shopping was needed, put classical music on the cassette player at low volume, and keep the books.

Before long, Cinnamon had made himself an indispensable presence in the office. Whether clients were due that day or not, he would put on a suit and tie and take up his position at the waiting-room desk. None of the clients complained about his not speaking. It never caused them any inconvenience, and if anything, they preferred it that way. He was the one who took their calls when they made appointments. They would state their preferred time and date, and he would knock on the desktop in response: once for "no" and twice for "yes". The women liked this conciseness. He was a young man of such classic features that he could have been turned into a sculpture and displayed in a museum, and unlike so many other handsome young men, he never undercut his image when he opened his mouth. The women would talk to him on their way in and out, and he would respond with a smile and a nod. These "conversations" relaxed them, relieving the tensions they had brought with them from the outer world and reducing the awkwardness they felt after their "fittings". Nor did Cinnamon himself, who ordinarily disliked contact with strangers, appear to find it painful to interact with the women.

At eighteen, Cinnamon got his driving licence. Nutmeg found a kindly driving instructor to give him private lessons, but Cinnamon himself had already been through every available instruction book and absorbed the details. All he needed was the practical know-how that couldn't be obtained from books, and this he mastered in a few days at the wheel. Once he had his licence, he pored over the used-car books and bought himself a Porsche Carrera, using as a down payment all the money he had saved working for his mother (none of which he ever had to use for living expenses). He made the engine shine, bought new parts through mail order, put new tyres on, and generally brought the car's condition to racing level. All he ever did with it, though, was drive it over the same short, jam-packed route every day from his home in Hiroo to the office in Akasaka, rarely exceeding forty miles an hour. This made it one of the rarer Porsche 911s in the world.

•

Nutmeg continued her work for more than seven years, during which time she lost three clients: the first was killed in a car accident; the second suffered "permanent expulsion" for a minor infraction; and the third went "far away" in connection with her husband's work. These were replaced by four new clients, all the same sort of fascinating middle-aged women who wore expensive clothing and used aliases. The work itself did not change during the seven years. She went on "fitting" her clients, and Cinnamon went on cleaning the office, keeping the books, and driving the Porsche. There was no progress, no retrogression, only the gradual ageing of everyone involved. Nutmeg was nearing fifty, and Cinnamon turned twenty. Cinnamon seemed to enjoy his work, but Nutmeg was gradually overcome by a sense of powerlessness. Over the years, she went on "fitting" the "something" that each of her clients carried within. She never fully understood what it was that she did for them, but she continued to do her best. The "somethings", meanwhile, were never cured. She could never make them go away; all that her curative powers could do was reduce their activity somewhat for a time. Within a few days (usually, from three to ten days), each "something" would start up again, advancing and retreating over the short span but growing unmistakably larger over time – like cancer cells. Nutmeg could feel them growing in her hands. They would tell her: You're wasting your time; no matter what you do, we are going to win in the end. And they were right. She had no hope of victory. All she could do was retard their progress to give her clients a few days of peace.

Nutmeg would often ask herself, "Is it not just these women? Do all the women of the world carry this kind of 'something' inside them? And why are the ones who come here all middle-aged women? Do I have a 'something' inside me as well?"

But Nutmeg did not really want to know the answers to her questions. All she could be sure of was that circumstances had somehow conspired to confine her to her fitting room. People needed her, and as long as they went on needing her, she could not get out. Sometimes her sense of powerlessness would be deep and terrible, and she would feel like an empty shell. She was being worn down, disappearing into a dark nothingness. At times like this, she would open herself to her quiet son, and Cinnamon would nod as he listened intently to his mother's words. He never said anything, but speaking to him like this enabled her to attain an odd kind of peace. She was not entirely alone, she felt, and not entirely powerless. How strange, she thought: I heal others, and Cinnamon heals me. But who heals Cinnamon? Is he like a black hole, absorbing all pain and loneliness by himself? One time – and only that once – she tried to search inside him by placing her hand on his forehead the way she did to her clients when she was "fitting" them. But she could feel nothing.

Before long, Nutmeg felt that she wanted to leave her work. "I don't have much strength left. If I keep this up, I will burn out completely. I'll have nothing left at all." But people continued to have an intense need for her "fitting". She could not bring herself to abandon her clients just to suit her own convenience.

Nutmeg found a successor during the summer of that year. The moment she saw the mark on the cheek of the young man who was sitting in front of a building in Shinjuku, she knew.

18

A Stupid Tree Frog Daughter
(May Kasahara's Point of View: 4)

•

Hi, again, Mr Wind-up Bird.

It's 2.30 in the morning. All my neighbours are sound asleep, but I can't sleep tonight, so I'm up, writing this letter to you. To tell you the truth, sleepless nights are as unusual for me as sumo wrestlers who look good in berets. Usually, I just slip right into sleep when the time comes, and slip right out when it's time to wake up. I do have an alarm clock, but I almost never use it. Every rare once in a while, though, this happens: I wake up in the middle of the night and can't get back to sleep.

I'm planning to stay at my desk, writing this letter to you, until I get sleepy, so I don't know if this is going to be a long letter or a short one. Of course, I never really know that anytime I write to you until I get to the end.

Anyway, it seems to me that the way most people go on living (I suppose there are a few exceptions), they think that the world or life (or whatever) is this place where everything is (or is supposed to be) basically logical and consistent. Talking with my neighbours here often makes me think that. Like, when something happens, whether it's a big event that affects the whole of society or something small and personal, people talk about it like, "Oh, well, of course, that happened because such and such," and most of the time people will agree and say, "Oh, sure, I see," but I just don't get it. "A is like this, so that's why B happened." I mean, that doesn't explain anything. It's like when you put instant rice pudding mix in a bowl in the microwave and push the button, and you take the cover off when it rings, and there you've got rice pudding. I mean, what happens in between the time when you push the switch and when the microwave rings? You can't tell what's going on under the cover. Maybe the instant rice pudding first turns into macaroni cheese in the darkness when nobody's looking and only then turns back into rice pudding. We think it's natural to get rice pudding after we put rice pudding mix in the microwave and the bell rings, but to me that's just a presumption. I would be kind of relieved if, every once in a while, after you put rice pudding mix in the microwave and it rang and you opened the top, you got macaroni cheese. I suppose I'd be shocked, of course, but I don't know, I think I'd be kind of relieved too. Or at least I think I wouldn't be so upset, because that would feel, in some way, a whole lot more real.

Why "more real"? Trying to explain that logically, in words, would be very, very, very hard, but maybe if you take the path my life has followed as an example and really think about it, you can see that it has had almost nothing about it that you could call "consistency". First of all, it's an absolute mystery how a daughter like me could have been born to two parents as boring as tree frogs. I know it's a little weird for me to be saying this, but I'm a lot more serious than the two of them combined. I'm not boasting or anything, it's just a fact. I don't mean to say that I'm any better than they are, but I am a more serious human being. If you met them, you'd know what I mean, Mr Wind-up Bird. Those people believe that the world is as consistent and explainable as the floor plan of a new house in a high-priced development, so if you do everything in a logical, consistent way, every-thing will turn out right in the end. That's why they get upset and sad and angry when I'm not like that.

Why was I born into this world as the child of such absolute dummies? And why didn't I turn into the same kind of stupid tree frog daughter even though I was raised by those people? I've been wondering and wondering about that ever since I can remember. But I can't explain it. It seems to me there ought to be a good reason, but it's a reason that I can't find. And there are tons of other things that don't have logical explanations. For example, "Why does everybody hate me?" I didn't do anything wrong. I was just living my life in the usual way. But then, all of a sudden, one day I noticed that nobody liked me. I don't understand it.

So then one disconnected thing led to another disconnected thing, and that's how all kinds of stuff happened. Like, I met the boy with the motorcycle and we had that stupid accident. The way I remember it – or the way those things are all lined up in my head – there's no "This happened this way, so naturally that happened that way." Every time the bell rings and I take off the cover, I seem to find something I've never seen before.

I don't have any idea what's happening to me, and before I know it I'm not going to school any more and I'm hanging around the house, and that's when I meet you, Mr Wind-up Bird. No, before that I'm doing surveys for a wig company. But why a wig company? That's another mystery. I can't remember. Maybe I hit my head in the accident, and the position of my brain got messed up. Or maybe the psychological shock of it started me covering up all kinds of memories, the way a squirrel hides a nut and forgets where he's buried it. (Have you ever seen that happen, Mr Wind-up Bird? I have. When I was little. I thought the stupid squirrel was sooo funny! It never occurred to me the same thing was going to happen to me.)

So anyhow, I started doing surveys for the wig company, and that's what gave me this fondness for wigs like they were my destiny or something. Talk about no connection! Why wigs and not stockings or rice scoops? If it had been stockings or rice scoops, I wouldn't be working hard in a wig factory like this. Right? And if I hadn't caused that stupid bike accident, I probably wouldn't have met you in the back alley that summer, and if you hadn't met me, you probably would never have known about the Miyawakis' well, so you wouldn't have got that mark on your face, and you wouldn't have got mixed up in all those strange things . . . probably. When I think about it like this, I can't help asking myself, "Where is there any logical consistency in the world?"

I don't know – maybe the world has two different kinds of people, and for one kind the world is this logical, rice pudding place, and for the other it's all hit-or-miss macaroni cheese. I bet if those tree frog parents of mine put rice pudding mix in the microwave and got macaroni cheese when the bell rang, they'd just tell themselves, "Oh, we must have put in macaroni cheese mix by mistake," or they'd take out the macaroni cheese and try to convince themselves, "This looks like macaroni cheese, but actually it's rice pudding." And if I tried to be nice and explain to them that sometimes, when you put in rice pudding mix, you get macaroni cheese, they would never believe me. They'd probably just get mad. Do you understand what I'm trying to tell you, Mr Wind-up Bird?

Remember when I kissed your mark that time? I've been thinking about that ever since I said goodbye to you last summer, thinking about it over and over, like a cat watching the rain fall, and wondering what was that all about? I don't think I can explain it myself, to tell you the truth. Sometime way in the future, maybe ten years or twenty years from now, if we have a chance to talk about it, and if I'm more grown up and a lot cleverer than I am now, I might be able to tell you what it meant. Right now, though, I'm sorry to say, I think I just don't have the ability, or the brains, to put it into the right words.

One thing I can tell you honestly, though, Mr Wind-up Bird, is that I like you better without the mark on your face. No; wait a minute; that's not fair. You didn't put the mark there on purpose. Maybe I should say that even without your mark, you're good enough for me. Is that it? No, that doesn't explain anything.

Here's what I think, Mr Wind-up Bird. That mark is maybe going to give you something important. But it also must be robbing you of something. Kind of like a trade-off. And if everybody keeps taking stuff from you like that, you're going to be worn away until there's nothing left of you. So, I don't know, I guess what I really want to say is that it wouldn't make any difference to me if you didn't have that thing.

Sometimes I think that the reason I'm sitting here making wigs like this every day is because I kissed your mark that time. It's because I did that that I made up my mind to leave that place, to get as far away as I could from you. I know I might be hurting you by saying this, but I think it's true. Still, though, it's because of that that I was finally able to find the place where I belong. So, in a sense, I am grateful to you, Mr Wind-up Bird. I don't suppose it's much fun to have somebody be "in a sense" grateful to you, though, is it?

So now I feel like I've said just about everything I have to say to you, Mr Wind-up Bird. It's almost 4 o'clock in the morning. I have to get up at 7.30, so maybe I'll be able to sleep three hours and a little bit. I hope I can get to sleep right away. Anyhow, I'm going to end this letter here. Goodbye, Mr Wind-up Bird. Please say a little prayer so I can get to sleep.

19

The Subterranean Labyrinth

•

Cinnamon's Two Doors

"There's a computer in that house, isn't there, Mr Okada? I don't know who's using it, though," said Ushikawa.

It was 9 o'clock at night, and I was sitting at the kitchen table, with the phone to my ear.

"There is," I said, and left it at that.

Ushikawa made a sniffling sound. "I know that much from my usual snooping," he said. "Of course, I'm not saying anything one way or another about the fact that you've got a computer there. Nowadays, anybody doing any kind of brainwork has to have a computer. There's nothing weird about it.

"To cut a long story short, though, the idea hit me that it might be good if I could contact you through the computer. So I looked into it, but damn, it's a hell of a lot more complicated than I imagined. Just calling up on an ordinary phone line wouldn't make the connection. Plus, you need a special password for access. No password, and the door doesn't budge. That did it for me."

I kept silent.

"Now, don't get me wrong, Mr Okada. I'm not trying to crawl inside your computer and fool around in there. I don't have anything like that in mind. With all the security you've got in place, I couldn't pull data out even if I wanted to. No, that was never an issue. All I have in mind is trying to set up a conversation between you and Ms Kumiko. I promised you I'd do that, remember, that I'd do what I could to help you and her talk to each other directly. It's been a long time since she left your house, and it's a bad idea to leave things hanging like this. The way it stands now, your life is probably just going to get weirder and weirder. It's always best for people to talk to each other face to face, to open themselves up. Otherwise, misunderstandings are bound to arise, and misunderstandings make people unhappy. . . . Anyhow, that's how I tried to appeal to Ms Kumiko. I did everything I could.

"But I just couldn't get her to agree. She insisted she wouldn't talk to you directly – not even on the phone (since a face-to-face meeting was out of the question). *Not even on the phone!* I was ready to give up. I tried every trick in the book, but her mind was made up. Like a rock."

Ushikawa paused for me to react, but I said nothing.

"Still, I couldn't just take her at her word and back off. Dr Wataya would really give it to me if I started acting like that. The other person can be a rock or a wall, but I'll find that one tiny point of compromise. That's our job: finding that point of compromise. If they won't sell you the refrigerator, make them sell you some ice. So I racked my brains trying to find some way to pull this off. Let me tell you, that's what makes us human – coming up with a million different ideas. So all of a sudden, a good one popped up in my foggy brain, like a star showing through a break in the clouds. 'That's it!' I told myself. 'Why not have a conversation on computer screens?' You know: put words on the screen with a keyboard. You can do that, can't you, Mr Okada?"

I had used a computer when I worked in the law firm, researching precedents, looking up personal data for clients, and communicating via E-mail. Kumiko had also used computers at work. The health food magazine she was an editor on had computer files on recipes and nutritional analyses.

"It wouldn't work on just any old computer," continued Ushikawa, "but with our machine and yours, you ought to be able to communicate at a pretty fast pace. Ms Kumiko says she's willing to talk with you that way. It was as much as I could get her to agree to. Exchanging messages real time, it would *almost* be like talking to each other. That's the one last point of compromise I could come up with. Squeezing wisdom out of a monkey. What do you say? You may not be too crazy about the idea, but I put my brains on the rack for that one. Let me tell you, it's tiring work thinking that hard with brains you don't even have!"

I shifted the receiver to my left hand.

"Hello? Mr Okada? Are you listening?"

"I'm listening," I said.

"All right, then: the one thing I need from you is the password to access your computer. Then I can set up a conversation between you and Ms Kumiko. What do you say?"

"I'd say there are some practical problems standing in the way."

"Oh? And what might those be?"

"Well, first of all, how can I be sure the other person is Kumiko? When you're talking on the computer screen, you can't see other people's faces or hear their voices. Someone else could be sitting at the keyboard, pretending to be Kumiko."

"I see what you mean," said Ushikawa, sounding impressed. "I never thought of that. But I'm sure there must be some way round it. Not to flatter you, but it's good to view things with scepticism, to have your doubts. 'I doubt, therefore I am.' All right, then: how about this? You start out by asking a question that only Ms Kumiko would know the answer to. If the other person comes up with the answer, it must be Kumiko. I mean, you lived together as man and wife for several years; there must be a few things that only the two of you would know."

What Ushikawa was saying made sense. "That would probably work," I said, "but I don't know the password. I've never touched that machine."

•

Nutmeg had told me that Cinnamon had customized every inch of the computer's system. He had compiled his own complex database and protected it from outside access with a secret code and other ingenious devices. Fingers on the keyboard, Cinnamon was absolute ruler over this three-dimensional subterranean labyrinth. He knew every one of its intertwining passages and could leap from one to another with the stroke of a key. For an uninformed invader (which is to say, anyone but Cinnamon) to grope his way through the labyrinth, past the alarms and traps, to where important data lay, would have taken months, according to Nutmeg. Not that the computer installed in the Residence was especially big: it was the same class of machine as the one in the Akasaka office. Both were hard-wired to the mainframe they had at home, though. There Cinnamon no doubt stored their client data and did their complex double bookkeeping, but I imagined that he kept something more in there than the secrets connected with the work that he and Nutmeg had done over the years.

What led me to believe this, was the depth of the commitment to his machine that Cinnamon displayed on occasion when he was in our special Residence. He normally stayed shut up in the small office he had there, but every now and then he would leave the door ajar, and I was able to observe him at work – not without a certain guilty sense of invading someone's privacy. He and his computer seemed to be moving together in an almost erotic union. After a burst of strokes on the keyboard, he would gaze at the screen, his mouth twisted in apparent dissatisfaction or curled with the suggestion of a smile. Sometimes he seemed deep in thought as he touched one key, then another, then another; and sometimes he ran his fingers over the keys with all the energy of a pianist playing a Liszt étude. As he engaged in silent conversation with his machine, he seemed to be peering through the screen of his monitor into another world, with which he shared a special intimacy. I couldn't help but feel that reality resided for him not so much in the earthly world but in his subterranean labyrinth. Perhaps in that world Cinnamon had a clear, ringing voice, with which he spoke eloquently and laughed and cried aloud.

·

"Can't I access your computer from the one here?" I asked Ushikawa. "Then you wouldn't need a password."

"No, that wouldn't work. Your transmissions might reach here, but transmissions from here wouldn't reach there. The problem is the password – the open sesame. Without that, there's nothing we can do. The door won't open for the wolf, no matter how hard he tries to disguise his voice. He can knock and say, 'Hi, it's me, your friend Rabbit,' but if he hasn't got the password, he gets turned away at the door. We're talking about an iron maiden here."

Ushikawa struck a match at his end and lit a cigarette. I pictured his snaggled yellow teeth and drooping mouth.

"It's a three-character alphanumeric password. You have ten seconds to input it after the prompt shows. Get it wrong three times, and access is denied, plus the alarm goes off. Not that there are any sirens that ring or anything, but the wolf leaves his footprints, so you know he was there. Clever, huh? If you calculate all possible permutations and combinations of twenty-six letters and ten numbers, it's practically infinite. You just have to know the password, or there's nothing you can do."

I thought this over for a time without replying.

"Any ideas, Mr Okada?"

After the client was driven away in the back seat of the Mercedes the following afternoon, I walked into Cinnamon's small office, sat down in front of his computer, and flipped the switch. The cool blue light of the monitor came on with a simple message:

`Enter password within ten seconds.`

I input the three-letter word that I had prepared:

`zoo`

The computer beeped once and displayed an error message:

`Incorrect password.`
`Enter password within ten seconds.`

The ten seconds started counting down on the screen. I changed to upper case and input the same letters:

`ZOO`

Again I was refused access:

`Incorrect password.`
`Enter correct password within ten seconds.`
`If incorrect password is input once more,`
`access will automatically be denied.`

Again the ten seconds began counting down on the screen. This time I made only the Z upper case. It was my last chance.

`Zoo`

Instead of an error message, a menu screen opened, with the instruction:

`Choose one of the following programmes.`

I released a long, slow breath, then began scrolling through the long list of programmes until I came to communications software. Highlighting this, I clicked the mouse.

`Choose one of the following programmes.`

I chose "Chat Mode" and clicked the mouse.

`Enter password within ten seconds.`

This was an important junction for Cinnamon to lock out access to his computer. And if the junction was important, the password itself ought to be important. I typed in:

`SUB`

The screen read:

`Incorrect password.`
`Input correct password within ten seconds.`

The countdown began: `10, 9, 8 . . .`

I tried the combination of upper- and lower-case letters that had worked the first time:

Sub

A prompt flashed on the screen:

Input telephone number.

I folded my arms and let my eyes take in this new message. Not bad. I had succeeded in opening two doors in Cinnamon's labyrinth. No, not bad at all. "Zoo" and "Sub" would do it. I clicked on "Exit" and returned to the main menu, then chose "Shutdown", which brought up the following options:

Record procedures in Operations File? Y/N (Y)

As instructed by Ushikawa, I chose "No" to avoid leaving a record of the procedures I had just executed.

The screen quietly died. I wiped the sweat from my forehead. After checking to be certain that I had left the keyboard and mouse exactly as I had found them, I moved away from the now cold monitor.

20

Nutmeg's Story

•

Nutmeg Akasaka took several months to tell me the story of her life. It was a long, long story, with many detours, so that what I am recording here is a very simplified (though not necessarily short) summary of the whole. I cannot claim with confidence that it contains the essence of her story, but it should at least convey the outline of important events that occurred at crucial points in her life.

•

Nutmeg and her mother escaped from Manchuria to Japan, their only valuables the jewellery they were able to wear on their bodies. They travelled up from the port of Sasebo to Yokohama, to stay with the mother's family, which had long owned an import-export business dealing primarily with Taiwan. Prosperous before the war, they had lost most of their business when Japan lost Taiwan. The father died of heart disease, and the family's second son, who had been second in command, was killed in an air raid just before the war ended. The eldest son left his teaching post to carry on the family business, but his temperament did not suit a life of commerce, and he was unable to recoup the family fortunes. They still had their comfortable house and land, but it was not a pleasant place for Nutmeg and her mother to live as extra mouths to feed during those strait-ened postwar years. They were always at pains to keep their presence as unobtrusive as possible, taking less than the others at mealtimes, waking earlier than the others each morning, taking on a greater share of the household chores. Every piece of clothing the young Nutmeg wore was a hand-me-down from her older cousins – gloves, socks, even underwear. For pencils, she collected the others' cast-off stubs. Just waking up in the morning was painful to her. The thought that a new day was starting was enough to make her chest hurt.

She wanted to get out of this house, to live alone with her mother somewhere where they didn't always have to feel constrained, even if it meant living in poverty. But her mother never tried to leave. "My mother had always been an active person," said Nutmeg, "but after we escaped from Manchuria, she was like an empty shell. It was as if the very strength to go on living had evaporated from inside her." She could no longer rouse herself to anything. All she could do was tell Nutmeg over and over about the happy times they used to have. This left Nutmeg to find for herself the resources to go on living.

Nutmeg did not dislike studying as such, but she had almost no interest in the courses they offered in high school. She couldn't believe that it would do her any good to stuff her head full of historical dates or the rules of English grammar or geometric formulas. What she wanted more than anything was to learn a useful skill and make herself independent as soon as possible. Her concerns were quite different from her classmates' comfortable enjoyment of school life.

The only thing she cared about was fashion. Her mind was filled with thoughts of clothing from morning to night. Not that she had the wherewithal to dress in style: she could only read and reread the fashion magazines she managed to find, and to fill notebooks with drawings of dresses in imitation of those she found in the magazines or clothes she had dreamed up herself. She had no idea what it was about the fancy dresses that so captivated her. Perhaps, she said, it came from her habit of always playing with the huge wardrobe that her mother had in Manchuria. Her mother was a genuine clotheshorse. She had had more kimonos and dresses than room in their chests to store them, and the young Nutmeg would always pull them out and touch them whenever she had a chance. Most of those dresses and kimonos had to remain in Manchuria when the two of them left, and whatever they were able to stuff into rucksacks they had to exchange along the way for food. Her mother would spread out the next dress to be traded, and sigh over it before letting it go.

"Designing clothes was my secret door to a different world," said Nutmeg, "a world that belonged only to me. In that world, imagination was everything. The better you were able to imagine what you wanted to imagine, the farther you could flee from reality. And what I really liked about it was that it was free. It didn't cost a thing. It was wonderful! But imagining beautiful clothes in my mind and transferring the images to paper was not just a way for me to leave reality behind and steep myself in dreams. I needed it to go on living. It was as natural and obvious to me as breathing. So I assumed that everyone else was doing it too. When I realized that everyone else was *not* doing it – that they couldn't do it even if they tried – I told myself, 'I'm different from other people, so the life I lead will have to be different from theirs.' "

Nutmeg left secondary school and transferred to a school of dressmaking. To raise the money for her tuition, she begged her mother to sell one of her last remaining pieces of jewellery. With that, she was able to study sewing and cutting and designing and other such useful skills for two years. When she graduated, she took an apartment and started living alone. She put herself through a professional fashion design school by waitressing in restaurants and taking odd jobs sewing and knitting. And when she had graduated from this school, she went to work for a manufacturer of quality ladies' garments, where she succeeded in getting herself assigned to the design department.

There was no question but that she had an original talent. Not only could she draw well, but her ideas and her point of view were different from those of other people. She had a clear image of precisely what she wanted to make, and it was not something she had borrowed from anyone else: it was always her own, and it always came out of her quite naturally. She pursued the tiny details of her image with all the intensity of a salmon swimming upstream through a great river to its source. She had no time for sleep. She loved her work and dreamed only of the day she could become an independent designer. She never thought about having fun outside of work: in fact, she didn't know how to do any of the things people did to have fun.

Before long, her bosses came to recognize the quality of her work and took an interest in her extravagant, free-flowing lines. Her years of apprenticeship thus came to an end, and she was given a free hand as the head of her own small section – a most unusual promotion.

Nutmeg went on to compile a magnificent record of accomplishment year after year. Her talent and energy attracted the interest of people not only within the company but throughout the industry. The world of fashion design was a closed world, but at the same time it was a fair one, a society ruled by competition. A designer's power was determined by one thing alone: the number of advance orders that came in for the clothing that he or she had designed. There was never any doubt about who had won and who had lost: the figures told the whole story. Nutmeg never felt that she was competing with anyone, but her record could not be denied.

She worked with total dedication until her late twenties. She met many people through her work, and several men showed an interest in her, but their relationships proved short and shallow. Nutmeg could never take a deep interest in living human beings. Her mind was filled with images of clothing, and a man's designs had a far more visceral impact on her than the man himself ever could.

When she turned twenty-seven, though, Nutmeg was introduced to a strange-looking man at an industry New Year's party. The man's features were regular enough, but his hair was a wild mass, and his nose and chin had the hard sharpness of stone tools. He looked more like some phony preacher than a designer of women's clothing. He was a year younger than Nutmeg, as thin as a wire, and had eyes of bottomless depth, from which he looked at people with an aggressive stare that seemed deliberately designed to make them feel uncomfortable. In his eyes, though, Nutmeg was able to see her own reflection. At the time, he was an unknown but up-and-coming designer, and the two were meeting for the first time. She had, of course, heard people talking about him. He had a unique talent, they said, but he was arrogant and egotistical and argumentative, liked by almost no one.

"We were two of a kind," she said. "Both born on the continent. He had also been repatriated after the war, in his case from Korea, stripped of possessions. His father had been a professional soldier, and they experienced serious poverty in the postwar years. His mother had died of typhus when he was very small, and I suppose that's what led to his strong interest in women's clothing. He did have talent, but he had no idea how to deal with people. Here he was, a designer of women's clothing, but when he came into a woman's presence, he would blush and behave crazily. In other words, we were both strays who had become separated from the herd."

They married the following year, 1963, and the child they gave birth to in the spring of the year after that (the year of the Tokyo Olympics) was Cinnamon. "His name *was* Cinnamon, wasn't it?" No sooner was

Cinnamon born than Nutmeg brought her mother into the house to take care of him. She herself had to work nonstop from morning till night and had no time to care for infants. Thus Cinnamon was more or less raised by his grandmother.

•

It was never clear to Nutmeg whether she had ever truly loved her husband as a man. She lacked any criterion by which to make such a judgment, and this was true for her husband also. What had brought them together was the power of a chance meeting and their shared passion for fashion design. Still, their first ten years together were fruitful for both. As soon as they were married, they left their respective companies and set up their own independent design studio in an apartment in a small, west-facing building just behind Aoyama Avenue. Poorly ventilated and lacking air-conditioning, the place was so hot in summer that the sweat would make their pencils slip from their grasps. The business did not go smoothly at first. Nutmeg and her husband both had an almost shocking lack of practical business sense, as a result of which they were easily duped by unscrupulous members of the industry, or they would fail to secure orders because they were ignorant of standard practice or would make obvious, simple mistakes. Their debts mounted to become so great that at one point it seemed the only solution would be to abscond. The breakthrough came when Nutmeg happened to meet a capable business manager who recognized their talent and could serve them with integrity. From that point on, the company developed so well that all their previous troubles began to seem like a bad dream. Their sales doubled each year until, by 1970, the little company they had started on a shoestring had become a miraculous success – so much so that it surprised even the arrogant, aloof young couple who had started it. They took on more staff, moved to a big building on the avenue, and opened their own shops in such fashionable neighbourhoods as the Ginza, Aoyama, and Shinjuku. Their original line of designer clothes often figured in the mass media and became widely known.

•

Once the company had reached a certain size, the way they divided work between themselves began to change. While designing and manufacturing clothes might be a creative process, it was also, unlike sculpting or novel writing, a business upon which the fortunes of many people depended. One could not simply stay at home and create whatever one liked. Someone would have to go out and present the company's "face" to the world. This need increased as the size of the company's transactions continued to grow. One of them would have to appear at parties and fashion shows to give little speeches and hobnob with the guests, and to be interviewed by the media. Nutmeg had no intention of taking on that role, and so her husband became the one to step forward. Just as poor at socializing as she was, he found the whole thing excruciating at first. He was unable to speak well in front of a lot of strangers, and would come home from each such event exhausted. After six months of this, however, he noticed that he was finding it less painful. He was still not much of a speaker, but people did not react to his brusque and awkward manner the way they had when he was young; now they seemed to be drawn to him. They took his curt style (which derived from his naturally introverted personality) as evidence not of arrogant aloofness but rather of a charming artistic temperament. He actually began to enjoy this new position in which he found himself, and before long he was being celebrated as a cultural hero of his time.

"You've probably heard his name," Nutmeg said. "But in fact, by then I was doing two-thirds of the design work myself. His bold, original ideas had taken off commercially, and he had already come up with more than enough of them to keep us going. It was my job to develop and expand them and give them form. No matter how large the company grew, we never hired other designers. Our support staff expanded, but the crucial part we did ourselves. All we wanted was to make the clothing we wanted to make, not worry about the people who would buy it. We did no market research or cost calculations or strategy planning. If we decided we wanted to make something a certain way, we designed it that way, used the best materials we could find, and took all the time we needed to make it. What other houses could do in two steps, we did in four. Where they used three yards of cloth, we used four. We personally inspected and passed every piece that left our shop. What didn't sell we disposed of. We sold nothing at discount. Our prices were on the high side, of course. Industry people thought we were crazy, but our clothing became a symbol of the era, along with Peter Max, Woodstock, Twiggy, *Easy Rider* and all that. We had so much fun designing clothes back then! We could do the wildest things, and our clients were right there with us. It was as if we had sprouted great big wings and could fly anywhere we liked."

•

Just as their business was getting into its stride, however, Nutmeg and her husband began to grow more distant. Even as they worked side by side, she would sense now and then that his heart was wandering somewhere far away. His eyes seemed to have lost that hungry gleam they once had. The violent streak that used to make him throw things now almost never surfaced. Instead, she would often find him staring off into space as if deep in thought. The two of them hardly ever talked outside the workplace, and the nights when he did not come home at all grew in number. Nutmeg sensed that he had several women in his life now, but this was not a source of pain for her. She thought of it as inevitable, because they had long since ceased having physical relations (mainly because Nutmeg had lost the desire for sex).

•

It was late in 1975, when Nutmeg was forty and Cinnamon eleven, that her husband was killed. His body was found in an Akasaka hotel room, slashed to bits. The maid found him when she used her pass key to enter the room for cleaning at 11 in the morning. The lavatory looked as if it had been the site of a blood bath. The body itself had been virtually drained dry, and it was missing its heart and stomach and liver and both kidneys and pancreas, as if whoever had killed him had cut those organs out and taken them somewhere in plastic bags or some such containers. The head had been severed from the torso and placed on the lid of the toilet, facing outward, the face chopped to mincemeat. The killer had apparently cut off and chopped up the head first, then set about collecting the organs.

To cut the organs out of a human being must have taken some exceptionally sharp implements and considerable technical skill. Several ribs had had to be cut through with a saw – a time-consuming and bloody operation. Nor was it clear why anyone would have gone to so much trouble.

Taken up with the holiday rush, the clerk at the front desk recalled only that Nutmeg's husband had checked into his twelfth-floor room at 10 o'clock the previous night with a woman – a pretty woman perhaps thirty years of age, wearing a red overcoat and not particularly tall. She had been carrying nothing more than a small purse. The bed showed signs of sexual activity. The hair and fluid recovered from the sheets were his pubic hair and semen. The room was full of fingerprints, but too many to be of use in the investigation. His small leather suitcase held only a change of underwear, a few toilet articles, a folder holding some work-related documents, and one magazine. More than one-hundred-thousand yen in cash and several credit cards remained in his wallet, but a note-book that he should have had was missing. There were no signs of a struggle in the room.

The police investigated all his known associates but could not come up with a woman who fit the hotel clerk's description. The few women they did find had no cause for deep-seated hatred or jealousy, and all had solid alibis. There were a good number of people who disliked him in the fashion world (not a world known for its warm, friendly atmosphere), but none who seemed to have hated him enough to kill him, and no one who would have had the technical training to cut six organs out of his body.

The murder of a well-known fashion designer was of course widely reported in the press, and with some sensationalism, but the police used a number of technicalities to suppress the information about the taking of the organs, in order to avoid the glare of publicity that would surround such a bizarre murder case. The prestigious hotel seems also to have exerted some pressure to keep its association with the affair to a mini-mum. Little more was released than the fact that he had been stabbed to death in one of their rooms. Rumours circulated for a while that there had been "something abnormal" involved, but nothing more specific ever emerged. The police conducted a massive investigation, but the killer was never caught, nor was a motive established.

"That hotel room is probably still sealed," said Nutmeg.

•

The spring of the year after her husband was killed, Nutmeg sold the company – complete with retail stores, inventory, and brand name – to a major fashion manufacturer. When the lawyer who had conducted the negotiations for her brought the contract, Nutmeg set her seal to it without a word and with hardly a glance at the sale price.

Once she had let the company go, Nutmeg discovered that all traces of her passion for designing clothes had evaporated. The intense stream of desire had dried up, where once it had been the meaning of her life. She would accept an occasional assignment and carry it off with all the skill of a first-rate professional, but without a trace of joy. It was like eating food that had no taste. She felt as if "they" had plucked out her own innards. Those who knew her former energy and skill remem-bered Nutmeg as a kind of legendary presence, and requests never ceased from such people, but apart from the very few that she could not refuse, she turned them down. Following the advice of her accountant, she invested her money in stocks and property, and her wealth expanded in those years of growth.

Not long after she sold the company, her mother died of heart disease. She was hosing the pavement outside the house on a hot August afternoon, when suddenly she complained she "felt bad". She lay down and slept, her snoring disturbingly loud, and soon she was dead. Nutmeg and Cinnamon were left alone in the world. Nutmeg closed herself up in the house for over a year, spending each day on the sofa, looking at the garden, as if trying to find all the peace and quiet that she had missed in her life thus far. Hardly eating, she would sleep ten hours a day. Cinnamon, who would normally have begun secondary school, took care of the house in his mother's stead, playing Mozart and Haydn sonatas between chores and studying several languages.

This nearly blank, quiet space in her life had gone on for a year when Nutmeg happened by chance to discover that she possessed a certain special "power", a strange ability of which she had no previous awareness. She imagined that it might have welled up inside her to replace the intense passion for design that had evaporated. And indeed, this power became her new profession, though it was not something she herself had sought out.

•

The first beneficiary of her strange power was the wife of a department store owner, a bright, energetic woman who had been an opera singer in her youth. She had recognized Nutmeg's talent long before she became a famous designer, and she had watched over her career. Without this woman's support, Nutmeg's company might have failed in its infancy. Because of their special relationship, Nutmeg agreed to help the woman and her daughter choose and coordinate their outfits for the daughter's wedding, a task that she did not find taxing.

Nutmeg and the woman were chatting as they waited for the daughter to be fitted when, without warning, the woman suddenly pressed her hands to her head and knelt down on the floor unsteadily. Nutmeg, horrified, grabbed her to keep her from falling and began stroking the woman's right temple. She did this by reflex, without thought, but no sooner had her palm started moving than she felt "a certain something" there, as if she were feeling an object inside a cloth bag.

Confused, Nutmeg closed her eyes and tried to think about something else. What came to her then was the zoo in Hsin-ching – the zoo on a day when it was closed and she was there all by herself, something only

478

she was permitted as the chief veterinary surgeon's daughter. That had been the happiest time of her life, when she was protected and loved and reassured. It was her earliest memory. The empty zoo. She thought of the smells and the brilliant light, and the shape of each cloud floating in the sky. She walked alone from cage to cage. The season was autumn, the sky high and clear, and flocks of Manchurian birds were winging from tree to tree. That had been her original world, a world that, in many senses, had been lost for ever. She did not know how much time passed during this reverie, but at last the woman raised herself to her full height and apologized to Nutmeg. She was still disoriented, but her headache seemed to have gone, she said. Some days later, Nutmeg was amazed to receive a far larger payment than she had anticipated for the job she had done.

The department store owner's wife called Nutmeg about a month later, inviting her out to lunch. After they had finished eating, she suggested that they go to her home, where she said to Nutmeg, "I wonder if you would mind putting your hand on my head the way you did before. There's something I want to check." Nutmeg had no particular reason to refuse. She sat next to the woman and placed her palm on the woman's temple. She could feel that same "something" she had felt before. To get a better sense of its shape, she concentrated all her attention on it, but the shape began to twist and change. *It's alive!* Nutmeg felt a twinge of fear. She closed her eyes and thought about the Hsin-ching zoo. This was not hard for her. All she had to do was bring to mind the story she had told Cinnamon and the scenes she had described for him. Her consciousness left her body, wandered for a while in the spaces between memory and story, then came back. When she regained consciousness, the woman took her hand and thanked her. Nutmeg asked nothing about what had just happened, and the woman offered no explanations. As before, Nutmeg felt a mild fatigue, and a light film of sweat clung to her forehead. When she left, the woman thanked her for taking the time and trouble to visit and tried to hand her an envelope containing money, but Nutmeg refused to take it – politely, but firmly. "This is not my job," she said, "and besides, you paid me too much last time." The woman did not insist.

Some weeks later, the woman introduced Nutmeg to another woman. This one was in her mid-forties. She was small and had sharp, sunken eyes. The clothing she wore was of exceptionally high quality, but apart from a silver wedding band, she wore no accessories. It was clear from the atmosphere she projected that she was no ordinary person. The department store owner's wife had told Nutmeg, "She wants you to do for her the same thing you did for me. Now, please don't refuse, and when she gives you money, don't say anything, just take it. In the long run, it will be an important thing for you – *and* for me."

Nutmeg went to an inner room with the woman and placed her palm on the woman's temple as she had done before. There was a different "something" inside this woman. It was stronger than the one inside the department store owner's wife, and its movements were more rapid. Nutmeg closed her eyes, held her breath, and tried to suppress the movement. She concentrated more strongly and pursued her memories with more tenacity. Burrowing into the tiniest folds she found there, she sent the warmth of her memories into the "something".

"And before I knew it, that had become my work," said Nutmeg. She realized that she had been enfolded by a great flow. And when he grew up, Cinnamon became his mother's assistant.

21

The Mystery of the Hanging House: 2

◆

SETAGAYA, TOKYO: THE PEOPLE OF THE HANGING HOUSE

Famous Politician's Shadow: Now You See It, Now You Don't

Amazing, Ingenious Cloak of Invisibility – What Secret Is It Hiding?

[From *The* ——— *Weekly*, November 21]

As first revealed in the October 7 issue of this magazine, there is a house in a quiet Setagaya residential neighbourhood known to locals as the "hanging house". All those who ever lived there have been visited by misfortune and ended their lives in suicide, the majority by hanging.

[Summary of earlier article omitted]

Our investigations have led us to only one solid fact: namely, that there is a brick wall standing at the end of every route we have taken in attempting to learn the identity of the new owner of the "hanging house". We managed to find the construction company that built the house, but all attempts to get information from them were rejected. The dummy company through which the land was purchased is legally 100% clean and offers no opening. The whole deal was set up with such ingenious attention to detail, we can only assume there was some reason for the fact.

One other thing that aroused our curiosity was the accounting firm that assisted in setting up the dummy company that bought the land. Our investigations have shown that the firm was established five years ago as a kind of shadow "subcontractor" to an accounting firm well known in political circles. The prominent accounting firm has several of these "subcontractors", each designed to handle a particular kind of job and to be dropped like a lizard's tail in case of trouble. The accounting firm itself has never been investigated by the Prosecutor's Office, but according to a political reporter for a certain major newspaper, "Its name has come up in any number of political scandals, so of course the authorities have their eye on it." It's not hard to guess, then, that there is some kind of connection between the new resident of the "hanging house" and some powerful politician. The high walls, the tight security using the latest electronic equipment, the leased black Mercedes, the cleverly set-up dummy company: this kind of know-how suggests to us the involvement of a major political figure.

Total Secrecy

Our news team did a survey of the movements into and out of the "hanging house" by the black Mercedes. In one ten-day period, the car made a total of twenty-one visits to the house, or approximately two visits per day. They observed a regular pattern to these visits. First, the car would show up at 9 o'clock in the morning and leave at 10.30. The driver was very punctual, with no more than five minutes' variation from day to day. In contrast to the predictability of these morning visits, however, the others were highly irregular. Most were recorded to have occurred between 1 and 3 in the afternoon, but the times in and out varied considerably. There was also considerable variation in the length of time the car would remain parked in the compound, from under twenty minutes to a full hour.

These facts have led us to the following suppositions:

1. The car's regular a.m. visits: These suggest that someone is "commuting" to this house. The identity of the "commuter" is unclear, however, owing to the black tinted glass used all around the car.

2. The car's irregular p.m. visits: These suggest the arrival of guests and are probably tailored to the guests' convenience. Whether these "guests" arrive singly or with others is unclear.

3. There seems to be no activity in the house at night. It is also unclear whether or not anyone lives there. From outside the property, it is impossible to tell if any lights are being used.

One more important point: the only thing to enter or leave the property during our ten-day survey was the black Mercedes. No other cars, no people on foot. Common sense tells us that something strange is going on here. The "someone" living in the house never goes out to shop or to go for a walk. People arrive and depart exclusively in the large Mercedes with tinted windows. In other words, *for some reason, they do not want their faces seen, under any circumstances.* What could be the reason for this? Why must they go to so much trouble and expense in order to do what they do in total secrecy?

We might add here that the front gate is the only way in and out of the property. A narrow alley runs behind the lot, but this leads nowhere. The only way into or out of this alley is through private property. According to the neighbours, none of the residents is presently using the alley, which is no doubt why the house has no gate to the back alley. The only thing there is the towering wall, like huge castle ramparts.

Several times during the ten days, the button on the intercom at the front gate was pushed by people who appeared to be newspaper canvassers or salesmen, but with no response whatever. If there was anyone inside, it is conceivable that a closed-circuit video camera was being used to screen visitors. There were no deliveries of mail or visits by any of the express services.

For these reasons, the only investigative route left open to us was to tail the Mercedes and determine its destination. Following the shiny, slow-moving car through city traffic was not difficult, but we could get only as far as

the entrance to the underground parking lot of a five-star Akasaka hotel. A uniformed guard was stationed there, and the only way in was with a special pass card, so our car was unable to follow the Mercedes inside. This particular hotel is the site of numerous international conferences, which means that many VIPs stay there, as do many famous entertainers from abroad. To ensure their security and privacy, the VIP car park is separate from that for ordinary guests, and several lifts have been reserved for VIPs' exclusive use, with no external indicators of their movement. This makes it possible for these special guests to check in and out unobtrusively. The Mercedes is apparently parked in one of the VIP spaces. According to the hotel management's brief and measured response to this magazine's inquiries, these special spaces are "ordinarily" leased at a special rate only to uniquely qualified corporate entities after a "thorough-going background check", but we were unable to obtain any detailed information on either the conditions of use or the users themselves.

The hotel has a shopping arcade, several cafés and restaurants, four wedding halls, and three conference halls, which means that it is in use day and night by large numbers of a wide variety of people. To determine the identities of the passengers in the Mercedes would be impossible without special authority. People could alight from the car, take one of the nearby exclusive elevators, get off at any floor they liked, and blend in with the crowd. It should be clear from all this that a system for maintaining absolute secrecy is solidly in place. We can glimpse here an almost excessive use of money and political power. As can be seen from the hotel management's explanation, it is no easy matter to lease and use one of these VIP parking spaces. Central to the need for "thoroughgoing background checks", no doubt, are the plans of security authorities charged with the protection of foreign dignitaries, which means that some political connections would have to be involved. Just having a lot of money would not be enough, though it goes without saying that all of this would take quite a lot of money.

[Omitted here: conjectures that the property is being used by a religious organization with the backing of a powerful politician]

22

Jellyfish from All Around the World

•

Things Metamorphosed

I sit down in front of Cinnamon's computer at the appointed time and use the password to access the communications programme. Then I input the numbers I've been given by Ushikawa. It will take five minutes for the circuits to connect. I start sipping the coffee I have prepared and concentrate on steadying my breathing. The coffee is tasteless, though, and the air I inhale has a harsh edge to it.

The computer beeps and a message appears on the screen, informing me that the connection has been made and the computer is ready for two-way communication. I specify that the charge for this call is to be reversed. If I am careful to prevent a record of this transaction from being made, I should be able to keep Cinnamon from finding out that I used the computer (though of this I am anything but confident: this is *his* labyrinth; I am nothing but a powerless stranger here).

A far longer time goes by than I had anticipated, but eventually the message appears that the other party has accepted the charges. Beyond this screen, at the far end of the cable that creeps through Tokyo's underground darkness, may be Kumiko. She, too, might be sitting before a monitor, with her hands on a keyboard. In reality, all I can see is my monitor, which sits there making a faint electronic squeal. I click on the box to select Send mode and type the words that I have been rehearsing over and over in my brain.

>I have one question for you. It's not much
of a question, but I need proof that it's really you out there. Here it is: The first time
we went out together, long before we were married, we went to the aquarium. I want you to
tell me what you were most fascinated to see
there.

I click on the symbol for sending the text (I want you to
tell me what you were most fascinated to see
there.↵). Then I switch to Receive mode.

The answer comes back after a short, silent interval. It is a short
answer.

>Jellyfish. Jellyfish from all around the
world.↵

My question and the answer to it are lined up on the upper and lower
halves of the screen. I stare at them for a while. Jellyfish from
all around the world.↵ It has to be Kumiko. The real Kumiko.
That very fact, though, serves only to fill me with pain. I feel as if my insides are being ripped out. *Why is this the only way that the two of us can talk
to each other?* I have no choice now but to accept it, though. And so I begin
typing.

>Let me start with the good news. The cat
came back this spring. All of a sudden. He was
a bit emaciated, but he was healthy and unharmed. He's stayed at home ever since. I know
I should have consulted you before I did this,
but I gave him a new name. Mackerel. Like the
fish. We're getting along together just fine.
This is good news, I guess.↵

A delay follows. I can't tell whether it is due to the time lag inherent
in this form of communication or a silence on Kumiko's part.

>I'm so happy to hear the cat is still
alive! I was worried about him.↵

I take a sip of coffee to moisten my mouth by now dry. Then I start
typing again.

>Now for the bad news. Actually, apart from
the fact that the cat is back, it seems that
everything else is going to be bad news. First
of all, I still haven't been able to solve any
riddles.

I reread what I have written, then continue to type.

First riddle: Where are you now? What are you doing there? Why do you continue to stay away from me? Why don't you want to see me? Is there some reason? I mean, there are so many things that you and I have to talk about face to face. Don't you think so?

It takes her some time to reply to this. I imagine her sitting in front of the keyboard, biting her lip and thinking. Finally, the cursor begins to dart across the screen in response to the movement of her fingers.

>Everything I wanted to say to you I wrote in the letter I sent. What I most want you to understand is that, in many ways, I am no longer the Kumiko you knew. People change for all sorts of reasons, and in some cases the transformation makes them go bad. That is why I don't want to see you. And that is why I don't want to come back to you.

The cursor halts and remains blinking in one place, searching for words. I keep my eyes fixed on it for ten seconds, twenty seconds, waiting for it to form new words on the screen. *The transformation makes them go bad?*

If possible, I would like you to forget about me as soon as you can. The best thing for both of us would be if you were to complete the formalities of our divorce and begin a whole new life. It doesn't matter where I am now or what I am doing. The most important thing is that, for whatever reason, you and I have already been separated into two entirely different worlds. And there is no way we can ever go back to being what we were. Please try to understand how painful it is for me to be communicating with you like this. You can't imagine how it tears me apart.

I reread Kumiko's words several times. I find in them no sign of hesitation, no suggestion that they come from anything but the deepest, most painful conviction. She has probably rehearsed them in her mind any number of times. But still, I have to find a way to shake this impenetrable wall of hers, if only to make it tremble. I go back to the keyboard.

>What you say is a little vague and diffi-
cult for me to grasp. You say you've gone
bad, but what exactly does that mean? I just
don't understand. Tomatoes go bad. Umbrellas
go bad. That I can understand. Tomatoes rot
and umbrellas get bent out of shape. But what
does it mean to say that you have "gone
bad"? It doesn't give me any clear image.
You said in your letter that you had sex
with somebody other than me, but could that
make you "go bad"? Yes, of course it was
a shock to me. But that is a little different
from making a human being "go bad", I would
say.↵

A long pause follows. I begin to worry that Kumiko has disappeared
somewhere. But then her letters begin to line up on the screen.

>You may be right, but there is more to it
than that.

Another silence follows. She is choosing her words with care, as if
pulling them out of a drawer.

That is just one manifestation. "Going bad"
is something that happens over a longer period
of time. It was something decided in advance,
without me, in a pitch-dark room, by someone
else. When I met and married you, it seemed to
me that I had a whole new set of possibilities. I hoped that I might be able to
escape through an opening somewhere. But it
seems that was just an illusion. There are
signs for everything, which is why I tried so
hard to find our cat when he disappeared that
time.

I keep staring at the message on the screen, but still no Send mark
appears. My own machine is still set to Receive. Kumiko is thinking
about what to write next. *"Going bad" is something that happens over a longer
period of time.* What is she trying to tell me? I concentrate my attention on
the screen, but all I find there is a kind of invisible wall. Once more the
letters begin to line up on the screen.

I want you to think about me this way if you
can: that I am slowly dying of an incurable

disease — one that causes my face and body to disintegrate little by little. This is just a metaphor, of course. My face and body are not disintegrating. But this is something very close to the truth. And that is why I don't want to show myself to you. I know that a vague metaphor like this is not going to help you understand everything about the situation in which I find myself. I don't expect it to convince you of the truth of what I am saying. I feel terrible about this, but there is simply nothing more I can say. All you can do is accept it.↵

An incurable disease.

I check to be sure that I am in the Send mode and start typing.

>If you say you want me to accept your metaphor, I don't mind accepting it. But there is one thing that I just cannot understand. Even supposing that you have, as you say, "gone bad" and that you have "an incurable disease", why of all people did you have to go to Noboru Wataya with it? Why didn't you stay here with me? Why aren't we together? Isn't that what we got married for?↵

Silence. I can almost feel its weight and hardness in my hands. I fold my hands on the desk and take several deep breaths. Then the answer comes.

>The reason I am here, like it or not, is because this is the proper place for me. This is where I have to be. I have no right to choose otherwise. Even if I wanted to see you, I couldn't do it. Do you think I DON'T want to see you?

There is a blank moment in which she seems to be holding her breath. Then her fingers start to move again.

So please, don't torture me about this any longer. If there is any one thing that you can do for me, it would be to forget about my existence as quickly as possible. Take those years that we lived together and wipe them from your memory as if they never existed. That, finally, is the best thing you can do for both of us. This is what I truly believe.↵

To this I reply:

>You say you want me to forget everything. You say you want me to leave you alone. But still, at the same time, from somewhere in this world, you are begging for my help. That voice is faint and distant, but I can hear it distinctly on quiet nights. It IS your voice: I'm sure of that. I can accept the fact that one Kumiko is trying hard to get away from me, and she probably has her reasons for doing so. But there is another Kumiko, who is trying just as hard to get close to me. That is what I truly believe. No matter what you may say to me here, I have to believe in the Kumiko who wants my help and is trying to get close to me. No matter what you tell me, no matter how legitimate your reasons, I can never just forget about you, I can never push the years we spent together out of my mind. I can't do it because they really happened, they are part of my life, and there is no way I can just erase them. That would be the same as erasing my own self. I have to know what legitimate reason there could be for doing such a thing.↵

Another blank period goes by. I can feel her silence through the monitor. Like heavy smoke, it creeps in through a corner of the screen and drifts across the floor. I know about these silences of Kumiko's. I've seen them, experienced them any number of times in our life together. She's holding her breath now, sitting in front of the computer screen with brows knit in total concentration. I reach out for my cup and take a sip of cold coffee. Then, with the empty cup between my hands, I hold my breath and stare at the screen the way Kumiko is doing. The two of us are linked together by the heavy bonds of silence that pass through the wall separating our two worlds. We need each other more than anything, I feel without a doubt.

>I don't know.↵

>Well, I DO know.

I set my coffee cup down and type as quickly as I can, as if to catch the fleeting tail of time.

I know this. I know that I want to find my way to where you are—you, the Kumiko who wants me to rescue her. What I do not know yet, unfortunately, is how to get there and what it is that's waiting for me there. In this whole long time since you left, I've lived with a feeling of having been thrown into absolute darkness. Slowly but surely, though, I am getting closer to the core, to that place where the core of things is located. I wanted to let you know that. I'm getting closer to where you are, and I intend to get closer still.↵

I rest my hands on the keyboard and wait for her answer.

>I don't understand any of this.

Kumiko types this and ends our conversation:

Goodbye.↵↵↵

•

The screen informs me that the other party has left the circuit. Our conversation is finished. Still, I go on staring at the screen, waiting for something to happen. Maybe Kumiko will change her mind and come back on-line. Maybe she'll think of something she forgot to say. But she does not come back. I give up after twenty minutes. I save the file, then go to the kitchen for a drink of cold water. I empty my mind for a while, breathing steadily by the refrigerator. A terrible quiet seems to have descended on everything. I feel as if the world is listening for my next thought. But I can't think of anything. Sorry, but I just can't think of anything.

I go back to the computer and sit there, carefully rereading our entire exchange on the glowing tube from beginning to end: what I said, what she said, what I said to that, what she said to that. The whole thing is still there on the screen, with graphic intensity. As my eyes follow the rows of characters she has made, I can hear her voice. I can recognize its rise and fall, the subtle tones and pauses. The cursor on the last line keeps up its blinking with all the regularity of a heartbeat, waiting with bated breath for the next word to be sent. But there is no next word.

After engraving the entire conversation in my mind (having decided I had better not print it out), I click on the box to exit communications mode. I direct the programme to leave no record in the operations file, and I cut the switch. The computer beeps, and the monitor goes dead white. The monotonous mechanical drone is swallowed up in the silence of the room, like a vivid dream ripped out by the hand of nothingness.

·

I don't know how much time has gone by since then. But when I realize where I am, I find myself staring at my hands lying on the table. They bear the marks of having had eyes sharply focused on them for a long time.

"Going bad" is something that happens over a longer period of time.

How long a period of time is that?

23

Counting Sheep

•

The Thing in the Centre of the Circle

A few days after Ushikawa's first visit, I asked Cinnamon to bring me a newspaper whenever he came to the Residence. It was time for me to start getting in touch with the reality of the outside world. Try as you might to avoid it, when it was time, they came for you.

Cinnamon nodded, and every day after that he would arrive with three newspapers.

I would look through the papers after breakfast. I had not bothered with newspapers for such a long time that they now struck me as strange – cold and empty. The stimulating smell of the ink gave me a headache, and the intensely black little gangs of type seemed to stab at my eyes. The layout and the headlines' type style and the tone of the writing seemed unreal to me. I often had to put the paper down, close my eyes, and release a sigh. It couldn't have been like this in the old days. Reading a newspaper must have been a far more ordinary experience than this. What had changed so much about them? Or rather, what had changed so much about *me*?

After I had been reading the papers for a while, I was able to achieve a clear understanding of one fact concerning Noboru Wataya: that he was constructing an ever more solid position for himself in society. At the same time that he was conducting an ambitious programme of political activity as one of the up-and-coming new members of the House of Representatives, he was also making constant public pronouncements as a magazine columnist and a commentator on TV. I would see his name everywhere. For some reason I could not fathom, people were listening to his opinions – and with ever-increasing enthusiasm. He was a new-comer to the political stage, but he was already being celebrated as one of the young politicians from whom great things could be expected. He was named the country's most popular politician in a poll conducted by a women's magazine. He was hailed as an activist intellectual, a new type of intelligent politician that had not been seen before.

When I had read as much as I could stand about current events and Noboru Wataya's prominent place in them, I turned to my growing collection of books on Manchukuo. Cinnamon had been bringing me everything he could find on the subject. Even here, though, I could not escape the shadow of Noboru Wataya. That day it emerged from the pages of a book on logistical problems. Published in 1978, the library copy had been borrowed only once before, when the book was new, and returned almost immediately. Perhaps only acquaintances of Lieutenant Mamiya were interested in logistical problems in Manchukuo.

As early as 1920, according to the author, Japan's imperial army was looking into the possibility of amassing a huge stock of winter survival gear in anticipation of all-out war with the Soviets. Equipping the army to fight in bitter cold was viewed as an urgent matter because they lacked the experience of having fought a real battle anywhere with such extreme winter cold as Siberia. If a border dispute led to a sudden declaration of war against the Soviet Union (which was by no means out of the question in those days), the army would be unprepared for a winter campaign. For this reason, a research team was established within the General Staff Office to prepare to fight a hypothetical war with the Soviet Union, the logistics section being charged with investigating the procurement of special winter clothing. In order to grasp what real cold was like, they went to the far northern island of Sakhalin, long a point of dispute with Tzarist Russia and then the Soviet Union, and used an actual fighting unit to test insulated boots and coats and under-wear. They ran thorough tests on equipment then in use by the Soviet Army and on the kind of clothing that Napoleon's army had used in its Russian campaign, reaching the conclusion that it would be impossible for the Japanese Army to survive a winter in Siberia with its present equipment. They estimated that some two-thirds of the foot soldiers on the front lines would be put out of commission by frostbite. The army's current survival gear had been manufactured with the gentler northern China winters in mind, and in addition there were too few kits to go round. The research team calculated the number of sheep necessary to manufacture sufficient effective winter clothing to outfit ten divisions (the joke making the rounds of the team then being that they were too busy counting sheep to sleep), and they submitted this in their report, along with estimates of the mechanical equipment that would be needed to process the wool.

The number of sheep on the Japanese home islands was insufficient for fighting an extended war in the northern territories against the Soviet Army in the event of economic sanctions or blockade against Japan, and thus it was imperative that Japan secure both a stable supply of wool (and of rabbit and other pelts) in the Manchuria-Mongolia region and the mechanical equipment for processing it, said the report. The man dispatched to make on-the-spot observations in Manchukuo in 1932, immediately after the founding of the puppet regime there, was a young technocrat newly graduated from the Military Staff College with a degree in logistics; his name was Yoshitaka Wataya.

Yoshitaka Wataya! This could only have been Noboru's uncle. There weren't that many Watayas in the world, and the name Yoshitaka was the clincher.

His mission was to calculate the time that would be needed before stable supplies of wool could be secured in Manchukuo. Yoshitaka Wataya seized upon this problem of cold-weather clothing as a model case for modern logistics and carried out an exhaustive numerical analysis.

When he was in Mukden, Yoshitaka Wataya sought an introduction to – and spent the entire night drinking and talking with – Lieutenant General Kanji Ishiwara.

Kanji Ishiwara. Another name I knew well. Noboru Wataya's uncle had been in touch with Kanji Ishiwara, the ringleader the year before of the staged Chinese attack on Japanese troops known as the "Manchurian Incident", the event that had enabled Japan to turn Manchuria into Manchukuo – and that later would prove to have been the first aggressive act in fifteen years of war.

Ishiwara had toured the continent and become convinced not only that all-out war with the Soviet Union was inevitable but that the key to winning that war lay in strengthening Japan's logistical position by rapidly industrializing the new empire of Manchukuo and establishing a self-sufficient economy. He presented his case to Yoshitaka Wataya with eloquence and passion. He argued, too, for the importance of bringing farmers from Japan to systematize Manchukuo's farming and cattle industries and to increase their efficiency.

Ishiwara was of the opinion that Japan should not turn Manchukuo into another undisguised Japanese colony, such as Korea or Taiwan, and should instead make Manchukuo a new model Asian nation. In his recognition that Manchukuo would serve as a logistical base for war against the Soviet Union – and even against the United States and England – Ishiwara was, however, admirably realistic. He believed that Japan was now the only Asian nation capable of fighting the coming war against the West (or, as he called it, the "Final War") and that the other countries had the duty to cooperate with Japan to secure their own liberation from the West. No other officer in the Imperial Army at that time had Ishiwara's profound interest in logistics combined with his great erudition. Most other Japanese officers dismissed logistics as an "effeminate" discipline, believing instead that the proper "way" for "his majesty's warriors" was to fight with bold self-abandonment no matter how ill-equipped they might be; that true martial glory lay in conquering a mighty foe when outnumbered and poorly armed. Strike the enemy and advance "too swiftly for supplies to keep up": that was the path of honour.

To Yoshitaka Wataya, the compleat technocrat, this was utter nonsense. Starting a long-term war without logistical backing was tantamount to suicide, in his view. The Soviets had vastly expanded and modernized their military capability through Stalin's five-year plan of intensive economic development. The five bloody years of the First World War had destroyed the old world's values, and mechanized war had revolutionized European thinking with regard to strategy and logistics. Having been stationed for two years in Berlin, Yoshitaka Wataya felt the truth of this in every bone of his body, but the mentality of the greater part of Japan's military men had not outgrown the intoxication of their victory in the Russo-Japanese War, nearly thirty years before.

Yoshitaka Wataya went home to Japan a devoted admirer of Ishiwara's arguments, his worldview, and the charismatic personality of the man himself, and their close relationship lasted many years. He often went to visit Ishiwara, even after the distinguished officer had been brought back from Manchuria to take command of the isolated fortress in Maizuru. Yoshitaka Wataya's precise and meticulous report on sheep farming and wool processing in Manchukuo was submitted to headquarters shortly after he returned to Japan, and it received high praise. With Japan's painful defeat in the 1939 battle of Nomonhan, however, and the strengthening of US and British economic sanctions, the military began to shift its attention southward, and the activities of the research team waging hypothetical war against the Soviet Union were allowed to peter out. Of course, one factor behind the decision to finish off the battle of Nomonhan quickly in early autumn and not allow it to develop into a full-scale war was the research team's conclusive report that "we are unable to wage a winter campaign against the Soviet Army given our current state of preparedness". As soon as the autumn winds began to blow, Imperial Headquarters, in a move unusual for the normally face-obsessed Japanese Army, washed its hands of the fighting and, through diplomatic negotiations, ceded the barren Hulunbuir Steppe to Outer Mongolian and Soviet troops.

In a footnote, the author pointed out that Yoshitaka Wataya had been banned from holding public office by MacArthur's Occupation after the war and for a time had lived in seclusion in his native Niigata, but he had been persuaded by the Conservative Party to run for office after the ban was lifted and served two terms in the Upper House before transferring to the Lower House. A calligraphic scroll of Kanji Ishiwara's hung on the wall of his office.

I had no idea what kind of Diet member Noboru Wataya's uncle had been or what he had accomplished as a politician. He did serve as a cabinet minister once, and he seems to have been highly influential with the people of his district, but he never became a leader in national politics. Now his political constituency had been inherited by his nephew, Noboru Wataya.

•

I put the book away and, folding my arms behind my head, stared out the window in the vague direction of the front gate. Soon the gate would open inwards and the Mercedes-Benz would appear, with Cinnamon at the wheel. He would be bringing another "client". These "clients" and I were linked by the mark on my cheek. Cinnamon's grandfather (Nutmeg's father) and I were also linked by the mark on my cheek. Cinnamon's grandfather and Lieutenant Mamiya were linked by the city of Hsin-ching. Lieutenant Mamiya and the clairvoyant Mr Honda were linked by their special duties on the Manchurian-Mongolian border, and Kumiko and I had been introduced to Mr Honda by Noboru Wataya's family. Lieutenant

Mamiya and I were linked by our experiences in our respective wells – his in Mongolia, mine on the property where I was now sitting. Also on this property had once lived an army officer who had commanded troops in China. All of these were linked as in a circle, at the centre of which stood prewar Manchuria, continental East Asia, and the short war of 1939 in Nomonhan. But why Kumiko and I should have been drawn into this historical chain of cause and effect I could not comprehend. All of these events had occurred long before Kumiko and I were born.

I sat at Cinnamon's desk and placed my hands on the keyboard. The feel of my fingers on the keys was still fresh from my conversation with Kumiko. That computer conversation had been monitored by Noboru Wataya, I was sure. He was trying to learn something from it. He certainly hadn't arranged for us to make contact that way out of the goodness of his heart. He and his men were almost certainly trying to use the access they had gained to Cinnamon's computer through the communications link to learn the secrets of this place. But I was not worried about that. The depths of this computer were the very depths of Cinnamon himself. And they had no way of knowing how incalculably deep that was.

24

The Signal Turns Red

◆

The Long Arm Reaches Out

Cinnamon was not alone when he arrived at 9 o'clock the next morning. Beside him in the passenger seat was his mother, Nutmeg Akasaka. She had not been here for over a month. She had arrived with Cinnamon unannounced that time too, had breakfast with me, and left after an hour or so of small talk.

Cinnamon hung up his jacket and, while listening to a Handel Concerto Grosso (for the third day in a row), he went to the kitchen to make tea and toast for his mother, who had not yet eaten breakfast. He always made perfect toast, like something out of a commercial. Then, while Cinnamon straightened up the kitchen as usual, Nutmeg and I sat at a small table, drinking tea. She ate only one slice of toast, with a little butter. Outside, a cold, sleety rain was falling. Nutmeg said little, and I said little – a few remarks about the weather. She seemed to have something she wanted to say, though. That much was clear from the look on her face and the way she spoke. She tore off stamp-sized pieces of toast and transported them, one at a time, to her mouth. We looked out at the rain now and then, as if it were our longtime mutual friend.

When Cinnamon had finished with the kitchen and started his cleaning, Nutmeg led me to the "fitting room". This one had been made to look exactly like the "fitting room" in the Akasaka office. The size and shape were almost identical. The window here also had two layers of curtains and was gloomy even during the day. The curtains were never open more than ten minutes at a time, while Cinnamon was cleaning the room. There was a leather sofa here, a glass vase, with flowers, on the table, and a tall floor lamp. In the middle of the room stood a large workbench, on which lay a pair of scissors, scraps of cloth, a wooden box stuffed with needles and thread, pencils, a design book (in which a few design sketches had been drawn), and several professional tools, the names and purposes of which I did not know. A large full-length mirror hung on the wall, and one corner of the room was partitioned off by a screen for changing. The clients who visited the Residence were always shown to this room.

Why Cinnamon and his mother had felt the need to make an exact reproduction of the original "fitting room" I had no idea. Here there was no need for such camouflage. Maybe they (and their clients) had become so accustomed to the look of the room in the Akasaka office that they were unable to come up with any new ideas for decorating this place. Of course, they could just as well ask, "What's wrong with a fitting room?" Whatever the reason for having it, I myself was pleased with it. It was the "fitting room", not any other room, and I felt a strange sense of security there, surrounded by all kinds of dressmaking tools. It was an unreal setting, but not an unnatural one.

Nutmeg bid me sit on the leather sofa and sat down next to me.

"So. How are you feeling?" she asked.

"Not bad," I answered.

Nutmeg was wearing a bright-green suit. The skirt was short, and the large hexagonal buttons came up to the throat like one of those old Nehru jackets. The shoulders had pads the size of bread rolls. The look reminded me of a science fiction movie I had seen a long time ago, set in the near future. Almost all the women in the movie wore suits like this and lived in a futuristic city.

Nutmeg's earrings were large plastic things the exact colour of her suit. They were a unique deep green that seemed to have been made from a combination of several colours, and had probably been ordered specially to match the suit. Or perhaps the opposite was true: the suit had been made to match the earrings – like making a niche in the wall the exact shape of a refrigerator. Maybe not a bad way to look at things, I thought. She had arrived wearing sunglasses, in spite of the rain, and their lenses had almost certainly been green. Her stockings were green too. Today was obviously green day.

With her usual series of smooth linked movements, Nutmeg drew a cigarette from her bag, put it in her mouth, and lit it with her cigarette lighter, curling her lip just a little. The lighter, at least, was not green but the expensive-looking slim gold one she always used. It did go very well with the green, though. Nutmeg then crossed her green-stockinged legs. Checking her knees, she adjusted her skirt. Then, as if it were an extension of her knees, she looked at my face.

"Not bad," I said again. "The same as always."

Nutmeg nodded. "You're not tired? You don't feel as if you need some rest?"

"No, not especially. I think I've become used to the work. It's a lot easier now than it was at first."

Nutmeg said nothing to that. The smoke of her cigarette rose straight up like an Indian fakir's magic rope, to be sucked in by the ceiling ventilator. As far as I knew, this ventilator was the world's quietest and most powerful.

"How are *you* doing?" I asked.

"Me?"

"Are *you* tired?"

Nutmeg looked at me. "Do I look tired?"

She had in fact looked tired to me from the moment our eyes first met. When I told her this, she gave a short sigh.

"There was another article about this place in a magazine that came out this morning – part of the 'Mystery of the Hanging House' series. Sounds like the title of a horror movie."

"That's the second one, isn't it?" I said.

"It certainly is," said Nutmeg. "And in fact, another magazine carried a related article not too long ago, but fortunately no one seems to have noticed the connection. *So far.*"

"Did something new come out? About us?"

She reached for an ashtray and stubbed out her cigarette. Then she gave her head a little shake. Her green earrings fluttered like butterflies in early spring.

"Not really," she said, then paused. "Who we are, what we're doing here: no one knows yet. I'll leave you a copy, so you can read it if you're interested. But what I'd really like to ask you about is something that somebody whispered to me the other day: that you have a brother-in-law who's a famous young politician. Is it true?"

"Unfortunately, it is," I said. "My wife's brother."

"Meaning the brother of the wife who is no longer with you?"

"That's right."

"I wonder if he's caught wind of what you're doing here?"

"He knows I come here every day and that I'm doing *something*. He hired somebody to investigate for him. I think he was worried about what I might be doing. But I don't think he's found out anything yet."

Nutmeg thought about my answer for a while. Then she raised her face to mine and asked, "You don't like this brother-in-law of yours very much, do you?"

"Not very much, no."

"And he doesn't like you."

"To put it mildly."

"And now he's worried about what you're doing here. Why is that?"

"If it comes out that his brother-in-law is involved in something suspicious, it could turn into a scandal for him. He's the man of the moment, after all. I suppose it's natural that he would worry about such things."

"So he couldn't be the one leaking information about this place to the mass media, then, could he?"

"To be quite honest, I don't know what Noboru Wataya has in mind. But common sense tells me he'd have nothing to gain by leaking things to the press. He'd be more likely to want to keep things under wraps."

For a long time, Nutmeg went on turning the slim gold lighter in her fingers. It looked like a gold windmill on a day with little wind.

"Why haven't you said anything to us about this brother-in-law of yours?" Nutmeg asked.

"It isn't just you. I try not to mention him to anybody," I said. "We haven't liked each other from the start, and now we practically hate each other. I wasn't hiding him from you. I just didn't think there was any need to bring up the subject."

Nutmeg sighed. "You should have told us."

"Maybe I should have," I said.

"I'm sure you can imagine what's involved here. We have clients coming to us from politics and business. *Powerful* people. And *famous* people. Their privacy *has* to be protected. That's why we've taken such extreme precautions. You know that much."

I nodded.

"Cinnamon has gone to a lot of time and trouble to put together the precise and complicated system we have for maintaining our secrecy – a labyrinth of dummy companies, accounts hidden under layers of camouflage, an anonymous parking space in that hotel in Akasaka, stringent management of the clientele, control of income and expenses, design of this house: his mind gave birth to all of this. Until now, the system has worked almost perfectly in accordance with his calculations. Of course, it takes a lot of money to support such a system, but money is no problem for us. The important thing is that the women who come to us can feel secure that they will be protected *absolutely*."

"What you're saying is that that security is being undermined."

"Yes, unfortunately."

Nutmeg picked up a box of cigarettes and took one out, but held it for a long time between her fingers without lighting it.

"And to make matters worse, I have this famous politician for a brother-in-law, which only increases the possibility of scandal."

"Exactly," said Nutmeg, curling her lip.

"So what is Cinnamon's analysis of the situation?"

"He's not saying anything. Like a big oyster on the bottom of the sea. He has burrowed inside himself and locked the door, and he's doing some serious thinking."

Nutmeg's eyes were fixed on mine. At last, as though recalling that it was there in her hand, she lit her cigarette. Then she said, "I still think about it a lot – about my husband and the way he was killed. Why did they have to murder him? Why did they have to smear the hotel room with blood and tear out his insides and take them away? I can't think of any reason for doing such a thing. My husband was not the kind of person who had to be killed in such an unusual way.

"But my husband's death is not the only thing. All these inexplicable events that have occurred in my life so far – the intense passion that welled up inside me for fashion design and the way it disappeared all of a sudden; the way Cinnamon stopped speaking; the way I became swept up in this strange work we do – it's as though they were all ingeniously programmed from the start for the very purpose of bringing me here, where I am today. It's a thought I can't seem to shake off. I feel as if my every move is being controlled by some kind of long arm that's reaching out from somewhere far away, and that my life has been nothing more than a convenient passageway for all these things moving through it."

The faint sounds of Cinnamon's vacuuming came from the next room. He was performing his tasks in his usual concentrated, systematic manner.

"Haven't you ever felt that way?" Nutmeg asked me.

"I don't feel that I've been 'swept up' in anything," I said. "I'm here now because it was necessary for me to be here."

"So you could blow the magic flute and find Kumiko?"

"That's right."

"You have something you're searching for," she said, slowly recrossing her green-stockinged legs. "And everything has its price."

I remained silent.

Then, at last, Nutmeg announced her conclusion: "We've decided not to bring any clients here for a while. It was Cinnamon's decision. Because of the magazine articles and your brother-in-law's appearance on the scene, the signal has changed from yellow to red. Yesterday we cancelled all remaining appointments, beginning with today's."

"How long will 'a while' be?"

"Until Cinnamon can patch the holes in the system and we can be sure that any crisis has been completely bypassed. Sorry, but we don't want to take any chances – none at all. Cinnamon will come here every day, as he always has, but there will be no more clients."

.

By the time Cinnamon and Nutmeg left, the morning rain had cleared. Half a dozen sparrows were washing their feathers in a puddle in the driveway. When Cinnamon's Mercedes disappeared and the automatic gate closed, I sat at the window, looking at the cloudy winter sky beyond the tree branches. Nutmeg's words came to mind: "some kind of long arm that's reaching out from somewhere far away." I imagined the arm reaching down from the dark, low-hanging clouds – like an illustration from a sinister picture book.

25

Triangular Ears

•

Sleigh Bells

I spent the rest of the day reading about Manchukuo. There was no need for me to hurry back home. Thinking I might be late, I had given Mackerel two days' worth of dried cat food when I left in the morning. He might not like it much, but at least he wouldn't starve. This made the thought of dragging myself home that much less appealing. I wanted to lie down and take a nap. I took a blanket and pillow from a cabinet, spread them on the sofa in the fitting room, and turned out the light. Then I lay down, closed my eyes, and began thinking about Mackerel. I wanted to fall asleep thinking about the cat. He was something that had *come back* to me. He had managed to come back to me from somewhere far away. That had to be a kind of blessing. As I lay there with my eyes closed, I thought about the soft touch of the pads on the underside of the cat's paws, the cold triangular ears, the pink tongue. In my mind, Mackerel had curled up and was sleeping quietly. I felt his warmth with the palm of my hand. I could hear his regular breathing. I was far more on edge than usual, but sleep came to me before too long, a deep sleep without dreams.

I awoke in the middle of the night. I thought I had heard sleigh bells somewhere far away, as in the background of Christmas music.

Sleigh bells?

I sat up on the sofa and felt for my watch on the coffee table. The luminous hands showed 1.30. I must have slept more soundly than I had expected to. I sat still and listened hard, but the only sound I could hear was the faint, dry thumping of my own heart. Maybe I had imagined the sleigh bells. Maybe I had been dreaming, after all. I decided, nevertheless, to check the house. I stepped into my slippers and padded into the kitchen. The sound grew more distinct when I left the room. It really did sound like sleigh bells, and it seemed to be coming from Cinnamon's office. I stood by the door for a while, listening, then gave a knock. Cinnamon might have come back to the Residence while I was sleeping. But there was no answer. I opened the door a crack and looked inside.

Somewhere around waist height in the darkness, I could see a whitish glow and a square shape. It was the glow of the computer screen, and the bell sound was the machine's repeated beeping (a new kind of beep, which I had not heard before). The computer was calling out to me. As if drawn towards it, I sat down in front of the glow and read the message on the screen:

`You have now gained access to the programme "The Wind-up Bird Chronicle". Choose a document (1-16).`

Someone had turned the computer on and accessed documents titled "The Wind-up Bird Chronicle". There should have been no one in the Residence besides me. Could someone have started it from outside the house? If so, it could only have been Cinnamon. "The Wind-up Bird Chronicle"?

The light, cheery sound, like sleigh bells, continued to emanate from the computer, as if it were Christmas morning. It seemed to be urging me to make a choice. After some hesitation, I picked number 8 for no particular reason. The ringing stopped, and a document opened on the screen like a horizontal scroll painting being spread out before me.

26

The Wind-up Bird Chronicle No. 8
(or, A Second Clumsy Massacre)

•

The veterinary surgeon woke before 6 a.m. After washing his face in cold water, he made himself breakfast. Daybreak came at an early hour in summer, and most of the animals in the zoo were already awake. The open window let in their cries and the breeze that carried their smells, which told him the weather without his having to look outside. This was part of his routine. He would first listen, then inhale the morning air, and so ready himself for each new day.

Today, however, should have been different from the day before. It *had* to be different. So many voices and smells had been lost! The tigers, the leopards, the wolves, the bears: all had been liquidated by soldiers the previous afternoon. Now, after a night of sleep, those events seemed like part of a sluggish nightmare he had had long ago. But he knew they had really happened. His ears still felt a dull ache from the roar of the soldiers' rifles. That could not be a dream. It was August now, the year was 1945, and he was here in the city of Hsin-ching, where the Soviet troops that had burst across the border were pressing closer every hour. This was reality – as real as the sink and toothbrush he saw in front of him.

The sound of the elephants' trumpeting gave him some sense of relief. Ah, yes – the elephants had survived. Fortunately, the young lieutenant in charge of the platoon had to remove the elephants from the list, thought the vet as he washed his face. Since coming to Manchuria, he had met any number of stiff-necked, fanatical young officers from his homeland, and the experience always left him shaken. Most of them were farmers' sons who had spent their youthful years in the depressed thirties, steeped in the tragedies of poverty, while a megalomaniac nationalism was hammered into their skulls. They would follow without a second thought the orders of a superior, no matter how outlandish. Commanded in the name of the emperor to dig a hole through the earth to Brazil, they would grab a shovel and set to work. Some people called this "purity", but the vet had other words for it. An urban doctor's son, educated in the relatively liberal atmosphere of the twenties, the vet could not understand those young officers. Shooting a couple of elephants with small arms should have been far easier than digging through the earth to Brazil, but the lieutenant in charge of the firing squad, though he spoke with a slight country accent, seemed to be a more normal human being than the other young officers the vet had met – better educated and more reasonable. The vet could sense this from the way the young man spoke and handled himself.

In any case, the elephants had not been killed, and the vet told himself he should be grateful. The soldiers, too, must have been glad to be spared the task. The Chinese workers may have regretted the omission – they had missed out on a lot of meat and ivory.

The vet boiled water in a kettle, soaked his beard in a hot towel, and shaved. Then he ate breakfast alone: tea, toast and butter. The food rations in Manchuria were far from sufficient, but compared with those elsewhere, they were generous. This was good news both for him and for the animals. The animals showed resentment at their reduced allowances of feed, but the situation here was far better than in Japanese homeland zoos, where foodstuffs had already run out. No one could predict the future, but for now, at least, both animals and humans were being spared the pain of extreme hunger.

He wondered how his wife and daughter were doing. If all went according to plan, their train should have arrived in Pusan by now. His cousin who worked for the railway company lived here, and until the vet's wife and daughter were able to board the transport ship that would carry them to Japan, they would stay with the cousin's family. The doctor missed seeing them when he woke up in the morning. He missed hearing their lively voices as they prepared breakfast. A hollow quiet ruled the house. This was no longer the home he loved, the place where he belonged. And yet, at the same time, he could not help feeling a certain strange joy at being left alone in this empty official residence; now he was able to sense the implacable power of fate in his very bones and flesh.

Fate itself was the doctor's own fatal disease. From his youngest days, he had had a lucid awareness that "I, as an individual, am living under the control of some outside force." This may have been owing to the vivid blue mark on his right cheek. When a child, he had hated this mark, this imprint that only he, and no one else, had to bear upon his flesh. He wanted to die whenever the other children taunted him or strangers stared at him. If only he could have cut away that part of his body with a knife! But as he matured, he came to a quiet acceptance of the mark on his face that would never go away. And this may have been a factor that helped form his attitude of resignation in all matters having to do with fate.

Most of the time, the power of fate played on like a quiet and monotonous ground bass, colouring only the edges of his life. Seldom was he reminded of its existence. But every once in a while, when the balance would shift (and what controlled the balance he never knew: he could discover no regularity in those shifts), the force would increase, plunging him into a state of near-paralytic resignation. At such times, he had no choice but to abandon everything and give himself up to the flow. He knew from experience that nothing he could do or think would ever change the situation. Fate would demand its portion, and until it received that portion, it would never go away. He believed this with his whole heart.

Not that he was a passive creature; indeed, he was more decisive than most, and he always saw his decisions through. In his profession, he was outstanding: a vet of exceptional skill, a tireless educator. He may have lacked a certain creative spark, but at school he had always achieved high marks and was chosen to be the leader of the class. In the workplace, too, others acknowledged his superiority, and his juniors always looked up to him. He was certainly no "fatalist", as most people use the word. And yet never once in his life had he experienced the unshakable certainty that he and he alone had arrived at a decision. He always had the feeling that fate had forced him to decide things to suit its own convenience. On occasion, after the momentary satisfaction of having decided something of his own free will, he would see that things had been determined beforehand by an external power cleverly camouflaged as free will, mere bait thrown in his path to lure him into behaving as he was meant to. The only things that he had decided for himself with complete independence were the kind of trivial matters which, on closer inspection, revealed themselves to require no decision making at all. He felt like a titular head of state who did nothing more than stamp the royal seal on documents at the behest of a regent who wielded all true power in the realm – like the emperor of this puppet empire of Manchukuo.

The doctor loved his wife and child. They were the most wonderful thing that had ever happened to him – especially his daughter, for whom his love bordered on obsession. For them, he would have gladly given up his life. Indeed, he had often imagined doing so, and the deaths he had endured for them in his mind seemed the sweetest deaths imaginable. At the same time, however, he would often come home from work and, seeing his wife and daughter there, think to himself, These people are, finally, separate human beings, with whom I have no connection. They were something other, something of which he had no true knowledge, something that existed in a place far away from the doctor himself. And whenever he felt this way, the thought would cross his mind that he himself had chosen neither of these people on his own – which did not prevent him from loving them unconditionally, without the slightest reservation. This was, for the doctor, a great paradox, an insoluble contradiction, a gigantic trap that had been set for him in his life.

The world he belonged to became far simpler, far easier to understand, though, once he was left alone in his residence at the zoo. All he had to think about was taking care of the animals. His wife and daughter were gone. There was no need to think about them for now. The vet and his fate could be alone together.

And it was fate above all, the gigantic power of fate, that held sway over the city of Hsin-ching in August of 1945 – not the Kwantung Army, not the Soviet Army, not the troops of the Communists or of the Kuomintang. Anyone could see that fate was the ruler here and that individual will counted for nothing. It was fate that had spared the elephants and buried the tigers and leopards and wolves and bears the day before. What would it bury now, and what would it spare? These were questions that no one could answer.

The doctor left his residence to prepare for the morning feeding. He assumed that no one would show up for work any more, but he found two

Chinese boys waiting for him in his office. He did not know them. They were thirteen or fourteen years old, had dark complexions and were skinny, with roving animal eyes. "They told us to help you," said one boy. The doctor nodded. He asked their names, but they made no reply. Their faces remained blank, as if they had not heard the question. These boys must have been sent by the Chinese people who had worked here until the day before. Those people had probably ended all contact with Japanese now, in anticipation of changes to come, but assumed that children would not be held accountable. The boys had been sent as a sign of goodwill. The workers knew that he could not care for the animals alone.

The vet gave each boy two biscuits, then put them to work helping him feed the animals. They led a mule-drawn cart from cage to cage, providing each animal with its particular feed and changing its water. Cleaning the cages was out of the question. The best they could manage was a quick hose-down to wash away the droppings. The zoo was closed, after all: no one would complain if it stank a little.

As it turned out, the absence of the tigers, leopards, bears and wolves made the job far easier. Caring for big carnivores was a major effort – and dangerous. As bad as the doctor felt when passing their empty cages, he could not suppress a sense of relief to have been spared that job.

They started the work at 8 o'clock and finished after 10. The boys then disappeared without a word. The vet felt exhausted from the hard physical labour. He went back to the office and reported to the zoo director that the animals had been fed.

.

Just before noon, the young lieutenant came back to the zoo, leading the same eight soldiers he had brought with him the day before. Fully armed again, they walked with a metallic clinking that could be heard far in advance of their arrival. Again their shirts were blackened with sweat, and again the cicadas were screaming in the trees. Today, however, they had not come to kill animals. The lieutenant saluted the director and said, "We need to know the current status of the zoo's usable carts and draft animals." The director informed him that they had exactly one mule and one wagon. "We contributed our only truck and two horses two weeks ago," he noted. The lieutenant nodded and announced that he was commandeering the mule and wagon, as per orders of Kwantung Army Headquarters.

"Wait just a minute," the vet interjected. "We need those to feed the animals twice a day. All our local people have disappeared. Without that mule and wagon, our animals will starve to death. Even *with* them, we can barely keep up."

"We're all just barely keeping up, sir," said the lieutenant, whose eyes were red and whose face was covered with stubble. "Our first priority is to defend the city. You can always let the animals out of their cages if need be. We've taken care of the dangerous meat-eaters. The others pose no security risk. These are military orders, sir. You'll just have to manage."

Cutting the discussion short, the lieutenant ordered his men to take the mule and wagon. When they were gone, the vet and the director looked at each other. The director sipped his tea, shook his head, and said nothing.

Four hours later, the soldiers were back with the mule and wagon, a filthy canvas tarpaulin covering the mounded contents of the wagon. The mule was panting, its hide foaming with the afternoon heat and the weight of the load. The eight soldiers marched four Chinese men ahead of them at bayonet point – young men, perhaps twenty years old, wearing baseball uniforms and with their hands tied behind their backs. The black-and-blue marks on their faces made it obvious that they had been severely beaten. The right eye of one man was swollen almost shut, and the bleeding lips of another had stained his baseball shirt bright red. The shirt fronts had nothing written on them, but there were small rectangles where the name patches had been torn off. The numbers on their backs were 1, 4, 7, and 9. The vet could not begin to imagine why, at such a time of crisis, four young Chinese men would be wearing baseball uniforms, or why they had been so badly beaten and dragged here by Japanese troops. The scene looked like something not of this world – a painting by a mental patient.

The lieutenant asked the zoo director if he had any picks and shovels he could let them use. The young officer looked even more pale and haggard than he had before. The vet led him and his men to a toolshed behind the office. The lieutenant chose two picks and two shovels for his men. Then he asked the vet to come with him, and leaving his men there, walked into a thicket beyond the road. The vet followed. Wherever the lieutenant walked, huge grasshoppers scattered. The smell of summer grass hung in the air. Mixed in with the deafening screams of cicadas, the sharp trumpeting of elephants now and then seemed to sound a distant warning.

The lieutenant walked on among the trees without speaking, until he found a kind of opening in the woods. The area had been earmarked for construction of a plaza for small animals that children could play with. The plan had been postponed indefinitely, however, when the worsening military situation caused a shortage of construction materials. The trees had been cleared away to make a circle of bare ground, and the sun illuminated this one part of the woods like stage lighting. The lieutenant stood in the centre of the circle and scanned the area. Then he dug at the ground with the heel of his boot.

"We're going to bivouac here for a while," he said, kneeling down and scooping up a handful of dirt.

The vet nodded in response. He had no idea why they had to bivouac in a zoo, but he decided not to ask. Here in Hsin-ching, experience had taught him never to question military men. Questions did nothing but make them angry, and in any case they never gave you a straight answer.

"First we dig a big hole here," the lieutenant said, as if speaking to himself. He stood up and took a pack of cigarettes from his shirt pocket. Putting a cigarette between his lips, he offered one to the doctor, then lit both with a match. The two concentrated on their smoking to fill the silence. Again the lieutenant began digging at the ground with his boot. He drew a kind of diagram in the earth, then rubbed it out. Finally, he asked the vet, "Where were you born?"

"In Kanagawa," the doctor said. "In a town called Ofuna, near the sea."

The lieutenant nodded.

"And where were you born?" the vet asked.

Instead of answering, the lieutenant narrowed his eyes and watched the smoke rising from between his fingers. No, it never pays to ask a military man questions, the vet told himself again. They like to ask questions, but they'll never give you an answer. They wouldn't give you the time of day – literally.

"There's a movie studio there," said the lieutenant.

It took the doctor a few seconds to realize the lieutenant was talking about Ofuna. "That's right. A big studio. I've never been inside, though."

The lieutenant dropped what was left of his cigarette on the ground and crushed it out. "I hope you make it back there," he said. "Of course, there's an ocean to cross between here and Japan. We'll probably all die over here." He kept his eyes on the ground as he spoke. "Tell me, Doctor, are you afraid of death?"

"I guess it depends on how you die," said the vet, after a moment's thought.

The lieutenant raised his eyes and looked at the vet as if his

513

curiosity had been aroused. He had apparently been expecting another answer. "You're right," he said. "It does depend on how you die."

The two remained silent for a time. The lieutenant looked as if he might fall asleep right there, standing up. He was obviously exhausted. A large grasshopper flew over them like a bird and disappeared into a distant clump of grass with a noisy beating of wings. The lieutenant looked at his watch.

"Time to get started," he said to no one in particular. Then he spoke to the vet. "I'd like you to stay around for a while. I might have to ask you to do me a favour."

The vet nodded.

·   ·

The soldiers led the Chinese prisoners to the opening in the woods and untied their hands. The corporal drew a large circle on the ground, using a baseball bat – though why a soldier would have a bat was a mystery to the vet – and ordered the prisoners in Japanese to dig a deep hole the size of the circle. With the picks and shovels, the four men in baseball uniforms started digging in silence. Half the squad stood guard over them, while the other half stretched out beneath the trees. They seemed to be in desperate need of sleep; no sooner had they hit the ground in full gear than they began snoring. The four soldiers who remained awake kept watch over the digging nearby, rifles resting on their hips, bayonets fixed, ready for immediate use. The lieutenant and the corporal took turns overseeing the work and napping under the trees.

It took less than an hour for the four Chinese prisoners to dig a hole some twelve feet across and deep enough to come up to their necks. One of the men asked for water, speaking in Japanese. The lieutenant nodded, and a soldier brought a bucket full of water. The four Chinese took turns ladling water from the bucket and gulping it down. They drank almost the entire bucketful. Their uniforms were smeared black with blood, mud, and sweat.

The lieutenant ordered two of the soldiers to pull the wagon over to the hole. The corporal yanked the tarpaulin off to reveal four dead men piled in the wagon. They wore the same baseball uniforms as the prisoners, and they, too, were obviously Chinese. They appeared to have been shot, and their uniforms were covered with black bloodstains. Large flies were beginning to swarm over the corpses. Judging from how dry the blood was, the doctor guessed they had been dead for close to twenty-four hours.

The lieutenant ordered the four Chinese who had dug the hole to throw the bodies into it. Without a word, faces blank, the men took the bodies out of the wagon and threw them, one at a time, into the hole. Each corpse landed with a dull thud. The numbers on the dead men's uniforms were 2, 5, 6 and 8. The vet committed them to memory.

When the four Chinese had finished throwing the bodies into the hole, the soldiers tied each man to a nearby tree. The lieutenant held up his wrist and studied his watch with a grim expression. Then he looked up towards a spot in the sky for a while, as if searching for something there. He looked like a stationmaster standing on the platform waiting for a hopelessly overdue train. But in fact he was looking at nothing at all. He was just allowing a certain amount of time to go by. Once he had accomplished that, he turned to the corporal and gave him curt orders to bayonet three of the four prisoners (numbers 1, 7 and 9).

Three soldiers were chosen and took up their positions in front of the three Chinese. The soldiers looked paler than the men they were about to kill. The Chinese looked too tired to hope for anything. The corporal offered each of them a smoke, but they refused. He put his cigarettes back into his shirt pocket.

Taking the vet with him, the lieutenant went to stand some distance from the other soldiers. "You'd better watch this," he said. "This is another way to die."

The vet nodded. The lieutenant is not saying this to me, he thought. He's saying it to himself.

In a gentle voice, the lieutenant explained, "Shooting them would be the simplest and most efficient way to kill them, but we have orders not to waste a single bullet – and certainly not to waste bullets killing Chinese. We're supposed to save our ammunition for the Russians. We'll just bayonet them, I suppose, but that's not as easy as it sounds. By the way, Doctor, did they teach you how to use a bayonet in the army?"

The doctor explained that as a cavalry vet, he had not been trained to use a bayonet.

"Well, the proper way to kill a man with a bayonet is this. First you thrust it in under the ribs – here." The lieutenant pointed to his own torso just above the stomach. "Then you drag the point in a big, deep circle inside him, to scramble the organs. Then you thrust upward to puncture the heart. You can't just stick it in and expect him to die. We soldiers have this drummed into us. Hand-to-hand combat using bayonets ranks right up there along with night assaults as the pride of the Imperial Army – mainly because it's a lot cheaper than tanks and planes and cannons. Of course, you can train all you want, but when all's said and done what you're stabbing is a straw doll, not a live human being. It doesn't bleed or scream or spill its guts on the ground. These soldiers have never actually killed a human being that way. And neither have I."

The lieutenant looked at the corporal and gave him a nod. The corporal barked his order to the three soldiers, who snapped to attention. Then they took a half-step back and thrust out their bayonets, each man aiming his blade at his prisoner. One of the prisoners (number 7) growled something in Chinese that sounded like a curse and gave a defiant spit – which never reached the ground but dribbled down the front of his baseball uniform.

At the sound of the next order, the three soldiers thrust their bayonets into the Chinese men with tremendous force. Then, as the lieutenant had said, they twisted the blades so as to rip the men's internal organs, and thrust the tips upward. The cries of the Chinese men were not very loud – more like deep sobs than screams, as if they were heaving out the breath left in their bodies all at once through a single opening. The soldiers pulled out their bayonets and stepped back. The corporal barked his order again, and the men repeated the procedure exactly as before – stabbing, twisting, thrusting upward, withdrawing. The vet watched in numbed silence, overtaken by the sense that he was beginning to split in two. He became simultaneously the stabber and the stabbed. He could feel both the impact of the bayonet as it entered his victim's body and the pain of having his internal organs slashed to bits.

It took much longer than he would have imagined for the Chinese men to die. Their sliced-up bodies poured prodigious amounts of blood onto the ground, but even with their organs shredded, they went on twitching for quite some time. The corporal used his own bayonet to cut the ropes that bound the men to the trees, and then he ordered the soldiers who had not participated in the killing to help drag the fallen bodies to the hole and throw them in. These corpses also made a dull thud on impact, but the doctor couldn't help feeling that the sound was different from that made by the earlier corpses – probably because they were not quite dead yet.

Now only the young Chinese prisoner with the number 4 on his shirt was left. The three pale-faced soldiers tore broad leaves from plants at their feet and proceeded to wipe their bloody bayonets. Not only blood but strange-coloured body fluids and chunks of flesh adhered to the blades. The men had to use many leaves to return the bayonets to their original bare-metal shine.

516

The vet wondered why only the one man, number 4, had been left alive, but he was not going to ask questions. The lieutenant lit another cigarette. He then offered one to the vet, who accepted it in silence and, after putting it between his lips, struck his own match. His hand did not tremble, but it seemed to have lost all feeling, as if he were wearing thick gloves.

"These men were cadets in the Manchukuo Army officer training school," said the lieutenant. "They refused to participate in the defence of Hsin-ching. They killed two of their Japanese instructors last night and tried to run away. We caught them during night patrol, killed four of them on the spot and captured the other four. Two more escaped in the dark." The lieutenant rubbed his beard with the palm of his hand. "They were trying to make their getaway in baseball uniforms. I guess they thought they'd be arrested as deserters if they wore their military uniforms. Or maybe they were afraid of what communist troops would do to them if they were caught in their Manchukuo uniforms. Anyway, all they had in their barracks to wear besides their cadet outfits were uniforms of the officer training school baseball team. So they tore off the names and tried to get away wearing these. I don't know if you know, but the school had a great team. They used to go to Taiwan and Korea for friendly games. That guy" – and here the lieutenant motioned towards the man tied to the tree – "was captain of the team and batted cleanup. We think he was the one who organized the getaway. He killed the two instructors with a bat. The instructors knew there was trouble in the barracks and weren't going to distribute weapons to the cadets until it was an absolute emergency. But they forgot about the baseball bats. Both of them had their skulls cracked open. They probably died instantly. Two perfect home runs. This is the bat."

The lieutenant asked the corporal to bring the bat to him. He passed the bat to the vet. The doctor took it in both hands and held it up in front of his face the way a player does when stepping into the batter's box. It was just an ordinary bat, not very well made, with a rough finish and an uneven grain. It was heavy, though, and well broken in. The handle was black with sweat. It didn't look like a bat that had recently been used to kill two human beings. After getting a feel for its weight, the vet handed it back to the lieutenant, who gave it a few easy swings, handling it like an expert.

"Do you play baseball?" the lieutenant asked the vet.

"All the time when I was a kid."

"Too grown up now?"

"No more baseball for me," the vet said, and he was on the verge of asking, "How about you, Lieutenant?" when he swallowed the words.

"I've been ordered to beat this guy to death with the same bat he used," the lieutenant said in a dry voice as he tapped the ground with the tip of the bat. "An eye for an eye, a tooth for a tooth. Just between you and me, I think the order stinks. What the hell good is it going to do to kill these guys? We don't have any planes left, we don't have any warships, our best troops are dead. Some kind of special new bomb wiped out the whole city of Hiroshima in a split second. We're either going to be swept out of Manchuria or we'll all be killed, and China will belong to the Chinese again. We've already killed a lot of Chinese, and adding a few bodies to the count isn't going to make any difference. But orders are orders. I'm a soldier, and I have to follow orders. We killed the tigers and leopards yesterday, and today we have to kill these guys. So take a good look, Doctor. This is another way for people to die. You're a doctor, so you're probably used to knives and blood and guts, but you've probably never seen anyone beaten to death with a baseball bat."

The lieutenant ordered the corporal to bring player number 4, the cleanup batter, to the edge of the hole. Once again they tied his hands behind his back, then they blindfolded him and forced him to kneel on the ground. He was a tall, well-built young man with massive arms the size of most people's thighs. The lieutenant called over one young soldier and handed him the bat. "Kill him with this," he said. The young soldier stood at attention and saluted before taking the bat, but having taken it in his hands, he just went on standing there, as if stupefied. He seemed unable to grasp the concept of beating a Chinese man to death with a baseball bat.

"Have you ever played baseball?" the lieutenant asked the young soldier (the one who would eventually have his skull split open with a shovel by a Soviet guard in a mine near Irkutsk).

"No, sir, never," replied the soldier, in a loud voice. Both the village in Hokkaido where he was born and the village in Manchuria where he grew up had been so poor that no family in either place could have afforded the luxury of a baseball or a bat. He had spent his boyhood running around the fields, catching dragonflies and playing at sword fighting with sticks. He had never in his life played baseball or even seen a game. This was the first time he had ever held a bat.

The lieutenant showed him how to hold the bat and taught him the basics of the swing, demonstrating himself a few times. "See? It's all in the hips," he grunted through clenched teeth. "Starting from the backswing, you twist from the waist down. The tip of the bat follows through naturally. Understand? If you concentrate too much on swinging the bat, your arms do all the work and you lose power. Swing from the hips."

The soldier didn't seem fully to comprehend the lieutenant's instructions, but he took off his heavy gear as ordered and practised his swing for a while. Everyone was watching him. The lieutenant placed his hands over the soldier's to help him adjust his grip. He was a good teacher. Before long, the soldier's swing, though somewhat awkward, was swishing through the air. What the young soldier lacked in skill he made up for in muscle power, having spent his days working on a farm.

"That's good enough," said the lieutenant, using his hat to wipe the sweat from his brow. "OK, now, try to do it in one good, clean swing. Don't let him suffer."

What he really wanted to say was, "I don't want to do this any more than you do. Who the hell could have thought of anything so stupid? Killing a guy with a baseball bat . . ." But an officer could never say such a thing to an enlisted man.

The soldier stepped up behind the blindfolded Chinese man where he knelt on the ground. When the soldier raised the bat, the strong rays of the setting sun cast the bat's long, thick shadow on the earth. This is so weird, thought the vet. The lieutenant was right: I've never seen a man killed with a baseball bat. The young soldier held the bat aloft for a long time. The doctor saw its tip shaking.

The lieutenant nodded to the soldier. With a deep breath, the soldier took a backswing, then smashed the bat with all his strength into the back of the Chinese cadet's head. He did it amazingly well. He swung his hips just as the lieutenant had taught him to, the bat made a direct hit behind the man's ear, and the bat followed through perfectly. There was a dull crushing sound as the skull shattered. The man himself made no sound. His body hung in the air for a moment in a strange pose, then flopped forward. He lay with his cheek on the ground, blood flowing from one ear. He did not move. The lieutenant looked at his watch. Still gripping the bat, the young soldier stared off into space, his mouth agape.

The lieutenant was a person who did things with great care. He waited for a full minute. When he was certain that the young Chinese man was not moving at all, he said to the vet, "Could you do me a favour and check to see that he's really dead?"

The vet nodded, walked over to where the young Chinese lay,

knelt down, and removed his blindfold. The man's eyes were open wide, the pupils turned upward, and bright-red blood was flowing from his ear. His half-opened mouth revealed the tongue lying tangled inside. The impact had left his neck twisted at a strange angle. The man's nostrils had expelled thick gobs of blood, making black stains on the dry ground. One especially alert – and large – fly had already burrowed its way into a nostril to lay eggs. Just to make sure, the vet took the man's wrist and felt for a pulse. There was no pulse – certainly not where there was supposed to be one. The young soldier had ended this burly man's life with a single swing of a bat – indeed, his first-ever swing of a bat. The vet glanced towards the lieutenant and nodded to signal that the man was, without a doubt, dead. Having completed his task, he was beginning slowly to rise to his full height, when it seemed to him that the sun shining on his back increased in intensity all of a sudden.

At that very moment, the young Chinese batter in uniform number 4 rose up into a sitting position, as if he had just woken up. Without the slightest uncertainty or hesitation – or so it seemed to those watching – he grabbed the doctor's wrist. It all happened in a split second. The vet could not understand: this man was dead, he was sure of it. But now, thanks to one last drop of life that seemed to well up from nowhere, the man was gripping the doctor's wrist with the strength of a steel vice. Eyelids stretched open to the limit, pupils still glaring upward, the man fell forward into the hole, dragging the doctor in after him. The doctor fell in on top of him and heard one of the man's ribs crack as his weight came down. Still the Chinese ballplayer continued to grip his wrist. The soldiers saw all this happening, but they were too stunned to do anything more than stand and watch. The lieutenant recovered first and leaped into the hole. He drew his pistol from his holster, placed the muzzle against the Chinese man's head, and pulled the trigger twice. Two sharp cracks rang out, and a large black hole opened in the man's temple. Now his life was completely gone, but still he refused to release the doctor's wrist. The lieutenant knelt down and, pistol in one hand, began the painstaking process of prying open the corpse's fingers one at a time. The vet lay there in the hole, surrounded by eight silent Chinese corpses in baseball uniforms. Down in the hole, the screeching of cicadas sounded very different from the way it sounded above ground.

Once the vet had been freed from the dead man's grasp, the soldiers pulled him and the lieutenant out of the grave. The vet squatted down on the grass and took several deep breaths. Then he looked at his wrist. The man's fingers had left five bright-red marks. On this hot August afternoon, the vet felt chilled to the core of his body. I'll never get rid of this coldness, he thought. That man was truly, seriously determined to take me with him wherever he was going.

The lieutenant reset the pistol's safety and slipped the gun into its holster. This was the first time he had ever fired a gun at a human being. But he tried not to think about it. The war would continue for a little while at least, and people would continue to die. He could leave the deep thinking for later. He wiped his sweaty right palm on his trousers, then ordered the soldiers who had not participated in the execution to fill in the hole. A huge swarm of flies had already taken custody of the pile of corpses.

The young soldier went on standing where he was, stupefied, gripping the bat. He couldn't seem to make his hands let go. The lieutenant and the corporal left him alone. He had seemed to be watching the whole bizarre series of events – the "dead" Chinese man grabbing the vet by the wrist, their falling into the grave, the lieutenant's leaping in and finishing him off, and now the other soldiers' filling in the hole. But in fact, he had not been watching any of it. He had been listening to the wind-up bird. As it had been the previous afternoon, the bird was in a tree somewhere, making that *creeeak, creeeak* sound as if winding a spring. The soldier looked up, trying to pinpoint the direction of the cries, but he could see no sign of the bird. He felt a slight sense of nausea at the back of his throat, though nothing as violent as yesterday's.

As he listened to the winding of the spring, the young soldier saw one fragmentary image after another rise up before him and fade away. After they were disarmed by the Soviets, the young paymaster lieutenant would be handed over to the Chinese and hanged for his part in these executions. The corporal would die of the plague in a Siberian concentration camp: he would be thrown into a quarantine shed and left there until dead, though in fact he had merely collapsed from malnutrition and had not contracted the plague – not, at least, until he was thrown into the shed. The vet with the mark on his face would die in an accident a year later. A civilian, he would be taken by the Soviets for cooperating with the military and sent to another Siberian camp to do hard labour. He would be working in a deep shaft in a Siberian coal mine when a flood would drown him, along with many soldiers. And I . . . , thought the young soldier with the bat in his hands, but he could not see his own future. He could not even see the events that were transpiring before his very eyes. He now closed his eyes and listened to the call of the wind-up bird.

Then, all at once, he thought of the ocean – the ocean he had seen from the deck of the ship that brought him from Japan to Manchuria. He had never seen the ocean before, nor had he seen it since. That had happened eight years ago. He could still remember the smell of the salt air. The ocean was one of the greatest things he had ever seen in his life – bigger and deeper than anything he had imagined. It changed its colour and shape and expression according to time and place and weather. It aroused a deep sadness in his heart, and at the same time it brought his heart peace and comfort. Would he ever see it again? He loosened his grip and let the bat fall to the ground. It made a dry sound as it struck the earth. After the bat left his hands, he felt a slight increase in his nausea.

The wind-up bird went on crying, but no one else could hear its call.

•

Here ended "The Wind-up Bird Chronicle No.8."

27

Cinnamon's Missing Links

•

Here ended "The Wind-up Bird Chronicle No. 8."

•

I exited the document to return to the original menu and clicked on "The Wind-up Bird Chronicle No. 9". I wanted to read the continuation of the story. But instead of a new document, I saw this message:

Access denied to "The Wind-up Bird Chronicle No. 9" based on Code R24.

Choose another document.

I chose No. 10, but with the same results.

Access denied to "The Wind-up Bird Chronicle No. 10" based on Code R24.

Choose another document.

The same thing happened with No. 11 – and with all the other documents, including No. 8. I had no idea what this "Code R24" was, but it was now blocking access to everything. At the moment I had opened "The Wind-up Bird Chronicle No. 8", I could probably have had access to any one of them, but No. 8 having been opened and closed, the doors were locked to all of them now. Maybe this programme did not permit access to more than one document at a time.

I sat in front of the computer, wondering what to do next. But there was nothing I could do next. This was a precisely organised world, which had been conceived in Cinnamon's mind and which functioned according to his principles. I did not know the rules of the game. I gave up trying and shut down the computer.

·

Without a doubt, "The Wind-up Bird Chronicle No. 8" was a story written by Cinnamon. He had input sixteen stories into the computer under the title "The Wind-up Bird Chronicle", and it just so happened that I had chosen and read No. 8. Judging from the length of the one story, sixteen such stories would have made a fairly thick book if set in type.

What could "No. 8" signify? The word "chronicle" in the title probably meant that the stories were related in chronological order, No. 8 following No. 7, No. 9 following No. 8, and so on. That was a reasonable assumption, if not necessarily true. They could just as well have been arranged in a different order. They might even run backward, from the present to the past. A bolder hypothesis might make them sixteen different versions of the same story told in parallel. In any case, the one I had chosen was a sequel to the story that Cinnamon's mother, Nutmeg, had told me about soldiers killing animals in the Hsin-ching zoo in August 1945. It was set in the same zoo on the following day, and again the central character was Nutmeg's father, Cinnamon's grandfather, the nameless vet.

I had no way of telling how much of the story was true. Was every bit of it Cinnamon's creation, or were parts of it based on actual events? Nutmeg had told me that "absolutely nothing" was known about what happened to her father after she saw him last. Which meant that the story could not be entirely true. Still, it was conceivable that some of the details were based on historical fact. It was possible that during such a time of chaos, a number of cadets from the Manchukuo Army officer training school were executed and buried in a hole in the Hsin-ching zoo and that the Japanese officer in charge of the operation had been executed after the war. Incidents of desertion and rebellion by Manchukuo Army troops were by no means rare at the time, and although it was rather strange to have the murdered Chinese cadets dressed in base-ball uniforms, this could have happened as well. Knowing such facts, Cinnamon might have combined them with the image he had of his grandfather and made up his own story.

But why had Cinnamon written such stories? And why *stories*? Why not some other form? And why had he found it necessary to use the word "chronicle" in the title? I thought about these things while sitting on the fitting room sofa, turning a coloured design pencil over and over in my hand.

I would have had to read all sixteen stories to find the answers to my questions, but even after a single reading of No. 8, I had some idea, however vague, of what Cinnamon was pursuing in his writing. He was engaged in a search for the meaning of his own existence. And he was hoping to find it by looking into the events that had preceded his birth.

To do that, Cinnamon had to fill in those blank spots in the past that he could not reach with his own hands. By using those hands to make a story, he was trying to supply the missing links. From the stories he had heard over and over again from his mother, he derived further stories in an attempt to re-create the enigmatic figure of his grandfather in a new setting. He inherited from his mother's stories the fundamental style that he used, unaltered, in his own stories: namely, the assumption that *fact may not be truth, and truth may not be factual.* The question of which parts of a story were factual and which were not was not a very important one for Cinnamon. The important question was not what his grandfather *did* but what his grandfather *might have done.* He learned the answer to this question as soon as he succeeded in telling the story.

His stories employed "wind-up bird" as a key phrase, and they almost certainly brought the narrative up to the present day in the form of a chronicle (or perhaps *not* in the form of a chronicle). But "wind-up bird" was not a term invented by Cinnamon. It was a phrase spoken by his mother, Nutmeg, in a story she told me in the Aoyama restaurant where we ate together. Nutmeg almost certainly did not know at that time that I had been given the name "Mr Wind-up Bird." Which meant that I was connected with their story through some chance combination of circumstances.

I could not be certain of this, however. Nutmeg could possibly have known that I was called "wind-up bird". The words might have affected her story (or, rather, *their* story), might have eaten their way into it on an unconscious level. This story jointly possessed by mother and son might not exist in a single fixed form but could go on changing and growing as a story does in oral transmission.

Whether by chance or not, the "wind-up bird" was a powerful presence in Cinnamon's story. The cry of this bird was audible only to certain special people, who were guided by it towards inevitable ruin. The will of human beings meant nothing, then, as the vet always seemed to feel. People were no more than dolls set on tabletops, the springs in their backs wound up tight, dolls set to move in ways they could not choose, moving in directions they could not choose. Nearly all within range of the wind-up bird's cry were ruined, lost. Most of them died, plunging over the edge of the table.

•

Cinnamon had very likely monitored my conversation with Kumiko. He probably knew everything that went on in this computer. He had waited until I had finished before presenting me with the story of "The Wind-up Bird Chronicle". This had not happened by chance or a sudden whim. Cinnamon had programmed the machine with a definite purpose in mind and shown me *one* story. He had also made sure I knew that there might possibly exist a whole, huge cluster of stories.

I lay down on the sofa and looked at the ceiling of the fitting room in the half-dark. The night was deep and heavy, the neighbourhood painfully quiet. The white ceiling looked like a thick white cap of ice that had been set on top of the room.

Cinnamon's grandfather, the nameless vet, and I had a number of unusual things in common – a mark on the face, a baseball bat, the cry of the wind-up bird. And then there was the lieutenant who appeared in Cinnamon's story: he reminded me of Lieutenant Mamiya. Lieutenant Mamiya had also been assigned to Kwantung Army Headquarters in Hsin-ching at that time. The real Lieutenant Mamiya, however, was not a paymaster officer but belonged to the mapmaking corps, and after the war he was not hanged (fate had denied him death) but returned to Japan, having lost his left hand in battle. Still, I could not shake off the impression that the officer who had directed the executions of the Chinese cadets had really been Lieutenant Mamiya. At least, if it *had* been Lieutenant Mamiya, it would not have been the least bit strange.

Then there was the problem of the baseball bats. Cinnamon knew that I kept a bat in the bottom of the well. Which meant that the image of the bat could have eaten its way into his story in the same way that the words "wind-up bird chronicle" could have. Even if this were true, however, there was still something about the bat that could not be explained so simply: the man with the guitar case who attacked me with the bat in the hallway of the abandoned apartment house. This was the man who had made a show of burning the palm of his hand with a candle flame in a bar in Sapporo and who later hit me with the bat, only to have me beat him with it. He was the one who had *surrendered* the bat to me.

And finally, why did I have burned into my face a mark the same shape and colour as that of Cinnamon's grandfather? Was this, too, something that came up in their story as a result of my presence having eaten its way into it? Did the actual vet really have a mark on his face? Nutmeg certainly had no need to make up such a thing in describing her father to me. The very thing that had led her to "find" me on the streets of Shinjuku was this mark that we possessed in common. Everything was intertwined, with the complexity of a three-dimensional puzzle – a puzzle in which truth was not necessarily fact and fact not necessarily truth.

•

I stood up from the sofa and went to Cinnamon's small office once again. I sat at the desk, elbows resting on the table, and stared at the computer screen. *Cinnamon was probably inside there.* In there, his silent words lived and breathed as stories. They could think and seek and grow and give off heat. But the screen before me remained as deep in death as the moon, hiding Cinnamon's words in a labyrinthine forest. Neither the monitor's screen nor Cinnamon himself, behind it, tried to tell me any more than I had already been told.

28

You Just Can' t Trust a House
(May Kasahara's Point of View: 5)

•

How are you, Mr Wind-up Bird?

I wrote at the end of my last letter that I had said just about everything I wanted to say to you – pretty much as if that were going to be it. Remember? I did some more thinking after that, though, and I started to get the feeling that I ought to write a little more. So here I am, creeping around in the middle of the night like a cockroach, sitting at my desk and writing to you again.

I don't know why, but I think about the Miyawaki family a lot these days – the poor Miyawakis who used to live in that vacant house, and then the debt collectors came after them, and they all went off and killed themselves. I'm pretty sure I read something about how only the eldest daughter didn't die and now nobody knows where she is. . . . Whether I'm working, or in the dining hall, or in my room listening to music and reading a book, the image of that family pops into my head. Not that I'm haunted by it or anything, but whenever there's an opening (and my head has lots of openings!) it comes creeping in and sticks around for a while, the way smoke from a bonfire can come in through the window. It's been happening all the time this past week or so.

I lived in our house on the alley from the time I was born, and I grew up looking at the house opposite. My window looks right at it. They gave me my own room when I started primary school. By then, the Miyawakis had already built their new house and were living in it. I could always see some member of the family in the house or yard, tons of clothes drying out at the back on nice days, the two girls there yelling out the name of their big, black German shepherd (what was his name?). And when the sun went down, the lights would come on inside the house, looking warm and cozy, and then later the lights would go out one at a time. The older girl took piano lessons, the younger one violin (the older one was older than me, the younger one younger). They'd have parties and things on birthdays and Christmas, and lots of friends would come over, and it was happy and lively there. People who have seen the place only when it was a vacant ruin couldn't imagine what it was like before.

I used to see Mr Miyawaki pruning trees and things at weekends. He seemed to enjoy doing all kinds of chores himself, things that took time, like cleaning the gutters or walking the dog or waxing his car. I'll never understand why some people enjoy those things, they're such a pain, but everybody's different, I guess, and I suppose every family ought to have at least one person like that. The whole family used to ski, so every winter they'd strap their skis to the roof of this big car and go off somewhere, looking like they were going to have the greatest time (I hate skiing myself, but anyhow).

This makes them sound like a typical, ordinary happy family, I suppose, but that's really just what they were: a typical, ordinary happy family. There was nothing about them whatsoever that would make you raise your eyebrows and say, "Yeah, OK, but what about that?"

People in the neighbourhood used to whisper, "I wouldn't live in a creepy place like that if you gave it to me free," but the Miyawakis lived such a peaceful life there, it could have been a picture in a frame without a speck of dust on it. They were the ones in the fairy tale who got to live "happily ever after". Compared to my family at least, they seemed to be living ten times as happily ever after. And the two girls seemed really nice whenever I met them. I used to wish that I had sisters like them. The whole family always seemed to be laughing – including the dog.

I could never have imagined that you could blink one day and all of this would be gone. But that's just what happened. One day I noticed that the whole family – the German shepherd included – had disappeared as if a gust of wind had just blown them away, leaving only the house behind. For a while – maybe a week – no one in the neighbourhood noticed that the Miyawakis had disappeared. It did cross my mind that it was strange the lights weren't coming on at night, but I figured they must be off on one of their family trips. Then my mother heard people saying that the Miyawakis seemed to have "absconded". I remember asking her to explain what the word meant. Nowadays we just say "run away", I suppose.

Whatever you call it, once the people who lived there had disappeared, the whole look of the house changed. It was almost creepy. I had never seen a vacant house before, so I didn't know what an ordinary vacant house looked like, but I guess I thought it would have a sad, beaten sort of look, like an abandoned dog or a cicada's cast-off shell. The Miyawakis' house, though, was nothing like that. It didn't look "beaten" at all. The minute the Miyawakis left, it got this know-nothing look on its face, like, "I've never heard of anybody called Miyawaki." At least that's how it looked to me. It was like some stupid, ungrateful dog. As soon as they were gone, it turned into this self-sufficient vacant house that had nothing at all to do with the Miyawaki family's happiness. It really made me mad! I mean, the house must have been just as happy as the rest of the family when the Miyawakis were there. I'm sure it enjoyed being cleaned so nicely and taken care of, and it wouldn't have existed at all if Mr Miyawaki hadn't been nice enough to build it in the first place. Don't you agree? You just can't trust a house.

You know as well as I do what the place was like after that, Mr Wind-up Bird. The house was abandoned, with no one to live in it, and all smeared with bird shit and stuff. That was all I had to look at from my window for years when I was at my desk, studying – or pretending to study. On clear days, rainy days, snowy days, or in typhoons, it was right there, outside my window, so I couldn't help but see it when I looked out. And strangely enough, as the years went by, I tried less and less not to notice it. I could – and often did – spend whole half hours at a time with my elbow on my desk, doing nothing but look at that vacant house. I don't know – not very long ago the place had been overflowing with laughter, and clean white clothes had been flapping in the wind like in a commercial for washing powder (I wouldn't say Mrs Miyawaki was "abnormal" or anything, but she liked to do laundry – way more than most ordinary people). All of that was gone in a flash, the yard was covered with weeds, and there was nobody left to remember the happy days of the Miyawaki family. To me that seemed sooo strange!

Let me just say this: I wasn't especially friendly with the Miyawaki family. In fact, I hardly ever talked to any of them, except to say "Hi" on the street. But because I spent so much time and energy watching them from my window every day, I felt as if the family's happy doings had become a part of me. You know how in the corner of a family photo there'll be a glimpse of this person who has nothing to do with them. So sometimes I get this feeling like part of me "absconded" with the Miyawakis and just disappeared. I guess that's pretty weird, huh, to feel like part of you is gone because it "absconded" with people you hardly know?

Since I've started telling you one weird thing, I might as well tell you another. Now, this one is really weird!

Lately, I sometimes feel like I have turned into Kumiko. I am actually Mrs Wind-up Bird, and I've run away from you for some reason and I'm hiding here in the mountains, working in a wig factory. For all kinds of complicated reasons, I have to use the name "May Kasahara" as an alias and wear this mask and pretend I'm not Kumiko. And you're just sitting there on that sad little veranda of yours, waiting for me to come back. I don't know – I really feel like that.

Tell me, Mr Wind-up Bird, do you ever get obsessed with these delusions? Not to boast or anything, but I do. All the time. Sometimes, when they're really bad, I'll spend the whole working day wrapped up in a cloud of delusion. Of course, I'm just performing these simple operations, so it doesn't get in the way of my work, but the other girls sometimes give me strange looks. Or maybe I say crazy things to myself out loud. I hate that, but it doesn't do any good to try and fight it. When a delusion wants to come, it comes, like a period. And you can't just meet it at the front door and say, "Sorry, I'm busy today, try me later." Anyway, I hope it doesn't bother you, Mr Wind-up Bird, that I sometimes pretend I'm Kumiko. I mean, I'm not doing it on purpose.

I'm getting really really really tired. I'm going to go to sleep now for three or four hours – I mean out cold – then get up and work hard from morning to night. I'll put in a good day making wigs with the other girls, listening to some kind of harmless music. Please don't worry about me. I'm good at doing all kinds of things even when I'm in the middle of a delusion. And in my own way, I'm saying little prayers for you, hoping that everything works out for you, that Kumiko comes back and you can have your quiet, happy life again.

Goodbye.

29

A Vacant House Is Born

•

The next morning, 9 o'clock came, then 10 o'clock, with no sign of Cinnamon. Nothing like this had ever happened before. He had never missed a single day, from the time I started "working" in this place. At exactly 9 o'clock each morning, the gate would open and the bright glare of the Mercedes' bonnet ornament would appear. This mundane yet theatrical appearance of Cinnamon would mark the clear beginning of each day for me. I had become accustomed to this fixed daily routine the way people become accustomed to gravity or barometric pressure. There was a kind of warmth to Cinnamon's punctilious regularity, something beyond mere mechanical predictability, something that gave me comfort and encouragement. Which is why a morning without Cinnamon's appearance was like a well-executed landscape painting that lacked a focal point.

I gave up waiting for him, left the window, and peeled myself an apple for breakfast. Then I peeked into Cinnamon's room to see if there might be any messages on the computer, but the screen was as dead as ever. All I could do was follow Cinnamon's example and listen to a tape of Baroque music while doing the laundry, vacuuming the floors, and cleaning windows. To kill time, I performed each function slowly and with excessive care, going so far as to clean the blades of the kitchen exhaust fan – but still the time refused to move.

I ran out of things to do by 11 o'clock, so I stretched out on the fitting room sofa and gave myself up to the languid flow of time. I tried to tell myself that Cinnamon had been delayed by some minor matter. Maybe the car had broken down, or he had been caught in an incredible traffic jam. But I knew that couldn't be true. I would have bet all I had on it. Cinnamon's car would never break down, and he always took the possibility of traffic jams into account. Plus, he had the car phone to call me on in case of an unforeseen emergency. No, Cinnamon was not here because he had *decided* not to come here.

•

I tried calling Nutmeg's Akasaka office just before 1, but there was no answer. I tried again and again, with the same result. Then I tried Ushikawa's office but got a message that the number had been disconnected. This was strange. I had called him at that number just two days earlier. I gave up and went back to the fitting room sofa. All of a sudden in the last two days there seemed to be a conspiracy against contact with me.

I went back to the window and peeked through the curtain. Two energetic-looking little winter birds had come to the yard and were perched on a branch, glancing wide-eyed. Then, as if they had suddenly become fed up with everything there, they flew off. Nothing else seemed to be moving. The Residence felt like a newly vacant house.

•

I did not go back there for the next five days. For some reason, I seemed to have lost any desire to go down into the well. I would be losing the well itself before long. The longest I could afford to keep the Residence going without clients was two months, so I ought to be using the well as much as possible while it was still mine. I felt stifled. All of a sudden, the place seemed wrong and unnatural.

I walked around aimlessly without going to the Residence. In the afternoons I would go to the Shinjuku west exit plaza and sit on my usual bench, killing time doing nothing in particular, but Nutmeg never appeared there. I went to her Akasaka office once, rang the bell by the lift and stared into the closed circuit camera, but no reply came. I was ready to give up. Nutmeg and Cinnamon had obviously decided to cut all ties with me. This strange mother and son had deserted the sinking ship for somewhere safer. The intensity of the sorrow this aroused in me took me by surprise. I felt as if I had been betrayed in the end by my own family.

30

Malta Kano's Tail

◆

Boris the Manskinner

In my dream (though I didn't know it was a dream), I was sitting across the table from Malta Kano, drinking tea. The rectangular room was too long and wide to see from end to end, and arranged in it in perfectly straight lines were five-hundred or more square tables. We sat at one of the tables in the middle, the only people there. Across the ceiling, as high as that of a Buddhist temple, stretched countless heavy beams, from all points of which there hung, like potted plants, objects that appeared to be toupees. A closer look showed me that they were human scalps. I could tell from the black blood on their undersides. They were newly taken scalps that had been hung from the beams to dry. I was afraid that the still-fresh blood might drip into our tea. Blood was dripping all around us like raindrops, the sound reverberating through the cavernous room. Only the scalps hanging above our table seemed to have dried enough for there to be no sign of blood dripping from them.

The tea was boiling hot. Placed beside the teaspoons in each of our saucers were three lurid lumps of green sugar. Malta Kano dropped two of the lumps into her tea and stirred, but they would not melt. A dog appeared from nowhere and sat down beside our table. Its face was that of Ushikawa. It was a big dog, with a chunky black body, but from the neck up it was Ushikawa, except that the shaggy black fur that covered the body also grew on the face and head. "Well, well, if it isn't Mr Okada," said the dog-shaped Ushikawa. "And will you look at this: a full head of hair. It grew there the second I turned into a dog. Amazing. I've got much bigger balls now than I used to have, and my stomach doesn't hurt any more. And look: No glasses! No clothes! I'm so happy! I can't believe I didn't think of this before. If only I had become a dog a long time ago! How about you, Mr Okada? Why don't you give it a try?"

Malta Kano picked up her one remaining green sugar lump and hurled it at the dog. The lump thudded into Ushikawa's forehead and drew ink-black blood that ran down Ushikawa's face. This seemed to cause Ushikawa no pain. Still smiling, without a word, he raised his tail and strode away. It was true: his testicles were grotesquely huge.

Malta Kano was wearing a trench coat. The lapels were closed tight across the front, but from the subtle fragrance of a woman's naked flesh I could tell she was wearing nothing underneath. She had her red vinyl hat on, of course. I lifted my cup and took a sip of tea, but it had no taste. It was hot, nothing more.

"I am so glad you could come," said Malta Kano, sounding genuinely relieved. Hearing it for the first time in quite a while, I thought her voice seemed somewhat brighter than before. "I called you for days, but you always seemed to be out. I was beginning to worry that something might have happened to you. Thank goodness you are all right. What a relief it was to hear your voice! In any case, I must apologize for having been out of touch so long. I can't go into detail about everything that has occurred in my life in the meantime, especially on the phone like this, so I will just summarize the important points. The main thing is that I have been travelling all this time. I came back a week ago. Mr Okada? Mr Okada? Can you hear me?"

"Yes, I can hear you," I said, realizing only then that I was holding a phone to my ear. Malta Kano, on her side of the table, was also holding a receiver. Her voice sounded like a bad connection on an international call.

"I was away from Japan the whole time, on the island of Malta in the Mediterranean. All of a sudden one day, the thought crossed my mind, 'Oh, yes! I must return to Malta and take myself near its water. The time for that has come!' This happened just after I last talked to you, Mr Okada. Do you remember that conversation? I was looking for Creta at the time. In any case, I really did not mean to be away from Japan so long. I was planning on two weeks or so. Which is why I did not contact you.

I told hardly anyone I was going, just boarded the plane with little more than the clothes I was wearing. Once I arrived, however, I found myself unable to leave. Have you ever been to Malta, Mr Okada?"

I said that I had not. I remembered having had virtually the same conversation with this same person some years before.

"Mr Okada? Mr Okada?"

"Yes, I'm still here," I said.

It seemed to me there was something I had to tell Malta Kano, but I could not remember what it was. It finally came back to me after I cocked my head and thought about it for a while. I switched hands on the receiver and said, "Oh, yes, there's something I've been meaning to call you about for a long time. The cat came back."

After four or five seconds of silence, Malta Kano said, "The cat came back?"

"Yes. Cat hunting was more or less what brought us together in the first place, so I thought I'd better let you know."

"When did the cat come back?"

"Early this spring. It's been with me ever since."

"Is there anything different about its appearance? Anything that has changed since before it disappeared?"

Changed?

"Come to think of it, I had the feeling that the shape of the tail was a little different," I said. "When I stroked the cat the day it came back, it seemed to me the tail used to have more of a bend in it. I could be wrong, though. I mean, it was gone for almost a year."

"You are sure it is the same cat?"

"Quite sure. I had that cat for a very long time. I'd know if it was the same one or not."

"I see," said Malta Kano. "To tell you the truth, though, I am sorry, but I have the cat's real tail right here."

Malta Kano put the receiver down on the table, then she stood and stripped off her coat. As I had suspected, she was wearing nothing underneath. The size of her breasts and the shape of her pubic hair were much the same as Creta Kano's. She did not remove her red vinyl hat. She turned and showed her back to me. There, to be sure, attached above her buttocks, was a cat's tail. Proportioned to her body, it was much larger than the original, but its shape was the same as Mackerel's tail. It had the same sharp bend at the tip, but this one was far more convincing than Mackerel's.

"Please take a close look," said Malta Kano. "This is the actual tail of the cat that disappeared. The one the cat has now is an imitation. It may look the same, but if you examine it closely, you will find that it is different."

I reached out to touch her tail, but she whipped it away from my hand. Then, still naked, she jumped up onto one of the tables. Into my extended palm fell a drop of blood from the ceiling. It was the same intense red as Malta Kano's vinyl hat.

"Creta Kano's baby's name is Corsica, Mr Okada," said Malta Kano from up on her table, her tail twitching sharply.

"Corsica?"

" 'No man is an island.' *That* Corsica," piped up the black dog, Ushikawa, from somewhere.

Creta Kano's baby?

I woke up, soaked in sweat.

•

It had been a very long time since I last had a dream so long and vivid and unified. And strange. My heart went on pounding audibly for a while after I woke up. I took a hot shower and changed into fresh pyjamas. The time was something after 1 in the morning, but I no longer felt sleepy. To calm myself, I took an old bottle of brandy from the back of the kitchen cabinet, poured a glass, and drank it down.

Then I went to the bedroom to look for Mackerel. The cat was curled up under the quilt, sound asleep. I peeled back the quilt and took the cat's tail in my hand to study its shape. I ran my fingers over it, trying to recall the exact angle of the bent tip, when the cat gave an annoyed stretch and went back to sleep. I could no longer say for sure that this was exactly the same tail the cat had had when it was called Noboru Wataya. Somehow, the tail on Malta Kano's bottom seemed far more like the real Noboru Wataya cat's tail. I could still vividly recall its shape and colour in the dream.

Creta Kano's baby's name is Corsica, Malta Kano had said in my dream.

•

I did not stray far from the house the next day. In the morning, I stocked up on food at the supermarket by the station and made myself lunch. I fed the cat some large fresh sardines. In the afternoon, I took a swim in the local pool. Not many people were there. They were probably busy with New Year's preparations. The ceiling speakers were playing Christmas music. I had swum a leisurely thousand metres when

I got cramp in my instep and decided to stop. The wall overlooking the pool bore a large Christmas ornament.

At home, I was surprised to find a letter for me – a thick one. I knew who had sent it without having to look at the return address. The only person who wrote to me in such a fine hand with an old-fashioned writing brush was Lieutenant Mamiya.

His letter opened with profuse apologies for his having allowed so much time to elapse since his last letter. He expressed himself with such extreme politeness that I almost felt I was the one who ought to apologize.

I have been wanting to tell you another part of my story and have thought for months about writing to you, but many things have come up to prevent me from sitting at my desk and taking pen in hand. Now, almost without my realizing it, the year has nearly run its course. I am growing old, however, and could die at any moment. I can't postpone the task indefinitely. This letter might be a long one – not too long for you, I hope, Mr Okada.

When I delivered Mr Honda's memento to you last summer, I told you a long story about my time in Mongolia, but in fact there is even more to tell – a "sequel," as it were. There were several reasons for not including this part when I told you my story last year. First of all, it would have made the tale too long if I had related it in its entirety. You may recall that I had some pressing business, and there simply wasn't time for me to tell you everything. Perhaps more important, I was still not emotionally prepared then to tell the rest of my story to anyone, to relate it fully and honestly.

After I left you, however, I realized that I should not have allowed practical matters to stand in the way. I should have told you everything to the very end without concealment.

I took a machine gun bullet during the fierce battle of August 13 1945, on the outskirts of Hailar, and as I lay on the ground I lost my left hand under the tracks of a Soviet T34 tank. They transferred me, unconscious, to the Soviet military hospital in Chita, where the surgeons managed to save my life. As I mentioned before, I had been attached to the Military Survey Corps of the Kwantung Army General Staff in Hsin-ching, which had been scheduled to withdraw to the rear as soon as the Soviet Union declared war on Japan. Determined to die, however, I had myself transferred to the Hailar unit, near the border, where I offered myself up as cannon fodder, attacking a Soviet tank with a land mine in my arms. As Mr Honda had prophesied on the banks of the Khalkha River, however, I was not able to die so easily. I lost only my hand, not my life. All the men under my command were, I believe, killed. We may have been acting under orders, but it was a stupid, suicidal attack. Our little portable mines couldn't have done a thing to a huge T34.

The only reason the Soviet Army took such good care of me was that, as I lay delirious, I said something in Russian. Or so they told me afterwards. I had studied basic Russian, as I have mentioned to you, and my post in the Hsin-ching General Staff Office gave me so much spare time, I used it to polish what I knew. I worked hard, so that by the time the war was winding down, I could carry on a fluent conversation in Russian. Many White Russians lived in Hsin-ching, and I knew a few Russian waitresses, so I was never at a loss for people to practise on. My Russian seems to have slipped out quite naturally while I was unconscious.

The Soviet Army was planning from the outset to send to Siberia any Japanese prisoners of war they took in occupying Manchuria, to use them as forced labourers as they had done with German soldiers after the fighting ended in Europe. The Soviets may have been on the winning side, but their economy was in a critical state after the long war, and the shortage of workers was a problem everywhere. Securing an adult male work force in the form of prisoners of war was one of their top priorities. For this, they would need interpreters, and the number of these was severely limited. When they saw that I seemed to be able to speak Russian, they shipped me to the hospital in Chita instead of letting me die. If I hadn't babbled something in Russian, I would have been left out there to die on the banks of the Hailar, and that would have been that. I would have been buried in an unmarked grave. Fate is such a mysterious thing!

After that, I was subjected to a gruelling investigation and given several months of ideological training before being sent to a Siberian coal mine to serve as an interpreter. I will omit the details of that period, but let me say this about my ideological training. As a student before the war, I had read several banned Marxist books, taking care to hide them from the police, and I was not entirely unsympathetic to the communist line, but I had seen too much to swallow it whole. Thanks to my work with intelligence, I knew very well the bloody history of oppression in Mongolia carried out by Stalin and his puppet dictators. Ever since the Revolution, they had sent tens of thousands of Lamaist priests and landowners and other forces of opposition to concentration camps, where they were cruelly liquidated. And the same kind of thing had happened in the Soviet Union itself. Even if I could have believed in the communist ideology, I could no longer believe in the people or the system that was responsible for putting that ideology and those principles into practice. I felt the same way about what we Japanese had done in Manchuria. I'm sure you can't imagine the number of Chinese labourers killed in the course of constructing the secret base at Hailar – killed with the express purpose of shutting them up, to protect the secrecy of the base's construction plans.

Besides, I had witnessed that hellish skinning carried out by the Russian officer and his Mongolian subordinates. I had been thrown into a Mongolian well, and in that strange, intense light I had lost any passion for living. How could someone like me believe in ideology and politics?

As an interpreter, I worked as a liaison between Japanese prisoners of war in the mine and their Soviet captors. I don't know what it was like in the other Siberian concentration camps, but in the mine where I worked, streams of people were dying every day. Not that there was any dearth of causes: malnutrition, overwork, cave-ins, floods, unsanitary conditions that gave rise to epidemics, winter cold of unbelievable harshness, violent guards, the brutal suppression of the mildest resistance. There were cases, too, of lynchings of Japanese by their fellow Japanese. What people felt for each other under such circumstances was hatred and doubt and fear and despair.

Whenever the number of deaths increased to the point where the labour force was declining, they would bring in whole trainloads of new prisoners of war. The men would be dressed in rags, emaciated, and a good quarter of them would die within the first few weeks, unable to withstand the harsh conditions in the mine. The dead would be thrown into abandoned mine shafts. It was impossible to dig graves for them all. The earth was frozen solid there year round. Shovels couldn't dent it. So the abandoned mine shafts were perfect for disposing of the dead. They were deep and dark, and because of the cold, there was no smell. Now and then, we would put a layer of coal over the bodies. When a shaft filled up, they would cap it with dirt and rocks, then move on to the next shaft.

The dead were not the only ones thrown into the shafts. Sometimes living men would be thrown in to teach the rest of us a lesson. Any Japanese soldier who showed signs of resistance would be taken out by Soviet guards and beaten to a pulp, his arms and legs broken before they dropped him to the bottom of the pit. To this day, I can still hear their pitiful screams. It was a living hell.

The mine was run as a major strategic facility by politburo members dispatched from Party Central and policed by the army with maximum security. The top man was said to be from Stalin's own hometown, a cold, hard party functionary still young and full of ambition. His only concern was to raise production figures. The consumption of labourers was a matter of indifference to him. As long as the production figures went up, Party Central would recognize his mine as exemplary and reward him with an expanded labour force. No matter how many workers died, they would always be replaced. To keep the figures rising, he would authorize the digging of veins that, under ordinary circumstances, would have been considered too dangerous to work. Naturally, the number of accidents continued to rise as well, but he didn't care about that.

The director was not the only coldhearted individual supervising the mine. Most of the guards inside the mine were former convicts, uneducated men of shocking cruelty and vindictiveness. They displayed no sign of sympathy or affection, as if, living out here at the edge of the earth, they had been transformed over the years by the frigid Siberian air into subhuman creatures. They had committed crimes and been sent to Siberian prisons, but now that they had served their long sentences, they no longer had homes or families to go back to. They had taken local wives, had children with them, and settled into the Siberian soil.

Japanese prisoners of war were not the only ones sent to work in the mine. There were many Russian criminals as well, political prisoners and former military officers who were victims of Stalin's purges. Not a few of these men were well-educated, refined individuals. Among the Russians were a very few women and children, probably the scattered remains of political prisoners' families. They would be put to work collecting rubbish, washing clothes, and other such tasks. Young women were often used as prostitutes. Besides the Russians, the trains would bring Poles, Hungarians and other foreigners, some with dusky skins (Armenians and Kurds, I should imagine). The camp was partitioned into three living areas: the largest one, where Japanese prisoners of war were kept together; the area for criminals and other prisoners of war; and the area for non-criminals. In this last there lived regular miners and mining professionals, officers and guards of the military guard detachment, some with families, and ordinary Russian citizens. There was also a large army post near the station. Prisoners of war and other prisoners were forbidden to leave their assigned areas. The areas were divided from each other by massive barbed-wire fences patrolled by soldiers carrying machine guns.

As a translator with liaison duties, I had to visit headquarters each day and was free to move from area to area as long as I showed my pass. Near headquarters was the railway station, and a kind of one-street town with a few shabby stores, a bar, and an inn for officials and high-ranking officers on inspection tours. The square was lined with horse troughs, and a big red flag of the USSR flew from a flagpole in the centre. Beneath the flag was parked an armoured vehicle, with a machine gun, against which there was always leaning a bored-looking young soldier in full military gear. The newly built military hospital was situated at the far end of the square, with a large statue of Joseph Stalin at its entrance.

There is a man I must tell you about now. I encountered him in the spring of 1947, probably around the beginning of May, when the snow had finally melted. A year and a half had already passed since I was sent to the mine. When I first saw him, the man was wearing the kind of uniform they gave to all the Russian prisoners. He was involved in repair work at the station with a group of some ten of his compatriots. They were breaking up rocks with sledgehammers and spreading the crushed rock over the roadway. The clanging of the hammers against the hard rocks reverberated throughout the area. I was on my way back from delivering a report to mine headquarters when I passed the station. The non-commissioned officer directing the work stopped me and ordered me to show my pass. I took it from my pocket and handed it to him. The sergeant, a large man, focused a suspicious gaze on the pass for some time, but he was obviously illiterate. He called over one of the prisoners at work on the road and told the man to read it aloud. This particular prisoner was different from the others in his group: he had the look of a well-educated man. And it was him. When I saw him, I could feel the blood drain from my face. I could hardly breathe – literally. I felt as if I were underwater, drowning. My breath would not come.

This educated prisoner was none other than the Russian officer who had ordered the Mongolian soldiers to skin Yamamoto alive on the bank of the Khalkha River. He was emaciated now, almost bald, and missing a front tooth. Instead of his spotless officer's uniform, he wore filthy prison garb, and instead of shiny boots, he wore cloth shoes that were full of holes. The lenses of his glasses were dirty and scratched, the frames were twisted. But it was the same man, without a doubt. There was no way I could have failed to recognize him. And he, in turn, was staring hard at me, his curiosity first aroused, no doubt, by my own stunned expression. Like him, I had also aged and wasted away in the nine intervening years. I even had a few white hairs now. But he seemed to recognize me nonetheless. A look of astonishment crossed his face. He must have assumed that I had rotted away in the bottom of a Mongolian well. And I, of course, never dreamed that I would run across him in a Siberian mining camp, wearing prisoner's garb.

A moment was all it took him to regain his composure and begin reading my pass in calm tones to the illiterate sergeant, who had a machine gun slung from his neck. He read my name, my job as translator, my qualification to move among camp areas, and so on. The sergeant returned my pass and signalled me with a jerk of the chin to go. I walked on a short way and turned around. The man was looking at me. He seemed to be wearing a faint smile, though it might have been my imagination. My legs were shaking, and I couldn't walk straight for a while. All the terror I had experienced nine years before had come back to me in an instant.

I imagined that the man had fallen from grace and been sent to this Siberian prison camp. Such things were not at all rare in the Soviet Union back then. Vicious struggles were going on within the government, the party and the military, and Stalin's pathological suspiciousness pursued the losers without mercy. Stripped of their positions, such men would be tried in kangaroo courts and either executed or sent to concentration camps, though finally which group was the more fortunate only a god could say. An escape from death led only to slave labour of unimaginable cruelty. We Japanese prisoners of war could at least hope to return to our homeland if we survived, but exiled Russians knew no such hope. Like the others, this man would end up with his bones rotting in the soil of Siberia.

Only one thing bothered me about him, and that was that he now knew my name and where to find me. Before the war, I had participated (unknowingly, to be sure) in that secret operation with the spy Yamamoto, crossing the Khalkha River into Mongolian territory for espionage activities. If the man should leak this information, it could put me in a very uncomfortable position. However, he did not inform on me. No, as I was to discover later, he had far more grandiose plans for me.

I spotted him a week later, outside the station. He was in chains still, wearing the same filthy prison clothes and cracking rocks with a hammer. I looked at him, and he looked at me. He rested his hammer on the ground and turned my way, standing as tall and straight as he had when in military uniform. This time, unmistakably, he wore a smile on his face – a faint smile, but still a smile, one suggesting a streak of cruelty that sent chills up my spine. It was the same expression he had worn as he watched Yamamoto being skinned alive. I said nothing and passed on.

I had one friend at the time among the officers in the camp's Soviet Army headquarters. Like me, he had specialized in geography in college (in Leningrad). We were the same age, and both of us were interested in making maps, so we would find pretexts now and then for indulging in a little shoptalk. He had a personal interest in the strategic maps of Manchuria that the Kwantung Army had been making. Of course, we couldn't have such conversations when his superiors were around. We had to snatch opportunities to enjoy this professional patter in their absence. Sometimes he would give me food or show me pictures of the wife and children he had left behind in Kiev. He was the only Russian I felt at all close to during the period I was interned in the Soviet Union.

One time, in an offhand manner, I asked him about the convicts working by the station. One man in particular had struck me as different from the usual inmate, I said; he looked as if he might once have held an important post. I described his appearance. The officer – whose name was Nikolai – said to me with a scowl, "That would be Boris the Manskinner. You'd better not have anything to do with him."

Why was that? I asked. Nikolai seemed hesitant to say more, but he knew I was in a position to do him favours, so reluctantly he told me how "Boris the Manskinner" had been sent to this mine. "Now, don't tell anyone I told you," he warned me. "That guy is dangerous. I'm not joking – they don't come any worse. I wouldn't touch him with a ten-foot pole."

This is what Nikolai told me. The real name of "Boris the Manskinner" was Boris Gromov. Just as I had imagined, he had been a major in the NKVD. They had assigned him to Ulan Bator as a military adviser in 1938, the year Choybalsan took power as prime minister. There he organized the Mongolian secret police, modelling it after Beria's NKVD, and he distinguished himself in suppressing counterrevolutionary forces. They would round people up, throw them into concentration camps, and torture them, liquidating anyone of whom they had the slightest suspicion.

As soon as the battle of Nomonhan ended and the Far Eastern crisis was averted, Boris was called back to Moscow and reassigned to Soviet-occupied Eastern Poland, where he worked on the purging of the old Polish Army. That is where he earned the nickname "Boris the Manskinner". Skinning people alive, using a man they said he brought with him from Mongolia, was his special form of torture. The Poles were scared to death of him, needless to say. Anyone forced to watch a skinning would confess everything without fail. When the German Army suddenly burst across the border and the war started with Germany, he pulled back from Poland to Moscow. Lots of people were arrested at that time on suspicion of having colluded with Hitler. They would be executed or sent to prison camps. Here, again, Boris distinguished himself as Beria's right-hand man, employing his special torture. Stalin and Beria had to cook up an internal-conspiracy theory, covering up their own responsibility for having failed to predict the Nazi invasion in order to solidify their leadership. A lot of people died for nothing while being cruelly tortured. Boris and his man were said to have skinned at least five people then, and rumour had it that he proudly displayed the skins on the walls of his office.

Boris may have been cruel, but he was also very careful, which is how he survived all the plots and purges. Beria loved him as a son. But this may have been what led him to become a little too sure of himself and to overstep the mark. The mistake he made was a fatal one. He arrested the commander of an armoured battalion on suspicion of having secret communications with one of Hitler's SS armoured battalions during a battle in the Ukraine. He killed the man after torturing him, poking hot irons into every opening – ears, nostrils, rectum, penis, whatever. But the officer turned out to be the nephew of a high-ranking Communist Party official. What's more, a thoroughgoing investigation by the Red Army General Staff showed the man to have been innocent of any wrongdoing. The party official blew up, of course, nor was the Red Army going to withdraw quietly after such a blot on its honour. Not even Beria was able to protect Boris this time. They stripped him of his rank, put him on trial, and sentenced both him and his Mongolian adjutant to death. The NKVD went to work though, and got his sentence reduced to hard labour in a concentration camp (though the Mongolian was *hanged). Beria sent a secret message to Boris in prison, promising to pull strings in the army and the party: he would get him out and restore him to power after he had served a year in the camp. At least this was how Nikolai had heard it.*

"So you see, Mamiya," Nikolai said to me, keeping his voice low, "everybody thinks Boris is going back to Moscow someday, that Beria is sure to save him before too long. It's true that Beria has to be careful: this camp is still run by the party and the army. But none of us can relax. The direction of the wind can shift just like that. And when it does, anybody who's given him a tough time here is in for it. The world may be full of idiots, but nobody's stupid enough to sign his own death warrant. We have to tiptoe around him. He's an honoured guest here. Of course, we can't give him servants and treat him as if he were in a hotel. For the sake of appearances, we have to put chains on his leg and give him a few rocks to crack, but in fact he has his own room and all the alcohol and tobacco he wants. If you ask me, he's like a poison snake. Keeping him alive is not going to do anybody any good. Somebody ought to sneak in there one night and slash his throat for him."

Another day when I was walking by the station, that big sergeant stopped me again. I started to take out my pass, but he shook his head and told me to go instead to the stationmaster's office. Puzzled, I did as I was told and found in the office not the stationmaster but Boris Gromov. He sat at the desk, drinking tea while waiting for me to arrive. I froze in the doorway. He no longer had leg irons on. With his hand, he gestured for me to come in.

"Nice to see you, Lieutenant Mamiya. It's been years," he said cheerily, flashing a big smile. He offered me a cigarette, but I shook my head.

"Nine years, to be precise," he continued, lighting up. "Or is it eight? Anyhow, it's wonderful to see you alive and well. What a joy to meet old friends! Especially after such a brutal war. Don't you agree? And how did you manage to get out of that well?"

I just stood there, saying nothing.

"All right, then, never mind. The important thing is that you did get out. And then you lost a hand somewhere. And then you learned to speak such fluent Russian! Wonderful, wonderful. You can always make do without a hand. What matters most is that you're alive."

"Not by choice," I replied.

Boris laughed aloud. "You're such an interesting fellow, Lieutenant Mamiya. You would choose not to live, and yet here you are, very much alive. Yes, a truly interesting fellow. But I am not so easily fooled. No ordinary man could have escaped from that deep well by himself – escaped and found his way back across the river to Manchuria. But don't worry. I won't tell anyone.

"Enough about you, though. Let me tell you about myself. As you can see, I lost my former position and am now a mere prisoner in a concentration camp. But I do not intend to stay here on the edge of the earth for ever, breaking rocks with a sledgehammer. I am as powerful as ever back at Party Central, and I am using that power to increase my power here day by day. And so I will tell you in all frankness that I want to have good relations with you Japanese prisoners of war. The productivity of this mine depends on you men – on your numbers and your hard work. We can accomplish nothing if we ignore your power, and that includes your own individual power, Lieutenant Mamiya. I want you to lend me some of what you have. You are a former intelligence officer of the Kwantung Army and a very brave man. You speak fluent Russian. If you would act as my liaison, I am in a position to do favours for yourself and your comrades. This is not a bad deal that I am offering you."

"I have never been a spy," I declared, "and I have no intention of becoming one now."

"I am not asking you to become a spy," Boris said, as if to calm me down. "All I'm saying is that I can make things easier for your people. I'm offering to improve relations, and I want you to be the go-between. Together, we can knock that shit-eating Georgian politburo son of a bitch out of his chair. I can do it, don't kid yourself. I'm sure you Japanese hate his guts. Once we get rid of him, you people will be able to have partial autonomy, you can form committees, you can run your own organization. Then at least you'll be able to stop the guards from dishing out brutal treatment anytime they like. That's what you've all been hoping for, isn't it?"

Boris was right about that. We had been appealing to the camp authorities about these matters for a long time, and they would always turn us down flat.

"And what do you want in return?" I asked.

"Almost nothing," he said, with a big smile, holding both arms out. "All I am looking for is close, friendly relations with you Japanese prisoners of war. I want to eliminate a few of my party comrades, my tovarishes, with whom it seems I am unable to achieve any understanding, and I need your people's coopera-tion to accomplish that. We have many interests in common, so why don't we join forces for our mutual benefit? What is it the Americans say? 'Give and take'? If you cooperate with me, I won't do anything to your disadvantage. I have no tricks up my sleeve. I know, of course, that I am in no position to ask you to like me. You and I share some unpleasant memories, to be sure. But appearances aside, I am a man of honour. I always keep my promises. So why don't we let bygones be bygones?

"Take a few days, think about my offer, and let me have a firm reply. I believe it's worth a try. You men have nothing to lose, don't you agree? Now, make sure you mention this only to people you are quite sure you can trust. A few of your men are informers working with the politburo member. Make sure they don't get wind of this. Things could turn sour if they found out. My power here is still somewhat limited."

I went back to my area and took one man aside to discuss Boris's offer. This fellow had been a lieutenant colonel in the army. He was a tough man with a sharp mind. Commander of a unit that had shut itself up in a Khingan Mountain fortress and refused to raise the white flag even after Japan's surrender, he was now the unofficial leader of the camp's Japanese prisoners of war, a force the Russians had to reckon with. Concealing the incident with Yamamoto on the banks of the Khalkha, I told him that Boris had been a high-ranking officer in the secret police and explained his offer. The colonel seemed interested in the idea of eliminating the present politburo member and securing some autonomy for the Japanese prisoners of war. I stressed that Boris was a cold-blooded and dangerous man, a past master of deceit and trickery who could not be taken at face value. "You may be right," said the colonel, "but so is our politburo friend: we have nothing to lose." And he was right. If something came out of the deal, it couldn't make things any worse for us than they already were, I thought. But I couldn't have been more wrong. Hell has no true bottom.

A few days later, I was able to arrange a private meeting between the colonel and Boris in a place away from prying eyes. I acted as interpreter. A secret pact resulted from their thirty-minute discussion, and the two shook hands. I have no way of knowing exactly what happened after that. The two avoided direct contact so as not to attract attention, and instead they seem to have engaged in a constant exchange of coded messages using some secret means of communication. This ended my role as intermediary. Which was fine with me. If possible, I wanted nothing more to do with Boris. Only later would I realize that such a thing was anything but possible.

As Boris had promised, about a month later, Party Central removed the Georgian politburo member from office and sent a new member to take his place two days after that. Another two days went by, and three Japanese prisoners of war were strangled during the night. They were found hanging from beams to make the deaths look like suicides, but these were clearly lynchings carried out by other Japanese. The three must have been the informers Boris had mentioned. There was never any investigation. By then, Boris had the camp in the palm of his hand.

31

The Bat Vanishes

•

The Thieving Magpie Returns

Wearing a sweater and coat, a woollen hat pulled down low almost to my eyes, I scaled the back wall and lowered myself into the alley. The sun would not be up for a while, and people were still asleep. I padded my way down the alley to the Residence.

Inside, the house was just as I had left it six days earlier, complete with dirty dishes in the sink. I found no written messages and nothing on the answering machine. The computer screen in Cinnamon's room was as cold and dead as before. The heating was keeping the place at normal room temperature. I took off my coat and gloves, then boiled a kettle and made myself some tea. I had a few biscuits and cheese for breakfast, washed the dishes in the sink, and put them away. Nine o'clock came, again with no sign of Cinnamon.

•

I went out to the yard, took the cover off the well, and leaned over to look inside. There was the same dense darkness. I knew the well now as if it were an extension of my own body: its darkness, its smell and its quiet were part of me. In a sense, I knew the well better than I knew Kumiko. Her memory was still fresh, of course. If I closed my eyes, I could bring back the details of her voice, her face, her body, the way she moved. I had lived in the same house with her for six years, after all. But still, I felt there were things about her that I could not bring back so clearly. Or perhaps I simply could not be sure that what I was remembering was correct – just as I could not recall with certainty the curve in the tail of the cat when he came back.

I sat on the edge of the well, thrust my hands into my coat pockets, and surveyed my surroundings once again. It felt as if a cold rain or snow might begin falling at any time. There was no wind, but the air had a deep chill to it. A flock of little birds raced back and forth across the sky in a complex pattern as if painting a hieroglyph, and then, with a rush, they were gone. Soon I heard the low rumble of a jet, but the plane stayed invisible above the thick layer of clouds. On such a dark, overcast day, I could go into the well without worrying that the sunlight would hurt my eyes when I came out.

Still, I went on sitting there for some time, doing nothing. I was in no hurry. The day had hardly begun. Noon would not be here for a while. I gave myself up to thoughts that came in no particular order as I sat on the edge of the well. Where had they taken the bird sculpture that used to be in this yard? Was it decorating another yard now, still urged on by an endless, pointless impulse to soar into the sky? Or had it been discarded as junk when the Miyawakis' house was demolished last summer? I recalled the piece fondly. Without the sculpture of the bird, I felt, the yard had lost a certain subtle balance.

When I ran out of thoughts, after 11, I climbed down the steel ladder into the well. I set foot on the well bottom and took a few deep breaths, as always, checking the air. It was the same as ever, smelling of mould but breathable. I felt for the bat where I had left it propped against the wall. *It was not there. It was not anywhere.* It had disappeared. Completely. Without a trace.

·

I lowered myself to the well floor and sat leaning against the wall, sighing.

Who could have taken the bat? Cinnamon was the only possibility. He was the only one who knew of its existence, and he was the only one who would think to climb down into the well. But what reason could he possibly have for taking the bat away? This was something I could not comprehend – one of many things I could not comprehend.

I had no choice today but to go ahead without the bat. That would be all right. The bat was after all just a kind of protective talisman. Not having it with me would pose no problem. I had managed to get into that room without it, hadn't I? Once I had presented these arguments to myself, I pulled on the rope that closed the lid of the well. I folded my hands on my knees and closed my eyes in the darkness.

As had happened last time, I was unable to achieve the mental concentration I wanted. All kinds of thoughts came crowding in, blocking the way. To get rid of them, I tried thinking about the pool – the twenty-five-metre indoor pool where I went for exercise. I imagined myself doing laps of the crawl there. I'm not aiming for speed, just using a quiet, steady stroke, over and over again. I bring my elbows out with a minimum of noise and splashing, then stroke gently, fingers first. I take water into my mouth and let it out slowly, as if breathing underwater. After a while, I feel my body flowing naturally through the water, as if riding on a soft wind. The only sound reaching my ears is that of my own regular breathing. I'm floating on the wind like a bird in the sky, looking down at the earth below. I see distant towns and tiny people and flowing rivers. A sense of calm envelops me, a feeling close to rapture. Swimming is one of the best things in my life. It has never solved any problems, but it has done no harm, and nothing has ever ruined it for me. Swimming.

Just then I heard something.

I realized I could hear a low, monotonous hum in the dark, something like the droning of insect wings. But the sound was too artificial, too mechanical, to be insect wings. It had subtle variations in frequency, like tuning changes in a shortwave broadcast. I held my breath and listened, trying to catch its direction. It seemed to be coming from a fixed point in the darkness and, at the same time, from inside my own head. The border between the two was almost impossible to determine in the deep darkness.

While concentrating all my attention on the sound, I fell asleep. I had no awareness of feeling sleepy before that happened. All of a sudden, I was asleep, as if I had been walking down a corridor with nothing particular on my mind when, without warning, I was dragged into an unknown room. How long this thick, mudlike stupor enveloped me I had no idea. It couldn't have been very long. It might have been just a moment. But when some kind of presence brought me back to consciousness, I knew I was in another darkness. The air was different, the temperature was different, the quality and depth of the darkness were different. This darkness was tainted with some kind of faint, opaque light. And a familiar sharp smell of pollen struck my nostrils. I was in that strange hotel room.

I raised my face, scanned my surroundings, held my breath.

I had come through the wall.

I was sitting on a carpeted floor, my back leaning against a cloth-covered wall. My hands were still folded on my knees. As fearful and deep as my sleep had been just a moment before, my wakefulness now was complete and lucid. The contrast was so extreme that it took a moment for my wakefulness to sink in. The quick contractions of my heart were plainly audible. There was no doubt about it. I was here. I had at last made it all the way into the room.

•

In the fine-grained, multi-veiled darkness, the room looked exactly as I remembered it. As my eyes became used to the darkness, though, I began to pick out slight differences. First, the telephone was in a different place. It had moved from the night table to the top of a pillow, in which it was now all but buried. Then I saw that the amount of whisky in the bottle had gone down. There was just a little left in the bottom now. All the ice in the bucket had melted and was now nothing but old, cloudy water. The glass was dry inside, and when I touched it I realized it was coated with white dust. I approached the bed, lifted the phone, and put the receiver to my ear. The line was dead. The room looked as if it had been abandoned, forgotten for a very long time. There was no sense of a human presence there. Only the flowers in the vase preserved their strange vividness.

There were signs that someone had been lying in the bed: the sheets and covers and pillows were in slight disarray. I pulled back the covers and checked for warmth, but there was none. No smell of perfume remained, either. Much time seemed to have elapsed since the person had left the bed. I sat on the edge of the bed, scanned the room again, and listened for sounds. But I heard nothing. The place was like an ancient tomb after grave robbers had carried off the body.

•

All of a sudden, the phone began to ring. My heart froze like a frightened cat. The air's sharp reverberations woke the floating grains of pollen, and the flower petals raised their faces in the darkness. How could the phone have been ringing? Only a few moments before, it had been as dead as a rock in the earth. I steadied my breathing, calmed the beating of my heart, and checked to make sure I was still there, in the room. I stretched out my hand, touched the receiver, and hesitated a moment before lifting it from its cradle. By then, the phone had rung three or perhaps four times.

"Hello." The phone went dead as I lifted the receiver. The irreversible heaviness of death weighed in my hand like a sandbag. "Hello," I said again, but my own dry voice came back to me unaltered, as if rebounding from a thick wall. I replaced the receiver, then picked it up again and listened. There was no sound. I sat on the edge of the bed, trying to control my breathing as I waited for the phone to ring again. It did not ring. I watched the grains in the air return to unconsciousness and sink into the darkness. I replayed the sound of the telephone in my mind. I was no longer entirely certain that it had rung at all. But if I let doubts like that creep in, there would have been no end to them. I had to draw a line somewhere. Otherwise, my very existence in this place would have been open to question. *The phone had rung; there could be no mistake.* And in the next instant, it had gone dead. I cleared my throat, but that sound, too, died instantly in the air.

I stood up and made a circuit of the room. I studied the floor, stared up at the ceiling, sat on the table, leaned against the wall, gave the door-knob a quick twist, flicked the switch of the floor lamp on and off. The doorknob didn't budge, of course, and the lamp was dead. The window was boarded from outside. I listened out for any sounds, but the silence was like a smooth, high wall. Still, I felt the presence of something trying to deceive me, as if the others were holding their breath, pressing them-selves flat against the wall, obliterating their skin colour to keep me from knowing they were there. So I pretended not to notice. We were very good at fooling each other. I cleared my throat again and touched my fingers to my lips.

I decided to inspect the room once more. I tried the floor lamp again, but it produced no light. I opened the whisky bottle and sniffed what was left inside. The smell was unchanged. Cutty Sark. I replaced the cap and returned the bottle to the table. I put the receiver to my ear one more time, but the phone could not have been any deader. I took a few slow steps to get a feel of the carpet against my shoes. I pressed my ear against the wall and concentrated all my attention in an attempt to hear any sounds that might have been coming through it, but there was, of course, nothing. I stepped to the door and, knowing that to do so was pointless, gave the knob a twist. It turned easily to the right. For a moment, I could not absorb this fact. Before, the knob had been so solid it could have been set in cement. I went back to square one and tried again, taking my hand from the knob, reaching out for it again, and turning it back and forth. It turned smoothly in my hand. This gave me the strangest feeling, as if my tongue were swelling inside my mouth.

The door was open.

I pulled the knob until the door swung open just enough for a blinding light to come streaming into the room. The bat. If only I had the bat, I would have felt more confident. *Oh, forget the bat!* I swung the door wide open. Checking left, then right, to be sure no one was there, I stepped outside. It was a long, carpeted corridor. A little way down the corridor, I could see a large vase filled with flowers. It was the vase I had hidden behind while the whistling waiter was knocking on this door. In my memory, the corridor was a long one, with many turns and branches along the way. I had managed to get here by coming across the waiter whistling his way down the corridor and following him. The number plate on the door had identified this as Room 208.

Stepping with care, I walked towards the vase. I hoped I could find my way to the lobby, where Noboru Wataya had been appearing on television. Many people had been in the lobby, moving to and fro. I might be able to find some clue there. But wandering through the hotel was like venturing into a vast desert without a compass. If I couldn't find the lobby and then was unable to find my way back to Room 208, I might be sealed up inside this labyrinthine place, unable to return to the real world.

But now was no time for hesitation. It could be my last chance. I had waited every day in the bottom of the well for six months, and now, at last, the door had opened before me. Besides, the well was going to be taken from me soon. If I failed now, all my time and effort would have been for nothing.

I turned several corners. My filthy tennis shoes moved without a sound over the carpet. I couldn't hear a thing – no voices, no music, no TV, not even a ventilator fan or a lift. The hotel was silent, like a ruin forgotten by time. I turned many corners and passed many doors. The corridor forked again and again, and I always turned right, on the assumption that if I chose to go back, I should be able to find the room by taking only lefts. By now, though, my sense of direction was gone. I felt no nearer to anything in particular. The numbers on the doors had no order, and they went by endlessly, so they were no help at all. They trickled away from my consciousness almost before they had registered in my memory. Now and then I felt I had passed some of them before. I came to a stop in the middle of the corridor and caught my breath. Was I circling back over and over the same territory, the way one does when lost in the woods?

•

As I stood there wondering what to do, I heard a familiar sound in the distance. It was the whistling waiter. He was in perfect tune. There was no one to match him. As before, he was whistling the overture to Rossini's *The Thieving Magpie* – not an easy tune to whistle, but it seemed to give him no trouble. I proceeded down the corridor in the direction of the whistling, which grew louder and clearer. He appeared to be heading in my direction. I found a good-sized pillar and hid behind it.

The waiter carried a silver tray again, with the usual bottle of Cutty Sark and an ice bucket and two glasses. He hurried past me, facing straight ahead, with an expression on his face that suggested he was entranced by the sound of his own whistling. He didn't look in my direction; he was in such a hurry that he couldn't spare a moment's wasted motion. *Everything is the same as before,* I thought. It seemed my flesh was being carried back in time.

As soon as the waiter passed me, I followed him. His silver tray bobbed pleasantly in time with the tune he was whistling, now and then catching the glare of a ceiling light. He repeated the melody of *The Thieving Magpie* over and over like a magic spell. What kind of opera *was The Thieving Magpie*? I wondered. All I knew about it was the monotonous melody of its overture and its mysterious title. We had a recording of the overture in the house when I was a boy. It had been conducted by Toscanini. Compared with Claudio Abbado's youthful, fluid, contemporary performance, Toscanini's had a blood-stirring intensity to it, like the slow strangulation of a powerful foe who has been downed after a violent battle. But was *The Thieving Magpie* really the story of a magpie that engaged in thievery? If things ever settled down, I would have to go to the library and look it up in an encyclopedia of music. I might even buy a complete recording of the opera if it was available. Or maybe not. I might not care to know the answers to these questions by then.

The whistling waiter continued walking straight ahead, with all the mechanical regularity of a robot, and I followed him at a fixed distance. I knew where he was going without even having to think about it. He was delivering the fresh bottle of Cutty Sark and the ice and glasses to Room 208. And indeed he came to a stop in front of Room 208. He shifted the tray to his left hand, checked the room number, drew himself up, and gave the door a perfunctory knock. Three knocks, then another three.

I couldn't tell whether there was any answer from within. I was hiding behind the vase, watching the waiter. Time passed, but the waiter went on standing to attention, as though attempting to challenge the limits of endurance. He did not knock again but waited for the door to open. Eventually, as if in answer to a prayer, the door began to open inwards.

32

The Job of Making Others Use Their Imaginations (The Story of Boris the Manskinner, Continued)

•

Boris kept his promise. We Japanese war prisoners were given partial autonomy and allowed to form a representative committee. The colonel was the committee chairman. From then on, the Russian guards, both civil and military, were ordered to cease their violent behaviour, and the committee became responsible for keeping order in the camp. As long as we caused no trouble and met our production quotas, they would leave us alone. That was the ostensible policy of the new politburo member (which is to say, the policy of Boris). These reforms, at first glance so democratic, should have been great news for us prisoners of war.

But things were not as simple as they seemed. Taken up with welcoming the new reforms, we were too stupid to see the cunning trap that Boris had set for us.

Supported by the secret police, Boris was in a far more powerful position than the new politburo member, and he proceeded to transform the camp and the town as he saw fit. Intrigue and terrorism became the order of the day. Boris chose the strongest and most vicious men from among the prisoners and the civilian guards (of which there was no small supply), trained them, and made them into his own personal bodyguards. Armed with guns and knives and clubs, this handpicked contingent would take care of anyone who resisted Boris, threatening and physically abusing them, sometimes even beating them to death on Boris's orders. No one could lay a hand on them. The soldiers sent from regular army units to guard the mine would pretend not to see what was happening under their noses. By then, not even the army could touch Boris. Soldiers stayed in the background, keeping watch over the railway station and their own barracks, adopting an attitude of indifference with regard to what went on in the mine and the camp.

Boris's favourite among his handpicked guard was a prisoner known as "The Tartar", who had supposedly been a Mongolian wrestling champion. The man stuck to Boris like a shadow. He had a big burn scar on his right cheek, which people said he had got during torture. Boris no longer wore prison clothes, and he moved into a neat little cottage that was kept clean for him by a woman inmate.

According to Nikolai (who was becoming more and more reluctant to talk about anything), several Russians he knew had simply disappeared in the night. Officially, they were listed as missing or having been involved in accidents, but there was no doubt they had been "taken care of" by Boris's henchmen. People's lives were now in danger if they failed to follow Boris's orders or if they merely failed to please him. A few men tried to complain directly to Party Central about the abuses going on in camp, but that was the last anyone ever saw of them. "I heard they even killed a little kid – a seven-year-old – to keep his parents in line. Beat him to death while they watched," Nikolai whispered to me, pale-faced.

At first Boris did nothing so crude as that in the Japanese zone. He concentrated his energies instead on gaining complete control over the Russian guards in the area and solidifying his foothold there. He seemed willing for the moment to leave the Japanese prisoners in charge of their own affairs. And so, for the first few months after the reform, we were able to enjoy a brief interval of peace. Those were tranquil days for us, a period of genuine calm. The committee was able to obtain some reduction in the harshness of the labour, however slight, and we no longer had to fear the violence of the guards. For the first time since our arrival, we were able to feel something like hope. People believed that things were going to get better.

Not that Boris was ignoring us during those few honeymoon months. He was quietly arranging his pieces to gain the greatest strategic advantage. He worked on the Japanese committee members individually, behind the scenes, using bribes or threats to bring them under his control. He avoided overt violence, proceeding with the utmost caution, and so no one noticed what he was doing. When we did finally notice, it was too late. Under the guise of granting us autonomy, he was throwing us off our guard while he fashioned a still more efficient system of control. There was an icy, diabolical precision to his calculations. He succeeded in eliminating random violence from our lives, only to replace it with a new kind of coldly calculated violence.

After six months of firming up his control structure, he changed direction and began applying pressure on us. His first victim was the man who had been the central figure on the committee: the colonel. He had confronted Boris directly to represent the interests of the Japanese prisoners of war on several issues, as a result of which he was eliminated. By that time, the colonel and a few of his cohorts were the only members of the committee who did not belong to Boris. They suffocated him one night, holding him down while one of them pressed a wet towel to his face. Boris ordered the job to be done, of course, though he never dirtied his own hands when it came to killing Japanese. He issued orders to the committee and had other Japanese do it. The colonel's death was written off simply as the result of illness. We all knew who had killed him, but no one could talk about it. We knew that Boris had spies among us, and we had to be careful what we said in front of anyone. After the colonel was murdered, the committee voted for Boris's handpicked candidate to fill his chair.

The work environment steadily deteriorated as a result of the change in the make-up of the committee, until eventually things were as bad as they had ever been. In exchange for our autonomy, we made arrangements with Boris concerning our production quotas, which became increasingly onerous. The quota was raised in stages, under one pretext or another, until finally the work forced upon us became harsher than ever. The number of accidents also escalated, and many Japanese soldiers lent their bones to the soil of a foreign land, victims of reckless mining practices. "Autonomy" meant only that we Japanese now had to oversee our own labour in place of the Russians who had once done it.

Discontent, of course, only blossomed among the prisoners of war. Where we had once had a little society that shared its sufferings equally, a sense of unfairness grew, and with it deep hatred and suspicion. Those who served Boris were given lighter duties and special privileges, while those who did not had to live a harsh life – if allowed to live at all. No one could raise his voice in complaint, for open resistance meant death. One might be thrown into an icy shed to die of cold and starvation, or have a wet towel pressed over one's face while asleep, or have the back of one's skull split open with a pick while working in the mine. Down there, you could end up at the bottom of a shaft. Nobody knew what went on in the darkness of the mine. People would just disappear.

I couldn't help feeling responsible for having brought Boris and the colonel together. Of course, if I hadn't become involved, Boris would have burrowed his way in among us sooner or later by some other route, with similar results, but such thoughts did little to ease my pain. I had made a terrible mistake.

One day I was summoned to the building that Boris used as his office. I had not seen him for a very long time. He sat at a desk, drinking tea, as he had been doing the time I saw him in the stationmaster's office. Behind him, standing to attention with a large-calibre automatic pistol in his belt, was The Tartar. When

I entered the room, Boris turned around to the Mongolian and signalled for him to leave. The two of us were alone together.

"So, then, Lieutenant Mamiya, I have kept my promise, you see."

Indeed, he had, I replied. What he said was unfortunately true. Everything he had promised me had come to pass. It was like a pact with the devil.

"You have your autonomy, and I have my power," he said with a smile, holding his arms out wide. "We both got what we wanted. Coal production has increased, and Moscow is happy. Who could ask for anything more? I am very grateful to you for having acted as my mediator, and I would like to do something for you in return."

There was no such need, I replied.

"Nor is there any need for you to be so distant, Lieutenant. The two of us go way back," said Boris, smiling. "I want you to work here with me. I want you to be my assistant. Unfortunately, this place has a critical shortage of men who can think. You may be missing a hand, but I can see that your sharp mind more than makes up for it. If you will work as my secretary, I would be most grateful and will do everything I can to see that you have as easy a time of it here as possible. That way, you will be sure to survive and make your way back to Japan. Working closely with me can only do you good."

Ordinarily, I would have rejected such an offer out of hand. I had no intention of selling out my comrades and securing an easy time of it for myself by working as Boris's assistant. And if turning him down meant that he would have me killed, that would have suited me fine. But the moment he presented his offer, I found a plan forming in my mind.

"What kind of work do you want me to do?" I asked.

What Boris had in mind for me was not a simple task. The number of chores waiting to be taken care of was huge, the single biggest job being the management of Boris's personal assets. Boris had been helping himself to a good forty per cent of the foodstuffs, clothing, and medical supplies being sent to the camp by Moscow and the International Red Cross, stashing them in secret storehouses, and selling them to various takers. He had also been sending off whole trainloads of coal through the black market. There was a chronic shortage of fuel, the demand for it endless. He would bribe railroad workers and the stationmaster, moving trains almost at will for his own profit. Food and money could make the soldiers guarding the trains shut their eyes to what he was doing. Thanks to such "business" methods, Boris had amassed an amazing fortune. He explained to me that it was ultimately intended as operating capital for the secret police. "Our activity", as he called it, required huge sums off the public record, and he was now engaged in "procuring" those secret funds. But this was a lie. Some of the money may have been finding its way to Moscow, but I was certain that well over half was being transformed into Boris's own personal fortune. As far as I could tell, he was sending the money to foreign bank accounts and buying gold.

For some inexplicable reason, he appeared to have complete faith in me. It seems not to have occurred to him that I might leak his secrets to the outside, which I now find very strange. He always treated his fellow Russians and other white men with the utmost suspicion, but towards Mongolians or Japanese he seemed to feel only the most open-handed trust. Perhaps he assumed that I could do him no harm even if I chose to reveal his secrets. First of all, whom could I reveal them to? Everyone around me was his collaborator or his underling, each with his own tiny share in Boris's huge illegal profits. And the only ones who suffered and died because Boris was diverting their food, clothing, and medicine for his own personal gain were the powerless inmates of the camp. Besides, all mail was censored, and all contact with outsiders was prohibited.

And so I became Boris's energetic and faithful private secretary. I completely overhauled his chaotic books and stock records, systematizing and clarifying the flow of goods and money. I created categorized ledgers that showed at a glance the amount and location of any one item and how its price was fluctuating. I compiled a long list of bribe takers and calculated the "necessary expenses" for each. I worked hard for Boris, from morning to night, as a result of which I lost the few friends I had. People thought of me (could not help but think of me) as a despicable human being, a man who had sold out to become Boris's faithful bootlicker. And sadly enough, they probably still think of me that way. Nikolai would no longer speak to me. The two or three other Japanese prisoners of war I had been close to would now turn away when they saw me coming. On the other hand, there were some who tried to approach me when they saw that I had become a favourite of Boris, but I would have nothing to do with them. Thus I became an isolated figure in the camp. Only the support of Boris kept me from being killed. No one could have got away with murdering one of his most prized possessions. People knew how cruel Boris could be; his fame as the "manskinner" had reached legendary proportions even here.

The more isolated I became, the more Boris came to trust me. He was happy with my efficient, systematic work habits, and he was not stinting in his praise.

"You are a very impressive man, Lieutenant Mamiya. Japan will be sure to recover from her postwar chaos as long as there are Japanese like you. My own country is hopeless. It was almost better under the tzars. At least the tzar didn't have to strain his empty head over a lot of theory. Lenin took whatever he could understand of Marx's theory and used it to his own advantage, and Stalin took *whatever he could understand of Lenin's theory (which wasn't much) and used it to his own advantage. The narrower a man's intellectual grasp, the more power he is able to grab in this country. I tell you, Lieutenant, there is only one way to survive here. And that is not to imagine anything. A Russian who uses his imagination is done for. I certainly never use mine. My job is to make others use their imaginations. That's my bread and butter. Make sure you keep that in mind. As long as you are in here, at least, picture my face if you ever start to imagine something, and say to yourself, 'No, don't do that. Imagining things can be fatal.' These are my golden words of advice to you. Leave the imagining to someone else."*

Half a year slipped by like this. Now the autumn of 1947 was drawing to a close, and I had become indispensable to Boris. I was in charge of the business side of his activities, while The Tartar was in charge of the violent side. The secret police had yet to summon Boris back to Moscow, but by then he no longer seemed to want to go back. He had more or less transformed the camp and the mine into his own inviolable territory, and there he lived in comfort, steadily amassing a huge fortune, protected by his own private army. Perhaps, too, rather than bring him back to the centre, the Moscow elite preferred to keep him there, firming their foothold in Siberia. A continual exchange of letters passed between Boris and Moscow – not using the post office, of course: they would arrive on the train, in the hands of secret messengers. These were always tall men with ice-cold eyes. The temperature in a room seemed to drop whenever one of them walked in.

Meanwhile, the prisoners working the mine continued to die in large numbers, their corpses thrown into mine shafts as before. Boris did a thoroughgoing assessment of each prisoner's potential, driving the physically weak ones hard and reducing their food rations at the outset so as to kill them off and reduce the number of mouths he had to feed. The food diverted from the weak went to the strong in order to raise productivity. Efficiency was everything in the camp: it was the law of the jungle, the survival of the fittest. And whenever the work force began to dwindle, freight cars would arrive packed with new convicts, like trainloads of cattle. Sometimes as much as twenty per cent of the "shipment" would die on the way, but that was of no concern to anyone. Most of the new convicts were Russians and Eastern Europeans brought in from the West. Fortunately for Boris, Stalin's politics of violence continued to function there.

My plan was to kill Boris. I knew, of course, that getting rid of this one man was no guarantee that our situation would improve in any way. It would continue to be one form of hell or another. But I simply could not allow the man to go on living in this world. As Nikolai had said, he was like a poisonous snake. Someone would have to cut his head off.

I was not afraid to die. If anything, I would have liked Boris to kill me as I killed him. But there could be no room for error. I had to wait for the one precise moment when I could have absolute confidence that I would kill him without fail, when I could end his life with a single shot. I continued to act the part of his loyal secretary as I waited for the chance to spring on my prey. But as I said earlier, Boris was an extremely cautious man. He kept The Tartar by his side day and night. And even if he should give me a chance to get him alone sometime, how was I to kill him, with my one hand and no weapon? Still I kept my vigil, waiting for the right moment. If there was a god anywhere in this world, I believed, the chance would come my way.

Early in 1948, a rumour spread through camp that the Japanese prisoners of war were finally going to be allowed to go home, that a ship would be sent to repatriate us in the spring. I asked Boris about it.

"It is true, Lieutenant Mamiya," he said. "The rumour is true. You will all be repatriated before very long. Thanks in part to world opinion, we will not be able to keep you working much longer. But I have a proposition for you, Lieutenant. How would you like to stay in this country, not as a prisoner of war but as a free Soviet citizen? You have served me well, and it will be very difficult for me to find a replacement for you. And you, for your part, will have a far more pleasant time of it if you stay with me than if you go back to endure hardship and poverty in Japan. They have nothing to eat, I am told. People are starving to death. Here you would have money, women, power – everything."

Boris made this proposal in all seriousness. He was aware that it could be dangerous to let me go, knowing his secrets as I did. If I turned him down, he might rub me out to keep me from talking. But I was not afraid. I thanked him for his kind offer but said that I preferred to return to Japan, being concerned about my parents and sister. Boris shrugged once and said nothing further.

The perfect chance to kill him presented itself to me one night in March, as the day of repatriation was drawing near. The Tartar had gone out, leaving me alone with Boris just before 9 o'clock at night. I was working on the books, as always, and Boris was at his desk, writing a letter. It was unusual for us to be in the office so late. He sipped a brandy now and then as he traced his fountain pen over the paper. On the coatrack hung Boris's leather coat, his hat, and his pistol in a leather holster. The pistol was not the typical Soviet Army-issue monster but a German-made Walther PPK. Boris was supposed to have taken it from a Nazi SS lieutenant colonel captured at the battle of the Danube Crossing. It had the lightning SS mark on the handle, and it was always clean and polished. I had often observed Boris working on the gun, and I knew that he kept it loaded, with eight shells in the magazine.

For him to have left the gun on the coatrack was most unusual. He was careful to have it close at hand whenever he was working, concealed in the drawer of the right-hand wing of his desk. That night, however, he had been in a very good, very talkative mood for some reason, and because of that, perhaps, he had not exercised his usual caution. It was the kind of chance I could never hope for again. Any number of times, I had rehearsed in my mind how, with my one hand, I would release the safety catch and send the first cartridge into the chamber. Now, making my decision, I stood and walked past the coatrack, pretending to go for a form. Involved in his letter writing, Boris did not look my way. As I passed by, I slipped the gun out of the holster. Its small size fit my palm perfectly, its outstanding workmanship obvious from its weight and balance. I stood before Boris and released the safety. Then, holding the pistol between my knees, I pulled the slide with my right hand, sending a cartridge into the chamber. With my thumb, I pulled the hammer back. When he heard the small, dry sound it made, Boris looked up, to find me aiming the gun at his face.

He shook his head and sighed.

"Too bad for you, Lieutenant, but the gun isn't loaded," he said after clicking the cap of his fountain pen into place. "You can tell by the weight. Give it a little shake up and down. Eight 7.65-millimetre cartridges weigh eighty grams."

I didn't believe him. Without hesitation, I pointed the muzzle at his forehead and pulled the trigger. The only sound was a click. He was right: it wasn't loaded. I put the gun down and bit my lip, unable to think. Boris opened the desk drawer and took out a handful of shells, holding them on his palm for me to see. He had trapped me. The whole thing had been a ruse.

"I have known for a long time that you wanted to kill me," he said softly. "You have imagined yourself doing it, pictured it in your head any number of times, am I right? I am certain I advised you long ago never to use your imagination. It can only cost you your life. Ah, well, never mind. There is simply no way that you could ever kill me."

Boris took two of the shells from his palm and threw them at my feet. They clattered across the floor to where I stood.

"Those are live shells," he said. "This is no trick. Put them in the gun and shoot me. It will be your last chance. If you really want to kill me, take careful aim. But if you miss, you must promise never to reveal my secrets. You must tell no one in the world what I have been doing here. This will be our little deal."

I nodded to him. I made my promise.

Holding the pistol between my knees again, I pressed the release button, took out the magazine, and loaded the two cartridges into it. This was no easy feat with one hand – a hand that was trembling all the while. Boris observed my movements with a cool expression on his face. There was even the hint of a smile there. Once

I had succeeded in thrusting the magazine back into the grip, I took aim between his eyes, forced my hand to stop trembling, and pulled the trigger. The room shook with the roar of the gun, but the bullet passed by Boris's ear and slammed into the wall. White, pulverized plaster flew in all directions. I had missed from only six feet away. I was not a poor marksman. When stationed in Hsin-ching, I had done my target practice with a great deal of enthusiasm. And although I had only my right hand now, it was stronger than that of most people, and the Walther was the kind of well-balanced pistol that let you take precise, steady aim. I could not believe that I had missed. Once again I cocked the hammer and took aim. I sucked in one deep breath and told myself, "You have to kill this man." By killing him, I could make it mean something that I had lived.

"Take steady aim, now, Lieutenant Mamiya. It's your last bullet." Boris was still smiling.

At that moment, The Tartar came running into the room, his big pistol drawn.

"Keep out of this," Boris barked at him. "Let Mamiya shoot me. And if he manages to kill me, do whatever you like."

The Tartar nodded and pointed the muzzle of his gun at me.

Gripping the Walther in my right hand, I thrust it straight out, aimed for the middle of Boris's contemptuous, confident smile, and coolly squeezed the trigger. The pistol kicked, but I held it steady. It was a perfectly executed shot. But again the bullet grazed Boris's head, this time smashing the wall clock behind him into a million pieces. Boris never so much as twitched an eyebrow. Leaning back in his chair, he went on staring at me with his snakelike eyes. The pistol crashed to the floor.

For a moment, no one moved or spoke. Soon, though, Boris left his chair and bent over to retrieve the Walther from where I had dropped it. After a long, thoughtful look at the pistol in his hand, he returned it to its holster on the coatrack. Then he patted my arm twice, as if to comfort me.

"I told you you couldn't kill me, didn't I?" Boris said. He took a pack of Camels from his pocket, put a cigarette between his lips, and lit it with his lighter. "There was nothing wrong with your shooting. It was just that you couldn't kill me. You aren't qualified to kill me. That is the only reason you missed your chance. And now, unfortunately, you will have to bear my curse back to your homeland. Listen: wherever you may be, you can never be happy. You will never love anyone or be loved by anyone. That is my curse. I will not kill you. But I do not spare you out of goodwill. I have killed many people over the years, and I will go on to kill many more. But I never kill anyone whom there is no need to kill. Goodbye, Lieutenant Mamiya. A week from now, you will leave this place for the port of Nakhodka. Bon voyage. The two of us will never meet again."

That was the last I ever saw of Boris the Manskinner. The week after that, I left the concentration camp behind and was shipped by train to Nakhodka. After many tortuous experiences there, I finally reached Japan at the beginning of the following year.

To tell you the truth, I have no idea what this long, strange story of mine will mean to you, Mr Okada. Perhaps it is nothing more than an old man's mutterings. But I wanted to – I had to – tell you my story. As you can see from having read my letter, I have lived my life in total defeat. I have lost. I am lost. I am qualified for nothing. Through the power of the curse, I love no one and am loved by no one. A walking shell, I will simply disappear into darkness. Having managed at long last, however, to pass my story on to you, Mr Okada, I will be able to disappear with some small degree of contentment.

May the life you lead be a good one, a life free of regrets.

33

A Dangerous Place

•

The People Watching Television

•

The Hollow Man

The door began to open. Holding the tray in both hands, the waiter gave a slight bow and went inside. I stayed in the shadows of the vase, waiting for him to come out and wondering what I would do when he did. I could go in as he came out. *There was definitely someone inside Room 208.* If things continued to develop as they had done before (which was just what was happening), the door should be unlocked. On the other hand, I could forget about the room for now and follow the waiter. That way, I could probably find my way to the place where he belonged.

I wavered between the two, but in the end I decided to follow the waiter. There was something dangerous lurking in Room 208, something that could have fatal consequences. I had all too clear a memory of the sharp rapping in the darkness and the violent white gleam of some knife-like thing. I had to be more careful. Let me first see where the waiter would lead me. Then I could come back to the room. But how was I supposed to do that? I thrust my hands into my pockets and found there, along with my wallet and change and handkerchief, a small ballpoint pen. I pulled the pen out and drew a line on my hand to make sure it had ink. I could use this to mark the walls as I followed the waiter. Then I could follow the marks back to the room. It should work.

The door opened and the waiter came out, empty handed. He had left everything inside the room, including the tray. After closing the door, he straightened himself and began whistling *The Thieving Magpie* as he hurried back along the route he had followed here. I stepped out from my place in the shadow of the big vase and followed him. Wherever the corridor forked, I made a small blue X on the cream-coloured wall. The waiter never looked back. There was something special about the way he walked. He could have been an entrant in the World Hotel Waiter Walking-Style Championship. His walk all but proclaimed, "This is how a hotel waiter is supposed to walk: head up, jaw thrust out, back straight, arms swinging rhythmically to the tune of *The Thieving Magpie*, taking long strides down the corridor." He turned many corners, went up and down many short flights of stairs, along stretches where the lighting was brighter or dimmer, past depressions in the walls that produced different kinds of shadows. I maintained a reasonable distance behind him to keep from being noticed, but following him was not particularly difficult. He might disappear for a moment as he turned a corner, but there was never any danger of my losing him, thanks to his vibrant whistling.

Just as a salmon migrating upstream eventually reaches a still pool, the waiter came out of the final corridor into the hotel lobby, the crowded lobby where I had seen Noboru Wataya on television. This time, however, the lobby was hushed, with only a handful of people sitting in front of a large television set, watching an NHK news broadcast. The waiter had stopped whistling as he neared the lobby, so as not to disturb people. Now he cut straight across the lobby floor and disappeared behind a door marked "Staff Only."

Pretending to be killing time, I ambled around the lobby, sat on a few different sofas, looked up at the ceiling, checked the thickness of the rug beneath my feet. Then I went to a pay phone and put in a coin. This phone was as dead as the one in the room had been. I picked up a hotel phone and punched in "208", but this phone was also dead.

After that, I went to sit in a chair away from where the people were watching television, to observe them unobtrusively. The group consisted of twelve people, nine men and three women, mostly in their thirties and forties, with two possibly in their early fifties. The men all wore suits or sports coats and conservative ties and leather shoes. Apart from some differences in height and weight, none had any distinguishing features. The three women were all in their early thirties, well dressed and carefully made up. They could have been on their way back from a school reunion, except that they sat separately and gave no indication of knowing each other. In fact, all the people in the group appeared to be strangers whose attention just happened to be locked on the same television screen. There were no exchanges of opinions or glances or nods.

I sat watching the news for a while from my place. The stories were of no special interest to me – a governor cutting a tape at the opening ceremony for a new road, children's crayons that had been discovered to contain a harmful substance, the death of a truckdriver who had been hit by a tourist bus in Asahikawa because of icy roads and reduced visibility in a major snowstorm, with injuries to several of the tourists on their way to a hot-spring resort. The announcer read each of the stories in turn in a restrained voice, as though dealing out low-numbered cards. I thought about the television in the home of Mr Honda, the fortune-teller. His set had always been tuned to NHK too.

These images of the news coming over the air were at the same time very real and very unreal to me. I felt sorry for the thirty-seven-year-old truckdriver who had died in the accident. No one wants to die in an agony of ruptured internal organs in a blizzard in Asahikawa. But I was not acquainted with the truckdriver, and he did not know me. And so my sympathy for him had nothing personal about it. I could feel only a generalized kind of sympathy for a fellow human being who had met with a sudden, violent death. That generalized emotion might be very real for me and at the same time not real at all. I turned my eyes from the television screen and surveyed the big, empty lobby once more. I found nothing there to focus on. There were no hotel staff members, and the small bar was not yet open. The only thing on the wall was a large oil painting of a mountain.

When I turned back to the television screen, there was a large close-up of a familiar face – Noboru Wataya's face. I sat up straight and turned my attention to the reporter's words. Something had happened to Noboru Wataya, but I had missed the beginning of the story. Soon the photo disappeared and the reporter appeared on-screen. He wore a tie and an overcoat, and he was standing at the entrance to a large building, with a mike in his hand.

". . . rushed to Tokyo Women's Medical University Hospital, where he is now in intensive care, but all we know is that he has not regained consciousness since his skull was fractured by an unknown assailant. Hospital authorities have refused to comment on whether or not his wounds are life-threatening. A detailed report on his condition is to be released later. Reporting from the main entrance of Tokyo Women's Medical University . . ."

And the broadcast returned to the studio, where the anchorman began to read a text that had just been handed to him. "According to reports just in, Representative Noboru Wataya has sustained severe injuries to the head in what appears to have been an attack on his life. The young assailant burst into his office in Tokyo's Minato District at 11.30 this morning and, in the presence of the persons whom Representative Wataya was meeting at the time, delivered several strong blows to the head with a baseball bat, inflicting severe injuries."

The screen showed a picture of the building that housed Noboru Wataya's office.

"The man had posed as a caller to Representative Wataya's office, concealing the bat inside a long cardboard mailing tube. Witnesses say the man pulled the bat out of the tube and attacked without a word of warning."

The screen showed the office where the crime had occurred. Chairs were scattered on the floor, and a black pool of blood could be seen nearby.

"The attack came so suddenly that neither Representative Wataya nor the others with him had a chance to resist. After checking to be certain that Representative Wataya was unconscious, the assailant left the scene, still holding the baseball bat. Witnesses say the man, approximately thirty years of age, was wearing a navy-blue coat, a woollen ski hat, also navy, and dark glasses. He was about five-foot nine and had a bruiselike mark on his right cheek. Police are looking for the man, who seems to have managed to lose himself without a trace in the crowds."

The screen showed police at the scene of the crime and then a lively Akasaka street scene.

Baseball bat? Mark on the face? I bit my lip.

"Noboru Wataya was a rising star among economists and political commentators when, this spring, he inherited the mantle of his uncle, longtime Diet member Yoshitaka Wataya, and was elected to the House of Representatives. Widely hailed since then as an influential young politician and polemicist, Noboru Wataya was someone of whom much was expected. Police are launching a two-pronged investigation into the crime, assuming that it could have been either politically motivated or some kind of personal vendetta. To repeat this late-breaking story: Noboru Wataya, prominent member of the House of

Representatives, has been rushed to the hospital with severe head injuries after an attack late this morning by an unknown assailant. Details on his condition are not known at this time. And now, in other news —"

Someone appeared to have switched off the television at that point. The announcer's voice was cut short, and silence enveloped the lobby. People began to relax their tensed postures. It was obvious that they had gathered in front of the television for the express purpose of hearing news about Noboru Wataya. No one moved after the set was switched off. No one made a sound.

Who could have hit Noboru Wataya with a bat? The description of the assailant sounded exactly like me – the navy coat and hat, the sunglasses, the mark on the cheek, height, age – and the baseball bat. I had kept my own bat in the bottom of the well for months, but it had disappeared. If that same bat was the one used to crush Noboru Wataya's skull, then someone must have taken it for that purpose.

Just then the eyes of one of the women in the group focused on me – a skinny, fishlike woman with prominent cheekbones. She wore white earrings in the very centre of her long earlobes. She had twisted around in her chair and sat in that position for a long time, watching me, never averting her gaze or changing her expression. Next the bald man sitting beside her, letting his eyes follow her line of vision, turned and looked at me. In height and build, he resembled the owner of the cleaning store by the station. One by one, the other people turned in my direction, as if becoming aware for the first time that I was there with them. Subjected to their unwavering stares, I could not help but be aware of my navy-blue jacket and hat, my five-foot nine-inch height, my age, and the mark on my right cheek. These people all seemed to know, too, that I was Noboru Wataya's brother-in-law and that I not only disliked but actively hated him. I could see it in their eyes. My grip tightened on the arm of my chair as I wondered what to do. I had not beaten Noboru Wataya with a baseball bat. I was not that kind of person, and besides, I no longer owned the bat. But they would never believe me, I was sure. They believed only what they saw on television.

I eased out of my chair and started for the corridor by which I had entered the lobby. I had to leave that place as soon as possible. I was not welcome there. I had taken only a few steps when I turned to see that several of the people had left their chairs and were coming after me. I sped up and cut straight across the lobby for the corridor. I had to find my way back to Room 208. The inside of my mouth was dry.

I had finally made it across the lobby and taken my first step into the corridor when, without a sound, all the lights in the hotel went out. A heavy curtain of blackness fell with the speed of an axe blow. Someone cried out behind me, the voice much closer than I would have expected, a stony hatred at its core.

I continued on in the darkness, edging forward cautiously with my hands against the wall. I had to get away from them. But then I bumped into a small table and knocked something over in the darkness, probably some kind of vase. It rolled, clattering, across the floor. The collision sent me down on all fours on the carpet. I scrambled to my feet and continued feeling my way along the corridor. Just then, the edge of my coat received a sharp yank, as if it had caught on a nail. It took me a moment to realize what was happening. Someone was pulling on my coat. Without hesitation, I slipped out of it and lunged ahead in the darkness. I felt my way around a corner, tripped up a staircase, and turned another corner, my head and shoulders bumping into things all the while. At one point, I missed my footing on a step and smashed my face against the wall. I felt no pain, though: only a dull twinge behind the eyes. I couldn't let them catch me here.

There was no light of any kind, not even the emergency lighting that was supposed to come on in hotels in case of a power failure. After tearing my way through this featureless darkness, I came to a halt, trying to catch my breath, and listened for sounds behind me. All I could hear, though, was the wild beating of my own heart. I knelt down for a moment's rest. They must have given up the chase. If I went any further in the darkness now, I would probably end up lost in the depths of the labyrinth. I decided to stay here, leaning against the wall, and try to calm myself.

Who could have turned out the lights? I couldn't believe it had been a coincidence. It had happened the very moment I stepped into the corridor as people were catching up with me. Most likely someone there had done it to rescue me from danger. I took my wool hat off, wiped the sweat from my face with my handkerchief, and put the hat back on. I was beginning to notice pain in different parts of my body, but I didn't seem to have any injuries as such. I looked at the luminous hands of my watch in the darkness, only to remember that the watch had stopped at 11.30. That was the time I climbed down into the well, and it was also the time that someone had beaten Noboru Wataya in his office with a baseball bat.

Could I have been the one who did it?

Down here in the darkness like this, that began to seem like one more theoretical possibility. Perhaps, up there, in the real world, I had struck him with the bat and injured him severely, and I was the only one who didn't know about it. Perhaps the intense hatred inside me had taken the initiative to walk over there without my knowing it and administer him a drubbing. Did I say *walk*? I would have had to take the Odakyu Line to Shinjuku and change there to the subway in order to get to Akasaka. Could I have done such a thing without being aware of it? No, certainly not – unless there existed another me.

"Mr Okada," someone said close by in the darkness.

My heart leaped into my throat. I had no idea where the voice had come from. My muscles tensed as I scanned the darkness, but of course I could see nothing.

"Mr Okada." The voice came again. A man's low voice. "Don't worry, Mr Okada, I'm on your side. We met here once before. Don't you remember?"

I did remember. I knew that voice. It belonged to the man with no face. But I had to be careful. I was not ready to answer.

"You have to leave this place as soon as possible, Mr Okada. They'll come to find you when the lights come on. Follow me: I know a shortcut."

The man switched on a penlight. It cast a small beam, but it was enough to show me where to step. "This way," the man urged. I scrambled up from the floor and hurried after him.

"You must be the one who turned out the lights for me, is that right?" I asked the man from behind.

He did not answer, but neither did he deny it.

"Thanks," I said. "It was a close call."

"They are very dangerous people," he said. "Much more dangerous than you think."

I asked him, "Was Noboru Wataya really injured in some kind of beating?"

"That is what they said on TV," the man replied, choosing his words carefully.

"I didn't do it, though," I said. "I was down a well at the time, alone."

"If you say so, I'm sure you are right," the man said matter-of-factly. He opened a door and, shining the torch on his feet, he began edging his way up the flight of stairs on the other side. It was such a long staircase that, halfway through the process, I lost track of whether we were climbing or descending. I was not even sure this was a staircase.

"Is there anyone who can swear that you were in the well at the time?" the man asked without turning around.

I said nothing. There was no such person.

"In that case, the wisest thing would be for you to run away. They have decided for themselves that you are the culprit."

"Who are 'they'?"

Reaching the top of the stairs, the man turned right and, after a short walk, opened a door and stepped out into a corridor. There he stopped to listen for sounds. "We have to hurry. Hold on to my jacket."

I grasped the bottom edge of his jacket as ordered.

The man with no face said, "Those people are always glued to the television set. That is why you are so greatly disliked here. They are very fond of your wife's elder brother."

"Do you know who I am?" I asked.

"Yes, of course I do."

"So, then, do you know where Kumiko is now?"

The man said nothing. I kept a firm grip on the tail of the man's coat, as if we were playing some kind of game in the dark, rushing around another corner, down a short staircase, through a small secret door, through a low-ceilinged hidden passageway, into yet another corridor. The strange, intricate route taken by the faceless man felt like an endless journey through the bowels of a huge bronze figure.

"Let me tell you this, Mr Okada. I don't know everything that happens here. This is a big place, and my area of responsibility centres on the lobby. There is a lot that I don't know anything about."

"Do you know about the whistling waiter?"

"No, I don't. There *are* no waiters here, whistling or otherwise. If you saw a waiter in here somewhere, he wasn't really a waiter: it was *something* pretending to be a waiter. I failed to ask you, but you wanted to go to Room 208, is that correct?"

"That is correct. I'm supposed to meet a certain woman there."

The man had nothing to say to that. He pressed for no details about the woman or what my business with her might be. He continued down the corridor with the confident stride of a man who knows his way around, dragging me like a tugboat along a complicated course.

Eventually, with no warning, he came to a stop in front of a door. I bumped into him from behind, practically knocking him over. His flesh, on impact, felt light and airy, as if I had bumped into an empty cicada shell. He quickly straightened himself and used his pocket torch to illuminate the number on the door: 208.

"This door is not locked," said the man. "Take this light with you. I can walk back in the dark. Lock the door when you go in, and don't open it to anyone. Whatever business you have, get it over with quickly and go back where you came from. This place is dangerous. You are an intruder here, and I am the only one on your side. Don't forget that."

"Who are you?" I asked.

The faceless man handed me the torch as if passing a baton. "I am the hollow man," he said. Faceless face towards me, he waited in the darkness for me to speak, but I could not find the right words. Eventually, without a sound, he disappeared. He was right in front of me one second, swallowed up by darkness the next. I shone the light in his direction, but only the dull white wall came out of the darkness.

.

As the man had said, the door to Room 208 was unlocked. The knob turned in my hand without a sound. I took the precaution of switching the torch off, then stepped in as quietly as I could. As before, the room was silent, and I could sense nothing moving inside. There was the faint crack of melting ice moving inside the ice bucket. I switched on the torch and turned to lock the door. The dry metallic tumbling of the lock sounded abnormally loud in the room. On the table in the centre stood the unopened bottle of Cutty Sark, clean glasses, and the bucket full of fresh ice. The silver-coloured tray beside the vase shot the beam of the torch back with a sensual gleam, as if it had been waiting for me for a very long time. In response, it seemed, the smell of the flowers' pollen became stronger for a moment. The air around me grew dense, and the pull of gravity seemed to increase. With my back against the door, I watched the movement around me in the beam of the torch.

This place is dangerous. You are an intruder here, and I am the only one on your side. Don't forget that.

"Don't shine that light on me," said a woman's voice in the inner room. "Do you promise not to shine that light on me?"

"I promise," I said.

34

The Light of a Firefly
•
Breaking the Spell
•
A World Where Alarm Clocks Ring in the Morning

"I promise," I said, but my voice had a certain artificial quality, as when you hear a recording of yourself speaking.

"I want to hear you say it: that you won't shine your light on me."

"I won't shine the light on you. I promise."

"Do you really promise? You're telling me the truth?"

"I'm telling you the truth. I won't break my promise."

"All right, then, what I'd *really* like you to do, if you don't mind, is pour two whiskys on the rocks and bring them over here. Lots of ice, please."

She spoke with the slightest hint of a playful, girlish lisp, but the voice itself belonged to a mature, sensual woman. I laid the penlight lengthways on the table and in its light went about pouring the two whiskys, taking a moment first to steady my breathing. I broke the seal on the Cutty Sark, used tongs to fill the two glasses, and poured the whisky over the ice cubes. I had to think clearly about each task my hands were performing. Large shadows played over the wall with every movement.

I walked into the inner room, holding the two whiskys in my right hand and lighting my way along the floor with the torch in my left. The air felt chillier than before. I must have worked up a sweat in my rush through the darkness, and was now beginning to cool off. I remembered that I had shed my coat along the way.

As promised, I turned out the light and slipped it into my pocket. Then, by feel, I placed one whisky on the night table and took my own with me to the armchair by the bed. In total darkness, I nonetheless remembered the layout of the room.

I seemed to hear the sliding of sheets against each other. She was raising herself in bed and leaning against the headboard, glass now in hand. She gave the glass a little shake, stirring the ice, and took a sip of whisky. In the darkness, these were all like sound effects in a radio play. I inhaled the aroma of the whisky in my hand, but I did not drink.

"It's been a long time," I said. My voice sounded somewhat more like my own than it had before.

"Has it?" she said. "I'm not sure what that means: 'time' or 'a long time'."

"As I recall, it's been exactly one year and five months," I said.

"Well, well," she said, unimpressed. "I can't recall . . . exactly."

I put my glass on the floor and crossed my legs. "You weren't here last time I came, were you?"

"Of course I was. Right here. In bed. I'm always here."

"But I'm sure I was in Room 208. This *is* Room 208, isn't it?"

She swirled the ice in her glass and gave a little laugh. "And *I'm* sure you weren't so sure. You were in *another* Room 208, that's for sure."

There was a certain unsteadiness in her voice which unsettled me. The alcohol might have been affecting her. I took my woollen cap off and laid it on my knee.

I said to her, "The phone was dead, you know."

"Yes, I know," she said, with a hint of resignation. "*They* cut it. They knew how I used to like to make calls."

"Are *they* the ones who are keeping you here?"

"Hmm, I wonder. I don't really know," she said, with a little laugh. The disturbance in the air made her voice quaver.

Facing in her direction, I said, "I've been thinking about you for a very long time. Ever since I was last here. Thinking about who you are and what you're doing here."

"Sounds like fun," she said.

"I imagined all sorts of possibilities, but I can't be sure of anything yet. I'm still at the imagining stage."

"Well, *well*," she said, as if impressed. "So you can't be sure of anything yet, you're still at the imagining stage."

"That's right," I said. "And I might as well tell you this: I think you're Kumiko. I didn't realize it at first, but I'm becoming more and more convinced."

"Oh, *are* you?" she said, after a moment's pause, sounding amused. "So I'm Kumiko, am I?"

For a moment, I lost all sense of direction, as if everything I was doing was off the mark: I had come to the wrong place to say the wrong things to the wrong person. It was all a waste of time, a meaningless detour. But I managed to set myself straight in the dark. To perform a check on reality, I fastened my hands on the hat in my lap.

"Yes, I think you are Kumiko. Because then all kinds of story lines work out. You kept calling me on the phone from here. You were trying to convey some kind of secret to me. A secret of Kumiko's. A secret that the real Kumiko in the real world couldn't bring herself to tell me. So you must have been doing it for her – in words like secret codes."

She said nothing for a while. She lifted her glass for another sip of whisky, then said, "I wonder. But if that's what you think, you may be right. Maybe I really am Kumiko. I'm still not sure, though. So, then, if it's true . . . if I really am Kumiko . . . I should be able to talk to you here through her voice. Isn't that right? It makes things a little complicated, but do you mind?"

"No, I don't mind," I said. Once more my voice seemed to have lost a degree of calm and some sense of reality.

She cleared her throat in the darkness. "Here goes, then. I wonder if it will work." Again she gave a little laugh. "It's not easy, though. Are you in a hurry? Can you stay here a while?"

"I don't really know," I said.

"Wait just a minute. Sorry. Ahem . . . I'll be ready in a minute."

I waited.

"*So. You came here looking for me. You wanted to see me, is that it?*" Kumiko's earnest voice resounded in the darkness.

I had not heard Kumiko's voice since that summer morning when I zipped her dress up. She had been wearing a new cologne behind the ears, cologne from someone else. She left the house that day and never came back. Whether the voice in the darkness was the real thing or a fake, it brought me back to that morning for a moment. I could smell the cologne and see the white skin of Kumiko's back. The memory was dense and heavy in the darkness – perhaps denser and heavier than in reality. I tightened my grip on my hat.

"Strictly speaking, I didn't come here to *see* you. I came here to *bring you back*," I said.

She released a little sigh in the darkness. "Why do you want so badly to bring me back?"

"Because I love you," I said. "And I know that you love me and want me."

"You sound pretty sure of yourself," said Kumiko – or Kumiko's voice. There was nothing derisive about her tone of voice – but nothing warm about it, either.

I heard the contents of the ice bucket in the next room shifting.

"I have to solve some riddles, though, if I'm going to get you back," I said.

"Isn't it a little late to be starting such things now? I thought you didn't have that much time."

She was right. There was not much time left and too much to think about. I wiped the sweat from my brow with the back of my hand. This was probably my last chance, I told myself. I had to *think*.

"I want you to help me," I said.

"I wonder," said Kumiko's voice. "I may not be able to help you. But I'm willing to try."

"The first question is why you had to leave me. I want to know the *real* reason. I know what your letter said – that you had become involved with another man. I read it, of course. And read it and read it and reread it. And I suppose it does offer some kind of explanation. But I can't believe it's the real reason. It doesn't quite ring true. I'm not saying it's a lie, but I can't help feeling it's nothing but a kind of metaphor."

"A metaphor?!" She sounded truly shocked. "Maybe I just don't get it, but if sleeping with other men is a metaphor for something, I'd like to know what."

"What I'm trying to say is that it seems to me to be nothing but an explanation for explanation's sake. It doesn't lead anywhere. It just traces the surface. The more I read your letter, the more I felt that. There must be some other reason that is more basic – more *real*. And it almost certainly involves Noboru Wataya."

I could feel her eyes focused on me in the darkness and was struck by the thought that she might be able to see me.

"Involves Noboru Wataya? How?" asked Kumiko's voice.

"Well, the events I've been through have been tremendously complicated. All kinds of characters have come on the scene, and strange things have happened one after another, to the point where, if I try to think about them in order, I lose track. Viewed from more of a distance, though, the thread running through them is perfectly clear. What it all boils down to is that you have gone over from my world to the world of Noboru Wataya. That shift is the important thing. Even if you did, in fact, have sex with another man or other men, that is a secondary matter. A front. That's what I'm trying to say."

She inclined her glass in the darkness. Staring hard at the source of the sound, I felt as if I could catch a faint glimpse of her movements, but this was obviously an illusion.

"People don't always send messages in order to communicate the truth, Mr Okada," she said. The voice was no longer Kumiko's. Neither was it the original girlish voice. This was a new voice, which belonged to someone else. It had a poised, intelligent ring to it. ". . . just as people don't always meet others in order to reveal their true selves. Do you grasp my meaning, Mr Okada?"

"But still, Kumiko was trying to communicate *something* to me. Whether or not it was the truth, she was looking to me for *something*, and *that* was the truth for me."

I sensed the darkness around me increasing in density, much as the evening tide comes to fullness without a sound. I had to hurry. I didn't have much time left. They might come looking for me here once the lights came back on. I decided to risk putting into words the thoughts that had been slowly forming in my mind.

"This is strictly the product of my own imagination, but I would guess that there was some kind of inherited tendency in the Wataya family bloodline. What kind of tendency I can't be sure, but it was some kind of tendency – something that you were afraid of. Which is why you were afraid of having children. When you became pregnant, you panicked because you were worried the tendency would show up in your own child. But you couldn't reveal the secret to me. The whole story started from there."

She said nothing but quietly placed her glass on the night table. I went on: "And your sister, I'm sure, didn't die from food poisoning. No, it was more unusual than that. The person responsible for her death was Noboru Wataya, and you know that for a fact. Your sister probably said something to you about it before she died, gave you some kind of warning. Noboru Wataya had some special power, and he knew how to find people who were responsive to that power and to draw something out of them. He must have used that power in a particularly violent way on Creta Kano. She was able, one way or another, to recover, but your sister was not. She lived in the same house, after all: she had nowhere to run to. She couldn't stand it any more and chose to die. Your parents have always kept her suicide a secret. Isn't that true?"

578

There was no reply. The woman kept quiet in an attempt to obliterate her presence in the darkness.

I went on: "How he managed to do it and what the occasion was I have no idea, but at some point Noboru Wataya increased his violent power geometrically. Through television and the other media, he gained the ability to train his magnified power on society at large. Now he is trying to bring out something that the great mass of people keep hidden in the darkness of their unconscious. He wants to use it for his own political advantage. It's a tremendously dangerous thing, this thing he is trying to draw out: it's fatally smeared with violence and blood, and it has a direct connection with the darkest depths of history, because its final effect is to destroy and obliterate people on a massive scale."

She sighed in the darkness. "I wonder if I could bother you to pour me another whisky?" she asked softly.

I walked over to the night table and picked up her empty glass. I could do that much in the dark without difficulty. I went into the other room and poured a fresh whisky on the rocks with the aid of the torch.

"What you just said was strictly the product of your own imagination, right?" she asked.

"That's right. I've strung a few ideas together," I said. "There's no way I can prove any of this. I don't have any basis for claiming that what I have said is true."

"But still, I'd like to hear the rest – if there *is* more to tell."

I went back into the inner room and put the glass on the night table. Then I switched off the torch and returned to my chair. I concentrated my attention on telling the rest of my story.

"You didn't know exactly what had happened to your sister, only that she had given you some kind of warning before she died. You were too young at the time to understand what it was about. But you *did* understand, in a vague sort of way. You knew that Noboru Wataya had somehow defiled and injured your sister. And you sensed the presence in your blood of some kind of dark secret, something from which you could not remain aloof. And so, in that house, you were always alone, always tense, struggling by yourself to live with your dormant, undefinable anxiety, like one of those jellyfish we saw in the aquarium.

"After you graduated from college – and after all the trouble with your family – you married me and left the Wataya house. Our life was serene, and with each day that went by, you were able, bit by bit, to forget your dark anxiety. You went out into society a new person, as you continued gradually to recover. For a while, it looked as though everything was going to work out for you. But, unfortunately, it wasn't that simple. At some point you noticed that you were being drawn, against your will, towards that dark force that you thought you had left behind. And when you realized what was happening, you became confused. You didn't know what to do. Which is why you went to talk to Noboru Wataya, hoping to learn the truth. And you sought out Malta Kano, hoping that she could give you help. It was only to me that you could not open up.

"I would guess that all this started after you became pregnant. That, I'm sure, was the turning point. Which is probably why I received my first warning from the guitar player in Sapporo the night you had the abortion. Getting pregnant may have stimulated and awakened the dormant something inside you. And that was exactly what Noboru Wataya had been waiting for. That may be the only way he is capable of committing sexually to a woman. That is why he was so determined to drag you back from my side to his, once that *tendency* began to surface in you. He had to have you. Noboru Wataya needed you to play the role your sister had once played for him."

When I had finished speaking, a deep silence came to fill the emptiness. I had given voice to everything that my imagination had taught me about Kumiko. Parts of it had come from vague thoughts I had had previously, and the rest had taken shape in my mind while I spoke in the darkness. Perhaps the power of darkness had filled in the blank spots in my imagination. Or perhaps this woman's presence had helped. Either way, there was no solid basis for what I had imagined.

"A very, very interesting story," said the woman. Again her voice had become the one with the girlish lisp. The speed with which her voice changed seemed to be increasing. "Well, well, well. So I left you to go into hiding with my defiled body. It's like Waterloo Bridge in the mist, Auld Lang Syne, Robert Taylor and Vivien Leigh —"

"I'm going to take you out of here," I said, cutting her off. "I'm going to take you home, to the world where you belong, where cats with bent tails live, and there are little backyards, and alarm clocks ring in the morning."

"And how are you going to do that?" the woman asked. "How are you going to take me out of here, Mr Okada?"

"The way they do in fairy tales," I said. "By breaking the spell."

"Oh, I see," said the voice. "But wait a minute, Mr Okada. You seem to think that I am Kumiko. You want to take me home as Kumiko. But what if I'm not Kumiko? What will you do then? You may be preparing to take home someone else entirely. Are you quite sure of what you're doing? Shouldn't you think it over one more time?"

I made a fist around the torch in my pocket. This couldn't possibly be anyone but Kumiko, I thought. But I couldn't prove it. It was ultimately nothing but a hypothesis. Sweat oozed from the hand in my pocket.

"I'm going to take you home," I said again, my voice dry. "That's what I came here to do."

I heard a movement in the sheets. She was changing her position in the bed.

"Can you say that for sure? Without a doubt?" she asked, pressing me for confirmation.

"Yes, I can say it for sure. *I'm going to take you home.*"

"And you have no second thoughts?"

"No, none. My mind is made up," I said.

She followed this with a long silence, as if checking the truth of something. Then, to mark the end of this stage of our conversation, she let out a long breath.

"I'm going to give you a present," she said. "It's not much of a present, but it may come in handy. Don't turn on the light now, but reach over here – very, very slowly – over to the night table."

I left my chair, and gauging the depth of the emptiness, I stretched my right hand out in the dark. I could feel the air's sharp thorns against my fingertips. And then I touched the thing. When I realized what it was, the air seemed to lodge in the back of my throat. The "present" was a baseball bat.

I took hold of the grip and held the bat out straight. It was almost certainly the bat I had taken from the young man with the guitar case. The grip and the weight were right. This had to be it. But as I felt it over more carefully, I found that there was something, some kind of debris, stuck to it just above the brand mark. It felt like a human hair. I took it between my fingertips. Judging from the thickness and hardness, it had to be a *real* human hair. Several such hairs were stuck to the bat, with what seemed to be congealed blood. Someone had used this bat to smash someone else – probably Noboru Wataya – in the head. It took an effort for me to expel the air caught in my throat.

"That *is* your bat, isn't it?" she asked.

"I think so," I said, struggling to keep calm. My voice had begun to take on a different tone in the deep darkness, as if someone lurking down here were speaking in my place. I cleared my throat, and after checking to be certain that the one speaking was the real me, I continued: "But somebody seems to have used this to beat someone."

The woman kept her mouth sealed. Sitting down, I lowered the bat and held it between my legs. "I'm sure you know what's going on," I said. "Somebody used this bat to crush Noboru Wataya's skull. The news I saw on TV was true. Noboru Wataya is in hospital in a critical condition. He might die."

"He's not going to die," said Kumiko's voice, without emotion. She might have been reporting a historical fact from a book. "He may not regain consciousness, though. He may just continue to wander through darkness, but what kind of darkness that would be, no one knows."

I felt for the glass at my feet and picked it up. I poured its contents into my mouth and, without thinking, swallowed. The tasteless liquid passed through my throat and down my gullet. I felt a chill for no reason, then an unpleasant sensation as if something far away were moving slowly in my direction through a long darkness. As I had known it would, my heart started beating faster.

"We don't have much time," I said. "Just tell me this if you can: where are we?"

"You've been here before, and you found the way in here – alive and unharmed. *You* should know where this is. And anyhow, it doesn't matter any more. The important thing —"

Just then there was a knock on the door – a hard, dry sound, like someone driving a nail into the wall, two loud raps followed by two more. It was the same knock I had heard before. The woman gasped.

"You've got to get out of here," she said, in a voice that was unmistakably Kumiko's. "If you go now, you can still pass through the wall."

I had no idea if what I was thinking was right or wrong, but I knew that as long as I was here, I had to defeat this thing. This was the war that I would have to fight.

"I'm not running away this time," I said to Kumiko. "I'm going to take you home."

I put my glass on the floor, put my woollen hat on, and took the bat from between my knees. Then I started slowly for the door.

35

Just a Real Knife
◆
The Thing That Had Been Prophesied

Lighting my way along the floor and keeping my steps soundless, I moved towards the door. The bat was in my right hand. I was still walking when the knocks came again: two knocks, then two more. Harder this time, and more violent. I pressed myself against the side wall where I would be hidden by the door when it opened. There I waited, keeping my breath in check.

When the sound of the knocks faded, a deep silence descended over everything again, as if nothing had happened. But I could feel the presence of someone on the other side of the door. This someone was standing there the way I was, keeping his breath in check and listening, try-ing to hear the sound of breathing or the beating of a heart, or to read the movement of a thought. I tried to keep my breath from agitating the sur-rounding air. *I am not here,* I told myself. I am not here. I am not anywhere.

The key turned in the lock. He performed each movement with the utmost caution, drawing out the time it took to perform any one act so that the sounds involved would become isolated from each other, their meaning lost. The doorknob turned, and this was followed by the almost imperceptible sound of hinges rotating. The contractions of my heart began to speed up. I tried to quell the disturbance this caused, but without success.

Someone came into the room, sending ripples through the air. I made a conscious effort to sharpen each of my five senses and caught the faint smell of a foreign body – a strange mixture of thick clothing, suppressed breathing, and overwrought nerves steeped in silence. Did he have the knife in his hand? I had to assume that he did. I remembered its vivid white gleam. Holding my breath, obliterating my presence, I tightened my grip on the bat.

Once inside, the someone closed the door and locked it. Then he stood there, back to the door, watching and waiting. My hands on the bat were drenched with sweat. I would have liked to wipe my palms on my trousers, but the slightest movement could have had fatal results. I brought to mind the sculpture that had stood in the garden of the abandoned Miyawaki house. In order to obliterate my presence here, I made myself one with that image of a bird. There, in the sun-drenched summer garden, I was the sculpture of a bird, frozen in space, glaring at the sky.

The someone had brought his own torch. He switched it on, and its straight, narrow beam cut through the darkness. The light was not strong. It came from the same kind of penlight I was carrying. I waited for the beam to pass me as he walked into the room, but he made no effort to move. The light began to pick out items in the room, one after another – the flowers in the vase, the silver tray lying on the table (giving off its sensual gleam), the sofa, the floor lamp. . . . It swung past my nose and came to rest on the floor a few inches beyond the tips of my shoes, licking every corner of the room like the tongue of a snake. I waited for what felt like an eternity. Fear and tension drilled into my consciousness with intense pain.

No thinking. You are not allowed to think, I told myself. *You are not allowed to use your imagination.* Lieutenant Mamiya had said that in his letter. *Imagining things here can be fatal.*

Finally, the torch beam began to move forward slowly, very slowly. The man seemed to be heading for the inner room. I tightened my grip on the bat. It was then I noticed that the sweat of my hands had dried. If anything, my hands were now too dry.

The man took one slow step forward, then stopped. Then one more. He seemed to be checking his footing. He was closer to me than ever now. I took a breath and held it. Two more steps, and he would be where I wanted him. Two more steps, and I would be able to put an end to this walking nightmare. But then, without warning, the light disappeared.

Total darkness swallowed everything again. He had turned off his torch. I tried to make my mind work quickly in the dark, but it would not work at all. An unfamiliar chill ran through me. He had realized that I was there.

Move, I told myself. *Don't just stand there.* I tried to dodge to the left, but my legs would not move. My feet were stuck to the floor, like the feet of the bird sculpture. I bent forward and barely managed to incline my stiffened upper body to the left. Just then, something slammed into my right shoulder, and something hard and cold as frozen rain stabbed me to the bone.

The impact seemed to revive me, and the paralysis disappeared from my legs. I sprang to the left and crouched in the darkness, feeling for my opponent. The blood was pounding through my body, every muscle and cell straining for oxygen. My right shoulder was going numb, but I had no pain. That would come later. I stayed absolutely still, and he did too. We faced each other in the darkness, holding our breaths. There was nothing to see, nothing to hear.

Again, without warning, the knife came. It slashed past my face like an attacking bee, the sharp point just catching my right cheek where the mark was. I could feel the skin tearing. No, he could not see me, either. If he could, he would have finished me off long before. I swung the bat in the darkness, aiming in the direction from which the knife had come, but it just swished through the air, striking nothing. The swing had been a good one, though, and the crisp sound helped me to loosen up somewhat. We were still an even match. The knife had cut me twice, but not badly. Neither of us could see the other. And though he had a knife, I had my bat.

Again, in our mutual blindness, breathing held in check, we felt each other out, waiting for some hint of movement. I could feel blood dripping down my face, but I was free of fear. *It's just a knife*, I said to myself. *It's just a cut.* I waited. I waited for the knife to come my way again. I could wait for ever. I drew my breath in and expelled it without a sound. *Come on!* I said to him in my mind. *Move!* I'm waiting for you to move. Stab me if you want to. I'm not afraid.

Again the knife came. It slashed the collar of my sweater. I could feel the point moving past my throat, but it didn't touch my skin. I twisted and jumped to the side, and almost too impatient to straighten up, I swung the bat through space. It caught him somewhere around the collarbone. Not enough to bring him down or break any bones, but I knew

I had hurt him. I could feel him recoil from the blow, and I heard a loud gasp. I took a short back-swing and went for him again – in the same direction at a slightly higher angle, where I had heard his breath draw in.

It was a perfect swing. I caught him somewhere high on the neck. There was a sickening sound of cracking bone. A third swing hit home – the skull – and sent him flying. He let out a strange sound and slumped to the floor. He lay there making little gasps, but those soon stopped. I closed my eyes and, without thinking, aimed one final swing in the direction of the sound. I didn't want to do it, but I had no choice. I had to finish him off: not out of hatred or even out of fear, but as something I simply had to do. I heard something crack open in the darkness like a piece of fruit. Like a watermelon. I stood still, gripping the bat, holding it out in front of me. Then I realized I was trembling. All over. And there was no way I could stop it. I took a step back and pulled the torch from my pocket.

"Don't!" cried a voice in the darkness. "Don't look at it!" Kumiko's voice was calling to me from the inner room, trying to stop me from looking. But I had to look. I had to see it. I had to know what it was, this thing in the centre of the darkness that I had just beaten to a pulp. Part of me understood what Kumiko was forbidding me to do. She was right: I shouldn't look at it. But I had the torch in my hand now, and that hand was moving on its own.

"Please, I'm begging you to stop!" she screamed. "Don't look at it if you want to take me home again!"

I clenched my teeth and quietly released the air I had locked in my lungs. Still the trembling would not subside. A sickening smell hung in the air – the smell of brains and violence and death. I had done this: I was the one who had made the air smell like this. I found the sofa and collapsed onto it. For a while, I fought against the nausea rising in my stomach, but the nausea won. I vomited everything in my stomach onto the carpet, and when that was gone I brought up stomach fluid, then air, and saliva. While vomiting, I dropped the bat on the floor. I could hear it rolling away in the darkness.

Once the spasms of my stomach began to subside, I wanted to take out my handkerchief to wipe my mouth, but I could not move my hand. I couldn't get up from the sofa. "Let's go home," I said towards the darkness of the inner room. "This is all over now. Let's go."

She didn't answer.

There was no one in there any more. I sank into the sofa and closed my eyes.

I could feel the strength going out of me – from my fingers, my shoulders, my neck, my legs. . . . The pain of my wounds began to fade as well. My body was losing all sense of mass and substance. But this gave me no anxiety, no fear at all. Without protest, I gave myself up – surrendered my flesh – to some huge, warm thing that came naturally to enfold me. I realized then that I was passing through the wall of jelly. All I had to do was give myself up to the gentle flow. *I'll never come back here again,* I said to myself as I moved through the wall. Everything had come to an end. *But where was Kumiko? Where did she go?* I was supposed to bring her back from the room. That was the reason I had killed the man. That was the reason I had to split his skull open like a watermelon. That was the reason I . . . But I couldn't think any more. My mind was sucked into a deep pool of nothingness.

·

When I came to, I was sitting in the darkness again. My back was against the wall, as always. I had returned to the bottom of the well.

But it was not the usual well bottom. There was something new here, something unfamiliar. I tried to gather my faculties to grasp what was going on. What was so different? But my senses were still in a state of near-total paralysis. I had only a partial, fragmentary sense of my surroundings. I felt as if, through some error, I had been deposited in the wrong container. After a time, though, I began to realize what it was.

Water. I was surrounded by water.

The well was no longer dry. I was sitting in water up to my waist. I took several deep breaths to calm myself. How could this be? The well was producing water – not cold water, though. If anything, it felt warm. I felt as if I were soaking in a heated pool. It then occurred to me to check my pocket. I wanted to know if the torch was still there. Had I brought it back with me from the other world? Was there any link between what had happened there and this reality? But my hand would not move. I couldn't even move my fingers. All strength had gone out of my arms and legs. It was impossible for me to stand.

I began a cool-headed assessment of my situation. First of all, the water came up only to my waist, so I didn't have to worry about drowning. True, I was unable to move, but that was probably because I had used up every ounce of strength. Once sufficient time had passed, my strength would come back. The knife wounds didn't seem very deep, and the paralysis at least saved me from having to suffer pain. The blood seemed to have stopped flowing from my cheek.

I leaned my head back against the wall and told myself, *It's OK, don't worry*. Everything had ended. All I had to do now was give my body some rest, then go back to my original world, the world above ground, where the sunlight overflowed. . . . But why had this well started producing water all of a sudden? It had been dried up, dead, for such a long time, yet now it had come back to life. Could this have some connection with what I had accomplished *there*? Yes, it probably did. Something might have loosened whatever it was that had been obstructing the vein of water.

•

Shortly after that, I encountered one ominous fact. At first I tried to resist accepting it as a fact. My mind came up with a range of possibilities that would enable me to do that. I tried to convince myself that it was a hallucination caused by the combination of darkness and fatigue. But in the end, I had to recognize the truth. However hard I attempted to deceive myself, it would not go away.

The water level was rising.

The water had risen now from my waist to the underside of my bent knees. It was happening slowly, but it was happening. I tried again to move my body. With a concentrated effort, I tried to squeeze out whatever strength I could manage, but it was useless. The most I could do was bend my neck a little. I looked overhead. The well lid was still solidly in place. I tried to look at the watch on my left wrist, without success.

The water was coming in from an opening – and with what seemed like increasing speed. Where it had been barely seeping in at first, it was now almost gushing. I could hear it. Soon it was up to my chest. How deep was it going to get?

Be careful of water, Mr Honda had said to me. I had not given any credence to his prophecy. True, I had not forgotten it, either (you don't forget anything as weird as that), but I had never taken it seriously. Mr Honda had been nothing more than a harmless episode for Kumiko and me. I would repeat his words as a joke now and then when something came up: "Be careful of water." And we would laugh. We were young, and we had no need for prophecies. Just living was itself an act of prophecy. But Mr Honda had been right. I almost wanted to laugh out loud. The water was rising, and I was in trouble.

I thought about May Kasahara. I used my imagination to picture her opening the well cover – with total reality and clarity. The image was so real and clear that I could have stepped right into it. I couldn't move my body, but my imagination still worked. What else could I do?

"Hey, Mr Wind-up Bird," said May Kasahara. Her voice reverberated up and down the well shaft. I hadn't realized that a well with water echoed more than one without water. "What are you doing down there? Thinking again?"

"I'm not doing any one thing in particular," I said, facing upward. "I haven't got time to explain now, but I can't move my body, and the water is rising in here. This isn't a dry well any more. I might drown."

"Poor Mr Wind-up Bird!" said May Kasahara. "You emptied yourself out trying so hard to save Kumiko. And you probably *did* save her. Right? And in the process, you saved lots of people. But you couldn't save yourself. And nobody else could save you. You used up your strength and your fate saving others. All your seeds were planted somewhere else, and now your bag is empty. Have you ever heard of anything so unfair? I feel sympathy for you, Mr Wind-up Bird, from the bottom of my heart. It's true. But, finally, it was a choice you made yourself. Do you know what I mean?"

"I do," I said.

I felt a dull throb in my right shoulder. It really happened, then, I told myself. The knife really cut me. It cut me as a real knife.

"Are you afraid to die, Mr Wind-up Bird?" asked May Kasahara.

"Sure I am," I said. I could hear my voice reverberating in the well. It was my voice, and at the same time it wasn't. "Sure I'm afraid when I think about dying down here in a dark well."

"Goodbye, then, poor Mr Wind-up Bird," said May Kasahara. "Sorry, there's nothing I can do for you. I'm far, far away."

"Goodbye, May Kasahara," I said. "You looked great in a bikini."

May Kasahara's voice was very quiet as she said, "Goodbye, poor Mr Wind-up Bird."

The well cover closed tightly again. The image faded. But nothing happened. The image was not linked to anything. I shouted towards the well mouth, *"May Kasahara, where are you now that I need you?"*

•

The water was up to my throat. Now it was wrapped around my neck like a noose. In anticipation, I was beginning to find it difficult to breathe. My heart, now underwater, was working hard to tick off the time that remained to it. At this rate, I would have another five minutes or so before the water covered my mouth and nose and started filling my lungs. There was no way I could win. I had brought this well back to life, and I would die in its rebirth. It was not a bad way to die, I told myself. The world is full of much worse ways to die.

I closed my eyes and tried to accept my impending death as calmly as I could. I struggled to overcome my fear. At least I was able to leave a few things behind. That was the one small bit of good news. I tried to smile, without much success. "I *am* afraid to die, though," I whispered to myself. These turned out to be my last words. They were not very impressive words, but it was too late to change them. The water was over my mouth now. Then it came to my nose. I stopped breathing. My lungs fought to suck in new air. But there was no more air. There was only lukewarm water.

I was dying. Like all the other people who live in this world.

36

The Story of the Duck People

•

Shadows and Tears

•

(May Kasahara's Point of View: 6)

Hi, again, Mr Wind-up Bird.

Hey, are these letters reaching you?

I mean, I've been writing you tons and tons of letters, and I'm starting to wonder if they ever arrive. The address I've been using is a "kind of" kind of thing, and I don't put a return address on the envelope, so maybe they're just piling up on the "little letter lost" shelf in a post office somewhere, unread and all covered with dust. Up to now, I figured: OK, if they're not getting through, they're not getting through, so what? I've been scratching away at these things, but the important thing was for me to put my thoughts down on paper. It's easy for me to write if I think I'm writing to you, Mr Wind-up Bird, I don't know why. Hey, yeah, why is that?

But this letter is one I really want you to read. I hope and pray it gets to you.

Now I'm going to write about the duck people. Yes, I know this is the first time I've mentioned them, but here goes.

I told you before how this factory I'm working in has this huge property, with woods and a pond and stuff. It's great for taking walks. The pond's a pretty big one, and that's where the duck people live, maybe twelve birds altogether. I don't know how their family is organized. I suppose they've got their internal arrangements, with some members getting along better with some and not so well with others, but I've never seen them fight.

It's December, so ice has started to form on the pond, but not such thick ice. Even when it's cold, there's still enough open water left for the ducks to swim around a little bit. When it's cold enough for thick ice, I'm told, some of the girls come here to ice-skate. Then the duck people (yes, I know it's a weird expression, but I've got into the habit of using it, so it just comes out) will have to go somewhere else. I don't like ice-skating, so I'm hoping there won't be any ice, but I don't think it's going to do any good. I mean, it gets really cold in this part of the country, so as long as they go on living here, the duck people are going to have to resign themselves to it.

I come here every weekend these days and kill time watching the duck people. When I'm doing that, two or three hours can go by before I know it. I go out in the cold, armed head to foot like some kind of polar-bear hunter: tights, hat, scarf, boots, fur-trimmed coat. And I spend hours sitting on a rock all by myself, chilling out, watching the duck people. Sometimes I feed them old bread. Of course, there's nobody else here with the time to do such crazy things.

You may not know this, Mr Wind-up Bird, but ducks are very pleasant people to spend time with. I never get tired of watching them. I'll never understand why everybody else bothers to go somewhere far away and pay good money to see some stupid movie instead of enjoying these people. Like sometimes they'll come flapping through the air and land on the ice, but their feet slide and they fall over. It's like a TV comedy! They make me laugh even with nobody else around. Of course, they're not clowning around trying to make me laugh. They're doing their best to live very serious lives, and they just happen to fall down sometimes. I think that's cool.

The duck people have these flat orange feet that are really cute, like they're wearing little kids' rain boots, but they're not made for walking on ice, I guess, because I see them slipping and sliding all over the place, and some even fall on their bottoms. They must not have non-slip treads. So winter is not really a fun season for the duck people. I wonder what they think, deep down inside, about ice and stuff. I bet they don't hate it all that much. It just seems that way to me from watching them. They look like they're living happily enough, even if it's winter, probably just grumbling to themselves, "Ice again? Oh, well . . ." That's another thing I really like about the duck people.

The pond is in the middle of the woods, far from everything. Nobody (but me, of course!) bothers to walk all the way over here at this time of year, except on unusually warm days. I walk down the path through the woods, and my boots crunch on the ice that's left from a recent snowfall. I see lots of birds all around. When I've got my collar up and my scarf wrapped round and round under my chin, and my breath makes white puffs in the air, and I've got a chunk of bread in my pocket, and I'm walking down the path in the woods, thinking about the duck people, I get this really warm, happy feeling, and it hits me that I haven't felt happy like this for a long, long time.

OK, that's enough about the duck people.

To tell you the truth, I woke up an hour ago from a dream about you, Mr Wind-up Bird, and I've been sitting here, writing you this letter. Right now it's (I look at my clock) exactly 2.18 a.m. I got into bed just before 10 o'clock, as usual, said "Good night, everybody" to the duck people, and fell fast asleep, but then, a little while ago, I woke up – bang! Actually, I'm not sure it was a dream. I mean, I don't remember anything I was dreaming about. Maybe I wasn't dreaming. But whatever it was, I heard your voice right next to my ear. You were calling to me over and over in this really loud voice. That's what shocked me awake.

The room wasn't dark when I opened my eyes. Moonlight was pouring through the window. This great big moon like a stainless-steel tray was hanging over the hill. It was so huge, it looked as if I could have reached out and written something on it. And the light coming in through the window looked like a big, white pool of water. I sat up in bed, racking my brains, trying to figure out what had just happened. Why had you been calling my name in such a sharp, clear voice? My heart kept pounding for the longest time. If I had been in my own house, I would have got dressed – even if it was the middle of the night – and run down the alley to your house, Mr Wind-up Bird. But out here, a million miles away in the mountains, I couldn't run anywhere, right?

So then you know what I did?

I got naked. Ahem. Don't ask me why. I'm really not sure myself. So just be quiet and listen to the rest. Anyhow, I took every stitch of clothing off and got out of bed. And I got down on my knees on the floor in the white moonlight. The heating was off and the room must have been cold, but I didn't feel cold. There was some kind of special something in the moonlight that was coming in at the window, and it was wrapping my body in a thin, protective, skin-tight film. At least that's how I felt. I just stayed there naked for a while, but then I took turns holding different parts of my body out to be bathed in the moonlight. I don't know, it just seemed like the most natural thing to do. The moonlight was so absolutely, incredibly beautiful that I couldn't not do it. My head and shoulders and arms and breasts and tummy and legs and bottom and, you know, around there: one after another, I dipped them in the moonlight, like taking a bath.

If somebody had seen me from outside, they'd have thought it was very, very strange. I must have looked like some kind of full-moon pervert going bonkers in the moonlight. But nobody saw me, of course. Though, come to think of *it, maybe that boy on the motorcycle was somewhere, looking at me. But that's OK. He's dead. If he wanted to look, and if he'd be satisfied with that, I'd be glad to let him see me.*

But anyhow, nobody was looking at me. I was doing it all alone in the moonlight. And every once in a while, I'd close my eyes and think about the duck people, who were probably sleeping near the pond somewhere. I'd think about the warm, happy feeling that the duck people and I had created together in the daytime. Because, finally, the duck people are an important kind of magic kind of protective amulet kind of thing for me.

I stayed kneeling there for a long time after that, just kneeling all alone, all naked, in the moonlight. The light gave my skin a magical colour, and it threw a sharp black shadow of my body across the floor, all the way to the wall. It didn't look like the shadow of my body, but one that belonged to a much more mature woman. It wasn't a virgin like me, it didn't have my corners and angles but was fuller and rounder, with much bigger breasts and nipples. But it was the shadow that I was making – just stretched out longer, with a different shape. When I moved, it moved. For a while, I tried moving in different ways and watching very, very carefully to see what the connection was between me and my shadow, trying to figure out why it should look so different. But I couldn't figure it out. The more I looked, the stranger it seemed.

Now, here comes the part that's really hard to explain, Mr Wind-up Bird. I doubt if I can do it, but here goes.

Well, to cut a long story short, all of a sudden I burst into tears. I mean, if it was in a screenplay or something, it'd go: "May Kasahara: Here, with no warning, covers face with hands, wails aloud, collapses in tears." But don't be too shocked. I've been hiding it from you all this time, but in fact, I'm the world's biggest cry-baby. I cry for anything. It's my secret weakness. So for me, the fact that I burst out crying for no reason at all was not such a surprise. Usually, though, I just have myself a little cry, and then I tell myself it's time to stop. I cry easily, but I stop just as easily. Tonight, though, I just couldn't stop. The cork popped, and that was that. I didn't know what had started me, so I didn't know how to stop myself. The tears just came gushing out, like blood from a huge wound. I couldn't believe the amount of tears I was producing. I seriously started to worry I might get dehydrated and turn into a mummy if this kept up.

I could actually see and hear my tears dripping down into the white pool of moonlight, where they were sucked in as if they had always been part of the light. As they fell, the tears caught the light of the moon and sparkled like beautiful crystals. Then I noticed that my shadow was crying too, shedding clear, sharp shadow tears. Have you ever seen the shadows of tears, Mr Wind-up Bird? They're nothing like ordinary shadows. Nothing at all. They come here from some other, distant world, especially for our hearts. Or maybe not. It struck me then that the tears my shadow was shedding might be the real thing, and the tears that I was shedding were just shadows. You don't get it, I'm sure, Mr Wind-up Bird. When a naked seventeen-year-old girl is shedding tears in the moonlight, anything can happen. It's true.

So that's what happened in this room about an hour ago. And now I'm sitting at my desk, writing a letter to you in pencil, Mr Wind-up Bird (with my clothes on, of course!).

Bye-bye, Mr Wind-up Bird. I don't quite know how to put this, but the duck people in the woods and I are praying for you to be warm and happy. If anything happens to you, don't hesitate to call me out loud again.

Good night.

37

Two Different Kinds of News

•

The Thing That Disappeared

"Cinnamon carried you here," said Nutmeg.

The first thing that came to me when I woke was pain, in different, twisted forms. The knife wound gave me pain, and all the joints and bones and muscles in my body gave me pain. Different parts of my body must have slammed up against things as I fled through the darkness. And yet the form of each of these different pains was still not quite right. They were somewhere close to pain, but they could not exactly be called pain.

Next I realized that I was stretched out on the fitting room sofa, wearing navy-blue pyjamas that I had never seen before and covered with a blanket. The curtains were open, and bright morning sun streamed through the window. I guessed it must be around 10 o'clock. There was fresh air here, and time that moved forward, but why such things existed I could not quite comprehend.

"Cinnamon brought you here," said Nutmeg. "Your wounds are not that bad. The one on your shoulder is fairly deep, but it didn't hit any major blood vessels, fortunately. The ones on your face are just scrapes. Cinnamon used a needle and thread to sew up the others so you won't have scars. He's good at that. You can take the stitches out yourself in a few days or have a doctor do it."

I tried to speak, but I couldn't make my voice work. All I could do was inhale and let the air out as a rasping sound.

"You'd better not try to move or talk yet," said Nutmeg. She was sitting on a nearby chair with her legs crossed. "Cinnamon says you were in the well too long – it was a very close call. But don't ask me what happened. I don't know a thing. I got a call in the middle of the night, phoned for a taxi, and flew over here. The details of what went on before that I just don't know. Your clothes were soaking wet and bloody. We threw them away."

Nutmeg was dressed more simply than usual, as if she had indeed rushed out of the house. She wore a cream-coloured cashmere sweater over a man's striped shirt, and a woollen skirt of olive green, no jewellery, and her hair was tied back. She looked a little tired but otherwise could have been a photo in a catalogue. She put a cigarette between her lips and lit it with her gold lighter, making the usual clean, dry click, then inhaling with eyes narrowed. I really had not died, I reassured myself when I heard the sound of the lighter. Cinnamon must have pulled me out of the well in the nick of time.

"Cinnamon understands things in a special way," said Nutmeg. "And unlike you or me, he is always thinking very deeply about the *potential* for things to happen. But not even *he* imagined that water would come back to the well so suddenly. It had simply not been among the many possibilities he had considered. And because of that, you almost lost your life. It was the first time I ever saw that boy panic."

She managed a little smile when she said that.

"He must really like you," she said.

I couldn't hear what she said after that. I felt an ache deep behind my eyes, and my eyelids grew heavy. I let them close, and I sank down into darkness as if on a lift ride.

·

It took two full days for my body to recover. Nutmeg stayed with me the whole time. I couldn't get up by myself, I couldn't speak, I could hardly eat. The most I could manage was a few sips of orange juice and a few slivers of canned peaches. Nutmeg would go home at night and come back in the morning. Which was fine, because I was out cold all night – and most of the day too. Sleep was obviously what I needed most for my recovery.

I never saw Cinnamon. He seemed to be consciously avoiding me. I would hear his car coming in through the gate whenever he dropped Nutmeg off or picked her up or delivered food or clothing – hear that special deep rumble that Porsche engines make, since he had stopped using the Mercedes – but he didn't come inside. He handed things to Nutmeg at the front door, then left.

"We'll be getting rid of this place soon," Nutmeg said to me. "I'll have to take care of the women again myself. Oh, well. I guess it's my fate. I'll just have to keep going until I'm all used up – empty. And you: you probably won't be having anything to do with us any more. When this is all over and you're well again, you'd better forget about us as soon as you can. Because . . . Oh, yes, I forgot to tell you. About your brother-in-law. Noboru Wataya."

Nutmeg brought a newspaper from the next room and unfolded it on the table. "Cinnamon brought this a little while ago. Your brother-in-law collapsed last night in Nagasaki. They took him to a hospital there, but he's been unconscious ever since. They don't know if he'll recover."

Nagasaki? I could hardly comprehend what she was saying. I wanted to speak, but the words would not come out. Noboru Wataya should have collapsed in Akasaka, not Nagasaki. Why Nagasaki?

"He gave a speech in Nagasaki," Nutmeg continued, "and he was having dinner with the organizers afterwards, when all of a sudden he went limp. They took him to a nearby hospital. They think it was some kind of stroke – probably some congenital weakness in a blood vessel in his brain. The paper says he'll be bedridden for some time, that even if he regains consciousness he probably won't be able to speak, so that's pretty much the end of his political career. What a shame: he was so young. I'll leave the paper here. You can read it when you're feeling better."

It took me a while to absorb these facts as facts. The images from the TV news I had seen in the hotel lobby were still too vividly burned into my brain – Noboru Wataya's office in Akasaka, the police all over the place, the front door of the hospital, the reporter grim, his voice tense. Little by little, though, I was able to convince myself that what I had seen was news that existed only in the *other world*. I had not, in actuality, in this world, beaten Noboru Wataya with a baseball bat. I would not, in actuality, be investigated by the police or arrested for the crime. He had collapsed in public, in full view, from a stroke. There was no crime involved, no possibility of a crime. This knowledge came to me as a great relief. After all, the assailant described on television had borne a startling resemblance to me, and I had no alibi.

There had to be some connection between my having beaten someone to death in the other world and Noboru Wataya's collapse. I clearly killed something inside him or something powerfully linked with him. He might have sensed that it was coming. What I had done, though, had failed to take Noboru Wataya's life. He had managed to survive on the brink of death. I should have pushed him over the brink. What would happen to Kumiko now? Would she be unable to break free while he was still alive? Would he continue to cast his spell over her from his unconscious darkness?

That was as far as my thoughts would take me. My own consciousness slipped away bit by bit, until I closed my eyes in sleep. I had a tense, fragmentary dream. Creta Kano was holding a baby to her breast. I could not see the baby's face. Creta Kano's hair was short, and she wore no make-up. She told me that the baby's name was Corsica and that half the baby's father was me, while the other half was Lieutenant Mamiya. She had not gone to Crete, she said, but had remained in Japan to bear and raise the child. She had only recently been able to find a new name for the baby, and now she was living a peaceful life growing vegetables in the hills of Hiroshima with Lieutenant Mamiya. None of this came as a surprise to me. In my dream, at least, I had foreseen it all.

"How has Malta Kano been since I last saw her?" I asked.

Creta Kano did not reply to this. Instead, she gave me a sad look, and then she disappeared.

•

On the morning of the third day, I was at last able to get out of bed by myself. Walking was still too hard for me, but I slowly regained the ability to speak. Nutmeg made me rice gruel. I ate that and a little fruit.

"How is the cat doing?" I asked her. This had been a matter of concern to me for some time.

"Don't worry, Cinnamon is looking after him. He goes to your house every day to feed him and change his water. The only thing you have to worry about is yourself."

"When are you going to get rid of this place?"

"As soon as we can. Probably sometime next month. I think you'll be seeing a little money from it too. We'll probably have to let it go for something less than we paid for it, so you won't get much, but your share should be a good percentage of what you paid on the mortgage. That should support you for a while. So you don't have to worry too much about money. You deserve it: after all, you worked hard here."

"Is this house going to be torn down?"

"Probably. And they'll fill in the well. Which seems like a waste now that it's producing water again, but nobody wants a big, old-fashioned well like that these days. They usually just put in a pipe and an electric pump. It's a lot more convenient, and it takes up less space."

"I don't suppose this place is jinxed any more," I said. "It'll be just an ordinary piece of property again, not the 'hanging house'."

"You may be right," said Nutmeg. She hesitated, then bit her lip. "But that no longer has anything to do with me or with you. Right? In any case, the important thing is for you to rest now and not bother with things that don't really matter. It will take a while until you're fully recovered."

Nutmeg showed me the article on Noboru Wataya in the morning paper she had brought with her. It was a small piece. Still unconscious, Noboru Wataya had been transferred from Nagasaki to a large university hospital in Tokyo, where he was in intensive care, his condition unchanged. The report said nothing more than that. What crossed my mind at that point was, of course, Kumiko. Where could she be? I had to get back home. But I still lacked the strength to walk such a distance.

I made it as far as the bathroom basin late the next morning and saw myself in the mirror for the first time in three days. I looked terrible – less like a tired living being than a well-preserved corpse. As Nutmeg had said, the cut on my cheek had been sewn up with professional-looking stitches, the edges of the wound held in good alignment by white thread. It was at least an inch in length but not very deep. It pulled if I tried to make a face, but there was little pain. I brushed my teeth and used an electric shaver on my beard. I couldn't trust myself to handle a razor yet. As the whiskers came off, I could hardly believe what I was seeing in the mirror. I put the shaver down and took a good look. The mark was gone. The man had cut my right cheek. Exactly where the mark had been. The cut was there all right, but the mark was gone. It had disappeared from my cheek without a trace.

.

During the night of the fifth day, I heard the faint sound of sleigh bells again. It was a little after 2 in the morning. I got up from the sofa, slipped a cardigan over my pyjamas, and left the fitting room. Passing through the kitchen, I went to Cinnamon's small office and peeked inside. Cinnamon was calling to me again from inside the computer. I sat down at the desk and read the message on the screen.

You have now gained access to the programme "The Wind-up Bird Chronicle". Choose a document (1-17).

I clicked on No. 17, and a document opened up before me.

38

The Wind-up Bird Chronicle No. 17
(Kumiko's Letter)

•

There are many things I have to tell you. To tell them all would take a very long time – maybe years. I should have opened up to you long ago, confessed everything to you, but unfortunately I lacked the courage to do so. And I still harboured the groundless hope that things would not turn out so badly. The result has been this nightmare for us both. It's all my fault. But it is also too late for explanations. We don't have enough time for that. So what I want to do here is tell you the most important thing first.

And that is, *I have to kill my brother, Noboru Wataya.*

I am going to go now to the hospital room where he is sleeping, to pull the plug on his life-support system. As his sister, I will be allowed to stay the night with him in place of a nurse. It will be a while before anyone notices that he has been disconnected. I got the doctor to show me yesterday how it works. I intend to wait until I am sure he is dead, and then I will give myself up to the police. I will tell them I did what I thought was right but offer no more explanation than that. I will probably be arrested on the spot and tried for murder. The media will leap in, and people will offer opinions on death with dignity and other such matters. But I will keep silent. I will offer no explanation or defence. There is only one truth in all this, and that is that I wanted to end the life of a single human being, Noboru Wataya. They will lock me up, but the prospect doesn't frighten me. I have already been through the worst.

•

If it hadn't been for you, I would have lost my mind long ago. I would have handed myself over, vacant, to someone else and fallen to a point beyond hope of recovery. My brother, Noboru Wataya, did exactly that to my sister many years ago, and she ended up killing herself. He defiled us both. Strictly speaking, he did not defile our bodies. What he did was even worse than that.

The freedom to do anything at all was taken from me, and I shut myself up in a dark room, alone. No one chained me down or set a guard to watch over me, but I could not have escaped. My brother held me with yet stronger chains and guards – chains and guards that were myself. I was the chain that bit into my ankle, and I was the ruthless guard that never slept. Inside me, of course, there was a self that wanted to escape, but at the same time there was a cowardly, debauched self that had given up all hope of ever being able to flee from there, and the first self could never dominate the second because I had been so defiled in mind and body. I had lost the right to go back to you – not just because I had been defiled by my brother, Noboru Wataya, but because, even before that, I had defiled myself irreparably.

I told you in my letter that I had slept with another man, but in that letter I was not telling the truth. I must confess the truth to you here. I did not sleep with just one man. I slept with many other men. Too many to count. I myself have no idea what caused me to do such a thing. Looking back upon it now, I think it may have been my brother's influence. He may have opened some kind of drawer inside me, taken out some kind of incomprehensible something, and made me give myself to one man after another. My brother had that kind of power, and as much as I hate to acknowledge it, the two of us were surely tied together in some dark place.

In any case, by the time my brother came to me, I had already defiled myself beyond all cleansing. In the end, I even contracted a venereal disease. In spite of all this, as I mentioned in my letter, I was never able to feel at the time that I was wronging you in any way. What I was doing seemed entirely natural to me – though I can only imagine that it was not the real me that felt that way. Could this be true, though? Is the answer really so simple? And if so, what, then, is the real me? Do I have any sound basis for concluding that the me who is now writing this letter is the "real me"? I was never able to believe all that firmly in my "self", nor am I able to today.

·

I often used to dream of you – vivid dreams with clear-cut stories. In these dreams, you were always searching desperately for me. We were in a kind of labyrinth, and you would come almost up to where I was standing. "Take one more step! I'm right here!" I wanted to shout, and if only you would find me and take me in your arms, the nightmare would end and everything would go back to the way it was. But I was never able to produce that shout. And you would miss me in the darkness and go straight past me and disappear. It was always like that. But still, those dreams helped and encouraged me. At least I knew I still had the power to dream. My brother couldn't prevent me from doing that. I was able to sense that you were doing everything in your power to draw nearer to me. Maybe someday you would find me, and hold me, and sweep away the filth that was clinging to me, and take me away from that place for ever. Maybe you would smash the curse and replace the seal so that the real me would never have to leave again. That was how I was able to keep a tiny flame of hope alive in that cold, dark place with no exit – how I was able to preserve the tiniest remnant of my own voice.

I received the password for access to this computer this afternoon. Someone sent it to me special delivery. I am sending you this message from the machine in my brother's office. I hope it reaches you.

·

I have run out of time. The taxi is waiting for me outside. I have to leave for the hospital now, to kill my brother and take my punishment. Strange, I no longer hate my brother. I am calm with the thought that I will have to obliterate his life from this world. I have to do it for his sake too. And to give my own life meaning.

Take good care of the cat. I can't tell you how happy I am that he is back. You say his name is Mackerel? I like that. He was always a symbol of something good that grew up between us. We should not have lost him when we did.

·

I can't write any more now. Goodbye.

39

Goodbye

♦

"I'm *so* sorry I couldn't show you the duck people, Mr Wind-up Bird!"

May Kasahara looked truly sorry.

She and I were sitting by the pond, looking at its thick cap of ice. It was a big pond, with thousands of little cuts on its surface from skating blades. May Kasahara had taken this Monday morning off work especially for me. I had intended to visit her on Sunday, but a train accident had made me a day late. May Kasahara had wrapped herself in a fur-lined coat. Her bright-blue woollen hat bore a geometrical design in white yarn and was topped with a little pom-pom. She had knitted the hat herself, and she said she would make one just like it for me before next winter. Her cheeks were red, her eyes as bright and clear as the surrounding air, which made me very happy: she was only seventeen, after all – the potential was there for almost limitless change.

"The duck people all moved somewhere else after the pond froze over. I'm sure you would have loved them. Come back in the spring, will you? I'll introduce you."

I smiled. I was wearing a duffle coat that was not quite warm enough, with a scarf wrapped up to my cheeks and my hands thrust in my pockets. A deep chill ran through the forest. Hard snow coated the ground. My trainers were sliding all over the place. I should have bought some kind of non-slip boots for this trip.

"So you're going to stay here a while longer?" I asked.

"I think so. I might want to go back to school after enough time has gone by. Or I might not. I don't know. I might just get married – no, not really." She smiled with a white puff of breath. "But anyhow, I'll stay for now. I need more time to think. About what I want to do, where I want to go. I want to take time and think about those things."

I nodded. "Maybe that's what you really ought to do," I said.

"Tell me, Mr Wind-up Bird, did you think about those kinds of things when you were my age?"

"Hmm. Maybe not. I must have thought about them a little bit, but I really don't remember thinking about things as seriously as you do. I suppose I just thought that if I went on living in the usual way, things would work themselves out all right. But they didn't, did they? Unfortunately."

May Kasahara looked me in the eye, a calm expression on her face. Then she laid her gloved hands on her lap, one on top of the other.

"So, in the end, they wouldn't let Kumiko out of jail?" she asked.

"She refused to be let out," I said. "She figured she'd be mobbed. Better to stay in jail, where she could have peace and quiet. She's not even seeing me. She doesn't want to see anyone until everything is settled."

"When does the trial start?"

"Sometime in the spring. Kumiko is pleading guilty. She's going to accept the verdict, whatever it is. It shouldn't be a long trial, and there's a good possibility of a suspended sentence – or, at worst, a light one."

May Kasahara picked up a stone at her feet and threw it towards the middle of the pond. It clattered across the ice to the other side.

"And you, Mr Wind-up Bird – you'll stay at home and wait for Kumiko again?"

I nodded.

"That's good . . . or is it?"

I made my own big white cloud in the cold air. "I don't know – I suppose it's how we worked things out."

It could have been a whole lot worse, I told myself.

Far off in the woods that surrounded the pond, a bird cried. I looked up and scanned the area, but there was nothing more to hear. Nothing to see. There was only the dry, hollow sound of a woodpecker drilling a hole in a tree trunk.

"If Kumiko and I have a child, I'm thinking of naming it Corsica," I said.

"What a great name!" said May Kasahara.

As the two of us walked through the woods side by side, May Kasahara took off her right glove and put her hand in my pocket. This reminded me of Kumiko. She often used to do the same thing when we walked together in the winter, so we could share a pocket on a cold day. I held May Kasahara's hand in my pocket. It was a small hand, and warm as a sequestered soul.

"You know, Mr Wind-up Bird, everybody's going to think we're lovers."

"You may be right."

"So tell me, did you read all my letters?"

"Your letters?" I had no idea what she was talking about. "Sorry, but I've never received a single letter from you. I got your address and phone number from your mother. Which wasn't easy: I had to stretch the truth quite a bit."

"Oh, no! Where did they all go? I must have written you five-hundred letters!" May Kasahara looked up to the heavens.

•

Late that afternoon, May Kasahara saw me all the way to the station. We took a bus into town, ate pizza at a restaurant near the station, and waited for the little three-carriage diesel train that finally pulled in. Two or three people stood around the big wood-burning stove that glowed red in the waiting room, but the two of us stayed out on the platform in the cold. A clear, hard-edged winter moon hung frozen in the sky. It was a young moon, with a sharp curve like a Chinese sword. Beneath that moon, May Kasahara stood on tiptoe and kissed me on the cheek. I could feel her cold, thin lips touch me where my mark had been.

"Goodbye, Mr Wind-up Bird," she murmured. "Thanks for coming all the way out here to see me."

Hands thrust deep in my pockets, I looked into her eyes. I didn't know what to say.

When the train came, she slipped her hat off, took one step back, and said to me, "If anything ever happens to you, Mr Wind-up Bird, just call out to me in a really loud voice, OK? To me and the duck people."

"Goodbye, May Kasahara," I said.

•

The arc of the moon stayed over my head long after the train had left the station, appearing and disappearing each time the train rounded a curve. I kept my eyes on the moon, and whenever that was lost to sight, I watched the lights of the little towns as they went past the window. I thought of May Kasahara, with her blue woollen hat, alone on the bus taking her back to her factory in the hills. Then I thought of the duck people, asleep in the grassy shadows somewhere. And finally, I thought of the world that I was heading back to.

"Goodbye, May Kasahara," I said. Goodbye, May Kasahara: may there always be something watching over you.

I closed my eyes and tried to sleep. But it was not until much later that I was able to get any real sleep. In a place far away from anyone or anywhere, I drifted off for a moment.

Works Consulted

◆

Alvin D. Coox, *Nomonhan: Japan Against Russia, 1939*, 2 vols (Stanford: Stanford University Press, 1985); Iwasaki Toshio, Yoshimoto Shin'ichirō, trans., *Nomonhan: sōgen no Nisso-sen, 1939*, 2 vols (Tokyo: Asahi shinbun sha, 1989).

Ezawa Akira, *Manshūkoku no shuto-keikaku: Tokyo no genzai to mirai o tou* (Tokyo: Nihon Keizai Hyōron sha, 1988).

Itō Keiichi, *Shizuka na Nomonhan* (Tokyo: Kōdansha bunko, 1986).

Amy Knight, *Beria, Stalin's First Lieutenant* (Princeton: Princeton University Press, 1993).

Kojima Jō, *Manshū teikoku*, 3 vols (Tokyo: Bunshun bunko, 1983).

Onda Jūhō, *Nomonhan sen: ningen no kiroku* (Tokyo: Gendaishi shuppan kai, Tokuma shoten, 1977).

Also available from Vintage

Haruki Murakami

AFTER THE QUAKE

'How does Murakami manage to make poetry while writing
of contemporary life and emotions? I am weak-kneed with
admiration'
Independent on Sunday

'Even in the slipperiest of Mr Murakami's stories, pinpoints
of detail flash out warm with life'
New York Times

The economy was booming. People had more money than
they knew what to do with. And then the earthquake struck.
For the characters in *after the quake*, the Kobe earthquake is
an echo from a past they buried long ago. Satsuki has a spent
thirty years hating one man: a lover who destroyed her
chances of having children. Did her desire for revenge cause
the earthquake? Junpei's estranged parents live in Kobe.
Should he contact them? Miyake left his family in Kobe to
make midnight bonfires on a beach hundreds of miles away.
Four-year-old Sala has nightmares that the Earthquake Man
is trying to stuff her inside a little box. Katagiri returns home
to find a giant frog in his apartment on a mission to save
Tokyo from a massive burrowing worm. 'When he gets
angry, he causes earthquakes,' says Frog. 'And right now he
is very, very angry.'

'Murakami is one of the best writers around'
Time Out

VINTAGE BOOKS
London

Also available from Vintage

Haruki Murakami

NORWEGIAN WOOD

'**Murakami must already rank among the world's greatest living novelists**'
Guardian

'Evocative, entertaining, sexy and funny; but then Murakami is one of the best writers around'
Time Out

'Such is the exquisite, gossamer construction of Murakami's writing that everything he chooses to describe trembles with symbolic possibility'
Guardian

When he hears her favourite Beatles song, Toru Watanabe recalls his first love Naoko, the girlfriend of his best friend Kizuki. Immediately he is transported back almost twenty years to his student days in Tokyo, adrift in a world of uneasy friendships, casual sex, passion, loss and desire – to a time when an impetuous young woman called Midori marches into his life and he has to choose between the future and the past.

'This book is undeniably hip, full of student uprisings, free love, booze and 1960s pop, it's also genuinely emotionally engaging, and describes the highs of adolescence as well as the lows'
Independent on Sunday

VINTAGE BOOKS
London

www.vintage-books.co.uk